AMERICAN ANTHEM

BJ HOFF

HARVEST HOUSE PUBLISHERS

EUGENE, OREGON

Verses marked NIV are taken from the HOLY BIBLE, NEW INTERNATIONAL VERSION®. NIV®. Copyright©1973, 1978, 1984 by the International Bible Society. Used by permission of Zondervan. All rights reserved.

Verses marked NASB are taken from the New American Standard Bible®, © 1960, 1962, 1963, 1968, 1971, 1972, 1973, 1975, 1977, 1995 by The Lockman Foundation. Used by permission. (www.Lockman.org)

Verses marked NLT are taken from the Holy Bible, New Living Translation, copyright ©1996, 2004. Used by permission of Tyndale House Publishers, Inc., Wheaton, IL 60189 USA. All rights reserved.

Verses marked NKJV are taken from the New King James Version. Copyright ©1982 by Thomas Nelson, Inc. Used by permission. All rights reserved.

Cover by Koechel Peterson & Associates, Inc., Minneapolis, Minnesota

Cover photos © wikimedia; Giorgio Gruizza, Andres Rodriguez / Fotolia; Photos.com / Greg Page

BJ Hoff: Published in association with the Books & Such Literary Agency, 52 Mission Circle, Suite 122, PMB 170, Santa Rosa, CA 95409-5370, *www.booksandsuch.biz.*

Previously published as the American Anthem trilogy: *Prelude, Cadence,* and *Jubilee.*

AMERICAN ANTHEM
Copyright © 2002/2003/2004 by BJ Hoff
Published by Harvest House Publishers
Eugene, Oregon 97402
www.harvesthousepublishers.com

Library of Congress Cataloging-in-Publication Data
American anthem / B.J. Hoff.
    p. cm.
    ISBN 978-0-7369-2646-1 (pbk.)
    1. Italian Americans—Fiction. 2. Immigrants—Fiction. 3. Singers—Fiction. 4. Blind musicians—Fiction. 5. Opera—Fiction. 6. New York (N.Y.)—Fiction. I. Hoff, B. J., 1940- Prelude. II. Hoff, B. J., 1940- Cadence. III. Hoff, B. J., 1940- Julbilee. IV. Title.
    PS3558.O34395A82 2009
    813'.54—dc22

                                                        2008040734

Printed in the United States of America

09 10 11 12 13 14 15 16 17 / RDM-SK / 10 9 8 7 6 5 4 3 2 1

My warmest thanks and appreciation to Harvest House Publishers for their interest in publishing this new, single-volume work of the three novels that made up the original series (The American Anthem). And as always, my deepest gratitude for their prayerful and ongoing support and encouragement.

BJ HOFF

American Anthem
Characters

MICHAEL EMMANUEL
Blind conductor-composer. Formerly an internationally acclaimed tenor.

SUSANNA FALLON
Sister of Michael Emmanuel's deceased wife. Michael's fiancée.

CATERINA EMMANUEL
Michael Emmanuel's daughter.

PAUL SANTI
Michael Emmanuel's cousin, assistant, and concertmaster of the orchestra.

LIAM AND MOIRA DEMPSEY
Husband and wife. Caretaker and housekeeper at the estate of Michael Emmanuel.

ROSA NAVARO
Renowned opera diva. Friend and neighbor of Michael Emmanuel.

∿

CONN AND VANGIE MACGOVERN
Husband and wife. Irish immigrants employed by Michael Emmanuel.

THE MACGOVERN CHILDREN
Aidan, Nell Grace, twins James (Seamus) and John (Sean), Emma, Baby William.

RENNY MAGEE
Orphaned street busker who emigrates from Ireland with the MacGoverns.

ANDREW CARMICHAEL
Physician from Scotland who devotes most of his medical practice to the impoverished of New York City.

BETHANY COLE
One of the first woman physicians in America. Andrew Carmichael's associate and fiancée.

∿

FRANK DONOVAN
Irish police sergeant and close friend to Andrew Carmichael.

MAYLEE
Abandoned child afflicted with premature aging disease.

MARY LAMBERT
Single mother of three children and recovering opium addict.

ROBERT WARBURTON
Prominent clergyman and lecturer. Andrew Carmichael's nemesis.

EDWARD FITCH
Son-in-law of Natalie Guthrie. Friend of Andrew Carmichael.

NATALIE GUTHRIE
Elderly mother-in-law of Edward Fitch. Patient of Andrew Carmichael.

By Mention or Brief Appearance:

FANNY J. CROSBY
Hymn writer and poet.

D. L. MOODY
Evangelist.

IRA SANKEY
Singer, songwriter, and partner of D. L. Moody.

Book One

PRELUDE

ANTHEM

Give my heart a voice
to tell the world about my Savior—
Give my soul a song that will ring
    out across the years,
A song that sings your boundless love
in sunshine or in shadow,
A psalm of praise for all my days,
through happiness or tears.
Make my life a melody
in tune with all creation—
Help me live in harmony
with every living thing.
Let my whole existence
be an anthem of rejoicing,
A prelude to eternal life
with you, my Lord and King.

—BJ HOFF

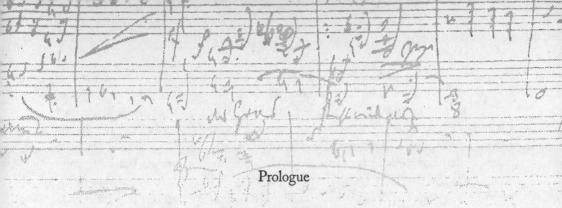

Prologue

CATCH THE DISTANT MUSIC

Blessed day when pure devotions
Rise to God on wings of love;
When we catch the distant music
Of the angel choirs above.

FANNY CROSBY

New York Harbor, 1846

Michael Emmanuel was eight years old when first he heard the Music.

It was an overcast day in mid-September. He was standing at the railing of the ship that would soon be taking him and his family home from their visit to America. Any moment now, the *Star Horizon* would cast off, leaving New York and the United States behind, and Michael wanted to store up all the memories he possibly could.

His parents stood a short distance away, talking with an elderly Italian gentleman they had met in the harbor. Michael turned back to watch the crush of people on the docks. Everyone seemed to be weeping or praying or shouting, all at the same time. Some stood with tears streaming down their cheeks, arms outstretched and hands extended, as if pleading to come along with those on board. Farther up the docks, a small band was playing, while just across the deck a priest led a small group of nuns in prayer.

The odor of tobacco smoke and ladies' lavender water mingled with the stench of floating garbage and the brackish smell of salt water. A hot, bitter taste filled Michael's mouth. As he stood on deck beneath a sky heavy with darkening clouds, he felt none of the same excitement that had rippled through him upon their arrival six weeks ago. Instead, a hollow ache wrung his heart at the thought of leaving this busy, boisterous land, where almost everything seemed big and noisy and new.

He had taken to America right from the beginning. Just this morning, before leaving their hotel, he had declared to his parents that one day he would return to live here. He already had *two* homes, after all, so why not three?

For as long as he could remember, they had spent most of the year in Italy, his father's land, staying in Ireland, his mother's country, for brief stints during the summer months. Michael liked both places, although Italy was his favorite "home." He liked the way the Tuscan sky glistened as the burning ball of the sun disappeared behind the mountains every evening. In Italy, there was always music playing and dogs barking in the streets and mothers leaning out of windows to call their children inside. In Ireland, everything—the towns, the people, the music—seemed overshadowed by a cloud. Even the wind seemed sad.

Suddenly, Michael realized that the ship had begun moving. They were putting out to sea, leaving America. As he watched, the harbor began to recede. Gradually, the people on the docks grew smaller, less distinct.

At that moment, something very strange occurred: there came to him the sound of music, a music unlike anything he had ever heard before. At first it was so quiet, so unexpected, that it might have been merely a sigh of the breeze or the lapping of the water beneath the ship. Or was the band in the harbor still playing?

Then, without warning, it began to hum and swell, growing louder, then louder still, until it seemed to leap across the water, heading directly toward him. Michael couldn't see where it was coming from. At some point, the wind had risen, and now it swept the deck, whistling through the rigging, whipping through the ropes and sails, diving in and out among the passengers at the rail.

The Music was everywhere now, falling out of the sky and marching across the water, like a vast army on the move or a great and majestic orchestra rising up from the ocean floor. Even the wind itself seemed to be singing!

As the sound built and surged, Michael could almost imagine that the doors to eternity had opened to let a band of angels come streaming through, singing and making thunderous music on a thousand instruments. And yet this music wasn't made of instruments or voices. It was neither—yet it was both. Just as it was both sweet and sad, brave and bold.

And beautiful. So beautiful.

It was everything Michael had ever imagined or felt or yearned for, but it was impossibly beyond his reach. It filled his ears, his head, his heart—filled him with such elation that he almost cried out in sheer delight.

One last mighty explosion of sound shook him from head to foot.

And then it was gone.

In a moment—even less, in a *heartbeat*—the Music died. And with it went the unutterable joy, leaving in its wake the most awful, sorrowful silence Michael had ever known.

At that instant, the sky really *did* open, not to release a chorus of angels, but instead to pour out a sudden, drenching rain. But Michael scarcely noticed. He was too intent on recapturing the Music that only seconds before had filled him to overflowing.

He turned and stumbled toward his parents, the rain pelting his face and stinging his skin. The other passengers also had begun to move in an effort to escape the downpour, and Michael found himself squeezed and pushed out of the way.

He was crying now, weeping as if he had lost his dearest treasure, and he could taste the salt from the spray of the ocean as it mingled with his tears. He shuddered, clutching his head with his hands as he tried to make his way through the crowd to his parents.

They saw him then and hurried to meet him, his father's arms encircling him protectively. "What is this, *mio figlio?* What has happened? Are you hurt?"

His mother stooped down and removed Michael's cap. She smoothed his hair and examined him as if searching for possible injuries.

The ship's whistle blasted, sending a white-hot knife of pain shooting through Michael's head. He cried aloud, tugging at his mother's sleeve. "Did you hear it, Mama? Papa? Did you hear the Music?" But he could tell by the way they were both staring at him that they had heard nothing.

His mother searched his face, then turned to look up at Papa.

"What music, Michael?" asked his father. "What music are you talking about?"

With the rain driving into his eyes and mouth, he tried to explain, to tell his parents what he had heard. He sobbed and stammered in his frustration. "I tried to catch it, don't you see, to keep it! I didn't want it to stop, not ever, but now it's gone!"

But he couldn't make them understand, and finally, exhausted, he let them lead him along the deck to their stateroom.

Much later, after his mother had brought him a light supper, Michael feigned sleep while his parents stood talking softly outside the door.

"What happened to him, Riccardo?" he heard his mama say. "What does it mean, this talk of *'catching the music'?*"

Michael rubbed his eyes, fighting the sleep crowding in on him.

"Who can say?" His father's voice was very soft. "Perhaps God has given the boy a gift. A vision."

"A *vision?* But he is only a child, Riccardo!"

His father said nothing for a moment. When he finally answered, he seemed to be speaking more to himself than to Mama. "In God's eyes, we are all children, are we not? And Michael—ah, *Saraid*, it seems to me that our son already soars closer to heaven than many grown men. Is it so unlikely that God would gift him in ways we cannot understand, allow him to hear something we cannot hear?"

"I don't understand this, Riccardo."

Mama sounded frightened, and Michael almost called out to her not to be afraid. The Music had been a wonderful thing, not something to fear. His pain had come from the glory of it, the inexpressible beauty and majesty of it.

And the *loss* of it.

"Music is the thing he loves best," Papa went on. "If God has indeed allowed Michael to hear a special music—perhaps even a *heavenly* music—"

He broke off, but Michael's mother prompted him. "What, Riccardo?"

"Then perhaps—" His voice faltered, then gained strength. "Perhaps our Michael has been chosen to be God's *trovatore*."

For the first time in hours, Michael felt the sadness lift and the ache in his head begin to drain away. His eyes were grainy from weeping and heavy with the need for sleep, but he heard his father's words, words he resolved to always remember:

"Perhaps our Michael has been chosen to be God's trovatore."

He felt as if he were floating, lulled into a distant world by the rhythmic rocking of the ship. His parents went on talking, their voices growing faint and far away. But the echo of that one truth continued to ring in his head and in his heart as he drifted off to sleep.

God's troubadour. *God's minstrel.*

1

SUSANNA:
BEGINNINGS AND ENDINGS

Home's not merely roof and room—
it needs something to endear it.

CHARLES SWAIN

Aboard the steamship Spain
New York Harbor, August 14, 1875

Was this an ending or a beginning?

Susanna Fallon had asked herself that question countless times since leaving Ireland, and now she was asking it again.

At first light, she had gathered on deck with the other passengers aboard the *Spain,* all of them eager for the sight of New York. Susanna wished she could believe that the sun rising over the sprawling American city heralded the dawn of an exciting future, a new life with new opportunities. But as the harbor came into view, any hopes she might have held for tomorrow threatened to sink. A flood of doubts rolled over her, vast and unfathomable as the ocean itself.

Susanna pulled her wrap tighter, watching as the ship slowly eased its way toward the pier. Floating garbage and debris littered the water, and she covered her nose and mouth against the stench. At the same time, a small barge angled up alongside them, and she could see an assembly of people thronging the smaller vessel, some waving at the passengers on the deck of the *Spain.*

"Why, look there, Mother—I believe some of our friends have come to meet us!"

Susanna recognized Mr. Moody's voice and turned to find him and Mrs. Moody, along with their children and the Sankeys, grouped just behind her. Nearby stood Dr. Carmichael, who had traveled to the States with the Moodys as a part of their entourage. Apparently, the Scottish physician had played some role or other in the British Isles crusades, although Susanna had never quite determined exactly what that role was.

"Ah, Miss Fallon, here we are at last!" boomed Mr. Moody. "How does it feel to be in America?"

The burly, bearded D. L. Moody and his wife were beaming at her, and Susanna attempted a smile in return. "In truth, Mr. Moody, the only thing I'm feeling at the moment is panic."

It struck Susanna that the American evangelist looked nearly as tired as he had when she'd first encountered him upon leaving Liverpool. And small wonder, given the fact that even aboard ship he had been continually attending to the needs of others.

His wife, who seemed to draw from a limitless supply of kindness, patted Susanna on the arm with a gloved hand. "You'll be just fine, dear," she murmured. "You're going to love America, you know. This is a splendid opportunity for you."

"Of course, it is!" Mr. Moody added, his tone enthusiastic. "Now, you did say there will be someone to meet you?"

Susanna nodded uncertainly. "That's what I was told, yes."

Mrs. Moody surprised her by pulling her into a quick embrace.

"We're so very glad we met you, Susanna. We'll be praying that everything goes well for you, dear. You're very brave, to come so far on behalf of your niece and brother-in-law. I know the Lord will look after you."

To her dismay, Susanna felt hot tears sting her eyes. Her chance meeting with the Moodys and the Sankeys had done much to ease her dread of the ocean voyage. Upon learning that she was a young Christian woman traveling alone, both couples had gone out of their way to look after her, inviting her to sit with them at mealtimes, answering her endless questions about the United States, and engaging her in frequent discussions about her own country of Ireland, as well as their common interest in music.

Even before the crossing, Susanna had learned a great deal about Mr. Moody and his "campaigns," as he referred to them. It seemed that the whole of the British Isles had been taken by surprise at the success of the Moody/Sankey meetings, not only in England and Scotland, but also in the heavily Protestant north of Ireland—and in the mostly Catholic south as well.

Susanna had been only one of thousands who had flocked to the early crusades. She could scarcely believe her good fortune a few months later when she found herself aboard the same ship as the American evangelists, who were returning to the States. To have the privilege of spending time with these esteemed spiritual leaders and their families had not only made the voyage less harrowing for her, but had actually given her a number of pleasurable hours.

Only now did the finality of their parting strike her. She was going to miss them greatly.

"I don't know how to thank you," she choked out, "all of you—for your kindness to me. I can't think what the crossing would have been like without you."

"Well, dear, it was awfully good of your brother-in-law to arrange first-class passage for you," said Mrs. Moody. "Otherwise, we might not have encountered one another at all. And how fortunate for you, to be spared the ordeal of traveling in steerage."

At the thought of the brother-in-law she had never met, Susanna tensed. Mrs. Moody, however, seemed not to notice. "I'm sure we'll see each other again, Susanna. There are plans for Mr. Moody to hold meetings in New York this fall."

"And if that works out," Mr. Moody put in, "we'll expect to see you in the very front row. Until then, you take special care, Miss Fallon, and just remember that your friends the Moodys and the Sankeys will be praying for you."

He paused, then drew a strong, encompassing arm around his wife and motioned that the Sankeys and Dr. Carmichael should move in closer. "In fact, we would like to pray for you right now, before we leave the ship."

And so they did, standing there on deck. Susanna had heard Mr. Moody pray before, of course: at their table before meals, at a shipboard worship service, and during the revival meetings she and her friend, Anna Kearns, had attended at the Exhibition Palace in Dublin. It seemed that when D. L. Moody prayed, he spoke directly with God, whom he obviously knew very well and approached boldly and eagerly, with an almost unheard-of confidence.

But to have this amazing man praying solely for *her* was an overwhelming experience entirely. By the final *Amen,* much of the strain that had been weighing on her for weeks seemed to melt away.

~

Once they disembarked and the Moodys and Sankeys had joined their welcoming party, Susanna's earlier apprehension returned in force.

The harbor was a different world. She found herself unable to move more than a few feet in any direction because of the throngs of people milling about. The noise was almost deafening—a harsh, unintelligible din of a dozen different languages, all flooding the docks at once. The shouts and laughter of sailors and passengers, the cries of greeting and wails of farewell, the pounding of feet on the planks as children ran and shoved their way among the grownups, the occasional blast from a ship's horn—all converged and hammered against Susanna's ears until she thought her head would split.

She stood there in the midst of this bedlam, not quite knowing what to do, fighting off a rising surge of panic. In that moment, she realized with a stark new clarity how utterly alone she was.

A man's voice sounded behind her. "*Signorina* Fallon?"

Startled, Susanna whipped around as if she'd been struck, ready to defend herself.

"You are Susanna Fallon?" he said.

He was young, with a fairly long, pleasant face and lively eyes behind his spectacles. And he was smiling at her, a wide, good-natured smile. He was also holding a bouquet of flowers and appeared not in the least threatening.

Susanna stared at him. The dark features, the Italian accent—it could be no one else.

But so young! According to Deirdre, Michael Emmanuel ought to be in his mid to late thirties by now. Yet he had called her by name.

"Mr. Emmanuel?" she ventured.

He gave his head a vigorous shake. "No, no! I am not Michael. I am Paul Santi, Michael's cousin. I have come to take you home."

"Home?" He nodded.·

"*Sì.*"

Whether it was fatigue or anxiety, Susanna's mind seemed to have gone suddenly dull. "I don't—how did you recognize me? How did you find me?"

"Your hat," he said, gesturing toward Susanna's bonnet. "Did you not write that you would be wearing a hat with blue ribbons?" His smile brightened even more. "These are for you," he said, "with Michael's compliments."

He thrust the lavish bouquet into Susanna's hands. "If you will come with me, *signorina,* we must first go there, to the depot." He pointed to a granite, fortresslike circular building. "Castle Garden," he added. "I will help you with the registration and the paperwork. Michael has already made arrangements for you to be passed through quickly. Do not worry about your luggage—I will take care of it. I have been through this myself, you see. I know exactly what to do."

Susanna glanced across the dock and saw the tall, kindly featured Dr. Carmichael standing there, watching them. For an instant, she was seized by an irrational desire to run toward the man, to flee the solicitude of this dark-eyed foreigner for the pleasant-natured physician and his link to the Moodys.

But she hardly knew Dr. Carmichael any better than she knew this Paul Santi. She must be mad entirely to think of throwing herself at the mercy of a man who was known to her only by his association with the Moodys—themselves strangers until a few days past.

Regaining her wits, she turned back to Paul Santi and, bearing her bouquet and a hard-won sense of determination, managed a careful smile and a civil word as he led her across the docks.

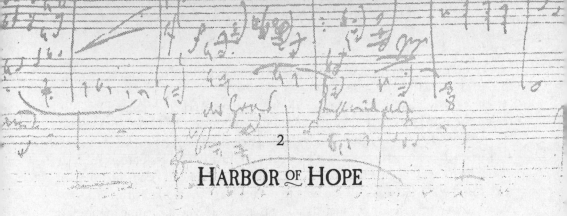

2

HARBOR OF HOPE

Hope of the world,
Afoot on dusty highways,
Showing to wandering souls
the path of light...

GEORGIA HARKNESS
FROM THE HYMN "HOPE OF THE WORLD"

Andrew Carmichael stood for a moment, taking in the sights and sounds around him.

No matter how many times he entered the harbor, it seemed new to him. Perhaps because of the ever-increasing flow of immigrants arriving each day, bringing with them their different languages and customs, their private struggles, their secret dreams. And their hopes that, in this land where others before them had found a future free of tyranny and despair, they, too, might build a new and better life for themselves and those they loved.

Andrew was convinced that no matter what brought them here by the thousands, what kept them here was hope. America offered a new kind of hope, one without boundaries. A hope that here, just beyond the walls of Castle Garden, waited opportunities that in their old land would have always remained just out of reach. Opportunities for success and happiness, and for the priceless gift of freedom.

And what kept *him* here? What had motivated him to leave his native Scotland with surprisingly few regrets, holding fast only to his memories of people who loved him and still prayed for him so faithfully? Why had America molded itself to his heart, to his very being, so tenaciously that he no longer thought of anywhere else but New York as *home?*

He smiled a little. Only the Lord knew the answer to such questions. And so far God had revealed little to Andrew about any divine plan for his life, other than the fact that it included trust. Trust and obedience.

It required a monumental amount of the former, Andrew thought, to generate the latter. At least in his case.

He sighed. It had been a fine trip. In the words of Andrew's father, D. L. had "reeled them in" by the thousands, and Andrew himself had benefited greatly from every service, every Bible study, every prayer meeting.

His decision to delay his return home and join D. L. and Ira Sankey midway through the crusade had been a sound one after all. He had been able to assist with the new converts, as well as seeing to the health of the workers. But as always, *he* had been ministered to as much as any of the seekers who had come to the altar. His soul had been nourished, his spirit renewed, his faith strengthened. He had also been reminded once more of the depth of God's grace in his own journey of forgiveness and restoration. And he was thankful.

But now he was home again, back on the shores of New York, preparing to return to his solitary flat and his cramped, dimly lighted office where too many patients crowded the waiting room, and too few possessed the means to pay their bills. Back to his own work.

He really had to get serious—immediately—about taking on an assistant, or perhaps even a partner, in his practice. He simply couldn't continue the exhausting routine to which he'd subjected himself over the past few years. But what manner of partner would be willing to share the kind of practice to which Andrew had committed himself? The search itself would be time-consuming and depleting. And in addition, a new partner would mean a new office—a larger space than the shoebox in which he now worked. When he considered the time and the effort it would require to locate both a partner and another office, the entire prospect seemed overwhelming.

Later. He would think about that later.

He flexed his neck and shoulders to ease the pain and stiffness that had settled into them, then glanced across the docks and saw Susanna Fallon, the young Irish woman the Moodys had befriended during the crossing. She was holding a bouquet and seemed to be deep in conversation with a slender, dark-haired fellow who smiled broadly and used his hands a great deal as he spoke.

When Miss Fallon happened to turn his way, Andrew touched his fingers to his cap and nodded. The young man looked to be a decent sort, and Miss Fallon was smiling, so after another moment Andrew gave a farewell nod and started off to hail a hack.

It was time to go home.

~

Paul Santi seemed a veritable tempest of energy and efficiency. Susanna found herself increasingly grateful for his assistance, for inside the enormous building all was confusion. Immigrants milled about everywhere, in the aisles or crowded together on benches, some sitting on boxes. The heat and humidity were stifling, and the odor of fear and unwashed bodies permeated the place. In the center of the building, a staff of a dozen important looking gentlemen engaged in what Paul Santi called the "registration process."

To her great relief, with the help of Paul Santi and an official who took over her arrangements, Susanna was whisked through the lines. It seemed no time at all before they had completed the questions and paperwork, then boarded the steamer that Paul Santi said would take them home.

Home. Susanna tried to ignore the twist in her stomach induced by the very mention of the word. Home was what she had left behind. Home was Ireland, her childhood, the family farm.

Whatever else might be waiting for her at the end of this reluctant journey, she could not bring herself to hope it would ever take the place of home.

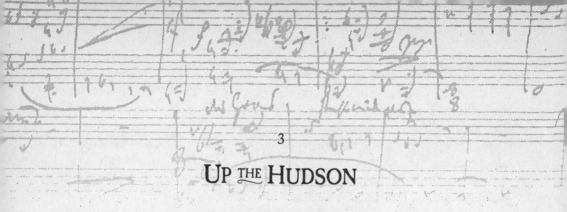

3

UP THE HUDSON

I am trusting Thee, Lord Jesus,
Trusting only Thee...

FRANCES R. HAVERGAL

Susanna Fallon endured the steamer ride up the Hudson River much as she might have suffered a trip to the gallows.

Her initial sense of relief that she'd been met by the pleasant-natured Paul Santi instead of her formidable brother-in-law had already given way to an escalating sense of dread. She was finally about to meet the man her sister had married in what Deirdre herself once called "a moment of madness." More than once she had questioned the wisdom of this new venture. Only the conviction that God's hand was in the entire experience—that and the thought of the motherless niece she had never seen—had brought her this far.

Deirdre's child, Caterina, was only three years old, still little more than a baby, and young enough to need the care and affection Susanna was eager to give. Even so, she harbored no illusions about her role in her niece's life, nor did she have any intention of trying to supplant Caterina's real mother.

Deirdre had been dead for over a year now, but surely the child would have retained some memory of her. Susanna had no desire to erase that memory. She meant only to assume her rightful role as the girl's aunt and, by doing so, offer her the love and guidance Deirdre would have provided had she lived.

Even Michael Emmanuel had insisted in his posts that his daughter needed Susanna. And the bitter reality was that Susanna needed a home. With her parents gone and the family's small dairy farm sold for debts, her choices had been few: stay in Ireland and hire on as a governess; make an undesirable, an *unthinkable*, marriage to Egan Dunn; or accept Michael Emmanuel's offer to come to America and make her home with him and Caterina.

And so here she was, installed on a ponderous steamboat, churning up a river that gouged its way through the wildest piece of countryside she had ever seen. Towering, rugged cliffs rose up on either side, and the low-hanging clouds of an August afternoon sky hovered overhead. She was about to commence an arrangement with a stranger she already distrusted, in spite of the fact that she didn't even know what the man looked like.

Perhaps, Susanna thought grimly, this was her own "moment of madness."

A sudden blast from the steamer's whistle jarred her out of her doleful thoughts. She looked toward the gorge stretching north, then raised her eyes to the massive rock cliffs and climbing woods that rose above them, on the east side of the river.

Beside her, Paul Santi gave a quick smile. "It is just beyond there," he said cheerfully, the words thick with his Italian accent as he pointed upward, to their right. "Bantry Hill."

Bantry Hill. Susanna swallowed against the hot taste of acid rising in her throat. Deirdre had named the place after their Ireland home, but her sister's letters had made it only too clear that she had never found the sort of happiness here she had known as a child on the farm back in Bantry.

When Susanna had first read Deirdre's glowing recollections of life on the farm, she had thought it a bit odd. Hadn't her sister been dead set on getting away from the farm and traveling all over the world? And now here she was reminiscing about a life she had been only too eager to leave.

Still, Susanna reasoned, she, too, had often daydreamed about exploring other places, in spite of her love for home. But she was different. She had never shared Deirdre's hunger for adventure, nor her boldness. Had it not been for the series of devastating events over the past year, she seriously doubted that she would ever have left Ireland.

Certainly not for so harsh a place as this appeared to be. Again she strained to look but could see only a huge, jagged cliff, dense with enormous old trees, their heavy-laden branches waving in the wind like green banners.

"The house cannot be seen from here," said Paul Santi. "Soon, though."

He really seemed quite kind. He had made numerous rather transparent attempts to put Susanna at ease during the journey up the river, talking animatedly about his life, his work, and his own experience of coming to a new land. Apparently, Santi was not only Michael Emmanuel's cousin, but functioned as his assistant as well. He had immigrated to the States only a few years ago, he explained, "at Michael's wish—and his expense."

Susanna turned away for a moment, closing her eyes to shut out the strange, austere landscape. A cooling mist from the river flowed over her. When she opened her eyes again, Paul Santi was watching her closely.

"This is…most difficult for you, no?" he said. "Such a big change. But it will be all right, you will see. Michael is so happy you are coming, and Caterina—she is fairly dancing with excitement! In no time at all you will be right at home with us."

Susanna managed a smile. "You live at Bantry Hill, too, Mr. Santi?"

"*Paul,*" he corrected with a nod. "*Sì,* Michael, he brought me across, and I have stayed with him and Cati ever since. I help him with the music, you see. I am his eyes, Michael says."

Susanna winced. In her anxiety over meeting her brother-in-law, she had temporarily forgotten his blindness. "I understand that he's quite a fine musician, in spite of...everything," she offered.

Again, Santi nodded, more eagerly this time. "Oh, yes, Michael is most gifted! He has built an orchestra"—he lifted a hand as if to grasp just the right word—"*superba.* He conducts. He composes also, *wonderful* music such as you have never heard! Even Bechtold says he is brilliant. Ah—but you must know all this from your sister."

Susanna bit back a caustic reply. Deirdre's letters had told her a great deal about Michael Emmanuel, indeed—but certainly nothing that would incline her to agree with Paul Santi's euphoric rhapsodizing about the man. She took a deep breath and forced a benign expression. "Is it true that he no longer sings?"

She knew the answer to the question but deliberately tried to keep Paul Santi talking. She intended to learn all she could about the man her sister had married, the man who only a few years past had been hailed as the "Voice of the Century."

Once extolled as the premier tenor of Europe, Michael Emmanuel had been well on his way to the same phenomenal success in America when a riding injury claimed his sight. So far as Susanna knew, he had never returned to the operatic stage.

Paul Santi's reply was slow in coming. "Michael sings mostly for Cati these days. And in the church, of course. But the opera—no."

Susanna studied Santi. He was a young man, probably in his midtwenties. He seemed a perpetually cheerful sort, alert and animated. It struck her as somewhat peculiar that, as best she could recall, Deirdre had never once mentioned him in her letters.

Now, for the first time since meeting him at the harbor, Susanna saw his features turn solemn.

"He left the opera because of his accident?" she prompted. Santi glanced at her, then looked away, straightening his eyeglasses a little with his index finger. "It is very difficult, singing and acting on a stage one cannot see."

"Yes, I'm sure it must be," Susanna replied, still watching him. "I can't imagine how he's managed to accomplish as much as he has, being at such a disadvantage."

Santi turned back to her. "Michael does not know...*disadvantage.* You will see.

Ah, here we are." He gestured toward the shore as the steamer began to maneuver toward the dock. "A short carriage ride, and we will be home."

Susanna looked around at the wilderness closing in on them, the fierce-looking cliffs and menacing sky. And once again she closed her eyes to ward off the sight of the wild, threatening landscape Paul Santi referred to as "home."

4

BANTRY HILL

It seemed life held
no future and no past but this.

LOLA RIDGE

Apparently, the carriage driver, Dempsey, was also a part of Michael Emmanuel's household.

Paul Santi's explanation seemed to indicate that Liam Dempsey was Michael's "man"—a combination of household manager and caretaker.

"Dempsey," Santi elaborated, "takes care of "—he paused and gave a light shrug—"everything. Whatever is needed, that is what Dempsey does."

Susanna might have been relieved to see another Irish face in this strange new world she had entered, had that face been more congenial. But Liam Dempsey could have soured new milk with his bushy-browed scowl and gruff, taciturn manner.

The road itself was no less forbidding. Narrow and rutted, it seemed all twists and sharp angles as the carriage wound upward, then upward still more.

The difficult road notwithstanding, Susanna had to concede that the late summer foliage on either side was glorious. Despite the heavy clouds and afternoon gloom, the trees blocked out almost all other views, and the farther uphill they went, the more spectacular the scenery became. Yet it was a fierce, savage kind of beauty, one that she suspected might turn utterly bleak with the onset of winter.

As if to confirm her thoughts, a gust of wind shook the carriage. "We will have a storm soon, I think," offered Paul Santi.

In spite of the sultry heat, Susanna shivered but didn't move away from the window. A moment later, she caught a glimpse of a lighthouse tower and its cupola, but it was quickly gone, lost behind the dense trees.

They drove on, for the most part in silence, jostling over the pits in the road as Dempsey urged the horses at a much faster clip than Susanna felt necessary, or even safe. Startled when they hit a particularly hard bump, she cried out.

Paul Santi gave her a quick smile. At that same instant, they went into a sharp turn. The carriage pitched, forcing Susanna to hug the door.

"The road is deplorable, I know," Santi said. "But we are almost there now."

Still shaken, Susanna caught her breath and tried to anchor her hat more securely. Her hand froze in its movement. This was quite possibly the very road on which Deirdre had met her death.

Chilled despite the August heat, she glanced out the window of the coach. Her nails dug through her thin gloves, into the palms of her hands as she turned to Paul Santi. "This road…is it—" She stopped, her voice faltering.

He looked at her, and Susanna saw understanding, then sympathy, dawn in his eyes. "Yes," he said softly. "But we have already passed…the site of the accident." He paused. "I'm so very sorry, *Signorina* Fallon. It didn't occur to me that you might want to stop—"

Susanna shook her head. "No, not today. Perhaps another time."

Eventually, she would want to see where Deirdre had died. But not just yet. For now, it was enough that she was finally about to meet her niece.

But she was also about to meet the man who had made her sister so unhappy—so altogether miserable, in fact, that she had fled her home, even her child, in the middle of a raging, late-night thunderstorm.

Susanna took in a deep breath, steadying herself for whatever was to come.

At last the carriage slowed. They were passing over an ancient, ivy-covered bridge, its stone walls crumbling in places.

Paul Santi gestured toward the window on his side. "You will see the house in a moment."

Susanna watched, but even after they left the bridge, she could see nothing other than a stand of towering pine trees. They approached a high stone wall, its gate supported by two monolithic stone pillars, and then, without warning, an immense manorial house rose dramatically into view.

Not a house—a *fortress*. Susanna caught a quick breath. No wonder Deirdre had found the place oppressive. Conspicuous in its austerity, Bantry Hill was more than a mansion, but stopped just short of being a castle. It looked to have been quarried from river rock that would withstand the passing of centuries. Given the elevation of the grounds, the steeply pitched roofs, and a tower of several stories that rose off the far end of the main dwelling, the place almost seemed to touch the low-hanging clouds that hovered over it.

As they drew closer, Susanna allowed that her initial impression might have been too severe. It still appeared to be quite a grand house, but not necessarily such a forbidding one. Elms and stately old beech trees, as well as maples and oaks surrounded the structure. And evergreens: she could never have imagined so many evergreen trees on a single property.

A wide, high-ceilinged portico with massive pillars and carved balustrades rimmed the front and as much as could be seen of the south side of the building. Large pieces of wicker with chintz cushions graced the rambling porch, along with baskets and urns of greenery and late summer flowers. A glassed-in conservatory flanked the south side of the house, opening onto terraced gardens and small glades.

Although Susanna couldn't see them from here, she knew from Deirdre's letters there would also be extensive fruit orchards in back of the grounds, and stables. For in spite of—or perhaps, as her sister had suggested, in *defiance* of—the riding accident that had blinded him, Michael Emmanuel had refused to give up his stable of fine horses.

They advanced toward the front of the house, and Susanna caught sight of a marble wishing well, then a child's white shingled playhouse. Her heart quickened at this reminder of her niece, and she found herself feeling a rush of anticipation. Then the coach finally came to a halt in front of the imposing stone stronghold, and her throat tightened with apprehension once again.

As if sensing her trepidation, Paul Santi lightly touched her gloved hand and gave her a reassuring smile. "Here we are at last," he said with convincing warmth. "Welcome home, Susanna. Welcome to Bantry Hill."

5

WELCOME HOME, DR. CARMICHAEL

But still our place is kept
and it will wait...

ADELAIDE A. PROCTER

A weary Andrew Carmichael surveyed his office with a practiced eye. Clearly his receptionist, Myrna Glover, had not been in for quite some time.

It took two trips to carry in the deliveries and newspapers that had been piled up in the small entryway. Inside, dust appeared to have bonded to the furniture, while various leaflets and advertisements lay tossed at random on the reception counter and across the waiting room. There was no sign that human hands had wielded a duster or a broom for several weeks.

Only the examining room appeared to be in order. That stood to reason, since Silas Webster and Phin Carey had seen to Andrew's patients at their own offices in his absence.

Andrew sighed. All Myrna had to do while he was gone was to bring in and sort the mail, tidy the reception area, and keep an eye on things. Little enough work for the pay.

He should have expected this. At her best, Myrna was lazy and indifferent; on her bad days, she was downright useless.

It would seem she had undergone an entire season of bad days.

Perhaps she had decided to seek other employment. If she hadn't, Andrew decided that he would suggest she do exactly that. Without delay.

He checked the small pharmacy, where for the most part he processed his own remedies and, finding things as he had left them, crossed to his office and sank down on the chair behind his massive oak desk—the one extravagance he had permitted himself last year.

If he hadn't been so tired, he would have got up and begun clearing things away. But he had been without food for several hours, and the dull throb that had been prodding at the base of his neck from early morning had sharpened to an ice pick, chipping away at the back of his skull, one piece at a time. He needed to go upstairs and rest before lifting a hand to anything else.

At the moment, however, the act of climbing the steps seemed more effort than he could manage. An ocean voyage might invigorate others, but not him. The sea air, followed by the onslaught of the city's heat, had set his joints to aching with a vengeance.

So with a deep sigh, he shrugged out of his suit coat, loosened his tie a little, and leaned back in the chair. The office was silent and muggy, and it was all too tempting to give into the fatigue and malaise that had settled over him. He could easily fall asleep right here at his desk, if only he didn't have so much to do...

⁓

"Doc! Wake up, Doc!"

Somebody was tugging at his arm as if it were a bell rope. Andrew jerked awake, his heart pounding. Dazed, he struggled to focus. For a moment he couldn't think where he was, only that the ship wasn't rocking.

"Please, Doc, you gotta come! Sergeant Donovan said for you to come *now!"*

Andrew's eyes felt as if someone had tossed sand in them. He stared at the little Negro boy with the dirty shirt, shook his head, and came fully alert. The child was Georgie Pride, a round-faced, wide-eyed youth who lived on the street and earned his keep by shining shoes or running errands for the merchants.

The clanging of fire bells and shouting in the street outside pierced the air, and he sat up. "Georgie? What is it?"

"Fire over to Mrs. Bedford's boardinghouse, Doc! Sergeant Donovan said you were back. Said you need to come!"

Andrew scrambled out of his chair. A glance at his pocket watch showed him it was close on three o'clock. He had slept for over two hours!

He looked around for his case, but Georgie already had it in hand. "C'mon, Doc!"

Not bothering with his suit coat, Andrew followed the boy out of the office. Outside, the acrid smell of smoke clung to the damp August heat like a singed veil. As they took off at a clip, a fire wagon passed them, bells clanging furiously, the horses snorting and pounding the cobbles. A frenzied mob of people surged down Fourth Avenue—men, women, and children, shouting to one another as they went.

Two dozen or more young working women resided at Gladys Bedford's board-inghouse. Andrew thought of them and picked up his pace even more, ignoring the hot shafts of pain that shot up his legs as he ran. By the time they reached

Third Avenue, his throat and mouth felt charred with the taste of smoke, and his eyes burned from the ash raining over the street.

The scene was a nightmare unleashed. The modest, three-story brick structure was surrounded by onlookers, with still more gathering nearby. In an instant, Andrew took in the dense black smoke spiraling above the building, the exploding bricks, the white, panicked faces at the windows on the third floor.

Most of the windows were open, and the screams of the women could be heard over the din in the street. Glass shattered, and Andrew looked to the side of the building just in time to see another window exploding.

The commotion spooked a horse standing in front of the building, and the animal went bolting down the street, dragging its empty buggy behind. Some of the bystanders were screaming, many weeping, while others merely stood gaping at the building as if transfixed.

Two fire wagons were on the scene by now, with men passing buckets and hoisting ladders. Frank Donovan was at the front of the boardinghouse, with two other policemen at the side, trying to push the crowd back.

Andrew sent the excited Georgie across the street. The boy protested, but Andrew jerked his head toward Seitzman's Bakery. "If you must watch, you do it from there," he ordered. "No closer. You're not to come back here, no matter what! Understand?"

He turned then and wedged his way through the crowd, heading for Frank Donovan. Flames were shooting up toward the roof. Women crowded at the upper windows, screaming and crying for help. Sparks and cinders rained down, and Andrew beat at the scorching ash with his hands as he made his way through the mob.

The policemen were shouting at the bystanders to get back, and although a few in the crowd began to retreat, most ignored the warnings and simply continued to stay where they were, gawking at the fire. At the front, Andrew saw Frank Donovan jump astride a dun-colored police mount. Hauling hard on the reins, the tall, powerful figure drove the horse down the edge of the crowd, shouting as only Frank could shout when enraged.

"Get back! Get back now, you bloodthirsty fools, or you'll be burnin' right along with the building! Move, I said!"

The big Irish police sergeant pulled a pistol and shot into the air. The horse reared and shook his head in an obvious attempt to lose the wild man on his back. But Frank Donovan rode on, pounding down the row of bystanders, shouting and shooting well over the heads of the crowd as he went.

Within seconds, the crowd had dispersed, most of them withdrawing to a safer distance, some even leaving the scene entirely, though grumbling and cursing as they went. A few, however, merely crossed the street and stood watching.

Frank reined his mount to a halt in front of Andrew. His mouth below the dark red mustache was set in a hard scowl as he holstered his gun. "Vultures!"

He spat the word out, swung down from the saddle, then turned on Andrew. "And what took *you* so long?"

"How did you know I was back?"

"Had one of the boyos watchin' your building now and then," the policeman replied. He grabbed Andrew's arm and yanked him back. "Watch yourself!"

His dark-eyed gaze swept Andrew head to toe, and he suddenly grinned, a flash of white in the smoke-blackened face. "Well, welcome home, Doc," he cracked, tipping his hat back on his head. "And about time, I'm thinkin'."

Andrew ignored the jibe, noticing for the first time the group of women huddled off to the side of the boardinghouse. Many looked disheveled, their faces sooty and streaked from weeping. Some stood holding each other, while others appeared to be dazed, perhaps even in shock.

He turned to Frank Donovan. "Lodgers?"

The policeman nodded. "Aye. None seem in a bad way. Just rattled some, as you'd expect."

"How bad is it, Frank?"

The other's mouth turned hard again. "Worst of the damage is to the building. Some of the lasses weren't home from work yet. Those who were, we got out in good time. But there's still a few upstairs. They'll have to jump, if the smoke don't get 'em first. The stairway is burning, and there's no steps down the back."

Andrew saw two firemen hurriedly stretching a safety net. Another, his face blackened, came vaulting out the door, shouting, "Hurry it up with that net! Everyone's out but the top floor, and they don't have long! We're losing it!"

"I should see to those women," Andrew said, starting off.

But Frank caught his arm. "No, you stay here. We'll need you for the jumpers. Dr. Cole has things in hand over there."

Andrew frowned. "Dr. Cole?"

The policeman was eyeing the crowd, but turned back to Andrew. "Ah, that's right. You haven't met our lady doc as yet, have you?"

"Dr. Cole is a *woman*?"

"Last time I looked," Frank said dryly. He motioned to one of his men to go around to the side of the building. "You'll have to wait for an introduction, I'm afraid."

Andrew turned and saw a small, fair-haired woman intent on examining a young girl's hands.

"Aye, that's herself," Frank said. "Dr. Cole—Dr. *Bethany* Cole. Right bonny for a lady doc, wouldn't you say?" Frank was watching him closely, his dark eyes glinting with a trace of amusement. "It's said that she—"

Abruptly, he broke off, his words swallowed up by the cries and shouts behind him as the women trapped inside the building began to jump.

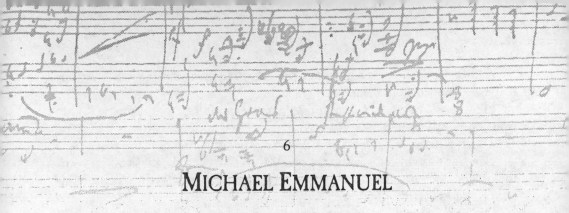

6

MICHAEL EMMANUEL

There was a man whom
Sorrow named his friend...

W. B. YEATS

Susanna had rehearsed her first meeting with Michael Emmanuel dozens of times, but now that the moment was here she felt suddenly panicked and wanted nothing more than to flee from it.

Paul Santi flung open the massive oak doors and stood back, waiting for her to step inside. Immediately she heard the laughter of children and what sounded like the barking of a very large dog. An instant later, an enormous wolfhound came barreling down the hallway, two shrieking little girls hot on his tail. Spying Susanna and Paul Santi, the dog came to an abrupt halt directly in front of them. The children, however, merely giggled and reversed directions, quickly disappearing down the hallway.

The wolfhound, a light fawn-colored giant with a deep chest, sat staring at Susanna. His tail whipped about in circles, his large head cocked to one side as he took her measure.

"*Signorina,* meet Gus," said Paul Santi, laughing as he reached to rub the big hound's ears. "He makes himself out to be the bully of Bantry Hill, but don't let him fool you. He is nothing more than an overgrown, overindulged *bambino.*"

The wolfhound shot Santi an indignant look at this uncommon lack of respect.

Susanna was no stranger to the great hounds of Ireland. Indeed, she fancied them and was thoroughly pleased to find one on the premises. Gus was by far the largest of the breed she had ever encountered. With only the slightest hesitation, she extended her hand to the dog, allowing him to examine her scent. He wasted no time in nuzzling the palm of her hand, his tail wagging with almost comic excitement.

31

Paul Santi clapped his hands together. "Ah! He likes you! He will give you no peace from now on, I fear."

"He's grand," Susanna said, smiling, grateful that, at least for the moment, the wolfhound had eased her nervousness.

"Those children—" she said, remembering the little girls.

"Caterina's playmates." Santi shrugged. "Cati will be in the music room with the others. There's a small birthday party for her today. That's why Michael did not come to the harbor with me."

"Oh, no!" Susanna brought a hand to her forehead. "I can't believe I forgot!"

But she had. In all the confusion and flurry of the past few weeks, she had completely overlooked the fact that her niece would turn four years old today.

"You mustn't trouble yourself," Paul Santi assured her. "Cati will understand, I assure you. Here, let's have your wrap, and I'll take you to her."

Susanna loosened her shawl and handed it to him, hoping he wouldn't notice its shabby condition. She took in the lofty vestibule that rose to a skylight three stories above and a magnificent staircase, its second-floor landing emphasized by a broad, stained-glass window with jewel-colored panes.

She was surprised at the lack of any visible ostentation. The house was cool—a welcome respite from the August heat. The walls were paneled in light mahogany, and the tall windows were draped only in sheer fabric, as if to allow as much light as possible. To the left, French doors stood open on a large drawing room, tastefully furnished. She caught a glimpse of a fireplace, framed by a wide mantel and colorful tiles.

Lush flowers, arranged carefully in porcelain vases, splashed the vestibule with bright hues, and a lovely Oriental carpet in delicate shades adorned its center. A restrained collection of oils and fine prints enhanced the overall air of gracious, but comfortable, living.

For a moment Susanna felt a vague sense of confusion. Deirdre had written of the house's "gloom" and "depressing atmosphere." But what she had seen so far shattered her preconceptions. She had been expecting the garish trappings of extreme wealth and luxury: ponderous furniture, perhaps, and tasteless accessories. Instead, her first glimpse of the house was actually inviting—and anything but dismal.

With the wolfhound loping along in front of them, Paul Santi led her down a long hallway, off which several rooms opened. Although some were only dimly lit, none were completely dark. They passed what was obviously the library, a thoroughly masculine-looking room, high-ceilinged and spacious, with walls of shelved books and an immense, octagonal desk.

The hallway was wide and well-lighted, and Paul Santi, lean and not much taller than Susanna, set a brisk pace for them.

Next to the library, they passed a room which looked to be an office, with a large, cluttered desk and more bookshelves lining the walls. Adjoining it—or more accurately, an extension of it—was another small study, crowded with storage cabinets and a variety of musical instrument cases.

It was obvious where the party was taking place. The hallway ended abruptly, converging on a large, open room from which poured a considerable commotion. Someone was playing a piano with great energy, accompanied by the uninhibited laughter of children.

They stopped just inside the doorway, and Susanna stood staring at the unlikely scene within. Only in the vaguest sense was she aware of the distinct Florentine flavor of the spacious room: the black-and-white marble floor, a variety of sculpted busts resting on pedestals, a few well-worn damask chairs, and several pieces of colorful Italian pottery.

Several musical instruments were scattered about the room, but her gaze quickly went to the splendid rosewood grand piano, at which a handsome, middle-aged woman was seated, pounding the keys with enthusiasm. At the end of the room, a circle of small children squealed and bobbed up and down around a dark-haired man who towered over them. Blindfolded, he was holding up a strip of paper and laughing as a little girl turned him round and round, then gave him a sound push toward the wall.

"Careful, Papa!" the child cried, then promptly covered her mouth with both hands, consumed with laughter.

At that instant, the wolfhound broke free and went charging into their midst, clearly intent on joining the fun.

Susanna realized at once that the little girl was her niece, Caterina. The tall, blindfolded man had to be her brother-in-law, Michael Emmanuel.

Yet for the very life of her, she could not comprehend why a man unable to see should be wearing a blindfold.

～

Suddenly the child turned toward the doorway, her eyes locking on Susanna.

She squealed and tugged at her father's hand, pulling him away from the wall. *"Papa! She's here! Aunt Susanna is here!"*

Smiling—and still blindfolded—Michael Emmanuel allowed himself to be hauled along by his daughter as she and the wolfhound came leaping across the room.

The little girl came to a breathless halt directly in front of Susanna, her dark, piquant features pinched with excitement. Finally, as if she could bear it no longer, she clasped her hands together in front of her face and gave a cry of pure delight. "Aunt Susanna! You *did* come! You are finally here!"

She was a wisp of a child with a wild mane of jet-black curls, a sprite dressed in yellow-and-white ruffled muslin and shiny black slippers laced with ribbons. Even if this had not been her niece, Susanna would have found it impossible to resist the dancing eyes and sharply defined features. She opened her arms, and without the slightest display of shyness, the little girl swooped into her embrace.

As she held her small niece snugly against her, Susanna was aware of Michael Emmanuel, who stood quietly waiting, the blindfold still in place.

Caterina pulled free just enough to look up at Susanna. "I knew you'd arrive in time for my birthday party, Aunt Susanna! I told Papa you would, didn't I, Papa? Did you know I am four years old today, Aunt Susanna?"

Susanna tried to apologize and explain why she hadn't brought a gift, but Caterina seemed not in the least disappointed. "*You* are my gift, Aunt Susanna! The best gift of all!"

Paul Santi moved to intervene. "Here, Cati, let your Aunt Susanna catch her breath. Your papa might also like to say hello, you know."

He went on then to offer a quick introduction, upon which Michael Emmanuel extended both hands to Susanna as if he could see exactly where she stood. Susanna hesitated an instant, then gave him her hand, which he clasped between his much larger ones.

"*Benvenuto alla nostra sede*, Susanna." *Welcome to our home.*

"Papa," Caterina said sternly, "you said we must speak English to Aunt Susanna, remember?"

Susanna smiled down at her niece. "It's all right, Caterina. I understand Italian—at least a little."

"Ah, of course, you would, with your music," said Michael Emmanuel. "But Caterina is right. We should speak the English most. We are Americans now."

He pressed Susanna's fingers lightly before releasing her hand. "We are delighted to have you with us, Susanna. I hope you will consider this your home."

Caterina broke in with a giggle. "Papa, you are still wearing the blindfold!"

He laughed and reached to remove the cloth from his eyes. Susanna was puzzled when his eyes remained closed even after he dropped the blindfold away. Puzzled, but oddly relieved.

She tried to study him without being too obvious, then remembered that his blindness would prevent his being aware of her scrutiny. Just as Deirdre had said, he was large enough to be intimidating. Yet he was not quite as Susanna had envisioned him. His voice was unexpectedly gentle, even mild, and his smile hinted of uncertainty. In truth, his overall demeanor seemed surprisingly void of the arrogance and flourish she had expected.

It came to her that there was also an air of something akin to sadness about the man, and again she felt an unsettling flicker of confusion.

"This child shows her papa no mercy," he said, ruffling his daughter's hair with one hand and dangling the blindfold from the other. "She insists I must follow the rules of the game like everyone else, even though I hardly have need of the blindfold." He dipped his head a little, adding, "And now, Caterina, you should go back to your guests, I think."

"But, Papa, I want to stay with Aunt Susanna!"

He shook his head. "Your aunt has only just now arrived. You will have all the time you wish to spend with her later. Besides, you must be polite to your guests. Go along now."

He turned to Paul Santi. "Would you mind keeping an eye on them, please, Pauli? Only for another half-hour or so."

The younger man rolled his eyes good-naturedly and smiled at Susanna. "If I must. Come along, Cati," he said, reaching for the girl's hand. "Let us see if I can find this donkey in need of a tail."

Still, Caterina hesitated. "Papa, you won't forget that I'm allowed to have supper with Aunt Susanna? My *birthday* supper."

Michael Emmanuel lifted his hands in a gesture of hopelessness. "How can you possibly think of supper? You and your friends have been eating all the afternoon!"

"Papa—"

He laughed. "*Sì*, of course, you will have supper with us. Go now. Your friends will be leaving soon."

He waited while Caterina scampered off with the wolfhound and Paul Santi firmly in tow, then turned back to Susanna. "If you are not too tired, Susanna, why don't we find a quiet place and talk a little before you go upstairs?"

Susanna looked at him. The last thing she wanted at the moment was a private conversation with this man, but he was already offering his arm.

Before she could respond, however, he turned, saying, "Ah, I almost forgot. There is someone else who is eager to meet you." He called to the woman seated at the piano. "Rosa, come meet Susanna."

Susanna studied the pianist as she approached, a strikingly attractive woman who appeared to be in her late forties. Her glossy dark hair was streaked with silver and brushed smoothly away from her face into a thick chignon, revealing strong features and dark, keen eyes that Susanna sensed would miss nothing. Not tall, she nevertheless conveyed a sense of utter confidence and authority.

The moment Michael Emmanuel introduced them, Susanna recognized the woman's name. Deirdre's letters had mentioned Rosa Navaro, the renowned opera diva who was both a neighbor and a close friend of the family.

"Welcome, Susanna," she said in a low, well-modulated voice, reaching for Susanna's hands. "How good it is that you have come. Caterina has been wild with impatience."

Susanna felt an instant of discomfort as she recalled that Deirdre had never trusted "the Navaro woman," had in fact thought her "meddlesome" and "presumptuous."

She battled for a moment with those conflicting feelings. Deirdre had often been unmercifully ruthless in her character assessments. Rare indeed was the person who won her sister's unqualified respect or admiration. Hadn't Susanna herself suffered more than her share of her sister's barbed criticisms?

Still, it seemed disloyal, somehow, to disregard entirely Deirdre's assessment of Rosa Navaro. And yet Susanna could not help responding to the warmth of the woman's greeting and the faint glint of humor in her dark eyes.

Looking into those eyes, Susanna decided that, for the moment at least, she would put her sister's remarks out of her mind. She smiled, meeting the other woman's welcome with a cordial greeting of her own.

The wolfhound skidded up just then, falling in beside Michael Emmanuel, who gave a quick flick of his hand. "Everything is under control, Gus," he said dryly. "You may stay with Caterina."

The dog apparently deemed Susanna a reliable companion for his master, for after only the slightest delay, he turned and trotted back to the party.

"If Rosa doesn't mind," said Michael Emmanuel, "we will leave her at the mercy of the children for now. The two of you can get better acquainted this evening. I took the liberty of planning a small supper," he explained. "Just a few friends, including Rosa."

Susanna had all she could do not to groan aloud. She felt almost limp with fatigue, wilted from the heat, and increasingly anxious to get away from her towering brother-in-law. She would have liked nothing better than to spend a quiet hour or so with Caterina and then retire early. Even so, she managed what she hoped was a polite, if not exactly enthusiastic, response.

Rosa Navaro gave her a quick look of understanding. "I'm sure Susanna is exhausted from the trip, Michael. You must allow her enough time for a good rest before evening."

"Oh...*sì*. Of course! If you would rather go upstairs right away, Susanna, we can talk later."

Susanna was sorely tempted to accept his suggestion. But she would have to face him sooner or later. Perhaps it would be best to simply have it over with. He would undoubtedly want to question her to some extent before allowing her to supervise Caterina, and she conceded, albeit grudgingly, that he was well within his rights to do so.

For that matter, she had her own questions to ask. So this time when he offered his arm, she took it.

7

A SOUL ALONE

So goes the lone of soul
amid the world...

DORA SHORTER SIGERSON

The drawing room was large but inviting and seemed to lend itself more to comfort than to formality. The windows were tall and narrow, the draperies a rich, golden hue, the sturdy but finely molded tables uncluttered with ornaments. Soft-toned Persian carpets were laid here and there over gleaming floors, while tapestry and damask chairs in cream and varying shades of brown added a feeling of warmth and coziness.

Michael Emmanuel waited until Susanna took a plump, comfortable chair in front of the fireplace before seating himself in a massive armchair opposite her. "What would you like, Susanna?" he said, ringing a small bell. "Tea or coffee? Or a cold drink, perhaps?"

Susanna clasped her hands in her lap, trying to still their trembling. "Tea would be fine, thank you."

They sat in silence until a small, middle-aged woman with a piercing stare arrived to serve their beverages and a tray of pastries. Michael Emmanuel introduced the woman as Mrs. Dempsey. The wife, no doubt, of the sour-faced driver who had brought them upriver.

The woman's demeanor toward her employer seemed surprisingly casual, more maternal than subservient, and after she left the room, Michael Emmanuel confirmed that she was no ordinary employee. "At one time, the Dempseys were neighbors and good friends to my grandparents in Ireland. Some years ago, I brought them here to work for me. They are like family, you see."

At some point he had slipped on a pair of dark glasses, and Susanna wondered why. It occurred to her that the glasses made him appear even more distant, less approachable. She found it almost impossible to think of this man as related to her in even the most obscure way. He was a forbidding, foreign stranger. And from what Deirdre had told her, his marriage to her sister had been a thoroughly unhappy, if not actually an *unholy,* alliance.

She caught herself resisting the urge to study him, in part because his very presence disturbed her. In addition, she feared that by observing him too closely, she might be guilty of taking advantage of his blindness.

Instead, she let her gaze wander aimlessly around the room, curious as to whether anything of Deirdre's influence might remain. Given her sister's fondness for the flamboyant, however, she saw nothing in the quiet charm of her surroundings that hinted of Deirdre's taste.

When she finally turned her attention back to Michael Emmanuel, she was again struck by the sense of *separateness* that seemed to hover about him. With his dark head bent low, a stoneware mug of steaming coffee cradled in both hands, he seemed almost removed from his surroundings, as though a kind of invisible barrier set him apart.

Susanna knew little about the man, only what Deirdre had written of him. His earlier mention of his Irish grandparents reminded her that he was indeed of mixed parentage: his mother had been Irish; his father, Italian. But in his appearance, as in his speech, the Mediterranean had clearly vanquished the Celt. There was no visible trace of the Irish in the arrogant Roman nose, the generous mouth, the darkly bearded face and dusky complexion.

Like his accent, and despite his claim of being "American now," the man was clearly Tuscan through and through.

He was, as Susanna had already observed, a very large man. She had been prepared for this, of course. In the first wild throes of her infatuation, Deirdre had spared no detail when she wrote of her new swain's "great stature," the "magnificent sweep of his shoulders," his "powerful and manly bearing."

In truth, Susanna, then still in her teens, had paid her sister's ravings little heed. Deirdre had always tended to be somewhat wild-eyed about her romances, of which there had been many. At the time, there had seemed no reason to believe that Michael Emmanuel's appeal would last any longer than that of his predecessors.

But Deirdre had surprised everyone by marrying her Italian suitor, supposedly at his insistence. Watching him now, Susanna found herself vaguely puzzled that this man had managed to capture her older sister's affection so completely, and in such a brief time.

Her confusion had little to do with his blindness, although the Deirdre she remembered surely would have found such an affliction disturbing, to say the least. Of course, he had not been blind when they married, and to be fair, Susanna had to concede that he did possess a certain dark handsomeness. Even now, in casual attire and with a somewhat rumpled appearance, he bore a kind of unstudied elegance that, combined with the dazzle and allure celebrity had always held for Deirdre, might easily have charmed her sister, especially in the beginning.

Still, he did not seem at all the type of man Deirdre would have ordinarily fallen for, certainly not the kind of man Susanna would have expected her to marry. Deirdre had always favored the slender, golden-haired, "aristocratic" types—the bloodless English squire sort of fellow. Indeed, most of her sister's beaus had been predictably alike: slim, fair-haired, pretentious—and, more often than not, drearily self-important.

Michael Emmanuel, however, was not only a startling physical contrast to the others, but had so far displayed none of the dash and debonair fussiness Deirdre had seemed to find so attractive. To the contrary, he appeared to be a solid, *earthy* type of man: quiet, self-contained, and without the "glitter" Susanna would have associated with a luminary of the music world.

Of course, she had met the man less than an hour ago. Appearances could be deceiving.

Deirdre had been deceived. And she had paid for it dearly. For no apparent reason, Susanna found herself remembering the early weeks when Michael Emmanuel had been, in Deirdre's words, "pursuing" her. It seemed that during that same time, an aspiring concert pianist had also caught her sister's fancy. Soon, however, all mention of the pianist was forgotten, and no other name but that of Michael Emmanuel filled Deirdre's letters. Unexpectedly came the image of a younger, laughing Deirdre, framed between two besotted suitors as they made their way down a dusty road to a penny fair. The truth was that Deirdre—at least in her adolescent years—had always loved being the center of attention. By her own admission she had thrived on the headiness, the feeling of power, that the pursuit by more than one beau seemed to give her.

And she had never hesitated to play one against the other as it suited her purposes.

Once again Susanna was assaulted by a sense of disloyalty, the same sense she had felt upon meeting Rosa Navaro. She forcibly shook off the unpleasant memory of her sister's youthful coquetry, reminding herself that she had never really known Deirdre as a mature woman, after all. Surely she would have changed a great deal since their final parting years before.

Still, Susanna couldn't completely dismiss the fact that Deirdre had written of her attraction to another man in the early days of her courtship with Michael Emmanuel. Perhaps, had her sister chosen differently, she might have found happiness.

She might even still be alive.

~

Michael had heard the reserve, the edge, in her voice almost from the beginning.

The girl resented him; that much was clear. Perhaps her resentment shouldn't baffle him. He had no way of knowing, after all, what Deirdre might have written to her younger sister over the years. Although she always insisted that she and Susanna were too far apart in age and too different in nature to be close, Michael knew many letters had been posted to Ireland throughout the months preceding Deirdre's death.

He drew a long breath. She was here—that was all that mattered for now. She had come, and he was convinced that Caterina would benefit greatly from the presence of a younger woman in her life, especially given the fact that Susanna was her aunt by blood.

There was no doubting Moira Dempsey's love for the child, but her advancing years and her household duties made it impossible for her to provide Caterina with the attention and understanding she would need in the years ahead.

Still, Susanna was very young. More than once Michael had wondered if at twenty-three she might not be *too* young for what would be required of her. She was little more than a girl herself. Yet he was asking her not only to become a member of their family, but to assume a highly responsible role as Caterina's companion and governess.

When he had first learned of Susanna's circumstances, it had seemed a perfect arrangement. Susanna was in need of a home, and Caterina, he believed, was in need of her aunt. He had prayed long and hard over the decision, and at the time he believed God's direction to be clearly given. Now that his plan had actually been set in motion, however, he was faced with the enormity of his decision. He could only hope he had not made a terrible mistake.

He took encouragement from the warmth he had heard in her tone toward Caterina—and in the firmness and steadiness he sensed, despite her youth and despite the fact that she must be overwhelmed and perhaps even a little frightened by her new circumstances. With that in mind, he determined he must be very careful in his behavior toward her. Still, there were things that needed to be discussed, matters to be explained and settled.

Before he had a chance to say anything, however, she took him off guard with a declaration of her own.

"I'm very anxious to hear about Deirdre," she said in a voice that made it clear she would not be denied. "I would like you to tell me how my sister died. And why."

Michael drew in a long breath. He had expected this, but not so soon, and not with such directness.

Very carefully, he set his coffee mug on the table. How much should he tell her? How much *could* he tell her, about the tragedy of her sister's death—and the travesty of his marriage?

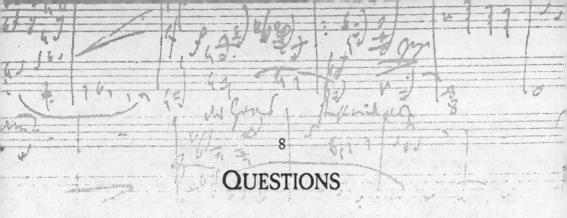

8

QUESTIONS

The hope of Truth grows stronger,
day by day...

JAMES RUSSELL LOWELL

Susanna could see him struggling for words. He set his cup down on the table, raked a hand through his unruly black hair—which was glazed with quite a lot of silver, she now noticed for the first time—and gripped his knees with both hands as he faced the cold fireplace.

"I did write to you of the accident—"

"You did," Susanna interrupted. "But—"

"The storm, the washed-out road—"

"Yes, but I need to know more than what you told me in your letters," she broke in again. "There must be more. You didn't actually—explain."

She clenched her hands even more tightly, ignoring the cup of tea on the table beside her. "I've yet to understand what Deirdre was doing on the road in such a terrible storm—and in the middle of the night."

Other than a slight clenching of his jaw, he gave no visible sign that he'd heard her, much less any indication that he intended to elaborate further.

"Surely you knew I would have questions," Susanna pressed. He turned his face slightly toward her.

"Of course," he said quietly. "But I think this is not the time that I should answer those questions. After you are rested and have had an opportunity to become more settled with us, perhaps then, we will talk."

Suspicion reared in Susanna, but she managed to check the retort that sprang to her lips. Clearly, he meant to put her off if she allowed it.

But why?

"Mr. Emmanuel—"

"Michael," he said with a slight turn of his hand.

"Michael," Susanna said tightly. "I understand that it might be difficult for you

to discuss this, but please try to imagine what it's been like for me. I had not seen my sister for years. When she died, I was an ocean removed. There was no chance to say good-bye. I couldn't even attend the burial." She caught a breath, then added, "I need to know how she died, what happened."

His features registered no change of emotion, except for a slight tightening about his mouth. "*Sì*, you are right that it is difficult for me to speak of this. And I know it must have been most painful for you, as well, to lose your sister when you are so far away. As for your questions, naturally I understand your need to know, but you must see that this is not the best time for us to discuss these things. I would prefer that we wait, please."

He would *prefer*—

Again, Susanna fought back an angry response. A confrontation was hardly the best way to begin her association with this man. Even though Deirdre had been gone for over a year now, and although he displayed no noticeable signs of grief, she had to allow for the possibility that he *might* still be in mourning.

But what about *her* grief? Ever since she'd made her decision to come to America, only her determination to finally learn the truth about Deirdre's death had eclipsed her eagerness to become a part of Caterina's life.

Now she was here. After one brief meeting with Caterina, she knew the child would easily win her heart. But it was blazingly evident that she would learn nothing more about the accident in which her sister had died until Michael Emmanuel was good and ready to tell her.

So, then—apparently he was just what Deirdre had made him out to be, an obstinate, difficult man. Bent on having his own way. Stubborn and unyielding.

Her earlier exhaustion suddenly renewed itself, and Susanna had to admit that even if she were so foolhardy as to instigate a skirmish with her daunting brother-in-law on her first day at Bantry Hill, she was far too depleted to carry it off. There would be time enough. He couldn't avoid her questions forever; she wouldn't allow it.

Sooner or later she would compel him to tell her everything. For the moment, however, perhaps he was right. Perhaps it would be best to have that discussion after she had rested and could think more clearly.

Besides, there was another subject waiting to be raised. "Very well," she said as evenly as she could manage. "I can wait. For now, perhaps we should discuss my position here, exactly what will be expected of me."

She could actually see him relax a little as he lifted his hands from his knees and flexed his fingers, then turned toward her. "I would hope, Susanna, that you will not think of this as a *position*. It is as I told you: I want you to consider this your home, and be a part of our family. We want very much that you should be happy here."

"I appreciate that," Susanna said. "But in our correspondence, we agreed that I would assume certain responsibilities with Caterina. Which, of course, I'm only too happy to do," she added quickly.

He lifted one hand in a casual gesture. Not for the first time, Susanna noticed his hands. Large as they were, there was nothing clumsy or coarse in their appearance; to the contrary, they conveyed an unexpected grace, a quality of refinement that somehow caused one to follow every gesture, every movement, no matter how slight.

She glanced quickly away.

"What I am hoping," he went on, "is that you will give Cati your companionship, your affection," he said. "You indicated that you might be willing to instruct her as well, to act as her governess if I wanted."

Susanna nodded, then remembered his blindness. "I should be more than willing to teach Caterina, if you like. I served as governess to the Maher children for a time, after the death of our parents—"

"Your father died only a few weeks after your mother," he put in. "That must have been most difficult for you."

Susanna's throat tightened at the memory of her parents. "Difficult, yes, but not all that much of a shock," she said softly. "They were very close, my parents. Once my mother was gone, my father seemed to fade almost overnight. He had been ill with his heart for a long time as it was. Without her, he simply—gave up."

Michael Emmanuel leaned toward her a little more. "To lose a parent is a great grief. I still remember the pain of losing my mother."

Susanna thought it strange that he would refer to his pain at the loss of his mother but not his wife. Still, they had been speaking of her parents, so perhaps she was making something of nothing.

Watching him, she was caught by the contrasts in his face. He looked younger than she'd expected, and in spite of the strength and ruggedness of his features, she thought she could detect faint touches of humor about his mouth. True, the unyielding set of his jaw attested to the stubbornness she had glimpsed earlier, but at the same time, her long-held notion of him as a hard, unkind man wavered slightly under the unexpected air of courtesy and even gentleness in his demeanor.

She was still unnerved by the dark glasses, the barrier they seemed to erect, the way they distanced him, precluding so much as a glimpse into his thoughts or emotions. It would be extremely difficult to gauge this man's feelings, unless he chose to reveal them. Either his sightless, unopened eyes or else the dark glasses would serve as closed shutters to his soul.

She realized with a start that he had apparently asked her a question.

"I'm sorry," she said, embarrassed that he might have caught her studying him so intently.

"Your music," he repeated. "I understand you are an accomplished pianist and organist."

"Not all that accomplished. Competent, perhaps." The fact was, Susanna loved both instruments with a passion, but in the face of Michael Emmanuel's genius, she knew whatever talent she possessed would surely shrink and seem lackluster, at best.

He smiled a little. "Well, please know that you are most welcome to use the piano in the music room. You will also find an adequate spinet in Caterina's playroom. She is trying to learn, so perhaps you will work with her a little?"

"Yes, I'd enjoy that." Susanna hesitated, feeling the need to reassure him as to her capability. "Just so you'll know, Mr.—*Michael*—I *am* a fairly experienced teacher. In both piano and organ, in addition to classroom curriculum. I would have tried to support myself with my teaching, but our community was poor, you see, and there was simply no interest or demand for an instructor. I could have gone to Dublin, of course, but when you wrote about Caterina—"

She suddenly realized she was rambling and broke off, leaving the rest unspoken.

"I'm sure it will be our good fortune that you chose to come here, Susanna." He paused. "You seem to have had the benefit of an excellent education. Yet Deirdre—" He stopped, as if the name of his deceased wife threatened to curb his tongue. "Deirdre admitted to little formal schooling, other than her music."

"That was her choice," Susanna said. Then, anxious that she not seem to speak ill of her sister, she hurried to explain. "We had sponsors—the Mahers—who were quite wealthy Anglo-Irish. They took an interest in us because of their fondness for our parents. Without them, any formal education would have been impossible. They offered Deirdre the same opportunities as they did me, but she chose to concentrate only on her singing."

"But you went further."

"Yes. I had a desire to teach. But even so, music was always very important to me."

Susanna cringed. She must sound like a mawkish schoolgirl.

But Michael Emmanuel merely smiled and gave a slight nod. "I think you will find Caterina to be very much like you in that respect." He paused. "So, tell me, do you also share…your sister's love of singing?"

"I—no. Deirdre had all the vocal talent in the family." Actually, Susanna found much joy in singing, as well as in playing the instruments. But she had always known her vocal talent to be smaller than Deirdre's, so she confined her singing to those times when she was completely alone and would not be compared to her sister.

In truth, it seemed that the balance scales had always tipped heavily to Deirdre's benefit, not only in terms of musical ability, but in appearance as well. Where Deirdre had been petite but buxom, Susanna was tall and too slender by far. Her sister had possessed the dramatic, attention-getting features and engaging personality most men could not resist. As for Susanna, boys her own age had usually treated her like a chum—or, worse still, like a sister—while older, more attractive men invariably seemed to shy away from her.

She had never measured up to her older sister in any capacity, nor did she delude herself that she ever would. And given her present situation, perhaps that wasn't such a bad thing. If Michael Emmanuel *was* still grieving for Deirdre, at least she would not serve as any sort of awkward or painful reminder of his loss.

"It would seem," said Michael Emmanuel, "that you are more than qualified to instruct Caterina. But let me emphasize that first of all I would like you to concentrate on feeling at home with us and learning to think of yourself as family. You are Caterina's aunt and, as such, will be accorded the respect of the entire household." He stopped, then added, "You will, however, be paid a fair wage for your responsibilities as her governess."

Susanna might have protested, had she not been so overcome with relief. She had feared being entirely dependent on her brother-in-law's largess, but now apparently she would actually be in a position to earn her keep. There was such a thing as being *too* proud, after all. She was a good teacher, and she knew it; she would accept whatever compensation he offered and be grateful for it. At some point, when Caterina was older, she could use any acquired savings to establish her own home and take responsibility for herself.

"Thank you," she said quietly. "That's very generous of you." She tasted her tea, found it cold, and set the cup back on the table.

"It will be of great help to have you here for Caterina," he said, leaning back in the chair and steepling his fingers in front of his chin. "Of necessity, I must sometimes travel. And during rehearsal, I occasionally stay in the city at night. Even when I'm here, at home," he continued, "I must work a great deal. It has been very difficult, to balance all the work and make certain Caterina isn't neglected."

He took a long sip of coffee, then went on. "You will find Cati an easy child to be with, I think," he said. "At the risk of sounding prideful, I believe my daughter to be very sweet-spirited, with a genuine interest in others and a desire to please."

He turned toward her with a rueful smile. "She is also incessantly curious, somewhat precocious, and can be a bit of a minx. At times she may try your patience."

"The Maher children I cared for were twin boys of eight years with unlimited energy—and boundless mischief," Susanna said dryly. "I somehow expect that Caterina will be a welcome change."

"Let us hope you feel the same in a few days," he said, still smiling.

He got to this feet then, indicating that their discussion was at an end. Susanna also stood, waiting for her "dismissal."

"I've kept you longer than I should have," he said. "I'll have Mrs. Dempsey show you to your rooms and help you get settled."

Susanna turned to go, but his voice, low with an unmistakable note of kindness, stopped her. "Susanna, if there is anything you need, you have only to ask. Supper is at seven, by the way, and we are very informal. Tonight, as I said, will be only family and a few close friends."

He stepped closer to her, and for an instant Susanna had the irrational thought that he was about to touch her. She suppressed a shudder and stepped back.

As if he had sensed her withdrawal, he also moved away. Immediately, he rang for the housekeeper, who appeared so quickly Susanna wondered if she'd been standing right outside the door.

Upon leaving the room, Susanna glanced back to see him standing at the fireplace. As she watched, he removed the dark glasses and slipped them into his coat pocket, then passed his hand over his eyes in a gesture that hinted of extreme weariness.

She hesitated, struck by an inexplicable twinge of self-reproach at the coldness and utter lack of courtesy she had shown this man, in spite of the graciousness—and generosity—he had displayed toward her. Shaken, her mind swimming with confusion and fatigue, she had to fight the urge to break into a run in her haste to escape him—and the troubling tumult of emotions he'd managed to set off in her.

9

AFTER THE FIRE

*She smiled and that transfigured me
And left me but a lout.*

W. B. YEATS

By late afternoon, the fire was out, and no lives had been lost. Most of the injuries ranged from smoke inhalation to a few minor burns. There were a number of sprained or broken limbs, but only one or two had suffered more serious injuries. Those who required further medical treatment had already been transported to the hospital by ambulance. The rest of the women, at least those who had nowhere else to go, were being packed into a police wagon and taken to one of the city jails for temporary shelter.

The building itself was still standing, but no one would be living there for a very long time. Andrew Carmichael and Frank Donovan both agreed, however, that all things considered, the situation could have been much worse.

As they stood talking and surveying the fallen bricks and other debris, Frank broke into a grin. Andrew, who was quite certain he had never been so tired in his life, was at a loss to imagine what Donovan found so amusing.

"Well, now, it strikes me, your honor," said the policeman, his always thick Irish accent more pronounced than ever, "that this is the first time I've ever seen you with so much as a wrinkled shirt collar, much less a dirty gob, don't you know. I wouldn't have thought you could look so downright disreputable, and that's the truth."

Andrew grinned. Frank Donovan was known as quite a ladies' man, with his arrogant good looks and more than a splash and dash of charm, which he could lay on ever so thick when he had a mind to. At the moment, however, his face, including the rakish mustache, was gray with smoke and soot.

Frank doffed his hat and flicked some ash from it, then settled it back on his head. "Aye, no doubt I'm a sorry sight as well. So, then—you'd like to meet the lady doc, I expect."

"Yes, of course. Is Dr. Cole a resident of the boardinghouse?"

Frank shook his head. "No. She has a flat near the square. Seems she heard the commotion on her way home and came to help. Come along, then, and you can make her acquaintance. Of course, you'll keep in mind that I'm rather taken with the woman myself. Not that an Irish cop would stand a chance with her kind."

Andrew attempted to smooth his hair, then pulled his handkerchief from his pocket and swiped at his face. "Her kind?"

Donovan wiped his face on the sleeve of his uniform. "I don't know what she's doing in this part of town, but I'd wager Dr. Bethany Cole's blood runs as blue as her eyes."

Andrew studied him for a moment. "Ever the cynic, aren't you?"

The policeman merely laughed.

Andrew liked Frank Donovan as much as he had ever liked another man. They had become fast and solid friends, but Frank made no secret of the fact that he thought Andrew outrageously naive where his fellowman was concerned. Naive, and perhaps even a little foolish. The "Missionary Medicine Man," Frank was fond of calling him.

The big policeman gave no quarter when it came to what he labeled the "dregs of humanity"—which in Frank's estimation included just about everybody "except for you and me, Doc, and at times I tend to worry about you."

If asked, Andrew would have been hard pressed to say exactly what it was about the big Irishman that he liked so much. They could scarcely have been more different. Other than the fact that they were both immigrants, they held almost nothing in common.

Andrew knew little of his friend's past, for Frank wasn't given to personal confidences. What little he did know he'd learned from others, and he suspected that many of the tales told about Frank Donovan were nothing but rumor. One story had it that Frank had come across as a stowaway when he was still a tyke, only to become one of the innumerable homeless waifs who wandered the notorious Five Points slum on the lower east side, shifting for themselves by indulging in petty thievery or running errands for the gang bosses.

According to that particular tale, Donovan had gotten mixed up in a gang only to be arrested for knifing a youthful rival, though he protested his innocence right up to the doors of the jail. It was said that a good-natured policeman had believed the boy's story and, after taking it upon himself to find the real assailant, had eventually gained Frank's release.

This was only one of the many colorful accounts Andrew had heard about Frank, and he had no way of knowing if it—or any of the other stories told about the man—contained a grain of truth. Nor did he care. What he did know was that Frank Donovan was the most thoroughly honest man he had ever come across. At times, that honesty could seem harsh, even brutal, but it was a trait that Andrew could not help but appreciate.

There was also a strength about the big Irishman that had nothing to do with his physical prowess. Donovan's brash courage and fortitude, combined with an uncommon sense of loyalty, made him a formidable foe and an incredible friend.

Andrew suspected that no matter what the big policeman might happen to come up against, he would prevail. Frank, no doubt, would describe himself far more simply with a single word: *hardheaded*.

And come to think of it, that probably summed him up about as well as anything.

~

It seemed to Andrew that Frank barely made it through the introductions without smirking.

Even with her hair and face dusted with ash, Dr. Bethany Cole was a pretty woman. No—she was more than pretty; she was *lovely*. Exceptionally lovely. Small with delicate features and hair the color of flax, she appeared too young to be a physician. Andrew saw in an instant why Frank had said what he did about her blood running blue. Everything about the woman bespoke *breeding*. She looked as if she would be far more at home serving tea in a Fifth Avenue drawing room than toting a doctor's bag around the squalid streets of Manhattan.

They exchanged somewhat awkward pleasantries, Frank taking it all in with that maddening grin of his.

"So, then, Dr. Cole—how long have you been in New York?" Andrew asked.

She had unusual eyes, he noted: startlingly large and remarkably blue, eyes that gave the impression of looking straight into one's soul. The thought disquieted Andrew, and he felt suddenly gawky and foolish, as if he had been transformed into a plowboy on the spot. Not to mention his "disreputable appearance," which Frank had so gleefully pointed out.

But Bethany Cole seemed not to notice. Perhaps he didn't look quite as disgraceful as Frank had intimated.

Or perhaps Dr. Cole was simply nearsighted. Come to think of it, she was peering up at him as if she might be just that.

"Actually, I haven't been here long at all," she said in a voice tinged with the well-modulated refinement of the upper class. "I arrived only a few weeks ago. From Philadelphia."

"So you're opening a practice here in New York?"

She lifted one delicate eyebrow. "Well—not just yet," she said, her tone dry. "I'm still—exploring the possibilities."

"I see. But you've applied for your hospital privileges, I expect?" Andrew thought her smile might have wavered slightly.

"I've applied, yes. So far, however, I haven't found a hospital interested in my particular skills."

Andrew knew only too well what she was insinuating. Most male physicians had no use whatsoever for women doctors—in fact considered the female "nature" itself unfit for the practice of medicine, aside from midwifery. Most of his contemporaries thought women should be barred from medicine altogether.

He did not share the popular opinion and, for some reason, found himself wanting to convey as much to Bethany Cole. "What about the Women's Infirmary? Have you spoken with them?"

She nodded. "As it happens, I'm already working at the Infirmary. But I'm still anxious to establish my own practice. I'll have to wait for that, however. I haven't a place or the means as yet to set up an office. Besides, I don't know the city well enough to decide where to locate."

Something tugged at the fringes of Andrew's mind, and had Frank not been standing there, arms crossed over his chest as he took in the exchange with more than a casual interest, he might have been able to verbalize it. As it was, however, he felt increasingly awkward and unable to concentrate on anything other than Bethany Cole's unnerving blue eyes and Frank Donovan's annoyingly insolent grin. So he simply stood there like a post, saying nothing.

Abruptly, Frank uncrossed his arms and made a move to leave. "Well, now, I expect I should see to my men. I'll just be leaving the two of you to your medical talk." With that, he doffed his hat, then set it back on his head at a rakish angle and left them alone.

Under Bethany Cole's steady scrutiny, Andrew suddenly found that he, too, was eager to get away. They made small talk for only another moment before he offered a clumsy good-bye and turned to go.

He could almost feel her inquisitive gaze following him. On an impulse he stopped and turned back to her. "Dr. Cole?"

She tilted her head a little, her expression quizzical. Andrew had never been given to acting impetuously. Yet something urged him on. He returned to offer her one of his calling cards, and as he did so, he studied her for a moment. "If you'd like," he said, "I might be able to help with those hospital privileges. If you're interested, that is."

She looked at the card he'd handed her, then at him. "Why—of course, I'd be interested."

Andrew swallowed against the slick of numbness creeping up his throat. "And about your practice—I might have an idea about that as well. If you'd like to… ah…stop by my office when it's convenient, we can discuss it."

He must sound like a dimwit—he *did* sound like a dimwit; he could hear it in his own voice. No doubt, she'd be too put off by him to venture anywhere *near* his office.

"Thank you," she said, still regarding him with a questioning look. "That's very kind of you, Dr. Carmichael. And, yes, I'll be sure to stop by your office." She paused. "Should I make an appointment?"

"An appointment? Oh...no, that's not necessary. Just...stop by anytime."

That said, Andrew again wished her a good day, turned quickly—nearly stumbling as he did—and made a hasty retreat to the front of the building.

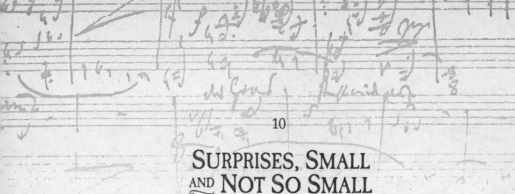

10

SURPRISES, SMALL AND NOT SO SMALL

Blessed day, so calm and restful,
Bringing joy and peace to all,
Linger yet in tranquil beauty
Ere the shades of evening fall.

FANNY CROSBY

Her rooms far surpassed any expectations Susanna might have had. Mrs. Dempsey opened the door onto a high-ceilinged, spacious chamber with frilly yellow curtains, an enormous four-poster decked with yellow and white linens, a wall of neatly shelved books, and an upholstered rocking chair so large and inviting Susanna could scarcely wait to try it.

The room's sunny atmosphere fortified Susanna in a way she wouldn't have thought possible. She brightened even more when she realized she was to have her own private water closet and dressing room. She would be living in absolute luxury compared to the small farmhouse where she had grown up. But when she looked at her battered trunk resting on the bench at the foot of the bed— conspicuous evidence of her straitened circumstances—she felt a sudden, unexpected longing for the simplicity of her home back in Ireland.

Mrs. Dempsey seemed not to notice. She pointed out the lovely view of the gardens from the window, and then instructed Susanna to have a "proper rest" before supper. Susanna declined the housekeeper's offer to help her unpack; the idea of a total stranger sorting through her few frayed garments and threadbare lingerie made her stomach clench.

She did try to express her appreciation for the room, but the housekeeper summarily dismissed her gratitude. "'Tis himself you'll want to be thanking. He was the one who saw to the fixings. He and the wee wane."

Taken aback, Susanna stared at her. "Mr... *Michael*, do you mean?"

"Aye, the *Maestro*, as they call him in these parts. Didn't he plan the job and see to it himself, he and the darling girl?" The housekeeper preened as if this evidence of her employer's generosity was a matter of personal pride.

Susanna waited until Mrs. Dempsey left the room to do a more thorough inspection. No detail seemed to have been spared in outfitting a room designed for the utmost in charm, coziness, and comfort. And it had been provided especially for her benefit—by Michael Emmanuel himself! The very idea left her feeling bewildered.

She forced herself to unpack her things before resting, hanging her few garments in a wardrobe twice the size she would need, then neatly stacking her personal items in the meticulously lined drawers of a highboy several inches taller than Susanna herself.

Finally spent, she sank down into the enormous rocking chair by the window. The late summer gardens below were splendid, but not formal. Instead of perfect designs, random quilts of color met her view. Like the gardens, those parts of the orchards that were visible appeared well-tended, but with no particular pattern or order.

For a time, Susanna closed her eyes, craving sleep. But she was too tense, too anxious about what might lie ahead, to thoroughly relax. Moreover, she was still trying to take in the fact that Michael Emmanuel had gone to so much trouble and expense on her account. A room decorated specifically with her in mind was the last thing she would have expected from what Deirdre had written of her "cold," "inconsiderate" husband.

All along she had expected to be treated like an impoverished relative—useful for looking after Caterina, but with no real place of her own in the household. She most certainly hadn't foreseen that anyone would have exerted even the slightest effort to make her feel *wanted* here.

Still, she couldn't help feeling suspicious of her brother-in-law's intentions and, consequently, hard-pressed to summon any real feelings of gratitude. The man Deirdre described in her letters had never acted unselfishly, but had been motivated solely by a desire to manipulate and control.

But why on earth would Michael Emmanuel attempt to manipulate *her*? She was already indebted to him, after all. He had paid her passage across, opened his home to her, even offered to pay her a wage. Certainly, there was no reason he should have gone to the additional expense of redecorating and furnishing a bedroom for her.

Susanna could make no sense of any of it, and finally her exhausted body had its way over her swimming thoughts. The next thing she knew Mrs. Dempsey was rapping at her door, informing her that supper would be served in twenty minutes.

To Susanna's relief, supper turned out to be just as Michael Emmanuel had promised: a small group, and a comfortably friendly one at that.

Paul Santi was there, of course, and Rosa Navaro, who was, Susanna learned during the course of the meal, a widow of several years. Also among those gathered about the enormous dining room table was a tall, intense Protestant pastor named Jeremy Holt and a Catholic priest whose thick head of silver hair made him appear, at first glance, to be older than closer inspection indicated. Everyone there called him Father Flynn, except for Michael Emmanuel and Pastor Holt, both of whom referred to him by his given name, Dermot. The pastor and the priest appeared to be great friends with each other, and with Michael Emmanuel as well.

What an uncommon thing such a friendship would be in Ireland!

The other member of the group was a petite, lively woman referred to as "Miss Fanny" by everyone there. Like Michael Emmanuel, she was also blind.

They were well into the meal before Susanna realized that "Miss Fanny" was none other than the acclaimed hymn writer, Fanny Crosby. She was a small woman, bedecked in an out-of-date suit and shiny, green-tinted eyeglasses, with a very large cross hanging around her neck. Miss Fanny looked to be middle-aged, but her chirpy voice and robust laugh made her seem much younger. Apparently, she had once been a teacher at the New York Institute for the Blind, the same institution where Michael had received instruction in Braille and other services for the blind after his accident. The two seemed to have become good friends, in addition to sharing a common passion for music.

It was obvious that all the dinner guests knew each other quite well, and yet Susanna felt no exclusion from their midst. To the contrary, they seemed to make a genuine effort to draw her in and put her at ease.

She was caught off guard entirely, however, when Michael Emmanuel stood, tapped lightly on his water glass, and said, "Although you met Susanna earlier as you arrived, now that we are all together, I would just like to say how pleased Caterina and I are that her aunt has come to make her home with us and be a part of our family."

Susanna, always uncomfortable with being the center of attention, felt the heat rise to her face. She was grateful when Miss Fanny spoke up. "I think we should ask the Lord's blessing on Susanna and your entire household, Michael. May I?"

With that, she bowed her head and offered a truly heart-warming prayer for Susanna, for Caterina, and for "our dear Michael." Susanna found herself deeply moved by the vivacious little woman's prayer on her behalf, by her obvious sincerity, and by what was clearly a close, very special relationship with her God.

"...May Susanna find this house to be more than a shelter, Lord. May she find here a new home, a true home, and may Your love and peace abide with her and all who dwell within."

After a collective and enthusiastic "Amen," Caterina immediately leaned toward Susanna to plant a quick kiss on her cheek. On her other side, Miss Fanny squeezed her hand. "You will be blessed here, Susanna. Just you wait and see! You've come to live with a wonderful family, you know."

Among the other surprises of the evening was the discovery that her enigmatic brother-in-law seemed to be a deeply spiritual man. He talked naturally with the others at the table about matters of faith, the church, and spirituality. Indeed, he and the two clergymen seemed to toss remarks back and forth with an ease and enthusiasm Susanna would have expected to find only among family members. Apparently, this kind of evening was fairly commonplace for them.

If she had thought about it at all, she would never have expected Michael Emmanuel to be a man of faith. Of all the things Deirdre had written about her husband, she had never once touched on this particular aspect of his character.

But, now that she thought about it, Deirdre had never exhibited any interest in spiritual matters herself.

Susanna was grateful for her companions' attempts to include her, but she nevertheless found it difficult to take in much of the conversation—in large part because of the bright and irresistible little girl seated at her side.

Back home, it would have been highly unlikely for such a young child to be included in an adult gathering. Of course, this was Caterina's birthday, and she really did conduct herself very much like a young lady—though a highly animated one. Her table manners were impeccable, and although she chattered away throughout the meal, making no secret of the fact that she found Susanna altogether fascinating, she paid immediate heed to her father if he happened to clear his throat or lift an eyebrow, as if to gently remind her that perhaps she might be monopolizing her aunt a bit too much.

For her part, however, Susanna relished her niece's prattle and the way her blue eyes virtually danced with every word and gesture. Caterina—"Cati," as her father and Paul Santi frequently referred to her—was an absolute delight of a child. Her high spirits seemed to infect everyone present, and Susanna was no exception.

Suddenly she realized, with a touch of surprise, that she was actually enjoying herself. She had even begun to feel more at peace about her arrangement with Michael Emmanuel—if not about the man himself.

∼

Sometime in the night, Susanna was awakened by the faint sound of music coming from downstairs. It took her a moment to recognize the soft strumming of a mandolin. She lay listening, strangely soothed by the plaintive melody, and within minutes she drifted back to sleep.

Later, she awakened again, this time roused by the clock in the downstairs hall striking one. Her head felt heavy, her eyes leaden, but the night had turned cool, and when the wind wailed outside her window, she stirred enough to pull the bedcovers up more snugly about her shoulders.

But just as she was about to doze off again, she heard something else, something that jarred her fully awake.

Footsteps.

She sat upright, instantly alert to the sounds in the hallway outside her room. She tensed as the footsteps grew nearer, then seemed to stop at the door to the room next to hers. Caterina's room.

The door creaked open, then closed again.

Chilled, Susanna held her breath, only to give a sigh of relief when she heard the soft chuffing of the big wolfhound. It was just Michael Emmanuel and the hound, she realized, checking on Caterina. Still, she didn't completely relax until the footsteps moved on and she heard a door close at the end of the hall.

The wind rattled her window, as if to remind her how secluded and removed from civilization this place called Bantry Hill really was.

She slumped back against the pillows, thinking about the music she had heard. Obviously, that, too, had been Michael. Apparently he was only now retiring, although he had appeared to be nearly as fatigued as she by the end of the evening.

Did he do this every night, she wondered? Stay up until all hours, wandering about the lonely halls with the wolfhound at his side?

Unexpectedly, the thought saddened her. Her emotions had been in turmoil ever since meeting her inscrutable brother-in-law. She had come here already distrustful of him, convinced that she would dislike him. Yet so far the man had exhibited none of the undesirable traits Deirdre had described, save for the possible display of stubbornness she had glimpsed earlier in the drawing room. In truth, he had been nothing but kindness itself since she'd arrived.

Susanna tried to will herself back to sleep, but the thought of that big, sightless man roaming about this cavernous mansion, alone except for his faithful wolfhound, kept her awake until long after the clock had chimed two.

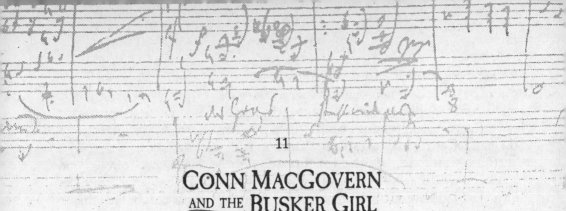

11

CONN MACGOVERN AND THE BUSKER GIRL

Winds and rain have *liberty* to enter freely
through the windows of half the houses—
the pigs have *liberty* to ramble about—
the landlord has *liberty* to take possession
of most of his tenements—
the silk-weaver has *liberty* to starve or beg.

BY AN AMERICAN DOCTOR IN THE LIBERTIES OF DUBLIN, MID-1800S

QUOTED IN *DEAR, DIRTY DUBLIN, A CITY IN DISTRESS*

BY JOSEPH O'BRIEN

Dublin, Ireland, September

Conn MacGovern was in a hurry this cold, rainy morning.

The good Lord willing, today would mark his last trek through the Liberties, his last look at the moldy, decaying buildings, where petticoats waved from the windows instead of curtains, and where the streets were strewn with vegetable and animal refuse, broken glass, and shattered dreams. Please, God, after today he would never again have to endure the rancid, foul stench that seemed to rise up like a poison fog from the streets, nor dodge the vermin-covered inhabitants and the starving, raggedy children come to beg.

Indeed, this was his last day in Dublin—his last day in *Ireland*—and though the thought stirred an entire tide of clashing emotions, his eagerness to put the slums behind him took precedence over the other feelings warring within. Had it not been for Baby Emma forgetting her rag dolly, he would be in the harbor with the rest of them now, waiting to board ship. But it would be a hardhearted man indeed who could resist the inconsolable wailing of his baby girl. So he had hurried back to the cellar flat to retrieve Dolly, now tucked safely inside his coat pocket.

Conn heard the shouts before he saw the small figure hunched down at the entrance to the alley. He stopped, struggling to take in the scene in front of him.

He recognized the girl almost immediately, though her face was partly concealed by her arms as if to ward off a blow. The shabby clothing that hung loosely on her and the crushed cap perched atop the tangled black hair gave her away at once: the young street busker called Patches—a name earned, most likely, from the multicolored pieces of material that decorated her baggy skirt.

But what was the girl doing here in the slums? She and her pack of vagabond musicians were usually to be found in the vicinity of Grafton or Henry Street, performing for whatever crowd and coin they could attract. There would be little chance of profits for them here in the Liberties, the most deplorable slum in Dublin.

Then Conn saw the cause of all the ruckus. Even though the alley was half hidden by shadows, there was no mistaking the other figure hulking over the girl—a woman grown, and quite a large woman at that. It took him only a second or two more to realize that the woman was beating on the scrawny little busker as if she meant to murder her entirely.

The sight of such unfair advantage fueled Conn's temper. He tore into a run, shouting as he went. "Hold off, there! Let up!"

He took the rain-slicked cobblestones in three wide leaps. Not until he was virtually on top of the woman did he recognize her. Nan Sweeney was an aging money lender—a sour old hag who lived like a pig in the heart of the Liberties and "employed" a number of the homeless ragamuffins from the streets to carry out her despicable deeds. It was said that Nan Sweeney would slice a throat as quick as a cheese and never give the act a second thought.

Conn took in the situation in a heartbeat. It was plain enough that the hatchet-faced old woman was in a rage with the young street musician. Her craggy face was distorted with fury, while the girl's sharply drawn features, though mottled with her own anger, could not quite mask the terror in her eyes.

Whatever the little monkey's crime, Conn reasoned, it could scarcely be license for such a thrashing.

He grabbed the woman's arm to haul her off the girl. "No more of that now!" he ordered. "Leave off."

The woman was as ugly as she was mean. She shook free of Conn, then turned on him with an upraised arm. For a moment, he thought she would go after him instead of the girl.

"You don't want to do that, old woman," he warned her.

The crone glared at him, but dropped her arm to her side.

"This is none of your business, man!"

Conn shrugged and gave her a nasty smile. "A mad old woman beating on a slip of a girl? I'm thinking to *make* it my business. And while I'm about it, Nan Sweeney, perhaps you'd care to explain what the girl has done to warrant such shameful treatment from you?"

Her fierce scowl changed not a bit. "And who might you be, sticking your big nose in where it don't belong?"

For all the woman's bravado and her considerable size, Conn topped her by a head and outweighed her by far. He also suspected she might not be half so fierce as she obviously fancied herself if her opponent were a man grown, rather than an underfed street urchin.

He brought his face close to hers, forcing himself to ignore the disgusting stench of her breath as he knuckled a fist under her sagging chin. "Conn MacGovern is the name, you old dragon. And you don't want to be stirring up trouble with me, I promise you. Now get yourself out of here before I forget you're an old woman and give you the trouncing you deserve."

The woman narrowed her eyes as if to challenge Conn, but he saw her uncertainty, and sure enough, she backed off a bit. "She's naught but a filthy, thieving little guttersnipe, is what she is! That's what you'd be defending, man? She *stole* from me, she did, the little mongrel!"

Conn couldn't think why he should be putting himself out for this "Patches" creature. Because of her, he was already late in meeting Vangie and the children at the docks. Vangie would be worried and worn to tears with the little ones. But he had watched the young busker's antics on the streets so many times that he seemed to have taken on the idiotic notion that he *knew* the girl. He even felt a kind of protectiveness for her.

No matter what she had done, he simply could not bring himself to abandon her to the malice of this deranged old woman.

He turned to the girl, still huddled against the wall like a shivering alley cat as she eyed him and Nan Sweeney with a baleful glare. For the first time Conn saw the ugly bruises that splotched the side of her face.

"Is it true, then?" he said, his tone more gruff than he'd intended. "Did you steal from this woman?"

"Stole my moneybag, she did!" Nan Sweeney ranted on. "Dirty little thief!"

The busker gave the woman a nasty scowl, then shot Conn an equally fierce look. "I was only after taking what was mine! 'Tis *her* that's the thief, and that's the truth!"

Her voice held the familiar roughness of the street ragamuffin, the words hurled rather than spoken. She stumbled to her feet, and when Conn saw her wince with pain at the effort, he realized that she had been hurt more badly than he'd first thought.

But it wasn't entirely this evidence of the girl's ill-treatment that tugged at his heart and stirred the desire to protect. In the shadows of his mind lurked the awareness that were it not for his strong back and his capacity for hard work, any one of his own children could just as easily be reduced to this girl's state, sleeping in alleyways, living the slum child's life, and risking health and hide by consorting with riffraff like Nan Sweeney.

Besides, there was something else about the girl—some vague, intangible quality that seemed to set the spindly little busker apart from the other strays who wandered the Dublin streets all hours of the day and night. As unlikely as it was, and despite her outrageous rags and that ridiculous mop of hair, an unaccountable aura of dignity seemed to hover about the girl.

All the same, why would she resort to thievery? Although the buskers were often dismissed as common beggars, Conn knew that many of them were skilled and clever enough at their trade to manage a fair living for themselves.

Every now and then one would stand out from the crowd as genuinely gifted. And since no one appreciated musicians more than the Irish, especially the Irish of Dublin City, even the poorest among a busker's audiences were inclined to be generous with their meager coin.

The small figure known as Patches was a great favorite. Of all the itinerant musicians, she was said to draw the largest crowds wherever she happened to perform. The little guttersnipe might be a wretched sight entirely—and perhaps a thief to boot—but she was one of the brightest buskers in Dublin. More than likely, there wasn't a stepdancer in the county she couldn't shame with her flying feet, funny old-fashioned shoes and all.

She was a natural mimic and had a way with the instruments, too: a fiddle or a simple tin whistle took on a kind of magic in her hands. And when she sang one of the sad old tunes, her voice seemed to squeeze a body's soul, wringing out all the secrets and sorrows long hidden and thought forgotten.

But perhaps more than anything else, what evoked Conn's nagging urge to help the girl was something behind those enormous eyes, something the hard glare of defiance could not quite mask. In the end, it was that hint of energy and keen intelligence that prevented him from turning his back on the pair and leaving them to slug it out as they would.

"Give her the moneybag," he ordered the busker in a tone that brooked no argument.

The girl glowered at him.

"*Do* it!" Conn warned. "Or I'll call the peelers on the pair of you."

Her glare didn't waver, but one hand slid behind her back. When she continued to hesitate, Conn narrowed his eyes and jabbed a finger in the direction of Nan Sweeney.

With a murderous look, the girl thrust the moneybag at her attacker.

The old woman fumbled to examine its contents. "No doubt the little cheat has taken most of the money out by now."

Conn gave her a nasty smile. "You've got it wrong, Nan. 'Tis *you* who are taking some of the money out. Now give the girl what's due her."

The woman turned on him, and her expression would have cowered a mad bull. "There be *nothing* due her!"

The girl lunged forward. "You bargained with me for a job, and I did what you said!"

Nan Sweeney lifted a threatening arm, but Conn grabbed her. "Pay her," he ordered. "Pay her what you owe, I said. And don't be lifting a hand to the girl again, or I'll scrape the streets with you myself, old woman or not."

She stared at him as if to take his measure, and Conn braced himself in case she swooped in on him. But after a few more seconds and a muffled curse, the woman dug into the bag, withdrew a few coins, and tossed them at the girl's feet.

"You didn't earn a bit of it, and well you know it, you little thief!"

Conn took a step toward the woman, and she quickly added in a grudging tone, "But I'll not have it said that Nan Sweeney don't pay for a job done."

The girl grinned at her, revealing a slight gap between her two front teeth, then bent to scoop up the coins at her feet.

"Get out," Conn snarled at the old woman. "Now."

She went stumbling out of the alley, muttering to herself about "thieving blackguards."

After a moment, Conn turned to the busker, who stood watching him, poised as if to run. "Now then, satisfy my curiosity," he said. "What, exactly, was this job the old harridan paid you to do?"

She stood, jingling the coins in her right hand as she watched him with a speculative expression. "I was to collect overdue rents from two of her tenants. And so I did. But then she refused to give me my take."

Conn stared at her, then burst out laughing. "What, you're such a fierce creature the landlords send you around to inspire fear in their debtors?"

She curled her lip. "Don't matter if they fear me or not. 'Tis old Nan they don't want set against them." She paused, and then, with the same streak of impudence she displayed when performing, added, "And what is it to you anyhow?"

Conn sobered. "Why would you lower yourself to work for the likes of Nan Sweeney?"

"I do as I please," she said with a shrug. Then she pulled her face into a look of distaste. "Though I'll not be turning a hand for old Nan Sweeney again, I can tell you. Refusing to pay me what we agreed, and her as rich as the queen herself! That's why I made off with the moneybag. I was only going to take what was mine and leave her the rest. But then she started in on me like the demented old witch she is. Would have murdered me entirely, I'll warrant."

Conn studied her, but she wouldn't quite meet his gaze. "Is that the truth, then?"

When she looked at him, the pale blue eyes had turned to ice chips. "Didn't I say it was so?"

"Beggin' your pardon, m'lady," Conn said with exaggerated sarcasm. "Far be it from me to question the word of such an upstanding citizen."

Her face flamed, but she made no reply.

"Where do you live?" Conn said.

"Wherever I choose," she shot back, turning on her heel as if to go.

"*Thank you very much, sir, for saving my neck and sparing me a thorough pounding,*" Conn taunted. "'*Tis ever so grateful I am, sir.*"

Slowly, she turned back to him. "Thank you very much, sir," she mimicked, yanking the tired-looking cap off her head and giving him a sweeping bow.

Conn shook his head, but to save him he could feel no real pique toward her, only a bit of amusement—and perhaps even a faint respect—for the little hoyden's insolence.

"How badly are you hurt?" he said, for he figured she'd taken a fair bruising.

She waved off the question. "How much could she hurt me, a crazy old woman like that?"

The girl had pride. Perhaps too much of it, Conn speculated. "Crazy old woman or not, you'd do well to stay out of her sight for a time. She'll be after evening the score with you, I'll wager."

She sniffed and gave a toss of her head, then scrunched her cap back into place.

Still amused by the girl's bravado, Conn speculated as to her age. When seen up close for the first time, he realized she might not be as young as he had thought when watching her perform at a distance. Given her diminutive size, she might pass for ten or eleven years, but he thought it more likely that she was close on twelve or even thirteen. "What's your name, lass?"

Again she tossed her head. "I'm called Patches," she replied archly.

"I know what you're called. But don't you have a proper name?"

She frowned at him as if he'd insulted her. "'Tis *Renny,*" she finally said. "I chose it myself. Renny Magee."

"What do you mean, you chose it yourself?"

She shrugged. "I got no folks. Never knew 'em. So I gave myself the name I fancied, and why shouldn't I?"

In spite of the roughness of her voice, she spoke with a certain flair Conn wouldn't have associated with one of the street orphans. In fact, he suspected the girl might have managed at least a token education for herself.

But here, what was he thinking? Standing about blathering with a busker girl when Vangie and the children were most likely wild for the sight of him by now.

"Well, Renny Magee," he said brusquely, "although it's been a grand experience, making your acquaintance, I must be away now. I've a boat to catch. But I don't mind telling you that I will miss your performances in America."

She gave him a questioning look and Conn nodded. "We are leaving today, my family and myself."

The thin, elfin face seemed suddenly transformed. "You're going to America?" she said, eyes shining with the kind of wonder ordinarily reserved for paying homage to royalty.

Again Conn gave a nod. "Aye, that I am. If the ship doesn't set sail and leave me behind, that is. My family is waiting for me at the docks, and late as I am, my wife will box my ears for certain."

The girl continued to look at Conn as if he were about to be knighted. "It must be a fine feeling entirely, leaving for America."

There was no mistaking the envy in her tone. Conn understood, though some of his own excitement had ebbed, now that the big day had arrived at last. Even Vangie, never one to back away from an adventure, had been showing her nerves this morning.

The thought of his wife roused him to action. She would be in a terrible state, Vangie would, thinking him murdered by robbers or run over in the street by a team of horses.

He stooped to retrieve his neckerchief and some papers the busker had apparently dropped during the altercation with Nan Sweeney. When he straightened, the girl had moved even closer and stood watching him with that same expression of envy and fascination.

Conn handed her her things, saying, "Well, then, look after yourself, young Renny Magee. I must be on my way."

The wide, glistening eyes seemed locked on his face as Conn gave her a farewell wave and started off, but her voice stopped him.

"Mister?"

Conn turned, waiting.

"I—did I hear you tell Nan Sweeney your name is MacGovern?"

"You did, and it is."

"Well—" She broke off, looking away from Conn as she shifted her weight from one foot to another and screwed up a corner of her mouth. "Well, then, Mr. MacGovern, I expect I ought to thank you for your help. Not many would have stopped as you did, I'm thinking."

The words tumbled out quickly, like pellets shot from a gun. Her face was flushed with crimson, her gaze locked on her own feet. Clearly, this Renny Magee was not overly familiar with even a simple thank-you. But then, perhaps she'd had few occasions in her young life to express her appreciation to another.

"You are very welcome, I'm sure," Conn said, unable to suppress a smile.

"And safe home," he added, wondering even as he said it if indeed Renny Magee, the girl called Patches, had a place to call home.

12

VANGIE

Had I the wealth that props the Saxon's reign,
Or the diamond crown that decks the King of Spain,
I'd yield them all if she kindly smiled on me...

ANONYMOUS, EIGHTEENTH-CENTURY

A punishing rain had set in by the time Conn reached the dock.

He was relieved to see that Vangie and the children had found shelter under a tarpaulin. Vangie held Baby Emma in her arms, while Nell Grace—who at seventeen looked more like her mother every day—had the twins well in tow, one on each side.

Aidan, the oldest, stood looking out over the docks with the same dark scowl he'd been wearing since the day Conn broke the news that they were leaving Ireland.

Aidan was a good lad, Vangie's joy and pride, her firstborn. But he was also a hothead. At nineteen, he was a man grown and seemed to believe himself called to challenge any and every decision his father made. He had kicked up a terrible fuss over the idea of going to America, so much so that he and Conn had scarcely spoken for weeks now.

Conn told himself that once the crossing was underway and Ireland behind them, the boy would surely come round and see the sense of things again.

For Vangie's sake, he hoped he was right.

The rain, uncommonly cold for this time of year, was falling harder now. Even so, Conn stood for a moment, drinking in the sight of his wife. The same rush of love that had made him a bumbling fool over her as a lad came rolling in on him again. It was always this way, even after more than twenty years of marriage and five children—seven, if he were to count the two gone to the angels in years past.

As he stood there, watching Vangie, her dark red hair blowing in the wind, her deep-set eyes searching the throng that lined the fence along the length of the dock—searching for *him*, Conn knew—he marveled, not for the first time, that the good Lord had blessed such a man as himself: a great, thick-necked oaf who had never been able to give the woman he loved anything more than hard times and shattered dreams.

With her vibrant beauty, still unfaded at thirty-seven years, her strength of spirit, and her good, true heart, his Vangie could have had any man she wanted—sure, a far better man than himself. But she had chosen him, Conn MacGovern, and, though he would always puzzle over his good fortune, he would never take it lightly.

Life had been hard for them right from the beginning. In the early years, they had merely scraped a living off the land, barely getting by, handing over almost all Conn's meager wages to the landlord. Yet they had somehow managed to be content with what they had, finding their fulfillment in each other, the children, their faith, and in the land itself.

But then had come the winter of the sickness. With never enough to pay for the medicines Vangie and the twins needed—not even enough to pay the rent—they had finally lost it all: the cabin, the land, the cow, and Vangie's hens. Indeed, they had lost everything but the clothes on their backs and their few poor pieces of furniture and pottery. And so they had moved to the city, to Dublin, where ever since they had lived like rabbits in a warren, boxed into two cramped rooms of a dreary hovel on the edge of the slums known as the Liberties.

Conn's reluctant decision that they must leave Ireland had nearly broken Vangie's heart and had all but destroyed his relationship with his son. More than once, Aidan had bitterly accused his father of betraying them all, of having no love for the land, no loyalty to their native country—and, worse still, no concern for his family's well-being.

In truth, it was Conn's concern for the family that had finally pushed him into the decision to emigrate, though of course the boy couldn't begin to imagine what that decision had cost his father. There were nights when, long after Vangie had fallen asleep, Conn lay wide awake, nearly frozen in his own anguish at the thought of leaving all he had ever known and taking his family across the formidable Atlantic.

The idea of starting over again, in a new country, among strangers—and he a man of forty years—filled him with almost as much dread as the possibility of watching his family starve to death on familiar soil. How many times had he been on the brink of throwing his resolve to the winds and announcing that they would not go to America, but would stay in Ireland after all?

Stay in Ireland and starve.

That was the reality that kept Conn from backing down and giving in to his son's continual haranguing. That, and Vangie's strength.

A weaker woman would have given up on him long before now, would have lost all hope and heart and left him to his own folly. But not his Vangie. When things had been at their worst and the future appeared most bleak, she had kept the family going—had kept *Conn* going, encouraging him to keep his faith in his dreams and in his Maker.

His wife's strength and unflagging faith had been the wind that buoyed Conn's own spirit, kept him from crumbling into the half-man, half-beast to which the English, if they had their way, would reduce every male in Ireland. Somehow Vangie had convinced him that the Almighty had not abandoned them—or the rest of the Irish. How often had she committed to him that she loved him more than everything in spite of the latest "setback," and would continue to love him, no matter what the future held?

But when Conn first voiced his intention to leave Ireland, even Vangie's confidence had plainly faltered. It had taken him days to persuade her that it was their best hope—most likely their *only* hope—of survival.

At first, she tried everything to talk him out of the idea, had pleaded with him, shrieked at him, threatened to leave him—indeed, she had aimed every weapon in her feminine arsenal at him—in a desperate attempt to convince him that his idea was madness itself. And then, without warning—and at the very moment Conn thought he might just as well give up the idea altogether—hadn't she announced that, despite her prayers that the Almighty would "let this cup pass from them," the good Lord had instead confirmed Conn's decision to her. Indeed, it seemed they were to go to America after all.

And that had been the end of her resistance—though not her fears, Conn knew. The apprehension still pinched her features as they made their plans, and the tears still welled up at almost any mention of leaving. But her God had spoken, and she would obey.

For Vangie, it was that simple, and always had been. So over the past several months, allowing themselves only the bare essentials needed to survive, they had managed to squeeze out enough from Conn's wages, Vangie's sewing money—and the sale of every item they could spare—to secure their passage. And now here they were, about to board the ship that would take them to their new life.

At that moment, he saw Vangie turn and catch sight of him. Her entire countenance brightened, and with a wave, Conn called out and started toward her.

⌒

Vangie saw him coming, and the worry that had been gnawing at her for the past hour immediately gave way to a flood of relief so powerful her legs very nearly buckled under her. She knew the Lord would have her entrust everything to Him. And most of the time, she managed to do just that. But, God forgive her, the hardest thing she faced at the beginning of each new day was to surrender her *family*, even to the One she knew to be merciful, the One she trusted with all her being. And now that Conn had made this life-changing decision—a decision that struck terror into her heart every time she thought of it—she found it nearly impossible not to worry, not to allow the weight of fear to crush the pinions of her faith.

She stepped away from the children a little, watching him hurry toward her, her big, good-looking husband—a "fine doorful of a man," as old Widow Dolan was wont to say—with that smuggler's smile and those sea-green eyes that could make her forgive him almost anything.

Not that there was much to forgive Conn MacGovern, she thought, warming with love at the sight of him. A woman would be a fool to wish for more in a husband than what she had found with Conn. He was no saint, and that was the truth, but he was a good man with a back carved from granite and a heart so soft the sight of an injured lark could bring him to tears. He was a strong, brawny man who could work from dawn till dark and bear the weight of two other men if need be, yet so light on his feet he could dance a jig on a spider's web and never tear it.

He was her husband, her best friend, her lover. After all these years, Vangie had only to look upon him and suddenly it was as if time itself had melted away and she was a young, lovesick girl again, and not the mother of five—including a son who was a man grown and a daughter about to pass into womanhood.

That's how it was *most* of the time.

For now, however, she firmly set aside her girlish foolishness and reminded herself that until this very moment she had been near sick to death with worry over the great *amadan*. And would you look at him now, hoofing his way toward her, late as a tinker's rent, yet smiling like the deadly charmer he fancied himself to be, and all the while expecting her to never mind his lingering.

Well, they would see about that. She gave Baby Emma a hoist and met her husband's foolish smile with a well-deserved glare.

"Ah, and so you have decided to favor us with your presence at last, Conn MacGovern!" she snapped at him. "I expect we should be counting ourselves blessed entirely that you showed up at all."

He had the good sense to look sheepish. "I'm sorry, my beauty, but it couldn't be helped. There was this girl, you see—well, you'll recall the one I mean, the little busker girl called Patches—she got herself into a stew of trouble, and so the only thing I could do was stop to help."

Vangie merely lifted an eyebrow.

"'Tis true," he said, reaching to give the baby's chin a tweak. "That miserable old witch Nan Sweeney was beating on the girl when I came along. Well, I couldn't simply pass on by and ignore the situation, now could I?"

Vangie pretended to scrutinize his broad, rakish features, but of course there was no question of his telling the truth. Conn couldn't lie to save his own hide, and wasn't she the better off for it?

She moved to shift the baby's weight to her other side, but Conn reached to take her to himself. Pleased, Emma chortled and grabbed at her daddy's nose. He pulled a face at her, which only made the tyke laugh that much more.

Vangie rubbed her back, which ached from standing in the damp so long with the weight of the baby upon her. She watched as Conn made a great show of producing the rag doll from his pocket, tickling Emma's nose with it. The baby squealed and buried her face in the doll's limp yarn hair.

He turned back to Vangie. "I am sorry, love," he said over the tyke's head. "I didn't mean to be so long."

Too weary to fuss at him, Vangie waved off his apology. "I was worried, is all. I want this over and done with."

She turned, a renewed wave of dread overtaking her as she stared at the steamer that would take them to America. Someone behind prodded them to move forward, and now they were in the thick of the passengers about to board.

Vangie looked to make certain the children were all accounted for, then again turned her gaze toward the ship. She felt Conn's large hand on her shoulder, steadying her. Unwilling to let him see the anguish and fear pressing in on her, she reached to cover his hand with her own.

"It will be well, love," he said softly, his breath warm against her hair. "'Tis the right thing we're doing."

Vangie didn't trust her voice to answer, instead merely nodded as they continued their march toward the vessel that waited to take them away from Ireland, from all that was known and familiar, to a place where only the Lord Himself knew what awaited them.

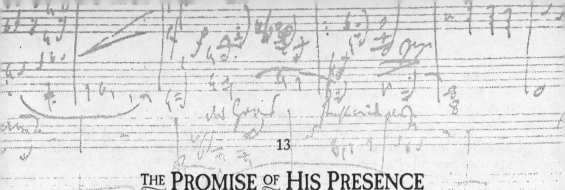

13

The Promise of His Presence

"For I know the plans I have for you,"
says the Lord.
"They are plans for good and not for
disaster, to give you a future and a hope."

JEREMIAH 29:11 (NLT)

They were in the thick of the passengers approaching the gangplank now, and there was no shelter from the bitter rain.

Vangie stopped long enough to turn around and make sure Conn had covered Baby Emma's face with her blanket. Immediately, she was shoved to the side by the driving crowd. Conn caught her arm, holding onto her as they continued toward the gangplank.

Now everything was confusion, a wild scramble as the steerage passengers rushed ahead. Children were screaming, women weeping, their men trying to shield them from those who would trample them outright in their haste to board and ensure themselves the best berths.

And all the while, the rain continued to batter the harbor with a vengeance.

Vangie saw a large, raw-boned woman and two strapping youths bearing down on the twins and Nell Grace, who had fallen behind.

"Nell Grace—behind you!" she called out to her daughter.

The girl looked at her, then turned, stumbling in her effort to keep the boys in tow. At the same time, Aidan left his place up ahead and came whipping through the mob, shoving his way to his sister and little brothers. He took James, the smaller of the twins, to himself, grabbing Nell Grace's arm with his free hand to buoy her and John along.

Vangie blinked against the tears burning her eyes. She tried to ignore the sick churning of her stomach as the reality of their departure slammed through her like a wrecking ball. By the time they neared the gangplank, her legs felt so brittle that it seemed the slightest movement would shatter her to pieces.

Sheer terror barreled down on her, and she bit her lip so fiercely she could taste her own blood. She felt Conn's hand tighten on her arm as if he had seen the surge of fear in her. Somehow she managed to force a smile for his benefit.

"Nothing matters so long as we're all together," she said, raising her voice above the pandemonium in an effort to reassure herself as well as her husband. "We have each other and the children. We will be all right."

He gave her a grateful smile and squeezed her arm. "We will, love," he said. "We will make out just fine. We are going to a better life, after all."

Vangie turned away so he couldn't see the panic struggling to overtake her. *Please let it be so!* She prayed silently. *Please let us be going to something better and not to our own destruction.*

She became gradually aware that the movement of the crowd had slowed and now was stopping altogether. People muttered among themselves, shifting the weight of their burdens as they speculated as to the reason for the delay. Finally, someone farther ahead passed back the word that a crew member had halted their progress until their numbers were called. There was much grumbling and scattered cursing, especially from some of the rougher men, but there was nothing to do for it but stand and wait in the relentless rain.

With Baby Emma still cuddled against him, Conn moved forward a little to stand between Aidan and Nell Grace and the twins. Vangie saw the hard, unyielding look Aidan gave his father, which Conn ignored.

They were so alike, the two of them. Aidan, the very image of his father, had inherited both Conn's good looks and bullheadedness. And Vangie loved him so deeply it made her heart ache.

She still remembered, as though it were yesterday, the night he had been born. Perhaps there was always a special bond between a mother and her firstborn son, especially when that son was so much like his da. The first moment she held him, he had stolen her heart entirely, and now, nearly a man grown, Aidan still never failed to warm her with his teasing and boyish laugh.

A laugh she had heard all too seldom in past months. Vangie sighed, her eyes going from husband to son. Why couldn't the two of them find their way to an agreement—or at the very least, a truce?

She watched her family for a moment, then let her gaze wander over the others who, like herself, stood drenched and miserable as they waited to board ship. Vangie saw her own fear reflected in the eyes of most of the women and in some of the men as well. Bony, whimpering children, some wearing little more than rags, clung to their parents, while young people who looked to be near the age of Aidan and Nell Grace shuffled their feet, as if anxious to get on with the adventure.

So many leaving. Leaving home and family and all they had ever known. Most would probably never set eyes on Ireland again, herself included. They were leaving their past, not knowing if they even had a future.

Vangie shuddered, fighting back tears. Suddenly from behind her, she felt a gentle touch on her shoulder. She turned to look, but there was no one except a gnarled old grandmother staring out into the distance, moaning softly to herself.

But something happened as Vangie stood watching, something not so much seen as *sensed*. It was as if all movement had ceased. The restless, querulous crowd fell silent, frozen in the moment like a painting, with the great ocean in front of them and the isle of home at their backs. Everything seemed to fade and grow still, leaving Vangie as a solitary observer, removed from the press of bodies all around her.

Again she was struck by the sensation of being touched. Vangie stood, scarcely breathing, her heart hammering as she saw, as if from a great distance, a kindly featured figure, dressed in homespun, moving among the crowd, murmuring to them, ruffling the hair of the children, consoling the women, encouraging the men, reassuring the elderly.

He laid a hand to their heads as he quietly made his way through the masses, and his every touch was like a blessing. With each step he took, an encompassing warmth and light seemed to radiate from him, overshadowing the fear of the voyage ahead, the dread of the waiting unknown, even the sting of the cold, slicing rain. A strong but gentle presence, he walked among them with a touch and a word of kindness like a benediction for them all. And no one seemed to acknowledge that he was even in their midst.

Then he was gone, and the crowd began to move forward again. The shouts of the crew could be heard over the wailing of the children and the futile attempts of their mothers to hush and comfort. A blast from the ship sounded, and somewhere in the distance the sound of a mournful fiddle could be heard.

Vangie had fallen behind her family and had to hurry to catch up. But now as she threaded her way through the throng of other passengers, there was a new firmness to her step. Her feet no longer felt leaden, and her heart no longer hammered with dread. Instead, a sweet, inexplicable peace enfolded her like a cloak as she pressed on.

She could not explain what had happened, but she knew what she had seen... she knew in her heart of hearts that she had not imagined it. That comforting presence, that caring touch, had been real—wonderfully, incredibly real.

It was a promise, and she seized upon it as such. A promise to cling to, not only for today, but for all the days to come. A promise to carry with her across the fierce Atlantic and into the new land they would one day call home.

A promise that, wherever she and her loved ones might venture, no matter how long their journey or how far their final destination, they did not go alone.

14

THE WATCH

She had the look of one who would
have gladly traded anything—
anything but her pride—
for the sweet taste of freedom...

FROM THE DIARY OF NELL GRACE MACGOVERN, 1875

Long after Conn MacGovern had disappeared from view, Renny Magee stood at the end of the alley staring at nothing in particular. Finally, she pulled her left hand free of her coat pocket and opened it to reveal the watch she had palmed from the street, where her rescuer had dropped it during his clash with Nan Sweeney.

Odd, he didn't look the sort to own such a fine piece. In truth, his attire had marked him as a man down on his luck, perhaps in circumstances not much better than Renny's own.

Not that her lot was all that bad. She got by, she did.

The timepiece's case was etched and carved all fancy-like, with strange, foreign-looking little houses and dragons and boats that made Renny think of some of the decorated knickknacks and baubles in the Chinaman's shop over on Henry Street.

After examining the watch's gold casing—at least it *looked* to be gold—she opened it to study the numerals and dials. Were it not for the frayed clothing MacGovern had been wearing, she would have thought she'd captured herself a real treasure.

Perhaps she should not be too quick to discount the watch's value. It looked to be expensive, perhaps *very* expensive.

Old Nan Sweeney would not see this particular piece, she wouldn't. Renny would take it to Henchy's, above the chandler's place. Most likely, the money-lender would pay more by half than that awful old woman would offer anyway. Not that she'd be foolish enough to go near to Old Nan again anytime soon.

Renny closed the case and stood flipping the watch from one hand to another

72

a few times. She was not entirely comfortable with the idea of keeping it. The thing was, when had anyone ever put himself out to help her before this day?

Aside from Thomas Lynch and one or two of the other buskers, she had no friends, not really. You couldn't trust anyone, and that was the truth. There was always someone on the prowl to pick your pocket or kick you about and take your money.

But Conn MacGovern had stood in for her, and him in a terrible rush on his way to the docks. Not only had the man put himself in harm's path for her, but he had treated her kindly enough, in a gruff sort of manner. Why, he had even said he'd miss her *performances*.

What if the watch was a family heirloom, something treasured and handed down now and again?

What if it was? That would make it all the more valuable.

Renny lifted the watch to look at it again, letting her fingers trace the engraving. The chafing at the back of her mind refused to go away. She looked down the street in the direction of the harbor, indecision sweeping through her.

Finally, propelled by an urgency that started her heart to thundering, she tore out of the alley and took off at a fierce run toward the docks.

～

The next few minutes were all confusion, with the crowd pressing forward like so many cattle prodded into movement, and members of the crew shouting commands and curses at them as if cattle they were indeed.

Conn saw Vangie weaving her way through a family with half a dozen children or more, trying to reach him. He was relieved to see that she was smiling. She no longer appeared quite so frightened and weary as she had only moments before. He flung out his arm above the heads of the little ones between them, grasping her hand and pulling her to him.

Immediately, the twins began hammering her with excited questions about the ship. Baby Emma squirmed in Conn's arms and reached for Vangie. Conn handed her over to her mother, then moved in front of them, using his large body as both shield and guide to propel his family through the crowd.

When a voice shrieked his name from behind, Conn whipped around to see who in this herd of strangers would be calling out to him. To his amazement, he saw the busker girl—Renny Magee—a fist stabbing the air as she snaked her way through the crowd, obviously intent on reaching him.

"Conn MacGovern! Ho! Conn MacGovern!"

Vangie looked at Conn, then turned to watch the girl. Conn stood staring, ignoring the people nearest him who had begun to grumble at the MacGoverns for impeding their movement. Indeed, his entire family had stopped where they were, gaping in bewilderment as a red-faced Renny Magee slipped almost effortlessly through the crowd and practically threw herself directly in front of Conn.

"What in heaven do you think you're doing, girl?"

Her cap was askew, both it and the shaggy hair beneath streaming with the rain, but she seemed completely indifferent to her wretched condition. Instead, she stood there, grinning at him as if she were altogether witless.

"Move along, man," a skinny, whiskered fellow complained, shoving Conn in his impatience to board the ship. "You're blocking the way, you are."

Conn glared at him, stepped aside a bit, then turned back to Renny. "What's this about, girl?"

The busker girl looked from him to Vangie and the children, then thrust out her hand, in which she held a watch.

His watch!

Instinctively, Conn reached inside his coat, but of course the watch was not there. It was cupped in the none-too-clean palm of Renny Magee.

"What are you doing with my *watch*?"

He fairly shouted at her—an accusation, not a question. It seemed she wasn't about to meet his gaze, but instead locked her eyes on something just over his shoulder. "You dropped it," she said, the rough-edged voice grating like a file along Conn's backbone.

He stared at her for a long moment. "I think not," he bit out. "You *stole* it; isn't that so, you little hoaxer? You stole my watch, and after my saving your neck at that!"

Renny Magee curled her lip and shot back, "Think what you like, MacGovern! But if I stole it as you say, then why did I run all this way to return it?"

Conn reached for the watch. She slapped it into his hand, and he stood eyeing her with disgust and no small measure of disappointment. "So Nan Sweeney was telling the truth after all. You *are* a thief! Have you no shame, girl?"

The pointed chin snapped up. "That old witch was *not* telling the truth!" Her face darkened. "Not…entirely, that is," she stammered. "It was as I said—I took from her only what was owed to me."

Conn lowered his head until he was in her face. "Well, my watch was not owing to you, you little guttersnipe! And you won't get by with it this time—I'll set the law on you for this."

He was surprised when Vangie put a hand to his arm to restrain him. "Conn—"

Still furious with the busker girl—and with himself for playing the fool to her chicanery—Conn ignored the note of caution in his wife's tone. "I'll handle this," he muttered.

But when he glanced around, he saw that his entire family was watching him and the girl: Aidan with his customary glare, Nell Grace and the twins with patent astonishment, and Vangie with a frown of disapproval. He also noticed that the other passengers had left them behind and were well on their way up the gangplank, while he stood listening to the lies of a sorry little trickster.

Still, he could not ignore the girl's flagrant thievery. The watch was the only thing of any value he had ever owned, and the Lord knew it would more than likely have to be sold when they reached America, to help them survive until he found work.

It was a fine piece, bestowed upon his Uncle Ryan for saving a landlord's daughter from certain death by drowning in an icy stream. Their uncle had left it to Conn's older brother, Taber, who had passed it on to Conn just before entering the priesthood.

Conn fancied the timepiece, had guarded it with his life.

The time might well come when it was the only thing that stood between his family and starvation. And now this scrawny, dirty-faced busker girl had pocketed it for herself.

"Conn—"

He turned, impatient with his wife's continued interference.

"She's only a girl," Vangie said quietly. "And isn't she returning the watch? There's no real harm done, after all. Besides," she added, "there's nothing to do for it now, except to thank her."

"*Thank* her—" Conn gaped at his wife, who lifted her chin a little and met his gaze straight on.

"She didn't *have* to bring it back," Vangie pointed out. "You probably wouldn't even have noticed it was gone until long after we set sail."

Speechless Conn continued to stare at her, ignoring the prickle of truth in her words.

"Conn, we have to go." Vangie inclined her head toward the ship. "'Tis not as if they'll wait for us."

He looked from his wife to Renny Magee. "Why would you do such a disgraceful thing, girl?"

For the first time, she seemed to show some sign of remorse. "I didn't *steal* it, MacGovern! I didn't!" she blurted out. "You *dropped* it, and that's the truth. I might have *thought* of keeping it—but only for a shake, I swear it!" The pale blue eyes met Conn's directly. "I brought it back, now didn't I?"

Conn studied her a few seconds more. "And am I supposed to reward your *honesty*, then?" he shot back.

The girl seemed to be deliberating as to whether she should say more. She shifted her weight from one foot to the other, lifted a hand to straighten her sodden cap a bit. She opened her mouth as if to speak, then seemed to think better of it.

Finally she found her voice. "I was thinking that if…if I did you a good turn, perhaps you'd allow me to go along with you and your family." She stopped, gulped in a deep breath, and added, "To America."

Conn reared back in astonishment. "Are you demented entirely, girl? Why on earth would you think such a thing?"

Her mouth tightened, but she didn't look away. "I'm wild to go, MacGovern. 'Tis all I've ever wanted to do, don't you see? But now there's more to it than that. If I stay in Dublin City, sooner or later Nan Sweeney will set her bullyboys on me, and they won't finish until they pound me to a puddle in the street! No one crosses old Nan without paying the piper."

She stopped and caught a breath, then went on. "I thought—if I returned your watch, I could convince you to take me with you. I'd work for you however long it took to pay my way, I would! I'm fit, and I'm as strong as any lad, I promise you."

"You are *daft*, is what you are!" Conn threw back at her. "As if I'd subject my family to the likes of you!"

Vangie gave his arm a hard yank, and when she spoke this time, her tone was much sharper than before. "Stop it, Conn! The girl says she's telling the truth, and you have your watch. Now let it be."

In truth, Conn had begun to feel a bit shamed by the way he had harangued the girl. But she *was* a thief, despite what was almost certainly an uncommon attack of conscience, not to mention her outrageous scheme to wangle her way aboard ship with his help.

Well, she could forget *that* idea. He might look the great *amadan,* but the little trickster would learn soon enough that he was not the dolt she apparently took him to be.

But what could have gotten into Vangie, to be rebuking him in front of the children so? It seemed for all the world that she was taking the little reprobate's side against him!

He shot the girl one more look of contempt, then swiped his hands in a gesture of disgust. "I have no more to say to you. You know what you did, and that's the end of it."

He would have walked away, but Vangie restrained him with a firm hand on his arm.

~

In spite of the girl's disreputable appearance—and even taking into account her thievery—Vangie couldn't help but feel sorry for her. The child's ridiculous clothes were in tatters, her hair looked a fright, and she was soaked all through. She also appeared to be none too clean. And that terrible fierce look of pain in her eyes when Conn had lashed out at her—

But what caught at Vangie's heart more than anything else was the girl's seemingly feverish desperation to go to America. Was she alone altogether, then, that she would take up so casually with a family of strangers—with a man she had robbed, or at least thought of robbing—simply to get away?

For an instant, Vangie almost felt guilty at her own reluctance to leave when the girl in front of her would obviously have traded places in an instant.

It occurred to her that the busker girl might be in trouble with the law. Perhaps the reason she was so intent on getting out of Ireland was because a gaol cell was waiting for her if she stayed.

And yet, she didn't seem a bad sort. Sure, this was no hardened felon.

"Please, MacGovern," the girl pressed again. "You won't be sorry for taking me—"

"Now you listen to me, girl!"

Conn had gone red in the face, and he was jabbing a finger at the girl as he began to revile her again—a sure sign that he was about to lose control of that wicked temper of his.

"Even if I were mad enough to pay any heed to your foolishness," he said, his words cutting the air like a blade, "which I assure you I am not, I couldn't take you with us! It takes money to go to America, or are you so thick-skulled you didn't know that?"

The girl paled, and Vangie was sure she was close to tears, but she stood her ground, not quite looking at Conn but clearly not about to let him cower her either. Vangie couldn't help but admire the youngster's grit.

"What, are you thinking the captain will simply tip his hat to your highness and welcome you aboard out of the goodness of his heart?" Conn ranted on. "You have to *pay* for passage, don't you know? I've sold near everything but the shirt off my back as it is, just to take my family across! I haven't the means to secure passage for a lying little thief like yourself as well!"

~

Vangie gripped his arm, obviously hoping to silence him. But it was not her touch that shamed him. It was Renny Magee herself, lifting her thin face to reveal an utterly stricken look. Conn felt a rush of self-reproach over his harshness with the girl.

Even so, there was no chance to make amends. Aidan chose that moment to step up and insinuate himself between Conn and the busker girl.

Nothing could have prepared Conn for what followed. "Give the girl my ticket, Da," his son said quietly. Conn froze, staring at his son without comprehension.

"What—"

The boy's lean face was that of a stranger, hard and cold and openly defiant. "Give her my ticket."

Conn clenched his fists, bracing himself against the pain roaring up the back of his skull as disbelief clashed with the rage already boiling inside him.

"Aye," Aidan said, his tone quiet but edged with challenge, "I mean what I say, and you know I do. She can have my passage, for I will not be using it."

15

THE PARTING

What brings death to one
brings life to another.

IRISH PROVERB

Aidan's low, even voice startled Vangie into silence.

Conn, obviously as stunned as she, stood as rigid as a rock, watching Aidan as the boy stepped up to him.

Without so much as a glance at the busker girl, Aidan faced his father. "Didn't I tell you from the first I wasn't going, Da? I only came with you today to help with the little ones and say good-bye."

"I'll not be listening to this!" Conn exploded, his features contorted with anger and incredulity.

"And isn't that just like you?" Aidan said, his voice still chillingly quiet. "You *never* listen. But this time you need to hear me, Da. I am *not* going with you. So if this girl wants to go, then she might just as well use my passage."

A terrible heaviness lodged in Vangie's chest, a weight so crushing it stole her breath away. Her mind flashed through scenes from the past nineteen years: Her infant son snuggled against her breast. Conn lifting the laughing boy over his head, swinging him about as if the two of them could sprout wings and fly. Aidan's tenth birthday, in better days, with the family gathered around him.

No. For the love of God, no! He couldn't mean to leave them now, to stay behind in Ireland while they traveled to America. They would lose him forever, never see him again in this life.

She desperately wanted to deny it, to shut her eyes to the truth she saw in her eldest son's face, to open them again to find that it had all been a terrible misunderstanding. But she knew. With a sick certainty, she knew that Aidan had set his mind to this, and there would be no changing it.

He *had* told them he would not go, told them repeatedly. And just as repeatedly, Conn had refused to listen.

And what about herself? She had been desperate to believe Conn when he insisted that the boy was simply talking to the wind, that he would never stay behind and watch his entire family set out without him. Hadn't she turned a deaf ear to her son as well?

Now, however, as she stood watching the boy challenge his father, she admitted to herself that she had never been quite convinced. Unlike Conn, who simply could not believe that in the end Aidan would actually defy him, Vangie had merely suppressed her fear that he might do exactly that. Perhaps if she had faced the inevitable from the beginning, then she would be better able to bear the pain now ripping through her.

She looked at her son and, as was so often the case, saw a younger Conn.

Indeed, the boy could have *been* Conn twenty years ago.

They were almost the same height, and although Aidan was the more slender of the two, he was already showing signs that in a few years he would grow as sturdy and hard-muscled as his father. He had the same sun-burnished copper hair, the same stubborn chin. The same fire in his eyes. The same pride: the fierce, hardheaded, at times irrational pride that clearly marked him as the son of Conn MacGovern.

God in heaven, how can I bear this?

She would surely go mad. And Conn—

Merciful Lord, it might destroy Conn entirely!

Quickly, she handed the baby to Nell Grace, then laid a hand on her son's arm. "Aidan—"

He turned to look at her, his expression going soft and regretful. "I'm sorry, Mother. Truly, I am. But I told you. I told you and him both. I can't go. 'Tis not for me."

"You young *fool!*" Conn shouted at him. "Do you have any idea at all what you're throwing away? You would actually stay in Ireland to starve while your entire family goes off without you? *Think,* boy! Your passage is paid! Do you really mean to throw away the only ticket to freedom you may ever have?"

"I don't call it freedom for a man to desert his country!" Aidan returned. "And I won't be throwing away my ticket, unless you're too stubborn to make use of it." He gestured toward the busker girl. "She wants to go with you. I don't. Take her."

"Do you really expect me to hand over your passage to *her?*" Conn flung an arm out toward Renny Magee, nearly striking the girl as he did so. "What, I'm to take a common little thief to America in place of my own *son?*"

He took a step toward Aidan, his face murderous. "You are *going,* do you hear me, boy? You will go with us if I have to pound you senseless and *throw* you onto that ship!"

Aidan's eyes went hard, and Vangie saw him knot his fists, but he never wavered. "I warn you, Da. Don't lay a hand on me! *Don't.*"

The ship's whistle pierced through the pouring rain. There was no time left to them now. No more time for talk, no time to beg or try to reason with them. If they didn't go aboard soon, none of them would be leaving Ireland this day.

But it mattered little how much time they had. Conn and Aidan would simply go on blasting each other with the pent-up fury and frustration that had been seething between them for weeks. And in the end nothing would change. There would only be more pain.

Conn lunged toward Aidan, who in turn gave his father a hard shove backward.

"No!" Vangie shouted, throwing herself between them. "No, Conn! You'll not do this. Aidan—stop it! Both of you, stop!"

They looked at her, then backed off—but only a little—as they stood glaring at each other.

"Conn," Vangie said, her voice trembling, "he *did* try to tell us. He said he wouldn't go. We didn't listen. We didn't *want* to listen!"

But even as she tried to defend her son, Vangie felt her heart begin to shatter.

She turned to Aidan. "I can't believe you mean to do this! Can you actually turn your back and walk away from us, son? From me? From your father, your sisters and brothers? The Lord knows when we'll see one another again, if ever! Aidan, *think!* Think what this will mean—to all of us!"

"I have thought about it, Mother." His voice gentled as he took Vangie's hand. "And, of course, I'll miss you. You know I will. But I'm not a boy anymore, can't you see? I'm a man grown, and I've a life of my own to live, without Da telling me how to live it—or where. And I don't choose to live my life in *America!*"

He fairly spat the word, as if the very taste of it would poison his mouth.

By now Aidan's face was a mask of barely controlled fury. "Either you give my passage to the busker girl or else toss it into the Atlantic," he grated out. "I don't *care* what you do with it, but I'll not be using it. If the day ever comes when I change my mind, I'll pay my own way across. But this is not that day."

Conn stood, shaking with scarcely restrained rage, as Aidan embraced the others, first Vangie, then Nell Grace, who by now was weeping openly. He kissed both her and Baby Emma on the tops of their heads before leaning down to the twins.

Vangie thought she would surely strangle on her grief as she watched him say good-bye to his little brothers.

"Be men for our mother, Seamus. Sean," he said, using their Irish names as he almost always did. "She will need you to be fine, good lads."

The two boys, similar in appearance though not quite identical, gazed up at their older brother with solemn, freckled faces. Johnny—Sean—whose hair was more golden than the copper fire of his father and two brothers—was clearly about to burst into tears, while James—Seamus—was already weeping. Even so, each of them managed to shake Aidan's hand.

And then the lad straightened and again faced his father. Vangie thought she would not survive the pain that knifed through her as she watched her son and her husband stand there staring at each other in unforgiving silence. In their pride and hotheaded stubbornness, they were so much alike, though neither would ever admit to it.

"Conn—*do* something!" she cried.

But he merely turned away, his face a mask of stone.

A swell of despair overcame Vangie, and she closed her eyes, unwilling to watch this final, heartless farewell between her husband and her son. When she again opened her eyes, Aidan had turned and was walking away, without so much as another word or a backward glance.

In that moment, a ray of light died somewhere in Vangie: the light that had been born with her eldest child, her darling boy. In its place remained only a cold, suffocating darkness, and she wondered how long it would take before it swallowed her whole.

Then she looked at Conn and realized with dreadful clarity that a light had gone out in her husband as well. It struck her that Conn's suffering might actually be more grievous than her own, for the bond between a man and his son was a fierce tie, more than blood and birthright, more than name and honor. A man saw in his son his own hopes, his dreams—his future. When Aidan turned his back on them this day, he not only rejected his father's authority, but he renounced Conn's dreams and brightest hopes as well.

Her head thundered as she watched her son walk away, his back erect, his shoulders squared. The ship's whistle sounded again. Her glance went to the busker girl for an instant. Then, ignoring the shrieking agony inside her, she made a decision.

"Conn," she choked out, "there is nothing left to do about Aidan. We can only pray that in time he will come to his senses and join us. But there *is* something we can do for that frightened child." She motioned toward the busker girl. "I think we should take her with us."

"For the love of heaven, woman!" he began to rail at her. "That *frightened child* stole my watch. Have you forgotten that? She's a *thief*, and who knows what else!"

"You don't know but what you *did* drop the watch, just as she said, Conn. All you know is that the girl *returned* it." Vangie gripped his thickly muscled forearm even harder. "And she *is* frightened! Look at her! Oh, Conn, listen to me—please! It's *wrong* to waste Aidan's passage, I tell you, wrong not to help that girl when we have it in our means to do so. Let her come with us."

He stared at her in open disbelief.

"I don't mean to simply give her the ticket for nothing," Vangie pressed. "We will see that she earns her way. She will work for the price of her passage."

He went on studying her, his eyes still brimming with bewildered anger. "You'd actually do this? You'd let a guttersnipe like her use our son's passage?"

Anger flared up in Vangie. "Our son doesn't *want* his passage! The girl does. She's begging to go. I say we take her. Let *something* worthwhile come of all this!"

"You mean it," he said, looking at her as if he scarcely knew her. "You actually mean to help the little thief."

"I do," Vangie said evenly. "What can be the harm?"

He let out an ugly laugh. "Oh, no harm, I'm sure, so long as she doesn't murder us all in our beds!"

"She's a child," Vangie shot back. "And perhaps a thief. But not a murderer, I think. She's just a poor girl looking for a future. Looking for some hope. We have it in our power to give her that hope, and I believe our Lord would have us do just that."

She pressed his arm, refusing to let him turn away from her. "I want to do this, Conn. We *need* to do this."

Conn's eyes brimmed with resentment as he glanced from Vangie to the girl. "What does it matter?" he said, giving a shrug. "Do as you like. Our son has gone mad, so why shouldn't the rest of us follow after?"

His tone was laced with bitterness as he went on. "But don't be expecting any thanks from the likes of her. And you would do well to forget any notion of her earning her way, I'll wager. She will no more step foot on deck before she disappears to work her mischief elsewhere; you wait and see if she doesn't."

"You may be right," Vangie said, too heartsick and exhausted to argue any further with him. "But at least we will have done what we could to help her. 'Tis not for us to take responsibility for what she does with that help. That's for our Lord to deal with."

He pulled his mouth into a hard line. "'Tis not for me to take any responsibility for her at all. This is your idea, not mine, Vangie. I will have no part in it."

⌒

A chant played over and over in Renny Magee's mind as she watched the two of them, MacGovern and his woman. *Let him say yes…let him say yes…*

Renny had reached the point where she believed her entire future might very well hang on what the MacGoverns decided. Despite the fact that she would have preferred to put Nan Sweeney completely out of her mind, she had not exaggerated her present situation. In truth, no one crossed old Nan and got away free. Nan would never let up until she had her justice. And old Nan's kind of justice was an ugly thing, as everyone knew. She was a terrible woman entirely.

This Mrs. MacGovern, now, she was a different sort, that much was clear. A good woman, Renny could tell. A tall, fine-looking woman with skin of rich cream and a grand head of hair the color of the bay at sunset. She had kind eyes, she did, but the way she was squaring off with her thickheaded husband gave

Renny high hopes that for all her kindness, she was more than a match for the man.

Even so, Renny cautioned herself not to be too hopeful. MacGovern had no reason to go easy on her, not with the bad business of the watch and all.

Just then, she saw them both glance in her direction. Renny held her breath as the woman turned and started toward her.

⌒

Vangie stood studying the thin-faced busker girl for a moment. "What's your name, child?"

"Renny Magee, missus."

"And how old are you, Renny?"

The girl shrugged. "Don't know, missus. I never knew my people, you see, so nobody ever told me how old I was."

Vangie looked at her more closely. "You're an orphan, then?"

"I am."

Vangie speculated that the girl was probably close on eleven or twelve, perhaps even older, though she was small and wretchedly thin for her age.

She drew a long breath, praying she was not making a terrible mistake. "Very well, then. My husband has agreed to allow you the use of our son's passage. But"—she lifted a hand to silence the girl's attempt to speak—"*but* you will not bring so much as a scrap of trouble or dishonor on yourself or upon this family for the duration of the crossing. My son's ticket is yours to use, but as of this moment you will conduct yourself with Christian decency, or my husband will have you put off the ship to your own destruction. Your hands will touch no other pockets except your own, and you will be obedient to what either my husband or I instruct you to do. Do you understand what I am saying, Renny Magee?"

The girl stared, her odd, pale blue eyes unnervingly steady, although Vangie sensed that she was restraining herself only with great effort. With one hand then, Renny Magee removed the sodden cap from her head and bowed slightly, as if in deference to a great lady. "I understand, missus," she said in a voice that was noticeably shaky. "And I'll not be a bit of trouble to you, my hand on it."

Vangie glanced at Conn and saw her own weary resignation reflected in his face. She would have no help from him; that much was plain.

She faced the girl again, injecting a note of sternness into her voice. "Since you will be traveling with us, you will take on your share of the work, is that understood? The children will have to be looked after. And there will be laundry—though I don't know as yet just how we will manage it. And mending. There is always mending with the children. Do you know how to sew, girl?" she asked abruptly, knowing the answer before she ever voiced the question.

Renny Magee glanced away. "I've never exactly tried my hand at it. But I can learn," she added hurriedly, looking back at Vangie. "I can learn most anything I set my mind to, and that's the truth."

"And learn you will. You will not be idle, miss."

Again the girl moved as if to speak—and again Vangie silenced her with a shake of her head. "When we reach America, you will continue to work for us no less than six months unless Mr. MacGovern says you may leave us sooner. Is that clear?"

"You've only to tell me what you want done, and I'll do it," said Renny Magee, now cracking a grin that revealed a pronounced space between her two front teeth. "For as long as you want."

Vangie was surprised to realize that the girl was almost fair when she smiled. Her piquant features took on a certain pertness that was somehow agreeable. She actually possessed a kind of impish charm in spite of her unkempt appearance.

But there was no more time for questions or a closer examination of Renny Magee. The ship gave a final warning blast, and a crew member shouted at them to get aboard or be left behind.

As they hurried up the gangplank, Conn in front, Renny Magee just behind him, Vangie turned to look back, irrationally hoping that perhaps Aidan might have lingered nearby to watch them go. But there was no glimpse of him. He was gone, and now they were leaving, too.

As the crew herded them belowdecks, Vangie struggled to regain the memory of what she had experienced in the harbor. They were not alone, she reminded herself. Nor was Aidan.

Perhaps not. But being alone wasn't the same as being lonely, and Vangie knew that without her son, her firstborn, she would always be lonely. Even in the midst of her family, she would be lonely.

She already was.

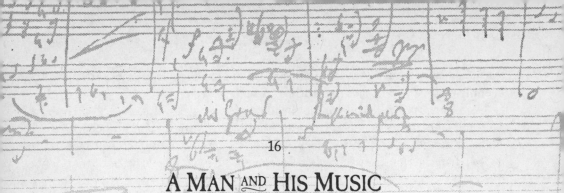

16

A MAN AND HIS MUSIC

In his music, consecrated,
The Divine is celebrated,
As his seeking heart embraces
Heaven's high and holy places.

ANONYMOUS

New York City

The theater shimmered with gaslight and candle glow, dimmed only by the reflection of the ladies' jewels and glistening gowns. A palpable sense of excitement hung over the concert hall, an anticipation so keen it could be felt above the shuffling and conversation of the audience.

"Papa will be coming out any minute now, Aunt Susanna! And he'll be so handsome! Wait and see!"

Seated between Caterina and Rosa Navaro in Michael's private box, Susanna smiled at her niece. She, too, was excited about the opening of tonight's concert. This would be her first time to attend a performance by Michael's orchestra, but that was not the sole reason for her anticipation.

In Dublin, she had often attended the symphony with the Mahers, her former employers. Her last outing with them had been over a year ago, but until tonight, she had had little time to reflect on the lack of music in her life, or the emptiness that lack engendered in her soul. Now, awaiting the concert, she realized how very much she had missed the experience.

Indeed, there had been precious little time to reflect on anything since she'd arrived in New York. The days had been filled with the effort of settling into her new home and acclimating herself to the routine of the household.

She had determined early on that considerable adaptability was expected from everyone at Bantry Hill, even from those who lived on the periphery of Michael Emmanuel's life. If she had once envisioned her brother-in-law as a brooding recluse, spending his days in self-imposed seclusion while he labored over his music and massaged his inflated ego, it hadn't taken long to send those preconceptions packing.

In truth, she had seen very little of Michael during the weeks since her arrival. He had been in rehearsal, staying in the city almost every night, some days coming home only long enough to spend a few hours with Caterina before rushing off again.

Other than what she'd learned from Deirdre's letters, Susanna had been forced to glean the little she knew about the man from Rosa Navaro and Caterina. Her own contact with him had been sporadic and at times frustrating. Although he was invariably gracious and never failed to show a concern for her comfort and well-being, he was most often preoccupied, even more remote than he'd been the day she'd first arrived at Bantry Hill.

More perturbing still, he had yet to offer a full explanation of Deirdre's death. By now, Susanna was almost convinced that he was deliberately avoiding the subject.

If that was his tactic—and she was increasingly suspicious that it was—he would soon realize that she wouldn't be put off indefinitely. He had promised her answers, and she had every intention of getting them.

She was determined to know what had happened to Deirdre. It was true that they had never been close; actually, there had been times when she wasn't even sure she *liked* her older sister. Nevertheless, they *had* been sisters, and there would be no peace for her until she learned the truth about Deirdre's death.

She had already decided that if Michael persisted in his evasion, she would take her questions elsewhere, perhaps to Rosa Navaro. She had even thought about going to the authorities but didn't quite know how to begin. Perhaps when Michael saw that she was a fair match for his stubbornness, he would finally give in and tell her everything.

And if he didn't?

She would face that particular dilemma only if and when it became necessary.

～

The concert hall quieted. The lights dimmed as the crimson velvet curtains opened on the orchestra. Paul Santi, the concertmaster, rose with his violin and gave the other musicians the note of A, and dissonance reigned until all the instruments swelled to total agreement.

Then silence again descended, and Paul exited the stage.

"There he is! There's Papa!" Caterina tugged at Susanna's sleeve, then bounced forward on the edge of her seat.

Susanna looked from the excited child to the stage, where Paul Santi was escorting Michael to the podium. The collective hush that had fallen over the audience now gave way to an unrestrained burst of applause as Michael took his place at the conductor's dais.

She saw him touch the toe of his left foot to the metal strip he used as a marker. He acknowledged the audience's welcome with a small bow and the quick, youthful smile that never failed to catch Susanna unawares. She had caught only brief glimpses of that smile, yet every time she encountered the sudden, unexpected expression of boyishness and warmth, she felt the same stab of confusion she'd known at their first meeting.

As it happened, Michael's stage presence was even more unsettling than his smile. Up until now, Susanna had seen him in only weekend or informal attire—often in his shirt sleeves or a worn sweater, his dark hair carelessly tousled, his demeanor sometimes brisk, sometimes relaxed, but always distant. She had come to think of him as a very casual man in his preferences, not much concerned with appearances and seemingly more inclined toward the natural than the artificial.

But the man on stage this evening was anything but casual. In truth, he was downright resplendent. In black tails and vivid white linen, he had forgone the dark glasses. The black, shaggy hair had been brushed to some semblance of control, the dark beard neatly trimmed, and with his towering height and Tuscan bearing, he was positively regal.

Susanna's throat constricted as she knotted her hands in her lap, acknowledging to herself, albeit grudgingly, that perhaps it wasn't so difficult after all to understand how Deirdre might have been dazzled by this man.

"Didn't I tell you, Aunt Susanna? Isn't Papa handsome?"

Caterina's loud whisper brought Susanna's thoughts back to the present. With her niece's small hand clasped warmly in her own, she smiled, then turned her attention back to the stage.

As she watched, Michael turned to the orchestra and gave an almost undetectable tapping of the baton. Then, with an authoritative lift of his wide shoulders, he signaled the musicians, and the three majestic chords of the overture to Mozart's opera *The Magic Flute* sounded.

The orchestra followed this overture with another, Gluck's *Alceste*, an intense, surging work of great nobility and depth. Then, with the assistance of Paul Santi, Michael again exited the stage, to return after only a moment or two.

He bowed again, then lifted his baton, and the first notes of the introduction to Beethoven's Seventh Symphony ascended and filled the hall. Susanna loved the Seventh but had been somewhat surprised at Michael's choice for the major work of the evening. She would have expected him to opt for the better-known and more ambitious Fifth or even the monumental Ninth. The Seventh was a more impetuous, emotional work, at times lively and deceptively lighthearted, then building to a frenzied, almost volcanic explosion of energy and power. It was also one of the tortured composer's more controversial, less predictable symphonies.

Critics often sought to offer an analysis of the work, but Susanna shared Michael's recently voiced opinion that the Seventh went *beyond* explanation, that perhaps the fact that it could not be explained or analyzed was actually a fundamental part of the work's appeal.

Now, watching him, it struck Susanna that the man on stage was quite possibly as unpredictable, as inscrutable, as the capricious symphony itself.

By the time the music reached the driving, marchlike second movement, Susanna had temporarily suspended her misgivings about her brother-in-law.

Indeed, she had almost lost sight of Michael and the orchestra as separate entities. The two had somehow become one, melding into a single mighty instrument of rhythm and motion and sound, sweeping the hall with a somber but heroic processional that made her pulse thunder and her spirit sing with the magnificence of it all.

"Is he using a score?" she whispered to Rosa Navaro, unable to comprehend how such a herculean work could possibly be transcribed to Braille.

The older woman offered her opera glasses to Susanna, saying, "Michael doesn't need a score. It's all here," she said, lightly tapping her own forehead, then her heart.

Incredible.

Susanna lifted the opera glasses to her eyes. Under the direction of a less brilliant conductor, the *Allegretto* could easily have become a funeral dirge, but Michael and his musicians had honed it to a persistent, exultant paean of praise.

She became aware that Caterina was gripping her hand more tightly, but when she looked, she saw that the child's gaze was riveted to the stage. The sight of the little girl so completely absorbed in the music gave Susanna an inordinate sense of pleasure, perhaps because it had been the same with her. She couldn't remember a time when music hadn't been an overwhelming, even spiritual experience for her.

Out of the corner of her eye, she noted that Rosa Navaro, to her left, was blinking furiously, as if trying to hold back tears of emotion. Indeed, many among the audience seemed to be fighting to keep their feelings in check as the orchestra unleashed the full force of Beethoven's colossal work.

She could see from Michael's profile that his eyes were closed, his face damp with perspiration. Susanna sensed that so absorbed was he in this bold epic of musical struggle and celebration that he was no longer a *conductor* of the music… he had in some incomprehensible way *become* the music.

As the insistent, driving pulse of the *Allegretto* finally gave way to the more exuberant *Presto*, a faint, collective sigh rose up from the audience. Susanna expelled a long breath to relieve her own tension; at the same time she felt Caterina relax the grip on her hand.

She could not help but be transfixed by the man at the podium. Not one of his movements was superfluous, from the slightest roll of the wrist to the powerful shuddering that seemed to run the length of his tall frame as he demanded—and received—the ultimate in musicianship from his orchestra.

There was no melodramatic posturing, no obvious air of self-aggrandizement or showmanship. Instead he appeared to be a man lifted out of himself, transported to a higher plane as he reached for some sublime but elusive splendor, some unseen touch of glory, while the music gathered force and became a power in and of itself.

By the time the orchestra had plunged into the *Finale,* an energized, abandoned outburst of power and exhilaration, Susanna felt certain that the entire audience, herself included, had been left breathless. Watching Michael, seeing the unmistakable signs of the intensity, the physical and emotional demands this particular work placed upon a conductor, she would not have been surprised had he collapsed before his final bow.

She leaped to her feet with the rest of the audience as a violent explosion of cheers and applause erupted. For an instant, Michael seemed to hesitate where he stood. When he turned to face the delirious crowd, he appeared almost stunned for a moment, as if he might be struggling to place his surroundings. But then the familiar winning smile broke forth, and he made a deep, sweeping bow of tribute to the orchestra.

He and Paul shook hands, and then at last he lifted his face toward the box and, smiling even wider, gave a deferential bow in their direction.

"Papa always bows to me at the end," Caterina said with obvious pride. Bouncing on the balls of her feet, she blew a kiss to the father who could not see her.

Flowers were flung wildly onto the stage, an enormous bouquet was presented, and the demand for an encore went up like a roar. Finally, Michael gave a consenting nod and turned back to the orchestra.

The piece they plunged into was new to Susanna. Her first thought was of a folk tune or an old world dance, but the music suddenly shifted to a medley that might have been martial in quality, had the rhythms not been so unrestrained. It ended with a hymnlike theme of great beauty, its final cadence sustained by the trumpets and horns and timpani. The entire work virtually shouted of something new, something distinctly and utterly American.

Again the audience rose to their feet in a wild ovation. Rosa Navaro touched Susanna's hand. "That was one of Michael's own compositions," she said. "Part of a larger work, a symphonic suite."

"Did you like it, Aunt Susanna?" Caterina piped in.

"It was wonderful," Susanna replied in all sincerity. "Your papa is a very gifted man."

The little girl's face dimpled in a wide smile as she gave a vigorous nod. "He's the cleverest man ever. And the best papa in the whole world, too!"

Susanna studied her niece for a moment. Caterina obviously adored her father.

Might her own feelings of distrust be unfounded after all? Could a man capable of such transcending emotion and brilliant artistry—and such obvious devotion to his child—also be capable of the kind of treachery of which she had long suspected him…and of which Deirdre had accused him?

Michael returned to the stage for two more encores. As Paul Santi led him to the wings for the final time, he seemed to falter and even stumble. Instinctively, Susanna lifted a hand out as if to steady him.

She caught herself, but not before Caterina had seen. "It's all right, Aunt Susanna," the little girl said, her features solemn. "You mustn't worry about Papa. He trips sometimes, but he never falls. Even if he should, everyone will pretend not to notice. They wouldn't want to hurt Papa's feelings, you see."

Susanna looked at the girl, sensing the total conviction with which she spoke. For one bittersweet moment she could see a reflection of herself in her niece's eyes. Like Caterina, she had adored her own father, had placed in him the same total, unshakable confidence, and had held the same childlike belief that others naturally revered him as she did.

But *her* father had been entirely worthy of a daughter's faith and devotion. For the sake of the trusting little girl beside her, she fervently hoped the same could be said of Michael Emmanuel.

Yet, somewhere at the outer fringes of her mind a dark, familiar whisper taunted her with the possibility that Caterina's confidence might just possibly be misplaced.

~

It was late when they boarded the night ferry. Only Rosa Navaro accompanied Susanna and Caterina up the river. Michael had stayed in the city, in preparation for the following night's concert.

They had barely settled themselves when Caterina, lulled by the darkness and the rocking of the boat, curled up next to Susanna and fell asleep.

In the dim glow of the lanterns, Rosa, seated across from them, smiled and nodded toward Caterina. "It seems that you have become very important to her."

Susanna smiled down at the sleeping little girl. "And she has become very important to me. She's really quite wonderful."

Rosa nodded. "The child needs you in her life, Susanna. It's good that the two of you have taken to each other so quickly."

Rosa's accent was mild, not nearly so pronounced as Michael's, but even in the soft shadows of the night, her strong, distinct features and snapping dark eyes were unmistakably Mediterranean. She lifted a hand to pat her hair, setting off a delicate chiming sound from the heavy gold bracelets encircling her wrist. Not for the first time, it occurred to Susanna that Rosa was really a very striking and exotic woman in appearance.

But it was Rosa Navaro's kindness she appreciated most. The opera diva had a warmth, a comfortable way about her that made her easy to be with and seemed to invite the confidence of others. Although Susanna hadn't forgotten some of the unpleasant things Deirdre had written about "that Navaro woman" in her letters, she chose to form her own conclusions—and she had decided to accept the friendship that Rosa seemed more than willing to offer.

"So, Susanna—did you enjoy the concert?"

Susanna blinked, hoping she hadn't been staring. "Oh, yes, very much."

Rosa nodded. "Nobody understands the Beethoven like Michael, I think. He is a brilliant musician."

Susanna studied her. "I wonder, though—doesn't he miss the opera? It must have been very difficult to give up such an illustrious career."

Rosa glanced away for a moment. "Michael finds his work with the orchestra fulfilling. He seems content."

"Did he stop performing because of his blindness?" Susanna knew she was pressing, but her curiosity overcame her customary reserve.

Rosa turned to look at her. "Only Michael could explain his reasons." She paused, then added, "I do know he wanted more time for his own music. Composing is very important to him."

"Yes...I'm sure it is."

Susanna deliberated over whether to raise any further questions. This woman was, after all, a good friend to Michael. She clearly doted on him, much as an older sister might. No doubt she would resent any attempt to pry into his personal life.

But what about *Deirdre's* life?

"Rosa?"

The older woman's expression had become somewhat guarded.

"Would you mind—I was hoping you might tell me more about Deirdre's accident. I've never really understood what, exactly, happened the night she died."

Rosa's normally open countenance now took on an unfamiliar, closed appearance. "But surely you already know about the accident, the buggy overturning—"

"Yes, I know about the buggy," Susanna said, catching a breath in an effort to curb her impatience. "What I *don't* know," she went on, choosing her words carefully, "is what Deirdre was *doing* in the buggy, at that time of night—in the middle of a thunderstorm."

The lantern light flickered, bathing Rosa's face in shadows as she turned her gaze downward. "You should ask Michael about this, Susanna."

"I *have* asked Michael about it—"

Caterina stirred just then, and Susanna broke off. But the child showed no sign of waking up.

"There never seems to be a...a *convenient* time for him to talk with me,"

Susanna continued. Even to her own ears, she sounded petulant, but Rosa's features remained unreadable. "He always insists it will have to wait until later."

"You must try to understand," Rosa replied. "No doubt it is still very difficult for Michael to speak of the accident. I think you will need to be patient, to wait."

"It seems to me that I *have* been patient," Susanna said, swallowing down her resentment. "I've been here for nearly a month now. How long should I have to wait?"

She realized her voice had risen, but although Caterina moved slightly, she slept on.

"Rosa," she tried again, "was my sister…happy? In the marriage, I mean?"

The older woman regarded Susanna with a studying look, then lifted a hand to smooth her hair. "How well did you know your sister, Susanna?"

Surprised by the question, Susanna stared at her. "I…we were sisters."

Rosa's gaze never wavered. "But there were a number of years between you. And you had been separated for some time, no?"

"Yes, that's true. But she *was* my sister. I cared about her. That's why I want— why I *need* to know what happened."

"These are not questions for me to answer, Susanna," Rosa replied, her tone firm but kind. "I'm sure Michael will explain. In time."

The ferry was docking now, and Caterina began to stir again. Susanna was surprised when Rosa reached to take her hand. "Give Michael time, Susanna. As difficult as it was for you to lose your sister, you must remember that he lost his wife."

In the carriage on the road home, they maintained a polite but meaningless exchange. Rosa's obvious reluctance to talk about Deirdre had only sharpened Susanna's suspicions. Where else could she go for the truth? She was beginning to feel as though she were locked outside a door to which there was no key— perhaps a door to which someone had deliberately *hidden* the key.

She stared out the carriage window into the thick darkness of the night, then glanced at the drowsy little girl snuggled against her. If only Caterina were older. Perhaps then she could learn the truth from her, the truth about what had really happened to her mother.

And *why* it had happened.

Suddenly weary, Susanna leaned her head back against the seat. She could feel Rosa's watchful gaze on her, but she closed her eyes and pretended to doze until she felt the carriage slow in its approach to the Navaro mansion.

Susanna straightened, careful not to rouse Caterina, who slept curled up like a kitten, her head in Susanna's lap. Rosa was smiling at both of them, but as she started to step from the carriage, she turned back and again reached to clasp Susanna's hand.

"Try to trust Michael, Susanna," she said, her dark eyes intent. "I'm sure that in his own time, he will tell you what you want to know. But if I may, I would caution you to be absolutely certain you want your questions answered."

She paused, still gripping Susanna's hand. "Sometimes," she said, "the answers to our questions are so painful to hear that we end up wishing we had never asked."

Then she was gone, leaving Susanna more disturbed than ever as she absently stroked Caterina's hair the rest of the way to Bantry Hill.

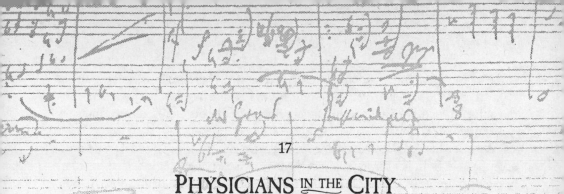

17

PHYSICIANS IN THE CITY

Your greatest challenge will not
necessarily be the attainment
of the title, "physician,"
but instead may well be the overcoming
of the opposition—
especially that of your "manly" colleagues—
once you attain that noble title.

IN A LETTER FROM DORSEY COLE TO HIS GRANDDAUGHTER, BETHANY

A cold autumn rain began early Monday morning, and by now Bethany Cole had begun to question her own common sense.

Although Uncle Marsh had offered a carriage, so far she had managed to get around the city just fine either by walking or using public transportation. Last night's change in the weather, however, reminded her that winter would be upon them in no time, and the walks she usually enjoyed would no longer be so pleasant.

Bethany enjoyed being self-sufficient—up to a point. She insisted on living in her own flat rather than rooming with her aunt and uncle, not only because she valued her privacy and wanted to fend for herself, but also because she was keenly aware of Aunt Mildred's feelings about "women who worked." Her aunt's resentment of Bethany's career included any attempt on the part of Uncle Marsh to make things a little easier for her. As far as Aunt Mildred was concerned, if Bethany wanted to be an "independent woman," she would be *completely* independent, with no assistance of any kind from her family.

Of course, Aunt Mildred was an incurable skinflint, so Bethany wouldn't have expected anything else.

Still, the Scriptures did counsel against pride. Being on her own was all well and good, but a day like this served to remind her that there might be such a thing as too *much* independence. At the moment, her umbrella was doing little to ward off the wind-driven rain, and by the time she reached the corner of Seventeenth and Fourth, her skirts were soggy, her boots were leaking, and she was chilled all through.

Without her small savings, she would have had to swallow her pride and accept a loan from her uncle—at least the loan of a carriage. Her inheritance from her grandparents was far more modest than Aunt Mildred probably thought, but at least she had something of her own to dip into, if necessary.

As she struggled to anchor the umbrella against the wind, Bethany scanned her surroundings as best she could. The neighborhood was reasonably pleasant and might even have been fashionable at one time. Now there were unmistakable signs that its more well-to-do residents had moved elsewhere—more than likely, farther north. Commercial establishments seemed to have taken over many of the spacious brick and stone houses.

Stormy as it was, the streets nevertheless teemed with Monday morning traffic, both pedestrian and carriage. A mix of workers and businessmen hurried along, darting in and out among the buggies and omnibuses, while the pungent smell of rain, sodden leaves, and horse droppings permeated the air.

Throughout the three-block walk from her apartment, Bethany had tried not to be too optimistic about Dr. Carmichael's invitation to stop by his office. It wasn't as if he had spoken of anything specific, after all. Still, she hoped she hadn't misunderstood him. He *had* alluded to the possibility that he might be able to help her in her efforts to set up a private practice, as well as in her ongoing struggle to obtain hospital privileges.

Hadn't he?

The hope of hospital privileges alone would have been enough to bring her calling long before now, but circumstances had intervened, and she'd found herself working almost around the clock for three weeks running. Influenza had drastically reduced the Infirmary's staff, and Bethany had more or less been living there, grabbing an hour's sleep whenever she could, eating whenever she thought of it.

In spite of the long hours of hard work and the lack of acceptance—or outright contempt—of many of her male colleagues, Bethany couldn't remember a time when she hadn't wanted to be a doctor. As a child, she had made patients of her baby dolls and every stray animal that happened to venture into the backyard. By the time she was in her teens, she had read all the way through her grandmother's household medical manual, going on to cajole her physician-grandfather into allowing her free access to *his* bookshelves. Within another year, she was pressing him to make her his assistant.

Wise man that he was, Dorsey Cole had gently but firmly resisted his grand-daughter's badgering. "Bethany, these days anyone can become a doctor. At least anyone can become a quack. But not just anyone can become a *good* doctor. If you really want to hang out a shingle alongside mine, then you must first equip yourself with a good education."

In his usual unhurried manner, he'd gone on to emphasize that a physician's knowledge should not be limited to diseases and injuries. "If you want to be a good doctor, you need a keen understanding of your patients' minds and hearts as well. To attain that kind of insight, you need to learn as much as possible about *people*, about life, and the world we live in."

Bethany adored the grandfather and grandmother who raised her after the train accident that killed her parents. She wanted to make them proud, and so, despite her youthful impatience, she had taken her grandfather's advice to heart. After the prerequisite education at Miss Haverhill's Feminine Academy—where she would have doubtless succumbed to total boredom had it not been for the good-humored mischief she and her companions foisted upon their roommates almost nightly—she left for the Women's Medical College of Pennsylvania.

She graduated first in her class. But as it happened, her grandfather had not lived long enough to take her into his practice. His health had been failing for some time even before she entered medical college, and shortly before graduation, he passed away. Not long after, her grandmother followed.

With both of them gone, Bethany couldn't imagine returning to the home where she'd grown up, much less taking over her grandfather's practice, which had diminished considerably with his poor health. Instead, she decided to settle in New York, not so much because her only surviving aunt and uncle lived here, but more because she believed the prospects for a woman physician might be greater in such a highly populated city. Almost immediately, she found a position at the New York Infirmary for Women and Children, allowing her to further expand her training under the founder, Dr. Elizabeth Blackwell, and other excellent women physicians, such as Dr. Mary Jacobi.

Even as both women encouraged Bethany in her efforts to establish her own practice and gain hospital privileges, they urged caution and patience. But Bethany had begun to realize that it was going to take something more than patience to achieve her goals here in New York. And that realization had driven her out on this wretchedly cold, wet morning. If there was any chance that Andrew Carmichael might be able—and willing—to help her, she was definitely going to listen to what he had to say.

As she approached the entrance of the aging brick building on Seventeenth Street, however, it occurred to her that after all this time the best she could probably hope for was that he hadn't completely forgotten about her by now.

⌒

Andrew Carmichael lifted a shoulder to catch the perspiration on his forehead, then tied off the last stitch at the corner of Charlie Duffy's left eye.

"You're very fortunate, Mr. Duffy," he said, adopting a stern tone. "You might have easily lost your eye, you know. That cut was way too close for comfort."

The old man nodded vigorously, his almost toothless grin breaking even wider. "Ah, but it was a grand fight, Doc! And wasn't that black-hearted scallywag more than a little surprised when I trounced him?"

Andrew suppressed a smile at his feisty patient. "Mr. Duffy, I'm not sure that a man of your years ought to be taking up a challenge, don't you see? Especially when it involves someone with a name like Dukes Neeson."

His patient cackled. "Call me Charlie, Doc! And don't you fret yourself a'tall about *me*. I can handle the likes of any knock-a-kneed Kerry-man! No doubt you're thinkin' I took the worst of it, but that would be because you ain't seen Dukes."

Andrew shook his head, no longer able to keep a straight face. "All the same, sir, the next time your bluff is called, I'd strongly suggest you walk away."

Charlie Duffy was sixty-five if he was a day and no bigger than an adolescent boy, but he clearly thought himself a man to be reckoned with. And perhaps he was at that, Andrew thought with wry amusement.

"No self-respecting Irisher ever walked away from an honest fight, Doc, no matter his years. Why, that good-for-nothing blackheart accused me of chatin', don't you know?"

The wizened little man sat up, and Andrew winced as dirty fingers traced a line over the wound he had just stitched.

"Nobody gets away with callin' Charlie Duffy a chate," his patient proclaimed, jutting out his chin. "And me who's never so much as dealt a false hand in me life."

Andrew helped the wiry little man off the table and shook his hand, taken aback by the surprising strength of the other's grip. "All the same, Mr. Duffy, in the future I hope you'll take care."

Charlie Duffy beamed up at Andrew as he touched his wound again. "You can count on it, Doc. And that's the truth."

He lifted a grimy paw in a kind of salute, then swaggered across the room.

⌒

Bethany Cole stepped into the waiting room, stopping just inside the door. Her first sense was one of confusion and disorder. Two long benches along the walls were lined with patients, leaving many others to stand. There were several children, some whimpering in their mother's arms, others scurrying back and forth across the room. None of the youngsters paid any heed to her as she entered, but their mothers took her measure with undisguised curiosity.

The odors of formaldehyde, alcohol, and other familiar chemicals hung over the room. There was also a strong indication that some little person was in serious need of a diaper change. A tall counter divided the modestly furnished waiting room from the reception area and examining doors. Bethany caught a glimpse of an unoccupied reception desk behind the counter. The windows were narrow and dusty, the wooden floor bare but reasonably clean. In the far corner, against an outside wall, an iron stove gave off an acrid odor of smoke, but a welcome warmth.

Bethany caught the sense of a much used, very *busy* room that suffered from a dearth of attention. A place where time, not necessarily money, accounted for the lack of neatness and attractive furnishings.

Clearly, she had come at a bad time. She chided herself for not thinking. First thing on Monday morning was definitely not the optimal hour to "drop by" a busy physician's office.

She felt a twinge of envy at the sight of the crowded waiting room. With all her heart, she longed to know both the burden and the blessing of an office filled to capacity with patients—*her* patients—waiting for her to employ her skills in their behalf. Out of habit, she had brought her medical case, and her fingers on the handle now itched to open it and go to work.

Annoyed with her own bad timing, she turned, intending to leave, then stopped when one of the surgery doors opened to reveal a spry looking little man with a black eye over which a row of neat stitches had been drawn. Right behind him stood Andrew Carmichael.

The physician saw her right away, his face registering surprise and, to Bethany's relief, recognition.

"Dr. Cole!"

The doctor's lab coat was wrinkled, the sleeves noticeably too short. A shock of dark hair fell over one eye. He appeared slightly rumpled and somewhat bemused. But at the moment, the only thing that mattered to Bethany was that he seemed genuinely pleased to see her.

He came the rest of the way into the waiting room, watching while his patient, a small, spindly-legged man, gave a jaunty wave and went out the door. Then he turned to Bethany. "Well, it's good to see you again, Dr. Cole. Nasty morning, though, isn't it?"

"I'm so sorry," Bethany burst out. "I can't believe I was foolish enough to come by on Monday morning. I wasn't thinking—"

"No, no, this is fine! I'd almost given up on your coming at all." A faint flush crept over his features, as if he'd suddenly realized he might have said too much.

Even on the day of the fire, when they'd first met, Bethany had sensed an unexpected awkwardness in this man. Not shyness, exactly, but something akin to it, and she'd wondered why that should be.

Andrew Carmichael looked to be in his mid to late thirties, and although he wasn't exactly a handsome man by contemporary standards, his long, clean-shaven face held a definite appeal and hinted of a strong, but pleasant character. According to the staff members at the Infirmary, he was held in high esteem, not only by his peers among New York's medical community, but by many of the missionary organizations throughout the city as well.

During the years since he'd settled in New York, the Scottish physician had apparently established himself as a brilliant and totally dedicated doctor, albeit somewhat unconventional in his lifestyle and treatment methods. Without exception, his name was spoken with the kind of respect and admiration usually reserved for much older, more elitist physicians.

He was also known to be a man with a heart for the underprivileged, taking the sort of unlikely risks most other physicians of his reputation would never have considered. It wasn't uncommon, her sources at the Infirmary told her, for Andrew Carmichael even to venture into the Five Points—the most abominable, dangerous slum area of the entire city—where he freely offered his skills to the poor wretches who threw themselves upon the mercy of the rare mission clinic in the district.

Bethany thought it peculiar that such a man would appear so unassuming and found herself liking him all the more for his lack of pretension.

She was also uncommonly pleased by the warmth of his greeting—he seemed utterly delighted to see her. She wasn't accustomed to others responding to her so spontaneously. She was aware of her natural reserve, especially with those outside her family or small circle of acquaintances. Admittedly, she tended to keep others at arm's length.

All the more reason she didn't want to impose. "Really," she began again, mindful by now of the unconcealed interest of the patients watching them, "I can see how busy you are. Why don't I come back another time?"

"Please don't leave." He came to stand a little closer to her. "You brought your case," he said, inclining his head toward her medical bag.

"I…yes. Force of habit, I suppose."

He nodded, studying her. "I…ah…don't suppose you'd like to lend a hand?" he said, giving a tip of his head to indicate the waiting patients.

Bethany stared at him. "You mean—*now*?"

His face creased in a smile that seemed to make the years drop away. "Of course, you'll have to use the dispensary," he said as if he had suggested the most natural thing imaginable. "Which is also the supply room. I've only one examining room, I'm afraid."

Bethany looked from Andrew Carmichael to the patients waiting for his attention: the restless infants and children, some clearly feverish; the elderly man and woman who sat holding hands at the end of the room; the little girl standing by the window, her right leg noticeably shorter than the left.

She turned back to him. "You're serious?"

He regarded her for a moment. "I've been told that you're an excellent physician,

Dr. Cole," he said, his expression holding what looked to be both challenge and expectation. "Would you agree?"

Bethany tightened her grip on her medical case, cast another glance at the crowded waiting room, then faced Andrew Carmichael, who was watching her intently. "Perhaps you might want to judge that for yourself," she replied.

Another disarming smile broke across his features as he made a sweeping motion of the waiting room with one hand. "Then choose your patient, Dr. Cole, and follow me."

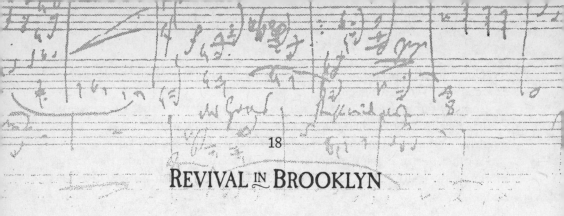

18

REVIVAL IN BROOKLYN

This is my story, this is my song,
Praising my Saviour all the day long.

FANNY CROSBY (FROM "BLESSED ASSURANCE")

October

Sergeant Frank Donovan couldn't think of anything he'd rather *not* be doing than attending a revival meeting, especially a revival meeting in Brooklyn.

To begin with, he didn't hold with revivals—not that he knew all that much about them, or needed to. Moreover, he didn't like Brooklyn. And he *did* know a good deal about Brooklyn. More than he wanted to.

He kept his peevishness to himself, however, as he led Miss Fanny Crosby down the aisle. Miss Fanny, of course, had no way of knowing that their encounter this evening was not mere chance. On this particular occasion, Eddie O'Malley had "accidentally" run into Miss Fanny in front of her Varick Street apartment and squired her to the ferry, where Frank—who "just happened to be going across to Brooklyn on police business"—escorted her the rest of the way to the revival.

Miss Fanny had become a special duty to the police force—and to the fire department, the railroad men, and a host of other city workers who had taken a serious interest in the well-being of the little lady who for years now had ministered to them all. No matter the weather, no matter how busy or exhausted she might happen to be—if indeed Miss Fanny even knew the meaning of the word *exhaustion*—she always had time for "her boys."

And they in turn looked after her safety, as well as they could without her knowing it. Frank doubted that, strong-willed and independent as she was, Miss Fanny would appreciate anyone fussing over her. No matter. It simply would not do to have the woman roaming about on her own in a crowd such as this, and her without the means to see what was going on right under her nose. So, with his captain's permission, he would be keeping an eye on her for the rest of the evening.

As far as Frank was concerned, if ever there was a saint walking, it was Fanny Crosby.

The woman seemed to be everywhere at once. Even the boys on the force were hard pressed to keep up with her. In spite of the fact that she couldn't see, Fanny Crosby was the liveliest, busiest woman Frank had ever met up with. If she wasn't scurrying about one of the Bowery missions, teaching a Bible study or telling stories to the children, she could be found visiting the sick at Bellevue or the orphan home or, more worrisome still, bustling here and there about Five Points—a leprous, disgraceful sore on the entire city of New York, and a place Frank Donovan would like to torch in its entirety.

Miss Fanny also was reputed to spend a great deal of time—although Frank could not imagine where she *found* the time—writing her poems and hymns. It was said the woman had written so many hymns that even *she* had lost count, and Frank could believe it. Those who knew her best claimed she gave away to the poor just about everything she made from her writing. And from the looks of the neighborhood where she lived, that might well have been so.

She had a husband, Miss Fanny did—a blind musician named Alexander Van Alstine. But theirs did not seem a conventional marriage, not in Frank's estimation. Miss Fanny continued to use her maiden name, and, even though she and her husband shared an apartment, they were seldom seen together socially. Apparently, they went about what they called "the Lord's work" in different ways, in different places.

That was their affair. For his part, Frank had resigned himself to tonight's event, which was being held, of all places, at a skating rink. It seemed that none of New York's churches were large enough to hold the mobs that packed these Moody/Sankey meetings.

As he might have predicted, Miss Fanny insisted on sitting as far down front as possible. "I might not be able to see what's going on," she explained cheerfully as they continued down the aisle, "but at least I'll be able to hear everything."

Frank found it necessary to flash his badge a few times, and more than once he had to shoulder their way through the crowd, but at last he delivered his charge safely to the third row center. When he would have taken his leave, however, with the excuse that he should stay in the back to keep an eye on the crowd, Miss Fanny gripped his hand and insisted he sit down beside her.

"Now, Sergeant, you told me yourself that you've never had the experience of hearing Mr. Moody preach."

"And that's the truth, Miss Fanny, but—"

As if she hadn't heard, she went right on. "Well, it's high time we remedied that, it seems to me. You'll be blessed, I promise you, by Mr. Moody's inspired preaching and Mr. Sankey's wonderful music." She smiled. "Oh, I'm so glad we ran into each other tonight! This is the Lord's doing; I'm sure of it."

For a little woman, Fanny Crosby was powerful strong. Frank tried in vain to remove his hand from her grasp. "The thing is, Miss Fanny, I'm on duty tonight, you see, so I really ought to stay where I can watch what's going on."

"Nonsense! Brooklyn isn't your jurisdiction, but even if it were, I'm sure the other men could handle things just fine without you. There's not going to be any trouble here tonight," she assured him. "This is a *revival* meeting, Sergeant! These are God's people. It may be a skating rink, but tonight it's the house of the Lord. Now you just sit yourself right down here beside me and prepare for a blessing. My other friends will be along any moment, and I want you to meet them."

Frank had yet to figure out why he found it so difficult to refuse a middle-aged blind woman. True, it was a rare occurrence entirely when Miss Fanny requested a favor. But when she did, it was sure to be accompanied by that sweet-mother smile of hers, and Frank knew right then and there he might just as well give up and do whatever she asked.

So with a somewhat exaggerated sigh, he plunked himself down onto the seat beside her. "I'll stay long enough to meet your friends," he said, "but then I'll need to be up and about."

He kept his tone firm, all the while hoping neither George Tully nor that weasel-faced Nestor Dillman from the Brooklyn force would witness his humiliation. Frank Donovan, perched right down front in a revival meeting, where no doubt some Protestant preacher was about to whip the crowd of thousands into an amen-shouting, hellfire-and-brimstone frenzy. He scarcely believed it of himself.

With that thought, he slid a little lower in his seat.

At the same time, Miss Fanny gave him yet another bright smile and a motherly pat on the hand.

~

With Michael at her side, Susanna stood in the aisle about halfway toward the front of the building, trying to catch a glimpse of Miss Fanny Crosby, whom they were to join this evening.

She could not have been more surprised when Michael asked if she'd like to accompany him tonight. A revival meeting wasn't exactly the kind of event with which she would have associated her bewildering brother-in-law, although his invitation didn't surprise her quite as much as it might have a few weeks ago.

As time passed, however, she found it increasingly difficult to believe that Michael's faith was superficial or somehow contrived for the sake of appearances. At first, Susanna, who had been raised Protestant by both parents, had assumed that Michael and his household would be Catholic. But according to Rosa, Michael's upbringing had been somewhat untraditional. Apparently his father, a practicing Catholic, and his mother, a Protestant from Northern Ireland, had exposed their son to each of their beliefs. Over the years he had explored both faiths for himself, eventually deciding on Protestantism, although he obviously maintained a wide circle of acquaintances among the Catholic faith.

In all aspects, he appeared to live an exemplary life, and his friends and associates—at least the ones Susanna had met—seemed genuinely fond of him, as did his small household staff. Certainly, there was no question but what he was a good father to Caterina. He was openly affectionate with his daughter and generous almost to a fault. Indeed, Susanna thought he might on occasion indulge the child just a little too much. Still, he seemed inclined to be firm and consistent in matters of discipline.

All things considered, Susanna supposed she shouldn't have found it peculiar that he'd be interested in a revival meeting. In any event, she had been pleased to no end when he invited her to come with him tonight. Not only was she looking forward to hearing Mr. Moody preach again, but she hoped to spend at least a few minutes with the Moodys and Sankeys after the meeting.

She turned to again scan the rows of seats behind them, then looked toward the front, wondering how they would ever find Miss Fanny in such a crowd. The building, which was actually a large skating rink, was packed with people, most already seated but many still milling about. There were few vacant seats to be seen, even though it was still early.

"Michael, perhaps you'd rather wait while I go and see—"

Just then, Susanna caught a glimpse of Miss Fanny's beribboned little hat and her dark glasses. "There she is. Close to the front. And it looks as though she's managed to save seats for us. This way," she said, taking Michael's arm to direct him.

Gus, the wolfhound, and Paul Santi had stayed at home tonight with Caterina, who was still recuperating from a nasty cold, so it was up to Susanna to serve as Michael's guide. She led him through the crowd as best she could, increasingly aware of how difficult this sort of situation must be for him. Even though he wore the dark glasses that should have alerted others to his disability, he still had to depend on someone—in this case, Susanna—to "part the waters" for him.

At first it had unnerved her a little, acting in this capacity. But Michael seemed inclined not to take himself—or his blindness—too seriously, and within minutes had managed to ease Susanna's anxiety by making light of her iron grip on his arm and her erratic stops and starts.

She was surprised to find Miss Fanny seated next to a uniformed policeman, whom she introduced as "Sergeant Donovan, my escort for the evening."

The policeman stood, his dark eyes flicking over Susanna, then darting to Michael with a sharp, inquisitive stare even as they shook hands. But their greetings were brief, for on the platform Mr. Sankey was already seating himself at a small, modest organ, ignoring the much larger and finer instrument nearby. Any chance for further conversation was lost when Mr. Moody entered the auditorium, along with an enormous choir which appeared to be at least two hundred voices strong.

Mr. Moody was just as Susanna remembered him: a burly, bearded figure of a man with extraordinarily kind eyes. He now walked directly to the platform and, with an upraised hand, led the assembly in prayer. Shortly afterward, Mr. Sankey began playing the organ and leading the crowd in the hymn "Hold the Fort."

From that moment on, the evening belonged to D. L. Moody, Ira Sankey, and the Lord.

⌒

Frank Donovan quickly excused himself to Miss Fanny as the man at the organ began to play and sing. He didn't go far, just off to the side at the end of their row.

Leaning against the wall as he listened, he had to admit that the music wasn't all that bad. The man Sankey had a big, rich voice and a way of delivering a song that was beginning to bore a hole in Frank's discomfort.

He glanced over at Miss Fanny who, as if she sensed him watching her, turned slightly and smiled in his direction. Frank sighed. It was hard to believe a saintly woman like herself would resort to such deviousness, but he couldn't shake the feeling that she'd known all along this evening's events weren't altogether accidental. Considering her subtle but ongoing concern for the state of his soul, she might well have engineered the whole evening herself, simply to get him under the roof with this pair of traveling evangelists.

He wouldn't put it past her. Not at all.

He shook his head, smiling to himself. He had a clear view of the blind man and the Fallon girl, whom Miss Fanny had introduced as Emmanuel's sister-in-law. Susanna Fallon was more than a little attractive, in a quiet sort of way. She was slender and fairly tall for a woman, with dark, soulful eyes and an interesting face, all framed by a tidy arrangement of heavy, chestnut hair shot with gold. She was young. *Too* young, Frank reminded himself ruefully. Obviously a churchgoer like the rest of the crowd, she held her songbook open, but she seemed to know the words mostly by heart as she sang along with everyone else.

Frank saw no resemblance to her deceased sister. Emmanuel's wife had been the bold, dramatic type who could snare a man at twenty paces and leave him babbling in the dust as she passed on by.

He would wager the girl was down on her luck. Her black dress appeared a bit worn, and there were no jewels. He wondered why her brother-in-law had brought her across. Perhaps with the intention of making her the next Mrs. Emmanuel?

Frank thought that unlikely, given her youth and decidedly unsophisticated appearance.

On the other hand, would a man who couldn't see be all that concerned with how a woman looked?

But Emmanuel's first wife had been a stunner, he remembered. He'd seen them together one night a few years back when he had duty on Broadway, near the opera house. They'd been surrounded by a crowd of admirers, but Frank had been close enough to get a good look at them and had asked Johnny Keenan who they were. At the time, he'd thought them a handsome pair, although the woman had appeared overly flashy, decked in her finery and enough jewels to light an entire city block. Still, she'd been a looker, no doubt about it.

Rumors had run rampant after the accident in which she died, but then rumors always ran rampant about theater people. Still, there *had* been talk of something strange. For one thing, you didn't find her kind driving her own buggy. She would have been *driven*. And taking off in the middle of the night during a fearsome thunderstorm—well, a number of the boyos had felt there was something wrong somewhere.

One thing was certain: the poor woman had met an ugly fate. Bernie Kehoe, one of the officers at the scene of the accident, told Frank that the buggy must have plunged a good twenty feet down before crashing against the rocks. According to Bernie, the Emmanuel woman had been thrown several feet from the buggy. Bernie said she'd looked for all the world like a busted doll when they found her.

Frank studied Emmanuel, wondering what a thing like that would do to a man. But his curiosity was quickly replaced by a surge of amazement as he saw Emmanuel suddenly throw back his head and begin to sing along with all the others.

Never in all his days had Frank Donovan heard anything like the sound that came out of that blind man's mouth. It was a wondrous thing entirely.

⁓

The familiar hesitation had begun to plague Michael as he stood listening to what had to be thousands of voices lifted in unrestrained praise. He seldom sang in public anymore, and even when he did, there was always that initial hesitancy, that springboard of indecision, until, no longer able to constrain himself, he gave in to a need which was, for him, as basic as food or drink.

Tonight's music had drawn him in with the force of a magnetic field. It was music that virtually *demanded* to be sung. The first time he had heard the new "gospel music," as some were calling it, he had been surprised by the strength of his own response. Far removed from the classical forms he knew and loved so well, it nevertheless held a unique appeal all its own. It was a music without class or ethnic distinctions, a music seemingly without sectarian ties or the confines of some of the older, more traditional structures. And yet in its rhythms and melodies, Michael could hear the wail and the cadence of the exile, the sorrowful lament and the plea for deliverance of the black slave, and the vigor, the ecstatic joy, and the call to glory of the camp meeting preacher.

This was a music evolved from diverse roots and mutual needs: a music of the common people who sought to worship, to praise, to plead, and to be one in the freedom of Christian love. Some called it heathenish. Others found it too personal, too self-centered. Many thought it nothing more than "message music," a trend that would never survive in the established church.

But Michael loved its lack of restraint and self-conscious convention, its spontaneity and free-flowing emotion, its inclusive embrace of the old and the new. This was the sound of *America*.

He had heard—only in part—a hint of this music years ago, when he had been but a boy, about to depart New York Harbor from his first visit to America. Something had happened to him that day, something too wondrous, too enormous for a child to grasp. Only years later had he finally come to accept that he had been given a kind of vision. Somehow he knew, without understanding how such a thing could be or why, that his Creator had given him a glimpse of a mighty, matchless music, a music that was as elusive as it was beautiful.

Ever since that day on the deck of the ship, he had been seeking the fulfillment of that early vision. And despite the years of frustrations and failures, the disappointments and defeats, he remained resolved to capture that divine spark, that it might ignite a flame and breathe its glory into his own work. It rang through his soul and echoed in his spirit, seeking—*demanding*—its own voice. This body of music would be his magnum opus, his greatest achievement—and the reason God had gifted him.

But for now, he was engulfed by the music at hand, a music that demanded to be sung.

And he simply could no longer resist its call.

~

"...This is my story, this is my song..."

"Blessed Assurance"—written by Miss Fanny—was quickly becoming one of Susanna's favorite hymns. She loved to sing it, and she loved to hear it sung. But the unexpected sound of Michael's voice as he joined the other voices filling the meeting place quickly silenced her.

She could not help but turn and stare. Before tonight, Susanna had only heard about the "Voice of the Century," the voice that was said to fill an amphitheater and thrill even the most world-weary audiences.

She had read of Michael's triumphs, but with nothing more than the curiosity of any other music lover. And of course in the early weeks of Deirdre's and his courtship, her sister had raved about her new suitor's "magnificent talent" and the unparalleled success that greeted him everywhere he performed.

But now, as she stood watching Michael, listening to him, her very soul shaken by his incredible voice, Susanna realized that neither the critics' reviews nor her sister's glowing accounts had been adequate to convey the wonder, the uniqueness of his extraordinary gift.

The truth was that mere words, no matter how eloquent or impassioned, couldn't possibly begin to express the inconceivable power—the *phenomenon*—of his singing. If God had arranged to give *glory* a voice, it might have sounded very much like the voice of Michael Emmanuel.

Vaguely, she was aware that others nearby had also stopped singing, some turning to look. Even Miss Fanny, although she didn't miss a note of her own, turned toward Michael with a broad smile of obvious delight, squeezing Susanna's hand as if to share the moment.

Michael, for his part, was absorbed by the music, completely unaware of the attention he was getting.

Susanna thought that the experience of being in the midst of thousands of voices raised in collective praise to their Creator would have been enough by itself to overwhelm her. But the sound of that glorious voice at her side as it lifted and soared above the entire auditorium was nothing short of breathtaking.

Transfixed, she could do nothing but stand and watch him. With his head thrown back, he looked as if his every sense was alive and ablaze with exultation.

Questions hurtled through her mind. With such a gift, how could anything—*anything*—have driven him from the world he had once conquered and made his own? What could possibly account for his turning away from the vast international audiences who had adored him, practically *enshrined* him, above all other musicians of his time?

Even as the questions gripped her, Susanna felt a sudden sickening—and wholly unexpected—wrench of dismay for all this man had lost. She fought to shake off the emotion. How could she feel so strongly for this baffling brother-in-law who had yet to provide her with even the most cursory of explanations for her sister's death?

Besides, she was quite certain he would not welcome her sympathy. On the contrary, he would most likely find it anathema. From what she had seen of Michael Emmanuel so far, she would expect him to have no desire, no need, for *anyone's* sympathy. As for her natural feelings of compassion for the man, she told herself firmly that it would be far more appropriate to sympathize with him for the loss of his wife—and, of course, the loss of his vision—rather than the loss of his career, no matter how spectacular it might have been.

But what about Michael himself? Susanna studied him, again recognizing the look of some profound and unfathomable joy enlivening his features. And she wondered—which among his many devastating losses had been most grievous to *him*?

19

DARK REMEMBRANCE

And, even yet, I dare not let it languish,
Dare not indulge in Memory's rapturous pain...

EMILY BRONTË

They visited with the Moodys and Sankeys for nearly half an hour, then took a late ferry. By the time they started for Bantry Hill, it was well after eleven. In the meantime, a cold wind had blown up, and with it a soaking rain.

In spite of the lateness of the hour, Susanna was still too exhilarated from the excitement of the evening to give in to fatigue. Michael sat in silence, his head resting against the back of the carriage seat, but Susanna knew he wasn't dozing.

She had become accustomed to his silences by now. There seemed to be no pattern to them, no predictability. They were just as likely to come in the midst of a crowded room as when they were alone together, which was rarely the case. He was never exactly rude. He would simply grow very still, occasionally for several minutes at a time. Although he seemed to be aware of his surroundings in a peripheral sense, it was obvious that for the most part he had distanced himself from those nearby.

Just then, the carriage bumped over a deep pit in the road, and he stirred. He straightened a little in the seat, stretching his arms out in front of him. "It's just as well that Caterina stayed behind tonight, no? She would be exhausted."

Susanna agreed, especially given the chill rain that had set in. "It's probably best that she stay in another day or two, I think, until her cold is completely gone."

Michael nodded, but said nothing more as he again leaned back and crossed his arms over his chest.

Just when Susanna had begun to think they would pass the rest of the drive in silence, the carriage took another jolt. She gave a sharp intake of breath. Michael uttered a sound of disgust and shook his head. "This road—*un disonore!* A disgrace."

Susanna looked at him, a coldness spreading over her. Did she only imagine that he winced, as if he'd realized that by mentioning the condition of the road he might have opened a door he would have preferred to leave closed?

"Michael—"

He cut her short. "I know," he said, giving a flick of his wrist. "We have not yet talked about the accident."

Susanna braced herself for another attempt on his part to evade the subject. "Don't you think it's time?" she ventured.

"*Sì,*" he said, surprising her. There was a long pause, then, "We will talk now, if you like."

His voice was low and tight, as if he were steeling himself for a dreaded ordeal. Susanna waited, still half expecting him to evade.

But apparently that wasn't his intention.

"We are very close to the site of the accident," he said quietly.

Susanna instinctively glanced out the window into the darkness. "How can you tell?"

His eyebrows lifted. "I know this road, of course. Every turn, every rise and fall of it. I know the exact place where it happened."

"What...*did* happen?" Susanna felt as if her throat were swollen shut. It was all she could do to force the words out.

As she waited, he drew in a long breath, leaned back, and turned his face slightly toward the carriage window. "It was raining," he said, his tone now more pensive than strained. "Even harder than tonight. A terrible storm. Thunder. Lightning. And wind—I remember the wind was particularly vicious. The road was already deeply rutted and slick from a week of much rain. In some places, large chunks had simply washed away."

He pressed a hand against his bearded face. "Deirdre drove the buggy herself," he went on, his voice thin. "She was not used to doing so. The police said she must have lost control in the turn." He paused, then added, "It's just ahead."

The hand against his face trembled slightly. "The buggy went over the side and crashed...down onto the rocks. Deirdre—"

He broke off, removed the dark glasses, and wiped a hand over his eyes as if caught up in the throes of some memory too excruciating to voice.

At that moment, they entered the deadly turn. Susanna held her breath until they came out of it. As if he, too, had been waiting until they passed the dreaded place, Michael dropped his hand away from his face and knotted it into a fist against the door panel.

"She was thrown from the buggy," he continued, his voice scarcely more than a murmur. "The police said she died instantly, from the impact of the fall."

A hot surge of nausea rose up in Susanna's throat. "But *why* was she alone?" she choked out. "You said she wasn't used to driving. What possessed her to do such a thing? And in the middle of the night, in such a storm—"

His expression was shuttered, revealing nothing of his feelings. He began to tap his fist against the door.

So long was his reply in coming that Susanna feared he meant not to answer at all. But finally he brought his hands to his knees as if to steady himself. "We had…an argument. A terrible argument."

For the life of her, Susanna couldn't imagine an argument so fierce that a woman would leave the house in a raging thunderstorm and drive off alone on a treacherous road.

As if he had read her thoughts, Michael hurried on. "Deirdre was very angry. I tried to reason with her, but—"

He stopped, making the slight turn of the wrist Susanna had come to recognize when he either couldn't find the words he wanted, or when no words seemed necessary.

"As I said, she was very angry." Again he straightened, replacing the dark glasses as he turned his face toward the window.

Susanna sat watching him, her mind racing. Obviously, raking up the memory of that awful night had been very difficult for him. And his explanation, as far as he'd taken it, seemed candid enough. Her instincts, however, told her he was leaving out as much as, if not more than, he'd divulged.

"But whatever were you arguing about that could have upset her so much?"

The moment the words escaped her lips, Susanna could have bit her tongue. She had no right to ask such a question, and she knew it.

He turned toward her, one eyebrow lifting in obvious annoyance.

"I'm sorry," Susanna said quickly, wringing her hands in her lap. "That was—that's none of my business. But, Michael—I'm only trying to understand what happened, what drove Deirdre to do such a reckless thing."

The line of his mouth tightened. "Married couples sometimes argue, Susanna. That is not such an uncommon thing."

"But their arguments don't usually end up with one of them dead!"

In the flickering light from the carriage lantern, he seemed to pale. "You wanted to know what happened, and I've told you. As for what we argued about, that is something I'm not willing to discuss."

Susanna stared at him, her impatience heating to frustration. "Michael—I already know Deirdre was unhappy, that your marriage was far from perfect. It's no great shock to hear that you fought. I'm simply trying to understand what happened, but it seems you don't want me to know!"

She hurled the words at him like stones, but he seemed unmoved.

The wind shook the carriage. The rain was coming in torrents now, beating against the roof and battering the doors as if trying to gain entrance. There were repeated crashes of thunder. Lightning streaked along the tree branches bending and whipping in the wind.

Susanna shuddered, unable to shut out the thought of Deirdre abroad on such a night as this, undoubtedly frightened, perhaps even terrified, as she fled the stone monolith of Bantry Hill in an effort to escape—

Escape *what*? Susanna studied the dark-featured man across from her who had again retreated into silence, his features set, his head bent low. Clearly, he had said all he meant to say.

Anger renewed itself and slammed through her as she groped for words to launch an attack on his stubborn silence. But just then, she realized the carriage was slowing. She turned to look and saw that they had already passed through the gate and were almost at the front of the house.

Something didn't seem right. She stared, at first unable to determine what was amiss. Then she realized.

"The lights," she said, more to herself than to Michael.

"What do you mean?"

"The house—there's too much light. It looks as if every lamp—"

She broke off as a blazing bolt of lightning cast the entire front of the house in an eerie incandescence. At the same time, the carriage quaked, slammed by a brutal gust of wind.

"*Caterina*—" The word was little more than a whisper on his lips, but even before the carriage came to a complete halt, Michael's hand was on the door.

The moment they stopped, he was out of the carriage, not waiting for Dempsey, hesitating only long enough to help Susanna down.

Susanna grabbed his arm, Dempsey following behind them.

Wind drove the rain against them, lashing their skin and clothing. Michael stumbled in his haste, but Susanna steadied him, and they went on.

By the time they reached the top of the porch steps, Moira Dempsey stood framed in the doorway. "Thanks be to God!" she burst out at the sight of them. "I thought you'd never get here!"

Paul Santi brushed by the housekeeper and took Michael's arm to hurry them inside. "It's Cati, Michael," he said without preamble as they shook the rain off their hair and coats onto the floor of the vestibule. "She seemed all right earlier, but now—she's very ill."

Michael raked both hands through his wet hair. "But she was better. What happened?"

Paul met Susanna's eyes for just an instant, and the worry she saw there chilled her far more than the water dripping down her face and hair.

Before Paul could answer, Moira Dempsey burst out, "'Tis the lung fever; I'm sure of it!" The woman stood wringing her hands, her mouth trembling. "She started in with the cough not long after you left, and she's scarcely stopped since, God help her. There's a wicked fever on her. She's that sick, lad. I did all I know to do, but it hasn't helped."

Michael paled. Then, throwing off his wet coat, he started for the stairway.

20

A LONG NIGHT

Till her eyes shine,
'Tis night within my heart.

RICHARD BRINSLEY SHERIDAN

They heard the hard, hacking cough before they even reached the landing.

Upstairs, the wolfhound was lying outside the door to Caterina's bedroom. The minute he saw them, he whimpered and got to his feet. Absently, Michael put a hand to the dog's head, ordering him to stay as they entered the bedroom.

Caterina was awake, pillows propped behind her. "Papa—"

Her attempted greeting set off a hard spasm of coughing.

Susanna went to one side of the bed, Michael to the other, where he scooped Caterina into his arms, holding her close and putting his cheek to her forehead.

"I'm sorry, Papa." The child's voice was hoarse and thick.

"Sorry?" Michael stroked her hair. "Why would you say such a thing?"

"I don't like to make you worry," Caterina managed between bouts of coughing.

Michael's composure seemed to slip for an instant as he rocked his daughter gently back and forth. "Papa isn't worried, *cara*. We will have Dr. Kent come and see to your cough. He will give you some medicine, and you will be well again. So why should I worry, eh?"

Caterina turned toward Susanna. "You look funny, Aunt Susanna," she said with a feeble smile. "You, too, Papa. Both of you are wet...like the ducks on the pond."

The few words seemed to exhaust her, and Michael drew her even closer as she was seized by yet another fit of coughing.

A knot settled in Susanna's chest at the familiar sound of that cough. She thought she recognized it.

She hoped she was wrong.

"Pauli?" Michael was saying. "Send Dempsey for Dr. Kent, please. Right away."

Paul started for the door, then suddenly turned back. "Michael—Dr. Kent is in hospital himself. Do you not remember? The stroke?"

Susanna saw Michael blanch. Caterina gasped and began to cough again, a loud, barking cough. Carefully, Michael lowered her to the bed and sat down beside her, stroking her forehead.

"She's so warm," he said, his voice low. "Too warm. We must have a doctor. But who?"

Paul gave a quick shrug of frustration. "We will have to find someone from the city."

Susanna's mind raced. A thought struck her, perhaps implausible. But Michael was right. They had to have a doctor.

"Michael—"

He turned toward her.

"I think I know what this is. The cough—it sounds like croup. I'm almost certain."

He frowned. "Croup? What is that?"

"It sometimes follows a bad cold. One of the Maher twins was susceptible to it. I remember what Mrs. Maher used to do. You understand, we'll still need a doctor, but perhaps we can ease the cough a little and make her more comfortable for a time. I'll just need a few things—"

"Pauli," said Michael, "help Mrs. Dempsey collect whatever Susanna needs. We will never get a doctor this time of night, but tell Liam to plan to leave first thing in the morning for the city, as early as possible."

On impulse, Susanna laid a hand on his arm. "Actually, Michael, I think I know a doctor who *might* come tonight." She sent Paul to fetch the items she'd need, then told Michael about Dr. Carmichael, the physician she'd met during the crossing. "He seemed such a good man, and the Moodys spoke so highly of him. He might remember me. Perhaps if I were to send a note, he would come."

Michael's strained expression seemed to ease slightly. "Where would Dempsey find this man?"

Susanna had to think a moment. "Seventeenth Street…yes, that was it. He mentioned that he was considering moving from East Seventeenth Street to somewhere with more office space."

"But surely he would not be in his office at this time of night."

Susanna frowned. "But he lives upstairs, over the office! I remember, because Mrs. Moody was often fussing at him that he ought to live somewhere else, where his patients can't find him at all hours."

Michael nodded. "Write the note, please, Susanna."

⌒

Within minutes Dempsey appeared at the door to get the note for Dr. Carmichael.

"I'll be leaving for the city now," the gruff Irishman announced. "Best not to wait. Even if the ferry's not running, there's always some fellow hanging about the dock, looking to make himself some extra money. I'll find a way."

"*Grazie,*" Michael replied, his voice strained. "Pay whatever you must, Liam. Paul, get him some money; would you please?"

When Dempsey was gone, Susanna made a tent of one of the bedsheets and explained to both Caterina and Michael—who of course couldn't see for himself—what she intended to do. By the time Paul returned with the bucket of hot water and lime she'd sent for, she was ready to begin.

"Now, Caterina, I'm going to get inside the tent with you, darling, and we'll breathe in the steamy fumes from this bucket, the two of us. I think it will ease that nasty cough."

For the next half-hour, Michael kept the fire going in the fireplace and Paul added hot water to the bucket every few minutes. Susanna held Caterina's hand as the child inhaled the vapor from the lime water.

The steam finally helped to lessen the coughing spasms enough that Caterina fell into a fitful sleep. Paul helped Susanna dispose of the wet sheets, then went downstairs to fetch some tea for all of them, leaving the room quiet for the first time since their return.

Susanna got up and took a towel to her wet hair. She could see Michael in the mirror, seated close beside the bed, holding Caterina's hand. His face was haggard with worry and fatigue.

Whatever else she might think about her cryptic brother-in-law, Susanna had to admit that there was no doubting his love for his little girl. Clearly, Caterina was the heart of Michael's life, the most important part of his world, and she could not help but feel a measure of softening toward him when she watched him with his daughter.

She could tell that he was praying. Susanna added yet another of her own silent pleas to his. The little niece with the ready smile and merry nature had become infinitely precious to her in a very short time. She couldn't imagine a single day without Caterina. If the child didn't make it—

She shook off the thought, refusing to give in to her fear. Caterina would be all right. This was only croup, after all. A common illness among young children, and one from which they almost always recovered.

Almost always. Unless it turned out to be what the old women back home called "the bad croup."

"I'm very thankful you were here, Susanna," Michael said softly from across the room. "You knew just what to do."

Susanna became aware that she'd been staring into the mirror, the towel still swathed around her hair. "This may not last, Michael. You understand that it's only a temporary measure?"

He nodded. "*Sì*, but it is something." He was silent for a moment, then said, "You care deeply for Caterina." It was a statement of fact, not a question.

Susanna swallowed, still watching his reflection in the mirror. "I love her as if she were my own."

"It would make Caterina so very happy to hear you say that." He paused and smiled a little. "It pleases me, too."

Susanna was unprepared for the warmth that stole over her at his words. She realized for the first time that in some inexplicable way, she *wanted* his approval, wanted to please him.

It was an entirely unexpected thought, and one that left her shaken and confused.

Why should she care whether Michael approved of her? This was the man who had somehow managed to make her sister so miserable that she'd referred to her marriage as a "disaster." Moreover, everything Susanna had learned so far led her to believe that Deirdre might well have been running away from Michael—and her marriage—the night she died.

She studied him in the mirror. It occurred to her that she still knew little more about Deirdre's accident than she'd known before she came here, other than the fact that there had been an argument—a particularly ugly one, apparently—and that Deirdre had driven off to her death. Up until tonight, Michael had managed to evade even the most superficial of explanations. Now, with his earlier account interrupted, she couldn't help but wonder how long it might be before he would again be willing to take up where he'd left off.

But before she could pursue her troubled thoughts any further, Caterina was gripped by a new, and even more violent, fit of coughing.

And this time, she seemed to be fighting with all her strength simply to breathe.

～

There was nothing unusual about a knock on Andrew Carmichael's door in the middle of the night. In fact, it was a rare night indeed when he managed more than four or five hours sleep. Fortunately, he had discovered while still in medical college that he could get along surprisingly well on very little sleep—a quality that had proved exceedingly valuable for one in his profession.

At the sound of someone pounding, he came instantly awake, fully alert. Quickly, he lighted the lamp on the table beside the bed. A glance across the room to the clock on the fireplace mantel showed that it was almost one-thirty.

It was still raining, a persistent, drumming rain that held little promise of slackening soon. Chilled, the doctor shivered a little as he threw on his bathrobe and half stumbled downstairs to the side entrance.

He felt uncommonly irritated—more so than usual—at being disturbed at such a late hour. The lingering effects of what he thought must have been a very pleasant dream clung to him like a subtle fragrance, and for a moment he resented the unknown intruder. Even so, he could hardly ignore the relentless pounding and go back to bed.

On the way downstairs, he became aware that the dream in question was of Dr. Bethany Cole. Now, there was an intrusion! The woman had been invading his mind at the most inopportune moments almost from the first day they'd met.

The thought of his attractive new associate fled, however, when he opened the door. The man standing on the stoop bore a strong resemblance to a walrus. Yes, definitely a walrus, complete with the heavy mustache. He was a hardy, thick-chested man, probably in his late fifties, with a bit of a droop to one eye.

"The name is Dempsey, sir," he said in a voice as rough as gravel. He thrust a piece of paper into Andrew's hand. "I was to deliver this note from Miss Susanna Fallon."

Andrew frowned, looking from the man with the Irish accent to the note in his hand. For a moment he couldn't think. Then it came to him. "Miss Fallon… oh, of course! Why, whatever is wrong? She's not ill, I hope?"

Even as he spoke, Andrew unfolded the stationery and read what appeared to be a hastily written note.

"Please forgive this imposition, Dr. Carmichael. I don't mean to presume on our brief acquaintanceship, but my four-year-old niece—the daughter of Mr. Michael Emmanuel—is very ill with what would seem to be a severe case of croup. I believe it is most critical that she receive medical attention right away, and Mr. Emmanuel's family physician is himself hospitalized. I do apologize for asking, but if you would be good enough to accompany Mr. Dempsey upriver, we'd be most grateful. We desperately need a trustworthy physician, and I naturally thought of you right away."

"Upriver?" Andrew questioned, glancing at the man called Dempsey.

"Aye, sir. Between Tarrytown and the Military Academy, it is. You know Mr. Emmanuel, sir?"

Andrew nodded, still studying the note. "The musician…yes, of course. That is, I know *of* him. That's right, now I remember, Miss Fallon told us about him and her niece."

He hesitated only a moment. "Well, step in out of the rain, man. I'll have to dress and get my bag."

The Irishman seemed relieved—and somewhat surprised. "You'll be coming, then, sir?"

Andrew cut a look at him. "Why, yes, of course." In truth, he hadn't thought of *not* going.

The sturdy Irishman stepped inside, cap in hand. He seemed unaware of the fact that he was thoroughly drenched.

"Come on up if you like," Andrew said, already starting up the steps.

"Thank you, sir. I'll be fine right here."

The man Dempsey was obviously a fellow of few words, which was just as well. This hour of the night Andrew wasn't much inclined toward conversation himself.

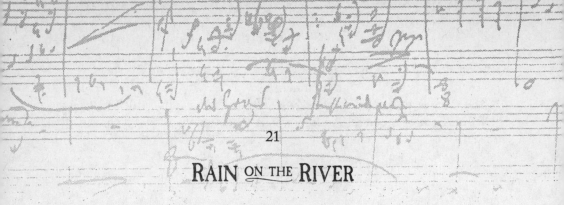

21

RAIN <u>ON THE</u> RIVER

If it be stormy,
Fear not the sea;
Jesus upon it
Is walking by thee.

JOSEPH SHERIDAN LEFANU

Susanna had tried everything she knew to do, but Caterina's racking cough only grew worse. She glanced across the room at the clock on the mantel. Nearly three-thirty. It seemed as if Dempsey had been gone all night.

Only with the greatest of effort had she managed to avoid utter panic. Michael, too, was clearly distraught. His hair was wild from raking his hands through it, and he had pulled at his tie so fiercely that both the tie and his collar hung askew.

"Michael, you should try to rest," Susanna said, raising her voice to make herself heard above Caterina's coughing.

He shook off the suggestion and got to his feet for yet another round of pacing the room. After a moment, he stopped in front of Susanna, extended a hand to her, and said, "Will you pray with me? Pray with me for Caterina."

Susanna studied him, her throat tight. For the first time since they'd come upstairs she could see him struggling with his faith. By now his fear seemed almost palpable, as was her own increasing dread. On impulse, she took his hand and went to stand with him beside Caterina's bed. With the rain drumming a relentless rhythm against the house and her heart hammering in painful counterpoint, they pleaded together for the child they both loved with all their hearts.

At some point, Susanna felt Michael's hand tighten on hers. At first she resisted, but only for an instant. His hand was strong and warm, and her growing panic, plus the need to be in harmony as they prayed, made it possible for her to put aside, at least for the moment, her misgivings and her doubts about him.

For now, all that really mattered was Caterina, and it seemed vital that they join their thoughts and their hearts as they approached the only One who could bring healing into this room tonight.

~

A few minutes later, Susanna went for a fresh pitcher of water. The rain had slackened by the time she made her way back to the bedroom, and the house had grown quiet, except for Caterina's continual hacking. The strangling cough pierced the night, sending one stab of pain after another shooting through Susanna.

The wolfhound saw her from his watchful position outside the room and lifted his great head in appeal. Even Gus was looking for a reassurance she couldn't offer. She stopped long enough to rub his ears and give him a word of encouragement.

She started to enter the bedroom, then hesitated. Michael had lifted Caterina from the bed and sat cradling her in the rocking chair by the window. His arms were wrapped securely around his daughter to help support her against the brutal coughing. Even as he hummed a soothing melody against her hair, his own face was a mask of despair and helplessness.

The sight of his stricken countenance and his unmistakable love for his daughter was almost Susanna's undoing. Something twisted inside her, and for a moment, forgetting that Michael could not see her distress, she turned away to collect herself before crossing the room to set the pitcher on the table.

The sound of voices downstairs startled her, and she sloshed water over the side of the bowl as she set it in place. Michael was already on his feet, still cradling Caterina in his arms.

"That must be Dempsey!" Susanna said. "I'll go."

Outside the room the wolfhound was poised at the top of the steps. He barked once, then turned to Susanna, as if waiting for a command from her.

"Quiet, Gus." A wave of relief swept over Susanna at the sight of the tall, rangy Dr. Carmichael ascending the steps while Paul waited in the vestibule with Dempsey, watching.

"Miss Fallon." Andrew Carmichael gave her a quick smile as he reached the top of the stairway.

"I can't thank you enough for coming, Dr. Carmichael! I know what a terrible imposition this is, but I couldn't think what else to do."

He waved off her apology and, at the sound of Caterina's coughing, glanced toward the bedroom. "Sounds as if she's having quite a time of it," he said, already starting down the hallway as Susanna hurried to keep pace with him.

"How long has she been this way?"

"All night," Susanna replied. "Mrs. Dempsey said she started not long after we left for Brooklyn, for the revival."

He looked at her. "You were at the meeting? So was I. In the wings, actually. One of the workers wasn't feeling well, so I stayed close by. Just in case."

They stopped just outside the bedroom door. "Now, then—tell me what you've done for her so far."

Susanna gave him a hasty account of her efforts, to which he nodded approval. "Good. Very good thinking. Well, let's go in."

Upon entering the room, the doctor stopped for only a moment before crossing to where Michael stood with Caterina in his arms.

Susanna quickly introduced them, and with great care Dr. Carmichael took Caterina from Michael. "Let's have a look, if I may," he said, lifting her onto the bed.

The child's frenzied coughing and unfocused gaze set off yet another spasm of alarm in Susanna. But Andrew Carmichael's good-natured features creased into a smile as he bent over the bed.

"I'm Dr. Carmichael, Caterina. I need to have a look at your throat, is that all right? It won't hurt a bit, I promise."

The girl's cheeks were stained with crimson, her eyes sunken, but she managed a faint smile and a nod. Even that small effort seem to ignite another round of hacking.

Susanna watched Andrew Carmichael closely as he checked Caterina's throat. She saw his expression turn somber, and in the stillness of the room she imagined everyone could hear her own heart pounding with apprehension.

⌒

The child's cough was so relentless it was all Andrew could do to manage even a cursory examination. But he was vastly relieved to find that it wasn't membranous croup, as he had feared when he first heard the cough. No, this was the plain old ordinary stuff—just an unusually severe case of it. More than likely the result of a bad cold but, hopefully, still treatable.

The girl's condition concerned him, however, for she was a slight little thing and clearly exhausted. When he listened to her heart, he knew at once the coughing was overtaxing it. He needed to get that cough under control, and at once.

Without turning, he asked Susanna Fallon to bring him a bowl of boiling water and a funnel. While she was gone, he gave the child a dose of quinine mixed with a little sugar. The quinine would do nothing for the cough, of course, but it would help to support her strength.

The girl's father stood beside the bed in silence, his hands knotted in fists at his sides. Reminding himself of the man's blindness, Andrew commenced to explain what he was doing. Emmanuel seemed eager to understand.

As soon as Susanna Fallon returned with the boiling water, Andrew mixed a tincture of benzoin in it and helped the child inhale it through the tin funnel.

"We're going to repeat this in a few minutes," he told them. "I should caution you that she might throw up at any time, but it's just as well if she does, so don't be alarmed."

Over the next hour, Andrew applied the benzoin treatment twice more, but saw scarce evidence of relief. Since Miss Fallon had already administered a steam tent, there was little else to try. The child was already much too weak; he wished he could have treated her sooner. He knew that to let this go on much longer would involve real risk to her heart and lungs.

There was only one other remedy left to him. In itself it contained an element of risk, but at this point he had no choice but to try.

He waited a few more minutes after the last inhalation of benzoin. Finally, when no relief seemed imminent, he stood. "All right, then," he said. "Let's wrap her in blankets. I'm going to take her outside."

The girl's father took on a look of horror, as if Andrew had threatened to drive a stake through his daughter's heart. "*Outside?*" he repeated, his voice strangled.

Susanna Fallon also went pale and opened her mouth as if to object.

Andrew understood their inevitable protests but tried to ignore their shock. There was really nothing else to do.

"It's a perfect night," he said by way of explanation. "The rain has stopped, but the air will still be moist. And this close to the river, we'll have fog. Those are excellent conditions. Just what we need right now."

He took in their faces, still frozen in doubt. "In extreme cases, such as Caterina's," he said carefully, "when nothing else works, quite often the night air will help. Now, there's no sign as yet of bronchitis or pneumonia, you see, so I think the risk is minimal. I strongly suggest we give this a go, Mr. Emmanuel. Quite frankly, there's little else left to do."

The girl's father seemed to be waiting for something more, while Susanna Fallon was studying Andrew closely. He met her gaze straight on, but gave a lift of his hands to show that he could not promise anything.

Meanwhile, the child took up another seizure of coughing.

Miss Fallon finally broke the silence. "Michael, we should at least try, don't you think? We can trust Dr. Carmichael."

At last the man nodded. But Andrew had the distinct feeling that if this didn't work, Michael Emmanuel—in spite of his blindness—would somehow make him pay. And it would not be a pleasant experience.

⌒

Outside, the night had grown calm. The rain seemed to be over, at least for the moment, and, just as Dr. Carmichael had predicted, a heavy fog was moving in.

The physician carried Caterina, bundled securely in blankets, onto the front lawn, where he stood, holding her and speaking softly of the beauty of her home and the night around them.

"I hope this is not a madman you have brought to our house," Michael said under his breath.

Susanna looked at him, but he didn't appear angry, merely skeptical.

"If you think about it," she said, "it makes perfect sense. The moist air, the fog—"

"Please, God, it will work," he said quietly.

Susanna heard the tremor in his voice and knew that he was trying his best to conceal his fear.

They stood that way, in silence, for what seemed a very long time, engulfed by the cool damp air. They could smell the river. The fog, acrid to the throat but somehow calming, drifted in and out among them and the trees. There was no sound except the faint rustle of leaves and the steady panting of the wolfhound, who stood at Michael's side, alert and seemingly poised for action.

It was a lonely, forsaken kind of silence, and Susanna shivered a little, not from the night air, but more from the sense of isolation that sometimes seemed to hang over Bantry Hill and this entire Hudson River Valley.

Andrew Carmichael had grown quiet now, too. Watching him as he stood with Caterina bundled securely against him, Susanna could see his lips moving only slightly.

She couldn't be sure, but she thought he was praying.

She had seen enough of the Scottish physician's interaction with the Moodys and the Sankeys to know that he was a deeply devout man. Still, it both surprised and comforted her to realize that a man of science and medicine looked to a higher power for the ultimate healing.

She seemed to lose all track of time. They might have been standing there for minutes or hours when she realized that Caterina had finally stopped coughing. Indeed, the child had grown completely silent.

Panic overtook Susanna. She heard Michael's sharp intake of breath and took his arm, as much to steady herself as him. But then she saw Andrew Carmichael's face in the flickering glow from the lantern, the slow smile breaking over his features as he studied Caterina.

After a moment, he lifted his face to the night sky and whispered something Susanna couldn't quite make out.

Suddenly the night no longer seemed lonely or forsaken. "She's all right, Michael," Susanna said, hurrying to reassure him. "Caterina is going to be all right."

He was trembling, and for a moment Susanna feared that he, too, had taken ill. But then she saw the dampness on his cheeks.

Moved, she reached for his hand, and when she did, he wrapped it securely between both his own, bringing it to his lips just for an instant. Taken completely off guard, Susanna would have yanked her hand away, but he restrained her with a gentle, firm clasp as he murmured something in Italian, then in English.

"You are a gift to us, Susanna. A gift of God. And I could not be more thankful for your presence in our lives."

Susanna swallowed hard. Her resolve to dislike—and distrust—this man began to bend like a slender reed in a windstorm. Even as her old emotions rose up in protest, she felt an unaccountable desire stir within her, a longing for things to be different between them.

For one yearning moment, she found herself wishing she could simply give up her suspicion, surrender her doubts, and put all the old questions to rest for once and for all.

Carefully then, he lowered her hand, loosening his grasp so that Susanna could move away if she chose. Instead, she lightly pressed his fingers with her own, took a deep breath, and led him across the grass to Dr. Carmichael and Caterina.

22

FAITH IN THE FACE OF FEAR

Our feet on the torrent's brink,
Our eyes on the cloud afar,
We fear the things we think,
Instead of the things that are.

JOHN BOYLE O'REILLY

Aboard the Jonathan Nye *on the way to America*

"Am I going to die, Mum?"

Vangie MacGovern dabbed the forehead of her fevered son with a damp cloth, forcing a smile for his benefit. "Ah, James, and what kind of talk is that, now? Of course you're not going to die! You've a cold in your chest, is all. Why, no doubt you'll be the first among us to see the shores of America. Here, now," she said, laying the cloth aside, "take a bit more of this broth."

She put the cup of barley water to his lips, but the boy turned his head away. "I don't like it, Mum. It smells."

Tears stung Vangie's eyes. "Please, James. You *must* take it. I know you don't like the taste, but just take a bit for Mother, won't you?"

He made no response to Vangie's coaxing, but simply closed his eyes. The boy had taken nothing since yesterday morning except a few sips of broth, and Vangie was at her wit's end. She had no enticements to offer him, no choice victuals that might tempt him. What with the dampness and lack of ventilation, even their basic provisions had spoiled long before they should have.

Grieved by her own helplessness, she turned to Nell Grace, who sat holding the sleeping Baby Emma in her arms. "Put the baby in her cradle and go and find your da," she told her daughter. "I can't think where he's wandered off to this time, but I'll wager if you follow the music, you'll find him."

The strains of a fiddle and a squeezebox could be heard coming from the dank compartment some called the galley. This was where many of their foodstuffs were stored, and where the women, disgusted with the foul fare served by the ship's cook, occasionally cooked their own meals over the fireplace. It was also where some of the steerage passengers had taken to gathering during the long days of the voyage to make their music and tell their tales in an attempt to ease the monotony of the journey and the growing despair that hung over them like a fetid cloud.

Some felt the merrymaking out of place, woefully inappropriate among the dark shadows and putrid stench of the ship's bowels. Conn, however, contended that the people must find their own escape from the relentless distress of the crossing, or else many would go mad.

Vangie agreed with him, but at the moment she felt as if she might be going mad herself.

She watched Nell Grace wind her way through the crowded passages between the bunks. A body could hardly navigate from one berth to the other without either bumping into a stranger or tripping over a protruding foot on the way.

It occurred to her that she had lost track of time. Their quarters were always dark, with nothing but a few flickering lanterns to scatter the shadows. Without a change in light to mark the hours, it was easy to become disoriented.

Here, too, Conn took the brighter side. They were fortunate, he said, to be among those sailing on an American ship rather than aboard one of the disgraceful British vessels. "At least our bunks won't be falling off the wall, and the water closets won't collapse with the first high wind."

He often compared their lot to that of the poor souls who made the crossing during the Great Hunger in the forties. "They were half-dead already when they boarded, but even if they hadn't been, the infernal British coffin ships would have finished them off. It is our good fortune, don't you see, to be making the journey in our full strength."

No doubt he knew whereof he spoke—and of course he meant well, trying to keep their spirits up. But at the moment, Vangie was feeling anything but fortunate. During the first week aboard ship, both she and Nell Grace had suffered fiercely with the seasickness; even Baby Emma had not been able to keep much in her stomach. Not long after, Conn and the twins had come down with colds and dysentery, along with half of the other steerage passengers. Now James had been taken with a fever.

It seemed as if the busker girl, Renny Magee, was the only one of them to escape the ravages of sea travel. Conn claimed the girl's devilry kept sickness at bay.

Lately, Vangie paid little heed to her husband's crankiness when it came to Renny Magee. Hadn't she seen the way his mouth twitched when the girl went barreling across the hold to retrieve the baby's rattle, or the faint creasing about his eyes when he came upon the lass entertaining the twins with one of the old tales about magic pigs or the great hound of Cuchullin?

The girl amused him, Vangie could tell. For her own part, she had to say that she was growing fond of Renny Magee. The busker girl had been as good as her word, not causing a bit of trouble, in fact bringing more help than harm to this odious voyage. She was especially good with the twins and Baby Emma.

Of course, Conn never much cared for admitting he was wrong, so it wasn't likely he would willingly concede any real virtue to the girl, certainly not until more time had passed. Even Vangie couldn't help but wonder what Renny might do once they left the ship. Would she keep her pledge to stay and work for them as they'd agreed, or would she simply disappear into the city, having accomplished the adventure she'd contrived for herself?

Vangie sighed and wrung the cloth in the basin. Only time would reveal the girl's true mettle. They wouldn't know what to expect from her until they arrived in America—which, according to some of the crew members, ought to be soon now. Within days.

There were things she ought to be doing in preparation, but she couldn't bring herself to leave James's side, sick as he was. She looked at her ailing boy, his face so thin and pale that even the band of freckles across his nose appeared to have faded. Drenched in perspiration, he jerked once, then again, in his troubled sleep.

Vangie shook her head as if to free herself of the panic clawing at her and began to sponge the boy's brow with renewed determination. "You must be getting well now, son," she murmured, speaking for her own benefit as much as for her son.

"You must be strong and fit for your first sight of America. Soon we will be leaving this terrible ship for our new life, and you'd not want to be missing a minute of that, would you? You must be brave and not give in to the fever, love. Our Lord will be taking the sickness away from you; I'm sure of it. God's healing hands are upon you at this very minute. You will be well, James. You will…"

Merciful Savior…I've already lost my firstborn son. Not another of my boys, please… not another…

Vangie knew she dared not give in to the ever-present fear that nagged her day and night. From the time she was a child, fear and its ugly accomplice, worry, had circled over her like buzzards waiting for their prey to drop. Only her faith had kept her a step beyond this plague of the spirit.

Even now, and her a woman with children grown, she could still fall victim to an entire host of fears that, unchecked, would all too easily freeze her spirit and paralyze her soul. Her husband credited her with far more grit than she actually possessed. Not for the world and everything in it would she have Conn or the children know that she was less than they thought her. In their eyes, her faith was unshakable, her strength inexhaustible.

And that's what she wanted them to believe, what she *needed* them to believe. Her only defense against this hidden weakness was her faith in the Almighty and the strength her family thought her to possess. As long as she could cling to God, and as long as her loved ones continued to confer on her the qualities she only wished she possessed, then Vangie could go on being everything they believed her to be, everything they needed her to be.

But God help her—and perhaps her family as well—if they should ever discover how slender was the thread that held her strength and faith intact.

~

Earlier, Conn had wandered across to the small galley next to steerage, where a few of the more able-bodied men had taken to making their music at night.

He was not a musician himself, but he could never resist the sound of a happy fiddle or a good Irish song. There had been a time when he and Vangie had danced with the other young people at the crossroads, and he had no doubt at all but what his wife could still outstep the best of them.

Shea Sullivan was fiddling a set of jigs when Conn ducked his head to pass through the doorway. One of the young McCormick lads was doing his best to keep up on the squeezebox, and in spite of the heaviness in Conn's chest, he couldn't stop his foot from taking up a tapping to the lively rhythm.

Except for two or three of the children, no one was dancing tonight. No surprise, that. Conn figured few had the energy or the heart left in them to dance.

His gaze traveled to the far end of the room, where Renny Magee sat, amusing a circle of youngsters. With her worn old cap crushed atop her head and a bit of flour dusting her features, the busker girl was giving forth the nonsensical lyrics and motions to a song about a constable and a goat that was smarter than the law.

More truth than lie in that particular song, Conn thought with a wry grin.

The lass was a natural mime. Indeed, Conn would concede that Renny Magee was likely adept at most any amusement, be it rendering a song or dancing a jig or playing a ditty on the tarnished tin whistle she carried around in her pocket. The girl was as cunning as a gombeen man and had as many tricks as a cart of monkeys, and that was the truth.

He knew the children—his own and the others aboard as well—did fancy the girl. And nothing would do Vangie but to defend the young hoyden. So, in order to avoid his wife's barbed remarks about his being such a hardhead, Conn had learned to restrain his sharp tongue about the little busker. Most of the time.

Besides, despite his misgivings about bringing her along, Renny Magee had proven to be quite a lot of help, not only to Vangie and their own brood, but to the other children in steerage as well. The girl was a constant source of entertainment. Her mercurial mind seemed to hold a limitless supply of diversions, and her energy was as boundless as her imagination.

Too bad, Conn told himself with grim amusement as he watched her, that the young scamp's code of honor was not honed nearly so fine as her inclination toward mischief.

He turned just then, catching sight of Nell Grace as she appeared in the doorway. In that moment, Conn was seized by an unexpected thought of Vangie at the same age. His daughter's hair was the same dark red, though easier tamed, and she had the same finely molded, sharply chiseled features as her mother. Though her loveliness was quieter, more subdued, than Vangie's fiery good looks, at seventeen the lass already carried herself with the same grace and lissome movements. As she stood there, her hand lifted to beckon him, she might have been Vangie herself, twenty years past.

Of all his children, this sweet daughter evoked in Conn a tenderness, a fierce protectiveness that almost bordered on the obsessive. He loved them all, but he feared most for Nell Grace. Her delicate beauty, her gentle nature, the innate goodness and innocence he had seen in her since childhood would make her easy prey for the vultures and despoilers of the world. Sometimes he wished he could shut her inside the fortress of her family's love and keep her there forever.

When he prayed for his children, he invariably found it harder to surrender Nell Grace to the good Lord's care than he did the others. It seemed that every plea for her safekeeping was accompanied by a wrenching anxiety, almost as if he must convince even the Almighty that the girl had greater need of God's protection than did the other, sturdier MacGovern offspring.

He didn't like to think what this said about his faith. Sure, Vangie would call him to task for his weak-kneed prayers. But then Vangie would not understand about doubting, especially about doubting their Lord.

All these thoughts coursed through him as he made his way across the room to his daughter. Her shadowed eyes betrayed her own fears and the reason she had been sent, and Conn chided himself. This night it was not Nell Grace who most needed the sheltering arms of their loving God.

⌒

Renny Magee watched MacGovern and Nell Grace leave the room. She knew at once why the girl had come for him, but forced herself to turn back to the children long enough to pull a comical face and make a hasty bow. Then she sped from the room.

As she plowed along the dark corridor that led to the bunks, it occurred to Renny that up until recently, any task she might have done for one of the MacGoverns, even Vangie, as the missus insisted she call her, would have been done with the thought of increasing her standing with MacGovern himself.

That was no longer the case. Now she did what was asked of her because of her feelings for them all. Unfamiliar feelings to which she could not give a name, but which seemed to be growing stronger—and more bewildering—with each day passing.

She had never known folks like the MacGoverns. These were people who seemed to actually *want* to be together, as if they found each other's company grand fun. They talked a lot and laughed a lot—and they seemed to hug a lot as well. Even when they scrapped—which the twins did with regularity—any one of them would defend the other in a heartbeat, should some rascal aboard the ship pose a threat.

Renny had noticed that the MacGoverns—especially Vangie—also spoke of "The Lord" as naturally as if the Almighty sat with them at table. They said their prayers *aloud*, not seeming to mind who else might be listening. They were keen on saying things such as "blessed" and "thanks be" and "if The Lord wills."

Why, MacGovern and his missus—Vangie—were so free with their conversation that they sometimes even said "I love you" to each other, not just to the children! Indeed, the man couldn't seem to walk across the room without smiling at his wife, and didn't he call her "my beauty" and hold her hand, even give her a squeeze when he thought no one else was about?

It seemed to Renny that the family treated her with uncommon decency, instead of haranguing her as if she were just another stray alley cat nobody wanted around. Well, except for MacGovern, of course, who still eyed her as if he half expected her to stick a shiv in his back every time she ventured within a hand's-breadth of him.

Now that she thought of it, though, even MacGovern tended to treat her well enough these days.

So perhaps it wasn't all that curious that she actually liked doing tasks for them, and found herself eager to be helping out more and more, instead of just seeing to what was expected of her.

Renny wished she could do something now. She wished with all her heart she could manage a way to help poor James get well and at the same time banish that awful look of terror from his mother's eyes.

Perhaps Vangie thought no one else had seen the way she held the boy with her eyes, as if he might slip away from her at any minute. She had a way, Vangie did, of not letting the others know she was afraid.

But Renny had seen enough fear in her time to recognize it for what it was. And Vangie was scared. Bad scared.

And with good reason, Renny allowed. The fever had wee James in a fierce grip, all right, and she didn't like the looks of the boy. Not at all.

Earlier today, she had heard Vangie praying for the boy, praying as if her heart might fly to pieces if The Lord didn't answer. So far, Renny had seen no sign of a reply.

It struck her that perhaps The Lord needed to be reminded about James a bit more often—perhaps as much as every hour or so. But Vangie had an awful lot to do as it was.

Renny was tempted to try her hand at the praying, but from the little she had heard, The Lord might not have any truck with a sinner like herself. Of course, she had only resorted to thievery when she was so hungry she couldn't bear it any longer, so hungry her stomach felt like the rats had been at it. Still, would the fact that she'd been near famished be an acceptable excuse to The Lord for the pockets she picked now and then? And what about the wrappers of fish she sometimes filched when the opportunity presented itself?

Vangie claimed God knew everything, that there was no keeping secrets from The Lord. If that was the case, no doubt He would turn a deaf ear to the words from the mouth of one such as herself.

Worse still, what if her boldness vexed Him and He took it out on the MacGoverns, them being associated with her as they were? Sure, she wouldn't want to do anything that might hurt James's chances for getting well.

No, Renny decided, she'd best not bother the Almighty with a sinful busker girl's prayer. She'd do better to keep her silence and stick to helping out in other ways, however she could.

She had reached the door to their quarters now, but stopped when she saw the whole family standing around James's bunk, holding hands and praying.

Renny Magee had been alone most of her life. She had lived on the streets of Dublin ever since she could remember. Even among the other buskers she had always been known as a loner. It had never much bothered her, being on her own. It was all she knew, after all.

But at this moment, watching from a distance as the MacGoverns joined ranks and prayed for their own, she had never felt more alone in her life.

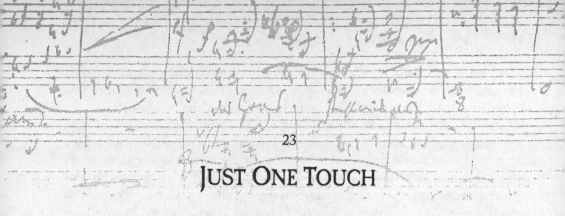

23

JUST ONE TOUCH

Prayer is the burden of a sigh,
The falling of a tear,
The upward glancing of an eye
When none but God is near.

JAMES MONTGOMERY

Throughout the long night, Renny did everything she could to help the MacGoverns. She changed the water beside James's bed as needed, fetched whatever they asked, and watched over Baby Emma so that Nell Grace could relieve Vangie.

No one, however, could coax Vangie into leaving the boy's side for more than a few moments. It seemed to Renny that Vangie was beginning to look almost as pale and wan as poor James.

Apparently, there was no ship's doctor aboard. One of the sailors had given MacGovern the excuse that the physician who would normally have traveled with them had to stay behind in Liverpool, due to some sort of emergency. When MacGovern demanded that one of the crewmen try to locate a doctor among the passengers above, he was told in no uncertain terms that they could not bother the first-class passengers with "the likes of a filthy Irisher."

MacGovern, of course, not one to swallow this sort of abuse easily, had made a terrible scene. Only Vangie's pleas—and the threat of lockup for the duration of the trip—had kept him from flying berserk at the man. Ever since then, he had done nothing but pace, his face set in a terrible fierce scowl.

Renny would warrant that MacGovern was not a man used to being scotched, and he was having a hard time of it, being helpless to aid his boy. Had it not been for upsetting Vangie even more, no doubt he would have been pounding the wall—or a crewman's head—with one of his big fists long before now.

At the moment, he had stopped his stomping back and forth to once again join Vangie and Nell Grace, who stood heads bowed, continuing their prayers for James. Some of the other steerage passengers, those not wary of infecting themselves, had come to add their petitions to those of the family.

Apparently, Christian folk believed that it took a great number of prayers from a large contingent of people to get anything worthwhile accomplished.

Renny was sitting between Johnny and the makeshift cradle of rags and straw that held Baby Emma. Both the boy and the baby were sleeping. Renny figured it must be two or three in the morning by now, if not later. Her view was blocked by the prayer circle, so she could not see James. But she knew all too well how he looked.

Her last sight of him had sent a creeping dread over her heart, for she realized with near certainty he would be gone by first light. She had seen the mask of death on others, had seen it often enough to believe the boy was only a short distance away from breathing his last.

Her eyes went to Vangie, and she could have wept at the raw fear and desperation ravaging the woman's face. Vangie knew. She knew her boy was dying, knew there was nothing to be done for him now.

There was no help to be had for James, and that was the truth. And yet she went on praying, Vangie did, as if any minute the door to heaven might open and pour out some wondrous potion on the boy that would rouse him from his fatal stupor and take the sickness away.

Renny sat watching a few minutes more, hammered by an entire riot of emotions. Suddenly, she knew what she must do. She could not—*would* not—put it off any longer. Taking pains to move quietly, she stood and, after reassuring herself that Johnny and the baby were still sound asleep, tiptoed down the aisle and out the door.

She went straight to the galley, which she knew would be deserted at this late hour. As she'd hoped, she found the place unoccupied. For a long time, Renny stood in the shadows, mustering her nerve. Finally, the blood pounding in her ears and her heart rising to her throat, she dropped down to her knees and propped her elbows on top of a small keg.

At first, she hesitated, uncertain and even fearful of what she was about to do. Would The Lord be offended by someone like herself having the cheek to come begging? Vangie and Nell Grace were big on talking about God's love and kindness, but so far Renny had seen little of either from Him. What if she angered Him? Would He strike back at her, punish her?

What if she prayed and James took even worse?

She shook off *that* thought after only a second or two. James couldn't possibly take worse. Wasn't he already dying? The worst that could happen was that The Lord might penalize *her* for being so bold where she had no right.

But even if she did rile Him, she had to try. She *had* to, for James's sake. And for Vangie's.

And so kneeling there in the shadows, on the cold, damp floor, she took a deep breath, bowed her head, and closed her eyes.

"Please, Lord...your Honor...my name is Renny Magee. You don't know me, any more than I know You, and I'm begging Your pardon ahead of time for bein' so bold, but I'd like to ask You a favor. Not for myself, you understand, but for James. James MacGovern. And perhaps I ought to tell You straight off that the favor is a big one..."

⌒

Conn stood in the dark corridor between their quarters and the galley, feeling more desperate than he had ever felt in his life.

They'd lost the two wee babes—one before she ever so much as saw the light of day, the other while only a few days old. Even so, bad as it had been, at least they had loved them but a brief time before their passing.

But Seamus, their wee James—eight years he had been with them now. Eight years of loving him and his brother, Johnny. Loving them and dreaming bright dreams for them and holding the highest of hopes for them.

And now to lose one of them? Was that how it was to end?

Dear God, it would be grief enough if he didn't have to look at Vangie's face and watch her heart break, piece by piece—what was left of it, that is, after leaving Aidan behind.

Two babes taken from her. One grown son as good as dead. How could she endure the loss of another?

He tried to pray, found that he had no words, could not summon enough strength or hope or faith to give voice to yet another supplication for his boy.

He knew he was not trusting as he should, not "clinging," as Vangie would say.

Never had he known such a terrible weakness before, such a hollowness in his soul. All this night he had felt as though *he* were the one who was slipping away, his life draining from him, little by little, like drops from a well going dry.

And Vangie—ah, he could no longer bear to meet her eyes. He felt the great failure of his life each time he looked at her, for he had brought her to this place and now could do nothing for her, not even comfort her.

Their son was dying. He knew it, and so did she. And yet Vangie went on hoping, went on praying and pleading and even *praising* the One who in an instant could stop this madness and give them back their James, their precious boy.

Aye, the Lord could do that.

If only He would.

Vangie had not as yet given up her hope. Nor would she, Conn knew, not until James had exhaled his last labored breath.

Conn hated himself for not being able to match his wife's faith with his own.

He ought to be drawing on every shred of strength left to him, every remnant of hope and faith he could muster. Not only for his son, but for Vangie. He should be strong for the both of them.

Instead, he was wandering about in the gloom like a man lost in a fog, aimless and without a thought of what to do. He was useless entirely.

He lumbered toward the galley, then stopped in the doorway at the scene that met his eyes. In the shadows, relieved only by the dim light flickering from the lantern beside the door, Renny Magee was kneeling.

It took Conn a moment to realize that the girl was praying.

Renny Magee, praying! He wouldn't have thought the little heathen even knew how!

He stood, scarcely breathing, not moving as he watched and listened in numb amazement.

"The thing is, Lord Sir, Vangie has already had to give up her one boy, the oldest—and 'twas me who gained the good from her loss, don't You see? His staying behind in Ireland made it possible for me to come to America. And now that we're almost there, James—well, sure, he's dying. I can tell from the looks of him. And so Vangie will lose another son, and her not yet recovered from her first grief.

"Do you really think that's fair, Lord Sir? Not that Vangie blames You for any of this, mind! Nothing of the sort. Vangie would never do that, although I confess I don't understand how she keeps from it at times. But even after all that's happened, 'tis clear she doesn't fault You for her sorrows.

"She's a good woman, Vangie is. But I expect You already know that. She's good to everyone, even to me, and myself a total stranger to her, and her husband believing I'm nothing but a common thief.

"It just seems to me that Vangie is entitled to something better than what she's had so far. She's a good mother, as You know, the kind of mother I'd have wanted for myself. She does love her children fiercely, as anyone can see, and her husband, too, although he is a hardheaded man, if ever I met one.

"All things considered, I have to wonder if You couldn't see fit to make James well again? I heard Vangie say to Nell Grace that all You would have to do is touch him, and the fever would leave for good. James would be well again.

"He's on fire, don't you see? If it's true that You could touch him and take the fire away, well…would that really be asking too much from you? Sure and a touch wouldn't require all that much effort, would it? Just one touch?

"And please, Lord Sir, I don't mean to rush You, but I'm afraid it might be too late even for You to do anything unless You do it quick like—right away if possible."

There was a long silence, and Conn thought perhaps she had finished. But then she started in once more, and even though he disliked himself for eavesdropping, he could not have moved away now if someone had tried to drag him.

"By the way, I expect it might be best if the family don't know I've talked to You. They might not like it, my speaking with You about James, what with MacGovern

thinking I'm a heathen. And perhaps I am, so if it's all the same to You, could we keep this between ourselves?"

She went on, but Conn, overcome, quietly turned and walked away. Nearly blinded from the tears that had welled up in his eyes, he trudged back down the dim corridor toward their quarters. As he went, he carried with him the sight of Renny Magee on her knees in the darkness, the sound of her childish but determined voice pleading on behalf of his dying son.

Renny Magee, whom he had berated time and time again as a thief, an abandoned child of the streets. He, too, had abandoned her, had deliberately made her feel unwanted and unwelcome.

Renny Magee, who believed he thought her a heathen and altogether worthless.

All this time, when he should have been modeling for her the unconditional love and mercy of their Savior, he had instead shown her only reproach and condemnation.

Self-disgust ripped through him, and he had to stop for a moment as bitter tears of shame spilled over, nearly blinding his eyes. "God forgive me," he whispered in the darkness. "I have been the worst kind of man. A cold, unfeeling, *hardheaded* man. And a poor excuse for a Christian as well."

He shook his head at his own poverty of spirit. "I have failed that child, Lord, and that's the truth." He faltered, his whisper echoing along the damp, dark walls. "God forgive me, I failed young Renny Magee. But somehow I believe—Lord, I *have* to believe—that even though I let her down, You *won't*."

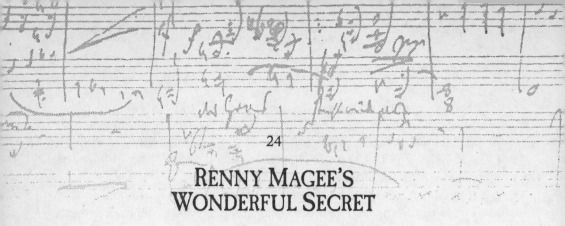

24

RENNY MAGEE'S
WONDERFUL SECRET

Oh could I tell, ye surely would believe it!
Oh could I only say what I have seen!

FREDERICK W. H. MYERS

It was nearly four o'clock in the morning when James's fever broke. The fire left the boy so quickly it was as if a cool, healing hand had passed over every inch of his burning body, absorbing the heat unto itself.

Conn was half dozing, sitting upright on his berth and leaning against the wall, when he heard Vangie cry out for him. He sprang to his feet so quickly he slammed his shoulder against the iron brace that fastened the bunk, sending a knife of pain shooting down his arm.

He reached James's bunk in a heartbeat. Vangie was kneeling by the boy, and Conn put a hand to her shoulder to steady her as he stood staring down at his son.

So it had come, then. What they had feared for days.

He began to tremble. Cold…he was so cold. He couldn't stop the shaking as he stood studying James's inert form. It occurred to him that the boy looked strangely serene.

He had to get a grip on himself, for Vangie's sake. "So, is he gone then?" he choked out, putting a hand to her shoulder. "Ah, you should have called me sooner, love."

"No, Conn!" Vangie lifted her face to him, and Conn saw that her eyes were wide and shining, not with grief-stricken tears, as he would have expected, but with a kind of wonder and something else, some peculiar kind of excitement.

"The fever is *gone*, Conn! James is only sleeping just now. He's better. Much better!"

Conn stared at her, then turned his gaze back to the boy for a closer look. Only then did he realize that James was indeed alive. Breathing deeply, evenly—peacefully—without the dreaded death rattle he had been expecting to hear all night.

Vangie reached for his hand, and Conn dropped to his knees beside her. "You're quite sure?" he choked out. "The fever is truly gone?"

She was weeping now, but through the tears her tired eyes glistened with unmistakable joy. "'Tis true, Conn. James is going to get well! Our boy is going to be all right, after all! God has answered our prayers, don't you see?"

"Aye, glory be to God," Conn said softly, his voice rough with emotion, his heart slamming against his chest as he watched his sleeping son. "But I can scarce believe *what* I see."

By now, Nell Grace and Johnny had come to join them. Like her mother, the girl was crying with stunned happiness, and Johnny was grinning down at his twin brother—and best chum—with huge delight.

Something struck Conn, and he glanced toward Renny Magee's bunk. The girl was simply lying there, watching them with those intense pale eyes of hers.

Conn couldn't be sure, for the lantern light was dim and flickering, but the lass appeared to be somewhat dazed. Her expression registered nothing except pure and utter amazement.

As Conn watched her, she met his eyes, but only for an instant before quickly glancing away.

She didn't want him to know, he realized. He remembered what he had overheard as she prayed. Why, the foolish little scamp, she actually feared they would be offended at the thought of her going to the Lord in James's behalf!

Somehow Conn understood that even now, with James obviously past the dark hour, the girl would want to keep her secret. He could see the shock in her face, the look of incredulity, the glint of something akin to panic, and he almost smiled, to think that Renny Magee could actually be struck speechless.

But why would she keep silent *now*? Oh, if James had died, God forbid, then in her confusion and ignorance, the girl might have possibly feared their disapproval—though her apprehension would have been unreasonable entirely.

Or would it have been?

But James *hadn't* died, and the real surprise was that the lass apparently was not going to try to steal a bit of the credit for his recovery.

He turned back to James, studying his son with damp eyes for a long time.

He would keep Renny Magee's secret all right, if that's how she wanted it. But not from Vangie. At another time, when they were alone, he would tell Vangie. He could not keep such a thing from her, not such a strange, unbelievable thing as this.

Regret came washing over him at the thought that he could not speak of this to the girl herself. He could not even thank her for caring so much about their boy that she would entreat a God she didn't know, a God who, Conn suspected, even frightened her.

But if he could not thank her directly, he could at least begin to treat her more decently. Perhaps he might even find a way to let her know that she was a heathen no longer in his eyes.

⌒

Later that morning, Renny sat holding Baby Emma, listening to the family's happy discussion about James.

He had awakened once and spoke with them, then almost immediately drifted off to sleep again. But there seemed no doubt that he was improving and would eventually be completely well again.

Renny did not know what to make of it. Certainly, it was no thanks to her. If MacGovern was right, she was a heathen, after all.

Perhaps it was nothing more than a…a *coincidence* entirely, James coming out of the fever as he had not long after she had prayed to the Lord.

It wasn't as if she were the *only* one who had prayed for the boy. In truth, the family had not *stopped* praying from the time the boy had taken ill, and a great number of others among the passengers—*good* people, *Christian* people—had prayed for James, too.

So she must not allow herself to make big out of little for her part in things. The fact that she had prayed, and in secret at that, could not possibly have had anything to do with James's recovery.

Indeed not.

But there was the matter of what James had said when he'd finally come round. The boy's words had left her head spinning.

"I felt the fire go out, Mum…"

When Vangie asked him what he meant, James told them of his dream.

"I dreamt I was on fire. It was like I was burning up, inside and out. It hurt awful bad, Mum! But then an angel came and touched me, soft-like, and took the fire away. Snuffed it right out of me! I could feel it going, I could. And all of a sudden, I felt…cool. Not cold, but just good, like when you come out of the river on a hot day and the wind blows on you while you're still all wet."

"…then an angel came and touched me…and took the fire away…"

Renny swallowed, hard. Her throat felt tight. She had no way of knowing what exactly had happened to James. But *something* had happened; that much was clear. Something unlike anything she could have imagined. Something strange. Very strange.

After a moment, she closed her eyes. Even if she dared not let herself believe that she had contributed in some way—no matter how small—to James's recovery, she reckoned it would only be polite to say *thank you.*

And so she did.

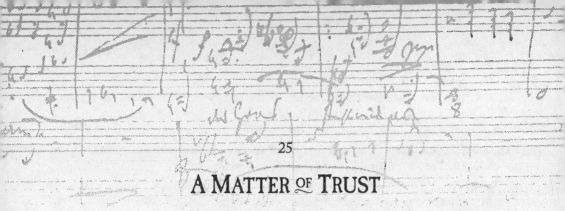

25

A MATTER OF TRUST

Lament for the land where the sun beams wander,
And shadows deeper than elsewhere fall...

JOHN SWANWICK DRENNAN

Bantry Hill

Today, Susanna decided, she would make the visit she had been putting off far too long.

Not that the delay had been entirely her doing. What with getting settled in and then Caterina's illness, there had been little time for anything other than managing the daily routine. But now there *was* time, and she intended to go while she could.

Shortly after breakfast, she went looking for Paul. She found him alone in Michael's office, putting some papers in order.

He looked up and, seeing her, broke into a wide smile. "Ah, Susanna! Come in! You are not taking your walk this morning?"

"Not yet," Susanna said, returning his smile. "Actually, I have a visit I'd like to make, and I was wondering if you might have time to drive me."

"Of course! Where would you like to go?"

"To Deirdre's grave," Susanna said, watching his reaction, "but I have no idea where she's buried."

His expression sobered. "The cemetery is not far. And, of course, I will be glad to take you."

"I thought—" Susanna stopped, then went on. "I thought perhaps we could also stop at the site of the accident. If you're quite sure it's not too much trouble."

He studied her for a moment, his usually lively features now altogether solemn. "It is no trouble at all. When would you like to leave?"

"Would it be convenient to go early this afternoon? Perhaps while Caterina is napping?"

"*Sì*, that would be very good. I will bring the buggy around front, say, at one o'clock."

"Thank you, Paul. I appreciate it."

Instantly, his expression brightened. "But it is my pleasure, Susanna! You never ask for anything. Never. I am more than happy to do something for you."

He *had* seemed pleased, Susanna thought on her way back upstairs. Not for the first time, it occurred to her that perhaps she should make more of an effort to get to know Paul Santi. In time, they might even become friends. He had certainly gone out of his way to make her feel at home since she arrived, often stopping to chat with her, inquire after her day, or inspect Caterina's latest drawings.

Not that he had ever indicated any sort of interest other than friendship. To the contrary, his behavior couldn't possibly be construed as anything but the natural courtesy and kindness he would have extended any other member of Michael's family.

At another time and under different circumstances, Susanna thought she might have responded more readily to his overtures toward friendship. She did enjoy Paul's company, especially since he never made things awkward by flirting or displaying any hint of romantic interest.

She had to smile a little at the very thought. Her experience with men was admittedly limited, but she couldn't help but think it would be *Paul*, not herself, who would find the idea of a "romantic interest" awkward—if not positively alarming.

Most of the time, he reminded her of a mischievous boy who entertained himself by amusing the entire household. His high energy and zany antics often made it difficult to remember that as concertmaster for the orchestra, he was an accomplished musician in his own right, not just Michael's assistant.

No matter how much he enjoyed playing the court jester, Susanna was convinced that back of his puckish high spirits there was a keen intelligence and sensitivity rarely glimpsed by anyone except those closest to him. Yet even though she liked Paul a great deal, she deliberately kept a certain distance from him. In truth, with the exception of Caterina, Susanna supposed it was fair to say that she kept a safe distance from everyone.

Perhaps her self-imposed reserve had to do with the fact that she could not shake the feeling of *impermanence* about her situation. After more than two months at Bantry Hill, she still could not completely relax, would not risk allowing herself to be seduced into a false sense of security. While she longed to share Caterina's life—at least until the girl was fully grown—a part of her lived in dread that circumstances might somehow dictate otherwise.

Outside Caterina's bedroom, she stood listening for a moment to the child's chatter, which was, of course, directed to Gus, the wolfhound. As she stood there, amused by her small niece's one-sided dialogue with the hound, something inside her gave an unexpected wrench at the thought of just how painful it would be to have to leave Caterina now, after becoming so fond of her, so involved in her life.

In an attempt to shake the melancholy that had been stalking her since daybreak, she went to tidy up her room a bit, then stood looking out the window. It was a sunny October morning, almost crystalline in its brightness and clarity of view. And yet Susanna had come to realize by now how quickly that could change. In fact, she half suspected that the gloom which sometimes hovered over her own spirit these days had much to do with the landscape itself.

There was a certain brooding secretiveness about this entire river valley, and Bantry Hill was in no way exempt from it. This was a world of dark, moldering estates, dense forests, and always the mighty river that gouged and wound its way through an almost surreal vastness. Magnificent but primitive, spectacular but formidable. It was all too easy to imagine that Bantry Hill might harbor some awful truth or terrible secret that, once revealed, would prove to be more than she could bear. Something that might even drive her away from this place—and from Caterina.

She hugged her arms to herself, as if to press the miasma of dread out of her body, out of her soul. With a sigh, she told herself it was simply her Celtic imagination running amok. The prospect of visiting her sister's grave had cast a pall over the entire morning.

On a day like this, she chided herself, her surroundings should inspire her, not depress her. She had no excuse for this shadowed, nagging sense of foreboding that darkened in the recesses of her spirit. She had a niece she adored, work she enjoyed, and people—like Paul Santi and Rosa Navaro—who seemed to care about her. God forgive her, what more could she want?

Without warning, the thought of Michael—the image of his darkly bearded face, the quick, brilliant warmth of his smile—caught her unawares, striking her like a blow and leaving her to reach out a hand to the window frame in order to steady herself.

After a moment she opened the window. Perhaps the morning air would clear her head. Leaning forward a little, she could see Michael and Paul standing just in back of the house. They seemed to be having a brisk, even heated, exchange, with much gesturing of the hands and waving of the arms—mannerisms Susanna had come to associate with the two men as typical of the Italian male.

Her first inclination was to close the window, or at least to step away. But when she heard her own name mentioned, her curiosity overcame her reservations about listening in, and she edged to the side of the window so she could hear better without being seen.

⁓

"*—But it is not right, Michael! You should tell Susanna the truth! You should have told her long before now!*"

Michael checked the impatient retort that rose to his lips. "And what should I tell her, Pauli? What exactly do I say to her, to Deirdre's sister, eh?"

"That is exactly the reason you should tell her the truth, Michael. Because she *is* Deirdre's sister. She has a right to know!"

"She has no *need* to know!"

"How can you be so sure? Is it really for you to judge?"

"Who else but I?" He could hear Paul's shallow breathing and knew he was debating on whether or not to continue. Michael gave him no chance. "You of all people should understand why I do not speak of this to Susanna. You were here, Pauli. You saw how it was with us."

There was a silence. Although Paul sounded more guarded, obviously he wasn't ready to desist. "Michael, you think you are protecting Susanna. But I wonder if it is not yourself you are trying to protect."

"And what is *that* supposed to mean?"

"Do you really not see what you are doing?"

"No, I do not *see* what I am doing," Michael shot back, his words laced with sarcasm. "Apparently, I must depend on you even for this."

Michael regretted his sharpness the instant the words left his lips. But he wasn't accustomed to criticism from Paul, except perhaps when it pertained to a difference of opinion over a music score, and he was surprised by how much it hurt. Paul was closer to him than a brother, yet he could not seem to understand why Michael had chosen to keep his silence about Deirdre. Instead, Paul saw his actions as unreasonable, even selfish.

"This is not right, Michael. It's not fair to Susanna! Why are you doing this? It is not like you to be deceitful."

Michael gave a long sigh, groping for patience.

"You are so intent on keeping the truth about that night—that one, terrible night—from Susanna, that you are keeping everything else from her as well, including—"

"Including *what*?" Michael bit out, losing the struggle to restrain his temper.

There was another silence. Then, "You care for her, Michael," Paul said quietly.

Michael tensed, knotted his fists at his side. "Enough, Pauli. You overstep."

"I see it, *cugino*. You care for Susanna, but you suffocate your feelings with your stubborn silence. And Susanna—"

"What about Susanna?"

When Paul finally answered, he sounded unexpectedly deflated. "Never mind. Perhaps you are right, I have spoken out of turn."

"*Sì, avete,*" Michael said tightly.

⌒

"Yes, you have…"

They had lapsed into Italian now, but even if Susanna hadn't understood their words, she could have detected the frustration in Paul's voice—and the tightly controlled anger in Michael's.

She waited another moment, then heard the back door slam as one or both of them came inside.

So Michael *hadn't* told her the truth about the night Deirdre died. At least not the *entire* truth. Indeed, it sounded as if he was hiding a great deal more than just the truth about the accident.

"You care for her. I see it."

Her heart leaped again, just as it had when she heard Paul speak those words. But obviously, Paul was wrong. If Michael really cared about her as something more than a friend—for that clearly was what Paul had insinuated—he wouldn't deliberately deceive her about her own sister. Would he?

"I wonder if it is not yourself you are trying to protect."

What had Paul meant by that accusation? At least, it had *sounded* like an accusation.

Suddenly, her every instinct urged Susanna to fly downstairs and confront Michael. She wanted to rip away those unnerving dark glasses and *demand* that he tell her everything. She wanted to lash out at him, to challenge him until that dark, inscrutable countenance finally showed some emotion, until he admitted that he had been in some way responsible for Deirdre's horrible death.

But of course she would do nothing of the kind. She could not face him and admit that she'd been eavesdropping, no matter how much she was tempted to do so. Nor could she go charging downstairs and provoke a scene that might prompt him to send her packing like the poor relative she was, leaving Caterina behind.

No, she could not risk arousing his anger to the point that he might actually banish her. Caterina had already lost her mother. God forbid that she should have to suffer yet another loss of one she loved.

And the child *did* love her. Susanna had no doubt of it.

She lowered the window, then began to pace the room. Could the truth, no matter how terrible it might be if fully known, really make all that much difference? She could not for the life of her fathom anything so horrible that it would prompt her to leave Bantry Hill—leave Caterina—of her own volition.

Finally, she sat down on the side of the bed, still struggling with the question as to whether anything—*anything*—she might learn about Michael himself, or Deirdre's death, could possibly be so heinous that she would allow it to drive her away from Caterina.

In the midst of her attempt to make a way through the quagmire of unanswered questions, yet *another* question—this one even more unsettling—came hurtling out of nowhere, startling her with its almost brutal force:

Was Caterina really the reason, the only reason, she was so resolved to stay at Bantry Hill? What part, exactly, did Michael play in her unwillingness to leave?

Shaken, Susanna sat unmoving, scarcely breathing, as she clasped and unclasped her hands. She must not, dare not, commit the folly of trying to answer that question.

Not now. Not ever.

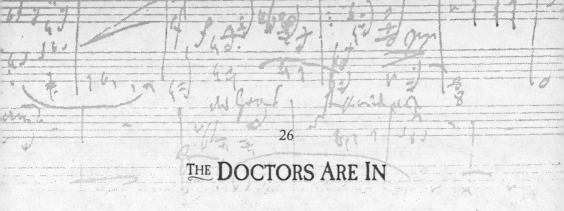

26

THE DOCTORS ARE IN

'Tis the human touch in this world that counts...

SPENCER MICHAEL FREE

New York City

Today was the first day the Drs. Carmichael and Cole would be seeing patients at their new location.

Loath to think that she might have been in any way responsible for Andrew's decision to relocate, Bethany finally accepted her new partner's insistence that the move had been inevitable for some time now, that she had merely provided the needed impetus for his taking action.

There was no denying that he had outgrown the building on East Seventeenth, and even though the new quarters were situated in a less desirable area, they were far more spacious. Besides, this was where Andrew Carmichael wanted to practice.

Bordered by Bleecker Street, Thompson Street, and the Bowery, the rambling brick building was located in the very heart of an immigrant district. Although many of the older structures in the area had once been homes to city merchants and businessmen, by now most had become commercial establishments and, more recently, settlement houses. Among them could be found temporary housing, as well as classrooms and workshops where English was taught and instruction provided in sewing, cooking, and other basic skills. Occasional clinics were set up for the poor, but these were makeshift at best and usually open to patients only a few days a month.

It hadn't taken Bethany long to realize that Andrew Carmichael had an intense burden for the underprivileged, especially the countless poor immigrants who spilled onto the shores of New York by the thousands. He had actually purchased the entire building on Elizabeth Street with the express purpose of moving both his office and his living quarters. His intention was clear: not only would he be available to his patients, he would also be living among them.

Bethany had been a little puzzled by the acquisition of the building, if not by the man's commitment. Andrew Carmichael couldn't be much past his midthirties—hardly old enough to have accumulated any real wealth. Besides, he kept his fees far too low to generate a lucrative income. Perhaps he was just unusually adept at saving. From what she knew of his lifestyle, it was modest, altogether unpretentious.

In fact, they had this in common; Bethany had never felt the need to own more than the basic necessities, except for her one extravagance—books. Nor had she ever been ensnared by the love of "things," desiring instead the freedom to practice medicine where the need was greatest, not necessarily where she could earn the most money. It seemed that here, too, her goals were highly compatible with those of her partner.

Her partner.

The fact that she could actually think of Andrew Carmichael in those terms was entirely his doing. Less than a month after they'd begun to practice together, he had informed Bethany that he preferred to acknowledge her as his *associate* rather than as his *assistant*.

The truth was, Bethany would have been grateful to serve as his assistant, at least for a time, so eager was she to set up a practice and secure hospital privileges. Andrew, however, refused to discuss it, pointing out that she had worked just as long and as hard as he had to gain her education and training—"most likely harder, considering the obstacles you've had to overcome in the medical community itself."

He insisted his need wasn't so much for an assistant as it was for a full-time partner, someone willing to carry an equal share of the increasing patient load. "Much as I dislike admitting it," he told her, his speech rhythmic with the faint Scottish burr Bethany had come to find rather charming, "I cannot seem to manage the work as I need to. So you see, there will be none of this 'assistant' business. You're my associate, and that's how it will be."

Even now, as Bethany stood scrutinizing the examining room—*her* examining room—she had to remind herself again that all this was real. She had worked so hard and had waited so long for her own private practice that she could scarcely take it in.

She heard Andrew clattering about in the adjoining examining room and smiled a little. Perhaps she ought to go offer to help him. The poor man did seem inclined toward disorder, even clumsiness at times.

She had worked until early evening the day before, arranging her instruments just so, stocking the cabinets with tins and bottles and boxes all neatly labeled, then lining the drawers with clean paper before filling them with an adequate supply of dressings, bandages, and towels. Now, with her white ticking apron starched and pressed, her hair tucked firmly into a knot at the nape of her neck, she was ready for whatever the day might bring.

Andrew, on the other hand, had made late calls on two patients the night before and consequently was only now readying his office and examining room. From the sound of things, he was *throwing* supplies in place rather than arranging them.

Bethany knew before she entered that she would most likely find him in a clean but rumpled laboratory coat, with a shock of dark hair falling over his forehead. As always, he would appear somewhat harried and impatient, although his impatience never seemed to be directed at her, only himself.

In fact, he was still in his shirt sleeves and down on his knees, scooping up an armful of bandages off the floor. He looked up as Bethany entered, giving her one of his diffident smiles as he scuttled to his feet, his free hand knocking an entire row of tin containers off the cabinet shelf in the process.

With some effort, Bethany kept a straight face as the tins went clattering to the floor. Andrew stared at the disarray, then, red-faced, gave a quick little shrug and a quirk of his mouth as he heaped the bandages on the examining table and bent to retrieve the scattered tins.

When Bethany knelt to help him, he muttered, not looking at her, "I should have done this last night, I expect."

"You were seeing patients last night," she reminded him. "I'll help you finish up."

Something about his lean profile, the dark head bent so seriously to his efforts—and so close to her—made the breath catch in Bethany's throat. More peculiar still was the sudden inclination to brush that rebellious wave of hair away from his forehead.

He turned to her then, their eyes meeting for an instant. Bethany quickly averted her gaze, but not before her pulse gave an unexpected leap.

"I'm really quite pathetic, aren't I?" he said.

Surprised, Bethany turned back to him, unable to stop a smile at the sight of his undue look of self-disgust.

"Don't be silly," she said, hurrying to scoop up the remainder of the tins. "It's just that you're in a rush, that's all."

It was then that she noticed his hands. His fingers were swollen, his knuckles red and inflamed, his movements stiff as he went on collecting the containers.

Bethany's stomach knotted. In that moment, she realized there was more to Andrew's ungainliness than haste or preoccupation, and it was suddenly anything but amusing. The slow, stiff gait as he ascended a flight of stairs, his tendency to drop things, the unusual paleness and fatigue that occasionally seemed to overtake him now took on new significance.

She said nothing, however, as she got to her feet. With a deliberate effort to keep her expression clear, she set the tins back in order, then refolded the towels and stacked them in the cabinet drawers.

When she turned, she found him watching her. He had donned his lab coat, its sleeves nearly an inch too short above his wrists. Not for the first time, it occurred to Bethany that with his considerable height, his long arms, and somewhat prominent nose, Andrew Carmichael was almost Lincolnesque—albeit more handsome-featured than the late president—in his appearance. Perhaps he was also just as stoic in his character.

She forced a smile. "Well," she said brightly, "it would seem that all we need now are some patients."

As if on cue, the bell above the entrance door rang, alerting them that someone had come into the office. They looked at each other, and both of them started for the door at the same time.

~

They had discussed the likelihood that they would see at least three or four new patients on their first day. Before noon they had ushered no less than a dozen through the doors.

By agreement, Bethany had seen to the women, while Andrew tended to the men. They had taken turns, also by agreement, in treating the children.

Andrew stood watching Bethany escort the last of their morning patients—a small girl dressed in little more than rags and her cadaverously thin mother—out the door. Word that a woman doctor had set up practice in the area seemed to have traveled fast, and Andrew suspected that after today the news would spread like a brush fire. Women simply did not want a male doctor attending them, especially in the more delicate female matters, such as gynecological problems and childbirth.

In deference to those women who did subject themselves to an examination, he always tried to be sensitive and exceedingly careful, even to the point of using a longer stethoscope than usual to maintain his distance from the patient. But these cursory physical examinations were unsatisfactory, to say the least.

Bethany had brought a solution to this dilemma. She seemed to easily gain the confidence of their female patients, even the most hesitant ones. A steady stream of women had already begun to show up at the old offices before the move, and Andrew had no doubt but what the same thing would happen here as well.

All told, there was simply no reckoning the difference she had made in the practice, not only by gaining the trust of the women patients as she had, but in the considerable workload she'd assumed all along. Andrew could not help but recognize a certain irony in the situation.

If he were to be altogether honest with himself, he supposed that in the beginning of their relationship, he might have entertained a fanciful thought of himself as some sort of modern-day knight, "rescuing" Bethany Cole by helping her obtain her hospital privileges, and at the same time secure a patient list of her own.

Saint Andrew. He smiled at his own foolishness. The fact was that *he* had been the one who needed rescuing.

And it seemed that the lovely Dr. Cole had done a fine job of it, in a very short time.

In any event, it was an immeasurable relief to know that entire families could now receive the medical treatment they needed and deserved. He had tried to do his best for *all* his patients, of course, but there was no denying an ongoing frustration in never being able to provide adequate care for the ever-increasing numbers who needed it, especially the women.

Of course, the truth was that he had never been all that comfortable with women, professionally or personally. His mother had died giving birth to him, leaving Andrew to be raised by his middle-aged clergyman father. There had been only an older brother, no sisters to bring even a touch of feminine influence to his youth. With the exception of his aging Aunt Cecily and a grandmother who died before he even reached his teens, nearly all the people in his life had been men.

He had been in love once, in his late twenties. Tragically, his somewhat frail Evelyn had died during a diphtheria epidemic before they could marry. After that, Andrew had withdrawn to his profession, the church, and his travels. More recently, of course, his own physical condition had become an issue, making him reluctant to even consider a new romantic interest.

Not that the opportunity had presented itself. Indeed, Bethany Cole was the first woman to evoke more than a passing interest in all that time.

In many ways, Bethany was a puzzle. At twenty-seven, she had gained an impressive education and quite a lot of experience. She seemed to attack any task she undertook with the same competence and conscientiousness she brought to every patient under her care. Yet she was an extremely feminine, attractive young woman with a bright, appealing personality.

More than once, Andrew had marveled that she hadn't married and wondered if there was someone in her life. A fiancé, perhaps? And if not, then *why* not?

He came to himself and realized she was standing with her back to the door, watching him with a faint smile.

"Well—it seems we managed our 'three or four' patients for the morning, Dr. Carmichael," she said.

"It does seem so, Dr. Cole," he replied. He became aware that he had been rubbing his hands together, kneading his fingers—an involuntary, almost mindless effort to assuage the pain. Quickly, he lowered them to his sides.

"Since the waiting room is finally empty," he said, "why don't we get away for lunch? There's just the place down the street."

Bethany looked dubious. "In this neighborhood?"

"I can see that I need to acquaint you more thoroughly with your new surroundings. You might be surprised at what's out there."

"I don't doubt that for a moment."

Andrew leaned against the counter, studying her—the fine, clearly drawn features and delicate complexion, the slight lift with which she carried her head, the always-correct posture—all of which virtually shouted upper class and breeding. "Whatever possessed you to do this, Bethany?"

She frowned. "Do what?"

Andrew took in the room with a quick sweeping motion of his hand. "Medicine. More to the point, why would you agree to practice in the thick of a settlement district, where you'll never earn anything more than a modest living, at best?"

"What possessed *you* to do it?" she countered.

He shrugged. "That's different altogether. I didn't have to fight the prejudice and resistance of an entire establishment. And I don't come from an upper-class background."

He hadn't meant for the last to slip out, and he could tell the remark had caught her unawares—and quite possibly annoyed her as well. "I'm sorry," he said quickly. "That was uncalled for—pure assumption on my part."

She was studying him with one uplifted eyebrow.

Again, Andrew attempted to apologize. "I *am* sorry, Bethany. As I said, I just assumed—"

With relief, he saw the ghost of a rueful smile touch her lips. "I'm not rich, if that's what you're thinking, Andrew."

"No, really, I didn't mean—"

She laughed. "It's all right. As I said, I am definitely not wealthy, although there was a time, I suppose, when my grandfather was. He came from a long line of bankers and philanthropists. Most of his family tried to discourage him from medicine. They thought it too *common*. Ultimately they more or less disowned him." She paused, smiling a little. "It didn't seem to bother him much. He was generally considered to be one of the finest surgeons and researchers in the country, but he had a distinct tendency to give away his earnings."

"What about your parents? I don't believe I've ever heard you mention them."

"They died in a train accident when I was very young. My grandparents raised me."

She said this without a trace of sentimentality, and Andrew sensed she had said all she meant to say about her family. Before she could change the subject, however, another thought struck him.

"Bethany—" He paused, thinking, then musing aloud. "Bethany *Cole*...your grandfather isn't Dorsey Cole, by any chance?"

She looked surprised, but pleased. "You knew my grandfather?"

"No, but of course, I know *of* him. I studied his papers on narcotics addiction after the war. In fact, I attended one of his lectures once when he visited Columbia. A brilliant man. Does he still practice?"

The light in her eyes dimmed slightly. "No, he died before I finished medical college."

"I'm sorry," said Andrew. "He must have been very proud that you chose to follow in his footsteps."

Her smile returned. "Yes, I think he was." She started for the door into the examining area, tugging at the ties of her apron. "He even permitted me to do an apprenticeship with him, which was probably the best—and definitely the most strenuous—part of my training."

She stopped, glancing back at the waiting room. "If this morning is an indication of things to come, Andrew, I think we may have to consider hiring a receptionist soon." .

"Quite right. And if you don't mind, I'll let you handle the interviewing. My last receptionist was a huge mistake. Perhaps you'll do better."

"I'll take care of it," she said briskly. "And now—about that lunch?"

Her gaze traveled down the front of his lab coat, at the blood spots left by a policeman with a stab wound.

Andrew tried to ignore the annoying way his heart had begun to race at the prospect of an hour alone with her, an hour without a room full of patients waiting for their attention. "I'll just change, and we'll go," he said.

He fumbled at the buttons on his coat, for once unable to blame his clumsiness on his swollen fingers.

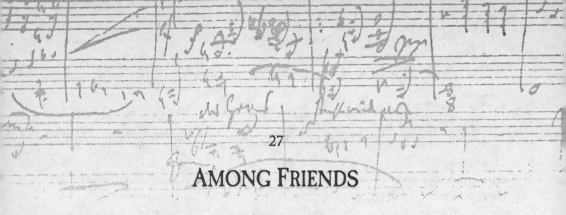

27

AMONG FRIENDS

Two are better than one,
because they have a good return for their work...

ECCLESIASTES 4:9 (NIV)

These are quite possibly the best potato pancakes I've ever tasted," Bethany declared, bringing the last bite to her mouth.

So much for her resolve not to finish everything on her plate.

"Didn't I tell you?" Andrew said, his tone smug as he stabbed another piece of German sausage. "The place may not look like much, but Axel's is a legend."

They sat on benches across from each other at a scarred wooden table. Bethany glanced around the small, dim room, the air of which was heavy with too many rich aromas to distinguish one from the other. Earlier, when they had come in, they'd had to wait for a table. Now she knew why.

Amid the clink of glasses and clatter of silverware, a variety of diners talked and laughed. Most of the patrons were dressed in business attire, but some men wore the work clothes of laborers, too.

A waiter in a butcher's apron appeared just then to suggest dessert. Bethany groaned aloud. "Do people really eat dessert after a meal like that?"

"Not I," Andrew said, waving off the waiter. He pushed his plate out of the way and leaned forward, folding his elbows on top of the table. "Tell me about Dr. Blackwell," he said. "What's she like?"

"Dr. Blackwell," replied Bethany, "defies description."

Elizabeth Blackwell had been the first woman in the United States to receive a medical degree. She had also created quite a scandal with her insistence on attending a male-dominated medical school because, at the time, the women's colleges didn't provide as high a quality of medical training as did the traditional universities. After finally graduating from Geneva Medical College—at the head of her class, no less—she had gone on to do advanced studies in London. When she returned to New York, with the help of her sister she established her own hospital: the New York Infirmary for Women and Children, where Bethany had received a part of her training while also serving on staff.

"Actually," Bethany said, "I've only met Dr. Elizabeth once, when she was here for a visit. She spends most of her time in London now. I know her sister, Dr. Emily, much better. And Dr. Jacobi as well."

"Yes, I know Dr. Jacobi, too. An excellent doctor. She's still teaching at the Infirmary, then?"

"Oh, yes. In fact, I more or less functioned as her assistant until recently. She's really remarkable, you know. In addition to her practice and her teaching, she's been busy setting up a children's dispensary at Mount Sinai. I've learned more from her about children's diseases than I ever did in medical college!"

"Good. I can promise you you'll put that knowledge to work sooner or later in our practice."

Bethany studied him. "Andrew," she said, "why haven't you told me about the rheumatism?"

A look of pained surprise darted over his features. As if by instinct, he dropped his hands to his lap, where they couldn't be seen, and glanced away. "I didn't realize you'd noticed."

"I wasn't sure until today," Bethany said. "So I'm right? It *is* rheumatism?"

"Rheumatoid arthritis, actually."

Bethany swallowed. "Acute?"

He tossed his head a little to flick the stubborn shock of hair away from his face. "No, chronic. With all the predictable symptoms."

"I'm sorry, Andrew."

"It doesn't interfere with my work," he said quickly, almost irritably. "You needn't worry about that."

"I'm not worried. But it must make things difficult at times." Bethany was careful to allow no hint of anything resembling sympathy to slip into her tone. She sensed he would be appalled if he suspected she felt sorry for him.

His shrug seemed casual enough, but he avoided meeting her eyes. "I apologize, Bethany. I know I should have told you before you agreed to come into the practice with me."

"Why didn't you?" she asked quietly.

He raised his head and looked at her. "That's fairly obvious, isn't it? I was afraid I might frighten you off."

"Oh, Andrew! Surely you don't believe that."

He sighed. "I wasn't being entirely selfish, Bethany. At least, I hope I wasn't, although I could hardly blame you for thinking otherwise. I really *did* believe I could be of help to you in your own efforts rather more quickly than if you tried going it alone." He paused. "Naturally, I'll understand if you want out."

Bethany frowned. "Don't be ridiculous. This makes no difference whatsoever."

His relief was unmistakable as he leaned forward and brought his hands back to the table. "You can't imagine how glad I am to hear you say that. And it truly *doesn't* affect my work."

"Stop apologizing, Andrew. Your work is exemplary. I should know that if anyone does. So…how long have you had it? The arthritis?"

He took a sip of water. "Several years, actually. It started when I was still in medical college. Although looking back, I think I had symptoms of it even before then."

"What do you do for it?" Bethany had no intention of prying, but her interest wasn't entirely professional. She had come to like Andrew Carmichael. She liked him a lot. She also admired him a great deal. Knowing how his particular disease could ravage the body, she hated to think what might lie ahead for him if the affliction progressed.

Again he shrugged. "I'm sure you already know there's not much one *can* do. Heat. Massage. The new salicylate treatments seem to help more than anything else. Of course, there are two schools of thought on whether exercise is helpful or harmful. I tend to think activity is best. At least that's been my experience."

"What about new research? Is there anything available?"

"Not very much, I'm afraid. I haven't run across anything lately that I didn't already know. The problem is, there seems to be a disadvantage for every potential benefit."

"What about these ocean crossings, Andrew? Don't you worry that being on the water so much might aggravate your condition? The dampness and cold can't be good for you."

He made a gesture with one hand as if to minimize the question. "I suppose it doesn't help, but I can't imagine giving up the traveling altogether."

"It's that important to you to be a part of the Moody campaigns?"

"It's a way I can help in the work." A faint smile tipped the corners of his mouth. "I'm no preacher, but I can at least help to take care of those who are."

"You feel that strongly about it?"

He regarded her with a look that made Bethany wonder if he thought she was being critical. She simply did not understand Andrew's commitment to these international "revivals."

The more she knew of Andrew Carmichael, the more she realized that something about Andrew's faith was different from her own. He tended to be reserved, even shy, in some situations, but there was a bedrock steadiness and strength to the man, both as a person and as a physician. In contrast, he displayed a kind of abandonment in his life that she could easily envy. As a believer, he was almost childlike. Enthusiastic. Even joyful. Devout. And completely nonsectarian. His interest and concern for people went beyond mere tolerance.

Andrew loved people. He loved them quietly, and sometimes even with a wry amusement. But he loved them. The impartial, unconditional treatment he extended to those around him on a daily basis exemplified a quality of life that Bethany had never before witnessed, except possibly in her grandfather.

His voice jarred her out of her thoughts, and she realized he was answering the question she'd asked.

"I know I'm not explaining this very well," he said, smiling a little. "No doubt you've noticed that I'm not all that good with words. But you see, traveling with D. L. began as my way of giving something back. There's always a need for a doctor's services during such a large, extended campaign. But D. L. Moody and Ira Sankey are doing their own kind of healing, it seems to me—an even more important kind of healing than I can offer as a physician—and it's gratifying and fulfilling for me to be a part of it, no matter how small a part. So if I'm uncomfortable for a few weeks as a result"—he gave a light shrug—"it's relative. It doesn't matter all that much."

Bethany found herself responding to his candor, his humility. "I must say, I admire you for it, Andrew. Even if I don't quite understand."

He frowned, then shook his head. "Don't admire me. The truth is that I gain far more from the Moody-Sankey campaigns than I could ever possibly *give*."

"Goodness, Andrew, it's not such a bad thing to be admired."

He regarded her with his usual warmth and good humor for a moment. Then his expression sobered. He reached across the table, and although he withdrew his hand at almost the same instant as he touched hers, the effect on Bethany was immediate—and unsettling.

"Believe me, Bethany, I covet your good opinion," he said softly. Their eyes locked for another second or two before he finally looked away.

"I didn't mean to embarrass you," Bethany said, feeling a need to lighten the moment. "I suppose I have a bad habit of sometimes saying what I think—*before* I think."

"No need to apologize," he said softly. "It's just that I wouldn't want you to think more highly of me than I deserve. You don't...there's a lot you don't know about me, Bethany."

"Secrets, Andrew?"

His entire expression changed, and she immediately wished she hadn't teased him. "I expect we all have our secrets," he said, his eyes darkening with some unreadable emotion.

Was it sorrow she saw reflected in his gaze? Bethany felt a sudden urgency to reassure him, though for what she couldn't have said. "Andrew, I just wanted you to understand that I respect you. As a physician. And as a person. And I want to be very clear on the fact that the arthritis makes absolutely no difference in our partnership." She paused, then added, "Or in our *friendship*."

Bethany was surprised by the ease with which the word rolled off her lips. But it was true. He was becoming more than a colleague. Even before today, she had sensed a subtle change taking place in their relationship, as if they'd moved beyond a professional alliance toward something more personal, something deeper…something that held a kind of promise.

A promise of what?

"You're quite sure?"

Bethany looked at him, and the softness of his gaze made her fumble for words.

"Yes. I'm quite sure."

His eyes held hers, and he swallowed with some difficulty. "I'm glad," he said. "And very relieved."

They sat quietly for a time, the companionable silence between two people who were becoming comfortable with each other.

"Bethany?"

She looked up.

"Are you…is there someone in your life? You've never said, but I've wondered. Are you engaged? Do you have a…commitment of any sort?"

His face was crimson, his hands occupied with wringing his napkin into a rope.

"Engaged?" Bethany stared at him. "No. No, I…there's no one."

He suddenly looked both relieved and embarrassed. "I confess that I find it nothing less than amazing, that some fellow hasn't put a ring on your finger by now."

"Well, there was someone, once. A long time ago."

He watched her closely. "What happened?"

Bethany hadn't expected that the memory would still hurt. Even so, she forced a note of lightness into her reply. "I finally realized he loved medicine more than he loved me." She paused and took a breath. "Not to mention the fact that a certain young debutante's father was only too willing to finance such a promising physician's career—if that promising physician happened to be his son-in-law."

He looked stricken. "I'm *sorry*, Bethany."

Bethany gave him a long, level gaze. "I'm not."

There. He could interpret that however he chose.

He finally mustered a smile, and it occurred to Bethany how dramatically even the faintest of smiles seemed to alter his entire countenance. Andrew wasn't exactly a handsome man. She supposed his face was a little too lean and long for classical good looks. But when he smiled, it was like the sun breaking through a stand of trees. She was increasingly coming to esteem that smile.

Later, outside the restaurant, he offered his arm, and Bethany took it. "Andrew?"

"Yes?"

"Will you be traveling again anytime soon?"

He looked down at her. "Why, no. Not for some months, actually."

"I'm glad," Bethany responded.

"Please don't be concerned about the workload, Bethany. I'll make certain that when I do travel, someone will be available to help with the practice. I wouldn't expect you to carry the entire patient load by yourself."

"It's not that," she said evenly, tightening her grasp on his arm just a little.

"No?" He gave her a quizzical look.

"I'm not concerned about the workload. I'm just glad you're not going away again soon."

"Oh," he said softly.

After a long pause, he cleared his throat. "I believe I'm glad, too."

With that, he tucked her arm a little more snugly against his side, and they walked down the street together toward their new office.

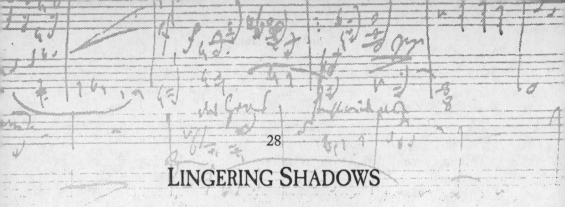

28

LINGERING SHADOWS

For the vision of hope is decayed,
Though the shadows still linger behind.

THOMAS DERMODY

Bantry Hill

But I'm not sleepy, Aunt Susanna. Why must I take a nap? Naps are for babies. And I am *not* a baby. I am four years old."

"Yes, I know, *alannah*, but remember what Dr. Carmichael said? A nap every day until he tells us otherwise. He wants to see you strong, even stronger than you were before your illness."

Susanna tucked the quilt snugly about Caterina's shoulders, then kissed her lightly on the forehead. "And you are quite right, miss, you are not a baby. You are growing up even as I watch, it seems."

Caterina, who never sulked for more than a moment or two, looked up and smiled. "Am I really, Aunt Susanna? You can *see* me growing?"

"Oh, indeed. I sometimes wonder where my wee girl has gone. Do you suppose someone might have taken her away and left a garden plant in her place, one that seems to be shooting up in front of my very eyes?"

The child giggled. "You're teasing, Aunt Susanna! I'm right here. And I don't feel any bigger than I was when you came."

Susanna smiled back at her. "Ah, but if you don't have your rest as Dr. Carmichael ordered, you might not grow at all, don't you see?"

"Couldn't I have another story first?"

Susanna could see the beginning signs of drowsiness in those deep blue eyes, so she shook her head firmly. "You have had two stories already, young lady. Perhaps tonight before bedtime we'll read another."

Caterina's expression turned solemn. "Papa is leaving. I don't like it when he's away."

"He won't be gone long. And didn't he promise to come say good-bye before he goes?"

"Yes. But I still wish he would stay home." She yawned. "I suppose I don't mind his being gone *quite* so much since you've come, though. I like having you here, Aunt Susanna."

The girl's eyes grew heavier, and Susanna touched another kiss to her forehead. "Thank you, sweet," she said quietly.

"Do you like it here with us, Aunt Susanna?"

The question was entirely unexpected, especially given the fact that the child could scarcely keep her eyes open.

"What kind of a question is that, Caterina? Of course, I like it here! I like being with you more than anything else I can imagine."

"I'm glad," said the little girl, her voice even thicker now. Her lashes fluttered as she closed her eyes. "Mama didn't, you know."

Susanna tensed. So rare was any reference to Deirdre by her daughter that the girl's words took her by complete surprise. "Whatever do you mean, Caterina? I'm sure your mother *loved* being with you."

Caterina didn't open her eyes, and Susanna had to strain to hear her reply. "No…she didn't…Mama didn't like us…very much…"

Susanna straightened. She felt suddenly chilled, as though the room itself had lost all warmth. She stood watching the sleeping child for another moment, then started for the door.

~

Susanna wished Paul had suggested two o'clock rather than one.

After getting Caterina settled, she'd gone to freshen her hair, then exchange her shoes for boots, in case the graveyard happened to be muddy. Consequently, she was in such a rush on her way out that she bumped into Michael, who was just coming inside.

The memory of the conversation she had overheard between him and Paul that morning caused her to feel even more awkward than usual in his presence. Awkward—and angry.

"I'm sorry, Michael," she said, an edge in her voice that even she could hear. "I didn't see you."

"Nor I you," he said with a smile.

"No, really—"

Susanna stared at him. As always, it took her a moment to realize that he was teasing. Although a touch of levity was hardly out of character for him, he never failed to surprise her when he made light of his blindness.

"And where are you off to in such a hurry?" he said, still smiling.

"I—" Susanna hesitated. She was reluctant to tell him where she was going, perhaps because of the way his facial expression typically altered at the very mention of Deirdre's name.

"I asked Paul to take me to the cemetery. I haven't had a chance as yet to visit Deirdre's grave, you see."

For a change, he wasn't wearing the dark glasses, although his eyes remained closed. Susanna watched him closely, and sure enough, his features tightened, if ever so slightly.

There were times when it almost defied belief, that this man—always so quiet-spoken, so gentle in his treatment of others, and, on the surface at least, so accepting and at peace with his own misfortune—could possibly be guilty of the deception she suspected. Other times, such as now, however, given his immobile countenance and the hard set to his mouth, she thought it might not be so unimaginable after all.

His tone was distant, impersonal when he replied. "You should insist that Paul take the buggy instead of the carriage. It is a most pleasant day."

On impulse, Susanna said, "Would you like to go with us?"

He was very still, and for a moment Susanna thought he wasn't going to answer. Then, averting his face slightly, he said, "No, you should be alone, I think."

Susanna waited, but he offered nothing more.

"Mrs. Dempsey will check on Caterina from time to time," she told him. "I won't be long."

He turned back to her. "Take as long as you like, Susanna," he said quietly. "I will be here until later this afternoon. Just so you know, I may stay in the city overnight, depending on how late we rehearse."

He hesitated as if he might add something more, but instead turned and started down the hall toward his office.

Susanna watched him walk away. Part of her seethed at his seemingly unshakable self-control. Another part tried in vain to ignore a stab of disappointment at the reminder that he would be leaving later.

What sort of madness was it, she wondered, to be continually torn by these opposing feelings about a man who, even after two months of living under his roof, remained a mystery? Was she ever to learn whether he was indeed the saint those closest to him believed him to be...or the fiend his wife had made him out to be?

∾

The graveyard rested at the very top of a high hill, no more than a mile distant from the house. It was one of the loveliest pieces of ground Susanna had ever seen. And one of the *loneliest*.

So this is how the wealthy bury their dead...

An unexpected swell of resentment rose up in her as she regarded the broad expanse of land, the ornate monuments, the grave sites decorated with extravagant floral arrangements or even objects of art. The hillside itself was rich and unmistakably fertile ground, planted with thick grass, its color now dulled by the approaching end of autumn. Broad, rolling reaches of land lay totally unused, but obviously well cared for.

Susanna found the place offensive, almost as if it had been desecrated by pagan symbols. In Ireland, land meant survival. At home, a piece of ground this large and opulent would have fed countless starving families. With such land as this, her parents could have made a comfortable living for a lifetime! Here in America, it was left to lie fallow, its only purpose to serve as burial grounds for the dead.

At one corner of the cemetery, just ahead, there was a small chapel that looked as if it would hold no more than thirty people. Either the services held there must be limited to a very few mourners, or else the building was used only as another empty memorial.

"This way, Susanna." Paul took her arm and led her to a grave near the far side of the cemetery.

Susanna stumbled on the uneven ground as they approached the monument. It had been hewn from marble, with an inset of an intricately embellished Celtic cross.

She was somewhat surprised to find a solitary grave rather than a family crypt. Given Michael's apparent wealth, she had half expected a more imposing burial site. Her sister's grave was one of the least pretentious she had seen so far. Not that she would have favored a more ostentatious stone; to the contrary, she found Deirdre's resting place more tasteful than many of the other more elaborate grave sites.

Paul continued to support her with his arm as they stopped beside the grave. Susanna's eyes locked on the words engraved at the base of the cross:

DEIRDRE FALLON EMMANUEL
WIFE AND MOTHER
1843–1874

Something about the stark simplicity of those few words, so utterly lacking in emotion or sentiment, tore at Susanna's heart. For the first time, the reality of her sister's death struck her full-force, and like a string under the tension of a tuning peg, she felt herself grow tight, tight to the point of snapping. Then the trembling began, a brittle, spasmodic shaking she couldn't control. She would not have been surprised if her very bones had fractured under the force of the tremors quaking through her.

Paul tightened his grasp on her arm. Offering no words, he simply stood beside her, lending his support in silence.

"The flowers?" she questioned, pointing to the simple arrangement of wildflowers decorating the grave.

"Michael sees to it that there are always flowers here. Dempsey maintains the grave at his direction."

There it was again, one of the many inexplicable contradictions that seemed to make up Michael Emmanuel's character. The man who could not bear to mention Deirdre's name was the same man who saw to it that fresh flowers adorned her grave.

She shook her head as if to clear away the confusion.

Until this moment Deirdre's death, although all too real in Susanna's mind, had never actually penetrated the depths of her emotions with its dreadful, irrevocable finality. But now, standing here beside this lonely mound of earth, beneath which rested the lifeless body of her only remaining family member, she seemed to hear, for the first time and the last, the thud of the coffin as it closed, signaling the end of her sister's all too brief life.

Deirdre...Wife and Mother...

Dead at thirty-one years of age. Survived by a husband who seemed hard-pressed to speak her name, and a daughter whose childish memory of her would soon wither and drop away like the flowers that adorned her mother's grave.

"If you like, I will leave you alone," Paul said quietly, giving her arm a reassuring squeeze. "Take as much time as you want."

Susanna nodded, and he walked away, turning down the path from which they had come. For a long time, she stood staring at Deirdre's monument. Finally, she knelt in the soft grass, warm in the afternoon sun. Her throat swollen, her heart heavy, she whispered a prayer for her sister.

When she got to her feet, she stood looking around the graveyard, then turned her attention back to the monument. Why hadn't Michael made more of an effort to personalize the stone? Had he cared so little that he hadn't even bothered to have a more loving memorial engraved—if not for his own consolation, then for Caterina's sake? Was this austere inscription yet another sign of his indifference to Deirdre?

The gravestone seemed too cold to Susanna, too austere. And yet wasn't it somehow in keeping with Michael's obvious resistance to Deirdre's memory, his attempts to shut out all evidence of her existence and their life together?

In the midst of her musings, Susanna searched for her own grief. What, exactly, did Deirdre's death mean to her? How did she really feel about the loss of the sister she had never known all that well?

With so many years between them, they had never been close. They had been sisters, but never friends. Susanna had been little more than a child when Deirdre had left home to pursue her dream of becoming an important singer. She'd returned some months later, discouraged and without further hopes, only to leave again, this time as a member of a small traveling musical company out of Dublin.

She had gone on to become a part, albeit a rather insignificant part, of the opera world. After that, she had never come home again to stay, only to visit, and then for a few days at most. When she *did* visit, it was always in the midst of a whirlwind of rapturous accounts of her latest role, or her latest male conquest—or, on occasion, in the throes of depression because a role was not going well or because there *was* no recent male conquest.

She had met Michael in London, married him in Italy, and from there accompanied him to New York. Long before then, any real affection or closeness she and Susanna might have shared had eroded during the long periods of separation. Only when her marriage began to go bad had Deirdre renewed her letter writing, penning one grim post after another to Susanna, each filled with her growing unhappiness and despondency—as well as tales of her husband's bad temper and selfishness.

Susanna surveyed the forlorn grave and the cemetery, its rows of solemn monuments and crypts so at odds with the bright, sunny afternoon. Most of the grief she was now experiencing, she realized, was due less to any real affection she might have once held for her sister than to a bitter sense of all that had been lost. The fleeting years apart, the hours and moments wasted, the irretrievable opportunities for growing closer. All the times they had never had...and now never would.

The sad reality was that she missed Deirdre more for what they had *not* been to each other than for what they *had* been.

In any event, all she could do for her sister now was to take care of her child and, at the same time, continue her search for the truth behind Deirdre's tragic death. That much she could do, *would* do.

The sun-swept graveyard had begun to darken with lengthening shadows. Finally, with unshed tears stinging her eyes, Susanna touched her gloved hand to the stone cross. "Good-bye, Deirdre," she murmured. "God give you peace."

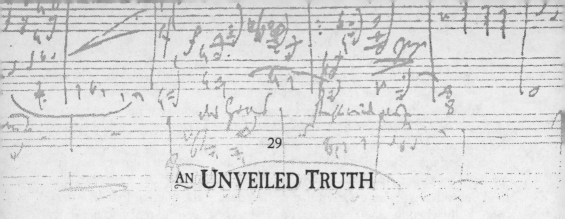

29

An Unveiled Truth

Even the truth may be bitter.

OLD IRISH SAYING

Does Michael bring Caterina to visit her mother's grave?" Susanna asked as they drove away from the cemetery.

Paul glanced at her, then turned quickly back to the road. "No, not often."

"Does he come at all?" Susanna pressed.

Paul's face took on a pinched expression as he clicked his tongue to step up the horse's pace a little. "No...I do not really know, Susanna."

"I see," she returned evenly. She was not in the least surprised that Paul would equivocate. More than likely, Michael didn't visit the cemetery at all.

They drove on, the silence between them thick with tension. Paul seemed different from his usual self this afternoon: quieter, more sober, as if he had much on his mind, and none of it pleasant. She wondered if he was still disturbed by his earlier argument with Michael.

As for herself, she felt completely drained, and her earlier melancholy had returned in force. She would have to shake off this dreary mood before going home to Caterina. It wasn't easy to conceal her feelings from her precocious niece; the child was uncommonly sensitive for one so young.

First, however, there was one last stop to make—this one, perhaps, even more difficult than the visit to Deirdre's grave.

The buggy slowed as Paul turned into a clearing on the left side of the road, just inside the turn.

Susanna looked around, a chill brushing the base of her neck. "This is where it happened?" she said, her voice low.

Paul nodded, and she started to get out.

"Wait," he cautioned, jumping down and hurrying around the buggy to help her.

Taking her arm, he led her across the road, where Susanna stood looking down the deadly drop. The rock-faced bluff pitched straight down for at least twenty feet or more before leveling off onto a kind of shelf, from which the ground again fell away to nothingness.

Instinctively, Susanna stepped back, and Paul's hand tightened on her arm. "The road was very muddy and slick that night, because of all the rain we'd had," he said, his voice tight. "Part of it had already washed away in a mud slide. The buggy went over here"—he inclined his head—"and landed there." He gestured to the shelf below.

"The ledge was enough to keep the buggy from going the rest of the way over the cliff, but even so—"

He didn't finish. He didn't have to. Susanna could imagine the rest. She could almost hear in her mind the clatter of the wheels, the shriek of the terrified horse, the sickening crunch of metal, Deirdre's screams...

The horror of that night came roaring in on her, and she shook her head as if to throw off the nightmare. Feeling ill, she turned and walked quickly away.

Paul followed. Back inside the buggy, they sat in silence, both of them staring straight ahead. The sun had slipped behind thickening clouds. No longer bright, the afternoon was tinged by what her mother had called "the long light," that wistful lengthening of shadows that hints of autumn's passing and winter's lurking.

A shudder seized Susanna, and for a moment she thought the same trembling that had gripped her back at the cemetery would overcome her again. She sat up straighter, stiffening her back as she tried to force from her mind the image of the cliff and what had happened there.

"They were very unhappy together, weren't they?"

He glanced at her, then looked away, his expression clearly uncomfortable. "That is not for me to say, Susanna."

"Apparently, it's not for *anyone* to say," Susanna shot back, provoked by the inevitable resistance that greeted any question she might ask about Deirdre.

"I'm well aware that Deirdre wasn't happy, Paul," she persisted. "She wrote to me often. Especially the last year, before...the accident. There was no mistaking her misery."

Paul sat in stony silence, his gaze straight ahead, as if he hadn't heard her.

"Why won't *anyone* tell me what happened?" Frustration pushed Susanna to the edge of her composure. "Deirdre died in an accident as inexplicable as it was tragic. She left her home—and her child—in the middle of the night in a terrible rainstorm! *Something* happened that night, something that must have made her take leave of her senses!"

She leaned toward him even more, and finally he turned to look at her as she went on. "She was my *sister*! I have a right to know what happened, yet no matter who I ask, I'm made to feel guilty *because* I ask! No one will tell me *anything*. Her own husband seems to choke on the very mention of her name! Why, Paul? Why should that be?"

His dark eyes behind the glasses were plainly troubled. "Susanna, I am so sorry," he said. "I know you must have many questions, but it should be Michael who answers them, not I. Still, it is so very difficult for him. Please try to understand."

By now Susanna's pulse was thundering, her head throbbing. "*Understand*?" she burst out. "I'm supposed to understand that it's difficult for Michael? Deirdre is *dead*, but I'm supposed to feel sorry for *Michael*, even though he refuses to tell me the truth about what happened to his own wife—to my *sister*!"

She heard the shrillness in her voice and groped for restraint, but she was shaking so badly her words spilled out in a staccato stammer. "I already know their marriage was troubled. You're not going to shock me. Deirdre told me in her letters how difficult Michael was to live with, how unreasonable he could be—"

Without warning, Paul swung around to stare at her, and whatever else she might have said froze on her lips. His face was white with fury, his eyes blazing.

"I should have known!" he ground out. "So—Deirdre told you that Michael made *her* unhappy?"

Momentarily stopped by this lightning change in him, Susanna could only sit and stare in astonishment.

"She said this?" he demanded.

"I…yes," Susanna admitted. "She was…wretchedly unhappy."

"Because of Michael," Paul repeated, his voice like that of a stranger in its hardness.

"Yes."

"And did she—"

Unexpectedly, he broke off, turning away from her. Susanna watched him drag in several long, uneven breaths and knot both hands into fists, bringing them to his temples as if to squeeze out some unbearable emotion as he stared mutely down at the floor of the buggy.

Her own anger temporarily deflected, Susanna managed to keep her tone level, even calm, when she spoke. "Paul, I understand your loyalty to Michael. He is your cousin, and you're very close, I know. But can't you try to understand what this is like for *me*? All I'm asking for is the truth. Not just bits and pieces of it, which is all Michael has ever offered me, but the entire truth. I'm not trying to pry. I don't mean to intrude on anyone's privacy. But is it really too much to ask that *someone* tell me what happened to Deirdre? And *why* it happened?"

At last he raised his face to look at her, and in that moment the pain she saw reflected there made Susanna question if she had gone too far.

"Michael has suffered, too, Susanna," Paul said, his tone quiet now. "He has suffered more than you can ever imagine. More than he would ever want you to know."

Susanna looked at him, wanting him to be right. She wanted to believe that Michael had indeed suffered because of Deirdre's death. She wanted to believe that he had cared enough to grieve for her, to agonize over his loss of her.

And yet how *could* she believe it, when everything Deirdre had written in her letters contradicted Paul's words? And when Michael himself seemed so intransigent in his silence?

She clutched at the rough wool of her skirt. Obviously, there was nothing more she could do to sway him. Like everyone else, Paul was determined to protect Michael.

She was about to suggest they leave when his voice cut through the quiet.

"I can see that I must tell you," he said, his tone heavy with resignation.

Susanna caught her breath at his words. A bleak, solemn look settled over his countenance. All light seemed to have fled his usually animated features as he faced her.

"God forgive me," he said, "for no doubt Michael will not. But this has gone on long enough. Too long. I think I must tell you, not only for your sake, but for Michael's sake as well." He paused, studying her. "But how much should I tell you, Susanna? How much do you really want to know?"

"Everything," she said firmly. "I want you to tell me everything."

He shook his head, and an expression of sorrow passed over his face. "No, I cannot do that. There are things of which only Michael can speak. But I will tell you what I can, and I warn you, Susanna, that even *that* may be more than you will want to hear."

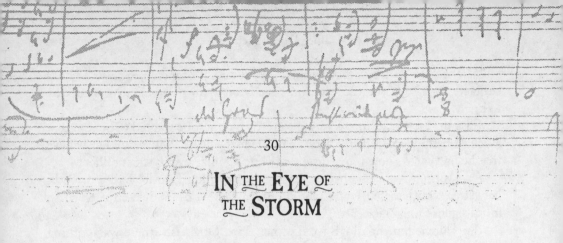

30

IN THE EYE OF THE STORM

When words are scarce,
they're seldom spent in vain;
For they breathe truth
that breathe their words in pain.

WILLIAM SHAKESPEARE

From the difficulty Paul seemed to have framing his words, Susanna was beginning to think that whatever he was about to say held the potential to either confirm her worst suspicions—or replace them with an entire set of new ones.

She watched as he removed his glasses and rubbed a hand over his eyes in a gesture of infinite weariness. When he finally spoke, even his voice sounded tired and leaden. "So...you knew the marriage was not good, that there was trouble between them—"

Susanna nodded. "Deirdre was very frank in her letters. More than once she told me their marriage was a failure."

His lips thinned. "The marriage was a *disaster*. A battlefield. And for a very long time."

"But *why*? Deirdre was so happy in the beginning—"

Paul looked at her. "Please, Susanna, you must let me tell you this in my own way, as best I can. And first, you must try to forget anything Deirdre may have written to you. There will be much you do not understand. Even after I have finished, you will no doubt have questions, but please realize that I can only tell you what I know. What I witnessed for myself. You are already aware that Michael will say nothing. Even now, he is not willing to speak against Deirdre. For Caterina's sake—and for his own reasons—he will keep his silence."

Reluctantly, Susanna nodded, indicating that he should go on.

"There was much trouble between Michael and Deirdre," he said heavily.

"Much trouble. Always they fought. Deirdre, you see, was always angry with Michael, and she would try to make him angry, too. She provoked him. Deliberately."

Susanna found it nearly impossible to remain silent in the face of such gross overstatement about Deirdre, an exaggeration that Michael surely must have fostered. But sensing that too many interruptions on her part would only distract Paul from the accounting he had begun, she resisted the temptation to object.

As if he could read her thoughts, Paul made a rueful smile. "You think I exaggerate about Deirdre, that I defend Michael and tell you only his side of things." He shook his head. "I am telling you the truth, Susanna. I know this is most difficult for you, but you must try to understand. Deirdre *hated* Michael."

At that, Susanna couldn't stop herself. "That's not true! She *never* wrote me anything of the sort. To the contrary, she said—"

Again he smiled, but it was bitter and utterly without humor. "That she was afraid of him, no? And what else? That Michael mistreated her? That he was a madman, with a vicious temper, and she lived in terror of what he might do to her?"

A terrible coldness began to seep through Susanna as she sat staring at him. The truth was, Deirdre *had* written those very things…and worse. Much worse.

"How—"

"How do I know what she told you?" His mouth twisted as though he had bitten down on something foul. "Because that's what she told *everybody*! Anyone who would listen." He glanced away. "Especially when she was drinking. As she almost always was."

Shock and outrage streaked through Susanna. "I won't *listen* to this! This is all Michael's doing, isn't it? He put you up to this—"

"Why would he do that?" Paul's retort was sharp, almost angry. "Why would Michael tell me what to say, when in truth he will be furious with me for saying *anything*?"

Then his expression gentled. He reached to touch her hand, but she pulled away.

"Susanna…I am so sorry. I know this must be very difficult for you. But you wanted to know…"

"I wanted the *truth,*" she bit out.

"And that is what I am trying to tell you," he said evenly. "But if you prefer that I not go on, I understand."

Susanna hesitated. Here, finally, was her first glimpse behind the door that up until this moment had been firmly shut to her. If she stopped him now, she might never have an opportunity like this again. And yet his words had already stirred up such a maelstrom of disbelief and doubt, such a tempest of anger and resentment in her, she couldn't imagine how she would deal with it all, much less whatever else she was about to hear.

But wasn't *not* knowing worse? And even if Paul's perspective had been colored by his affection for Michael, he was at least making a sincere effort to be honest with her. So absolute was the integrity that emanated from Paul Santi that there could be no question of his deliberately twisting or tainting the truth. Not even for Michael.

So she swallowed hard and turned back to him, waiting. "Go on," she said. "Please."

He nodded. "Before I say more, I think I should tell you that Michael has always believed Deirdre had a…a *sickness*. That she was ill." He put a hand to his head. "In her mind."

"Are you saying he thought she was mentally ill?"

He delayed his reply, obviously considering his words. "*Sì*, but not because he meant to make…ah…the *excuse* for her, you see. He truly did believe this. And perhaps he was right. Perhaps to do the things Deirdre did, she would have had to be ill. Michael said that Deirdre was…that she could not control the drinking. And when she drank, she did things—she became very difficult. She hurt many people—especially Michael."

He paused, his voice dropping. "You say that Deirdre wrote to you of how Michael had hurt her. But the truth, Susanna, is that Deirdre hurt *Michael*. And Caterina. She hurt Caterina as well."

Despite the mildness of the day, a chill shuddered through Susanna. Questions and doubts came rushing in on her. And yet watching him, seeing her own hurt reflected in his eyes, sensing how difficult, even *painful*, this was for him, she found it impossible not to believe him.

"The fights were terrible," he went on in the same strained voice. "And Michael is a man who, I can tell you, resists an argument. Always, he has sought peace in his life. But Deirdre would give him no peace."

"You're painting a very cruel picture of my sister, Paul," Susanna said, her voice thin.

"*Sì*, it must seem so to you, I know. But the truth is sometimes a bitter thing, Susanna. And I will not lie to you: Deirdre could be a very cruel person."

All the uneasy memories and reluctant recollections that had begun to crowd her thoughts of late now collided with Paul's bitter narrative, battering her with the force of a tidal wall. For a split second Susanna thought she might suffocate under the weight of her own emotions. But she managed to nod an indication that he should continue.

"Michael tried—for a long time he tried—to save their marriage. To help Deirdre stop the drinking. But Deirdre, she did not want to be helped; she did not want to save the marriage. She wanted a divorce."

Susanna looked up. "A *divorce*? Deirdre never mentioned a divorce in her letters."

He shrugged. "Nevertheless, it is what she wanted. She asked him for a divorce often. All the time."

"But surely after his accident—"

He laughed, a short, strangled sound. "After Michael's accident, she *demanded* a divorce."

Susanna forced herself to take deep, steadying breaths, fighting off one wave of nausea after another. "But by then they had Caterina."

"*Sì*, they did." Paul's tone was almost plaintive. "But Deirdre never wanted Caterina, you see. She meant to leave both Michael and Cati."

"*No!*" The fierceness of her response surprised Susanna. "Deirdre wouldn't have abandoned her own child—"

"But of course she would have abandoned her! Caterina was little more than a nuisance to Deirdre!"

Paul's words cracked like the lash of a whip, startling Susanna. Her arms felt numb, and she began to rub them with a hard, bruising roughness.

"Susanna? I'm sorry, I think I must say no more. This is too difficult for you. I am hurting you—"

"I'm all right," Susanna said shortly. She wasn't, of course. She wanted to pummel him with her fists for inflicting these hideous images onto her, even as the entire sum of her own fears began to materialize in her mind.

The stone of pain in her midsection might crush her in half at any moment. But she couldn't let him stop. Not now. "I have to know," she whispered.

He sighed and started in again. "I will tell you what Michael believed. This he told me himself, that Deirdre had never loved him, not even from the beginning."

"No, I—that's simply not true, Paul! She absolutely *raved* about him in her early letters. She *adored* him—"

"Perhaps she adored what he represented to her," Paul interrupted, an edge to his voice, "but Michael is convinced that for Deirdre, it was nothing more than a brief infatuation, that in truth she *used* him. As she might have used a rung on a ladder to get where she wanted to go."

Susanna stared at him, struggling *not* to believe. "That's unfair! Deirdre wouldn't have married him simply to advance her career—"

She stopped. Her heart gave a hollow thud, and her own words echoed in her ears as she remembered a day in the past. A sweet, warm summer's day at the farm, when Deirdre had been about to leave home for a tour with a small theater company...

They had ventured down to the stream behind the old Mannion place and were sitting on the bank, splashing their bare feet in the water. Deirdre had just announced, somewhat pointedly, that on this particular trip she would be traveling in the same company with Donal Malone, an older man from the village, fairly well known in the county as a gifted baritone and an above-average actor.

He had also been sweet on Deirdre for some time.

"You don't want to be telling Papa that old Donal Malone is going along," Susanna warned her, only half teasing.

"It's not as if we'll be traveling *alone* together," said Deirdre. "We'll be with all the other members of the troupe. Not that I'd mind being alone with Donal."

Susanna had responded like a typical adolescent, giving an exaggerated shudder and a curl of her lip. "Donal Malone is an old man!"

"He's just past *forty*, you little eejit. That's hardly old. Not that it's any of your affair."

"He has a belly, and his hair is always greasy. I'll wager he uses fish oil on it." When Deirdre didn't react, she pressed, "You wouldn't let him *touch* you, would you?"

Deirdre had simply given her a look of disdain—a look that made it clear Susanna was still a child and, at the moment, a tiresome one. "Donal is thick with Thom Drummond, the director," Deirdre said archly. "It never hurts to have a man of influence take a fancy to you. I'll let the poor fool chew on my ear all he wants if he can boost my standing in the company."

Susanna fervently wished she could dismiss the memory as nothing more than mere girlish foolishness. Instead, she found herself cringing with sympathy for Michael. Even then, her sister had displayed a blatant tendency to manipulate. Was it really so difficult to believe that Deirdre had refined her skills even more in that particular area as she matured? If that was the case, what an incredibly painful—and humiliating—discovery it must have been for Michael, to realize he'd been nothing more than a means to an end.

Paul was watching her. "I am only telling you what Michael believed, Susanna," he said. "And he believed that he had been—used. Especially when—"

He stopped abruptly, frowning as if uncertain how to proceed.

"When *what*?"

"When the affairs began."

"Affairs?" Susanna flinched as if she'd been struck. "She was *unfaithful* to him?"

Paul was staring at something in the distance now, his jaw tight. He had begun to pull at the frame of his eyeglasses so viciously Susanna expected them to snap in his hands.

Abruptly, he replaced the glasses and turned toward her. In that moment, Susanna encountered an expression of such bitterness, such misery, that she knew she had not yet heard the worst of it.

"There is no kind way to tell you something like this, Susanna, so I will simply say it: Deirdre was openly promiscuous. She cuckolded Michael almost from the time they came to New York."

Susanna felt the blood drain from her head. The cold that had earlier enveloped her now seemed to turn inward with a fierce, numbing blast. She felt Paul's eyes on her, watching her as if he feared she would faint.

"Do you have *any* idea how difficult this is for me to accept?" she choked out.

No matter what else Deirdre might have done, Susanna simply couldn't believe that her sister had actually been capable of such baseness, such...*depravity*.

And yet every instinct within her seemed to shout that Paul would never lie about such a thing. As unbelievable and vile as it was, he was telling the truth.

And so she sat, mute, her mind reeling, her heart aching, and listened to the rest of it.

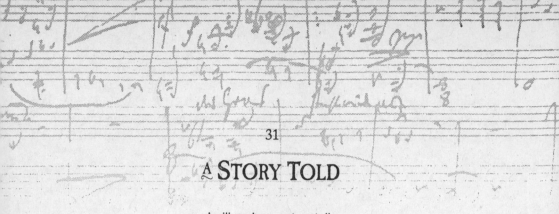

31

A STORY TOLD

I will my heavy story tell...

W. B. YEATS

Susanna couldn't have said when she turned the final corner of her lingering suspicions and doubts. She knew only that she could now *see* the truth evolving, like a distorted collage being formed even as she watched, as pieces of her own unsettling memories converged with Paul's devastating narrative. One after another her fragmented recollections came together, finding their place among the heartbreaking images Paul was painting for her. Having accepted the irrefutable reality of her sister's shame, she now unlocked the closed places in her mind and prepared herself to hear whatever was left to be told, no matter how grievously it might wound.

Stunned and trembling, she listened to the evidence against a sister whose debauchery had eventually robbed her of all reason, morality, and self-respect, only to leave her a dissipated virago who ultimately brought the worst sort of scandal down upon her husband and herself.

She listened in silence, her heart breaking even as a part of her raged inwardly for the awful destruction wreaked by her sister upon the very ones who loved her most. She learned of the ways Deirdre had shamelessly used Michael and his influence in the operatic world to foster her own career, while all the time Michael knew her voice suffered the lack of brilliance and power that might have eventually brought her true greatness.

And when he left the world that Deirdre had been so desperate to conquer, she had viewed his abdication as a kind of personal betrayal, foisting upon him even more bitterness, more resentment, more vicious attacks.

She heard with shuddering revulsion of the ongoing trysts with other men that had continued right up to the disgraceful affair in which Deirdre had been involved at the time of Michael's accident...and her death.

She bled inside to hear that her sister had turned away from her own child.

Having never wanted Caterina, she punished Michael by punishing his child with her sharp tongue and scolding derision, indeed punishing the girl so cruelly Michael had begun to fear she might actually resort to physical abuse.

When Paul was loath to continue, offering to spare her any further demoralizing details, Susanna insisted he go on. And so she sat listening with mounting horror as he told her of the sick and demented "pranks" Deirdre had perpetrated on Michael after he lost his sight—often just before an orchestra performance or a social event: despicable tactics which caused him such humiliation and embarrassment that eventually he could scarcely bring himself to leave the house.

She listened, she anguished, and she quietly wept. By the time Paul reached the night of Deirdre's death, Susanna felt stricken with such misery she thought she could not bear to hear the rest of it. But she knew she must. There was no way in the world she could live without knowing what had happened that terrible night.

"The night she died," she choked out, "had she been drinking?"

Paul nodded, his face engraved with the stark, grim lines of remembered pain. "Most of the day. Earlier in the evening, I heard her and Michael arguing. She was determined to go out, was demanding that Dempsey take her to the ferry so she could go to the city. But Michael had already alerted Dempsey and me that we were not to drive her anywhere, not under any circumstances.

"It was a terrible night," he went on. "A dangerous night. The roads were treacherous at best. But apparently Michael's attempts to keep her from leaving only made her that much more determined. I was in the back, in my office, but I could hear them. Some time later, Deirdre went upstairs, and I thought she had retired for the night."

He leaned forward on the seat of the buggy, his expression doleful as the mild breeze blowing over the mountain ruffled his hair. "I was wrong," he said. "Much later—I think it was nearly midnight—I was reading in my room when I heard them again. Downstairs, in the music room. Deirdre was screaming, and Michael was shouting—an uncommon thing for him. I heard a crash, the sound of something breaking. I got up and went to Caterina's room. Cati was terrified of those drunken rages," he explained. "I didn't want that she should wake up alone."

His face ravaged, he faltered in his account. Susanna very nearly told him to stop. Her heart ached, not only for Caterina, for the fear and bewilderment the child must have endured, but for Paul as well. She could see what this was doing to him, that it was as painful for him to relive as it was for her to hear for the first time. But he quickly regained his composure and went on.

"Caterina was awake and very frightened. I wanted to go downstairs, for by then Deirdre had gone wild, screaming like a madwoman, and we could hear glass shattering. I was afraid of what might happen—"

He stopped to take a breath. "Michael had instructed me I should never interfere. Deirdre never liked me anyway—she resented anyone Michael cared about—and I was afraid I would only make things worse if I tried to intervene. So I stayed upstairs with Caterina.

"A few minutes later, I heard Deirdre in the vestibule, raving, screaming at Michael, that he was trying to keep her a prisoner. Then I heard the front door slam.

"Soon, Michael called for me and Dempsey. I left Caterina and went downstairs. Michael was beside himself. Dempsey and I left as quickly as we could get the carriage horses harnessed. Michael was insisting he would go with us, but we convinced him to stay at the house, with Caterina."

He looked at her. "Later, we were much relieved that he had stayed behind." He stopped, his expression bleak. He seemed to shudder, and his voice faded until Susanna had to strain to hear. "We were too late. She had gone off the road."

He motioned to the bluff. "She was dead by the time we reached her."

Susanna sat totally still, tugging at her hands, unable to breathe as she watched Paul, now hunched over, his hands gripping his knees.

His harsh words sliced through the silence. "She was going to another man that night. She told Michael so. She often did that, tormented him about the other men—"

He broke off, shaking his head. "Michael tried to stop her, but he couldn't. He could never stop her when she was like that. No one could stop her…"

His words drifted off. Susanna was seized by a peculiar sense of unreality, as if she'd been caught up in the middle of someone else's nightmare.

Paul straightened, leaned toward her a little. He seemed calmer now, quieter. "Michael tried many times to help Deirdre. He took her once to a…a *sanitarium*. But she refused to stay. He also brought doctors to her, at Bantry Hill. But she defied them. Michael did everything he could think to do. But Deirdre—it was as if she did not want to be helped. Perhaps Michael was right, after all. Perhaps she was sick in her mind. I never understood. None of it. The drinking, the affairs, the…craziness. And all the time he never so much as lifted a hand to her. Some men—" He looked at Susanna. "Some men would have *killed* her!"

There was a question Susanna had to ask, although she thought she already knew the answer. "Did Michael…did he love her? Ever?"

Paul turned to look at her, his gaze steady—and exceedingly sad. "*Sì*, of course he loved her. Even at the end, he loved her, although perhaps, it was a different kind of love by then. One of pity, no? But without love, how could he suffer such abuse, such disgrace, and still stay with her, even try to help her? But his love, his attempts to help—nothing was enough. Nothing was ever enough for Deirdre."

When Susanna made no reply, he added, "I'm sorry, Susanna. So very sorry you had to learn these things about your sister. I can only imagine how painful it is for you."

"Well," Susanna said, her voice thick, "at least I finally know…the truth."

For a time she sat, unmoving, unable to speak. She glanced away, too dazed to think, too numb to even try to absorb everything he had told her. Yet a grim certainty ran through her. He had spoken the truth.

Paul leaned toward her, his gaze seeking hers as if searching for evidence of further doubt on her part. "Susanna, what I have told you is the truth. I have exaggerated nothing. It is all true."

Slowly, Susanna raised her head. She saw reflected in his dark eyes his concern for her, as well as the fundamental honesty she had always recognized, and in spite of her reluctance to accept the terrible burden he had just shared with her, she knew she had no choice but to believe him. He wasn't lying. More than likely, Paul Santi wasn't even *capable* of deception.

"It's all right, Paul. I...need to thank you for telling me. I had to know."

Still, it was simply too much to take in, all at once. There was so much she couldn't grasp, so much she couldn't comprehend. She wondered if she would ever be able to understand what had actually happened to Deirdre, what had gone wrong, in her marriage...her life.

Did she even *want* to understand? Could she bear it?

"I will take you home now," said Paul, his tone gentle. He hesitated. "Are you all right, Susanna?"

Susanna looked at him, then managed a nod. But she wondered if indeed she would ever be all right again.

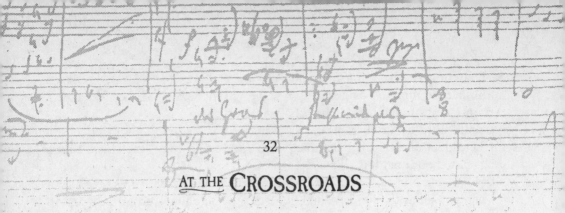

32

AT THE CROSSROADS

Still heavy is thy heart?
Still sink thy spirits down?
Cast off the weight, let fear depart,
And every care be gone.

PAUL GERHARDT (TRANSLATED BY JOHN WESLEY)

They pulled up to the front of the house, but although the wind had turned much cooler, neither made any attempt to get out of the buggy.

Susanna glanced at the porch, then looked away. She was utterly exhausted, weary to the point of weakness, yet reluctant to go inside and face Michael.

"So," she said quietly, turning to Paul, "what made you finally decide to tell me?"

"I realized that Michael would not...*could* not," he replied.

Susanna slowly shook her head. "I still don't understand why."

"Michael meant only to shield you, Susanna," he answered. "To protect your memories of Deirdre and spare you pain. And I think, perhaps, without realizing it, he meant to protect himself as well."

Susanna frowned. "What do you mean?"

His expression became thoughtful as he studied her. "Have you not seen, Susanna, that Michael is coming to have much affection for you?"

Susanna tensed. At the moment, the last thing she wanted to hear was how Michael might feel about *her*. She had yet to get past his turbulent relationship with *Deirdre*. Even so, something stirred inside her at Paul's words.

She diverted her gaze, saying nothing.

"Perhaps," Paul went on in spite of her silence, "Michael has been blind in more ways than one."

She stared at him, surprised that he would refer to Michael's blindness in such a way.

"I believe you are becoming very important to Michael," he went on, his expression solemn. "And when I see the two of you together, I wonder if he is not becoming important to you."

Susanna suddenly felt as if she were suffocating. "Don't, Paul. Not now. I can't deal with anything more right now. Surely, you understand that."

He held up a hand, palm outward, shaking his head. "Wait—please, Susanna. I do not mean to cause you further distress. Naturally, any feelings between you and Michael are none of my business. I am merely trying to answer your question. I know, because Michael told me so, that he was determined not to damage your memory of Deirdre. But I think it is also possible that he was afraid—afraid the truth might turn you against *him*."

"That's ridiculous."

"Is it?" He searched her eyes. "Michael knew that Deirdre was writing often to you. Don't you think he at least suspected *what* she was writing? He sensed almost from the time of your arrival that you distrusted him. Perhaps he thought that if you knew the truth, you would find it unforgivable, that he could not somehow help Deirdre, that he could not save his own wife."

As Susanna considered his words, uneasiness began to snake through her. What he was driving at seemed uncomfortably close to something she was reluctant to admit, to Paul, perhaps even to herself. "But his evasion only made me more suspicious," she said, not quite meeting his eyes.

"*Sì*, I understand that, and you understand it. But Michael did not. I think he might have been afraid you would even blame him for Deirdre's death. That you might think him somehow responsible."

"I *never*—"

The denial died on her lips. In truth, because of Deirdre's letters and Michael's entrenched silence, she *had* suspected Michael of deception at the very least, had even wondered if somehow he might not have played a part in Deirdre's death.

She framed her face with her hands, trying to knead away the pain drilling at her temples.

"Susanna, I have never gone against Michael," Paul said, his voice low. "Not until today. But when I realized that by withholding the truth from you, he was only fostering more and more doubt on your part, I felt I had to do something."

She sensed him watching her, waiting, and she finally looked up.

"I had seen that he was coming to care for you," he went on. "Yet I also saw that his silence was erecting a barrier, allowing you to think the worst of him. In time, I feared it would create even more grief for him, and he has had enough grief for any man, enough for a lifetime. I simply could not watch him continue to wound you—or himself—any longer."

His searching gaze unnerved Susanna. She turned from him and sat staring at the stone front of Bantry Hill. But she heard every word he spoke as he continued.

"Michael is a man of God, not a man of deceit, Susanna. I think somehow you know this. It is true, he is a very complex man, difficult to understand. But more than anything else, he is a *good* man, a godly man who wants nothing more than what is best for the people he loves. Michael is a man who lives for God, for his family, and for his music."

A question occurred to Susanna, and she turned back to him. "You said that Deirdre used Michael to advance her own career, that she took it as a personal betrayal when he left the opera. Was Deirdre the reason he left? Was she responsible for that, too?"

He shook his head. "No. She resented him for it, of course. When he gave up his own career, it took much away from Deirdre as well, for it meant Michael would no longer be in a position to exert influence in her behalf. But, no, that is something apart from Deirdre, something I can't explain."

"More secrets?" The words were out before Susanna could call them back, and she cringed at the bitterness she heard in her own voice.

Paul impaled her with an indicting look of great sadness. "No, Susanna. Michael makes no secret of that part of his life, but it is very complicated. Even now, I am not certain I understand it myself. But I'm sure Michael would tell you about it if you were to ask."

He continued to watch her, his expression gentle but measuring. "I wish you could allow yourself to know Michael as he really is, Susanna. Could you not give him this much grace, to begin again, and at least accept the friendship he would like to offer you?"

Could she? Now that she knew the truth, could she bring herself to start over, this time without the preconceptions, the suspicions that had very nearly poisoned her judgment of Michael, her feelings about him, even her life at Bantry Hill?

Susanna looked at Paul and saw the intensity behind his words, the depth of emotion in his appeal—not for himself, but for Michael, whom he loved. She wished she could answer as he obviously wanted her to. Instead, she could manage only the weakest reassurance.

"I don't know, Paul. I need time. There's so much I need to think about. I feel—"

She broke off. How *did* she feel? Apart from the hurt and the confusion, the anger and shock engendered by Paul's accounting of Deirdre's lies and the immorality that had spilled over to bring pain to everyone who loved her—apart from all that, how did she feel?

The acid of self-pity threatened to eat through her soul. For the moment she could think of nothing except the losses she had suffered in such a brief time. Her sister. Her parents. Her home. Even her *country*.

And as of today, she had lost Deirdre *twice:* once to death, and then again to truth.

While they had never been truly close, they had always been tied by the bonds of blood and memory that made them sisters. Not only had death broken those bonds, it had also destroyed any chance for reconciliation, any hope for developing a real relationship. Even when Deirdre had finally reached out to her, confided in her, it had all been a lie, making the pain of her loss doubly bitter.

Suddenly, as if he had sensed her thoughts, Paul touched her hand, saying, "You have lost a great deal, Susanna. It must be a terrible grief, to lose your family as you have, to leave your home for a life among strangers, and now this. I cannot tell you how much I wish I could make things easier for you."

Susanna looked at him, seeing the genuine kindness, the desire to help, even to heal, that brimmed in his eyes. But Paul could *not* help, could not heal, could not make things easier. She was the only one who could begin to move beyond the loss and the lies, the hurt and the disillusionment, and eventually forge her way toward something better.

At that instant, Susanna knew that she stood at a crossroads. She could choose to hold on to *yesterday*, to what might have been, with all its heartache. She could barricade herself behind a past that could never be restored, allowing that past to overshadow the present and consume any hope for the future. Or she could move forward, slowly but deliberately, committing one step at a time to God and whatever plan He might hold for her life.

In short, she could retreat or she could go forward. And she recognized with piercing clarity the sacrifices, the responsibilities, inherent to either choice.

"We have been gone a long time," Paul said. "Michael will be worried by now."

Susanna turned to see the massive front doors of the house swing open to reveal Michael, standing there, tall and dark and solemn, his face lifted slightly as if he was listening for something. She watched him for another moment, then shifted her attention back to Paul.

"He needn't know you've told me," she said.

Paul had been about to step out of the buggy, but now swung around to look at her. "What?"

"You're worried that Michael will be upset when he learns you told me about Deirdre." She put a hand to his arm. "But it's all right. Michael doesn't need to know just yet."

"Susanna, he will have to know—"

"But not today," she said firmly. "And you needn't be the one to tell him. I'll tell him myself. When the time is right, I'll explain."

Paul's face creased in a smile of unmistakable relief. "*Grazie*! Thank you, Susanna."

She closed her eyes for a second or two, then opened them and drew in a deep, bracing breath of the cool air coming up off the river. Again she turned toward the house and saw that Caterina had come to the door and was now at Michael's side, waving and bouncing from one foot to the other. Michael, too, lifted a hand in greeting.

Susanna sat staring for a long time at the man and the little girl framed in the doorway, waiting.

Waiting for Paul.

Waiting for her.

And in that moment, though her heart was still heavy, her spirit still wounded, she stepped away from the crossroads. She made a decision.

Summoning all her courage, Susanna lifted her face and prepared to take the first step on the road that pointed to the future. The road that led to Bantry Hill, and whatever waited beyond.

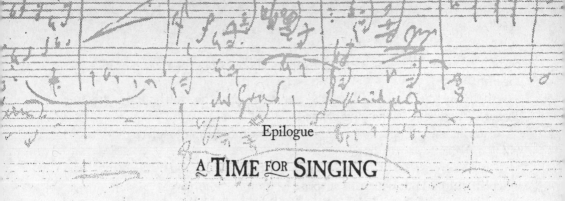

Epilogue

A TIME FOR SINGING

But should the surges rise,
And rest delay to come,
Blest be the tempest, kind the storm,
Which drives us nearer home.

AUGUSTUS M. TOPLADY

November

Thanksgiving was still two days away, but for over a week now Caterina had been urging Susanna to help her learn some "new piano pieces for Christmas." The suggestion that they might at least wait until the calendar was turned to December was invariably met with such a patent look of disappointment that Susanna could hardly refuse.

So on this snowy November evening they were ensconced in the music room, Caterina at the piano keyboard with Susanna on a chair beside her. The girl had not as yet progressed beyond a basic treble melody line, but with the confidence of youth she had assured Susanna that by Christmas she would be playing "parts."

Given her niece's stubborn bent and obvious musical aptitude, Susanna had no reason to doubt that declaration. Nor was she surprised when Caterina showed no particular preference for the simpler music of the season. She had already detected in her somewhat precocious niece a distinct taste for challenge, so when the child insisted on adding "Angels from the Realms of Glory" to her limited repertoire—in part because its composer, Henry Smart, had been "blind like Papa"—Susanna merely resigned herself to the task at hand.

Near the end of their practice time, her pupil turned to Susanna, her piquant features set in a decisive expression. "On Christmas Eve," she announced, "I'm going to play my new hymn for Papa and tell him all about it. Or do you think he already knows its—'history'?" she asked, imitating Susanna's earlier use of the word.

"Well, your papa does know a great deal about music, *alannah*. But I'm quite certain he would be pleased to learn more about whatever you choose to play for him."

At that moment Michael walked into the room, the wolfhound at his side. "What is this about Papa being pleased?"

Caterina put a finger to her lips as if to warn Susanna to silence. "We can't tell you, Papa. It's a surprise!"

"Ah—a surprise!" Michael said, smiling as he came to stand by the piano. "And when shall I find out what this surprise is, hmm? Tomorrow?"

"Not tomorrow," Caterina said, cupping her chin in her hands, clearly prepared to play out this exchange as long as possible.

"The next day then?"

"No, not the next day either!"

Michael feigned a frown. "Why do you tease your papa so? You know I am impatient when it comes to surprises."

Caterina giggled. "You will have to wait a long time for *this* surprise, Papa! Maybe as long as Christmas!"

"*Christmas?*" Michael reared back a little and drew a hand over his forehead with great dramatic flair. "*Impossibile!* I think you must tell me now! This very minute! Else, I will have to squeeze it out of you!"

With that, he made a lunge for her. She squealed, but went willingly. Susanna, by now accustomed to these evening roughhouse matches, quickly got out of their way and went to sit by the fire. The wolfhound, never one to be left out, charged directly into the middle of the fracas, and for the next ten minutes pandemonium reigned, with much shrieking and barking and laughter.

Michael was the first to give over. Lumbering to his feet, he lifted both hands in a mock plea for mercy. "Enough! I am too old for this!"

"Then let's sing," Caterina said agreeably.

"How can I sing when you have exhausted me?" But even as he teased, Michael felt for the piano stool and lowered himself onto it.

"Play carols, Papa," Caterina instructed.

"*Christmas* carols? Cati, it is not yet Thanksgiving!"

"That doesn't matter," she said firmly. "It's snowing, so it *looks* like Christmas. I don't see why we can't sing Christmas carols all the time. Christmas doesn't last long enough to hold all the songs I like."

Michael turned in Susanna's direction and smiled. "A good point, no?" He then launched into a rousing version of "O Come, All Ye Faithful," and Caterina immediately piped in. Soon they were both singing, though Michael obviously kept his voice restrained so he wouldn't overwhelm Caterina's childish efforts.

As if to make sure Susanna wasn't left out, Gus, the wolfhound, ambled over and plopped down beside her chair to share the fire. On cue, Susanna rubbed his great head as she sat watching Michael and Caterina.

She had grown fond of their evenings in the music room. These days Michael seldom stayed in the city. Clearly, he enjoyed being at home with his daughter, and just as clearly, Caterina delighted in his presence.

Susanna didn't always join them, intent on giving the two of them as much time alone together as possible. But of late it seemed that one or the other would come looking for her if she didn't make an appearance. By now she had to admit she'd be disappointed if they happened to forget her.

There were times of contentment for Susanna. Indeed, it surprised her to realize just how contented she *was*. Gradually, a subtle peace had settled over her relationship with Michael. As yet, she hadn't told him of Paul's disclosure. If he ever questioned what accounted for the fact that she no longer tried to quiz him about Deirdre, he gave no indication. Perhaps he was simply relieved to have an end to her incessant questions. Whatever the case, he clearly welcomed this unexpected truce and meant to leave well enough alone.

In truth, it seemed that they were, at the least, becoming friends. If Susanna occasionally felt a vague, disturbing longing for something more—or sensed that Michael did—she deliberately refused to attach anything other than a fleeting thought to it.

For now, she wanted only what she had: the joy of loving Caterina and being loved in return; the opportunity to live a quiet, fulfilling life in a place where she felt cared for and safe and even *needed;* and the dignity of knowing she was earning her livelihood rather than depending on Michael's largess.

At first she had questioned whether she would ever be able to put aside Paul's shattering revelations about Deirdre. She wondered if the awful things she had learned would be engraved upon her mind forever, like a searing, indelible brand. The reality of all she had lost threatened to mire her in a fog of despair.

Like Job in the Scriptures, she had attempted to counter desolation with faith: "*The Lord gave, and the Lord has taken away.*" It had been more difficult to add the final "*Blessed be the name of the Lord.*"

But as the days passed, she became more and more caught up in Caterina's— and Michael's—busy world. The continuous flow of responsibilities and new experiences gave her no time for brooding, no opportunity for dwelling on the past. And so, almost without her realizing it, a quiet restoration had begun.

In a way she had never before experienced, she began to feel the assurance of God's love for her. Like a dawning sun, the healing warmth spread over her days. As she went about taking care of Caterina, she became increasingly aware that she, too, was being cared for—attended by a love that urged her past the gloom of disappointment and hurt into a better place, a brighter place.

Sometimes she could even think of Deirdre without the accompanying stab of pain or the sick sense of shame and betrayal. She lived, after all, caught up in the swift current of a child's needs, engulfed by a little girl's love and laughter and affection.

And always, there was the music. That same healing love that moved through other parts of her life was also present in the music, coloring and enriching her world, nourishing her spirit and feeding her soul.

Absently she stroked the wolfhound's crisp coat, her gaze returning to Michael and Caterina. Michael kept drifting in and out of Italian as he attempted to teach Caterina the melody line of what sounded like a child's cradle song. It was a sweet, charming little piece, a simple tune.

Caterina's black curls fell about her face. Michael now stood behind her, his hand covering the little girl's on the keyboard. As Susanna watched them, the ancient words of Job, at the beginning of his story, again echoed in her mind: *"The Lord gave, and the Lord has taken away. Blessed be the name of the Lord."*

But this time she also heard, even more clearly, the words that came near the end of Job's trial: *"And the Lord gave Job twice as much as he had before..."*

With her eyes still locked on Michael and his child, Susanna felt an awareness rise up in her soul—an awareness infused by the same indescribable, divine love that had carried her through the past weeks. And in that moment she realized that although she had lost much, she had been given more.

Michael turned just then, smiling. "Come join us, Susanna."

"Yes, Aunt Susanna! Please! Come sing with us!"

Susanna hesitated. Ordinarily, she limited her participation to simply watching from across the room or occasionally accompanying them as they sang. But they insisted, so she rose and went to join them.

When she would have taken the piano stool, however, Caterina stopped her. "No, Aunt Susanna. I want to play 'Joy to the World'! You sing with Papa."

Always too inhibited to add her voice to Michael's, Susanna simply hummed along as he began to sing. Caterina also chimed in, continuing to play the melody with great deliberation.

At some point Michael had placed one hand on his daughter's shoulder, and now extended the other hand to Susanna. She hesitated only a moment before clasping it.

She had stopped humming and was only half listening when, unexpectedly, her thoughts went back to the day she had stood on the deck of the ship bringing her to America. She remembered the chill of excitement—and fear—that had seized her as she glimpsed New York Harbor for the first time. All the intervening months fell away, and she recalled with startling clarity the question that had been in her mind that day, the question that had nagged at her all the way across the Atlantic:

Was this an ending or a beginning?

For one shining instant Susanna heard the answer to that question ring out above the words and the music of the familiar carol. She had finally begun to move beyond the past, to accept and even exult in the present, to look forward to the future.

Suddenly, eagerly, Susanna began to sing. Michael turned and smiled at her, tightening his grasp on her hand. In that moment, all her old apprehensions vanished, and she lifted her voice in harmony with the voices of her new family.

She had her answer.

Bantry Hill was both an ending *and* a beginning.

It was also home.

BOOK TWO

CADENCE

It matters not
If the world has heard
Or approves or understands...
The only applause
We're meant to seek
Is that of nail-scarred hands.

—BJ HOFF

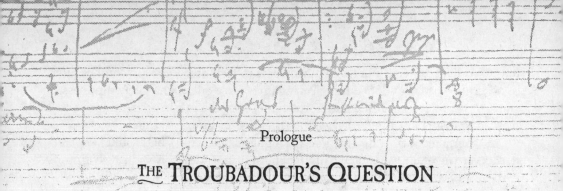

Prologue

THE TROUBADOUR'S QUESTION

'Tis past; 'tis gone. That fairy dream
Of happiness is o'er;
And we the music of thy voice
Perhaps may hear no more.

**FANNY CROSBY, FROM A TRIBUTE WRITTEN FOR JENNY LIND,
THE "SWEDISH NIGHTINGALE," UPON HER VISIT
TO THE NEW YORK INSTITUTION FOR THE BLIND**

New York City, 1869

B*ravo! Magnìfico!"* The curtain fell on the final act of *Il Trovatore* to a deafening
ovation, and the auditorium quaked under the riotous explosion.

Michael Emmanuel made yet another deep, sweeping bow as bouquets were
flung onto the stage and the applause and cheers grew more frenzied. The theater
blazed with prismed light refracted by crystal chandeliers and diamonds worn
by the ladies in the crowd. Even the gold filigree of the walls and cornices shone
lustrous, as if reflecting the fire and passion of the enthusiastic crowd.

Michael had performed the part of *Manrico* the troubadour on many stages,
in many countries, to much acclaim. But never had he been lavished with more
adulation and fervor than here in America's greatest city.

The crowd began to chant *"Trovatore, Trovatore!"* calling out the name like a
mantra until he obligingly took another bow. Twice more the curtain rose and
fell, but this exuberant audience seemed to have no intention of letting him
go. As he stood at center stage taking his bows, the cries of the crowd washing
over him like a flood, he struggled to recapture even the slightest semblance of
the elation that once would have accompanied such a triumphant performance.
Instead, another feeling, all too familiar, drew in on him, engulfing him with a
suffocating closeness. A wound in some dark hidden place, torn wider with each
performance, had become a deep, aching pit of yearning—a yearning for some
nameless, indescribable…*something*.

The critics and the international press often spoke of Michael as having "the music world at his feet," but lately it had come to feel more like a predator at his back. His joy had abandoned him, leaving in its place only a gnawing emptiness. The crowds, the acclaim, the glitter, the fame, even the music itself—none of it seemed to matter any longer. It held no meaning for him, no value.

In that moment, a wildly irrational thought seized him. What would happen if, this very night, he were to take his final bow, turn, and simply walk away from it all—the years of study and preparation, the relentless discipline and drill, the never-ending rehearsals and performances and unceasing demands on his time and energy?

The adulation of the crowds. The sense of power. The celebrity. The glory.

Could he leave it all behind? What would it do to him? How would it change him?

Would he be a different man? A lesser man?

Or would he somehow become a *better* man?

His mind reeled with the idea, and he found it impossible to recapture reason, to return to himself. The sea of faces dimmed; the clamor of applause receded. His throat tightened. Scarcely breathing, he waited for some cold touch of dread to descend on him, or at least some sense of impending loss and grief. But nothing happened. He felt nothing but the nagging weight of fatigue, the exhausting aimlessness that had plagued him for months now.

Suddenly he thought of Deirdre. He had been questioning what such a radical change might do to *him*. Now he could not help but wonder what it might do to his wife.

Instinctively, he glanced toward the wings, but Deirdre wasn't there. She still blamed Michael for her failure to secure the role of *Leonora*. Incensed by his "betrayal" of her—his refusal, for the first time, to use his influence on her behalf—she hadn't shown up at the theater since the day he had told her that Annabella Antolini had been signed for the coveted soprano's role.

If he were to quit, to leave the world of opera altogether, Deirdre would never forgive him. Never. There would be no end to her fury. She would believe—and perhaps rightly so—that his defection would strike the final blow to her already downward-spiraling career.

He was suddenly jerked back to his surroundings as a young assistant placed a bouquet of roses in his arms. Michael stared at the flowers, then at the boy. Finally, he managed a forced smile and gave another brief, wooden bow to the audience.

When the curtain came down once again, he stumbled from the stage. Ignoring his manager and the others milling about in the wings, he raced to his dressing room, closed the door with a firm thud, and turned the key.

1

A STIRRING IN THE HEART

There is a murmur in my heart...

EDWARD DOWDEN

Bantry Hill Estate, Hudson River Valley
Late November 1875

No, no! *Assolutamente non!* I cannot do this, Michael!"

"Pauli, listen to me! I told you, Dempsey will be with you the entire time. He and the handler will see to the horse. You will have nothing to do except to sign the papers."

"I do not like the horses, Michael! You know I do not like the horses!"

"You need not *like* the horse, Pauli! The handler has been paid to bring him from the ship to the stables. You will simply go with Dempsey in case he should need your help."

"What *help*? I would be of no help!"

Susanna, on her way down the hall in search of some clean sketch paper for Caterina, stopped short at the sound of raised voices coming from Michael's office. She wasn't intentionally eavesdropping, but it would have been impossible not to overhear the boisterous dialogue taking place between Michael and Paul Santi.

Neither of the two men sounded angry, merely persistent. Some of their exchange was in English, some in Italian, but Susanna understood enough to gather that Michael had a new horse arriving at the harbor and was insisting that Paul accompany Dempsey to claim the animal.

Clearly, Paul had other ideas.

"You know I am no good with the horses, Michael."

"I know you are *afraid* of the horses, Pauli."

"No, not afraid. *Terrified.* I am terrified of the nasty beasts! You know this—and the horses know it also!"

"I am not asking you to *ride* the horse, Pauli, merely to go with Dempsey."

"Why does Dempsey need *anyone* to go with him? Why can he not go alone?"

"I *told* you. There will be papers to sign." Michael lowered his voice. "Have you forgotten that Liam cannot read?"

Silence. Then, "Oh, all right, all right! I will go! But you remember, *cugino:* if your precious horse ends up in the ocean and me with him, my death will be on your head!"

Susanna smiled. She was used to these impassioned outbursts by the lively young Italian. Paul and Michael frequently sparred, but seldom about anything of real importance. She suspected that some of their disputes were deliberately instigated—sometimes by Paul, sometimes by Michael—simply because both of them enjoyed the verbal fencing. Michael often sounded amused during their contests, and it was common to see them both laughing and pounding each other good-naturedly on the back only minutes later, like schoolboys pleased with their own cleverness.

Just then Paul emerged from Michael's office, caught sight of her, and threw up his hands. "Why do I bother, I wonder? Always he wins!"

"What have you gotten yourself into this time?"

Paul rolled his eyes, giving a palms-up gesture of futility. "This is not *my* idea, you can be sure! It's all Michael's doing. He insists that I go with Dempsey to the harbor to fetch one of his ill-tempered beasts!"

Michael appeared in the doorway, dressed in a dark wool jacket and white shirt—more businesslike apparel than he usually wore at home. Was he going away again? Susanna tried to suppress a pang of disappointment at the thought.

He wore his dark glasses, too, and she wondered whether he had put them on for her benefit. He seldom wore the glasses except in her presence, a fact that she found increasingly puzzling—and annoying.

"Paul would have me believe I endanger his life by sending him to the docks," Michael said. "The truth is, I suspect he's eager to go, to avoid working this afternoon."

Paul feigned an injured look. "Susanna," he said solemnly, "if I do not return, I would like you to have my violin."

"But I don't *play* the violin, Paul."

"All the same, I want you to have it. In my memory."

"Well, that's very kind of you, Paul." She imitated his grave tone. "You can be sure I'll pray for your safe return."

"You see," Paul said to Michael, "even Susanna knows you have placed my life at great risk."

One eyebrow went up as Michael crossed his arms over his chest. "I believe Dempsey is waiting for you."

"You are a hard man, Michael."

"So you have said. Many times. Now go."

"*Sì*, I go." Paul shot an impish smile at Susanna, then hurried off down the hall.

Susanna watched him go, relieved that Michael and his cousin were obviously back to normal in their relationship. She had developed a genuine fondness for Paul Santi, a bond forged the day Paul finally divulged to Susanna what Michael had refused to reveal about her sister.

It had been Paul who explained about Deirdre's alcoholism, her turbulent and disastrous marriage to Michael, and the events that had led up to her death on the treacherous mountain road after a violent argument. Convinced that by withholding the truth from Susanna, Michael would only inflict more pain on her and, ultimately, on himself, Paul had told Susanna what Michael would not, risking his own relationship with the cousin he revered.

When he learned that Paul had broken his confidence about Deirdre and their marriage, Michael had been furious, bitterly denouncing Paul for a deliberate betrayal of trust. Only after much explanation and persuasion on Susanna's part did Michael finally move past his anger and accept that Paul had acted with honorable intentions. Paul had seen what Michael could not: that in his efforts to keep Susanna's memories of her sister untarnished, Michael was actually hurting her, fostering a distorted image of Deirdre, and encouraging Susanna's increasing suspicion of himself.

To Susanna's vast relief, the two had finally reconciled. There seemed to be no lingering evidence of the rift between them.

She suddenly realized that Michael was still standing in the doorway, waiting.

"I...I was looking for some fresh drawing paper for Caterina," she said, embarrassed by her own woolgathering. "She seems to have used up her entire stock."

"In here." He motioned Susanna into his office. "Cati likes very much to draw, no? Does she have any particular ability, do you think?"

"Actually, I think she shows quite a lot of skill for one so young. But, then, Caterina seems to do extremely well in whatever she attempts," Susanna said. "Except perhaps for her sewing."

"So I have heard," he said dryly. "Just so you'll know, Rosa, too, has tried to interest Cati in the sewing, also with no success."

Susanna smiled to herself. Rosa Navaro, the famed opera star, had long been a close friend of the family—a neighbor and a surrogate aunt to Michael's daughter. Caterina adored her; if even Rosa could not interest Caterina in sewing, it might well be a hopeless cause.

Susanna waited as he crossed the room and opened the door of a floor-to-ceiling storage cabinet. As deftly as if he could see the shelves, he retrieved a thick pad of paper and handed it to her. "She likes best to draw the animals, no?"

"Yes. Horses are her favorite subject."

"Sì, she loves the horses. Already she rides well." He paused. "And you, Susanna? Do you ride?"

"Oh, no! No, I've never ridden. I'm afraid I share Paul's apprehension about horses. I've always been rather frightened of them."

"Ah, but there is nothing to be afraid of," he said, coming around to his desk and resting his hands on the back of the chair. "We must respect them, of course. But there is no need for fear."

He paused. "You think it strange that I would say such a thing."

It was a statement, not a question. And indeed, Susanna had been thinking exactly that, given the riding accident that had caused his blindness. Deirdre had written only the sketchiest of details about the incident: apparently Michael had been jumping his favorite horse when a pheasant flew out of a hedge and startled him. The horse's forelegs had become tangled in the hedge, and he failed to clear the jump. Michael was thrown, striking his head against a rock. According to the doctors, the blow caused irreparable damage to his optic nerve, blinding him for life.

Michael nodded as if he had read her thoughts. "What happened to me is most likely the reason for Paul's fear. But it wasn't the horse's fault. It was simply an accident."

He indicated that Susanna should sit down, and he lowered himself into the chair behind the desk and shuffled some papers out of his way. Although the dark glasses tended to put her off, his blindness evoked no feelings of pity for him. Sympathy, perhaps—after all, life must be much more difficult for him than for those who could see. But not pity. To the contrary, she felt admiration that he could live so fully, so *generously,* in spite of the obvious difficulties his disability presented.

But, then, Michael defied just about every preconceived notion she'd ever held of him. He was a man of many facets, a different kind of man entirely from what she once feared he might be.

He was also a man who could, with absolutely no warning, kindle feelings that confused and agitated her. She was attracted to him. Strongly attracted, in a way she had never before experienced. Consequently, she found herself torn between trying to avoid him and wanting to be near him.

According to Paul, the attraction wasn't entirely one-sided. Michael, he insisted, was coming to have "much affection" for Susanna. So far, Susanna had managed not to delve too deeply into the implications of this remark. Nevertheless, she couldn't entirely dismiss the quick dart of excitement that grazed her heart. Could Paul possibly be right? And if so...

She realized with a start where her thoughts were leading her and felt a sudden urgency to distance herself from the man across the desk. She stood so abruptly that her chair almost tipped over. "Well...," she stammered, "I expect I should be getting back upstairs to Caterina. She'll be wondering what's become of me."

Michael got to his feet, his expression puzzled as he lifted a hand to delay her. "I was about to ask you if you would mind working with me this afternoon.

Paul will be away, and I'd like to follow the Braille through the new sections of the *Anthem*. It would help me very much if you would play the piano so I can concentrate on the score."

Susanna's old uncertainty, the familiar feelings of ineptness, surfaced immediately, and she hesitated.

"If you'd rather not—"

"No...no, it's not that. I'll be glad to help. If I can, that is."

He smiled a little. "When will you ever dismiss this foolish sense of inadequacy, Susanna? You are much more accomplished than you're willing to credit yourself. Indeed, I suspect if I could ever catch you unawares, I would discover that you are a most gifted pianist. But every time I enter the room you stop playing."

Susanna couldn't think how to reply. Michael's incomparable musicianship intimidated her to the point that whatever ability she *might* possess invariably froze in his presence. It was one thing to accompany him and Caterina during one of their lighthearted evening songfests, but quite another to perform music of a more serious nature for Michael alone—especially one of his own compositions.

"I'll be in the music room most of the afternoon. Why don't you come down after Caterina is settled in for her nap?"

For a moment, Susanna found herself staring, caught up in the warmth of his smile, the stubborn wave of dark hair that tumbled over his forehead, the breadth of his shoulders, the strength of his features that could soften when least expected—

She blinked, forcing herself to answer. "That won't be too late? I mean—aren't you going away?"

He frowned. "Going away?"

"I thought perhaps you were going downriver..."

He passed a hand over the sleeve of his coat, shaking his head. "No, not tonight. I'll be at home tonight."

Susanna's earlier disappointment vanished. "Well...all right then." She paused to clear her throat. "I'll just take this paper up to Caterina, and come down later."

"*Grazie*, Susanna."

It was impossible, of course, no more than a fanciful notion. But Susanna almost felt as though he were watching her as she left his office and started down the hall.

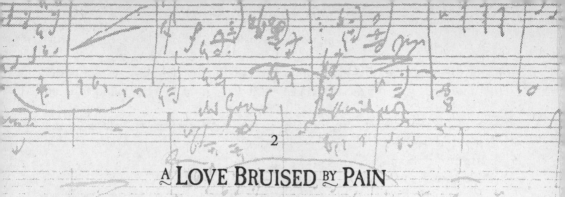

2

A LOVE BRUISED BY PAIN

Many days you have lingered
around my cabin door!
Oh! Hard Times, come again no more!

STEPHEN FOSTER

New York City

Conn MacGovern got up and pulled back the blanket between the sleeping quarters and the other half of the room that served as the kitchen. Vangie was already at her work, even though it wasn't yet daylight.

She sat at the table, bent low over the sewing, her hair falling free as she worked by the flickering light of an oil lamp. Conn stood watching her for a moment, his throat tight, his mouth sour with bitterness.

Whatever had possessed him to bring her here? This "house" was nothing but a hovel, a dilapidated shack of board and tin and tarpaper, squeezed among dozens of others just like it, or worse. The golden streets of America had turned out to be paths of mud and garbage, and the promise of a "job for every man" nothing but a lie.

Close on two months now they had been here, and so far he had found no work. Nothing more than an occasional odd job to help pay the rent. Were it not for Vangie's sewing and the pittance Nell Grace earned making artificial flowers, they wouldn't even have a roof over their heads.

Had his dreams of America been nothing more than folly after all? There sat his wife, crooking her spine and straining her eyes over piecework that paid a pitiful poor wage. His children were sleeping in broken-down beds in a cold and drafty room where, come winter, they would surely be taken with the rheumatism or even pneumonia.

Nell Grace was actually thinking of hiring herself out as a servant at one of the big houses uptown, though he would hear none of that foolishness. There was never enough to manage anything more than mere survival, not even with

Renny Magee's meager findings from the discards in the alleys or the occasional coin she earned from entertaining a paltry audience on the street.

A worm of self-pity twisted in his gut. What more had he ever wanted, after all, than a patch of good land, a few animals, and a free man's sun on his back? And just see where his foolish dreaming had landed them all: in the heart of a godforsaken slum where people piled their waste in the streets like animals and drank water that tasted as if it had been drawn from a poisoned well.

Better they had stayed in Ireland than this! At least in Dublin they hadn't feared for their lives every time they stepped out of the house.

He sighed. Vangie turned and saw him watching her.

Conn tried to smile but failed. "You ought not be working in the dark, love." He buckled his belt and made an effort to smooth his hair with his hands before crossing the room to her. "Won't you be ruining your eyesight altogether?"

She lifted her face for his kiss. "I could do this in my sleep," she said. "And what are you about today?"

Conn heard the note of caution in her voice. She knew him so well, knew how it seared his pride, this going out in search of a job day after day only to return home empty-handed. "I'll be going back to the docks," he said, forcing a cheerful tone. "Sooner or later I'm bound to get on if I show up every day."

"You have the right of it there. As soon as they get a look at you, they'll see that you can do the work of three men, and won't they be hiring you on the spot?"

Leave it to Vangie to put a good face on things, he thought with a rush of gratitude. Her unfaltering faith in him was all that kept him going at times, and that was the truth.

"Your breakfast is ready," she said. "You go and wash, and I'll dish it up."

When Conn returned to the table, she had set a bowl of stirabout and a chunk of yesterday's soda bread at his place.

"I heard Nell Grace getting dressed, but the boys are still asleep," she said. "Renny has already gone off on one of her excursions. I do wish she wouldn't venture out on her own so, in the dark. Who knows what might become of the girl out in the streets by herself?"

"That one can take care of herself well enough. Only a fool would go and tangle with the likes of Renny Magee."

He adopted a gruff tone, but in fact he felt a certain peculiar pride in the girl's cheeky resourcefulness. Even so, he hoped he was right about her fending for herself. She was a rascal, she was, but though she fancied herself fierce enough to stand off a battalion of Brits, she was but a slip of a girl and hardly a match for some of the vile bounders afoot on the streets of New York.

Just then Baby Emma appeared in the gap between the curtains, her rag dolly tucked under her arm. She came trundling over to Conn to be picked up, and he swept her into his arms, tousling the mop of golden red curls as she nuzzled her head under his chin. She was warm and sweet, her skin still flushed from sleep, and in spite of his earlier dour mood, love spread over him like a soft cloak.

As he sat there, dandling his baby girl on his lap and watching his beauty of a wife, Conn thought about his two sons sleeping healthy and whole in their bed and the grown daughter who was an incredible gift to them all. How could he forget, even for a moment, the undeserved goodness of his life?

But directly on the heels of his remorse came the grievous thought of the lad they had left behind: Aidan, his eldest son.

Well, that had not been *his* doing, now had it? He'd had his passage, bought and paid for. But as the boy himself was wont to remind them with his bold tongue, he was a man grown, he was, and could live his life the way he wanted. His ticket to America had meant so little to him he'd been willing to give it up to Renny Magee, a total stranger, an itinerant street busker.

And hadn't they all tried to make him see the foolhardiness of his action?

Aye, but perhaps there was something more a father could have done, had he not lost his temper and washed his hands of his own son.

Conn clenched his jaw, recalling Aidan's warning that they might meet with more trouble in America than anything they had ever known in Ireland. What a bitter thing it would be if his son turned out to be right.

Vangie still held it against him that he had not been able to coax Aidan into coming with them. No doubt she thought if he had tried harder, he might have changed the boy's mind. But Aidan had made his choice, and that was the end of it. There was no purpose in dredging up the pain time and again. They had enough to worry over as it was.

Vangie was keen on reminding him that worry was a sin, that the answer to their prayers might not come quickly, but it would come *eventually* if they maintained their faith. Conn wanted to believe, as his wife did, that it was only a matter of time before something good found its way to them. But he had never been a patient man, and it was a hard thing entirely to have patience in the face of his family's growing need.

"In God's time," Vangie would say. "It will happen in God's time."

He could only hope that God's time would come soon, for he did not see how they could go on as they were much longer.

⌒

With Baby Emma in her arms, Vangie cracked the door enough to watch Conn trudge off down the street, his hands in his pockets, his cap pushed back on his head. Love for him welled up in her, but it was a love bruised by pain. The pain of watching her husband's pride drain away, day after day, like the lifeblood trickling from a mortal wound.

Conn was a proud man. Too proud, some might say. But he was also a good man, a man who looked after his family and took seriously his responsibilities as a husband and father. He had never been one for the drink, nor had she ever known him to cast a roving eye, although the women were quick enough to eye *him*. Gambling held no appeal for him, and he routinely handed his pay over to her before it had so much as warmed his palm. Back home, he had been known for his honesty and his willingness to lend a hand to his neighbors. By any account, he was a man to respect.

He was not, however, a man meant to be idle. It was bitter enough for a man like Conn to be unemployed, but to see his wife and daughter working when he could not must chafe his very soul. Vangie had seen the anger—and the anguish—that flared in his eyes when he walked into the room and saw her and Nell Grace at their respective tasks, and him with nothing to do. She knew all too well the toll this was wreaking on him, and the knowing wrenched her heart.

If only Aidan had come with them, perhaps things would have been different...

Impatiently, she shook off the thought. What would have been different? Then *both* of them would have been looking for work. A lot of help that would be to Conn.

But at least she would have had the comfort of her son. If Conn's temper hadn't been so quick that last day in the harbor, perhaps he might have been able to talk some sense into Aidan and persuade him to come with them after all.

The nails of both hands dug into her palms until she wondered that she didn't draw blood. She had to stop this puzzling over what they might have done— what *Conn* might have done—to keep Aidan from staying behind. Had to stop wishing for what might have been.

Had to stop blaming Conn for their son's willfulness. She turned away from the door and set the baby to the floor beside the table, giving her a tin cup and spoon to play with. Nell Grace came into the room, her dark red hair tied neatly back with a piece of ribbon. "Morning, Mum. I'll dress Emma if you like."

"There's no hurry. You have your breakfast first so you can get on with your work. The boys will be up soon, and we'll need to clear a place for them to eat."

As if she could read the worry in Vangie's face, Nell Grace came to put a hand to her arm. "Da will find a job any day now, I'm sure. He just needs to find the right place, is all. A place where someone can recognize a man's worth for what it is."

Vangie turned to look at her, surprised but grateful for this thinly veiled attempt to lift her spirits. "Aye, the both of us know that, now don't we? 'Tis himself we need to convince."

Nell Grace smiled a little as she sat down to her bowl of stirabout. "You could convince Da of just about anything, I expect."

Vangie looked at her. "Is that so?"

"It is," Nell Grace said, not looking up. "Doesn't he dote on your every word? I only hope the man I marry will be as taken with my opinions as Da is yours."

"And aren't you a bit too young just yet, miss, to be thinking about the man you will one day marry?"

Nell Grace lifted one delicate eyebrow. "Tell me again, Mum, for I forget— how old were you when you married Da?"

Vangie's attempted frown crumbled under her daughter's mischievous grin. "You know very well I was exactly the age you are now. Seventeen years. But didn't it only make things harder for us, being wed so young? I want better for you."

Nell Grace regarded her with a long, unsettling look. "Then you want more for me than I want for myself. I couldn't imagine anything much better than being married to a man who would look at me the way Da looks at you, and after twenty years at that."

Vangie felt herself flush. *"Fuist!* Such foolish talk, and to your mother! You'd best finish your breakfast and tend to your flowers, miss."

She went to start the dishes, but after a moment stole a glance at Nell Grace, who already seemed to have forgotten their exchange and now sat eating, absorbed in her own thoughts.

Vangie smiled as she turned back to the dishes. Nell Grace was right. Despite the struggles and drudgery that had filled so many of their years together, what she had with Conn MacGovern was something other women could search for a lifetime over and never find.

In truth, she wouldn't have traded even the hardest times for a different life with someone else. She was blessed even when burdened. The thought both shamed her and quickened the struggling hope within her heart. And suddenly even the chill that clung to the cabin walls seemed to give way to an unfamiliar warmth, a warmth that had nothing to do with the stingy bit of fire fighting to stay alive in the aged stove.

Vangie felt a tug on her skirts and looked down to see Baby Emma reaching up for her. Quickly she dried her hands and lifted the toddler into her arms, burying her face in the cloud of red-gold curls that so distinctly marked the offspring of Conn MacGovern.

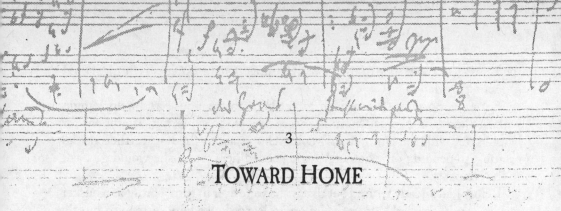

3

TOWARD HOME

Let others delight mid new pleasures to roam,
But give me, oh, give me, the pleasures of home!

JOHN HOWARD PAYNE

By midmorning, Renny Magee was hotfooting it back toward the house. Already she had dodged two drunken reprobates, a filthy old woman with not a tooth in her head, and a gaggle of swaggering bullies too young for whiskers, but who clearly fancied themselves men to be reckoned with.

Of course, they hadn't counted on Renny Magee. Just because she was slight and thin as a whip, their type almost always made the mistake of assuming she was also frail and weak—and perhaps simpleminded as well.

She grinned to herself at the thought of how she had easily showed them up for the great lumpheads they were. Like most of the other tomfools who lurked about Bottle Alley, the boyos she'd met up with this morning had been neither clever enough nor quick enough to so much as give her a good chase. She'd outrun the lot of them in a shake without ever losing a breath.

Her morning foraging had not been a colossal success, but at least she had more to show for her efforts than what she'd started out with. She had crammed her pockets with some sizable scraps of material salvaged from the bins behind the German tailor's shop on Broadway. As clever as Vangie was with a needle, she would put the colorful pieces to good use.

The best of her booty was a perfectly good wooden chair, which someone had discarded in back of one of the row houses. A coat of paint, and it would look as good as new. She had also come across one of yesterday's papers, clean as could be, which MacGovern would appreciate. He enjoyed his newspapers, he did.

Today she had gone as far as East Fourteenth Street, scouting for open parks and other sites where a busker might attract a crowd. Renny had gotten to know this end of the city fairly well by now, venturing into a new neighborhood every chance she got. Based on what she'd seen so far, she figured the district called the Bowery would be one of the more likely areas where a street performer could attract a crowd.

For now, however, she needed to get back to the house and help Vangie with the boys and Emma. Mornings were devoted to exploring; afternoons for helping out with the children and doing chores about the house. Then in the evening, depending on whether Vangie needed her or not, she would go back to the streets.

Renny had already figured out that if she were ever to turn a profit as a busker in New York, she had a great deal more to learn. Folks here seemed to mostly want songs and stories about the lands from which they'd come and this new land where they'd settled.

Not so in Ireland. There they hankered for the old tales, the legends of the ancient heroes and fairies and favorite saints. Back home, it had been as easy as chasing a hare out of the bushes to entertain a crowd on the street. A tune, a tale, and dancing feet had enabled Renny to make out just fine. Why, she could have gone anywhere in Dublin—in the entire surrounding countryside, for that matter—and earned a respectable wage for her efforts.

This place, though, was a city of foreigners. These people were strangers, with sundry origins and varied histories. How was she to learn such a jumbled mix of stories and legends, not to mention the different songs each clan boasted as their own? In two months of roaming about the littered streets and fetid alleys, Renny had taken in all she could, but in truth she was woefully ignorant of the different sects that made up this sprawling city.

New York was a stewpot of foreign faces and foreign tongues. The music was strange, the food even stranger. She was coming to recognize some of the more distinctive features of the Italian peddlers, or the small Oriental folk who hobbled down the lanes with their hands clasped as if in prayer, or the solemn-faced Hebrews who hurried along in pairs, always looking to and fro. But although she was learning her way about the city, she felt as if she'd only begun to scratch the surface. Why, the very sounds of New York—not to mention the astonishing sights and revolting smells—were enough to confuse a scholar. Such shrieking and screaming and cursing and caterwauling the likes of which she had never heard! It seemed to Renny that, for the most part, these New Yorkers were a demented lot entirely.

Demented or not, she meant to soak up all she could about them. And she needed to do it as quickly as possible, if she were to earn her own keep and help out the MacGoverns. Things were hard for them right now, and Renny meant to do whatever she could to ease Vangie's worries and the needs of the children.

If only she could read...

Her mind raced as she hauled the chair along behind her, heading down Mulberry Street. If she could read, there would be no limit to what she could learn. If she could only access the newspapers—and perhaps even books—why then, she would surely find everything she needed to know and then some.

The MacGoverns could read, every one of them—except for Baby Emma, of course. Even the twins knew their letters and a number of words, and them only eight years old. Apparently, MacGovern himself, who claimed to have had an educated da, had taught his entire family, including Vangie.

So far Renny had been able to keep her inability to read a secret. None of her chums back home had been able to read, either, and such things hadn't mattered on the streets of Dublin. But she was beginning to realize that, here in America, a person who could not so much as read a newspaper was at a definite disadvantage.

She had briefly considered asking Vangie to teach her. Or perhaps Nell Grace. But they were always so busy, tending to their piecework and the household tasks and the children. She couldn't imagine presuming on them to spend time helping *her*. Why should they?

Besides, the very thought of revealing her *disadvantage* to anyone—even to Vangie—made Renny's skin heat with shame. No doubt it would make her even smaller, poorer, somehow, in their eyes, were they to know the truth.

It cut against the grain for Renny to ask for help. With few exceptions, she depended on no one but herself.

She despised admitting that there was anything—anything at all—that she could not manage quite well on her own. But when it came to the reading, if she didn't make her problem known to someone, then how could she ever hope to learn? No matter how resourceful she happened to be, she couldn't fathom how she could teach herself to read.

She slowed her steps, hefting the chair onto her shoulders as she turned the corner to Baxter Street and home.

Home. Was that really how she thought of her present situation, then? The rickety shack with the tarpaper roof, perched in the midst of all the other shanties just like it. Had this really become *home* to her?

In truth, Renny had never had a real home, so it was difficult for her to understand exactly *what* she felt, or was supposed to feel, about the place she shared with the MacGoverns. Yet she did like the sound of the word. *Home.* She liked the snug feeling that came whenever she said it aloud. Sometimes she would repeat it over and over to herself, savoring it as if it had a taste all its own.

But she was hard-pressed to find the right words to define it. A roof over her head. A mattress on the floor alongside the baby's cradle. Food on the table, no matter how plain the fare or how scanty the portions. A place where she didn't have to fear the shadows that moved about in the night, where she could sleep without a brick clutched in her hand for protection.

And yet it was more than that. Home, for Renny, was the MacGoverns.

But only, she reminded herself, as long as she was under her pledge to them.

Six months. That's what she had committed, to stay with them for six months in exchange for her passage to America.

She considered six months quite a long enough period of time to be obligated to anyone. She had her own life to live, her own future to see to. She had not come to America just to fetch and carry for the MacGoverns, no matter how decent to her they might be. Renny Magee was not meant to be anyone's *property*.

Indeed not. And that being the case, she would do well not to attach too much importance to her present circumstances. In a relatively short time, having kept her commitment, she would be free to go her own way. No doubt the MacGoverns would be as pleased to see the last of her as she would be to leave them behind.

And yet the thought of her eventual freedom failed to kindle in her the sense of anticipation and excitement it once had. Still, she had four months left to go before she could reclaim her independence—a considerable length of time. It was only natural she wouldn't yet feel any real eagerness at the prospect. For now, she would simply do the work expected of her and bide her time. When the day finally arrived that she could once again be responsible to no one but herself, she expected she would scarcely be able to contain her enthusiasm.

The house was in sight now, and as the morning fog lifted to reveal the small, leaning shack at the edge of the row, Renny stepped up her pace. Vangie would have saved her a bowl of stirabout, and there would be water heating on the stove for the dark tea the MacGoverns fancied.

All in all, Renny decided, the day was looking fine.

4

SOMETHING OF GENIUS, SOMETHING OF GOD

Sweet blind singer over the sea,
Tuneful and jubilant, how can it be,
That the songs of gladness, which float so far,
As if they fell from an evening star,
Are the notes of one who may never see
"visible music" of flower and tree.

FRANCES RIDLEY HAVERGAL

Every day for weeks now, Caterina had taken to coaxing the old Irish tales from Susanna. Today was no exception. So, after lunch, with Gus the wolfhound dozing at the foot of the bed, Susanna spun yet another of the mythic tales, this one about the lazy princess and her three aunts.

"...And although the girl was lovely as the day itself and had three mysterious helpers to aid her in winning the prince, she was lazy to the point of despair. No doubt when she grew older and was no longer so fair, she would pay a dear price for her slothfulness..."

By the time the story was finished, Caterina was asleep. Susanna watched her for a moment. For the most part, the little girl seemed to have regained her strength, but two successive bouts of croup had left their mark. There were still times when the child seemed to tire too easily, times when her color wasn't quite as it ought to be. Susanna thought it was probably a good thing that Dr. Carmichael would be stopping by later in the week to check on her.

Finally, she went to her own bedroom to freshen up before going downstairs. She had barely managed to brush her hair and smooth her collar when she heard the sound of the piano coming from the music room. Apparently, Michael was already at work.

She hurried down the steps, anchoring her hair clasp as she went. By the time she reached the end of the hallway, the music of the piano had changed to that of the mandolin. With it came Michael's voice, honeyed and light.

Susanna stopped to listen just outside the music room, marveling at the tones that seemed to flow with such ease, such perfection. He was singing what sounded like an Italian folk song, a tune infused with sunlight and rolling hills and peaceful pastures.

Through the doorway, Susanna studied him. He sat on the window seat, the late afternoon sun casting a dappled glow on his features. He had changed to a scarlet-colored shirt of soft wool, which only intensified his dark good looks. With his eyes closed, his strong profile haloed by the light streaming through the window, he appeared younger, less formidable. Perhaps even vulnerable. And undeniably handsome.

At almost the exact moment she walked into the room, he stopped playing, unfolded himself from the window seat, and stood, smiling. "Ah, Susanna, you are here." He laid the mandolin on the window seat. *"Buono."*

There seemed to be no such thing as sneaking up on Michael, despite his blindness. And yet it both pleased Susanna and unsettled her that he always seemed to know the instant she entered a room.

"I'm sorry it took me so long. Caterina wanted a story."

He waved off her apology. As he reached for the dark glasses in his shirt pocket and slipped them on, Susanna felt a familiar sting of irritation. Why was it he never seemed compelled to wear the glasses in the presence of others, only with her? It was almost as if he felt a need to *shield* himself from her.

Susanna suddenly felt awkward and uncertain. "Michael…I don't know how much help I can be—"

Before she could finish, he motioned her to the piano stool. Susanna eyed the Bösendorfer's keyboard with a mixture of anxiety and anticipation. She loved to play this magnificent instrument, yet she was so tense that for a moment she could only sit and stare at the smooth ivory keys before her.

Michael, of course, could not see her agitation. He leaned over her shoulder to place a pad of manuscript against the music rack, and Susanna gave an involuntary shiver.

"If you would play this for me and then make notation, please? Paul will render the Braille later."

The section he pointed to was several pages into the score and barely legible. Susanna did the best she could, disconcerted as she was by his voice.

And his nearness.

After she'd finished the notation in a shaky hand, he asked her to go back and play from the beginning. Susanna looked at him, then turned back to the manuscript, flipping through the first few pages. The first part had already been roughly scored for orchestra, but soon melded into a primary melody line with just some harmony and miscellaneous notes.

She eased her shoulders, flexed her fingers, and willed herself to relax. This was no concert hall, she reminded herself, and she was not a performer. She was merely helping Michael through some initial stages of his own music.

"Remember, Michael, I'm no virtuoso—"

"I know, I know. So you have said. Just...ah...play it as you like for now. In parts or with accompaniment. However you like."

At first Susanna had no conception of what she was playing, no real awareness of anything except the cool smoothness of the ivory under her fingertips, the absolute purity of sound as she pressed each key. She did exactly as she was told, initially playing one part at a time while Michael, still standing directly behind her, hummed a little and occasionally uttered, "No, that's not it," or, "Ah, yes! That's exactly what I want there."

It took Susanna a few minutes to realize he wasn't commenting on her playing, but rather on his own composition. The first time she brought together all the parts, she both felt and heard the stiffness in her technique, the utter lack of color and emotion in her playing, and she cringed.

But Michael didn't seem to notice. He merely went on humming, occasionally murmuring to himself. Then he moved around and began to tap lightly on the side of the piano to spur her on to a brisker, more strident rhythm.

The longer she played, the more the music began to reach out to her, beckoning her, drawing her out of herself. She started, caught off guard when Michael moved behind her and began to tap her shoulders with both hands, urging her forward, driving her on. After a moment, however, she lost her self-consciousness, and her fingers seemed to fly over the keyboard, improvising, adding, drawing forth an extensive accompaniment to the notes on the pages. The force of the music infused her spirit, raising her to the level of performance such glorious music demanded. The sounds and rhythms marched and danced, filling Susanna's soul, transforming the room into a concert hall, the Bösendorfer into an entire orchestra.

This was Michael's newest work, the *American Anthem*. He rarely spoke of it to her, but she had heard him and Paul working on it together, knew he often labored over it long hours into the night. Twice he had incorporated excerpts from it into the orchestra's concert program.

A distinctly nationalistic flavor ran through the work, as if it had been woven by the people of many nations, striving to form a whole. Although symphonic in its structure and complexity, it was an *earthy* folk music.

But more than anything else, it was a music of the spirit. Triumphant and rejoicing, it proclaimed a mighty faith, yet in places it was imbued with such plaintive melodies and sweetness it brought a kind of yearning to the soul.

Too quickly, it ended.

Susanna reached the end of the pages in front of her, her hands clinging to the last chord as she sat in stunned disbelief. The work was not even half complete;

obviously, it was destined to be a huge, expansive score. But even in its unfinished and preliminary state, it left her both exhausted and exhilarated, her pulse thundering, her mind racing.

On occasion, Susanna had caught such a strong sense of a composer through his music that she felt as if she *knew* him, or had at least caught a glimpse of his heart. So it was at this moment. She was convinced that she had heard the song of Michael's soul in his music. She had heard something of genius, certainly, but even more, she had heard something of God.

She felt acutely disappointed, even stricken, by the music's *incompleteness*. It was like being held captive by the power of a thundering, monumental story—only to find that it was a story without end.

Then she came to herself and realized that Michael's hands still rested on her shoulders.

The strength and warmth of his hands stole the breath from her, even as the *Anthem* had left her breathless. She tensed, and he dropped his hands away, leaving Susanna to wonder at the inexplicable feeling of abandonment that followed.

~

Michael heard her catch her breath, felt her stiffen beneath his touch. Immediately he released her, but too late. She jerked to her feet, made a hasty apology, and left the room.

He hadn't meant to offend her. In truth, he'd been so caught up in the music and her interpretation of it that his actions had been more instinctive than deliberate.

Yet more than once he'd been seized with a strong urge to touch her. Whenever she took his arm to guide him, or drew close enough that he caught the sunny scent of her hair, he would find himself overwhelmed by the desire to pull her closer. But always he stopped himself in time. He had no way of knowing whether she might welcome the familiarity or shrink from it. Or slap his face.

Now, standing alone at the piano, he wondered why he found it so difficult to sense Susanna's feelings. True, he was often frustrated by his inability to assess facial expressions, but he considered himself reasonably intuitive. Despite the blindness, he believed he was capable—at least in most circumstances—of gauging another person's response to him.

Not so with Susanna.

Just when he thought she might be warming to him, if only as a friend, he would hear a distance in her voice. He could never be quite certain whether she genuinely wanted to be with him, or simply tolerated him as she might have endured the attendance of a tiresome but unavoidable employer.

The very possibility made him cringe.

Michael found the idea of being *tolerated* just as abhorrent as being *pitied*. And to be tolerated by a woman who could make his head swim simply by entering a room was more than he could bring himself to face.

On the other hand, perhaps he was expecting too much. Given Susanna's earlier suspicion of him—induced in part by Deirdre's blatant lies, but also by his own attempts to conceal the truth—perhaps the fact that they had progressed as far as they had was no small achievement. At least she no longer seemed to mistrust him, no longer openly avoided him. At times, in fact, he could almost bring himself to believe that she was becoming...fond of him.

Of course, that might be nothing more than wishful thinking on his part. Or self-delusion.

Or abject foolishness.

Why should Susanna be even remotely attracted to him? He was blind. Years older than she. And as best he could recall his own shaggy reflection in the mirror, not exactly the stuff a young girl's romantic dreams were made of.

Worse, he had been her sister's husband, in a marriage that had been *disastrous*. When Susanna first arrived at Bantry Hill, Michael had attributed her coolness not only to her distrust of him, but also to the difficulty of her position. She was the sister of his deceased wife, yet she had been separated from Deirdre for years and had never even met him—her brother-in-law—until her arrival in America. Even her relationship with Caterina was complicated by the fact that she was not only the child's aunt and companion, but in addition functioned as a kind of nursemaid and governess.

Susanna had been thrust into a household of strangers in a foreign country, to live under the same roof with a man she didn't trust, a man who, for all she knew at the time, had made her sister's life one of unhappiness and tragedy. Such a situation would have strained the endurance of the most rugged, intractable personality, much less that of one so young and—unless he was badly mistaken—so unsophisticated and tenderhearted. And yet she *had* endured, and had come to trust him.

But even if she no longer suspected him of being the monster Deirdre had apparently made him out to be, Susanna might never be able to feel more than a passionless regard for him. A sisterly affection, at best.

The very idea brought up a swell of revulsion in Michael's throat. The role of elder brother might be more appealing than that of barbarian, but it was most definitely not the role he would choose to play in Susanna's life.

And what about Paul? Was it possible that Susanna and Paul might be attracted to each other? Paul could not speak of Susanna with anything less than admiration and warmth. And as for Susanna, even without the ability to see them together, he could sense that she held Paul in extremely high regard, that she genuinely liked him.

Everyone liked Paul, he reminded himself. How could they not? Pauli was lively, quick-witted, sensitive. What was there about him *not* to like?

Young girls seemed always to find Paul appealing, with his boyish charm and courtly manners, his zest for life. His youth...

Michael shook his head. *Santo cielo,* he himself was only thirty-seven! Not yet ready to be put out to pasture!

Then another thought occurred to him. Perhaps Susanna's awkwardness in his presence had nothing to do with him, and everything to do with her own background. Because of her steady nature, her considerable education, and the maturity that seemed to far outdistance her actual age, Michael tended to forget just how sheltered Susanna's life must have been. As the youngest daughter of parents who made their living from a small farm, she had no doubt lived a rustic existence—simple, quiet, and remote.

He had the impression—mostly from Deirdre—that their early lives had centered primarily around church and immediate family. The rebellious Deirdre apparently had broken out of that vacuum, managing to escape the isolation of the dairy farm.

Hadn't she often taunted him with tales of her various wild escapades, her many beaus, and the libertine company she'd kept, unbeknownst to her family? These stories might have been overblown, even fabricated, but Michael had no doubt that Deirdre would have found a way to create an active social life for herself.

The opposite was probably true of Susanna. He suspected she had stayed close to home, ill at ease with most people—especially men—and he doubted she had ever been romantically involved with anyone, at least not seriously.

If he was right, might that not account for at least some of the uneasiness he sensed in her when they were together? Granted, things were better between them now, but there were still times when she seemed uncomfortable, as if she couldn't wait to get away.

For his part, Michael sensed a major battle going on between his brain and his heart. He wanted to protect her, to shelter her. He wanted to know her better. He wanted to encourage her, to build her confidence, to help her realize her natural gift for music.

He wanted to hold her.

At various times, Susanna displayed the curiosity of a child, the idealism of a young girl, the reasoning of a scholar, and the bedrock steadiness of a saint. She had a way of laughing that made him wish for more, an enthusiasm that could strip away his well-placed defenses, a joy that lifted his heaviness of spirit, and a quiet faith that seemed to have been tried both by intellect and experience. She was guileless but not naive, agreeable but not complacent, practical but never predictable.

She could exasperate him one minute with a noncommittal remark about a piece of music, only to disarm him a moment later with an unsolicited but surprisingly insightful observation about the composer's intention for that music.

In spite of her youth, she was far more complex than any woman he had ever known. She was as fascinating as she was complicated, as frustrating as she was delightful.

The truth, rather than striking him like a thunderbolt, had been creeping in on him for weeks now, a stealthy but insistent shadow. He didn't know whether to moan with despair or sneer at his own foolishness.

For the first time in years—and against any common sense his infuriatingly romantic, Tuscan-Irish spirit might claim—he was falling in love.

In love with Susanna.

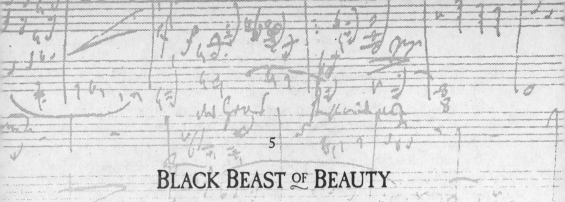

5

BLACK BEAST OF BEAUTY

Opportunity often shows its face in an
odd and most unlikely place...

IRISH PROVERB

The wind blew raw with winter riding on it when the word came down once again: no jobs today.

Conn was cold and sore discouraged, yet could not bring himself to leave the harbor. The thought of the worry in Vangie's eyes kept him ambling about the docks long after he had an excuse for being there. She was doing her best to keep their spirits up, but Conn knew too well the look of desperation that would greet him when he walked through the door again with empty pockets.

Hands shoved inside his jacket, he stood staring at the big ships rocking in the water. Crewmen roamed the decks: laughing, shouting, cursing, herding passengers aboard, or slinging their gear over their shoulders as they prepared to disembark. Nearby, a raggedy child wailed, clinging to the skirts of a mother wasted from starvation or illness. At a blast from a ship's horn, the child squalled even louder, but the mother turned her face away, paying no heed.

The usual assortment of immigrants milled about, anxiously searching for a familiar face or someone who would show them where to go. A dozen different languages could be heard, but—Irish was the most prevalent—here a Kerryman's sharp accent, there a Donegal lilt.

Conn knew he ought to go into the city and try some of the factories again, but hopelessness settled over him like a sodden blanket, thwarting his intentions and draining his strength. After countless weeks of trudging the streets and haunting the warehouses, hadn't he tried every possible place where work might be found? And all in vain. There was simply nowhere else to go.

The sound of a loud commotion farther up the docks caught his attention. He looked, but could see only a raucous crowd gathered near the pier. He turned to go, but stopped again when he heard a sound that chilled his blood.

A horse, screaming, wild with panic and pain. He had heard the sound too many times not to recognize it.

He shouldered his way through the crowd and saw two men trying to lead a big, powerful-looking stallion off a rusting, blistered ship. The great beast was savage in his resistance. He was a magnificent brute, midnight black and strongly muscled, but the fine, elegant head was encased in an iron muzzle, which the horse was fighting with a vengeance.

As Conn watched, the stallion reared, striking out with deadly hooves when one of the men attempted to restrain him.

Conn looked around. Close-by—but not *too* close, he noticed—stood a slender young fellow seemingly intent on the goings-on. He had the dusky skin and features of an Italian, but was dressed too fine for any Italian immigrant Conn had ever met up with.

At the moment, the lad looked a mite pale. Once he opened his mouth as if to call out something to the men struggling with the stallion, but the words seemed to die in his throat as he stood gawking at the scene before him.

Conn turned his attention back to the horse. The crowd was heckling the two men, shouting and jeering at their lame efforts to subdue the stallion. The handler was about to lose control, while the other, a thickset, middle-aged fellow with a drooping mustache, was clearly out of his element as he attempted to calm the animal. The poor beast was crazy with fear, no mistake about it. He wanted nothing more than to free himself, and he would kill anyone who happened to get in his way.

The jibes and catcalls, the confinement of the muzzle, and the inept efforts of the men trying to handle him had obviously served to fire the stallion's madness. When the fool hauling on the lead rope turned to bring a whip crashing down on the animal's lathered flank, Conn felt the beast's primal rage explode inside himself.

Every muscle in the horse's body seemed to knot with the effort to break free. He reared and hammered the boards with his mighty hooves. Ears pinned flat against his head, he swung toward the man on his left, then the other.

Scarcely realizing what he was doing, Conn wedged his way to the front of the crowd, stopping when he saw the stallion throw the handler off balance with a furious shake of his head. The ferret-faced man bellowed a loud curse as he jumped sideways. "I'll have no more truck with that black devil!" he roared. "This is as far as I go!"

Turning, he flung the whip down and stomped away, leaving the older man nearly helpless to control the stallion. As if he sensed the man's fear, the horse exploded in fresh fury, giving a vicious scream, lunging and heaving as he tried to wrest himself free.

Conn didn't think, but merely reacted. He threw himself past the crowd, yanked the lead from the gray-haired man, and shoved him out of the way.

Gleaming with sweat, the stallion lashed out with his powerful hooves at this new adversary. But Conn gamboled around him, staying out of his way, giving him no target as he continued to grip the lead rope.

The stallion shook his head, spraying saliva through the muzzle, but in spite of the animal's resistance, Conn managed to keep a firm grasp on the rope. The great black beast eyed him with raw malice as Conn began to speak in broken fragments of the old Irish tongue. He kept his voice quiet but steady, dropping it lower still as he coaxed and murmured to the enraged animal. When the horse dipped his head toward Conn as if to threaten him, Conn drew a step nearer to let the stallion catch his scent.

The sight of such a magnificent beast in that cruel iron contraption was a grief in itself, and Conn burned to free the animal from its confines. But for the moment, he had no choice. Trying to remove the muzzle would likely cost him a hand or an arm.

His shoulders ached from the strain, but he managed to retain his hold. By now the two were engaged in a deadly dance of power, each intent on forcing the other to capitulate. And all the while, Conn continued his low Irish drone, his eyes locked with those of the stallion.

Finally, the horse's wildness began to cool. Conn breathed a little easier as he saw the bunched muscles relax a bit. But those malevolent eyes followed his every move as he slowly and ever so carefully moved one hand to the horse's crest.

Immediately, the stallion froze, ears flattened, eyes glinting.

Conn stopped, then tried again. And again. On his third attempt the horse, though still guarded, seemed to realize this man meant him no harm, that he could tolerate his touch. For several minutes, Conn stroked him, first one side and then the other.

With his hand resting on the horse's withers, he stood, quietly waiting, until the stallion's skin ceased rippling and the dark eyes lost their wildness. Slowly, then, Conn unlocked the muzzle and carefully peeled it away, groaning to see the damage that had been done to that elegant head.

Ugly, seeping sores had formed from weeks of constant chafing. The animal had to be in absolute misery.

Conn felt the blood rush to his own head, pain hammering at his temples as he beheld what had been done to this noble beast. He could almost feel the animal's relief, to be finally shed of his torment.

Keeping a firm hold on the rope, he turned to the middle-aged man and his younger companion. "This horse needs attention right away. Those sores are infected."

The older man nodded and stood regarding Conn with a speculative expression. "We've lost the handler, as you saw for yourself," he said in a gravelly voice. "I've no idea how we'll get the animal upriver."

Another Irishman, Conn realized the moment the man opened his mouth. But, then, was there anyone in New York City who was *not* Irish?

He continued to stroke the stallion's back. Though still guarded and tense, the animal was at least standing quietly enough for now and no longer seemed bent on killing him.

"You work on the docks, do you?" asked the Irishman.

Conn shook his head. "There's no work to be had on the docks of late. At least, that's what we're told."

"So you're needing work then, are you?"

"Aye, that I am. Needing it in a bad way," Conn admitted. "I've found no job since we arrived, other than a bit of day labor, nothing that lasts."

"Dublin born, are you?"

"Not at all," Conn replied. "We're from the country—at least we were, until we had to move into Dublin City to survive. The wife and I were both born and raised in County Kildare."

The man nodded. From under his heavy eyebrows, his gaze traveled from Conn to the stallion, and then back to Conn. "You know horses."

It was a statement of fact, not a question. Conn nodded. "I do. I was a stable hand for a time, when I was a boy, and later I handled and took care of the stables for a fine trainer. One of Ireland's best." He glanced at the stallion. "This, now, is surely a magnificent beast."

The other man turned to look at his younger companion, who raised his eyebrows.

The Irishman turned back to Conn. "You would be well paid if you were to go along with us upriver and handle the horse."

Conn stared at the man. "Now, d'you mean? Today?"

The older man nodded. "We need to be leaving right away. And this lad and myself are no match for that devil."

Conn's hand must have tightened on the stallion's back. The animal snorted, head lifting as his ears flattened again.

Instantly Conn gentled his touch, and the horse settled down again.

Conn looked from the stallion to the Irishman. "I expect I could go," he finally said. "But I'd have to be letting the wife know. She'll fret something terrible if I don't turn up before dark."

"Send one of the boyos with a message," the other man suggested, jerking his head toward a group of young boys playing along the pier. "I'll pay."

The Irishman watched Conn with an expression that seemed to indicate he had more to say. After a moment, he tipped his cap forward a little and crossed his sturdy arms over his chest. "'Tis not for me to be offering anything for certain, you understand, but you might give a thought to talking with my employer when we arrive. We lost our trainer and stableman some time back, and he's in need of a man he can count on." He stopped. "He wants a good man with the horses as soon as possible, especially with this spawn of the devil arriving. There might be a job for you if you're interested."

Conn's heart leaped to his throat. "Is that so now?"

"'Tis. As I said, I can't make any promises, but after seeing the way you handled this ill-tempered beast, I'd be willing to vouch for you."

He paused, eyeing Conn for another second or two, then added, "My employer won't stand for a drinker or a scrapper."

"Man, I am neither."

The older man's eyes held Conn's for a moment more. Then he raised a hand and gave a sharp whistle to hail one of the boys at the pier. Three came running, and he dispatched the quickest of them with a coin and the message Conn repeated for Vangie.

"All right, then," the man said, turning back to Conn. "Do what you must with that black *pooka* and let us be on our way."

"How do I call you?" Conn asked.

"The name is Dempsey. And this here is Paul Santi. He's cousin to my employer, Mr. Emmanuel."

"And the horse, does he have a name?"

"Aye, as I was told, he's to be called 'Amerigo.'"

Conn turned away from the other two and looked at the stallion straight on, deliberately masking his sympathy for the animal, which was still a grand piece of horseflesh in spite of the evident abuse. The black beast eyed him in turn, his ears pricked.

"So, then—*Amerigo*—" Conn said, "will you come with me like a gentleman or must we be having it out again?"

The dark eyes shifted, and for a moment Conn braced himself for yet another skirmish. But finally the black stallion gave a princely toss of his head, snorted, then, quieted, as if in concession to Conn's authority.

Conn watched him, strangely moved and even saddened to see the horse's grudging submission. "I know, big fella," he said softly in the stallion's ear. "I know how this must gall you. 'Tis a bitter thing to have no say in your own welfare, to be treated as nothing more than a piece of meat, your only value the strength of your back and what you can earn for your greedy master."

He paused as the dark, world-weary gaze seemed to take his measure. "I promise you this, Amerigo," he said, his voice lower still. "You give me no grief, and you will get none from me. You will find that I am a fair man." He paused. "We will hope the same can be said of your new owner."

As they left the docks, Conn's mind played the Irishman's words over again. *"There might be a job for you if you're interested..."* He tried not to get his hopes too high, but how could he *not* hope? After all this time—all the disappointments and discouragement, the roads that seemed to lead to nowhere, the bitter taste of failure on his tongue from morning till night—what else did he have *but* hope?

Was it possible that this big, mean-looking beast might actually turn out to be more blessing than curse?

It was all he could do not to laugh aloud at such an unlikely idea.

Especially when he saw the hot-tempered *pooka* glaring at him as if he'd like nothing better than to dismantle Conn's head from his shoulders.

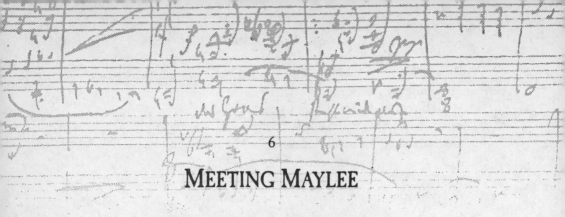

6

MEETING MAYLEE

Somewhere there waiteth in this world of ours
For one lone soul, another lonely soul—
Each chasing each through all the weary hours,
And meeting strangely at one sudden goal...

EDWIN ARNOLD

After they closed the office for the afternoon, Dr. Bethany Cole and Dr. Andrew Carmichael settled themselves in the buggy, pulled their lap robes snugly around them, and set off for Mulberry Street.

The raw wind held a threat of sleet or snow, but Bethany had finally managed to convince Andrew that she didn't mind the cold. In fact, she actually enjoyed it—up to a point. What she really liked was the opportunity to study the busy city streets. New York was like an ongoing stage play, featuring new dramas with new actors and different scenes around every corner. Her fascination with the city never ceased.

At the moment she was following with great interest the progress of a pig and an extremely large black-and-tan dog as they made their way down Elizabeth Street. At first glance, she'd thought the pair seemed unlikely friends, but on closer inspection she saw that one was actually trying to muscle the other out of the street. When they reached the corner, the pig staked out a heap of garbage for his own, attacking it with zeal. When the dog pushed in as if to share a meal, Bethany assumed the pig, smaller by half, would simply leave the spoils and move on. Instead, the fierce little creature turned on the dog with such aggression that the startled hound took off as if he'd been attacked by a wild boar.

Bethany laughed, and Andrew, who had also been following the implausible scene, joined her. Once they were past, Bethany turned to him. "You said you'd tell me about the patients we're calling on this afternoon."

He nodded. "Have you heard of Michael Emmanuel?"

"The musician? Of course. He's a patient?"

"No, his little girl. She had a bad case of croup some time back. Had it twice, in fact—both very nasty bouts. She seems to be doing nicely now, but I stop in on occasion, just to check on her."

"But you actually *know* Michael Emmanuel? We're going to his *home*?"

Andrew shot her an amused look, and Bethany realized she must have sounded like an awe-struck schoolgirl. "Sorry. I suppose I'm something of a fan. I attended his opening concert this season. I also heard him sing once, in Philadelphia, before his accident. He was incredible! What a terrible thing to happen to him, losing his sight."

Andrew nodded. "I never had the opportunity to hear him sing, but I seldom miss one of the orchestra's concerts, if I can help it. Well—you'll meet him this afternoon, and I think you'll like him very much. He's quite a remarkable man. They live upriver, so we'll make that our final call of the day."

"I must say, I'm impressed, Andrew. I had no idea when I came to work with you that I'd be meeting celebrities."

"Much as I covet your admiration," he said dryly, "I expect Michael Emmanuel is the only celebrity you'll be meeting through your association with me. As you've undoubtedly noticed by now, my patient list inclines toward a more modest social class. And in that regard, I should fill you in on our first call."

He reined in, allowing an omnibus to pass ahead of them. "Let's just say that while Caterina Emmanuel will no doubt *steal* your heart, I'm afraid our next patient will more than likely *break* your heart."

~

The orphanage was a bleak, three-story building on Mulberry Street with half a dozen sagging steps leading up to the front door. The windows were small and narrow, the roof in need of repair. Beneath a dull afternoon sky and devoid of any hint of color or greenery, the place reminded Bethany of every sorry-looking, grim institution she had ever encountered.

Inside, the long, uncarpeted hallways were cold and dim and quiet—too quiet for a place where children lived. The bare walls were relieved only by peeling paint and an occasional gouge in the plaster, and the few windows were narrow and uncurtained. But although the air was stale, it was noticeably free of the unpleasant mix of odors often associated with similar establishments.

"I suppose it *could* be more depressing, though it would take some doing," she said in a near-whisper. Something about the Cora Wylie Children's Home discouraged a normal tone of voice.

"I know." Andrew's voice was hushed as well. "But it's not really as bad as it looks. The place needs renovating, of course, but that takes money, and there's never enough for the essentials, much less a healthy infusion of light and color.

Still, there's an excellent staff here: qualified and compassionate. I can assure you, that's not always the case among the metropolitan children's homes."

They passed three little girls who were being shepherded down the hall by an older companion. They all smiled at Andrew, and the older girl made a reply to his greeting. For Bethany, they had only curious looks.

At the end of the corridor, Andrew took her arm and guided her to the hallway on the left. "This way. Maylee is in a room to herself."

This was a shorter corridor, and as they approached the room at the very end on the right, Andrew pressed Bethany's arm to slow their progress.

"Just a reminder that Maylee is extremely bright and perceptive," he said. "She's not hard of hearing or slow-witted or any of the things people sometimes assume when they meet her for the first time."

With a quick glance in Bethany's direction, Andrew rapped lightly on the door, identifying himself but not waiting for a response before pushing the door open onto a small, neat room. Its corners were shadowed in the weak gray light seeping through a solitary window, but the bedding and curtains splashed color enough to dispel the gloom.

"Dr. Carmichael!"

"Well, Maylee, how are we today?"

Andrew motioned Bethany closer, and she went to stand beside him. "This is Dr. Cole, Maylee," he said, reaching to take the child's hand. "I told you about her last time I was here. Dr. Cole will be working with me from now on."

"Hello, Maylee. I'm very pleased to meet you." Bethany smiled and held the child's gaze. At this moment, she was thankful Andrew had taken the time to prepare her for this first meeting.

Maylee sat in the middle of a small iron bed, surrounded by pillows and a stack of books. She was even smaller than Bethany had expected—tiny and delicate, almost doll-like. Her face was thin and wrinkled, with small, sharp features and almost no eyebrows or lashes. Only a few wisps of snowy white hair dusted her scalp. Her elbows and knees appeared painfully swollen, and her hands exhibited the "liver spots" associated with the elderly.

She appeared to be an extremely small, wizened old lady.

She was eleven years old.

Bethany's heart wrenched in pity. She had never seen a disease like this before.

"You did it again, Dr. Carmichael!" Maylee exclaimed. "You asked me how *we* are doing today. Why do doctors and nurses always say 'we'? There's only one of me, after all."

Without waiting for a reply, Maylee turned her attention to Bethany. "Hello, Dr. Cole. How do you like working with Dr. Carmichael? Is he *very* difficult?"

The girl's voice was thin and high-pitched, but Bethany found herself immediately captivated by her smile and the distinct glint of humor dancing in her eyes. She reminded Bethany of a bright little bird, alert and eager.

"Well, I would say that Dr. Carmichael is actually quite easy to get along with," she replied. "*Most* of the time."

"And is he a *good* doctor?"

"Oh, he's an excellent doctor, I assure you," Bethany said with a straight face. "But hasn't he already told you that?"

Maylee threw her hands up and giggled. "Yes! Often!"

"That's just about enough from you two," said Andrew. He feigned an indignant look. "I would hope for a little more respect from my own associate and my favorite patient. Now then, Maylee—let's just have a look at you and listen to your heart, shall we?"

"See? You did it again! We can't *both* have a look at me and listen to my heart, now can we?"

Andrew summoned a stern expression as he removed the stethoscope from his medical case. "I was speaking of Dr. Cole and myself. Do you know what 'precocious' means, young lady?"

"Maturing early? Advanced for my age?" Maylee burst out laughing.

Bethany marveled that this child could find humor in her condition. That she could actually laugh at herself, given what she must endure, was nothing short of astonishing.

Apparently there was no research—at least none that Andrew had been able to come up with—dealing with a disorder such as Maylee's. He was at a complete loss as to any form of treatment. Two other physicians who had consulted on her condition leaned toward the influence of external agents, but Andrew strongly believed Maylee's disease to be the result of some sort of genetic mutation.

Bethany had seen the helplessness in his eyes when he told her about Maylee. Now, after meeting the child for herself, she understood his frustration. As physicians, there should be something they could do, some sort of treatment that would at least improve the quality of her life—a life that was certain to be woefully brief.

The painful reality was that the girl was aging at an incredible pace, and there was nothing anyone could do to stop it. Given her present rate of decline, Andrew projected that Maylee could not possibly live more than another year, if that.

At Andrew's suggestion, and with Maylee's consent, Bethany listened to the girl's heart and checked her pulse. The readings reflected the vitals of an elderly woman rather than those of an eleven-year-old child.

Andrew resumed his examination, this time concentrating on the girl's swollen and obviously tender joints. Maylee warmed to him—indeed, seemed to blossom under his attention. And Bethany remembered something else Andrew had told her about the unfortunate child: although she lived in an institution among dozens of other children, for all intents and purposes she lived alone.

It wasn't so much that the other children shunned her. To the contrary, Maylee was accepted and well-liked by the others. But given her physical limitations, especially the increasing stiffness of her joints and the fatigue that resulted from the slightest exertion, the girl found it all but impossible to participate in the normal activities of childhood.

She continued to study her lessons and played quietly by herself in her room. Sometimes, when she was strong enough, she would entertain one or two of the younger children by reading to them or telling them stories. What seemed to bring the girl more comfort and enjoyment than anything else were her books. Books, Andrew had told Bethany, were Maylee's best friends.

But how wretchedly unfair that books should be the child's *only* friends.

~

Later, after leaving the orphanage and starting for the ferry, Andrew seemed unusually pensive. Bethany was struggling with her own emotions, and neither spoke for several minutes.

The visit with Maylee had left her filled with a chafing pain that was anything but "professional." In fact, she couldn't remember that she had ever felt such a mixture of anguish—and anger—about a patient.

"Are you all right?" Andrew asked quietly.

Bethany cleared her throat. "It's so unfair! Isn't there *anything* we can do?"

He gave a long sigh. "Believe me, Bethany, I share your frustration. This is one of those times when I feel more like a failure than a physician."

Bethany looked at his swollen hands grasping the reins and saw that they were trembling.

"I've read every text, written to everyone I can think of, including some friends in Europe—anyone who might know something I don't. But not a one of them has ever seen a case like Maylee's. It's as if she's the only child ever to be afflicted in such a manner. The only thing I've found that helps at all, so far as the swelling and the discomfort, is what I take myself. Salicylic acid. That at least seems to give her some temporary relief."

Bethany's gaze traveled from his hands to his lean profile. His expression was uncommonly strained. "Do you ever get angry, Andrew?"

He nodded, not looking at her. "More often than you might think."

"But who do you get angry *with*?"

"With myself, I suppose. For not knowing enough, not being able to do enough. Or sometimes I suppose I simply get angry with *life* in general. For being so unfair."

"But not with God."

"God didn't do this to Maylee, Bethany."

"Then who did?" Outrage welled up in her and overflowed. It wasn't as if she hadn't attended critically ill or dying children before today. Even in the short time she'd been practicing medicine, she had encountered far too many cases that kept her awake nights.

But the disorder that would eventually claim Maylee's life seemed especially cruel. A little girl shouldn't have to go through such an ordeal. She shouldn't have to watch herself turn into an old woman before she reached puberty. She shouldn't have to hear the doctor she obviously admired and trusted admit that he could do nothing—absolutely nothing—to help her.

A child should not have to die before she'd had a chance to live.

"Don't you ever question God, Andrew? Don't you ever wonder how to reconcile what we're taught about God's goodness, His compassion, when you see some of the terrible, ugly—*heartless*—things that happen to people? To innocent children?"

He turned to look at her. "Do I ever question why God allows these things? Yes, of course I do. How could any physician *not* question? But do I believe God is some sort of a vindictive spirit wielding His power on a whim—blessing some and cursing others? No. I don't for a minute believe He inflicted Maylee with this condition. He loves her more than that."

"He may not have caused it, but he *could* prevent it! If God loves her so much, then why doesn't He simply take it from her? Or at least provide a means of mitigating the symptoms and easing her misery?"

Andrew's reply was slow in coming. "He could have prevented the Cross, too," he said quietly, "but He didn't. I suppose if we could explain *that*, we could explain just about anything."

He turned to her again, his expression still solemn, but gentle. "I don't have an answer for you, Bethany. I can't even answer many of my own questions. The only thing I know for certain is that God's love is beyond our comprehension. In fact, it seems to me that His love is as much a mystery as His will. As to why He does what He does or doesn't do what we think He should do—well, I suppose that's where faith comes in. Sometimes there's simply nothing else to do but trust Him."

Bethany stared at him. One of the fundamental differences between Andrew's faith and her own was that his seemed to be inextricably woven into everything he did. He stepped boldly into the arena of life, went head to head with its injustices and evils, its challenges and struggles, securely armed with his faith. If he succeeded at what he attempted, then God was good and to be thanked. If he failed, well, God was *still* good and to be thanked. Simply because he was God.

Bethany, on the other hand, was more likely to leave her faith behind the lines for fear it wouldn't withstand the blows of battle. Her resolve, her own strength of will, and her stubborn refusal to concede defeat kept her going. Or so she had once believed.

Now she wasn't so sure. "I'm not like you, Andrew," she said hesitantly. "My faith is no match for yours. I have so many questions—"

He regarded her with a tilt of his head and a curious look. "Do you really think I don't? And how do we go about measuring faith, Bethany? That seems to me a futile effort altogether. We can't know very much about our faith at all until we find ourselves in a situation that tests it. Then, I expect we're often surprised by what we discover. About our faith—and ourselves."

His next words seemed carefully considered. "You asked me a moment ago if I ever question God. I think what I question is *life*, not God. It seems to me that life itself prompts continual questions. But the more I question, the more I find myself believing that the answer to all my questions is God. In fact, it seems to me that He's the *only* answer that can be trusted."

He shrugged and gave a self-conscious smile. "Sorry. I didn't mean to go on."

Bethany made no reply. Although she was reluctant to admit that she didn't quite understand what he was getting at, he had certainly given her something to think about. At the moment, however, the only thing that seemed to be registering was the realization that she no longer felt like shaking her fist at heaven and shouting *Why?*

Andrew reached to take her hand. "If it's any consolation, Bethany, I do understand. I'm not exactly a stranger to doubt or frustration."

"Andrew—you couldn't possibly understand how I feel. You're simply too good a man."

A look of dismay darted across his features.

"You've said that before, and it's not so." His tone was unnaturally sharp. "I'm not a 'good man,' Bethany. Not at all. Not like you think."

Bethany smiled to herself but kept silent. She had no intention of involving herself in a debate with Andrew about his character. For one thing, he was far too modest to admit to the admirable traits she saw in him. And for another, she wasn't ready to risk letting him see the strength of her feelings for him.

Although she wasn't at all sure how much longer she could manage to conceal those feelings.

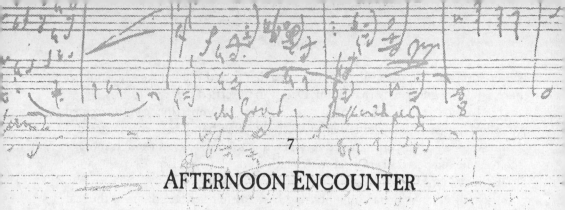

7

AFTERNOON ENCOUNTER

A copper-skinned six-footer,
Hewn out of the rock.

JOSEPH CAMPBELL

They were nearing the docks on the way to the ferry when they encountered Sergeant Frank Donovan. He was standing near the entrance to the harbor, stabbing the air with an index finger as he harangued a group of young boys.

Andrew drew the buggy to a stop and called out to him. The sergeant turned, his disagreeable expression clearing after a second or two. He made a gesture that they should wait, then turned and dispatched the youths huddled nearby with a chop of his hand.

"And it's a cell for the lot of you if I catch you bedevilin' old man Potkin again!" he shouted after them.

He approached the buggy, rapping his night stick against the palm of one hand. "And what would two of our city's most eminent physicians be doing in this part of town?" He doffed his hat to Bethany with a smile that made his dark eyes dance. "On a mission of mercy, are we?"

"Actually, we're on the way to the ferry, you rascal," said Andrew. "Dr. Cole and I are going upriver on a call."

The police sergeant fastened his full attention on Bethany, and she forced a smile in return. Donovan was tall, like Andrew. A big strapping Irishman, he gave off such an air of hardness and strength that he might have been hewn from a slab of granite.

And something about his eyes led Bethany to believe that he could be just as cold.

Andrew's friendship with this man puzzled her. She couldn't imagine how he and Frank Donovan could have possibly been more different. Andrew's strength and quiet masculinity seemed to derive from a deep inner peace—a *stillness* within himself—while the Irish police sergeant struck her as a man burning with energy.

Whether it was a fiery nature or raw power that fueled the flames, she couldn't have said. She knew only that Frank Donovan unsettled her.

He had a way of looking at her that bordered on impertinence but stopped just short of being downright offensive. On the other hand, his behavior toward Andrew appeared to be prompted by a genuine fondness, even though most of the time he tempered his respect with a biting edge of cynicism.

"Upriver, eh? Hobnobbing with the gentry, are we?"

The policeman was watching her, and Bethany felt her face flame at the realization that he'd caught her staring. She forced herself to meet his gaze straight on, and he lifted a dark eyebrow in an expression of wry amusement—as if he were completely aware of her discomfiture and enjoying it immensely.

"Not everyone up the river is gentry, Frank," Andrew was saying. "Actually, we're calling at the Emmanuel estate, up near West Point."

"Emmanuel? The blind man?"

For just an instant, Bethany detected a glint of irritation in Andrew's eyes. "Michael Emmanuel, yes," he said. "The *musician*."

"How did you get mixed up with *him*?"

Andrew knitted his brows together in a dark frown. "His daughter is my patient, Frank. I'm not 'mixed up' with him."

Frank Donovan crossed his arms over his chest and tipped his hat farther back on his head. His gaze traveled to Bethany, then back to Andrew. "No need to get tetchy, Doc. You do seem to get yourself hooked up with some strange company at times, is all."

"I suppose I do, but you can be sure there's nothing in the least strange about Michael Emmanuel. He's an interesting man, and his daughter is quite a delightful child."

The policeman regarded him with a thoughtful look. "That may be, Doc, but there was a bit of talk at the time of the wife's accident, you might recall."

"There's always talk, Frank. And seldom much truth behind it."

Donovan shrugged. Turning to Bethany, he again lifted his hat to her. "Well, then, I won't be keeping you from your patients. You two have a care now."

Without another word, he turned and walked away.

Andrew shook his head, smiling a little.

"Have you been friends long?" Bethany said after a long silence.

"A few years now." Andrew paused. "I know Frank can be aggravating at times. But he's a good man, really. A fine policeman, an *honest* one. And he has more courage than ten men—perhaps too much for his own good."

When Bethany made no reply, he added, "He doesn't mean any harm. It's just his way."

She shot him a dubious look.

"Really," he insisted. "Once you get to know him, you'll see what I mean. Frank just takes some getting used to."

Bethany had no intention of getting used to Frank Donovan. There was a *hardness* about the man that never failed to put her off. He always seemed to be darkly amused by his surroundings, but Bethany didn't for a minute believe he was as shallow as he pretended to be. To the contrary, she suspected that the Irish police sergeant possessed an intellect every bit as formidable as the courage Andrew had referred to—and a temper that could turn downright nasty if provoked.

And there was something else, something she couldn't quite define. The few times she had been around Frank Donovan, there had been a moment—albeit fleeting—when his behavior toward her seemed to reflect, not so much contempt or dislike, but *suspicion*. As if he didn't quite trust her.

Andrew, of course, hadn't noticed. Andrew seldom saw anything but the good in others. In fact, for a man of his intelligence and experience, he often seemed surprisingly *unworldly*, perhaps even a little naive.

An inexplicable trait, but one she found endearing. And also, at times, exasperating.

∽

Andrew watched Bethany closely, secretly glad that she didn't seem to take to Frank Donovan. Perhaps he should have made more of an effort to point out his friend's good points.

But in truth, he was relieved. Frank, after all, did have a way with women. Andrew didn't really begrudge him the ease with which he attracted the ladies, although he *had* occasionally wondered what it would be like to have a dash of Frank's appeal.

Most of the time, however, Andrew actually found Frank's "Irish charm" rather amusing; he even enjoyed teasing him about it every now and then. But this was one time he was glad that Frank's charm hadn't worked its magic.

Andrew held no false illusions about himself. He knew he was a rather plain, decidedly awkward man. Awkward physically and, at least around women, awkward socially as well.

He hadn't minded all that much. Not until he'd met Bethany. Even then, he had been almost glad when she brought up the subject of his arthritis. After all, if she attributed his ungainliness to the disease, she might not realize that even if he didn't have an ache or a pain about him, he'd probably still be a bit of a dolt. At least around her.

He glanced at her again. She was studying the ships in the harbor, and he took advantage of the moment to indulge in an unhurried view of her profile—which to his way of thinking was nothing short of a work of art.

When she turned and favored him with an unexpectedly bright smile, he whipped his head around so hard he felt his neck crack.

Oh, he was in a fine fix, all right. A fine fix, indeed. He only hoped Frank didn't catch on to the state he was in.

Andrew counted him as his closest friend, but the thought of Frank's merciless teasing made him shudder. The man could be downright relentless when he caught hold of something that amused him. And the idea of Andrew being smitten with a woman like Bethany Cole would almost certainly strike Frank as a huge joke.

And rightly so, he thought grimly.

~

Michael Emmanuel had insisted they stay for dinner, so it was nearly nine when they boarded the ferry. The mist-laced wind off the river made the night seem even colder. Bethany secured her scarf more snugly about her neck as they settled themselves for the ride.

"Well," she said, as much to herself as to Andrew, "so much for preconceptions."

Andrew tugged at the collar of his coat. "Preconceptions?"

Bethany nodded. "Michael Emmanuel. And Susanna. I had them pictured altogether different from the way they are."

"What were you expecting?"

Bethany furrowed her brow. What *had* she expected? Certainly not the unaffected ease with which the blind musician had hosted their evening. Nor the surprising quietness and gentleness of the voice that had once thrilled thousands. As for Susanna, Bethany had taken immediately to the young woman's warm demeanor and her quick, friendly smile.

"I would never have guessed Michael Emmanuel would be so…comfortable. So easy to be with. He seems so unaffected, so unimpressed with himself. And I really liked Susanna. She's lovely, isn't she?"

Before Andrew could reply, Bethany added, "She's much younger than I thought she'd be, but she has a steadiness about her that makes her seem older, somehow. And I sensed that she might like to be friends."

"No doubt it gets rather lonely for her up here, isolated as they are. Especially since she's relatively new to the area. To the *country*."

"It's like something from a novel."

"What's like something from a novel?"

"Their story." She turned to look at him. "Really, Andrew—think about it. The sister of a man's deceased wife travels across the ocean to care for a child she's never seen and ends up falling in love with her famous brother-in-law."

Andrew snapped his head around to stare at her. "Why on earth would you think Susanna's in love with Michael?"

Bethany rolled her eyes. Men. You had to hit them over the head with a board sometimes. "Surely you've seen the way she looks at him?"

His eyes grew wider still. "No, I can't say that I have." He paused. "How *does* she look at him?"

Bethany sighed. She didn't consider herself a romantic, not in the least, but there was something about Michael and Susanna that had captured her interest—and her imagination.

"Just take my word for it, Andrew. Susanna Fallon is in love with her brother-in-law. And Michael is in love with her. It's just that neither of them knows it yet."

He laughed. "You seem awfully sure of yourself. Is this some sort of womanly intuition, or are you really as positive as you sound?"

"Both. You'll see."

"I think you might be dangerous," he said, shaking his head. "A physician who also reads minds."

"It has nothing to do with reading minds. It's simply a matter of being aware of those around you. The way they look at each other. Or *don't* look at each other. The way they touch. Or don't touch. A change in the tone of voice."

She went on, intrigued by her own discovery. "I wonder if Michael knows he tends to flush a little every time Susanna opens her mouth. If the man could see, he'd never take his eyes off her. Yes, he's definitely smitten."

The faint amusement that had brimmed in Andrew's eyes only an instant before now gave way to a look that could only be described as startled. Whatever accounted for the change, he seemed to recover quickly.

"Dangerous," he repeated with a nod. "Definitely dangerous." He nodded firmly, then added, "You did like them, though?"

"Oh, goodness, yes! They're absolutely delightful! I can understand how you and Michael might become fast friends. You think a great deal alike."

Indeed, it struck Bethany that Andrew's friendship with Michael Emmanuel made much more sense than the high regard in which he seemed to hold that awful Frank Donovan.

The thought of the annoying Irish policeman brought a question to mind. "Andrew, what did Frank Donovan mean today, about there being 'talk' when Michael's wife died?"

Andrew didn't answer right away. "It was all gossip, really. You know how people like to speculate on the misfortunes of the famous. Michael's wife was killed in a carriage accident not far from their home. Because of the lateness of the hour and the fact that she was alone, there were some rather wild rumors going round. There was a terrible thunderstorm that night, and no one could quite figure why a woman would have been out alone in such weather." He stopped. "Some of the rumors hinted that there was trouble between her and Michael, that in fact she was having an affair at the time."

Bethany shuddered. "How awful. As if he hasn't had enough tragedy."

"Yes, well, as I said, there was a great deal of gossip, but I have no idea if there was any truth in it."

He seemed eager to change the subject. "I believe Susanna was greatly impressed with you," he said. "Did you notice how many questions she asked about our work—about *your* work?"

Bethany rolled her eyes. "In truth, I don't want Susanna to be *impressed* with me. I'd like it better if we could just be friends." She paused. "Actually, I hope we can be friends with both Susanna *and* Michael. And that little Caterina—what a charmer *she* is! They're a delightful family."

"But they're *not* a family," Andrew reminded her quietly. "Not really."

"True," she said. "But that could change."

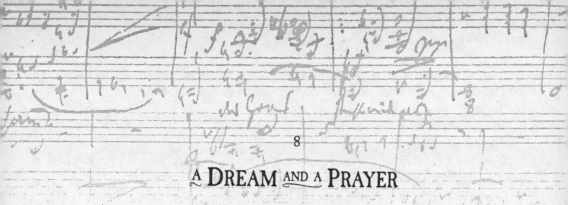

8

A Dream and a Prayer

I prayed for good fortune...
God gave me dreams.
I dreamed of high places...
God gave me wings.

NELL GRACE MACGOVERN

By the looks of him, a body might have thought that the man had either gone daft entirely or else was deep in his cups.

Since Conn MacGovern had never been a man for the drink, Vangie could only conclude that some sort of derangement had suddenly descended upon her husband.

He swept through the door like a mad Viking, an idiotic grin plastered from ear to ear, his face as red as if he had eaten live coals for supper. Now that Vangie knew he was not lying dead in a ditch, the dread that had been building inside her all evening gave way to anger.

"Where have you been, man? I've been out of my mind with worry!"

For a moment he looked puzzled. "I sent a boy—"

"A boy who said you would be away a few hours! In case you haven't noticed, it's suppertime! And a *late* suppertime at that!"

To her amazement, he laughed. A deep, full-throated, booming laugh of a kind Vangie had not heard from him in an age. And then he came charging toward her, lifting her from her feet and swinging her around until the room swam in front her.

"*Conn!* Stop it now! Stop it, you great *amadan*! What's come over you?"

The twins were seated round the table, with Baby Emma in her chair between them. Renny Magee was putting wood on the stove, while Nell Grace ladled soup into the younger ones' bowls. All as one, they stopped to gape, first at their father, then at Vangie. Wee Emma clapped her hands and shrieked, as if she thought the antics of her parents were grand fun.

No more had the words left her mouth than it occurred to Vangie that only one thing could be responsible for the high spirits of her husband.

"Conn?"

"A job, love! I have me a job!"

Vangie gave a small cry. "You don't!"

"Ah, but I do! And not just any job, my beauty! Oh, no, not at all. A grand job it is, and with a fine place for us to live as well!"

Vangie held her breath, afraid to believe.

He sobered a bit then. "'Tis the truth, love. I'd not joke about something as big as this."

Vangie knew then that it was so. She knew it from the beam of confidence she had not seen in his eyes for much too long a time, knew it from the scarcely remembered lift of his shoulders, the strong thrust of his chin, and the way he was looking at her as if he had at last brought her a basket of joy instead of yet another bucket of despair.

"Oh, glory be to God," she choked out, barely able to stand without buckling.

"Well, tell us, man! Tell us everything!"

~

And so tell them he did, and took great delight in the telling. Conn perched himself by the fire and rubbed his hands together in anticipation. He deliberately drew out his tale, gaining great satisfaction as he watched the astonished faces of his wife and children, who were circled about him as if he held court. He stopped to answer their eager questions, sparing no detail, for hadn't it been a long time indeed since he'd had anything worthwhile to relate to them, much less an account that would bring such excitement to their eyes?

"An *estate*, do you say?" This from Vangie.

"Oh, love—wait until you see it! You can't imagine! Why, it's even grander than the Lighton Mansion back home!"

"It *isn't*!"

"I give you my word, the place is a palace!"

"And you are quite sure that we are to come, too, Da?" Nell Grace asked, her eyes enormous and shining. "There's truly room for us all?"

"'Tis just as I told you. You don't think I'd be going without you, now do you?" Conn reached a hand to his daughter's hair.

"It seems that years ago the estate belonged to a wealthy old man," he went on to explain. "In addition to the big house, there's another lodging on the property, where the caretaker and his wife used to live. It's empty now. The present manager and his wife—the Dempseys, who came across from Ireland just as we did—live in the big house. The caretaker's place is where we will be living. 'Tis a fine, sturdy house, it is, well-built and clean. And doesn't it even have a few pieces of furniture for our use?"

"It's too much to take in, Conn! Can this truly be happening to us?"

"Ah, there's more, love," he assured her. "But first let me tell you about my new employer, Mr. Emmanuel—they call him the Maestro, him being a great musician, you see. He's an Italian man, did I say that? And in spite of his obviously being very well-to-do, he doesn't seem a bit puffed up about himself, not at all. In fact, I'd say he's a real gentleman, exceedingly well-educated and fine-spoken." He stopped. "Poor fellow, though. According to Dempsey, the Maestro lost his wife only last year in a carriage accident."

"How awful!" said Vangie.

"It is that. He has his little girl, though," Conn continued, "a lass of four years. His sister-in-law lives there, too, as well as a cousin—a young Italian fellow who nearly died right in the middle of the harbor from fear of the stallion."

He smiled at the recollection of the boy's pasty face and boggling eyes. "And then there's the older couple I mentioned. Dempsey manages the place, and his wife does the cooking and the cleaning. But the two of them are getting along in years, and Mr. Emmanuel is after making things a bit easier for them. When he discovered that I had a wife and a grown daughter—not to mention two healthy sons—who would be willing to work, he seemed pleased altogether."

He paused to catch his breath. "Did I tell you the man is blind?"

"*Blind?*" Vangie cried. "Oh, the poor man! And him having lost his wife as well. So much sorrow for him to bear, Conn."

Conn nodded. "Aye, but he's not a man who wears his feelings on the outside. He strikes me as the type who keeps his own counsel. He's very soft-spoken and I suspect he's quiet-natured all through. Dempsey says he's a man of great intellect, with the music and all—a famous man at that."

"Oh, Da!" Nell Grace stared at him as if he had risen an extra foot in height even as she watched. "And to think he employed you right then and there as he did! He must place great faith in you."

"And why wouldn't he?" Vangie said. "It's clear this Mr. Emmanuel knows quality when he sees it."

She immediately clapped a hand over her mouth. "But he can't see you at all! Oh, Conn, what if I say something as foolish as that in front of the man, God forbid?"

Then she smiled at him, her eyes shining. "Well, but whether he can see or not, 'tis obvious he could sense the kind of man you are."

Conn fought down a surge of pleasure at the pride glowing in his wife's eyes. In truth, he couldn't quite forget the way his new employer had made him feel during their discussion. "Well," he said, "the Maestro did consult with his man, Dempsey, and with his cousin as well, in private, before he offered me the position.

But only for a short time. Indeed, it seemed to me that he had made up his mind before he conferred with them. And I would have to say"—Conn realized at that instant just how much it pleased him to say it—"that he treated me almost as an equal throughout the entire interview. He treated me with *respect*, Vangie. As one man to another."

Conn's heart threatened to melt at the sight of his wife's damp eyes, her trembling smile. He pulled both her and Nell Grace close, putting an arm around each of them. "It would seem that the good Lord has answered our prayers," he said, feigning a gruff tone to conceal his own unreliable emotions. "I have a job, and we are to have a new home. And not in this wretched city, but in a place where there is land and clean air."

"And *horses*!" put in James. "Don't forget the horses, Da!"

"Well, now, it's not likely I would be forgetting the horses, son." Conn tousled the lad's hair. "Seeing as how it's a horse I have to thank for getting me this job in the first place!"

⁓

Renny had hovered near the stove throughout the entire exchange, her feelings going into a spin as she heard MacGovern's spirited account of his day.

It was plain that the lot of them had forgotten her presence, not that she would have expected anything else, what with them being so stirred up over MacGovern's big news.

And it *was* big news indeed, no doubt about it. Vangie was all a-tremble. Nell Grace, the quiet one of the household, had more questions than a judge, while the twins exerted their energy by thumping each other on the head like wee simpletons. Through it all, Baby Emma fought to stay awake so she could emit an occasional squeal.

As for MacGovern, well, he was about to rip a seam, so full of himself was he at the moment.

Renny was glad for them all, she truly was. One look at Vangie, her face brilliant with this new joy, was enough to make Renny's own heart swell to bursting. And in truth, it was fine to see the worry lines eased a bit from MacGovern's rough features, as well. He was a good man, if a hard one, and he did dote on his family, every one of them.

Aye, this was a good thing altogether, and she mustn't mind that they would almost certainly be cutting her loose now. She could hardly expect a place among them in their new situation. More than likely, MacGovern would not give a thought to the bargain they had struck back in Ireland, but would be relieved to be shut of her, and the sooner the better.

She was assuring herself that she would be grateful to get on with her own life when she noticed himself and Vangie looking in her direction, speaking in low tones to each other. As she watched, MacGovern gave Vangie's shoulder a bit of a squeeze, then crossed the room toward Renny.

She held her breath, steeling herself for what she was about to hear. She hadn't thought it would come so soon. Couldn't he have waited for a spell, at least until the next day, before giving her the brush? Did he have to be in such an infernal hurry?

MacGovern crossed his sturdy arms over his chest and stood studying her with that keen-eyed look. When he finally spoke, it was with the gruff tone she had become accustomed to. But his words were not what she had expected.

"What with all the excitement, Renny Magee, I might have forgotten to mention that we will expect you to accompany us to our new home."

The cold, hollow place inside Renny suddenly felt the sun. She swiped at the fringe of hair falling over her eyes and stared at him. "You…mean to take me with you?"

"Of course, we'll be taking you with us. As I recall, we had an agreement, did we not? That you would stay with us no less than six months in return for Aidan's passage?"

Renny nodded. "Aye, that's so."

"And isn't it only the decent, Christian thing, to keep your word, once a bargain is sealed?"

Renny's gaze locked with his. "'Tis."

"Then that is that, it seems to me." He uncrossed his arms and hitched his thumbs in his belt. "Unless you can think of a good reason why you should not come along with us, that is."

"No!" Renny blurted out the word like a shot. "A bargain is a bargain. But—"

"But *what*?" he said, his eyes narrowing.

"You're quite certain—there's a place for me? There will be work for me, so that I can earn my keep, I mean? Vangie will still…need me?"

"Sure, you've seen how it is with us. There is always work enough." MacGovern regarded her with a long, thorough look. "You will be assisting me in the stables and on the grounds, as well as helping Vangie. You will not be idle, girl, I promise you that."

Renny pulled her most sober expression, as if to consider his words for another moment. "Then I will go with you," she said, her tone as solemn as a banker's pledge.

"Well, now," said MacGovern, his expression equally grave. "That is a great relief to us all, I am sure."

9

WHEN HOPE AND FEAR COLLIDE

Our feet on the torrent's brink,
Our eyes on the cloud afar,
We fear the things we think,
Instead of the things that are.

JOHN BOYLE O'REILLY

Early December

M ichael?"
Michael straightened, tucking the lap robe more snugly about his legs. It was cold, even inside the carriage, though he had scarcely noticed until now. He'd been too absorbed in his thoughts about this evening's rehearsal, the Christmas concert, Susanna...

Most of all, Susanna.

He turned slightly to face Paul, who sat across from him.

"Michael, are you all right?"

"Of course. I was just...thinking."

"You are still planning to stay in the city tonight, no? Since rehearsal will no doubt go longer than usual."

"No, I've changed my mind. I think we should go back tonight."

"But it will be late. And even colder by then. Snowing, perhaps."

Michael could hear Paul's resistance to the idea of taking the ferry twice on such a night. Paul hated the New York winters.

"Tomorrow the MacGovern family will be arriving. I should be there. But you can stay at the hotel tonight, if you like."

After a long silence, Paul made a valiant reply. "No, I will go back with you."

"We have had this conversation before, Pauli. I can manage the ferry alone."

Paul muttered something, then started in on a different subject. "You're very serious today, *cugino*. What occupies you so? Not the program, surely. It is going well. We will be ready in good time."

"No, I'm very satisfied. There was much improvement at last night's rehearsal."

"Then what is it?"

Michael delayed his reply just long enough that Paul answered for him. "Ah. Susanna. You are thinking of Susanna."

It was not a question. And there was no mistaking the note of smugness in Paul's voice.

Michael made no attempt to confirm or deny, but Paul was clearly not going to be put off by his silence. "So, I was right. It *is* Susanna."

Michael gave an exaggerated sigh, but he already knew it would take more than a show of impatience to stifle the other's curiosity.

Then, strictly on impulse, he surprised himself by shooting a question at Paul. "What does she look like?"

When Paul hesitated, Michael prompted him. "Susanna—what does she look like?"

"You have asked me this before."

"Then I am asking again."

"Hmm. But to describe Susanna is not such an easy thing."

Paul was obviously enjoying this.

"You may spare me the dramatics, *cugino*."

"*Sì*. Well...Susanna is like...*una principéssa!*"

"A princess? High praise," Michael said dryly. "And exactly *how* is Susanna like a princess?"

"She has a...stillness about her. The way she walks, holds her head, her every movement. She has...much grace. Even a kind of elegance."

Michael had actually sensed the grace, the "stillness" Paul referred to. For the first time in years, there was peace in his home. The kind of peace he had longed for—for himself, for Caterina, for his entire household.

And Susanna had brought this peace.

"As I have told you before," Paul rambled on, "Susanna is very attractive. But hers is more a...*quiet* loveliness. There is no pretension about her."

"But she doesn't know she's attractive," Michael said, more to himself than to Paul. "She thinks she is plain."

"Ah, but she is mistaken! Susanna is not plain. Not by any means."

Michael knew he was pressing, but couldn't seem to stop himself. "So, then—Susanna is both pretty and poised," he said, trying for a casual note.

"It's fortunate, I think, that you are a musician, *cugino*, for you are certainly no poet."

He leaned back against the seat. "What color is her hair?"

"Ah, yes. Susanna's hair. It is...the color of honey. Like honey, with streaks of the sun. And she has, what do you call them? The *freckles*. Freckles on her nose. Only a few. Perhaps four or five."

Something in this whimsical reply set Michael on edge. Paul had actually *counted* the freckles on Susanna's nose? It seemed an unwarranted intimacy. Intrusive—presumptuous, even—for Paul to have studied Susanna so closely.

When he could not...

And then he recognized the scalding bilge that came crashing over him. He was jealous. Jealous of Paul.

This wasn't the first time he had wondered if his cousin might not have feelings for Susanna—or she for him. Nor was this the first time he had felt this same resentment at the thought. Paul could *see* Susanna, could look into her eyes, observe her movements, her reactions. Paul didn't have to depend on some questionable sixth sense to interpret Susanna's feelings. Paul was—

Michael stopped himself. How could he be so childish as to resent *Paul*, whom he loved like a brother? He was being unreasonable, and he knew it. A jealous, petulant schoolboy spoiling for a fight.

Overcome with self-disgust, Michael dragged one hand through his hair. He had thought himself finished with the ugly business of jealousy once and for all. He had battled it throughout most of his marriage. He would not—*could* not— allow it to shred his spirit again. And certainly not because of Paul. The bitter taste of self-reproach remained on his tongue.

Paul was still reciting Susanna's virtues. "What more can I say? She is lovely. Very lovely. But I think you are right, that she does not realize this. Always she makes less of herself. She...diminishes herself, even her music. I wonder why."

Before Michael could venture a reply, Paul offered his own. "Perhaps...because Deirdre seemed to cast such a bright light, Susanna became accustomed to walking in her sister's shadow."

Michael swallowed against the knot in his throat.

"I wonder, Michael—why do you always ask me about Susanna's appearance? Why have you not looked at her for yourself by now?"

The question, typical of Paul's directness, caught Michael completely off guard. "With my hands?"

"*Sì.* As you do with others."

"I suppose," he said, searching for an answer, "because I've never felt quite free to do so. I'm not at all sure Susanna would be...comfortable with the idea. So I have not presumed."

But, oh, how he had wanted to! Wanted to take her face between his hands, to trace the line of her temples, her chin, touch her hair, to look at her and see her in the only way left to him—with his touch, and with his heart. Yet something had always stopped him.

"I don't believe you would be presuming, *cugino*. I believe you are mistaken about what Susanna wants."

Michael frowned. "Meaning, I suppose, that you *do* know what she wants."

"I know what I see."

And Michael could not see.

Abruptly, he lifted a hand to put an end to the exchange. "I need to concentrate now on the music," he said, turning toward the carriage door.

But he couldn't concentrate on the music. He could think only of Susanna, of his adolescent jealousy, of the revulsion engendered by his own pettiness.

His life was spiraling out of control. And all because of Susanna.

How had his feelings for her managed to engulf him so subtly, yet so completely? When, exactly, had he first begun to listen for the sound of that low, modulated voice, so thoroughly Irish despite the British overtones of her uncommon education?

When had he come to recognize the moment she entered a room simply by the soft rustling of her skirts and her faint but unforgettable fragrance, like a dusting of rose petals?

How had she slipped so quietly into his life, become such an essential part of him, stirring in him the beginnings of a desire—a *need*—to love again...and the incredible hope that he actually could?

And what was he going to do about it, now that it had happened?

If Paul was right about Susanna's feelings, the impossible had suddenly become possible, and for an instant Michael was paralyzed by a need to protect himself. The memory of Deirdre's betrayal came roaring in on him in all its stark, tearing ugliness, its soul-destroying anguish.

How would he ever find the courage to open himself up to another person again, to risk another failure, another loss? His marriage to Deirdre had for years stripped him of his self-respect, his pride, his very manhood. Did he seriously believe that he was ready to try again, that he was even *capable* of trying again to love, to trust, to build a life together...with Deirdre's sister?

10

NIGHT MUSIC

The high that proved too high,
the heroic for earth too hard,
The passion that left the ground
to lose itself in the sky,
Are music sent up to God.

ROBERT BROWNING

Susanna had been restless all evening. Since dusk, an uncommon stillness had engulfed the house and the grounds. The air itself seemed hushed with expectation, as if waiting for something to happen.

It was well after eleven when she felt the change settle over the night. She had let her hair down and sat brushing it in front of the vanity when the wind suddenly blew up with a wail like a wounded beast rising from the river. Almost immediately a volley of sleet followed, pounding against the house with a vengeance.

She hurried to close the shutters, then went to secure the ones in Caterina's bedroom as well. Gus, the wolfhound, lying at the foot of the bed, lifted his great head and looked at her. Susanna took a moment to rub his ears, then made certain that Caterina was well covered and sleeping soundly before returning to her own room.

Moira Dempsey had warned her about the fierce winter storms that often whipped through the valley, but the ferocity of the wind never failed to put Susanna on edge. Tonight, the awareness that both Michael and Paul were gone made her feel even more anxious and isolated than usual.

Not so long ago, she would have felt *relieved* knowing Michael was away.

How quickly things could change…

She was as fidgety as if she'd consumed an entire pot of tea and knew she might just as well give up all thought of sleep, at least until the storm passed.

With a rueful glance at her nightclothes laid out on the bed, she put down her hairbrush, got up, and went to the window.

There was nothing to be seen, of course—nothing but darkness and bits of icy filigree on the windowpane. She stood listening as the sleet went on beating against the house. The gutters babbled with melting ice—a sound she'd found soothing in her childhood. But tonight, that musical murmur was accompanied by the sharp percussion of tree limbs cracking in the wind, and the ferocity of the storm unnerved her.

She went into the hallway. The gas lamps cast the length of the long narrow corridor in shadows. The door to Caterina's bedroom was ajar, and the wolfhound stuck his head out just enough to satisfy himself that it was only Susanna before turning and going back inside.

Somewhere something banged, and Susanna jumped. But when the noise continued, she recognized it as the loose shutter at the drawing room window and hurried downstairs to close it. Dempsey had been grumbling about the annoyance a few nights past but hadn't gotten around to fixing it yet.

After closing the shutter, she left the room and stood for a moment in the vestibule, unable to decide what to do. She wasn't accustomed to wandering about at so late an hour, when the rest of the household was abed. The storm battering the house and the night creaks of the large old mansion all around her made her feel peculiarly small. Vulnerable. Even *alien*, as if she didn't actually belong here.

Foolishness. It was just a house, just a storm. Still, she would be glad when tomorrow came and the MacGovern family would arrive. There was a husband and wife—and children. Perhaps Bantry Hill would no longer seem so austere, with more children about.

And the MacGoverns were Irish. Ever since Michael had told her about them, she had found herself entertaining hopes that she and Mrs. MacGovern might become friends. The longer she was here, the more she missed the companionship of other women. Rosa Navaro visited as often as she could and made every attempt to be kind, but most of the time she was almost as busy as Michael. She traveled a great deal, and even when she was at home, she was most often involved with her private students or some civic event.

Moira Dempsey had been decent enough to her, but the housekeeper was aging right before Susanna's eyes and seemed either unwilling or unable to expend the effort a real friendship would require. Not to mention Susanna's bewildering suspicion that the woman harbored some sort of resentment toward her. Occasionally she would make a sour remark about "too much education" or "those who get above their raising." "Uppity" was the word she used to describe these unidentified pretenders to a higher plane. And more confusing still was the baleful look the woman would occasionally fix on Susanna when she and Michael were together—a look that seemed to border on distrust.

Susanna knew the Dempseys held great affection for Michael; indeed, their behavior toward him was almost like that of doting parents with a favorite son. But why their fondness for Michael should translate to resentment of her was a puzzle.

She finally willed herself to move, starting down the hall. In spite of the gas lights, the rooms all the way down were dark and unwelcoming, and the house was cold. Moira Dempsey didn't hold with the "extravagance" of leaving a fire in an unoccupied space, so before leaving her room, Susanna had grabbed a shawl to throw over her gingham shirtwaist. Now she gathered it more snugly around her shoulders against the chill.

On impulse, she headed for the music room. She would build a fire, she decided, and she would play. When nothing else could still the unrest in her, music would. Neither the smell of wood smoke nor the sound of the piano was likely to rouse the Dempseys, who slept at the opposite end of the house, and if Caterina happened to wake, she would merely turn over and go back to sleep.

Michael had told her to use the room whenever she liked, after all.

First she laid a fire, knowing the large, drafty room with its high ceilings and tall windows would take some time to heat.

As she sat down at the piano, she felt oddly shy, almost like an intruder. It wasn't as if the keyboard were foreign to her; she accompanied Caterina and Michael when they sometimes sang together in the evenings and played for Caterina's lessons. On occasion she even helped Michael with his composing.

But it was different coming to the magnificent instrument alone, with no purpose except to please herself, and with the luxury of knowing she could play whatever she liked with no one to listen.

At first, she touched the cool ivory keys tentatively, as if they might crack under too much pressure. She roamed over the bass, its rich timbre calling forth a sigh of satisfaction from her. After a few arpeggios, she ran the scales, grimacing at the stiffness of her fingers from lack of practice. Finally, she slipped into a Bach invention. After that, there was nothing else in the room for her except the piano and the music.

At the conclusion of the Bach, she moved to Chopin, as she always did when seeking an emotional—or even a physical—release. The delicate, fragile composer, whose sentimentality often belied the storm in his soul, never failed to absorb her with his elegant and brilliant artistry, flawless even in the most intense, anguishing passages.

At first she sought the grace and peace of the nocturnes, but it took only a few moments to realize that she wanted more than the simple tranquillity of the night songs. Like the storm roaring down over the river valley, a tempest seemed to be gathering in her spirit. She needed to empty herself of the turbulence—or else tame it.

She turned away from the nocturnes and tried the G-minor Ballade—a mistake, she knew almost at once, because she was clumsy and out of form. She could not maintain the intensity and passion of the piece, nor could she endure its tragic undertones.

At any other time she might have stopped then and there, frustrated by her own lack of discipline, but by now she was beyond quitting. Her agitation had built a fire in her that even the music seemed powerless to contain. She dived headlong into the tempestuous C-minor etude—the *Revolutionary*. It was more an *attack* than an interpretation, but Susanna didn't care. This was not intended for the ears of an audience, after all—indeed, not even for her own ears, but more for her heart and her spirit.

Encouraged that she had not entirely decimated the great Pole's creation with her rusty technique, she next went to the *Military Polonaise*. In her present fever, she was ready to do battle, but she was also growing tired, and the demands of the polonaise worked to still the storm.

Fatigue set in as she began the *Fantaisie-Impromptu*, a work personally disliked by Chopin himself, but for some reason a favorite of Susanna's—perhaps for the very extravagance of emotion the music's composer had disdained.

Her fingers caressed the keys now, her pulse slowing as the chaos in her spirit dissipated. As inept and out of practice as she knew herself to be, the aching melody of the *Fantaisie* nevertheless adhered itself to her soul, sweeping her up and carrying her along, making her a part of the music.

She completed the piece and rested for a moment. The effort demanded by the music had drained much of the day's tension from her. And even through the fatigue, an unexpected sense of elation infused her. She felt revived and strengthened.

Her glance came to rest on the manuscript on top of the piano—Michael's *American Anthem*—and she reached for it, flipping through the first few pages. Paul's musical notation was neat and precise, and, knowing him, Susanna felt certain he took great pains to transcribe every note and dynamic exactly as Michael communicated it.

After a slight hesitation, she chose a portion of the manuscript she hadn't yet played through and propped it on the music rack in front of her. She remembered the afternoon she'd first played a portion of the music at Michael's direction, how enthralled she had been at the genius that blazed from each page. What a thrill it must be, to perform a magnificent work such as this—an unparalleled experience, surely.

She began to play; forgetting about her inadequacies, she gave herself up to the music. From childhood, she had possessed a keen ability to "hear" sounds in her inner ear, even to re-create complicated musical structures in her mind. But when she tried to imagine the ultimate performance of this work, she could never capture more than a faint echo of its greatness. For now, she could only content herself with what she was able to reproduce at the keyboard, and even that was enough to move her to tears.

No matter how confusing her emotions toward Michael might be, when it came to his incredible musicianship, she could only stand in awe. It was more than artistry, more than skill, or even genius. Something far less tangible, something indescribable, marked Michael's music. Rosa Navaro and Miss Fanny Crosby would call it *anointing*, the touch of the Divine.

When she had first come to Bantry Hill, Susanna might well have scorned the thought, but no longer. Dwelling under Michael's roof, observing the way he lived his life, seeing the father he was to Caterina—and being a recipient of the kindness and grace he extended so freely—had finally compelled her to turn from the suspicion and distrust that had molded her earlier opinion of him.

Eventually, as she was drawn more and more into his life—and especially into his music, which was almost like being drawn into his soul—she'd had to concede that this man, whom her own sister had despised and even tormented, was a *good* man. A man of integrity and faith and a generous spirit. A man to respect.

And a man she feared she was growing to love.

⁓

Michael brushed the icy rain from his hair as he stood outside the closed doors to the music room. He had waited a long time to hear Susanna play like this—unobserved, free, abandoned.

Although the Chopin was rough in places and her technique not entirely under control, he warmed to the fire with which she imbued the latter part of the C-minor etude, the *Revolutionary*. Chopin was not one of Michael's favorites. He admired his unwavering perfectionism and artistry, but much of the composer's music was too fussy for his personal taste. As for the *Revolutionary*, the only time the tempestuous piece failed to annoy him was when he was in excessively high spirits.

But that was before tonight. He found himself captivated by Susanna's interpretation of the piece. A kind of angry defiance drove her. More than that, she seemed to sense what most pianists—even Michael himself—tended to forget or ignore about the puzzling combinations of emotion that characterized Chopin's work and made him unique. Critics often pointed to Michael's own mix of Italian and Irish in an attempt to analyze the varied palette his heritage inevitably brought to his music. In the same way, Chopin, while most passionate about his native Poland, had inherited from both his French father and his Polish mother the traits that contributed to his genius. Strict form and passion, lyricism and bravura, whimsy and melancholy—an entire spectrum of attributes worked together to shape the composer's music and no doubt accounted for the brilliance others might imitate but could never emulate.

Susanna managed to unearth this diversity in her playing, and yet she considered herself, in her own words, merely "competent." What could possibly account for her skewed self-perception, her conviction that her musicianship was somehow lacking? Had she never performed for anyone but herself? Had no one ever recognized her gift and affirmed it?

Surely, if no one else had realized, Deirdre would have. And yet once, when he'd questioned Deirdre about her younger sister, she had carelessly discredited Susanna's musical skills as "pedestrian, at best."

But of course, she would have. In Deirdre's estimation, the abilities of all others paled in the light of her own.

Scarcely aware of what he was doing, Michael followed her through the music, instinctively directing her now and then, nodding his head with pleasure and approval. He thought he could hear her begin to tire a little by the time she ended the *Polonaise* and turned to the dreamier *Fantaisie*. There was a long silence, then the rustling of paper and, thinking she had finished, he reached for the doorknob. But he stopped when she suddenly launched into a portion of his own *Anthem*—the *cantare* section, in which he had developed a blend of brief works from various nations, a multicultural set of hymns as well as selections incorporating the newer gospel music form.

Michael's pulse began to race with excitement.

Somehow, she heard what *he* had heard as it poured from his spirit. In her playing were the same subtleties of emotion, the same reaching and receiving, a soaring past the limits, then a subsiding. The separateness and the coming together, the divisions and the harmony...

She *understood*. She had found a link to his heart, his spirit, and was now pouring out her perceptions into the music and, in so doing, giving him a glimpse into his own soul.

And hers.

A thrill of elation seized him as the music with which he had so long struggled and experimented echoed behind the closed doors. Hearing her grasp and deliver what he had created only made him burn even more to move forward, to continue the work, to go on discovering and creating and refining.

Moreover, the realization of Susanna's understanding, her *partnership* in this, his most important venture, brought her closer to him. Hearing her play helped him to know her...and made him wish to know her even better, to know everything that made her...*Susanna*.

And with that realization came an urgency to make her grasp and accept her own ability—her *exceptional* ability. Her gift. Always, when he tried to convince her, she would dismiss him with either an awkward protest or a pretense of amusement, as if he were merely being foolish. And always he retreated, fearful of exerting unwanted pressure.

Perhaps Susanna suffered from her own sort of blindness: an inability to see herself as she really was. He wanted to find a way to make her believe him, to help her comprehend what he had sensed the first time he had ever heard her at the keyboard.

Perhaps there *was* a way. A way that might benefit them both, even bring them closer together.

At last, silence fell behind the doors, and, taking a deep breath, Michael slipped the dark glasses from his pocket, put them on, and walked quickly into the room.

~

"*Brava,* Susanna! Well done."

Susanna turned to see Michael standing in the doorway. He was still dressed as he had been earlier in the day, in soft gray tweeds and a black sweater.

Humiliation flooded through her. How much had he heard? "Michael—I thought you were staying in the city."

"I decided I should come back." He walked the rest of the way into the room, not stopping until he reached the piano. "The MacGoverns are moving in tomorrow. I didn't want to be away when they arrived."

"Oh—yes. Yes, I...should have reminded you...I'm glad you remembered." She closed the keyboard and twisted her hands in her lap. "I...perhaps I shouldn't have come down so late. I couldn't sleep...I didn't think there was any danger of waking anyone."

He dismissed her concerns with a wave of his hand. "Don't apologize. As I told you, Susanna, the piano is for your use anytime you wish. I enjoyed your music." He paused. "I must tell you, Susanna—the more I hear you play, the more I believe you are just the person I am looking for."

When she didn't answer, he went on. "For some time now," he said, "I have been in need of a dependable pianist and organist for the orchestra. Someone who would be willing to work with us full-time. I believe you would be perfect."

Susanna sat dumbstruck, staring at him in disbelief. "Well," she finally managed, "I'm relieved to see that you couldn't have been listening very long."

"I expected you to say something like that," he said, smiling. "Actually, I have been listening for quite some time, and I am entirely serious. I continue to use guests on a temporary basis because I have yet to find the right person for a permanent position. I would like it very much if you would consider my offer."

"You can't be serious! You *know* I'm not capable."

"I know nothing of the kind," he said evenly. "I believe you are exactly what I am looking for. In fact, I *know* you are. But we have discussed your abilities before, no? My challenge is to convince *you* of what I already know."

He *was* serious. Or else somewhat mad.

"You really don't understand," she said, trying to steady her voice. He had triggered a disturbing mix of panic—and something akin to hunger—in her.

"Even if I *were* capable—which I know very well I'm not, no matter what you say—I could never carry it off. I literally freeze when I have to perform. I've always been that way—I *hate* being in front of an audience! I'd humiliate myself. I couldn't possibly do what you're suggesting."

Susanna hadn't meant to be *quite* so truthful and was mortified by her outburst. But perhaps it was for the best. His suggestion was unthinkable.

"I would never pressure you to do something you truly do not want to do, Susanna. And I understand about the stage fright. I was once acquainted with that particular demon myself."

When Susanna attempted to voice a protest, he ignored her. "It's true," he said. "You'd be surprised. But I learned that stage fright can be managed, even turned to your benefit. You can master the fear by confronting it—and relying on God to complete the work He's begun in you. I know you trust God's faithfulness, and if you trust my musical instincts at all, then believe me when I tell you that you have the ability to do this."

"Michael—I've told you before—"

"*Siete dotati!* Do you not hear me? You are *gifted.* Truly gifted! Why can you not accept what I tell you? Susanna, listen to me, please. We are friends now, are we not?"

"Friends? Yes. Yes, of course."

"And so then, do you trust me—as your friend?"

Confused, Susanna watched him closely, even as she searched her heart for the answer. "Yes, Michael," she said softly. "I trust you."

"And you trust my ability as a musician, no?"

"Oh, Michael, you *know* I do! You're an *incredible* musician—"

He waved off anything else she might have said. "Then I ask you to trust my *judgment.* As a musician. As your friend. And as someone who...cares for you and wants only your best. Can you do that, just for this moment?"

He was leaning over her, his damp hair falling over his forehead, the dark glasses securely in place. Then, without waiting for her to reply, he extended his hands toward her.

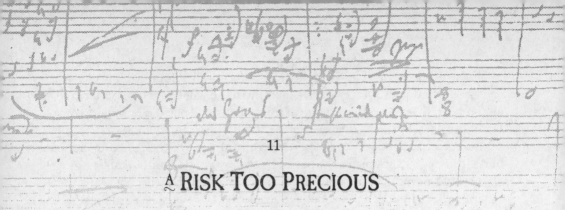

11

A RISK TOO PRECIOUS

Is this my dream, or the truth?

W. B. YEATS

I can help you. We will work together," Michael said, clasping her hands in his.

Susanna had no idea what he meant, and she was far too aware of the warmth and strength of his hands to think clearly. Something had shifted between them. A boundary had blurred. The moment she admitted that she trusted him, the reins of restraint—which had provided not only a pattern for behavior but, at least for Susanna, a kind of self-protection—seemed to have slackened.

She wondered if Michael felt it, too, but if he did he gave no sign. He seemed more intent on keeping her immobile, as if he feared she might bolt from the room.

If he only knew...

Susanna had no desire to be anyplace but where she stood. Close to him, so close she could count every line in his face, except for those concealed by the dark glasses. Close enough to see the silver in his hair. Close enough...to be overwhelmed by the closeness.

And then she realized what he was saying, and the feeling quickly dissipated.

"...The orchestra will perform the *Anthem* in sections—in movements—until it's completed. I have need of someone for the piano. Or organ perhaps. You play both. And I would not rush you. I promise to work with you until you feel ready. We can—"

"No."

Above the glasses, his dark brows knitted together. "Susanna, I can help you. I can help you gain confidence, lose the stage fright—"

"*No*, Michael." She forced the words through gritted teeth as she freed her hands from his.

"But you could be—you have so much to offer—"

Something in Susanna seemed to wilt, to shrink and die, like a blossom too frail to survive. She should have known. Why had she ever imagined she could be enough for a man like Michael?

What she heard him saying was that he wanted to change her, make her into something more than what she was. But why had she expected anything else? He lived in a different world from anything she had ever known.

And he was accustomed to a different kind of woman, a kind of woman she couldn't even pretend to be. He had fallen for Deirdre, hadn't he? Deirdre, who had glittered like the brightest jewel, with a zest for life and a sense of the dramatic that bedazzled every man she met. Deirdre, who had always been so *alive*. Whatever else she might have been, Deirdre was never dull, never timid. Audiences hadn't intimidated her—they energized her. Nothing was ever too large, too grand for Deirdre. She rode through life like a princess royal, driving her own chariot, trampling beneath her wheels anything—or anyone—that got in her way.

A man like Michael would hardly be interested in a country mouse who turned to pudding at the very thought of mingling in a crowd, much less walking onto a stage.

"I can't do what you want, Michael. I'm sorry."

"But how can you know this unless you try? I don't understand."

He seemed genuinely puzzled, and for an instant Susanna found herself torn between self-doubt and the desire to please him. But there was a gaping chasm between where she wished she could go and the conviction that she could actually make the leap.

No more had the inner struggle begun than she felt a surge of anger at herself. Was she really so hungry for his approval, his affection, that she would actually wish to become someone else? Someone like Deirdre?

She had never entertained the least desire for greatness. Her entire life had been unexceptional. Indeed, she knew herself to be just an ordinary person, had no thought of ever being anything else.

But she couldn't expect Michael to understand that. Everything he *did* was extraordinary. He basked in the spotlight of success and glamour and celebrity. Even after the loss of his eyesight and the demise of his operatic career, he still enjoyed the life of a hugely popular, successful musician. Renowned, respected, and revered, how could he possibly understand why she wanted no part of that world?

In truth, Susanna wasn't at all sure she understood it herself.

"Susanna?"

He was waiting for some sort of an explanation. But how did she go about explaining her very *nature*?

Frustrated and confused, she fumbled for the right words. "Michael, this isn't something I can explain. Please, can't you just accept the fact that what you're asking goes against everything I am? I'm simply not made that way."

"And you think I want to change you."

Susanna bit back a reply. That was *exactly* what she thought.

"This is not about *changing* you, Susanna. I meant only to help you overcome an unwarranted lack of confidence. Possibly I can be more objective about your abilities than you. You are much more gifted than you realize." He paused. "But perhaps for me it is a selfish thing as well, because I would like very much for you to be a part of what I do."

His voice dropped even more, and she strained to hear him over the moaning wind and the rattle of sleet on the windows. "Susanna, believe me, I have no desire to change you. You are..." He hesitated. "I would not change you for anything."

Susanna searched his face for any sign of insincerity. But without eye contact, it was impossible to read his intent. What she *did* know was that Michael was not an impulsive man. Yet she had the distinct feeling that he had just spoken on impulse.

She saw that he was clenching and unclenching his fists. Watching him, sensing his discomfort, Susanna felt her resistance waver. Her pique with him, and with herself, began to drain away.

"It's not that I don't value your opinion, Michael. To the contrary, I'm flattered that you would even consider me, and I'm sorry—"

He shook his head and lifted a hand to stop her. "You need not apologize. It's not my intention to make you uncomfortable or try to coax you into doing something you don't want to do. I respect your wishes. But if the time should ever come...if you should ever change your mind, you will tell me?"

"Of course," Susanna said, unable to imagine such a time.

"Susanna," he said, moving a little closer, "would you allow me to...look at you?" He lifted his hands, palms outward.

Completely unprepared for this, Susanna felt her throat constrict. Tom Donoghue, her mother's cousin, had been blind. And the Widow Blaine. What Michael was asking was a fairly common practice for the unsighted, the only way they could "see" another's features. But with Michael, it seemed more significant. More intimate.

Her hesitation was just enough to make him step back. "If you would prefer that I not—"

"No, I...don't mind."

When he still delayed, she tried for a lighter, more casual tone. "It's fine, Michael. Really." Then a brash thought seized her. "One thing—"

"*Sì?*"

"I wonder—would you please do something for *me*?"

He tilted his head and waited.

"Would you *please* take off those glasses?" The words spilled out all at once. "You never wear them with anyone except me, though I can't think why! In truth—it hurts my feelings."

For a moment he seemed to freeze, and Susanna cringed, ashamed of her crassness. She had made him angry, and she wouldn't have blamed him if he had bludgeoned her with a scathing retort. But even as she braced herself, he slowly lifted a hand, removed the dark glasses, and slipped them into his pocket.

His eyes remained closed. "Just so you'll know, Susanna," he said, his voice exceedingly quiet as he stood facing her, "I never intended to hurt your feelings. I wear the glasses in order that I *not* offend you."

Susanna held her breath, her nails digging into her hands. After the accident Deirdre had written that his eyes were scarred. Ugly, even *frightening*.

And then he opened his eyes.

They were beautiful. Blue crystals, deeply set and thickly lashed. They lacked focus, of course, but this merely gave him a contemplative, intense expression that conveyed a depth of feeling she would not have thought possible.

There were no scars, no disfigurement of any kind.

It was inconceivable that Deirdre would have lied about this, too. And yet the evidence of her sister's pitiless deceit stood before her.

Oh, Deirdre…Deirdre…how could you?

"I am not offended by your blindness, Michael," she managed to say. "How could you have thought I would be?"

He shrugged, but Susanna already knew the answer. "What did Deirdre tell you?" she said.

He stilled, lifted a hand to one temple, then passed it over his face. "My eyes—"

"Your eyes are perfect. But that's not what Deirdre said, is it?"

He paled, silence his only reply.

"Surely Paul told you the truth? Rosa? Someone…"

"*Sì*. Of course. But even after they convinced me, Deirdre insisted I wear the glasses. She hated the blindness." He paused. "But, Susanna, I wear them on other occasions, not only with you. I almost always wear them in a crowd—especially in an unfamiliar setting. I am a large man. I could easily hurt someone if we should collide. The glasses, at least, call attention to the fact that I cannot see where I'm going. You understand?"

Always, it seemed, he thought of others before himself. And this was the man Deirdre had repeatedly called "selfish." "Inconsiderate."

When she spoke again, her voice trembled. "I didn't realize…"

"You prefer I not wear the glasses when we are together?"

Susanna's gaze went to his eyes, and in that instant she was struck by the irrational sensation that he was looking directly at her. She swallowed, then shook her head as if to expel the feeling. "I think—yes, I think I'd rather you didn't."

"So, then—I won't."

Inordinately pleased by his quick response, Susanna moved to close the distance between them, lifted her face, and waited. "Yes...well, then..."

He dipped his head, resting his hands lightly on her shoulders.

"Michael?"

He hesitated.

"I'm nothing like Deirdre," she blurted out.

His countenance went solemn. "I know," he said softly.

"People never took us for sisters, unless they knew us. I don't resemble her in the least." She stopped. "I'm quite plain."

Why had she felt the need to tell him that? He would find out for himself soon enough, after all.

His mouth quirked. "That is not what I have been told."

"But it's true—"

"Susanna?"

"Yes?"

"Hush now."

Susanna drew in a sharp breath and closed her eyes, holding her breath as he began to trace the oval of her face with his fingertips.

It was an unsettling experience—but not unpleasant. As Michael himself had stated, he was quite a big man, and when he conducted the orchestra or embellished his speech with dramatic gestures, Susanna invariably caught a sense of great power in his hands. She hadn't expected such gentleness. But as he molded her face with his fingers and began to skim every feature, his touch was light and deft—and in no way overly familiar.

"You need not hold your breath, Susanna."

At the note of amusement in his voice, she opened her eyes and found him smiling as he continued his exploration. Once he nodded, as if his touch had confirmed what he already knew. His expression intent now, he continued to trace her features.

His fingertips were calloused—from the mandolin, she supposed. And from gardening—Michael loved to work in the gardens. He brushed over her forehead, lightly winging out from her eyes, even seeming to take note of her eyelashes before moving down over her cheekbones and the hollows beneath them. Susanna tensed, but he allowed his thumbs to graze the corners of her mouth only for a second before briefly skimming his fingertips along her jawline.

He fanned his hands outward, noting the length of her hair, and only then did Susanna remember that she hadn't bothered to put it up again. Heat rose to her face, but of course he couldn't see her disarray. Somehow, the thought didn't help.

Finally, he gave a slight nod—Susanna thought he might have sighed as well, though she couldn't imagine why. She was keenly aware of his hands clasping her shoulders, just as keenly aware that she didn't really want him to release her.

"Thank you, Susanna."

There was a huskiness, a tenderness in his voice she had never heard, a softness to his features she had never seen, but she tried not to attach too much importance to either.

"You are wrong, you know," he said, his voice even lower now. Susanna looked at him.

"What?"

He was still smiling. "You are not in the least *plain*."

And it occurred to Susanna that, for the first time in her life, she didn't *feel* plain.

And then he bent to touch his lips to her forehead. In that moment, her last slender thread of caution pulled free and dropped away. The kiss, in its gentleness and poignancy...and *carefulness*...seemed more like a benediction. She did not so much feel herself kissed...as *blessed*.

~

Michael had been almost overcome by her closeness. Both elated and unnerved, he stood stunned by the force of his own feelings. The cool softness of her skin under his fingertips and the subtle fragrance of roses he had come to identify with her very nearly distracted him from "seeing her," being able to form his own image of her appearance rather than depending on Paul to convey that image to him.

And now he knew why he had refrained for so long. Her features were delicate but distinct, her face thin, but not gaunt. Her youthful skin was cool and silken. He grew almost dizzy when he realized her hair fell free, when he tested the weight of it. *Honey*, Paul had said. Her hair was the color of honey.

Feelings he had suppressed for years blazed up in him: a deep, humming pleasure in her loveliness, a loveliness of which she was completely unaware. The unfettered lightness of simply being close to her, being in her presence. The wrench of pain at the very thought of parting from her.

Still holding her, he struggled to clear his head. He couldn't bring himself just yet to let her go. Whatever boundary had stood between them seemed to be gone. It was a moment that signaled either a crossing or a retreat. They were poised at the edge of what was safe and familiar, facing each other across an unknown terrain. They could back away and maintain the amicable, comfortable relationship they had forged—a relationship without risk, for the most part. Or they could cross over into a new province where nothing was charted, nothing was absolute.

Only a few years ago, he would have pursued her, courted her, with all the confidence and arrogance of a youthful buccaneer. But the disaster of his marriage, the tragedy of Deirdre's death—and, yes, the loss of his sight—all stood between the man he had once been and the man he was now.

He could not afford the luxury of daydreams or assumptions where Susanna was concerned. God had healed him, restored him to wholeness, that was true. But there were parts of him, deep and hidden, that were still bruised from the years of rejection and humiliation—and from the soul-shattering realization that he had allowed himself to be used by a woman who had never loved him, who had simply seen him as a means to an end.

But Susanna was, as she herself had said, "nothing like Deirdre." She was totally without guile. And perhaps it wasn't only her directness and lack of pretension that inspired his trust. Perhaps the fact that in the beginning *she* had so obviously mistrusted *him* made it easier for him to sweep his own doubts and suspicions aside.

Still, he was afraid. Afraid to risk, unwilling to chance losing her friendship, her acceptance of him. He would rather have *something* than nothing.

And as much as he wanted to be completely free with Susanna—free to love her, to hope that she might come to love him—in his spirit he knew this wasn't the time. What they had right now, at this moment, was too precious to risk. She brightened his world and lighted his life and brought grace and joy and peace to his existence. For now, that must be enough.

Even so, he could not stop himself from bending to touch his lips to her forehead in a light, decidedly chaste kiss.

And she did not pull away.

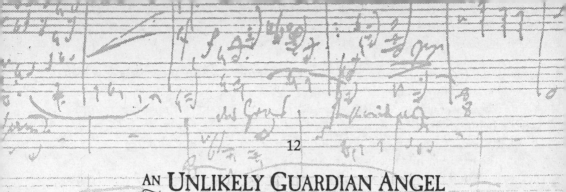

12

An Unlikely Guardian Angel

Some have entertained angels
without knowing it.

HEBREWS 13:2 (NASB)

Andrew Carmichael was alone in the dispensary, measuring medicines and filling bottles when the office bell rang. He glanced up, wiped a hand over the front of his laboratory coat, and went out into the waiting room.

It was going on five, a miserable evening with a punishing wind and a mixture of ice and snow. A blast blew into the waiting room as soon as he opened the door.

The woman who stood before him was quite different from the usual run of patients who showed up on his doorstep. She wore a tastefully designed hooded cloak that had probably cost more than the sum total of his accounts due. Although her face was partially concealed by the fur trim of the hood, he could see that she was a woman of refined features.

"Are you Dr. Carmichael?" she asked in a breathless voice.

Andrew nodded, quickly standing aside to let her enter.

She stepped inside at once, glancing about the waiting room. She was a small woman, scarcely reaching Andrew's shoulder, but something in her bearing gave the impression of greater stature.

"How can I help you?"

She withdrew a piece of paper from her handbag and gave it to Andrew. "I wondered if you would be good enough to call at this…residence. I believe you will find a need for your services there."

Andrew looked at her, then at the paper. It was an address on Mulberry Street, a particularly wretched area of shanties and log hovels.

He glanced up to find the woman watching him closely.

"You'll be paid whatever you require, of course," she said. "I'll send my driver around tomorrow to take care of your fee, and if further visits are necessary, you've only to give him your bill."

"May I ask who the patient is?" Andrew said, puzzled by the lack of information being offered.

"Patients," she corrected. "You'll find a woman and young children."

"The entire family needs treatment?"

The hood had fallen away from her face, and Andrew saw that she was probably in her forties, an attractive woman in an unpretentious sort of way.

"I…I'm not sure," she replied. "The mother, for certain, and the youngest child. Perhaps all of them." She lowered her eyes.

"This situation—is it urgent?"

She still didn't look at him. "I believe it may be, yes. Could you possibly go today, Doctor?"

Andrew studied her. Despite the quiet elegance of her features, she appeared drawn, as if she hadn't slept well for some time.

"I—yes," he said. "I expect I can arrange to go yet this evening."

The tautness of her features gave way to a look of unmistakable relief. "Thank you so much."

"May I have the mother's name, please?"

She hesitated, swallowing with some difficulty. "Lambert. Mary Lambert."

"Is she a relative?"

Something flickered in her eyes. "No," she said, her tone unexpectedly sharp.

Abruptly, she turned to go, but Andrew stopped her with another question. "And may I have *your* name, Mrs.—"

"I don't believe that's necessary."

Andrew was tempted to press, but decided against it. He had a sense that her self-control was exceedingly fragile.

"Very well, then," he said. "I'll look in on the family later this evening and see how I can help."

She only half turned, inclining her head and murmuring a word of gratitude before hurrying out the door.

Andrew stepped outside just long enough to watch a driver clad in black carefully hand the woman into a handsome—but not ostentatious—carriage. The sting of the wind and the ice-laced snow drove him back inside before he could see which way they went.

As he finished up his work in the dispensary, he decided to wait for Bethany's return from the children's home before making his call on the Lamberts. As usual, she'd insisted on walking, though he had urged her to take the buggy. Of course, it hadn't been this cold and wet when she set out, and Bethany seldom chose to ride when she could walk. She could be stubborn at times.

He smiled a little at the thought. After locking the medicine cabinet, he went to wash his hands. The hot pain in his swollen wrists and fingers warned him that an outing in this weather would do the arthritis no good, but there had been no mistaking the importance of his mysterious visitor's request. Quite simply, he hadn't the heart to refuse.

His gaze went to the medicine cabinet, lingering there for a moment until a shudder seized him and he turned away. With an angry toss of the towel, he wheeled toward the door.

Perhaps he should take the buggy and pick up Bethany on his way to Mulberry Street. But it was after five, and the streets would be crowded. He was almost sure to miss her in passing. Besides, he was fairly certain she'd want to make the call with him once she returned.

He decided to wait, hoping she would turn up soon.

⁓

Bethany was thankful with every treacherous step that she had had the foresight to wear her boots. The streets were slippery, darkness was drawing in fast, and impatient pedestrians weren't inclined to give one another much room.

She should have listened to Andrew. Hadn't he warned her the weather was going to turn nasty before dark?

She was about to turn the corner onto Mott Street when a wiry little man wearing a fisherman's cap and a baggy overcoat jostled by her, nearly shoving her into the street. She had no more righted herself and started off again when a gaggle of shopgirls came sloshing toward her, laughing and poking at each other, seemingly oblivious to her approach. In an effort to avoid them, Bethany darted sideways into the street and only barely escaped being struck by a coal wagon. The driver cursed at her, splashing her with dirty water as he rumbled on.

Incensed by now, she stood glaring at the back of the rickety wagon. Someone behind her gave a shout, and almost too late she turned to see one of the police department's Black Marias hurtling toward her. She sidestepped it just in time, though she turned her ankle in the process.

The vehicle clanged to a stop, and Bethany hobbled backward, skidding and nearly falling on a patch of ice.

"Dr. Cole!"

Bethany gritted her teeth as she recognized the policeman hanging onto the side of the Black Maria. She was wet and shivering, and she wanted nothing so much as to get back to the office. The last person she wanted to see right now was Sergeant Frank Donovan.

The big policeman jumped down and raked her over with a quick scowl. "You all right?" he said, not waiting for a reply before adding, "You're drenched."

"No, I'm not all right," she snapped. "And, yes, I'm drenched."

He grinned at her. "Well, unless you're out for an evening stroll, I think you'd best let me give you a ride." He jabbed a thumb over his shoulder in the direction of the police wagon. Before Bethany could reply, he took her arm and began propelling her toward the wagon. "It might be a bit rank inside, but it's dry for all that. And you look as if you could use some drying out."

She yanked her arm free. "Thank you, Sergeant, I can manage. I haven't that much farther to go."

He ignored her, encircling her waist and sweeping her up to the inside of the wagon, then jumping in behind her. "Doc would have my hide if he knew I'd left you on your own in this weather. What was he thinking, anyway, sending you out in this?"

Bethany glared at him. "Andrew—Dr. Carmichael—didn't *send* me out, Sergeant. It was entirely my decision."

"Ah. But not a very smart one, if you don't mind my saying so." He gave a whistle, then shouted at the driver of the wagon.

"You can sit on the floor if you want," Donovan said as they hauled off down the street.

Bethany looked around at the foul interior of the Black Maria. "I'll stand, thank you," she replied with forced civility.

"As you like. So, then—what brings you out on such a wretched day?"

Bethany had the feeling he was deliberately trying to annoy her. The last place she wanted to be was inside this disgusting wagon with Frank Donovan, but she refused to give him the satisfaction of amusing himself at her expense.

"We have a patient at the orphanage," she said, keeping her voice cool and steady. "The weather hadn't turned this bad when I left the office, so I decided to walk."

"I see." He regarded her with a detached, clinical expression. "Well, how do you like your work by now, Dr. Cole? Not quite what you're used to, I expect."

"And just what exactly do you think I'm used to, Sergeant?"

His dark eyes snapped with insolence. "Whatever it was, I doubt it was anything much like the Bowery."

"As a matter of fact, I find our practice very rewarding. We're obviously needed here."

Frank Donovan rolled his tongue along the inside of his cheek. "I'll not argue that you're needed. All the same, I can't help wondering what possesses a woman like you to become a sawbones in the first place. And to set up practice in a neighborhood like this—" He broke off, shaking his head.

"A woman like me?" Bethany countered. "And exactly what kind of woman might that be?"

An impudent smile played at his lips beneath the dark red mustache. "Well, now, it strikes me that an attractive young woman of good family—as you obviously are—would find it more suitable being a doctor's *wife* rather than being the *doctor.*" He paused. "You wouldn't be one of those women's rights females, would you? Sure, and you don't look much like the rest of 'em."

Bethany held her temper only by an iron act of will. "Are you goading me on purpose, Sergeant, or are you really as boorish as you seem to want me to believe?"

He gave a harsh laugh. "I've offended you. I apologize, Dr. Cole—that wasn't my intention. Not at all."

His apology was a farce, and they both knew it.

"You needn't apologize, Sergeant. I didn't make it through medical college by being thin-skinned. Unfortunately, my chosen profession has more than its share of buffoons."

Again he laughed, even harder this time. "I do admire your spirit, Dr. Cole. No wonder Doc is so smitten with you. I doubt he's ever met up with your kind before."

"My *kind*?"

"Ah, now, don't get yourself in a twist," he said, doffing his hat and affecting an unconvincing look of remorse. "I didn't mean any harm. But it's true about Doc, you know. The poor fella is as love-struck as any man I've ever seen."

Bethany groped for a last remnant of self-control. "You know, Sergeant, Andrew—Dr. Carmichael—considers you a friend. To save me, I can't imagine why."

Without warning, the policeman's mouth went hard. "Oh, I'm Doc's friend, right enough. Don't you be doubting it. That's why I'm more than a little concerned about him."

Bethany frowned at him. "What are you talking about?"

"I think you know exactly what I'm talking about." He leaned against the wall of the wagon and crossed his arms over his chest. "Doc is a very trusting sort, as you may have noticed. Indeed, if there is such a thing in this infernal town, the man's an innocent entirely."

In a flash of insight, Bethany realized that despite his crudeness, his rough demeanor, and his cutting cynicism, Frank Donovan *was* a friend to Andrew. Not only a friend, but his self-appointed protector as well.

And just as clearly, she understood something else: Donovan was protecting Andrew from her. He considered *her* a threat to his friend.

Her anger boiled to the surface, and she turned on Donovan. "Just what is it about me that you don't approve of, Sergeant? What exactly do you think I'm going to do to Andrew? Stab him in the back with my scalpel? Run off with all the exorbitant fees we're bringing in?"

His mouth twisted into a humorless smile. "Now, Dr. Cole, I think you know exactly how it is with Doc where you're concerned. The poor man is so besotted with you he can't find his own tongue when you're close-by. Why, he'd open a vein for you if you so much as crooked your little finger at him."

Bethany stared at him in astonishment. "That's the most ridiculous—"

"I think not," he said, his tone sharp as he uncrossed his arms and slipped his hands into his pockets. "Mind, now, Lady Doc—I'm no fool. And neither," he added with a calculating look, "are you."

Bethany had just opened her mouth to reply when a sudden, unwelcome realization siphoned the strength of her outrage.

Donovan was right.

The occasional moments of attraction that had passed between her and Andrew early in their relationship had deepened almost daily. At least she sensed that to be the case with Andrew.

But what about her own feelings?

"That's what I thought."

She stiffened at the sound of Frank Donovan's mocking voice, the look of utter contempt in his eyes.

"You know full well you're going to hurt him. Oh, not on purpose, perhaps. But you'll hurt him all the same."

"What I know is that you're badly out of line, Sergeant."

"If you have any feelings for the man—and I'm not saying you don't—you'd be doing him a kindness by letting him know just where you stand. Somehow, you don't quite strike me as a woman with a yen to settle down and tend to the hearth fire while Doc goes about his work of healing. You'd rather be toting your own medical bag around town alongside of him. You don't want to be *any* man's wife, do you?"

His tone turned even more caustic as he went on. "Even if you don't admit it, I think you know that one of these days—and maybe not too far off—Doc's going to need a wife more than he needs a *business partner.* He's going to need someone to take care of *him* instead of taking care of everybody *else.*"

When she did not respond, his lip turned up in a sneer. "Come on, you know how it is with him! Faith, woman, you *work* with him every day. You've seen his hands, the stiffness in his legs—the way he can barely make it up a flight of stairs on a bad day! He's getting worse all the time; even I can see it! The man is more likely than not to end up an invalid eventually. *Isn't* he?"

Stricken, Bethany could only stare at him. He'd seen more than she would have thought. And yet...it was becoming difficult *not* to see. Andrew was getting worse. Some days he could scarcely manage to stitch a wound.

Bethany forced herself to stand there, trying to breathe evenly, to show no reaction. Not for the world would she give this...rube...the satisfaction of knowing he had triggered an unexpected, unsettling rush of bewilderment.

She had her life in order. Her education was complete. Her career was underway. She had a practice, an office, and a growing list of patients. And, thanks to Andrew, she had finally obtained hospital privileges.

Indeed, she had everything she had ever wanted, everything she had dreamed of and hoped for since she was a schoolgirl. Her life was satisfyingly full; she had no need for more. There was no *room* for anything more.

But thanks to Andrew's so-called *friend*, she could feel her complacency beginning to slip away. In its place rose a boiling cloud of confusion, conflicting emotions, and questions she wasn't yet ready to answer. Not even to herself.

Why had she ever gotten into this disgusting, squalid wagon with Frank Donovan anyway? And why couldn't he have simply kept his unsolicited opinions to himself?

"Here we are, then. I'll just stop in and say hello."

He jumped easily from the wagon and reached to help Bethany down, flashing a smile that didn't quite mask the flinty edge in his expression.

As he set her to the ground, he held her a moment longer than necessary, his gaze raking her face. "I meant no offense, Dr. Cole," he said, his tone oddly impersonal and detached. "Just looking out for a friend."

Bethany tugged free of him. "And is Andrew aware, Sergeant, that you've appointed yourself his guardian angel?"

He burst out laughing. "I hardly think so. It's not likely that anyone—even a saint like Doc—would ever mistake me for an angel!"

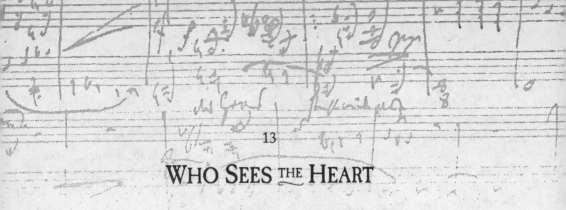

13

WHO SEES THE HEART

Give me, O God, the understanding heart.

GEORGIA HARKNESS

Too late, Andrew recognized the searing flash of resentment that shot through him.

Any jealousy on his part was wholly irrational. Frank had made it clear upon entering that their meeting had been merely a chance encounter, and Bethany followed up by explaining in greater detail.

And yet the sight of them together had unsettled him. He despised himself for such an adolescent reaction, especially since it had to do with a friend. This was *Frank*, after all.

Andrew had never seen any indication that Frank might harbor an attraction for Bethany. The man hardly lacked for feminine companionship—the ladies seemed to fall at his feet anytime he passed by.

Well, a certain *kind* of lady, at any rate.

Bethany's appeal was, on the other hand, of a quieter, more subtle nature than that which Frank typically seemed to favor.

Still, what a striking pair they made! Bethany with her fair, patrician loveliness in contrast to Frank's dashing, flamboyant good looks.

With relief he noted that Bethany distanced herself from Frank as soon as they entered the waiting room. He greeted both of them with as much enthusiasm as he could muster, and was just about to speak to Bethany about his mysterious visitor and her urgent request that he visit this Mary Lambert and her children. But the door opened again, this time to admit the petite blind hymn writer, Miss Fanny Crosby.

Ordinarily, Andrew would be glad to see Miss Fanny. But he had the call pending on Mulberry Street, and he was anxious to get away. Stifling his impatience, he went to her. "Miss Fanny! What in the world are you doing out in this weather?"

"Why, I'm paying you a visit, of course, Andrew." She smiled at his fussing and brushed the light coating of snow from her shoulders. "Aren't you glad to see me?"

She stood in the middle of the waiting room, her head slightly lifted as if she were listening to something in the distance. "Who else is here, I wonder?"

Frank made his presence known, as did Bethany, while Andrew helped Miss Fanny remove her coat. "I'm always glad to see you," he assured her, leading her to a chair beside the iron stove that warmed the room. "But you ought to be scolded for venturing out on such a day. Please tell me you're not on foot!"

"Oh, listen to you! As if I'm not used to being out in worse weather than this. But, no, I'm not walking. Or at least I didn't walk *here*. Ben Drummond gave me a ride from the Women's Mission House. I decided I could use a brief respite to warm up a bit, so I decided to stop and visit with you for a spell."

"Well, we're very glad you did." Andrew forced a smile at Bethany over the top of their visitor's head.

Miss Fanny gave him a motherly pat on the hand, then turned in the direction of Frank Donovan. "Sergeant, I stopped at the precinct house earlier today to check on the boys, and I heard all about patrolman McNally's lovely bride and their wedding, bless them both."

"Aye," Frank said, drawing a little closer. "Patrick went and tied the knot at last."

"Yes, well, I keep praying for a good Christian woman to bring you to your senses as well. A man your age needs to be thinking of settling down."

Frank grinned and winked at Andrew. "Now, Miss Fanny, what would you know about my age?"

She waved a hand as if to dismiss his prattle. "I know a good deal more about you than you might expect, Frank Donovan. I know, for example, that you fancy yourself quite the rascal. But I also know that even a rascal can be saved from his own foolishness by the good Lord—and a good woman."

Before Frank could make a comeback, Miss Fanny turned toward Bethany. "Dr. Cole, I was at the children's home this morning, and dear little Maylee told me about your frequent visits to her. And yours, too, Andrew. Bless you both for taking an interest in the child."

Her expression grew more solemn. "But I wonder how she is, really. She never complains, you know. Not a word."

Bethany glanced at Andrew before replying. "Maylee is fairly stable for now, Miss Fanny. But...you understand she'll never be well. Her condition is degenerative."

"I know," said Miss Fanny with a sigh. "And I pray for the poor child daily. She simply breaks my heart. But do you know, the sweet girl would much rather sing me a song about Jesus than talk about herself. How our dear Lord must cherish her!"

They made light conversation for a few minutes. Then Miss Fanny got to her feet, saying, "Well, Sergeant, Dr. Cole seems to have survived her jaunt in your foul-smelling old wagon well enough, so perhaps I could impose on you to deliver me to my apartment?"

Frank replaced his hat, tipping it to the back of his head with one finger. "It would be my pleasure, Miss Fanny, but I have to say, I don't understand why your husband didn't keep you at home in the first place. Days like this aren't fit for you to be out."

Andrew watched the two of them as the diminutive Miss Fanny took Frank's arm. "Van is my husband, Sergeant, not my guardian. Besides, he has his work to do, and I have mine. The Lord takes very good care of us."

She smiled up at him. "But thank you all the same for your concern. You're a good man."

Frank looked at Andrew and lifted an eyebrow. "We both know better than that, Miss Fanny."

"Oh, would you listen to yourself! The trouble with you, Frank Donovan, is that you really don't know *what* kind of a man you are. One of these days, when you stop running long enough, the Lord is going to get hold of you, and then you'll realize what I've been trying to tell you all along."

"Now don't you start on me, Miss Fanny," Frank grumbled. "You know I won't argue with you."

Still holding on to his arm as they started for the door, Miss Fanny gave a wave to Andrew and Bethany. "And I expect I must be the only person in New York who can claim that distinction. Well, come along now. It's time I was getting home."

~

As soon as the door shut behind them, Andrew turned to Bethany. "I have a call to make. I thought you might want to go with me, although I feel I should tell you that I have no idea what it's all about."

Andrew went on to explain then about his strange visitor. "I don't know what to expect," he finished, "so if you're tired and would rather not go—"

"No, I'm going with you. It sounds intriguing." She was already collecting her coat and her medical bag. "You said the entire family might need treatment?"

Andrew nodded, shrugging into his own coat. "It's possible, although she didn't seem to know for certain."

"And she didn't tell you anything else? Not even her name?"

"Nothing more." He stood thinking a moment, then opened the door and looked out. "I think we'll take a hack. I don't know about you, but an open buggy ride in this weather doesn't hold much appeal for me this evening."

"So long as you pay the fare." She grinned at him.

"Yes, well I'm feeling extravagant."

"Imagine that," she said, whirling about and starting for the door. "And you a Scot."

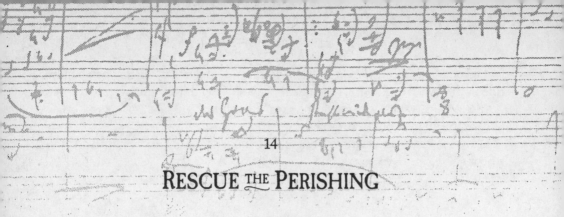

14

RESCUE THE PERISHING

Down in the human heart,
Crushed by the tempter,
Feelings lie buried that grace can restore:
Touched by a loving heart,
Wakened by kindness,
Chords that were broken will vibrate once more.

FANNY CROSBY (FROM "RESCUE THE PERISHING")

Bethany had been mired in a slough of despondency ever since her visit to Maylee.

The encounter with Frank Donovan had only intensified her gloomy feelings. For the most part, she thought she'd managed to conceal her dark mood from Andrew, but the sight that greeted them when they walked into the hovel on Mulberry Street depressed her already low spirits even further.

A boy of twelve or thirteen opened the door and stood staring at them with bleak eyes. After hearing Andrew's explanation as to their call, he stepped aside for them to enter, then went to stand in a dim corner of the room, arms crossed over his thin chest.

Bethany tried to be discreet as she scanned their surroundings. Two small girls huddled close together under a pile of rags on a rude, unpainted bedstead with nothing but straw ticking for a mattress. Directly across the room from the bed, a small, fragile woman lay uncovered and shivering on a sagging divan, muttering and ranting to herself.

Next to a narrow basin, a dilapidated cupboard leaned against one wall and appeared to hold two or three tin cups, some unmatched plates, and a piece of stone crockery. The only other furniture in the room was a scarred wooden chair. The lone window was merely a hole without glass, stuffed with rags. There was no fire, and the room was cold and damp. Permeating the dreary surroundings was a strong stench of sickness and neglect.

Bethany looked at Andrew and saw that his mouth was white rimmed, his features drawn tight. He was angry. As angry as she had ever seen him.

He made a gesture that he would see to the woman on the divan, so Bethany went to the little girls in the corner.

And all the while, the boy with the sharp features and inscrutable expression stood watching them in silence.

~

It took Andrew only seconds to recognize an opium addict in the throes of early withdrawal. The woman's eyes shot open at his approach, but in spite of the sly, almost calculating furtiveness, he could see that she was disoriented.

Clad only in a tattered nightdress, she was emaciated, her hair wet with perspiration and matted about her face. The stench that engulfed her person and the entire corner of the room was nearly overwhelming. She was trembling so hard the divan shook beneath her.

The minute Andrew reached her, she kicked out with both legs and began to flail her arms in front of her. He turned his face away for a moment, drew in a long breath, and willed himself not to condemn her.

But the woman sprawled before him was a bad dream with which he was all too familiar.

"Mrs. Lambert?"

She continued to thrash about and moan.

Andrew waited, but she showed no sign of quieting. "Mary? Can you hear me?"

She squeezed her eyes shut and threw her hands over her face. Andrew bent over her. "Mary, I'm a doctor. I've come to help you."

He reached to brush the tangled hair away from her face, but with an unexpected show of strength, she struck out at him, knocking his hand away.

Andrew persevered, even though the very sight of her made him want to retch. Not with nausea; he'd overcome that hazard of his profession years ago. But Mary Lambert dredged up something much deeper, much darker. Something he would have preferred to keep buried forever.

Suddenly impatient with himself, he straightened and turned to Bethany. "I'm going to need help with her. See if you can calm her down," he said as Bethany approached. "Otherwise, we'll have to restrain her long enough for an examination."

Bethany hesitated only a moment before seating herself on the edge of the divan. She grasped one flailing hand and brought it to rest on her lap. At the same time, she began to murmur words of reassurance to the woman.

Almost instantly, Mary Lambert stopped her thrashing about, obviously distracted by Bethany's soft voice and firm touch.

"Now, Mary, we need you to be very quiet so Dr. Carmichael can examine you. We're here to help you."

The woman squirmed but continued to watch Bethany with wary eyes.

"You're very ill, Mary. And so are your children. We're here to help. But we need you to help us as well."

"What about the girls?" Andrew asked as he adjusted his stethoscope.

"They're both severely malnourished," Bethany told him. "I suspect the younger of the two may have pneumonia. They're dehydrated, of course, and feverish. They need to be hospitalized right away."

With her free hand, Mary Lambert reached as if to knock Andrew's stethoscope away, but Bethany intercepted her move, and she dropped her hand without protest.

As Bethany continued to soothe the woman, Andrew made a brief but thorough assessment of her condition. He found exactly what he had expected. She was badly jaundiced. Her pulse was racing, her heartbeat fast and erratic. Twice she wrenched herself into a fetal position, gripping her abdomen with one hand as if to squeeze off the cramps he knew she was having. By now she was thoroughly drenched with sweat, and she'd taken to muttering again—something about spiders and rats. She was delusional.

No surprise there, either.

He checked both her arms and saw the needle tracks that indicated she was injecting the narcotic instead of smoking it. Like her little girls, she was malnourished and close to dehydration. Her stomach was undoubtedly empty by now, so he went ahead and gave her a minimum dose of strychnine for her heart, then prepared a bromide of soda to help quiet her, although at the moment there was no combativeness about her, no attempt to block his treatment.

Andrew was keenly aware of the boy watching from the corner of the room. "Fetch me a blanket, son. And a cold cloth."

The boy didn't move. "We don't have no blankets."

Andrew and Bethany exchanged glances.

"Some rags then," Andrew said. "Your mother needs to be kept warm."

Finally the boy pushed himself away from the wall and disappeared behind the curtain separating one room from the other. When he returned, he held a thin coat and a wet gray rag.

"This is all I could find," he said, handing Andrew the coat without looking at him.

Anger shot through Andrew. *Money for opium, but not for blankets…*

He covered Mary Lambert as best he could with the coat, then left Bethany to bathe the woman's face and hands with the dirty cloth.

Andrew motioned the boy to one side. "What about you, lad?" he said quietly. "Have you been ill, too?"

The youth shook his head. "I'm okay."

"How long has it been since you've eaten, son?"

The youth shrugged but made no reply.

Andrew sighed at the lack of response. "Does your mother drink liquor, too? With the opium?"

The boy darted a glance across the room at his mother, then turned back to Andrew. He blinked once, and Andrew recognized his attempt to keep his feelings well under wraps.

"Sometimes. Not always."

"How long has she been like this?" said Andrew.

"Like she is now?" The youth shrugged. "Three or four days, I guess. Before that she was sick a lot." He paused. "But she weren't never—out of her head, not until lately."

"Has she been using opium for very long?"

The boy hesitated. "A year or so. Maybe more."

"What about your father?"

In an instant, the impassive expression disappeared, replaced by a look of such raw hatred Andrew felt as if he'd been struck.

"We don't have a father," the boy bit out.

Andrew regarded him curiously. "What's your name, son?"

"Robert."

"Why do you say you have no father, Robert? Are your parents separated? Divorced?"

A look of loathing swept over the boy's face. "They weren't never married. He just comes down here every now and then. When he gets tired of his *real* missus."

Andrew's chest tightened at the shame and anger in young Robert Lambert's eyes. "He doesn't provide for you at all?"

The boy gave a contemptuous laugh. "There's what he *provides*." He gestured toward his mother. "Not that he ever gave us that much to begin with. She had to work and all, when she still could. But at least she used to spend the money he gave her for food and rent. Lately, though, she's spent it all on the opium and the drink." He glanced away. "Landlord is threatening to throw us out now."

"Does he still come here—your father?"

The boy shook his head, a look of contempt darkening his features. "He ain't been around for months now."

Andrew tried to think. He knew what had to be done, but he wondered how the boy would react. "I need to confer with Dr. Cole a moment," he said, leaving the boy and returning to Bethany and Mary Lambert.

Bethany looked up at him. "I've never seen anything like this before. What's wrong with her, Andrew?"

"A lot of things. Liver disease for one, I expect. Anemia. Withdrawal. She's in a bad way."

"Withdrawal?"

"Opium," Andrew said shortly. "And alcohol."

He caught a glimpse of disgust, but Bethany was too professional to give sway to her feelings for long.

Andrew turned and gestured to Robert Lambert. "Your mother and your sisters will have to go to the hospital, son. I'm going to make arrangements to have them moved to Bellevue."

As the boy approached, his previous stoicism seemed to fall away. A look of panic flickered in his eyes. "All of them?"

Andrew nodded.

"But we don't have money for any hospital!"

Instinctively, Andrew put a hand on his arm. "Don't worry about the money. They'll be taken care of; I'll see to it. There's really no choice, Robert."

He hesitated. "You need a place to stay as well, and I know of one. Whittaker House. It's run by a pastor named Ted Whittaker and his family, and—"

"I'll not stay in any preacher's house!"

Andrew glanced at Bethany, then at the youth. "What do you have against preachers, Robert?"

"*He's* a preacher!"

The boy's words didn't register right away. "Who's a preacher?"

"*Him!*" Robert's face was splotched, his eyes blazing. "Our *father!*"

The room seemed to grow very still. "Your...father is a pastor?" Andrew said softly, struggling to take in the lad's meaning. "Who—what's his name?"

"Warburton. *Robert* Warburton." The boy spit the words from his mouth as if they were laced with poison. "She named me for him!"

Andrew stared at him in numb astonishment. It must be coincidence. Another Robert Warburton.

"You're quite certain—he's a pastor?"

"He talked about it often enough. Bragging on his big church and all the traveling he has to do and the speeches he's asked to make and the books he writes. Oh, he's a preacher all right!"

A big church. Speeches. Books. It couldn't be—but it *had* to be. Robert Warburton. Pastor of one of the largest, most influential congregations in the city—in the *state*. A man looked up to by hundreds, perhaps even thousands, as if he were a saint.

Robert Warburton...

Bethany touched Andrew's arm and he saw the recognition in her eyes. Most likely, just about everyone knew who Robert Warburton was.

A thought struck him, and he turned to the boy. "Robert, do you have family in the city? A grandmother, perhaps?"

The boy frowned. "Mama's not from here. Her folks are back in Ohio." He paused. "She told us she wanted to be an actress. That's why she moved here.

Only she couldn't get a job and was down on her luck. I guess that's when she took up with *him*."

Andrew's mind groped for answers. With no family in the city, who was the woman who had sent him here? And *why* had she sent him, if she and the Lambert family weren't even related?

"I'll be all right just stayin' here," the boy said.

"You can't possibly stay here," Bethany said firmly before Andrew could make a reply. "You've no food. No heat. And you said yourself the landlord was threatening eviction. No, Robert, Dr. Carmichael is right. Besides, I promise you, you'll like Whittaker House. Ted Whittaker is a young man himself, with a wonderful family. All the boys who live there seem to like it. It's a good place." She paused. "That's where you need to go, Robert. At least for now."

Andrew looked at Robert and saw him gazing at Bethany with something akin to awe. What sort of effect might Bethany have on a youth like Robert Lambert—a boy trapped in the midst of squalor and despair, with a mother who had become something less than human to him? Bethany, with her impeccable dress, her exquisite, delicate features, her loveliness—not to mention the almost maternal tone she was taking with him.

And where had that maternal tone come from? He hadn't heard it before, not even with Maylee.

"You'll need to stay with your mother and your sisters," Bethany went on, "until we can arrange for an ambulance. I'll wait here with you while Dr. Carmichael takes care of all the arrangements. Then he and I will take you to Whittaker House."

Robert looked from one to the other. "You'll both go with me?"

"Of course we will."

Robert studied her as if he were searching for some additional reassurance. Finally, he thrust his hands into his pockets and nodded. "All right, then."

"Good." Bethany smiled at him, and Andrew—not for the first time—counted himself blessed to have her at his side. Bethany could usually persuade just about any patient of *anything*.

He thought that might be particularly true if the patient happened to be male.

15

TO STEP ASIDE IS HUMAN

Then gently scan your brother man,
Still gentler sister woman;
Tho' they may gang a kennin wrang
To step aside is human...
One point must still be greatly dark,
The moving why they do it;
And just as lamely can ye mark
How far perhaps they rue it.

ROBERT BURNS

The hack was nearing Bethany's apartment, and she had yet to utter more than a few words since leaving Whittaker House. The experience with Mary Lambert and her children had proven difficult for both of them, Andrew sensed, but even more of an ordeal for Bethany than for himself. He was having serious doubts about whether he should have asked her to accompany him, and he voiced those regrets.

"Don't be ridiculous," she said with a frown. "I have no intention of avoiding the difficult calls because I'm a woman. I thought you knew me better than that by now."

Andrew took her hand. "It has nothing to do with your being a woman. But I couldn't help seeing how it distressed you, and I could have handled the call on my own. Asking you to come was pure selfishness on my part. I simply wanted you with me."

She glanced down at their clasped hands but made no attempt to pull away. "You said you'd read my grandfather's papers on narcotic addiction?"

Andrew nodded.

"Well, so did I. But since much of his research concentrated on the War years and the soldiers who became addicted to painkillers after being injured, I suppose I've assumed that addiction was mostly confined to men. Seeing Mary Lambert and what the opium has done to her disturbed me. It seemed worse, somehow, to encounter a woman—a mother with obviously neglected children—in that awful condition."

Something dark and troubling squeezed Andrew's chest, but he couldn't quite bring himself to reply, not just yet.

"No doubt you think I'm naive," she went on, "and perhaps I am."

"No," Andrew said. "Not at all. We don't hear very much about women becoming addicted to liquor or narcotics," he said. "Nevertheless, it's all too common. Especially in the slum districts. I've seen it time and time again. Women or men—it's a vicious, devastating evil."

He should tell her. He should tell her now. This was as good a time as any, and eventually she would have to know. She had confided in him, after all. She'd been open and candid with him about many things in her life. The longer they were together, the more she seemed to open her thoughts, her memories, her feelings to him. But how did he begin? And how could he face what he would surely see in her eyes once she knew the truth?

He pulled in a deep breath. On impulse, he squeezed her hand, saying, "It's late, and neither of us has eaten since noon. Why don't we stop at Upton's and have a late supper?"

"Oh, you read my mind! A decent meal and a cup of tea will go far to lift my spirits; I'm sure of it."

Andrew forced a smile to mask the sick awareness that what he planned to tell her over supper would almost certainly do anything *but* lift her spirits.

~

"Andrew, you've scarcely eaten at all. I thought you were hungry."

They were midway through a late dinner at Upton's, and Andrew still hadn't initiated the conversation he'd been dreading. He pushed his food around on his plate, not answering her.

Bethany gave a long sigh and put her own fork down. "I can't get them out of my mind either," she said. "And do you know what I find myself thinking, Andrew?"

He looked up.

"I can't help but wonder about the church."

"What do you mean?"

"When I see a case like Mary Lambert—and when I realize that there must be tragedies like this all throughout the city—I have to question how it happened, how it came to this. There are also *churches* throughout the city, filled with people who claim to abhor poverty and neglected children and godless parents. How does an entire family come to utter ruin without the church *doing* something about it?"

She clenched one hand into a fist. "Worse still, if the Lambert boy was right, it was Robert Warburton—a *clergyman*—who led Mary Lambert into this appalling state! How could a man—a pastor—do such a thing and live with himself? With his *wife*?"

"Don't you think *we* are the church?"

She frowned and leaned forward a little. "What?"

"You and I. And anyone else who's willing to take Christ's mercy to the world." Andrew pushed his plate away. "*People* make up the church, Bethany, and *people* are inclined to forget about the Mary Lamberts of this world. The problems seem so overwhelming that even people who *do* care feel as if they can't do anything to change the situation. They forget that one person *can* make a difference. That's where it has to begin: with one person."

He stopped, raking a hand over the back of his neck. A fiery shaft of pain shot up his arm, and he caught his breath before going on. "For the most part, we assume that one person can't make a difference, and so we leave it up to 'other people'—those who are 'in charge' of that sort of thing: the clergy, the benevolent societies, the physicians. But the truth is, there aren't nearly enough 'other people' to do the job. And for those of us who *do* try to help, there's never enough time or energy to do as much as we'd like."

Again he paused and leaned back with a sigh. "Sooner or later, fatigue and discouragement set in. At least that's how it is for me. At times, when I think about all the poverty and illness and hopelessness in this city, I can't help but become frustrated with my limitations. And my own self-centeredness."

Bethany leaned forward. "If there's anything you're *not*, Andrew Carmichael, it's self-centered. You're the most selfless person I've ever known."

Andrew cringed inwardly at the compliment, especially since he had vowed to set the record straight tonight. He braced himself to change the subject.

As it happened, she did it for him.

"I need you to teach me all you know about addiction, Andrew," she said. "I want to learn as much as I can."

Andrew knotted his hands together. "Surely, with your grandfather's studies and expertise in that area—"

She interrupted with a shake of her head. "I'm not talking about what I've learned from books and papers. Yes, I've read as much as I could about various addictions, but I've had no real experience in treating them. Obviously, you have. After tonight, I can see that I need to know more."

Andrew swallowed against the dryness in his mouth. She had opened the door to the very subject he'd intended to raise—and now he wanted nothing so much as a way to avoid it.

But before he could utter a single word, he looked up to see a young patrolman named Liam MacGrath bearing down on their table.

"Evenin', Dr. Cole," the policeman said, doffing his hat to Bethany. "Dr.

Carmichael. Sergeant Donovan said if you weren't at your office or at home I might find you here or over to Axel's. You're needed down at Paradise Square."

Andrew scraped his chair back and retrieved his medical case. "What's happened?"

"Big explosion at the powder factory. We got several with real bad burns."

"We'll need transportation," Bethany said matter-of-factly as she got to her feet, her case in hand. "We took a hack here."

The young patrolman looked at her. "Well, now, I don't mind tellin' you, Dr. Cole, Paradise Square is no place for a lady."

Bethany fixed a look on him and smiled. "I appreciate your concern, Officer, but I've been there before. Will you drive us?"

The policeman darted a glance at Andrew.

One look at Bethany's face and Andrew knew better than to try to dissuade her. Paradise Square was as foul a place as any city ever harbored, but by now most of the rogues and rabble who peopled the area had come to recognize Bethany and himself—indeed, seemed to hold a grudging respect for them. Besides, it sounded as if they would both be needed.

"She's right," he conceded. "We should be on our way."

Not until they had left the restaurant and were nearing the infamous Five Points district did it strike Andrew that only the most craven of cowards would welcome the squalor of Paradise Square as a means of withholding the truth from the woman he loved.

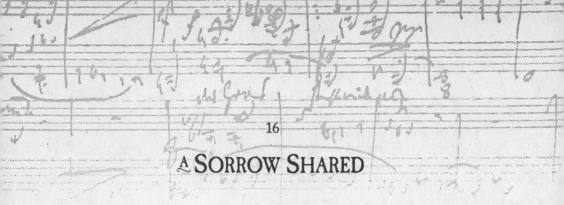

16

A SORROW SHARED

Too long a sacrifice
Can make a stone of the heart.

W. B. YEATS

In the snug little caretaker's house at Bantry Hill, Vangie MacGovern lay beside her husband, watching him as he slept. He was peaceful as a boy, smiling in his dreams.

Here it was, three weeks before Christmas, and Vangie was still hiding his rightful gift from him.

It was becoming harder and harder not to tell him. Soon he would guess. She had been in the family way too many times for him to be entirely ignorant of the signs.

And why *hadn't* she told him? With each of the other children, she had been eager to make the announcement. She would have thought she would be even more impatient with this one. This would be their *American* child after all. Their first child born out from under the English boot of persecution. Their first child born to freedom.

The enormity of her deceit gnawed at her. By not sharing the news with Conn, she was depriving him of the elation he experienced each time he learned that a new babe was on the way. He had every right to share this joy, and she had no right to withhold it.

Yet she continued to keep silent. God forgive her, for some inexplicable and no doubt sinful reason, she did not *want* to see her husband's joy, that familiar light of happiness and pride that always accompanied such news.

What kind of wicked, ungrateful woman had she become? It wasn't that she resented the babe. To the contrary, she had already begun to experience that familiar rush of love and fierce protectiveness for a new life growing inside her. No matter how many times she might give birth, each time was a wonder, an incomparable gift.

No, she could never resent her own child. It was *Conn* she resented.

The truth had been lurking at the edges of her mind for days, but she had kept it at bay. Now she was confronted with the full force of its shame and fury. How could she possibly resent her husband for loving her and for giving her yet another expression of that love? Hadn't she been blessed more than any woman had a right to be? To be married to a man who still loved her with all the passion of his manhood and the fullness of his heart after more than twenty years—surely she should be overcome with happiness and gratitude, not filled with resentment and bitterness.

The crux of her mutinous feelings toward her husband was Aidan, of course. She still resented Conn for the way he had set his head—and his heart—against their oldest son. She had begged him to write to the boy and initiate a reconciliation. Surely if Aidan knew of their unexpected good fortune, and if he could be convinced that Conn wanted him here, *needed* him here, then he would join them. But Conn met her every plea with the same hardheaded refusal. He simply would not take the first step.

And so day after day, week after week, the stone in Vangie's heart—the stone that stood between her love for her husband and her forgiveness of him—seemed to grow harder and more resistant.

She had written her own letters to Aidan, a number of them. But no reply had come, not so much as a note. And Vangie knew with a sick certainty that a reply would *never* come unless Conn himself made the first move to break down the wall between himself and their son. And how likely was that, himself the stubborn fool?

Vangie feared she might never see her oldest son again. And for that, she could not bring herself to forgive her husband.

Both the pain and the unforgiveness burned in her day and night. Like a pool of acid eating away at her insides, little by little, joy by joy, dream by dream. She could find little more than drudgery in the very act of living. The anticipation of a new baby couldn't fill the void of her firstborn's absence any more than her love for her husband could bridge the widening gap between them.

Conn stirred in his sleep and moved to draw her closer to him. But Vangie resisted, lying still until at last, overcome by the soul sickness dredging up in her with a vengeance, she rose and left their bed.

～

Renny Magee lay awake on her cot in the narrow loft, listening to the night sounds of the river and the rising wind. She could tell by the draft coming through the window that the air had turned sharply colder.

At first she thought the strange noise below was merely the wind keening through the pine trees at the side of the house. She burrowed deeper under the bed covers. But after a moment more, she heard the sound again and sat up, listening.

It wasn't the wind. Someone was in the kitchen, directly below her.

Someone weeping.

She hesitated only a minute before flinging the covers aside and, shivering in the cold, tiptoed down the wooden steps from the loft in her stocking feet.

At the doorway to the kitchen, she stopped short. There was no light in the room, save for a candle flickering weakly on the shelf of the cupboard near the window. Still, she could see Vangie, sitting alone at the table, her head resting on her arms, her slender shoulders rising and falling as she wept.

Dread immobilized Renny as she stood watching. What terrible thing had happened? But then it struck her that Vangie would hardly be weeping alone at the kitchen table had some awful event occurred. In times of difficulty, members of the MacGovern family didn't keep to themselves, but drew together.

The sight of the strong, kindhearted Vangie sorrowing in the lonely silence of the night pierced Renny's heart like a darning needle. Yet she resisted the fierce desire to cross the room and offer comfort. Vangie would most likely not welcome an intrusion upon her solitude.

And so she backed away, hovering just outside the door where she wouldn't be seen, half in fear of what had brought Vangie to such a state of despair, half in despondency at the awareness that it was not her place to approach this woman she loved as she might have loved her own mother…had she ever known what it was to *have* a mother.

~

Conn woke from a restless sleep to find Vangie gone from their bed.

After another moment he heard her in the kitchen, weeping. He rose to go to her, then stopped, sinking back onto the mattress. This wasn't the first time she had left their bed in the middle of the night.

And he knew why. She meant to conceal her pain from him.

Apparently, she believed he didn't hear her sobbing alone in the kitchen, didn't see the evidence of her sadness in her swollen eyes at the breakfast table. She continued to pretend that all was well, that she was happy and content in their new home. But to his own grief, Conn knew better. For a long time now, Vangie had kept a part of herself closed, shut away from him, even when they made love.

There was a place in her reserved for someone else, he knew. An empty place that not even the depth of his love, the needs of the children, and the richness of their life here on this sprawling, wondrous piece of land could ever fill. It was Aidan's place, and it was growing inside her, growing to such proportions that Conn feared before long it might shut out all else, including him.

At last he turned and, even though the urge to go to her was almost more than he could bear, he fought against it. He couldn't bring himself to face her resentment yet again, to see the accusation in her eyes. He knew what she wanted from him, and although he would have moved mountains for her, sure, there would be no moving Aidan. He had seen it in his son's face that day on the docks, when he'd turned and walked away from them, from all of them, even his mother. The boy had made his choice, and he had chosen Ireland over his own family.

What could be done about such a son?

Besides, did Vangie really think this was easy for *him*? Didn't she realize that the knife in her heart sliced as deeply into his own? Aidan was *his* son, too. Didn't she understand that the loss of their son was as much his loss as hers?

There was nothing more he could say to her that he hadn't already said, nothing to ease her pain or purge her resentment toward him. Surely in time, she would come to see that there was nothing either of them could do. Aidan would come to America only if and when *he* wanted to come, and until then they might just as well let go of the boy.

He considered himself a man, after all, so let him be a man. They had their other children to care for. The good Lord knew that in itself was a full-time job.

Conn sighed. Morning would come soon, and he'd have to be up and ready to work. And so he buried his head in the pillows, trying to drown out the heartbreaking sound of his wife's unhappiness, even as he attempted to ignore his own.

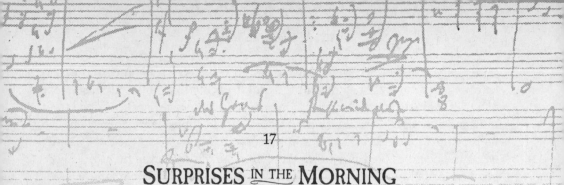

17

SURPRISES IN THE MORNING

A little love, a little trust,
A soft impulse, a sudden dream...

STOPFORD A. BROOKE

Christmas was less than three weeks away, and the orchestra would perform its annual holiday concert—the final concert of the year—in just ten days.

Susanna had been seeing evidence of Michael's usual pre-performance tension for days now. This morning, however, he seemed more energized than edgy, consuming his breakfast in a rush and replying to Caterina's questions in a vague and disjointed fashion. None of this was like him at all; Michael was a man who typically savored not only his food, but mealtime itself, taking advantage of the time at the table to enjoy Caterina's chatter.

Come to think of it, Caterina was also acting peculiar. Instead of Susanna having to call her at least twice before she stirred, she had appeared in the hallway a little before seven, still in her nightgown and wrapper, but wide awake and fairly dancing with high spirits.

By the time they were finished with breakfast, Susanna was convinced that both Michael and Caterina were indeed behaving oddly, as if they were conspiring together. Caterina kept darting glances at Susanna with a puckish smile, and several times she left her chair to whisper in her father's ear, despite Susanna's pointed remarks about rudeness.

Normally Michael would have reprimanded his daughter for such conduct, but this morning he appeared to be enjoying her mischief. And Caterina, the little minx, was clearly intent on taking full advantage of her father's indulgence.

They had taken to eating their morning meal in the small breakfast room off the kitchen instead of in the dining room. Susanna herself had suggested the change; both Michael and Caterina seemed less restrained in the small, cheerful setting that looked out onto the gardens. Besides, the vast dining hall was too stuffy a setting for breakfast. Since Paul was almost always up and about before the rest of the household and rarely sat down for the morning meal, it was normally just the three of them at the table.

As Michael's time with his daughter was limited, Susanna had offered more than once to take her meal alone, but in truth she had been pleased when Michael wouldn't hear of it. She looked forward to these early-morning times with him and Caterina. Michael also seemed to enjoy beginning the day in this fashion. He was more relaxed and animated at breakfast than at any other time.

Susanna admired the way he so diligently reserved a part of his mornings and as many evenings as possible for his daughter. His travels back and forth to the city and the hours he spent locked up in the music room cut deeply into his time with Caterina, but he was never neglectful. To the contrary, he made every effort to give her his undivided attention—and affection—as often as possible. As for Caterina, she seemed to take her father's busy life in stride, while clearly thriving on the time they *did* spend together.

Michael pushed his chair back from the table and stood. "I trust the two of you have not forgotten this evening?"

His question prompted a muffled giggle from Caterina, which her father quickly silenced with one raised eyebrow.

"No, of course not," Susanna replied. "Is Paul still planning to meet us at the ferry and take us to the hotel?"

"*Sì*. Cati seems bent on dressing in her finest, but if you would prefer not to, Susanna, that's quite all right."

Susanna's "finest" was the black wool dress she had brought with her from home—not quite shabby, but undeniably well-worn. Still, even if she could afford it, which she definitely could not, a new dress would have been an unnecessary extravagance for a simple dinner after rehearsal. Her black dress would do perfectly well.

Still puzzled by his and Caterina's odd behavior this morning, Susanna caught herself—just for a moment—wondering…

But, no, neither of them could possibly know about today. Caterina had pried her birth date out of her once, but that had been many weeks ago. The girl was bright, but surely too young to remember a date for so long a time. Besides, even if she *had* remembered, it was foolish entirely to think that Michael might make an effort to acknowledge it.

Unless Caterina had coaxed…

Really, she was being *too* foolish. Still, it was rather nice, even *pretending* that someone might remember her birthday.

She watched as Michael bent to press a good-bye kiss on the top of Caterina's head. Immediately the child leaped from her chair and whipped around to him. "I wish it were tonight right *now*, Papa!" she burst out, flinging her arms about his waist.

"Someday soon, *mia figlia*," he said dryly, "I hope for you to make the acquaintance of a virtue called 'patience.'"

"But I know about patience, Papa," she said, still clinging to him. "Mrs. Dempsey says it means not to rush the cook or we'll eat the potatoes raw."

He chuckled. "Mrs. Dempsey is a wise woman, no?"

"She also taught me a poem about patience."

"Ah! And I expect you are about to recite it."

Caterina tilted her head, curls bouncing, and looked up at him: *"Patience is a virtue. Have it if you can. It's rarely seen in woman—and never in a man."*

Michael's dark brows shot up in surprise. Then he threw back his head and laughed.

Beaming, the child turned to look at Susanna.

"I think it's time for our morning devotions, miss," she said sternly, then lost the struggle to keep a solemn expression.

Michael tugged at a lock of his daughter's dark hair. "I must get ready to leave," he said. "I will see you this evening."

Caterina was watching Susanna closely, the fingers of one hand pressed against her lips as if to contain another giggle. Yes, there was definitely some sort of collusion between the child and her father. She rose from her chair and started to follow Caterina out of the room.

Michael, however, stopped them. "Caterina, I need to speak with your Aunt Susanna for a moment. You go along to your room and wait for her."

The little girl frowned, glancing from her father to Susanna, but finally went bouncing out of the room, looking back only once.

"I wanted to talk with you about this before I raise the subject with Caterina," Michael said, gesturing that Susanna should again sit down.

His lighthearted demeanor had sobered.

"Is something wrong?" Susanna asked.

He shook his head, taking a chair across the table from her. "No, but there is something I want to discuss with you, something that will involve you just as much as it will Caterina or myself. I want to know how you feel about it before I initiate anything or bring it up to Caterina."

Exceedingly curious, Susanna listened carefully, her astonishment growing as he told her what he wanted to do, indeed what he felt God was *calling* him to do.

When he had finished, he paused for only a second or two. "What do you think? Would you be willing that I should do this? And to help out if needed?"

Susanna wiped the dampness from her eyes. "I think it's a wonderful idea," she said quietly. "And of course, I'll help however I can."

"And do you think Caterina will agree?"

"Oh, Michael, you know she will! Caterina has a generous heart entirely. And I have no doubt but what she'll be more help than you can imagine."

Slowly, he nodded and smiled. "I think you are right. We will tell her together, no?"

He sought her hand across the table. "Thank you for understanding, Susanna."

Susanna looked at their clasped hands. After so long a time, they had moved from suspicion to acceptance, from acceptance to trust, from trust to friendship. And now they had come together as allies in a common cause.

He squeezed her hand as if he had read her thoughts. How could such a simple touch, Susanna wondered, make her heart feel as if it were overflowing with warm oil?

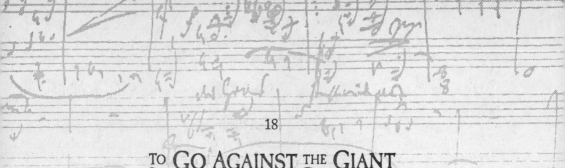

18

TO GO AGAINST THE GIANT

Use well the moment; what the hour
Brings for thy use is in thy power;
And what thou best canst understand
Is just the thing lies nearest to thy hand.

JOHANN W. VON GOETHE

During the first few minutes of rehearsal, Susanna found it difficult to concentrate. Her thoughts kept drifting to Michael and the surprise he'd revealed after breakfast. If she had had any remaining doubts about the kind of man he was, what he had divulged to her this morning would have erased them all.

She could never say this to Michael—he had a way of deflecting any praise that came to him—but Susanna was deeply moved by the thought of what he meant to do. It was a good thing, even a *noble* thing. She found herself genuinely enthusiastic about the experience ahead—and inordinately pleased that Michael had placed so much confidence in her cooperation.

But for now, she really needed to pay attention to what was happening on stage. In addition to the orchestra, Michael had assembled three choirs: two large choirs from local churches and a smaller but highly talented children's choir from several of the city's shelter houses. They could not have been more diverse.

Watching Michael work was a fascinating experience. Most of the time he seemed relaxed, even casual with his people, and their high regard for him was obvious. Even so, in spite of his informal bearing, he insisted not only on perfection, but on total involvement in the music. Under Michael's baton, no musician dared to daydream or indulge in idle chatter with a neighbor.

He had built a magnificent orchestra, one that rarely received anything but the highest of praise from the critics. There were exceptions, of course. One or two columnists seemed incapable of anything but the most scathing reviews—not only of the orchestra, but of Michael himself. He routinely discarded those reviews that were transparently personal, petty, or spiteful, but seemed to pay close heed to the comments of the few critics he respected, even if their judgments were less than glowing. Clearly, he was not a man to grow complacent with his own abilities or accomplishments.

Susanna's gaze roamed over the orchestra and the choirs. It was an awesome array of talent, yet with every number rehearsed, she became more keenly aware of the absence of an organist. Up until now, the rehearsal had consisted mostly of varied renderings of seasonal carols—some from other countries—and a number of traditional selections, such as Schubert's "Mille Cherubini in Coro" and "Jesu Joy of Man's Desiring." Michael typically developed his own arrangements, even for the simplest Christmas carol, so perhaps he had purposely omitted the organ. But when he instructed just before the break that they would end the rehearsal with "For unto Us a Child Is Born" and the "Hallelujah Chorus" from the *Messiah*, she fully expected an organist to arrive on the scene, albeit late.

During the break, Caterina went running up to the stage, where Paul and Michael still lingered, engaged in some private discussion. Michael smiled when his daughter tugged on his coattails, then lifted her into his arms as the few orchestra members remaining on stage came over to them.

Susanna watched with wry amusement as Caterina proceeded to charm them all with her dimples and laughter. After another moment, Michael set her to her feet, and she led him down the stage steps to the front row, where Susanna was seated.

"So—how are we doing?" he said, sitting down beside her. "Do you have any suggestions?"

"Papa, may I go play the harp?" Caterina begged.

"Don't interrupt, Cati," said Michael. Then he nodded. "Only for a moment. We will be starting again soon."

He smiled at Susanna. "One time it is the harp, next the cello," he said as Caterina scampered off. "I think she means to play all the instruments in the orchestra."

"Like her papa," Susanna said. It was true: Michael seemed capable of playing whatever instrument he chose, although at home he clearly favored the simple mandolin.

He gave a turn of the wrist, saying, "But we will hope that Caterina plays them *well*. Her papa is a virtuoso with none." He paused, his expression growing more serious. "Speaking of virtuosos, I need to ask if you would be willing to help us a little before we finish today."

Instantly, Susanna's guard shot up.

"Now, before you say no, let me explain. I would have asked you at the beginning of the rehearsal, but I knew you would think I arranged it on purpose—and I promise you, Susanna, I did no such thing."

"Arranged *what*?"

He hesitated, as if reluctant to explain.

"Arranged what, Michael?" she repeated sternly.

As if he could feel her scrutiny, he turned his face away. "It seems that Christopher Redding, our organist…ah, what has happened is…that he fell on the ice yesterday afternoon and broke not only his ankle, but a wrist as well. I thought perhaps you might consider helping us. For this evening, at least."

Susanna stared at him, speechless. An unexpected twinge of excitement was immediately swallowed up by a surge of annoyance and disappointment as she remembered his and Caterina's behavior of the morning: the sly smiles and furtive whispers between the two. To think she had actually allowed herself to believe, even for a moment, that they might have been plotting something…special.

"Do you really expect me to believe you didn't plan this?"

He turned back to her with an infuriating ghost of a smile.

"You see," he said, "I knew what you would think."

"Then you also knew what I would say."

He shrugged, a gesture that merely heated Susanna's irritation.

"You can't possibly think I would humiliate myself in front of all these people."

Paul and Caterina had left the stage and now stood watching them, Caterina with eyes wide and curious, Paul with his gaze averted, as if trying to pretend he wasn't listening.

But Susanna was beyond the point of caring.

"Michael, I haven't been near an organ for nearly a year! And I've never played an organ like *that*!" Forgetting Michael's blindness for the moment, Susanna stabbed her index finger toward the immense grand organ at the far right of the stage—a massive instrument with five manuals in addition to the pedals. An organ like this would surely intimidate all but the most outstanding of musicians.

And she had been longing to get her hands on it all evening…

She shook her head as if to banish the treacherous thought.

"But you once played for the worship at your church," Michael pointed out.

"That was ages ago! And a poor excuse of an instrument it was at that. Certainly nothing like that behemoth on stage."

His jaw clenched in a stubborn look, and he murmured something about it being "just an organ."

"It is most assuredly not '*just* an organ,'" Susanna shot back.

"But only for this evening," he said, his tone deceptively mild. "You need not play—how do you call it?—full organ. If you would merely accompany us as best you can. Otherwise the rehearsal will not be what it should."

Was there no end to his attempt to manipulate? "And I suppose your Mr. Redding will be fully recovered in time for the concert? He must have quite an impressive capacity for healing."

Michael's expression turned sheepish, but he made no reply.

Susanna shook her head. "I simply cannot believe you did this. And to bring Caterina into it as well! So *this* was what all the whispering and scheming at breakfast was about."

"But, Aunt Susanna—that's not what we were whispering about—"

"Caterina—" Michael's tone was unusually sharp.

"Well, we weren't," the child repeated with uncharacteristic sullenness. "I didn't know anything about Mr. Redding."

Susanna looked from one to the other. Michael's expression was impassive, closed, but Caterina's lower lip could not have protruded any farther, and tears glistened in her eyes. Could Susanna possibly be mistaken about Michael's having deliberately contrived this scenario?

"I'm sorry you think I would try to deceive you in such a way," Michael said quietly. "The truth is that I only learned of Redding's accident when I arrived this afternoon. As I told you, I was hesitant to approach you about the organ. I was fairly certain that you would react…just as you have."

Paul, obviously bent on redeeming the situation, gave Susanna a look of appeal. "It is true, Susanna. Redding's son brought the word of his accident only moments before rehearsal began." He paused. "As a member of the orchestra, I wish, of course, that you would reconsider. We do feel the lack of the organ. It would be a great help if you would play for us. And it's not as if you would be a soloist. Why, with the instruments and all the voices you would scarcely be noticed!"

Susanna lifted an eyebrow at this; they both knew the likelihood of the organ not being noticed.

"But if you really feel incapable, I understand," Paul added with a cherubic expression.

"I don't know that I'm *incapable*." Susanna was growing nearly as exasperated with Paul as she was with Michael. "I expect with some warning I could have managed. But even the most accomplished of organists, which I would never pretend to be, needs to practice."

"But of course," Paul quickly agreed. "It would take a long time—perhaps weeks?—before you would feel competent, no?"

"Not *weeks*," Susanna said. "But certainly a few *days*. It hardly matters in any event. You need someone sooner than I could be prepared."

Michael broke in then. "*Sì*, as you said, there is no possibility that Redding would be back with us in only a few days. I admit that I probably *was* hoping that if I could convince you to assist us today—and if you managed well enough—then you might consider playing for the concert itself."

"Michael, we've talked about this before—"

He nodded. "I know, I know. And I do understand your fear—"

"I'm not—it's not *fear*. Not exactly." Susanna bit her lower lip. Several times. "All right. It *is* fear. But you can't possibly understand what it's like for me."

"As I have told you before, I *do* understand."

"I know what you told me, but—"

"But aren't you brave, Aunt Susanna?"

Susanna turned to look at her niece.

"When we read the story about David and Goliath, you said that being brave doesn't mean we're not afraid. It means doing what we're supposed to do even if we *are* afraid."

Susanna stared at her niece. Caterina was gazing up at her with the uncompromising, guileless look of a child who has found a truth, made it her own, and now decided to test it.

She saw the look on Paul's face—not smug, exactly, but definitely keen to hear her reply. Michael, too, was obviously curious as to how she would answer Caterina.

But Caterina had not finished. "You said David was probably *very* afraid of Goliath, because he was just a boy and Goliath was a *giant*. But David went to meet Goliath anyway, and God helped him. And if the organ is like a big, scary giant…"

If Michael had not been blind, his gaze would have easily burned a hole through Susanna. And in Paul's eyes, she encountered a distinct glint of challenge.

To her surprise, Michael moved to ease the tension, lifting his hand as if to put a halt to any further discussion. "I understand, Susanna. You simply do not feel…ready…to do this. So, then, we will stop trying to coerce you and get back to rehearsal."

"But, Papa—"

Michael shook his head. "It is enough, Caterina. Your Aunt Susanna has said no. We will speak no more about it."

"Thank you, Michael."

Throughout the remainder of rehearsal, Susanna could feel Caterina watching her. The little girl's disappointment pierced her heart. And she knew that, because of her stubbornness, Handel's crowning achievement would suffer for the lack of an organ's depth and richness.

But Michael had it coming. He had attempted to trick her into doing something he knew she wouldn't want to do. All her earlier warm thoughts toward him went flying from her mind, replaced by a cold, wrenching disappointment of her own.

Still, no matter how she tried to justify her resistance to his maneuvering, her excuses seemed to bounce off the wall of her conscience. They all added up to nothing more than fear. The fear of calling attention to herself. The fear of failing—failing not only the expectations of those who were counting on her, but failing the music itself. The fear of not being…*adequate*.

It was a fear that even she could not explain, so how could she expect anyone else to understand it? Least of all a man who almost certainly had never felt inadequate in his life.

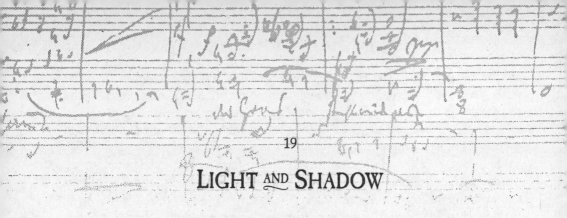

19

LIGHT AND SHADOW

My heart is like a trembling leaf
carried by the wind.

ANONYMOUS

For the past hour, Bethany Cole's mood had seesawed from exasperation to anticipation so many times she was getting a headache.

The exasperation stemmed from the time and effort spent on decking herself out in an exceptionally uncomfortable dinner dress and a new hair style, which she immediately decided made her look somewhat like a ferret.

By the time she removed some of the froufrou from the dress and secured her hair to its usual nape-of-the-neck twist, her hands were trembling. She felt three kinds of fool for working herself into a state over what should have been nothing more than a pleasant evening among friends.

As for her earlier anticipation, it had been all but swept away by her impatience with herself. This was not some sort of a…a rendezvous, after all, but simply a social gathering to which Andrew had offered to escort her.

And wasn't Andrew the reason she was so jumpy in the first place? He seemed bent on making more of the occasion than it really was. He had even sent her flowers, for goodness' sake! Not to mention the fact that, with all the time she'd wasted fussing over her appearance, she could have seen a few more patients or even made hospital rounds. Certainly, she could have accomplished something more worthwhile than giving herself a roaring case of hives.

Not that she actually had hives just yet, but if she didn't calm down and stop fussing over her appearance, it could still happen.

And wouldn't that be just fine and dandy? No doubt poor Andrew would be positively elated at the thought of escorting a red, bumpy-faced partner into Gaulerio's elegant dining room.

She took one more quick glance in the mirror, deciding not for the first time that her hair was too pale—was it just the light, or was she starting to go gray around her temples? And one side of her neckline was draped lower than the other. Well, it was too late to do anything about that. Leaning closer to the mirror, she jabbed another hairpin into the back of her hair—and discovered a spot on the tip of her nose, a blemish that she was quite certain had not been there a minute before.

She groaned, slapped some more talc over her face, and resigned herself to the dismaying fact that she was going to be a huge disappointment, if not an all-out embarrassment, to poor Andrew.

But why did she keep thinking of him as "poor Andrew," when this entire debacle was all his doing anyway?

⁓

Andrew Carmichael fumbled with his neckcloth, finally giving up in utter frustration.

He should have left the office earlier. He had insisted that Bethany take some extra time, sending her off a good hour and a half before they usually closed up. Now he wished he had left when she did. But the three patients remaining in the waiting room had all seemed serious enough to warrant attention, so he had stayed.

So much for allowing some extra time for himself tonight. As it was, he'd barely managed to shave and change clothes.

Bethany, of course, would be absolutely lovely. As always. Which raised the question he'd been asking himself all day: given the fact that Bethany Cole would steal the breath from any man at twenty paces, why on earth had she agreed to accompany him tonight?

What a picture they must make to anyone else: the Princess and the Peasant.

Beauty and the Beast.

He actually groaned in self-disgust. What had ever possessed him to think that Bethany might *want* to spend an entire evening with him? She spent most of her days with him as it was.

Had she consented only because they were associates? Did she view tonight as just another event to be endured because they were partners?

Or had she simply not been able to think of an excuse quickly enough to beg off?

Anxiety tore at him even more as he recalled the conversation he'd had only last week with Frank Donovan. Frank's cynicism often rankled him, but on this particular occasion, he had found his friend's sarcasm particularly annoying. In truth, Frank's remarks had hurt, and hurt deeply. And yet his barbs had held such a ring of truth that Andrew had actually found himself fighting off a kind of bleak despondency for days after.

Frank had come to the office just as patient hours were over, and Bethany was on her way out. Andrew had watched her leave, not realizing that Frank was watching *him*.

When he turned back, Frank's face was creased with a smirk. "Ah, Doc, you're in a bad way, it seems to me."

Andrew had known exactly what Frank was getting at, but he'd managed to feign a questioning look.

Frank shook his head. "I don't reckon there is a sorrier sight than a man in love."

"Frank..."

"Have you given this sufficient thought, Doc?"

Frank's abrupt change in tone, from his usual wry banter to this unexpected gravity, caught Andrew off guard. "Have I given *what* sufficient thought?"

"Have you considered the consequences if things don't work out?"

"Am I supposed to know what you mean?"

"Oh, come on, Doc! You know what I'm talking about. You're in love with the woman, and that's the truth."

Andrew felt mortified. Had he been that transparent? And if he had, what business was it of Frank's?

"Even if you were right—and I'm not saying you are—shouldn't you let me worry about it?" He forced a short laugh. "I'm not exactly wet behind the ears anymore, you know."

Frank had a most irritating way of eyeing a man as if he were nothing shy of a fool. "Well, that's true enough, Doc. But you wouldn't be the first man to go diggin' yourself a grave with the wrong shovel. If you take my meaning."

Andrew frowned but said nothing.

"I'd hate to see you make a bad mistake, is all."

Andrew clenched his fists at his sides.

"The thing is, Doc, if it's settlin' down to home and hearth fire you're wanting, I confess I don't quite see that happening with your Dr. Cole. She may be a fine doctor—by all accounts, she is exactly that—but can you honestly see the woman with a passel of young'uns hangin' on to her skirts while she stirs the soup?"

For the first time in their friendship, Andrew found himself angry with Frank Donovan. No, more than angry—furious. Frank's intentions might be the best; he might sincerely believe he was doing nothing more than looking out for a friend, but that did nothing to cool Andrew's anger. This time Frank had gone too far.

Andrew gave a shrug, intending to put an end to the conversation before he said something he might later regret.

As it turned out, it was Frank who brought the exchange to a halt. With an idle wave of his hand and in a tone thick with exaggerated Irish, he said, "Ah, well, 'tis none of my business after all, is it now? I'm naught but a thickheaded mick who needs to mind his own affairs."

They parted with an unresolved—and unfamiliar—tension between them. They hadn't encountered each other since, but Andrew knew how it would be when they did. They would make an attempt at small talk, pretending nothing had happened, but the tension would still hang between them until either time or circumstance managed to expel it.

He quit fiddling with his tie and picked up his hairbrush. His hands were so swollen he could scarcely manage the brush, but he made one more hasty attempt to coax his hair into place. He had never thought much about his hair one way or the other. Lately, however, he bemoaned the color, an odd shade, neither brown nor black, rather like the bark of a tree.

And that dreadful forelock that simply would not be constrained; had he been a woman, he could have anchored it in place with a hairpin, but as it was, he went about most of the time looking like a one-eyed sailor.

He passed a hand down his nose. The hawkish, too prominent beak of the Carmichael men was definitely not one of the familial traits he might have coveted.

By now he was thoroughly disgusted with himself. This was a simple evening out with friends, not some sort of a…a tryst. And yet he'd made a royal botch of things when he asked Bethany if he could escort her, and then gone on to compound his humiliation by behaving like a lovesick poet most of the week. Sending her flowers this afternoon, for goodness' sake, and insisting she take time away from the office when he would have really preferred to have her there—had needed her there, in fact.

He'd rather just call the whole thing off. But of course that was impossible. Then he really *would* make himself out a total fool.

He swiped the stubborn lock of hair away from his forehead and grabbed his coat and gloves from the back of the chair. He looked for his scarf, found it at his feet, then struggled to pull his gloves on over his swollen knuckles. Finally, stomach churning, he left the room, uttering a hasty prayer as he went that he wouldn't knock anything over at dinner to embarrass himself or Bethany.

At least one piece of news he had saved for tonight was almost guaranteed to please her. And he hoped she'd also like the surprise he'd planned for after dinner.

All in all, it would be a lovely evening, except…except for what he planned to tell her later—something he *must* tell her. Tonight.

20

SUSANNA'S SURPRISE

He that is down needs fear no fall,
He that is low, no pride.

JOHN BUNYAN

Susanna was still smarting from the scene back at the concert hall when they walked into Gaulerio's restaurant. The setting that greeted her, however, caused her to forget everything else—for the moment, at least.

This was Michael's favorite eating place, and Paul's as well. Gaulerio's was known to be a favorite meeting and dining establishment for many among the music community. Even so, Susanna was surprised at the lack of gilt and glitter. Instead, the restaurant had a quiet elegance, warmed by a great deal of wood and rich tones of burgundy and deep blue. The room was illuminated with candles and low-hanging chandeliers.

Although every table seemed to be occupied, the sounds of conversation and the clink of silver and china were unobtrusive, muffled by the thick floor coverings and heavy draperies.

A small, trim man with a neat mustache rushed up to them. "Ah, *Maestro! Benvenuto, benvenuto!* We were beginning to think you had abandoned us!"

Michael laughed. "Surely you know better than that, Enrico."

Enrico greeted Paul just as effusively, then bowed low to Caterina. "Ah, the *principéssa!* See how quickly you are growing up!"

The three men exchanged a few words in rapid Italian before Michael took Susanna's arm and introduced her as "*Signorina* Fallon—Caterina's Aunt Susanna."

With a huge smile and a sweeping bow, Enrico kissed Susanna's hand, then said something in Italian too quickly for her to catch. Straightening, he turned to Michael and took his arm. "Everything is ready, *Maestro*. We will go upstairs now."

Michael and Paul, obviously well-known here, had to stop several times before reaching the stairway to acknowledge greetings from the various diners. A number of men stood to shake hands, while the women, Susanna noticed, watched Michael closely with unconcealed interest.

At the top of the stairs, Enrico led them down a narrow hallway and flung open the paneled double doors at the end. "Here we are! Come, please!"

Caterina scampered ahead of her, and Paul, too, moved quickly forward. Susanna started into the room, then stopped. At the same time, Paul's good-natured face split into a wide smile as he stood watching Susanna.

Directly ahead of her, a small group was gathered around a large oval table, lavishly decorated with winter greenery, candles, and sparkling china. Nearby, on a smaller table, several brightly colored, beribboned packages were heaped.

Susanna stared in astonishment. Rosa Navaro was there, along with Dr. Cole and Dr. Carmichael. Pastor Holt. Even Miss Fanny Crosby had come. The moment they caught sight of her, they all stood, laughing and applauding. "Happy Birthday, Susanna!"

Caterina danced circles around her. "Did we surprise you, Aunt Susanna?" she piped. "*Did* we?"

Susanna smiled down at Caterina and took her hand. "How clever you are, *alannah*. And how well you kept your secret—you and your papa!"

"Papa did all the work," Caterina said with the utmost seriousness. "He and Cousin Paul."

"Well...I'm very grateful. This is a wonderful surprise."

Susanna didn't trust herself to so much as glance at Michael.

This, then, was what he and Caterina had been whispering about this morning. Not a scheme to replace the missing organist, not a ploy to "advance" her to a place where she had no desire to be. A party.

A surprise party. For her.

Michael had been telling the truth, after all. Just as Caterina insisted. And fool that she was, she had made a scene, humiliated herself, disappointed Caterina—and embarrassed Michael.

Susanna wished she could fall through the floor, so great was her self-reproach. Two things struck her in that instant: she was dismayed at how quickly the old mistrust of Michael could reappear, confounding her other feelings for him; and at the same time she was shaken by a surge of relief, in spite of her shame, to realize that she'd misjudged him so badly.

"Michael," she said, her voice low as she turned to him, "I didn't know...this morning, when you and Caterina—"

"*Sì*. I know," he said, his tone quiet and unmistakably sad.

She had mistrusted him, misunderstood him, hurt him. He was *still* hurting—she could hear it in his voice, see it in the slump of his shoulders, the white lines that bracketed his eyes.

"I don't know what to say. I'm sorry...so sorry...for thinking—"

"It's all right, Susanna. Come—we should go in now." He waved off her apology, but his demeanor was restrained, his expression inscrutable.

"I must talk with you later."

. He offered his arm as if he hadn't heard her. "Your friends are waiting."

~

Somehow Susanna managed to ignore her raw feelings as the evening progressed. The heaviness in her heart seemed to recede in the laughter and the warmth around the table, and at one point she realized she was actually enjoying herself.

If Michael bore her any grudge, no one would have guessed. He was his usual affable, congenial self, greeting all their guests and drawing Andrew Carmichael aside for a private word. No one else seemed to notice that he seldom spoke directly to her, that he avoided even the most casual touch of the hand or brush of the sleeve when passing a dish or a condiment her way.

The only bad moment came after all the gifts had been opened. There was a soft indigo shawl from Rosa, a delicate, lace-edged handkerchief from Miss Fanny, and a pair of fawn-colored gloves and matching neck scarf from Dr. Cole and Dr. Carmichael. From Paul she received copies of Miss Alcott's *Little Women* and *Little Men,* and Caterina presented her with a portrait she had painted—a remarkably realistic likeness of Gus, the wolfhound.

Only after all the other gifts had been opened and an elegantly decorated cake had been served did Michael surprise her by quietly pushing a gift wrapped in shimmering paper and satin ribbons in front of her.

Susanna looked at the package, then at Michael. Her fingers trembled as she loosened the ribbons and pulled the paper from an exquisite ivory jewelry box. The lid was adorned with an intricately carved minstrel's harp, also in ivory.

She caught a sharp breath. "Oh…how *beautiful!*"

Bethany Cole and Rosa echoed her sentiment, while Paul described the gift in detail to Miss Fanny.

Caterina tugged at her sleeve. "It plays *music,* Aunt Susanna!"

Susanna wound the spring, and "Dear Harp of My Country" by Ireland's own poet, Thomas Moore, began to chime its plaintive melody in bell-like tones.

Susanna's eyes filled, as did her heart. Her gaze went to Michael, who sat quietly, his lips curved in a faint smile.

"It's…*exquisite,* Michael."

"It was my mother's," he said softly. "My papa gave it to her when I was born."

She stared at him, shaken by the value his words attached to the gift, a gift she would have counted as highly precious even without its personal significance to Michael.

"It's...the most wonderful gift ever. I don't know what to say."

"I hoped you would like it," he said simply.

Like it? Susanna felt like weeping. She was thrilled that he had chosen to give her something that obviously meant a great deal to him. And yet the personal nature of the gift only served to sharpen her feelings of guilt.

She looked around the table and saw the well-meaning but curious smiles. Somehow she managed a smile of her own.

"Thank you...so much, every one of you. This has to be the most special birthday party I've ever had."

In truth, it was the *only* birthday party she'd ever had. At home, there had never been enough money for such extravagance. The enormity of what Michael had done for her, the trouble he'd gone to for her, overwhelmed her anew.

She should probably say more, especially to Michael, but she couldn't think of a thing that wouldn't have sounded gauche or mawkish. "I'm truly grateful for your kindness," was all she could manage.

The buzz of conversation and laughter rose again as they shared the birthday cake. When the evening ended, Susanna felt almost relieved. She had enjoyed herself, certainly, and she appreciated the kindness of these friends whom she had known for only a brief time. But the collision of her emotions was taking its toll on her, physically and emotionally. She felt depleted by the time they left the restaurant. All she wanted was to get away and be by herself.

Because of the snow, Michael had arranged in advance for rooms at a nearby hotel; they would be staying in the city the rest of the night. This thwarted any chance for a conversation with him, but Susanna thought it might be just as well. She didn't think she could possibly muster the energy for a coherent exchange with anyone tonight, especially Michael.

Yet she couldn't bear the thought of leaving things so...*bruised* and strained. So in the lobby of the hotel, she drew him aside with the intention of thanking him once more for the party and, of course, for the gift.

She struggled for the right words, but they came out awkward and disjointed. "Michael...I don't know how to thank you. For tonight. I've never...nobody has ever done anything like this for me. And the music box...I'll cherish it. Always. Truly, I will. It means—it's very special."

"That's why I wanted you to have it, Susanna," he said quietly. "Because you, too, are very...special."

Without giving her time to reply, he brought her hand to his lips, then released her. "*Buona notte,* Susanna. I hope you rest well. Would you take me to Paul now, please?"

It was impossible to gauge Michael's emotions when his feelings were shuttered as they were now. Susanna did hear the note of weariness in his voice when he said good night, however, and sensed that he, also, was ready to end the evening.

⌒

Later, after Caterina and Rosa had retired, Susanna walked into the sitting room of their suite and stood at the window, looking out. The snow, still falling, muffled the usual night sounds, wrapping everything in an otherworldly stillness, the kind of quiet that seems to slow the passing of hours and calm even the most restless of hearts.

But Susanna's heart would not be quieted tonight. Only an hour ago, she had been craving solitude. Now that she had it, a sense of abandonment and isolation crept over her. She stood at the window, weighing every word that had passed between her and Michael earlier in the evening.

Why, she wondered, had she been so quick to judge Michael's motives, so resistant to his encouragement? What was the source of her self-doubts, her sense of inadequacy? She treasured the gift of music more than almost anything else in life. But until now, she had never allowed herself to confront her fear of failure for what it really was.

Earlier, Caterina's childish but incisive words had ambushed her, opening up something in Susanna that, at the time, she had known she must examine more closely when she could. Those words came back to her now, unsettling her just as much as they had before:

"...but aren't you brave, Aunt Susanna? You said that being brave doesn't mean we're not afraid. It means doing what we're supposed to do even if we are afraid."

As she allowed her thoughts to slip back across the years, Susanna knew it would be all too easy to blame Deirdre for the fear and insecurities that had plagued her for as long as she could remember. Her sister had never let her forget that *she* was the *artiste,* Susanna the *plebeian.* Contemptuous of Susanna's timidity, Deirdre had dubbed her "Mouse" and disparaged her every attempt at accomplishment.

Susanna had tried to rationalize Deirdre's behavior as typical of the older sibling lording it over the younger. But she knew better. Even as a child, Deirdre had been spiteful toward Susanna, as if any recognition of her sister diminished her own share of the limelight.

And yet despite her vindictiveness, Deirdre was not to blame for Susanna's weaknesses. In truth, Susanna knew that what she had become was what she had made of herself.

In admitting her fear of failure, recognizing her own inadequacies, she had contented herself with the shadows, avoiding even the slightest pursuit of prominence or status. She had made excuses to avoid taking a risk. The place she had claimed for herself, the place where she was most comfortable, was in the background.

She had long thought of it as humility. Now she saw it was false humility.

For years she had convinced herself that the "Christian way" was to avoid any form of self-aggrandizement, when in fact she had simply been avoiding any possibility of failure. Rather than pursuing and developing the gifts God had bestowed upon her, like the unfaithful steward she had *buried* them. She had been not only ungrateful, but *unfaithful*.

And yet how did one distinguish genuine humility—a virtue God not only approved but even commanded—from a desire to be "safe," a deliberate attempt to stay backstage out of fear of failure?

Susanna already knew the answer. What she had claimed as humility was utter selfishness. Self-deception on a grand scale. Even when she *knew* herself capable, she refused to try, refused to risk. She hadn't been exhibiting Christian virtue at all. She had merely wrapped herself in a cocoon, protected herself from the possible humiliation of not being perfect.

All her life, from girlhood to womanhood, she had chosen safety over adventure, security over opportunity, contentment over change. Deirdre might have fed her self-doubts, might have even chipped away at her confidence, but Susanna knew that she, and she alone, was ultimately responsible for this stifling of the spirit. She had placed restraints upon herself. She had let herself become the "Mouse" her sister despised.

And in one blistering moment of insight, she realized that she was also the only one who could free herself from that confinement.

But even if she *wanted* that freedom, was she willing to pay the price for it? *Could* she pay it? It would mean changing the way she saw herself, what she believed about herself. It might even mean changing her life.

"No, Caterina—" she whispered the answer to her niece's question—"I'm not brave. I don't even know if I *want* to be brave. Or if I can."

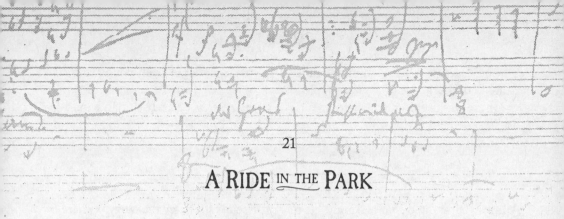

21

A RIDE IN THE PARK

What if the dream came true?

PADRAIC PEARSE

Frank Donovan holstered his gun, donned his coat and hat, and took the steps two at a time as he left his second-floor rooms.

He still had to pick up his mount at the stables and see to Tommy Brennaman. He had plenty of time, but he planned to have himself a bite of supper before going on duty.

No doubt Brennaman would show up late as usual. If the rookie patrolman were not such a good hand with the horses, Frank would have done his best to get him booted off the force long before now. He always had an excuse, did Tommy, and a lame one at that.

Well, Frank intended to tell him the way of things tonight once and for all. There were other men who could handle a horse. He'd had just about enough of Brennaman's slouching.

It was still snowing, coming down even heavier now, and snow made the job just that much harder. The only good thing about it was that it covered up some of the garbage heaped in the streets and made the pigs run slower than usual.

In all likelihood the park would be busy. Everyone and his brother would be out on an evening like this, to test the skating or have themselves a sleigh ride. For himself, he wouldn't like to be on the ice just yet, in case it wasn't quite safe. But that wouldn't stop a host of eejits from giving it a try.

His mood blackened still more as he tramped across the street at the Orphan Asylum. Ordinarily he wouldn't have volunteered for park duty, especially on a night such as this—it was well off his beat. But most of the precincts were short on men due to a particularly beastly wave of grippe, and since he had nothing better to do, Frank had opted to take an extra shift or two.

After all, there was something to be said for trotting a fine horse around the park in the snow while watching a gaggle of pretty young girls on their skates.

One never knew when he might be called upon to rescue some lovely young thing from a fall on the ice or a runaway sleigh.

There was nothing like a hero to a lassie in distress. Even an Irishman would do.

If she were desperate enough, that is.

⁓

Andrew had hinted that he might have a surprise for her after the party. When they pulled up to the park and got out of the buggy, the first thing Bethany saw was a sleek, dark green sleigh, the body trimmed with red and gold stripes. Two midnight black horses, their harness bells jingling in the light wind, stood pawing at the snow.

Bethany whipped around and found Andrew smiling at her. "Oh! Andrew! This is the surprise?"

"You're pleased?"

"*Pleased*? This is incredible." The snow crunched under her feet as she went over to the sleigh and peeked inside for a closer look at the figured carpet, the crimson velvet seats and braided trim. She ran her hand over one of the ornamental plumes and then turned back to him. "How did you ever think of such a thing?"

He shrugged. "I just thought you might enjoy it."

"But where did you get it?"

"I rented it. It's ours for the rest of the evening."

Bethany looked back to the sleigh, then lifted her face to catch the snowflakes drifting down. She caught Andrew's arm. "Well, what are we waiting for?"

Laughing, he helped her into the sleigh and settled her snugly under an enormous bearskin blanket before going around to the other side. Bethany had never been in the park before tonight, had only passed by it on occasion. To her delight, she found it was lovely: elegantly landscaped and well-maintained, its hills and meadows blanketed in white, and trees that looked to be sprinkled with diamonds of ice.

She was surprised to see crowds almost everywhere they passed. "I had no idea so many people would be out on a night like this."

"Winter is one of the favorite times for park goers," he said. "The big thing in the winter is ice skating on the lakes and ponds—and sleigh riding, of course. Central Park has become one of the city's most popular recreational spots."

Sleighs were everywhere, filling the night with the sound of harness and bells and laughter. Men tipped their hats and women smiled and nodded as they passed by each other on the track. Dozens of people thronged one of the lakes, skating in singles or couples or entire family groups.

"Do you skate, Andrew?"

He smiled a little as if reminiscing, but shook his head. "Not for years. There was a pond near my home, in Scotland. When I was a boy, my sister and I used to skate there. I doubt I'd be able to stay on my feet now, after so long a time."

"You have a sister? You've never said."

His expression sobered. "Jean was several years older than I. She married after I left home, but died in childbirth not long after I came across."

"I'm sorry." Bethany studied his profile. "It occurs to me that you really haven't told me very much about your childhood or your family, even though I've told you all about mine."

"There's not that much to tell. I grew up in Glasgow, as you know, had a perfectly ordinary childhood. My father still lives there. He's a clergyman. My mother passed on when I was still a boy. Jean took over and ran the household after that. And mothered me."

Still watching him, Bethany felt a twinge of sympathy. She knew what it was like to grow up as the only child among adults. While it had certain benefits, it could also be lonely.

As if he'd read her thoughts, he said, "How was it for you, Bethany, growing up without brothers or sisters?"

"I didn't mind. Not usually. Oh, there were times when I would have liked a brother or sister, but for the most part I was content." She ducked her head sheepishly. "It's not all bad, really—being the center of everyone's attention."

Andrew raised an eyebrow. "Somehow you don't strike me as the kind who enjoys attention all that much."

He paused for a moment, and his next remark caught Bethany off guard. "I've heard that one who grows up as an only child often wants a large family after marriage."

"Is that a question?"

"Well…no, not necessarily," he replied, not looking at her.

An unpleasant thought filtered through Bethany's mind: the memory of Frank Donovan's accusations about the unlikeliness of her domestic—and maternal—aspirations. "I suppose I haven't thought much about the future. I always seem to be so focused on the present."

He nodded. "I think perhaps you and I are a lot alike in that respect. There's always so much to do—"

"And never enough time in which to do it," she finished. "Unless you have the energy and the initiative of Miss Fanny Crosby, who I find to be absolutely amazing! Honestly, Andrew, however does she manage to do everything she does?"

"She is a wonder."

"Of course, she has no family depending on her," Bethany mused. "That would allow her more time for her work." She reached to tuck a strand of hair back under her hat. "I understand she and her husband tend to go their separate ways."

"Where their work is concerned, that's true. But they're devoted to each other."

"Her husband is blind, too, isn't he?"

"He is. In fact, I believe they met when they were both at the Institute for the Blind. Mr. Van Alstyne teaches, but not at the Institute. He's a music teacher and a church organist as well. A very gifted man, so I've heard."

"Van Alstyne? But I thought Miss Fanny's name was Crosby?"

"That's her maiden name. I believe they agreed that she would continue using it. Perhaps because of her music—that's how everyone knows her."

She shook her head. "Well, I'm absolutely in awe of both of them. Accomplishing so much, in spite of the fact that they can't see."

"It seems to me you needn't take a backseat to anyone when it comes to accomplishment. I'd say you've managed rather well yourself."

Bethany waved off the compliment. "Some days I feel as though I'm not accomplishing *anything*," she said with a sigh. "Especially when it comes to the patients I can't help."

"You're thinking of Maylee."

"Yes, I *hate* not being able to do anything for her, Andrew! She's such a wonderful child. She's smart, she's curious about everything, and she has the sweetest spirit. And yet just look at what she's forced to endure—and who knows what still lies ahead for her!"

"But you *have* helped her, Bethany. More than you realize. She absolutely delights in your visits, you know. She tells me all about them every time I stop by. You've given her something she's never had before."

Bethany frowned at him.

"Don't you see? You've become her friend. I think any little girl could count herself blessed to have someone like you in her life. I'm not so sure but what you haven't become a kind of mother figure to her as well."

"Goodness, I hope not! I don't consider myself a model for motherhood, not by any stretch of the imagination!"

"You're always so hard on yourself, Bethany. I happen to think you'd make a wonderful mother!"

Clearly, he'd spoken on impulse. He went crimson the moment the words left his lips.

"Well…be that as it may," said Bethany, feeling awkward, "I have no particular ambitions in that direction."

Andrew suddenly seemed intent on the horses pulling the sleigh. "Never?"

"I wouldn't say 'never.' I haven't actually thought that far ahead. What about you, Andrew?"

"Me?"

"You'd obviously be a good family man. Why haven't *you* ever married?"

He kept his eyes fixed straight ahead. "I don't necessarily prefer things this way," he said evenly. "But with the practice…and my health…"

Their eyes met, and Bethany recalled Frank Donovan's words about Andrew's condition, how it would eventually grow worse. And in that wistful, uncertain gaze she saw that Andrew also feared that, in time, he might become a burden.

She wanted to say something to reassure him, encourage him. But she knew too much about the possible progression of his disease to try to put a good face on it.

Thankfully, his unfailing sense of humor came to the rescue. "Besides," he said, a ghost of a smile touching his lips, "why would any woman willingly marry a doctor?"

"Why would any *man* marry a doctor, for that matter?" she tossed back recklessly.

"Perhaps doctors should only marry doctors?" he said, not quite meeting her gaze.

He let the question hang. Bethany decided not to touch it.

⌒

Frank Donovan saw them from the hillside. Doc and Lady Doc, as he'd come to think of them.

Still mounted, he saw them drive by in their fancy sleigh as they came round the near side of the lake. Doc had himself a fine-looking hat on, and Dr. Cole was decked out like one of the swell-looking matrons from the carriage trade.

Except that Dr. Bethany Cole looked nothing at all like a matron.

He cracked a grim smile. Maybe he would ride down and catch up with them, say hello.

But then he remembered that things weren't quite as they had been between him and Doc. And Dr. Cole, of course, froze up at the very sight of him.

So he stayed where he was, watching, as their sleigh began to slow down, not far from one of the snow-covered arbors near the lake.

⌒

Neither of them spoke for two or three minutes more. Finally, Andrew cleared his throat. "About Maylee—I have something to tell you."

Bethany sat up straighter, immediately interested. "You've learned something new about her condition?"

He shook his head. "I only wish that were the case. But I think this will please you, all the same. Do you remember the night we were at Bantry Hill, the night we told Michael and Susanna about Maylee?"

"Of course. I remember how sympathetic they were."

"Yes, well, last week Michael asked me to take him to visit her."

"What a nice gesture. But then, Michael is a very kind man."

"As it happens, it was more than a gesture. Michael has suggested that Maylee come and live at Bantry Hill."

"Andrew! He can't be serious?"

"Oh, he's very serious. Michael isn't a man to make idle propositions. He was quite taken with Maylee—you should have seen how well they hit it off right from the start. When he pulled me aside at the party tonight, he said he'd spent considerable time in prayer and discussed it with Susanna. They haven't told Caterina yet, but Michael is sure she'll be delighted."

"But why would he do such a thing?" Bethany frowned in disbelief. "Does Michael really understand Maylee's condition, that she's going to require more and more care eventually, and that she won't ever be well?"

"I assure you, Michael understands. I made certain of that. As to why he's willing to do this, why he *wants* to do it"—he smiled a little—"all he would say was that God had put it on his heart. He's quite resolved."

"How amazing!"

Andrew slowed the horses and turned in toward the lake. "Let's watch the skaters for a bit, shall we? Or are you too cold?"

"No, I'm fine," Bethany said, distracted. "Does Maylee know about this?"

"Not yet. I thought you'd want to be with me when I tell her. Perhaps we can go and see her tomorrow."

He paused. "This will be a good thing for her, Bethany. There's certainly room for her at Bantry Hill, and Michael says she'll have plenty of attention and care. In addition to Susanna and the Dempseys, he's employed a new man and his family from Ireland. They're already living there, on the premises. There's a wife and a grown daughter, and they've agreed to help with Maylee."

"He's thought this through, then? You're quite certain?"

Andrew leaned back against the seat of the sleigh. "He seems to have considered everything very carefully," he said. "He's already broached the subject with the MacGoverns—that's the family he recently hired on. And as I said, he's discussed it with Susanna and by now, I'm sure, with Caterina, too. Actually, he makes it sound as if the lot of them are looking forward to having Maylee there." He paused. "This means she'll have a real home, Bethany. She won't have to spend what's left of her life in an institution."

According to Andrew, Maylee's parents had abandoned her when she was still a toddler. Once they realized they had a desperately ill child on their hands, they had deposited her at a church door and fled. The cruelty of that abandonment never ceased to anger Bethany.

She suspected that Andrew had been praying about Maylee's situation for some time now. As a matter of fact, so had she, although God hardly needed her prayers when He had Andrew's.

She scanned their surroundings for a moment. The park looked like one of those lithographs by Mr. Currier and Mr. Ives: the skaters on the lake, the trees, some of which had grown quite tall, the rustic, snow-covered arbors, and in the distance the graceful Bow Bridge. Were it not for the crowds of people everywhere, they could have been in the country instead of a city park.

Bethany knew that Andrew came here sometimes, when he wanted to get away by himself, just to sit and think…or perhaps to pray. There had been a time when keeping company with such a godly man, a man given to speaking of God and prayer and spiritual things as easily as others spoke of politics or banking might have intimidated Bethany. But no longer. Andrew might be a man of faith, but he was thoroughly down to earth.

She respected him as she had no other man except for her grandfather, but she was no longer quite so daunted by his faith as she had once been. Actually, Andrew himself was the one who had helped her realize that she needn't be some sort of a spiritual giant to prove herself a Christian, that it was enough to love God, to trust Him, and be obedient to His will.

"I'm no more important to God than you are," he continued to impress upon her. "And my prayers carry no more weight with the Almighty than do yours."

Abruptly, Bethany turned to him. "How do you pray for Maylee, Andrew? If you don't mind my asking, that is."

"Of course, I don't mind," he said quietly. "Well, naturally I continue to pray for her healing. But mostly I've prayed for *comfort* for her—for a place where she'll be truly wanted and loved. I've often wished I could take care of her myself, but I'm so seldom at home—"

Bethany nodded. "Don't think the idea hasn't occurred to me, too. But neither of us is in a position to give her full-time care."

Her mind was racing. "Monitoring her care will be an ongoing need. That will mean frequent trips upriver."

"We can manage that, don't you think?"

"Traveling to Bantry Hill would hardly be a burden. You know I love going there. I still can't comprehend Michael doing this," Bethany went on. "And for a child he's only just met."

"I don't know that we can ever understand someone like Michael." Andrew flexed the fingers of one gloved hand, then the other, as if to ease the stiffness. "I *do* know he's a man of genuine compassion—a kind of compassion so rare that surely it can't be anything but a gift. A *God* gift. I must say I admire him tremendously."

They were sitting very close together now. Bethany looked into his face—the strong features, the boyish shock of hair falling over his forehead, the faint web of lines at the corners of his eyes. Something tugged at her heart. When had he become so much more than a colleague? More than a friend?

When had he come to mean more to her than she was comfortable admitting, even to herself?

On impulse, she closed the small distance between them, touching her lips to his lean, clean-shaven cheek. "And *I* admire *you*, Andrew Carmichael."

He turned an endearing shade of pink. "For what?"

"For caring so much about a lonely little girl. And for being—" She paused. "Just...for being yourself."

His gaze fell upon her, intense with unspoken questions. Then without warning, this man—her partner in medicine, her closest friend, her only confidant—slowly removed his hat and lowered his face to hers.

He kissed her with uncommon gentleness, one corner of her mouth, then the other. Slowly, she touched his cheek, and he turned into her touch, then took her face between his hands and kissed her again.

In that moment Bethany's complacency with the order of her life, the fullness and satisfaction and independence she'd been so certain her career would bring, seemed to lift away like a mist rising over the frozen lake. She felt herself take a sharp turn and step onto a new pathway. Her present began to fade and recede until the only thing she could see was a future with Andrew.

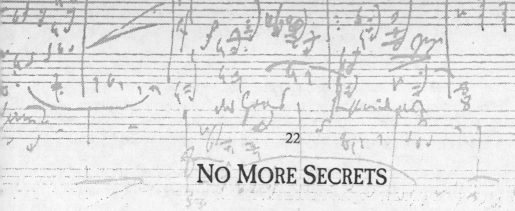

22

No More Secrets

To think, the fullness my yearning heart
has long been seeking was here then, and
still abides, in your safekeeping.

ANONYMOUS

Frank had almost changed his mind about approaching them, had actually started to move the horse slowly down the snow-covered hill. But he drew to a sharp halt when he saw what they were about, saw Doc remove his hat, draw her close, and dip his head toward hers.

Something tightened in his chest, and a taste as bitter as salt water burned his mouth as he watched them. He hadn't meant to spy, but for a moment he couldn't look away, even though his pulse was beating in his ears like a drumroll.

He had known jealousy only once before in his life, but it had been nothing like this scalding, squeezing sense of being pushed away, an impotent outsider. The awareness of what was happening to him took him completely off guard, and, shaken, he struggled to rein in his treacherous feelings.

In truth, he was envious of *both* of them: Doc, because he had obviously claimed for himself the heart of a woman Frank could only admire...and desire... at a distance; and Bethany Cole, because she now wielded even more influence with the only man Frank Donovan had ever called a *friend*.

Slammed by a wall of emotions he couldn't begin to understand—didn't *want* to understand—he hauled his mount around and took off in a fury, throwing snow before and behind him as he charged up the hill.

~

Andrew drew back. "We need to talk," he said, his voice unsteady. "But not at the risk of your freezing to death. Let's find a coffee shop."

Bethany hesitated, then looked around. "Over there," she said, pointing to a snow-hooded arbor, ringed by benches beneath its canopy.

"Aren't you cold?"

"No, I'm fine. It's so beautiful here, I'd rather stay outside."

They left the sleigh, stopping to buy a bag of hot roasted chestnuts before claiming one of the benches that faced the bridge. Gas lamps and carriage lanterns cast their soft glow into the night, dappling the riding paths and hillsides with light and shadow.

They were secluded, surrounded by dense vines, trees, and shrubbery frosted with snow. It seemed that everyone else in the park was either on the ice or circling the lake in a sleigh.

Bethany bit into a chestnut, mindful of Andrew's eyes on her. She felt uncommonly nervous. The chestnut seemed to lodge in her throat. She glanced at Andrew to see that he wasn't eating at all, just watching her. For some reason, she couldn't quite face him yet.

In a matter of moments, everything had changed.

The problem was, she wasn't sure she *wanted* things to change. Nevertheless, one of them probably needed to say something.

~

"Bethany, I've never told you exactly how I feel about you, but I expect by now you know."

Andrew cringed. His voice sounded as if it were coming from someone else. It was too loud, his tone too formal. His words spilled out too quickly, as though he were desperate to say everything at once and get it over with. He knew his face must be crimson, and not from the cold.

"You've...probably known for some time," he repeated lamely. "Certainly before tonight."

Bethany turned to look at him, her eyes wide and searching. "You've become very important to me, Bethany. I care for you. Deeply. You already know that. But I haven't wanted to bring this up until I was...until I knew—"

"If *I* care for *you*?" she finished for him.

He nodded, holding his breath. "That, too, but there's more—"

"Andrew, of course, I care for you. Surely, you've realized that." Her lips curved in just the faintest hint of a smile, and she lifted her hand as if she might touch him, but instead dropped it back to her lap.

"I had...hoped."

He moved to tuck a stray lock of hair back under her hat, then traced one side of her face with the back of his hand. "You are so incredibly lovely," he said, nearly strangling on the words. "I never get enough of just...looking at you."

"Now you're embarrassing me," she said, but Andrew thought she looked pleased. And she moved closer to him.

He caught her hand and held it. "Bethany, there are things I need to tell you.

Now, before we talk about anything else. I've been meaning to tell you for some time, but I keep putting it off, afraid—"

"Andrew, I'm just not sure—"

He put up a hand to interrupt her. "I think I know what you're going to say, Bethany, and I understand."

Frank Donovan's warning echoed in his mind. *"If it's settlin' down to home and hearth fire you're wanting, I confess I don't quite see that happening with your Dr. Cole…Can you honestly see the woman with a passel of young'uns hangin' on to her skirts while she stirs the soup?"*

Before she could say anything more, he hurried to reassure her. "I wouldn't ask you to give up…anything, Bethany."

She frowned. "What are you talking about?"

"I wouldn't expect you to give up medicine," he said, the words pouring out in a rush. "Surely you know I would *never* ask that of you! If we were to…if we were married…I wouldn't for a minute expect you to stop practicing."

"Andrew—are you asking me to marry you?"

"I…well, not yet. I mean, yes. Yes, I am, but there's something else I want to tell you before—"

"I should think so."

"What?"

"I believe it's common to at least mention the word 'love' before proposing marriage."

Andrew reared back. "Well, of *course*, I *love* you! I've already admitted that—"

"No, as a matter of fact, you haven't."

Andrew felt his face flame. "I…must have *thought* about saying it so often that I just assumed I had."

She shook her head, her lips pressed together.

"Well, now I have."

"So you have." Her eyes glinted with humor.

"I realize I'm no prize, Bethany. Believe me, it's taken every shred of nerve I have simply to get to this point. But I'd be—"

"Andrew—"

He stopped, waiting.

"Let's both admit that I'm not exactly any prize either. At least not for a man who wants a more…*traditional* marriage. I couldn't give up medicine, Andrew. I simply couldn't. I've worked too long, too hard—"

"I know you have, and you're an excellent doctor," he interrupted. "You love medicine—"

"Yes, I do—"

"And I love *you* too much to ask you to give up anything that means so much to you—"

"And what if we should have children?"

That set him back. Still, it was a perfectly legitimate question. "I'd like children, of course—eventually—but it *would* mean your taking time off from the practice—"

"But not necessarily giving it up altogether."

"Oh, no. Of course not. We'd...work it out."

She said nothing for a moment, but he could tell she was thinking. As much as he hated to give her anything else to think about, he knew he must.

"Bethany, there's the matter of my health—"

~

She tried to preserve a calm front, but inside she was churning. She should have known he would raise the issue himself, wouldn't leave it to her. And ever since Frank Donovan had drilled her with his cynical diatribe that day in the police wagon, she had played this very question over and over in her mind. But now that she knew that he loved her—and that *she* loved him—she could no more give him up because of his poor health than she could have struck him and left him to die.

"Your health isn't an issue with me, Andrew."

"Perhaps it should be. It will most likely get worse, Bethany. We both know that."

She nodded. "I won't lie to you, Andrew. Of course your health worries me. But it worries me because I care for you, and because I *hate* the idea of your being in pain. But this illness is a *part* of you. And if I'm to be a part of your life, then we'll face everything together. Including the arthritis."

It struck her then that she wasn't simply reassuring him or trying to convince herself. What she was saying was true—as true as her love for Andrew. Frank Donovan had been wrong.

Very wrong.

"Think about this, Andrew: if it were turned around, if *I* were to be afflicted with an ongoing illness, would you want me any less? Would you reject me?"

"Of course not!"

"Well, then?"

He nodded, his gaze never leaving hers. "Point taken. And I won't deny it's a huge relief to me. But there's something else, Bethany. Something I should have told you long ago, and certainly before I asked you to marry me."

Bethany laughed. "My goodness, Andrew, you certainly are taking a long time getting around to proposing to me."

But he didn't share her laughter. He looked pale, the shadow of his beard darker than before. His eyes smoldered with pain. For a moment Bethany wondered if the arthritis had flared, but she sensed that this was a different kind of pain—and that whatever he was about to say might be of a far more devastating nature than the issue of his health.

When he began to speak, he looked…and sounded…weak. Weak and miserable. In spite of the cold, perspiration lined his forehead and upper lip, and his hands were trembling visibly.

"You can't imagine how I hate telling you this. I'd give anything if I didn't have to, but then I wouldn't be able to live with myself."

He stared out across the park in the direction of the bridge. "I need you to know that when I've finished, I will completely understand if you want nothing more to do with me. Perhaps you won't even want to practice with me. No matter what else has happened between us, no matter what's been said tonight, you owe me nothing. No commitment."

"Andrew, nothing could be so bad that I'd walk away from you." Bethany spoke the words, but his bleak stare sent a chill coursing through her. He hadn't replaced his hat, and he began to run it around and around between his fingers.

"Do you remember the day we talked about your grandfather? I told you I'd read some of his papers on narcotics addiction?"

Bethany nodded.

"In truth, I'd read everything I could get my hands on about the subject, not just your grandfather's research. But medical curiosity wasn't my reason for studying your grandfather's publications."

Bethany watched him, a cold knot forming deep inside her as he went on.

"I was an addict, Bethany. I was addicted to opium."

His tone was as wooden as before, but his eyes were heavy with shame. They sat staring at each other for one long, terrible moment as Bethany fought to hold on to her composure.

"*How?*"

"Are you quite sure you want to hear this?" Andrew's voice was still flat, but his features were sculpted in anguish.

"Whether I *want* to hear it is beside the point. I think I *must* hear it."

His eyes went over her face, and then slowly, he nodded.

"It began when I was still in medical college. One of the faculty physicians—well-intentioned, I'm sure, but careless, now that I look back on it—started me on small doses of opium, to help me manage the pain. This was at the outset of the arthritis, when the symptoms were absolutely brutal, and he'd seen that I was having a bad time of it. But I was determined not to give up my training, and so, meaning to help, he saw to it that I could get however much of the drug I needed, to see me through. As I said, he no doubt meant well, even though he had to know the risk. Before I knew what was happening—"

"You became addicted."

He nodded, and she could almost feel his misery.

"It begins so innocently," he went on. "For many, it's as simple as purchasing a few compounds from the chemist to ease some sort of physical distress. Or in far too many cases—like mine—a physician who means only to help initiates a deadly cycle. But it almost always ends up the same way: one becomes enslaved by the very thing that was meant to free him of the pain."

"But obviously, you're not still addicted. You've taken a cure—"

His head came up, and he let out a sharp, bitter laugh. "An addict is never *cured*, Bethany. Not completely. You know that." He wiped a hand over his mouth. "I will always be an addict. A *former* addict, God willing, but an addict, all the same."

"I can't…it's almost impossible for me to imagine you…that way…"

"You wouldn't have liked me very much, that's certain. I despised *myself* during that time. Every day I promised myself I'd quit. But when I tried"—he shook his head—"I was scrambling for more of the stuff within hours."

"How…did you overcome it?"

"Cold abstinence."

His words came out like bullets, and the turbulence of emotion in his face made Bethany shudder.

He pressed on. "About the same time that I realized what was happening to me, that I had become dependent, my roommate also became aware. Somehow or other he managed to get permission for both of us to leave the college for several days. He took me to his parents' home in Edinburgh, where he made preparations and then locked both of us inside an attic room."

"I scarcely made it through the first stage. The second stage was pure torture—I'll spare you the details."

"No," Bethany said quietly. "Tell me. I want to know everything you went through."

His features contorted, but he nodded. "Every nerve, every muscle feels as though it's been scraped raw and then left to burn in the sun. Nausea, abdominal cramps, fever, unbearable spasms that set your entire body to shaking—" He stopped, closing his eyes for a moment.

"It's as if everything in you is twisted and crushed and pulled apart. You think you're dying and pray you will. And the entire time this is going on, you know you're not just battling for your health or your sanity—you're battling for your very *soul*."

"Oh, Andrew," Bethany whispered. "How did you ever bear it?"

He made a lame attempt at a smile, but it quickly fell apart. "Well—let's just say I'll be forever grateful to Charles Gordon. My roommate. For his perception and his prayers and his strong back. He kept me from taking a leap from the attic window more than once. And he stormed heaven on my behalf for days. Not to mention all the abuse he put up with in the meantime." He stopped. "I owe him a debt I could never repay. He literally saved my life."

Bethany's mind felt numb. "I'm sorry you had to go through all that, Andrew."

He turned his face toward hers. "Not half as sorry as I am that I had to *tell* you about it. I saw your shock and revulsion the night we went to see Mary Lambert, and from that time on I lived in terror that I'd see the same thing on your face once you knew about me.

"I'm ashamed for you to know about that time in my life, Bethany. All I can do is promise you that it's over. Completely over. But perhaps…that doesn't matter. The very fact that it happened is no doubt enough to shake your faith in me."

Slowly, Bethany took his face between her hands, holding him steady and making him look at her. "Don't insult me, Andrew," she said. "It would be a poor kind of love indeed that would allow the past to destroy the present and the future. I'm sorry for what you endured, and I hate it that you had to go through that, but it doesn't change the way I feel about you."

Please, God, let it be the truth, she thought fiercely. *Let me be strong enough to put this terrible thing behind us and never look back.*

She could. Of course, she could. The man she had kissed only moments before wasn't the same man as that young college student. Awful as the experience must have been for him, it took an incredible measure of courage and strength to go through what he did and survive it. The very fact that he *had* fought it and overcome it only confirmed her measure of the man. In time, she would be able to look at him and never think of the other.

She *would*…

"I have to ask you this," he said, his voice almost a whisper. "Now that you know—how *do* you feel about me?"

Their faces were so close they shared a breath. "I believe I've already mentioned the word *love*, Andrew."

Snow was falling again, and the wind blew a spray of it inside the arbor. Andrew freed one hand to brush away a stray snowflake from the corner of her mouth. "You're quite sure?"

"Sure enough that I believe I just might marry you, Andrew Carmichael."

A slow smile worked its way across his features. "Do you mean that?"

"Oh, I mean it all right. There's just one thing—"

His smile wavered. "What would that be?"

"Are you ever going to get around to *asking* me?"

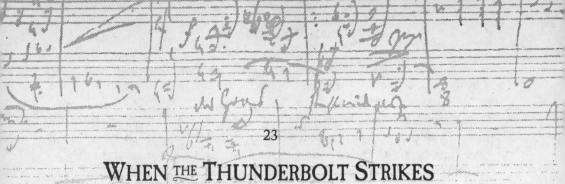

23

WHEN THE THUNDERBOLT STRIKES

Whiter she than the lily,
Than beauty more fair,
Sweeter voiced than the violin,
More lightsome than the sun;
Yet beyond all that
Her nobleness, her mind—
O God Who art in Heaven,
Relieve my pain!

ANONYMOUS, 19TH CENTURY, TRANSLATED BY PADRAIC PEARSE

For several mornings now Paul Santi had watched, hoping to catch a glimpse of Conn MacGovern's daughter when she came outside.

Sometimes she appeared at the front of the house, sweeping the porch or picking up stray playthings. Other mornings she would walk out back to toss food to the chickens or to play with one of the cats living in the stables.

So far, Paul had resisted any attempt to engage her in conversation. This morning, however, as he stood on the brow of the upward slope that separated the main house from the caretaker's cottage, she actually started up the hillside, in pursuit of a black-and-white kitten, now bounding toward Paul as fast as its tiny legs would carry it.

The girl stopped halfway up the rise, her gaze going from the kitten to Paul as if she couldn't quite make up her mind what to do. On impulse, Paul reached down and scooped up the small creature before it could dodge past him. After another second or two, the MacGovern girl again started toward him.

With every step of her approach, Paul could see that she was even more lovely than she'd appeared at a distance. Her hair was a cloud of auburn, though not quite so fiery as her mother's. She was slender enough to appear fragile but carried herself with the purposeful, fluid grace of Mrs. MacGovern, a strikingly attractive woman in her own right.

Only a few feet away, she halted again. Paul smiled, hoping to reassure her that he was entirely harmless as he closed the distance between them.

"Yours?" he said, placing the kitten in her arms.

She shook her head without meeting his eyes, snuggling the kitten against her. For one irrational moment, Paul found himself envying the small creature.

"Well, *he* thinks he's yours," he said. "Or at least he would like to be."

Finally, she smiled, and Paul felt as if a vial of sunshine had been poured out over his head like a blessing.

"His mother is one of the stable cats," she said shyly. "But I've rather...adopted him, you see."

Her soft voice, tuned by the lilting Irish accent, was sheer melody to Paul's ear. And those eyes! As shining and as brilliant as the most priceless of emeralds!

He knew he was staring like a great *stupido*, but when he tried to speak, he seemed to have lost his voice.

"You are Mr. Emmanuel's cousin," she said, reminding Paul that in addition to acting like a fool, he was also being rude.

"*Sì*," he managed. "*Mi scusi*. Forgive me. I am Paul Santi. And you are Mr. MacGovern's daughter." He cringed at the realization that he sounded like a foolish schoolboy.

But she was still smiling at him, so perhaps she was not put off by his awkwardness after all.

"Your father—I speak with him each day. Michael says Mr. MacGovern has already proven himself to be invaluable." He cleared his throat. "We—all of us—are very glad that you and your family are here."

She looked down, and Paul had all he could do not to lay his hand on top of her head to find out if her hair felt as silken as it looked.

At that moment he glanced toward the cottage, only to see Conn MacGovern standing on the front porch, watching them. MacGovern was a big man who typically looked at Paul with an expression of mild contempt. No doubt the Irish trainer had taken note of the fact that Paul, unlike Michael and MacGovern himself, preferred to keep his distance from the horses.

Paul was finding it difficult to concentrate, his attention going from the girl standing only inches away from him to her father, who had stepped off the porch and now stood in the yard, arms crossed over his brawny chest, watching them intently.

"Ah...your father," Paul said, inclining his head in MacGovern's direction.

She turned to look, and at the same time MacGovern called to her.

Nell Grace. It suited her, Paul decided.

When she turned back to him, she shot him another quick smile. "I'd best be away now."

"Yes...of course. I...may I say that I'm very pleased to have finally met you, Miss MacGovern," Paul managed to say.

She turned and hurried back down the hill, the kitten watching Paul over her shoulder.

He saw her exchange words with her father, then go around toward the barn. MacGovern followed her, taking her by one arm—not a rough gesture but one of protective firmness all the same. MacGovern glanced back at him once, and although they were too far apart to gauge his expression, Paul felt almost certain that the big Irishman's glare would have withered the grapes on a vine.

But he would think about MacGovern later. Nothing must be allowed to spoil this momentous morning, which quite possibly might turn out to be the most important day of his life.

The thunderbolt. He had been struck by the thunderbolt.

At long last, love had come.

Inside the cottage, Conn stood with his back to the sink, finishing his second cup of tea, scalding hot and strong enough to make his ears ring, the way he liked it. No one except Vangie could make tea to please him.

He watched her spoon some stirabout into Baby Emma's mouth, at the same time attempting to quiet the twins, who were far more interested in pestering each other than in finishing their breakfast. Renny Magee was already off to the stables, and Nell Grace had headed for the back of the house the minute she returned from shutting the kitten inside the barn. No doubt to bury herself in her books or her writing pad.

He knew he had embarrassed the lass, but though he dreaded her tears almost as much as those of her mother, he was not about to tolerate her carrying on with that cheeky Italian fellow. He had just come back from saddling the stallion for his employer's early morning ride when he'd spotted the two of them, Nell Grace and that Santi *gorsoon*, standing on the hillside blathering as though they'd known each other most of their days. The thought of that young sneak skulking about after Nell Grace had set his blood to boiling.

To his surprise and annoyance, Vangie had seemed altogether unperturbed when he told her. Determined that she should understand, and growing impatient with the twins' antics, he now ordered them to get their coats and wait outside for the school wagon.

"I don't see why we have to go to school anyway," grumbled Sean, who only the week before had informed his parents that he was an American and now preferred to be called *Johnny*.

"You have to go to school so you'll not be a cabbagehead the rest of your life," said his twin brother, punching him in the ribs.

James was the darker of the two, his hair a deeper red, his skin not quite so pale. When it came to mischief, however, it seemed to Conn that they were perfectly matched.

"That'll do!" he warned. He took a step toward them, and they went scrambling for their coats.

"If you learn nothing else at school," Conn grumbled, "perhaps you'll acquire the means to behave like civilized children instead of troublesome little heathens."

The twins glanced at each other, eyes glinting, but Conn gave them a look that quickly cut short even the thought of a snicker.

"Your lunch, boys," Vangie said before they made it to the door. Sean—*Johnny,* Conn reminded himself—came back to grab their pail off the table, aiming a kiss at his mother's cheek that barely connected before he again dashed out the door. James watched, then he, too, darted across the room to kiss his mother good-bye.

The instant Vangie set Baby Emma to the floor, the child promptly trundled over to Conn. He picked her up and swung her about a couple of times, then off she went behind the stove to play with the wooden blocks her brothers had carved and polished for her.

"Those two," Conn said with a sigh, sitting down beside Vangie at the table. "I don't like to think of the trouble they'll bring when they're older."

"They're good boys. Give thanks they're in good health and have plenty of life in them."

"Oh, I'm thankful enough for that. It's the mischief in them that worries me."

"They're but eight years old, don't forget." She paused. "What happened between you and Nell Grace?"

"She was up the way with that Italian fellow."

"Mr. Emmanuel?"

"No, no, the skinny one. The one with the smart talk and the yellow streak."

"Conn! You don't even know the lad."

"I know what I see. He's all talk, that one is. He won't even go near the horses." Conn scowled. "I say, never trust a man who doesn't take to the horses."

Vangie looked at him, then shook her head. "Conn MacGovern, sometimes I could just box your ears."

"What?" Conn couldn't believe it. She was vexed with *him*! "You can't mean you approve of the girl cavorting with his kind!"

"*Cavorting*? Oh, Conn, would you listen to yourself, you great oaf! I thought you said Nell Grace was merely *talking* with the lad. Sure, there's nothing wrong with that!"

"She ought not to be anywhere near him. Or any other boyo, for that matter! The girl is only seventeen, after all."

Vangie was eyeing him as if he'd grown an extra head. She didn't understand; that was the thing. What did she know about untrustworthy men, after all?

"You can be such a dolt at times," she said matter-of-factly. "Have you forgotten, then, that I was only seventeen when we were *married*?"

"That was different," he said, and of course it was.

"Different, indeed," she muttered. "And your point is, I expect, that the young man at the Big House is Italian instead of Irish."

"Exactly."

"He would also appear to be respectful and well-mannered. A gentleman, from what I've seen of him."

Conn frowned. "I wouldn't be knowing anything about that."

"No, indeed you would not."

Conn couldn't make out her tone, but from the look in her eye it wasn't in his favor.

"He's well-educated as well. You can hear it in his speech." She brushed some crumbs off the edge of the table into her hand.

Conn shrugged. What good was education if a man had no backbone?

"And he's obviously from good people," Vangie went on. "Mr. Emmanuel is a good man, a *Christian* man. You said so yourself. And the boy is his cousin, isn't that so?"

"Be that as it may—"

She arched an eyebrow. "I don't see the harm in Nell Grace making conversation with the lad. She needs friends, especially missing her brother as she does."

They locked gazes a moment more, then she looked away. There seemed to be no understanding Vangie these days. One minute she would dissolve into tears if he disagreed with her even on the least of matters, but then just as quickly she would turn all fire and smoke, taking him to task for a misspoken word.

Still, he'd rather have her vexed with him for his thickheadedness than hollow-eyed with sorrow. Aye, better her fussing than her weeping, and that was the truth.

He leaned forward to plant a quick kiss on her cheek. When she made no response, he got up from the chair and glanced at his pocket watch. "I'd best be getting back to the stables. Himself will be wanting his ride soon."

He stood over her, hesitating, uncertain as to whether he ought to say what was still on his mind. But he was the man of the house, after all. "So, then—you'll keep Nell Grace away from that Santi fellow?"

Her chin went up. "I'll do no such thing. Our girl is not a child any longer, Conn, and it's time you realized it. Nell Grace is at an age where she has the right to speak with anyone she chooses. And she's not a foolish girl. We can trust her judgment, it seems to me."

Confused now, for it was a rare thing entirely for Vangie to openly defy him, Conn went for his coat. He was reluctant to leave things as they were, but couldn't think how to handle her when she was in such a state.

Once at the door, however, he turned back. "Even so," he said, determined to make his point, "no good can come of letting a boyo like that slaver after her. And him a coward at that."

She shook her head, not looking at him as she rose from the table.

"Well, then," he finally said, "I'll be in by noonday."

Conn stepped outside, closing the door behind him. There was no explaining the strangeness in Vangie this morning. For a few moments he had glimpsed the fire he had always admired in her. Indeed, he almost welcomed her impatience with him. But nearly as quickly as the sparks had flared, the heaviness had returned, taking the light from her eyes and the color from her cheeks.

He could not bear the sorrow that seemed to hover over her of late, would have done most anything to restore her spirit. And indeed, though she couldn't know, he *had* tried to do something about it. Still, one thing he would not tolerate, no matter what Vangie had to say: no daughter of his was going to have any truck with a useless fellow like that cousin of Mr. Emmanuel's.

Nell Grace deserved better than a great *gorsoon* who was so unmanly as to be afraid of the horses.

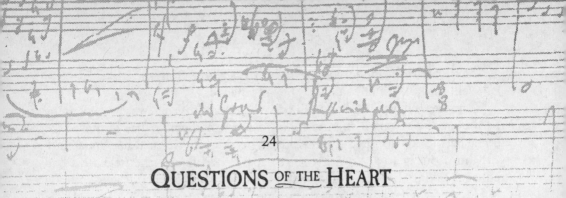

24

QUESTIONS OF THE HEART

So simple is the heart of man,
So ready for new hope and joy...

STOPFORD A. BROOKE

The morning was raw and blustery, and the wind stung Michael's cheeks as he cantered across the rolling fields surrounding Bantry Hill, but he didn't mind the cold.

Today he was on Mehab, the Arabian he had bought from Rosa Navaro after her husband's death. At his side, Conn MacGovern rode Yasmin, a mare the trainer favored.

Michael had promised himself that by Christmas he would be riding Amerigo, the contentious stallion he had imported from Ireland, but that remained to be seen. MacGovern had worked wonders in gentling the horse and building his trust, but the stallion was still unpredictable, and seemed to enjoy trying to outwit both his trainer and his owner when they least expected it.

Mehab, on the other hand, responded instantly to the slightest pressure of rein or knee, the subtlest shifting of Michael's weight. MacGovern kept to his left, and although Michael sensed his presence, the trainer's comfortable silence allowed Michael the illusion of riding alone, just himself and the magnificent Arabian.

He threw his head back and breathed in the chill morning air, mixed with a faint scent of horseflesh and leather. Downhill and back up again, his body became one with the horse. He leaned into the reins, urging Mehab into full gallop, his heart beating in time with the drumming cadence of the horse's movement.

A fire blew to life in Michael's veins, a passion much like the rush he felt when he stood onstage and conducted his orchestra. Riding was music—the singing of the wind, the percussion of hoof on turf, the pounding tempo of nature in all its glory. He could feel the Arabian's muscles flowing beneath him like a swiftly running stream, and together they cut a path through the frosty morning as if they were flying.

At last, at the top of a high hill, he reined in and stood waiting for Conn MacGovern to catch up. Mehab snorted and pranced, then quieted as MacGovern cantered the mare up the hill to Michael's side.

Michael had quickly come to respect his new employee, especially MacGovern's love of the land and his willingness to undertake even the meanest of jobs. He sensed in the sturdy Irish immigrant a rock-solid integrity, coupled with a lively bent toward humor. Moreover, the man never seemed the least uncomfortable with Michael's blindness.

Now MacGovern drew his horse to a stop and let out a laugh. "It'd be a great *amadan* indeed who'd wager against you, now wouldn't it, sir? Remind me never to bet my week's wage on any race you'd run."

Michael grinned in MacGovern's direction. "Ah, but if you had been on Amerigo—"

"If I'd been on Amerigo, Mr. Emmanuel, I'd be lying dead in a ditch by now, and that's the truth. But he's coming right along, and you'll be riding him yourself soon."

"Thanks to your training." Michael reached down to slap Mehab's neck. "I'm very pleased to have you and your family here at Bantry Hill, MacGovern."

"No more pleased than we are, sir."

"And your wife and children are settling in well? The house is suitable?"

"Faith, sir, it's much more than suitable. It's a palace compared to that dismal shack we had in the city."

"Good," Michael said. "If you need anything, be sure and let me know."

They turned and started back, trotting side by side. Silence stretched between them for a time, broken only by the clopping of hooves on the turf and the snorting and blowing of the horses.

Then MacGovern cleared his throat. "If you don't mind my asking, sir, it's… well, it's uncommon to see a blind man such as yourself daring to ride. Especially when—"

"Especially when I lost my sight in a riding accident?" Michael turned toward MacGovern and chuckled. "News travels quickly at Bantry Hill, I see."

"Begging your pardon, sir, I didn't mean to—"

Michael dismissed his apology with the wave of a hand. "It's all right. No doubt some think I'm completely mad to keep riding. But my passion for horses came early, when I was a boy in Tuscany. A man doesn't give up a thing like that easily."

"'Tis true, sir," MacGovern said. "I know for myself, I rarely feel so much a man as when I'm sitting a fine horse."

Michael nodded. "After the accident, a number of well-meaning people tried to convince me not to ride again. Even Paul questioned my judgment. I had a difficult time explaining to him why riding was so important to me."

MacGovern did not reply to this, but Michael heard him take in a deep breath and exhale it heavily. At last he spoke again. "Speaking of that young helper of yours—he's your cousin, is he?"

"Paul? *Sì*, Pauli is my cousin—and my assistant. He is also concertmaster with the orchestra."

"Concertmaster, eh?"

Michael heard the lack of understanding in MacGovern's tone.

"That sounds like an important job for such a young fellow."

"It is a most important position, yes, and he *is* very young for so much responsibility—only twenty-seven. But Paul is an excellent musician. In many ways, he is invaluable to me. He is—how do you say it—my 'right arm.'"

"Twenty-seven? Is that a fact now? I wouldn't have thought it." He paused. "He's not a married man?"

"Married? No, Paul is not married."

"I've noticed the lad seems…a bit shy of the horses. Unlike yourself, sir."

"That's true. Pauli does not share my love of riding."

MacGovern said nothing, but Michael heard him mutter something under his breath. They urged the horses forward in an easy canter, and did not speak again until they reined to a stop near the stables.

Michael dismounted, gave Mehab an affectionate pat, and handed the reins over to MacGovern.

"It is because of me that Paul has no love of the horses," he offered.

"Sir?"

"Because of the accident," Michael said. "Pauli never had any real interest in riding, even before then. But the accident only made things worse. Since then, he cannot bring himself to trust a horse. Any horse."

"I see."

Michael thought he detected a kind of grudging understanding in MacGovern's voice, and perhaps a trace of awkwardness as well, for having raised the subject of the accident at all. The exchange seemed peculiar, to say the least, and he wondered where it was leading.

Apparently, he wasn't to know.

"Well, then, here comes the lad now, sir," MacGovern said abruptly. "I'd best be on my way and tend to the horses."

Michael frowned. Why had MacGovern taken off in such a rush, as if he was deliberately avoiding Paul?

Perhaps Paul had done something to provoke the man, although given Paul's diligent avoidance of the stables, he couldn't think how.

Michael didn't raise the subject of MacGovern right away. Paul was getting ready to leave for the ferry, but first had some questions about the evening's rehearsal. He was standing in as conductor tonight, as he did on occasion, to give Michael a break.

Only after they'd gone to Michael's office and discussed the selections that still needed the most work did Michael make an attempt to satisfy his curiosity.

"Is there a problem between you and MacGovern that I should know about?"

There was a distinct delay in his cousin's reply. "MacGovern? No, not at all. Why—should there be a problem between MacGovern and me?"

The hesitation only made Michael more curious. "He was asking about you this morning, that's all."

"MacGovern was asking about *me*? Why?"

Michael shrugged. "I have no idea. He seemed very interested in you for some reason."

There was a long silence. "He...he *did* see me talking with his daughter this morning. Perhaps he does not approve?"

"Ah. His daughter." So that was it. Michael smiled to himself. "And is she pretty, *Signorina* MacGovern? Hmm?"

"*Em bella!* She is—beyond description!"

Michael's interest sharpened. "And how old is this young lady?"

"How old? I have no idea. What—does that matter?"

Michael shrugged. "I was just wondering why MacGovern asked *your* age."

"My age? What did you tell him?"

"I told him the *truth,* of course. You are twenty-seven, are you not?"

"*Sì*. But did he mind that I am so old?"

"*Old?* " Michael laughed. "I should be so old, *cugino!*"

"His daughter is...very young, I think," Paul said, a touch of uncertainty in his voice. "Perhaps MacGovern thinks I am too old for her."

"Very possibly," Michael said, poker-faced. He enjoyed needling his cousin almost as much as Paul enjoyed teasing *him.* "But it seemed to me that he was more concerned about your lack of affection for the horses."

"The *horses?*" Paul sighed. "Of course. MacGovern has seen that I do not like the horses. No doubt he holds that against me."

"Mm. Perhaps you should spend more time in the stables, Pauli."

"I will do whatever it takes," the younger man said solemnly. "Anything at all."

Michael leaned forward across the desk. "Paul? You're serious?"

Again Paul sighed. "It is the thunderbolt, Michael," he said, his voice grave and heavy with significance.

Relief coiled through Michael. If Paul's affections ever *had* been directed toward Susanna, that was clearly no longer the case.

"Paul, how well do you know this girl?"

"We met only this morning," his cousin said, his voice dreamy. "But I know, Michael. I *know!*" He stopped. "It is the thunderbolt, I tell you. You will pray for me, yes?"

"To be sure," Michael said dryly.

He heard Paul rise from his chair. "Thank you, Michael!" he burst out, grasping Michael's hand across the desk. "You understand that this is difficult for me. I know nothing about women! I have never been in love. Not until now."

"Paul," Michael cautioned, "you only spoke to the girl this morning—"

"That is true, but as I told you—"

"*Sì.* The *thunderbolt.* It would seem that I must begin to pray at once."

"I knew you would understand, *cugino!*" Paul paused, and when he resumed, his voice held an edge of sly humor. "But of course, you *would* understand. It is the same for you and Susanna, no?"

Michael frowned. *"Che cosa?"*

"Oh...nothing. I meant nothing." He sounded even more cagey.

"I think you meant *something.*"

Paul remained silent, but Michael could feel his scrutiny. "Out with it, Pauli."

"With you, Michael, one is never certain. But with Susanna, one can tell..."

Michael lifted an eyebrow. *"Must* you speak in riddles always, Pauli? One can tell *what?*"

"You know. That she cares for you."

Michael swallowed. "Clearly, the *thunderbolt* has struck your brain as well as your heart."

There was a long silence. When Paul spoke again, the teasing note had left his voice. "You cannot see the way Susanna looks at you, Michael. But *I* have seen."

An unbidden rush of hope swept over Michael, so strong he very nearly gave himself away. He quickly reminded himself that Paul was caught up in the throes of a romantic seizure and might well be seeing his own infatuation in everyone else.

Paul came around the desk and put a hand to Michael's arm. "Michael—forgive me if I speak out of turn. I know I often do. But I also know what I see. With Susanna, there is much feeling for you. And I think it is the same with you, but for some reason the two of you are determined to fight against it."

"Susanna still doesn't trust me," Michael ventured quietly. "Have you forgotten the incident at rehearsal, how quickly she suspected the worst when she thought I had conspired against her?"

"No, I have not forgotten. But I think perhaps you make too much of what was nothing more than a bad coincidence."

Michael started to interrupt, but Paul stopped him. "Listen to me, Michael. Susanna may have jumped to conclusions, but you told me yourself that she apologized. Or at least attempted to, once she realized that she had misunderstood. She admitted her mistake. Why can you not simply accept the incident for what it was? It was not that important, Michael, except in your mind. You are so... thin-skinned...where Susanna is concerned."

Michael weighed Paul's words, and something in him resonated to his cousin's defense of Susanna. No doubt he *had* made too much of what had merely been a misunderstanding. But it had been such a *painful* misunderstanding...

He heard Paul mutter a sound of frustration, though when he spoke his words were conciliatory. "I apologize if I have made you angry, Michael."

Distracted by the confusion simmering in him, Michael waved off his cousin's apology. "I'm not angry."

And he wasn't. At least, not with Paul.

If he was angry with anyone, it was with himself, for the morass of his emotions, the uncertainty of his judgment. And he was also angry with Deirdre. It was a futile, misdirected, and wholly irrational anger, he knew, but at times he felt as if his dead wife would always be a barrier between him and any possible chance to love again. Because of Deirdre, Susanna would never fully trust him. And because of Deirdre, his *own* capacity for trust had been so badly fractured he wasn't sure that even love would ever be enough to heal the breach.

He clenched his hands at his side, then reached for the back of the chair, swaying a little on his feet. Since the accident, he was occasionally plagued by vertigo, and now it swept over him.

"Michael—"

He heard the alarm in Paul's voice and lifted a hand. "It's nothing. I'm all right." He sank down onto the chair, waiting for his head to clear. "You should go now or you'll miss the ferry."

"But—"

"I'm fine, Pauli. A little dizzy, that's all. It will pass in a moment. Go on now."

After Paul left, Michael sat, not moving, with his head in his hands. In spite of his best intentions, his mind wandered back to Paul's words about Susanna: "*...you have not seen the way Susanna looks at you...but I have seen...she cares for you...*"

And what if Paul was right? What then?

He sighed. He, too, had been struck by the thunderbolt.

But in his case, the lightning had brought not only the revelation of love, but the recognition of its futility as well.

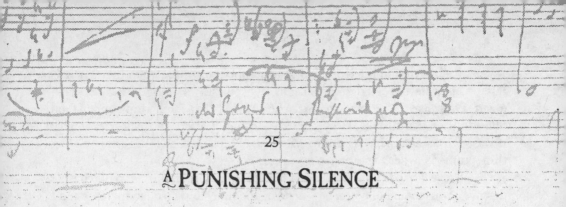

25

A PUNISHING SILENCE

I was mute with silence,
I held my peace even from good;
And my sorrow was stirred up...

PSALM 39:2 (NKJV)

When Conn returned to the house for the midday meal, he found only Nell Grace and Baby Emma in the kitchen. Nell Grace was stirring something on the stove—cabbage soup, from the smell of it—while the tyke played near her feet. There was no sign of Vangie.

"Where's your mother?"

Even before he asked, he knew something was amiss. At this time of day, he never walked into the kitchen but what Vangie wasn't either at the stove or the sink, putting the finishing touches to their meal.

Nell Grace's expression was troubled as she inclined her head toward the rear of the house. "Out back," she said. "I think she's sick, Da."

Conn immediately started for the outhouse, only to find Vangie a few feet from the back door, crouched on her haunches, head down, her hair hanging in her face.

"Vangie!" He hurried to her, dropped down at her side, and put his arms around her. In spite of the cold, she wore only a shawl, and he could feel her trembling.

"What is it, love? What's wrong?"

She shook her head as if too weak to reply.

"Let me get you inside. It's too cold for you to be out here like this."

He drew her up, alarmed when her hair fell away from her face and he saw how pale she was. She looked as if she might faint at any instant. Suddenly a spasm shook her, and she wrenched herself from his arms to go to her knees again. She gagged, but nothing came up. She moaned, but it was more a sob.

As Conn stood there, watching her and feeling helpless entirely, it struck him

330

that this was familiar. He had seen Vangie like this before—many times, in fact. His mind registered the memory, and a thrill of excitement shot through him, only to give way to a pang of hurt pride. If he was right, then why wouldn't she have told him by now?

But this wasn't the time for questions. He bent to steady her. "Better now, love?"

She nodded and let him raise her to her feet and help her inside. In the kitchen, Nell Grace followed their movement with worried eyes, while little Emma whimpered for her mama.

"Your mother will be all right," Conn told them. "She just needs to lie down for a bit. She's feeling poorly."

In the bedroom, he lifted her onto the bed, covered her, and then sat down beside her. She was still shaking, but when Conn reached to pull an extra quilt up from the foot of the bed and tuck it around her shoulders, she turned her face away, saying nothing.

He watched her for a long time, wanting to touch her but sensing her withdrawal from him. "Why haven't you told me, Vangie?" he said quietly.

She turned a dull look on him, then shrugged and quickly glanced away. "I was waiting…to be sure."

Conn studied her. "As I recall, with the others you knew quite some time before ever the sickness set in."

She didn't answer, didn't even look at him. He took the hand clutching the bed linens and found it limp and cold.

"Vangie?"

At last she turned and met his eyes. Conn was taken aback at the hard look to her, as if she was angry with him.

"Is it that you don't want the babe?" He could barely get the words out. A heaviness had lodged in his chest, and he was beginning to feel sick himself as his mind scrambled to make sense of Vangie's behavior.

"'Tis not that I don't want it."

"What then?" He pressed her fingers, trying to ignore the alarm welling up in him.

The look she turned on him made the hair at the back of his neck stand on end. Her gaze seemed to burn right through him with something he had never seen in Vangie's eyes before, not even in the heat of their worst arguments. He felt himself indicted, censured for some unknown crime.

But just when he thought she was about to lash out at him for whatever dire offense he had committed, she again turned away. Conn thought she looked to be caught up in the effort of making a particularly difficult, even a grudging, decision.

"I…wasn't certain how you'd feel about it," she said. "With Emma scarcely out of didies herself."

She was lying. Vangie knew exactly how he'd feel about a new babe, how he had *always* felt. That was what hurt the most. By not telling him, she was keeping from him something she *knew* would give him pleasure. It was as if she had deliberately chosen to withhold a blessing.

He moistened his lips against the dry sourness in his mouth. "I would feel the way I have always felt, Vangie. Proud and happy. Has there ever been a time when I *didn't* feel so, once I learned a new babe was on the way?"

She dragged her gaze back to him. "I thought it might be…different now. We're not young anymore, after all."

Conn stared at her. Was she serious? "Not *young*?" he said, trying to make light. "And were we so much younger, then, when Baby Emma was conceived?"

His words brought not even the trace of a smile to her lips. "That was different."

"Oh, I see. And *how* was it different?" Conn felt his temper begin to heat, even though he sensed that the worst thing he could do at this moment would be to allow himself to get angry. "I confess you're confusing me, love. I don't understand what it is you're trying to tell me."

She regarded him with a look that made Conn feel as if she had already judged him guilty of some terrible crime. "You wouldn't understand even if I explained it to you."

Her words were laced with a mixture of weariness and resignation. She didn't look well, not at all. Possibly, any discussion of whatever wrong she thought he had committed ought to wait until she had rested.

Yet he couldn't bring himself to simply let this go. He would have been relieved to learn that her condition accounted for the recent mood changes and erratic behavior. But the way she was looking at him! She had nearly admitted that there *was* something wrong, and that, whatever it was, she considered it beyond his understanding. Was it merely the pregnancy affecting her emotions, or was she actually turning against him because of some imagined sin on his part?

"*Help* me understand, then, Vangie. Sure, and you know by now that I can't bear it when you shut me out."

Conn thought he saw a faint trace of regret in her face. But when he moved closer to her, she flinched and pulled her hand away.

She was still as stone as she looked at him. "I suppose I meant to punish you," she said in a chillingly impassive voice.

Conn reared back, gaping at her. "*Punish* me? For what?"

"For Aidan." Her eyes were so fierce upon him that Conn felt as if his soul had been seared.

"It's because of you I've lost my son."

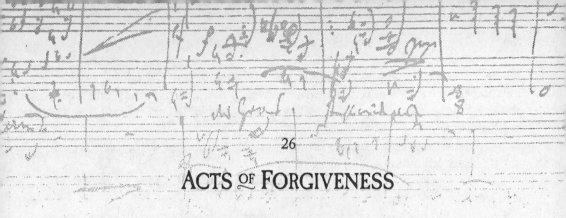

26

ACTS OF FORGIVENESS

For a man to be himself,
he must know himself.

IRISH SAYING

Vangie could see the battle taking place in Conn. She watched every stage of it: the flaring of his temper, his struggle to control it, his inclination to deny everything she said.

An angry red stain splotched his cheeks, and his mouth twisted with the effort of containing an explosion of self-defense. To her surprise, though, he said nothing, at least not right away. Instead he sat staring at her, his eyes boring into her as if he meant to scale every layer away until he could see into her mind and her heart.

"You believe that?" he finally said, his voice hoarse. "You believe it's my fault that Aidan stayed behind?"

"I *know* it's your fault!" Vangie pushed herself up on her elbows, facing him. "I also know that even if we had stayed in Ireland, Aidan would have left us. Our son is a man grown, but you insisted on treating him like a disobedient schoolboy. You never once gave him credit for anything he did, Conn! All you ever did was criticize him for not doing it your way!"

Vangie stopped to catch a breath, but she wasn't finished. Her nausea had subsided, but now the anger and resentment and bitterness that had built up for months came pouring out of her like poison out of a newly lanced abscess. "Perhaps if you had just once admitted to yourself that Aidan was a *man* and entitled to live his own life, he wouldn't have been half so eager to get away from us. From *you*! And even now, knowing the pain his absence has brought upon me—and don't think I haven't seen your own pain—you *still* won't give over and mend your differences with the boy. You won't even *try*!"

Even as the words ripped out of her, Vangie knew she wasn't being altogether fair. Aidan was every bit as stubborn as his father, and just as headstrong and rebellious as was common to a lad his age. But she had kept her churning feelings to herself too long and was now consumed by the need to make Conn face the fact that he wasn't entirely blameless for the troubles between himself and their son.

Still, when she saw his heavy shoulders sag, his features go slack, she wished she had been less venomous in her attack.

"Why haven't you brought this up before now?" he said, his tone as wounded as his eyes.

Vangie held his gaze, saw the pain ravaging his face, but would not allow herself to soften. "What good would it have done?" she countered. "You'd only accuse me of being 'overwrought' because I'm in the family way."

He frowned, his mouth set in a stubborn line, but Vangie could tell she'd struck a nerve.

"What more could I have done, then?" he said, his expression bleak. "Didn't I try to talk him out of his lunacy, even up to the time we were ready to board? Didn't I try to stop him from staying behind?"

"You did, Conn. But it was too late. Too much had passed between the two of you to undo it in a few moments. By then, Aidan was full to bursting with the need to get away and be on his own, where we wouldn't always be so close at hand, ordering his life."

"Where *I* wouldn't be so close at hand, is what you mean."

"Aye, that *is* what I mean. But even after we came across, didn't I beg you to write to the boy and try to make peace? It just might have made a difference, had a letter come from your hand instead of always being written in mine."

"If he was as set against me as you claim, I can't think a letter would have made any difference at all."

"But you could have *tried*, Conn! You could have *tried*! I don't know if I can ever forgive you for not *trying*!"

Her words came out as a wail, and Vangie cringed both at the sound of her own voice, and at the agonized look on Conn's features. But didn't the great oaf have some of this coming at last?

Yet, when he gazed at her so, his face lined with old sorrows and the slow dawning of a new wisdom, when she met his eyes and saw nothing there but regret and love—love for *her*—Vangie found it exceedingly difficult to stay angry with the man.

He got to his feet and stood looking down at her as if trying to decide what to say next. Fortunately, they were no longer bellowing at each other when Renny Magee banged upon the bedroom door and called out to them.

At Conn's grudging, "Come," the girl crashed into the room, waving an envelope.

"The post just came!" she announced, her voice shrill with excitement. "There's a letter! Miss Fallon said I should bring it to you."

"A letter?" Vangie repeated.

Conn reached for it, but Renny Magee charged toward the bed and thrust the letter directly at Vangie. The girl stood there then, clearly bent on learning, if not the contents of the letter, at least the identity of its sender.

Conn shot a dark look at the girl, but Vangie ignored the both of them. *"Aidan!"* she choked out. "'Tis from Aidan!"

She scarcely noticed when Conn hauled himself to his feet and with a jab of his thumb motioned for Renny Magee to follow him out of the room.

Well, let him go, then. If he was so stubborn that he wouldn't read a letter from his own son—the son they hadn't heard from in months—then let him just go and sulk.

Her heart pounding with anticipation, Vangie propped her pillow behind her, opened the letter with trembling hands, and began to read.

⌒

Minutes later, when Conn came back into the room, she had not moved, but sat clasping the letter with both hands against her heart as she wept.

"Why didn't you tell me?" she choked out. "All this time I've begged you to write to him—and you never said a word! Why? Why didn't you tell me you *had* written to him?"

Conn sat down beside her. "I thought it would be cruel to raise your hopes." He paused, his eyes going to the letter still clutched in her hands. "What does he say, then?"

Watching him, Vangie handed him the letter. "You read it," she told him. "I want to hear it again, and if you read it, it will be almost like hearing it from himself."

Conn looked at her, then took the letter and began to read.

⌒

Dear Mother,

I suppose by now you know that Da wrote to me some time past. In truth, I was relieved to hear from him, for I hated having the hard feelings between us.

I have missed all of you more than I would have thought possible, and now that I know Da is not still set against me, I am making plans for my own journey to America. I have been working, and soon I will be able to pay my own way across.

I cannot tell you exactly when I will come, for I still have to make arrangements to leave my job, and there are some other matters I must attend to. But it should be soon.

No doubt the twin terrors have found new mischief to get themselves into, and I expect Baby Emma is getting big. Has Nell Grace caught herself a fellow yet? Tell them all I am truly anxious to see them, and that includes Da.

And tell them I am coming soon. Just as soon as I can.

Your devoted son,
Aidan MacGovern

By the time Conn finished reading the letter, Vangie was weeping again.

"Oh, Conn," she said, grasping his arm, "he's coming! Aidan is truly coming! Finally, we'll all be together again!"

Conn patted her hand. "Aye, love. We'll all be together again. Will that make you happy then, Vangie?"

She leaned toward him. "I can't think of anything that would make me happier!" She paused. "Conn...the things I said to you—"

He shook his head. "Never mind that. We both know I deserved to hear everything you had to say."

"No, that's not true." She studied him, and to his surprise a faint smile appeared, though the tears were still streaming down her face. "Perhaps you deserved...*some* of it. But not all."

She opened her arms to him then, and with a long, shaky sigh of relief, Conn gathered her to him and buried his face in her hair.

"Oh, Conn," she murmured against his shoulder. "Now we'll have our family together at last. Aidan, our new babe—all our children—under our roof again. That's how things are supposed to be."

Aye, that's how things were supposed to be, Conn thought. And this was how things were supposed to be between him and Vangie. This was how things should *always* be.

He understood, perhaps better than she thought he did, how difficult, how agonizing, this situation had been for Vangie. As a child, her father had deserted them, and after the death of her mother from heart failure, Vangie and her three sisters—all of them but wee girls—had been separated and passed around to different relatives to raise, none of whom wanted an extra mouth to feed. Her early years had been years of fear and abandonment, years of never feeling "whole" because of the way her family had been torn apart. When she was grown and agreed to marry Conn, she had made him promise that they would have a large family, and that, no matter what, nothing would ever divide them.

Conn had done his best to keep his word; staying behind had been Aidan's idea, after all. But as time passed and he saw the way Aidan's absence was tearing at her heart, he knew he had to do something—whatever it took—to reunite them.

As he held her, he tried to convince himself that he was grateful for the joy

Aidan's letter had brought Vangie. And *him*. He, too, was happy the boy was coming across. He tried to put down the vague uneasiness gnawing at the back of his mind, but something about the boy's letter nagged at him. In truth, he hadn't expected it to be this easy. All along, he'd worried that Aidan would either ignore the "peace offering" Conn's letter was meant to be and not reply at all, or else he would make his father beg—and Conn wasn't at all sure he had it in him to beg his eldest son, not even for Vangie's sake.

But here was the reply, and it had come fairly quickly at that—seemingly a genuine response that held an olive branch of its own. And here was his wife, happy and content in his arms. So why was he acting like a fool, instead of making the most of the moment?

With one finger under her chin, he tipped her face up to his. "And so I am forgiven, then?" he said, only half-teasing. "Great *amadan* that I am?"

Her eyes still glistened with tears, but these were new tears, tears of happiness. "I don't think you're an *amadan* at all," Vangie said softly. "I think you're a good man and a wonderful husband. And as for forgiveness, I should be asking yours, Conn MacGovern."

Conn frowned. "For what, love?"

"For keeping the announcement of our new babe from you. It was a terrible cruel thing to do."

He kissed her—carefully, for he was already feeling the need to protect her. "You are forgiven, Evangeline MacGovern. And now, seeing that we're both forgiven, do you think I might have a bite to eat? 'Tis starving I am."

To his dismay, Vangie turned a pale shade of gray. "Oh, did you have to mention food, Conn MacGovern?"

Before he could help her stand, she was out of the bed and on her way to the back door, not even stopping in the kitchen to tell their lasses the big news.

There were times, it did seem, when a husband could do nothing right.

27

A STEP TOWARD TRUST

I do not ask for any crown
But that which all may win;
Nor try to conquer any world
Except the one within.
Be Thou my guide until I find
Led by a tender hand,
The happy kingdom in myself
And dare to take command.

LOUISA MAY ALCOTT

Frustrated that there had not been an opportunity to make a thorough apology to Michael after the night of her birthday, Susanna was determined to seek him out before any more time had transpired. After three days, she finally summoned the courage to approach him.

Finding the opportunity, however, was another matter. He had stayed in the city the two days following her birthday, returning so late last night that Susanna and the rest of the household had already retired. He made an unusually brief appearance at breakfast this morning, only long enough to talk briefly with Caterina while he hurried through a few bites of food. Although he had been painstakingly polite to Susanna, they exchanged only two or three sentences before he excused himself.

Apparently, he was going to be at home tonight. Earlier that morning, Paul had mentioned that he would be taking the evening rehearsal in Michael's place. If she were going to speak with him—and Susanna was feeling an increasing urgency to do so—this evening might be her best chance.

It had been a busy day—busier than usual. In addition to her everyday responsibilities with Caterina, Susanna was overseeing the preparation of one of the guest rooms, making a final check of the medications and other supplies Dr. Carmichael had suggested, and tending to other details in anticipation of their new guest's arrival. The child, Maylee, would be coming just before Christmas, and Susanna wanted everything to be ready for her.

She had not met Maylee yet, but Michael's accounting of the poor child's condition wrenched Susanna's heart and made her eager to see the girl settled here at Bantry Hill, where she could have as much attention and care as she needed. Caterina was excited about having "a new friend" on the premises, although Michael had cautioned that Maylee would not likely have the stamina to be a playmate.

To Caterina's credit, she had taken this to heart and then made a remarkable observation: "Well, I'm happy that she's coming anyway, because she will probably feel better here, since she'll get lots of love and good food."

The only one who seemed less than happy about having a new child around the house was Moira Dempsey, but then Susanna was beginning to think that Moira was content only when she had something to complain about.

As the day wore on, Susanna sensed that Michael was deliberately avoiding her. After his usual morning ride, he retreated to his office, taking his midday meal there as well. He worked through the rest of the afternoon until supper, after which he told Susanna he would see to Caterina's bedtime.

By nine that night Susanna had had enough. She *would* talk with him—now, tonight, before he had a chance to start the same routine over again the next day.

She was headed downstairs on her way to Michael's office when she stopped outside the kitchen to pick up a piece of cookie. A deposit, no doubt, from Caterina or even the wolfhound, since they tended to travel as a pair. The kitchen door was partially open, and a voice from inside arrested her. She was a little ashamed to be eavesdropping, but when she heard her own name, she couldn't bring herself to leave. She held her breath and pressed herself against the wall.

"She'll not be staying here; don't think for a minute she will." It was Moira, in her usual caustic tone.

Her husband answered, his voice gruff. "You don't know that."

"She might stay for now, if she has designs on him, as I suspect she does. But you watch. That'll change soon enough. Who's to say but what she's not the same turn as the sister, after all?"

Susanna cringed at the comparison with Deirdre. But to her surprise, Liam Dempsey came to her defense. "This one's not at all like the other. She seems a good enough sort. The wee wane dotes on her, and she turns a steady hand to her work. And doesn't the man have a right to a bit of happiness? The Lord knows he's had little enough of it these past years."

"Even if she means well, she's too young," Moira insisted. "A girl like that is not going to tie herself down with a blind man and a child for long! You mark my words, she'll not be staying! And there he'll be again."

"'Tis none of our affair, woman!" Liam growled. "You worry too much!"

"And wasn't I right about the other one?" Moira shot back. "Didn't I tell you what *she* was, early on?"

"Aye. But I've been married to you long enough to know you're not right *all* the time, and this is one of those times, I'll wager."

Susanna stood staring at the kitchen door for a second or two more, then quickly turned and retraced her steps. She went into the library and stood at the window, fuming. How dare Moira Dempsey assume she was anything like Deirdre, simply because they were sisters! She had done nothing to earn the woman's suspicion and contempt. And yet...

The Dempseys *had* known Michael since he was a boy, and Moira obviously considered herself a surrogate mother to him. Not only had she been a part of his childhood, but she would have experienced the difficult years after his accident when he'd endured both blindness and a devastating marriage. She would have witnessed much of the anguish and humiliation Deirdre had brought upon him.

Even though Susanna was shocked at the animosity that apparently fueled Moira's disapproval, once she calmed, she had to concede that perhaps in the housekeeper's place she would have reacted the same. The woman did not know her, after all. How could she be expected to trust Susanna's motives or her actions where Michael was concerned? Nothing but time—most likely a great deal of time—would win Moira Dempsey over.

She left the library and went in search of Michael, still mulling over the conversation. She hated being the object of someone's distrust. More distressing still was the awareness that Moira's suspicion was based on nothing but the deceit of another person—in this case, Susanna's own sister.

And wasn't this very nearly the position in which she had placed Michael?

The realization slammed her like a hammer blow, and she stopped in the middle of the hallway. From the beginning she had been unable to trust Michael, and all because of Deirdre. Her own suspicions had been based entirely on what she'd been told by her sister—whose deceit had been monumental.

Down the hallway, she heard noises from the music room and started in that direction. Just as she reached the door, she heard a dissonant crash, like a cat jumping on the piano keys. Then a loud thud.

She found Michael on his knees near the piano. Manuscript pages were scattered everywhere, and he frowned and muttered to himself as he vainly tried to sort through them. He looked unusually disheveled, his hair tousled, his tie askew, his face flushed.

Rarely had Susanna seen a flare of the proverbial "artist's temperament" in Michael—that volatile emotionalism and passion of one completely consumed by his work, or the blistering flash of impatience when the work did not go well. For the most part, despite the limitations his blindness imposed on him, he almost always maintained an enviable calm, a reserve of self-control she never would have expected to find in so complicated and gifted a man.

She wasn't sure she really believed there *was* such a thing as the "artist's temperament," but if there was, Michael certainly didn't seem to fit the mold. This was one time, however, when his even disposition had clearly abandoned him.

She hesitated at the door, waiting for the right moment to enter.

His head came up. "Susanna?"

"Yes." She walked the rest of the way into the room. "Can I help?"

Without waiting for him to answer, she stooped down and began picking up random manuscript sheets from the floor, glancing at them to see what they were.

"*Grazie,*" he said. "I was foolish enough to think I could manage this without Paul."

"What sort of order do these belong in?"

He sighed. "I had two stacks and managed to drop them both. One section is partially coded—but not numbered. The rest is Paul's notation. Everything is out of order."

"Why don't you let me do this?" Susanna offered, already beginning to sort the pages numbered in Paul's neat hand from those coded in the New York Point for the blind, which Michael used for his personal reference. "I'll just separate the Braille sheets and put Paul's in order."

"Ah. *Grazie,*" he said again.

He pushed himself up to one knee, staying there as if he could watch Susanna's progress. His closeness unnerved her and made her hurry even more.

"Was it terribly hard for you?" she asked, attempting to make conversation as a means of easing the awkwardness between them. "Learning to use Braille?"

He hesitated, then nodded. "It was not easy. I think for children, it is probably a little easier. Their reading and writing habits are not so well-formed yet. Becoming blind as an adult is much like beginning a new life."

He said it without so much as a trace of self-pity. Susanna looked at him. He seemed weary to the point of exhaustion, and in that instant she felt as if she might suffocate with love for him.

Love. How studiously she had avoided that word! Yet how easily it seemed to slip into her thoughts of late.

Flustered, she glanced away and finished scooping up the manuscript as quickly as she could.

"There," she said, "I think I've got it back together the way it should be."

They stood, and for a moment they faced each other, Michael's hand on her arm, his head bent low.

"Michael...I wonder if we could talk," Susanna ventured. "I...want to apologize for the other night. There hasn't been time—"

Unexpectedly, he lifted his hand as if he would touch her face, but didn't. "There is no need."

"There *is* a need," Susanna insisted. "Please, can't we just...talk?"

"Susanna—"

"Michael, I have something I need to tell you, but there's something else I need to say first. *Please*, just let me say it!"

He frowned in surprise at her outburst, but stood waiting, his features taut, as if he were apprehensive about what was coming.

"Can we—" Susanna glanced toward the settee in front of the fireplace. "Can we sit down?"

"*Sì*. Of course."

He was in his shirt sleeves but moved now to shrug into the jacket tossed on top of the piano before crossing the room. Susanna followed him, watching as he stooped to punch up the fire: his broad back, his great mane of dark hair, his easy movements. Emotion seized her again, and she had to look away.

He racked the poker and joined her on the small sofa. "So, then, what is it you wanted to tell me?"

"About the other night. I want to explain why I acted as I did—"

"You did explain," he broke in. "And I told you, I understand."

"Oh, Michael, will you please stop being so...*forgiving*!"

One dark eyebrow lifted, but he said nothing.

"You're always so kind to me." Susanna's voice rose. "But I don't deserve your kindness this time, don't you see? I'm trying to tell you that I'm dreadfully sorry, really I am, about what happened. I've no idea why I jumped to the conclusion I did. I know you better than to think you'd deliberately deceive me. You wouldn't. It was foolish and unfair, and I still can't believe I acted as I did. You have every right to be upset with me—"

"But I'm *not* upset with you, Susanna."

"Well, you *should* be! I jumped to conclusions, I accused you of a perfectly awful thing. Can you forgive me? And please, don't just say you do! Don't be kind! I need to know you really *do* forgive me, if you can."

He sat utterly still, his expression thoughtful, as if he was choosing his words with deliberate care. "Of course, I forgive you, Susanna," he said softly. "But you're wrong in thinking it was all your fault. I should have told you about Christopher's accident before rehearsal. But I suspected you would accuse me of deliberately taking advantage—"

"And that's exactly what I *did* accuse you of! It probably wouldn't have made any difference *when* you told me, I would have—"

He lifted a hand to stop her. "But more than likely, you would not have been so quick to assume what you did if I had simply explained beforehand. That was my fault, not yours."

Finally, some of the tension began to seep out of Susanna and she managed a deep breath. "It should never have happened. I...don't really know why—"

"Is it so difficult for you to trust me, Susanna, even now?"

"Oh, Michael, no! I *do* trust you! It's so much easier, so natural, to trust—"

Susanna stopped, putting a hand to her mouth to stop the words she had almost blurted out: *"It's so much easier, so natural, to trust someone you love..."*

"I would like to believe that, Susanna. But I can't help wondering...why now?"

"I've changed," Susanna managed to say. "I can't explain, but I *have* changed. And there's something else—"

She stopped, trying to quell her nervousness. What was she letting herself in for? But she had promised herself—and God—that she was going to *try*.

"If you want, I'm willing to help with the concert. I'll...play the organ. If I can, that is. I'll at least try."

He leaned forward so suddenly the sofa pitched under his weight, and the smile that slowly spread over his features made Susanna feel as if she'd just handed him a rare and precious gift.

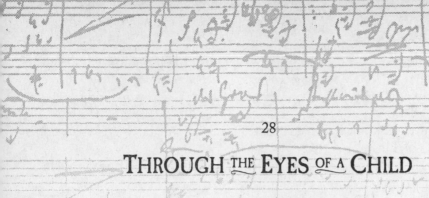

28

THROUGH THE EYES OF A CHILD

Truth cannot hide from the eyes of a child.

ANONYMOUS

S o...what changed your mind?"

"It's not that I haven't *wanted* to help you, Michael. I *have*. I can't tell you how many times I've refused to do something I really wanted to do." Susanna paused. "Because I was always afraid. Afraid I'd fail."

She went on, struggling to explain about the safe place she had made for herself by always staying in the background, never undertaking anything beyond her capabilities, and the false humility she had birthed and nurtured through the years.

She *hated* being this honest with Michael, recoiled at letting him see just what a pitiful coward she had been...and perhaps still was, if truth were told. She would much rather have had his respect, even his admiration—but it seemed important that she make as honest an explanation as she could manage.

She thought it futile entirely to mention Deirdre's attempts to diminish her, so she didn't. Her sister's contempt had not created Susanna's inadequacies and fear of failure, after all, but had only added to the weaknesses already there. Only in letting slip the nickname Deirdre had given her—"Mouse"—did she hint at her sister's ongoing abasement. And when she saw Michael's countenance tighten, she hurried on, giving him no time to respond.

"It was Caterina, I suppose, who finally helped me come to realize what I had done to myself all these years."

"Cati?" he said with a look of surprise.

"Yes. When she brought up David and Goliath at the rehearsal, it triggered something in me, something that forced me to confront what I'd done to myself." She paused. "Children often have a way of...*mining* truth from a grownup's heart."

Michael smiled a little and nodded. "I, too, have sometimes had to confront a truth because of one of my precocious daughter's incisive questions."

~

Caterina had flung one of those "incisive questions" at him only that evening, after he had heard her prayers and tucked her into bed.

He had bent over to kiss her good night when the question came. "Papa? Why are you unhappy with Aunt Susanna?"

"But I am *not* unhappy with Aunt Susanna. Where did you get such an idea, Cati?"

"You hardly talked to her today," Caterina had replied, her tone uncommonly solemn. "And when you did, Aunt Susanna looked…worried. And you sounded like you do with me sometimes when I've done something to make you unhappy."

He took her hand. "I've been very busy, Cati. Too busy. But I promise you, I'm not unhappy. Not with Aunt Susanna nor with anyone else."

A long sigh escaped her—a very *adult* sigh. "Do you like Aunt Susanna, Papa?"

"Such questions tonight! What is going on in that clever little head, eh? Of course, I like Aunt Susanna. I like her very much. Don't you?"

"I *love* her!" Caterina said fiercely. "I love her more than anyone else in the world except for you!"

"Good. I hope you have told her so. She would like hearing it, I know."

"Have *you* told her, Papa? Does she know you like her?"

"Well…it is…different for grownups," Michael stammered. "We do not always speak of such things."

"Why not? Don't you think Aunt Susanna would want to know you like her? She likes *you*. A lot. I can tell."

"And how is it that you know this, hmm?"

"When she looks at you, I can see it. I think Aunt Susanna likes you almost as much as I do."

Caterina was just a child, Michael reasoned. A child who loved her father and her Aunt Susanna with all her heart. Even so, her words made him lose his breath for an instant, wishing that *he* could see how Susanna looked at him.

~

Susanna watched Michael retreat and wondered where he'd gone. Michael was a man who needed quiet as much as food and water, and somehow he seemed to have carved out a place within himself where he could withdraw—even in the middle of a crowd or an ongoing conversation.

She had grown accustomed to his silences, but in light of what she'd been trying to tell him, she wished he hadn't picked *now* to turn inward.

"Michael?"

He straightened. "I'm sorry, Susanna. I was thinking about what you said. About Caterina. What else did you say?"

"Yes, well, I was saying that even though I'm familiar with most of the music you're doing for the Christmas concert, your arrangements will be altogether new to me. And there's so little time left—only a few days. I'd have to practice a great deal, but where? I can't very well go into the city every day and leave Caterina."

"That need not be a problem. Saint Catherine's has a fine organ. I'm sure Dermot would be more than happy for you to use it for your practice."

"Dermot?"

"Dermot Flynn. You met him your first evening here, remember? He's the priest at Saint Catherine's. It's close, not quite a mile away. And you needn't worry about Caterina. Moira will be here, even if Paul and I are gone. Perhaps Caterina could go with you sometimes. I'm sure she'd like that."

As Susanna listened, Michael proceeded to work everything out, precisely and thoroughly. And Susanna began to realize that she had lost any hope of a way out.

Perhaps this was God's way of making His will perfectly clear.

With a bit of help from Michael.

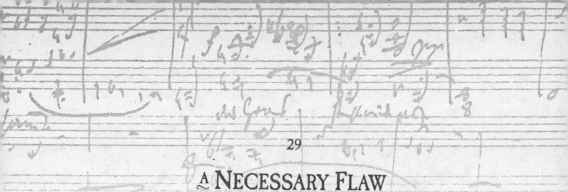

29

A NECESSARY FLAW

I have sought, but I seek it vainly,
That one lost chord divine,
That came from the soul of the Organ
And entered into mine.

ADELAIDE A. PROCTER

O nly three days remained until the concert. In addition to spending hours at Saint Catherine's every day in practice, Susanna also had to help ready the house for Christmas. Decorations were constructed and put up; preliminary baking had begun, with Moira Dempsey feverishly supervising every move made in the kitchen; gifts were prepared—some homemade, others purchased; and Caterina insisted on adding a new Christmas carol to her repertoire on a biweekly basis, which of course required extra instruction.

Susanna felt as if she were living in a whirlwind. By now it was difficult to believe there had ever been a time when a concert didn't loom like a waiting storm and every hour of the day wasn't filled with too much work to do.

The world outside might just as well have not existed, so frenzied and all-absorbing was life at Bantry Hill. Most of the news she managed to glean came through discussions between Michael and Paul about events going on in the city or her own random reading of the newspapers.

Apparently the Tilton-Beecher scandal still dominated the gossip circles, even though a mistrial had been declared the previous year and Henry Ward Beecher had been exonerated by his congregation. The famous Brooklyn preacher and brother of Harriet Beecher Stowe had been accused of adultery with the wife of one of his parishioners—a parishioner who also happened to be his closest friend. But then Mr. Beecher seemed to be the subject of more than one scandal. Apparently, there was much speculation that the clergyman was also involved in the rising spiritualism movement—especially with its women.

Susanna had the feeling there might be more to this story than what Michael and Paul discussed in her presence. She had read mention in the newspapers about the character of some of the women who participated in the spiritualist groups springing up all over New York State, and their reputations were questionable at best.

Indeed, scandal seemed to be the leading fodder for the newspaper mills these days. In addition to the tales about Beecher, there was also the recent news that the infamous "Boss" Tweed, the leading, albeit corrupt, political force in the city of New York for years, had escaped from jail and was on his way to Cuba.

Some journalists were having a field day exposing all manner of disgraceful tales from within the women's suffrage movement—everything from rumors of its members advocating "free love" to accusations that some were actively campaigning against marriage and motherhood.

Even President Grant and his administration weren't exempt from the rumors of scandal. So rampant were stories of debauchery and corruption that Susanna had almost resolved to simply give up reading the papers altogether. And she rather wished Paul would do the same before he inadvertently brought up one of the unsavory news reports in Caterina's hearing.

In truth, she had precious little time for leisure reading these days. As Liam drove her to Saint Catherine's for her afternoon practice, she spent most of the ride there ticking off all the things she still had to do afterward. She found herself feeling a great deal more harried and distracted since she'd agreed to take part in the Christmas concert.

So distracted, in fact, that she had to ask Liam to repeat himself as he deposited her at the walkway to the church.

"I said himself will be coming along with me when I return."

"Michael?"

"Aye. We've some errands to tend to, so we'll be stopping for you afterward."

Susanna nodded absently, already turning and starting for the front doors. She hoped Michael didn't show up early; she wasn't ready for him to hear her progress just yet. In fact, she was beginning to wonder just how much *progress* she was actually making. She had left the church yesterday altogether frustrated, keenly regretting all the months she'd gone without touching an organ. Her efforts to regain her former technique and agility seemed to be taking an inordinate length of time.

The music itself wasn't all that difficult. Even though Michael's arrangements were new to her, they were fairly easy to follow and blessedly practical in construction. But her legs ached from using muscles that hadn't been exercised in over a year, and her playing was still wooden, not merely in physical dexterity, but in emotion.

The organ at Saint Catherine's wasn't so grand as the one she'd be playing in the concert hall, but it was still daunting, even in its simplicity. An organ was a mighty, formidable instrument at the best of times. An exacting taskmaster. And, when the organist was not at her best, more foe than friend.

Much later in the afternoon, she was making her fifth—or was it her sixth?—pass through the "Hallelujah Chorus" and finding it every bit as stiff and as unemotional as her preceding attempts. Tired, discouraged, and demoralized, she uttered a cry of frustration and deliberately slammed the final chord in an angry thud. She ripped her music from the rack and sat pressing it to her chest, her head down, tears streaming from her eyes.

The fact that she was crying only served to heighten her self-disgust, for she had never by nature been a *weeper.* Even as a child she had always taken pride in maintaining her composure. But at the moment she was weary beyond words and furious with herself, that she had agreed to this—this impossible undertaking. She hated the organ. She hated the music. And she hated weeping. All of which only made the tears come even harder.

When a pair of strong hands clasped her shoulders, she whipped around, sending her music flying. "Michael! How long have you been here?"

She winced at the accusatory tone in her voice, but if he noticed, he gave no indication. "I came through the back," he said, evading her question about how long he'd been listening. "Why are you so upset?"

"I'm not."

"I see." He paused. "Then why are you so angry?"

Susanna stood, then stooped down to retrieve her music. "I am angry with *myself,*" she said between clenched teeth, "because I've committed to do something of which I'm obviously incapable. And if you've been here very long, you know exactly what I'm talking about. I'm *never* going to be able to do justice to this music by the time of the concert."

She straightened to find him standing quietly, his head tilted to one side as if he was giving her his closest attention.

"I'm—it's as if I'm made of wood when I try to play. I don't understand it! The music isn't all that difficult, and yet I'm murdering it entirely!"

"Come, sit down."

Reluctantly, Susanna followed him to the front pew and sat down beside him. "Michael—"

"First, you are not...*murdering* the music, Susanna. You are placing too great a demand on yourself and creating an unreasonable tension. It is not the music that is thwarting you, but your own expectations. And perhaps a part of that is my fault."

"It's hardly your fault that I play like a clumsy schoolgirl!"

"You do not play like a clumsy schoolgirl. You play like a highly gifted young woman, even a professional—but one who has set for herself an impossible goal. A goal of nothing less than perfection."

He continued to speak, using his hands as much as his voice as he attempted to make his point. "Now that you have agreed to do this, you are determined to do it *perfectly*. But because the time in which you must achieve this self-imposed perfection is unrealistic, you're becoming tense and disillusioned with your own abilities. You will do just fine when the orchestra surrounds you and you can forget any limitations you now imagine—for they are negligible and will go completely unnoticed once you join the other musicians. You will see. God will then imbue your music with...*spirit* and power. He will enable it to soar."

Susanna sat staring at him. With her music tucked under one arm, she lifted her other hand to wipe away the dampness from her cheeks. "How can you know that?"

"I know." He shrugged. "No music is perfect. No performance is, either. I would not *allow* my people to perform the music without *some* imperfection, no matter how small."

"But your orchestra is *wonderful*! I've never heard the slightest mistake when they perform. Never."

"The fact that you have not heard a mistake doesn't mean it isn't there. There is always a flaw. A small dissonance somewhere, at least once. Always." He gave a cryptic smile. "I insist on it."

Susanna stared at him. "You insist on a *flaw*?"

"*Sì*. It is my way of reminding them—and myself—that no one and nothing is perfect except God." He stopped, his expression all seriousness as he added, "Of course, I allow for only *one* flaw. No more."

"Well," Susanna said dryly, "I expect you won't have to worry about anything being perfect as long as *I'm* a part of the orchestra."

He reached to touch her face. "If it were up to me, you would *always* be a part of the orchestra."

He stood then and helped her to her feet. "Remind me to tell Dermot he needs to heat his church. This sanctuary is unconscionably cold. Come now, let's go home and have a fire and something hot to drink."

Susanna took his arm but hesitated before starting up the aisle. "Michael...I want to be sure you know that I'm not trying to back out of the concert. I *want* to do this for you, really I do! But—"

He turned toward her. "No, Susanna. You must not do this for *me*. You must do it for *you*. Do you understand?"

The intensity in his voice surprised her. Before she could reply, he added, "This is between you and God. Like a covenant. Do this for Him, and for yourself. He wants you to see that He has gifted you...and called you for this. He wants to show you that in spite of your fear and feelings of inadequacy, you can trust Him to be faithful in helping you to fulfill that calling. No matter what."

"How can you know that?" The same question she had asked before.

He smiled, then gave the same reply as before. "I *know*."

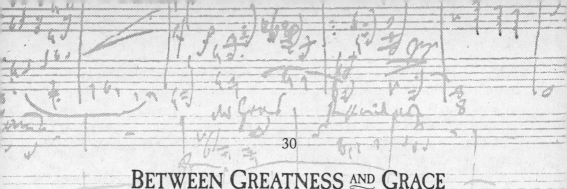

30

BETWEEN GREATNESS AND GRACE

Life's but a walking shadow, a poor player
That struts and frets his hour upon the stage...

WILLIAM SHAKESPEARE

Michael never held rehearsal the day before a concert. "Just as the music must have its silences, its rests," he said, "the musicians themselves must also rest."

But tonight, with the concert looming less than twenty-four hours away, Susanna did not feel rested. Instead, she stood at her bedroom window thinking with grim irony that Michael might as well have held rehearsal. A *long* rehearsal. She wouldn't be getting any sleep tonight, and no doubt would feel even more lightheaded and queasy tomorrow.

She hadn't even bothered to change into her nightclothes. Earlier she had tried to read, but she could have been staring at a blank page for all the good it did. She did manage to write a letter to the Mahers, her former employers, but barely remembered what she'd written. She had checked on Caterina three times and found both her and the wolfhound sleeping soundly. Now, unable to think of anything else to do, she decided to go downstairs and fix some warm milk. She didn't particularly *like* warm milk, and wasn't at all convinced it encouraged sleep. Still, it was worth trying.

Besides, the kitchen was comfortable and inviting—when Moira wasn't there. It was certainly the warmest room in the house. Susanna usually kept her distance when the housekeeper was working. It would be nice, she decided, to have it all to herself for a change.

But when she approached, she was surprised to see the door open and light filtering out into the hallway. The Dempseys usually retired much earlier than this. Perhaps Moira was working on some special Christmas delicacy. Tentatively, she stepped into the room. It was softly lit by candles, and a cheerful fire blazed and crackled in the enormous stone fireplace.

Michael sat at the kitchen table. In front of him was a plate of bread and cheese, and he was drinking something from a cup. He pushed his chair back and stood the instant he heard her footsteps.

"Susanna?"

"Yes. Sit down, Michael. What are you doing?"

"Indulging myself." He smiled sheepishly, brushing the front of his sweater as if to dispel any crumbs. "You couldn't sleep either?"

"No. I didn't really expect to. But surely *you* don't get nervous the night before a concert?"

"Come in, please. Join me. I heated some milk—have some with me. And something to eat? Paul said you scarcely touched your supper."

"Paul is too observant for his own good." Susanna poured herself a cup of milk and went to sit down across the table from him.

"So...*do* you get nervous before a concert?"

He shook his head. "At the moment I am excited. I had a letter from my father today. It seems he is finally coming to visit."

"Oh, Michael, that's wonderful! How long has it been since you've seen him?"

"A long time. Years. I have been trying to convince him to come here and stay, but he insists this will be only a visit. Perhaps once he is here I can change his mind."

"When is he coming?"

"Not until spring. Sometime around the end of March or early in April, I think. I haven't told Caterina yet. She will badger me incessantly once she knows."

"Well, I'm very happy for you. You'll have to tell me what you'd like me to do to help prepare for his visit."

"That is not your responsibility, Susanna," he said firmly. "You are not a part of the household *staff*—you are Caterina's aunt."

"But I *want* to help."

"Probably you can help most by keeping Caterina from driving all of us to lunacy once she learns the news. She has been wild to meet her grandpapa."

"They've never met? Then she *will* be thrilled. What a splendid opportunity for both of them."

He nodded. "But now I will answer your question. About the stage fright. I don't get nervous, no. I pray much about it, however," he added with a wry grin.

"I find it odd that you would be even the slightest bit tense," Susanna said. "You always look so completely calm when you're conducting." She took a sip of milk. "I'm terrified, of course. I suppose I'll be even worse tomorrow."

He nodded, although Susanna was quite sure he couldn't comprehend what she was feeling.

"You told me once that you understood about stage fright," she said. "But I can't imagine why."

He shrugged. "I don't have stage fright with the orchestra, because when we perform, I become one with them. But when I was still singing—" He raised his eyebrows. "I know about 'terrified,' I assure you."

"I certainly can't think *why*. Your success was legendary."

"The fear was as real to me as it is to you. It happened every time I went on stage. Sometimes I became physically ill and thought I could not possibly go on."

"But you always did…"

He nodded slightly. "But not always *willingly*."

"Is that why you quit singing? Or was it because of the blindness?"

He was about to take a sip of milk, but the cup didn't quite make it to his mouth. It stopped in midair, and he frowned.

"Forgive me," Susanna said quickly. "That's really none of my business."

"*E'niente.*" He shrugged. "Actually, it was neither. God helped me to function in spite of the stage fright. That's why I can be so certain He will do the same for you. As for the blindness—I left the opera *before* the accident."

"*Before*? But *why*? I'd just assumed—" She stopped. "Deirdre?"

"It's not easy to explain."

"I shouldn't have asked—"

"No, no, it's all right." He tilted his head. "But are you sure you want to hear this?"

"Only if you want to tell me."

Slowly, he nodded, then clasped his hands on top of the table. "I know that Paul told you about Deirdre and me."

Susanna hadn't expected him to bring up the subject of his marriage. "Michael, there's no need—"

He lifted a hand. "It's all right, Susanna."

She sank back against the chair, watching him. His face had grown taut, his expression intense. The creases at the corners of his eyes seemed more deeply drawn, his mouth tighter. His hands, always elegant and expressive, clenched, then unclenched and began to move as he spoke.

~

"To fail in one's marriage—this is a hard thing, a very hard thing for a man to live with. But the truth is that Deirdre was never happy with me. I was not a good husband for her. It was a mistake for us to marry. We barely knew each other. But she wanted it that way, and I…well, I was impulsive then, too. But from the beginning we were very different. Later, things changed even more. I changed. And so did Deirdre.

"She needed more, much more, than I could give her. Deirdre, I think, was driven," he said quietly. "She had a kind of hunger in her, a need, that nothing seemed to fill. She was always searching for more. And when she didn't find it, when she could not have what she thought she wanted, she would grow angry. Very angry. Ultimately, she wanted a much different kind of life from what we had, much different than I could endure.

"She loved the opera, you understand? More than anything, she loved the life of the theater: to perform, to be surrounded by people, to be adored. She had so much ambition, so great a passion, that at times she simply overwhelmed me. I felt as if I were drowning."

He brought his hands to his face, kneading his temples as if his head ached. "We were, as I said, very different. We believed in different things, wanted different things. But at the time, I tried to tell myself that we were *not* so different after all."

He got to his feet and went to stand with his back to the fire. His hair fell forward as he stood there, his head dipped low, his hands clasped behind his back. "I must tell you things about myself I would rather you not know," he said with a rueful smile. "I would prefer that you think the best of me. But—"

He shrugged, then went on. "For some years before Deirdre and I met—and during much of our marriage—I had...great success. And I enjoyed it; it was—" He made a circular motion with his hand. "It made my head spin. There was the money, of course. There was always much money. More than I needed, more than I could spend. And the celebrity—ah, the crowds! With every role I sang, every stage I walked onto, I felt more and more the adulation of the people, the audience. And the excitement of the lifestyle: travel, new experiences—this was important to me, especially as a young man. I was very restless, never satisfied. Much like Deirdre, no?"

Susanna noticed that the longer he spoke, the more pronounced became his accent—and the more strained his expression.

"So...I, too, was driven, you see. I possessed a different kind of hunger, but a hunger all the same. More than anything else, what drove me was the music. Always the music. Always, I searched for something I had heard—in my head, in my heart, when I was but a child. Something I knew I was meant to create, or discover, yet something always just out of reach.

"I later came to realize that as a child I had been given a kind of *vision*, a glimpse of God's plan for my life—I am almost embarrassed to tell you this, it sounds so presumptuous—but it is true, nevertheless. Then as I grew older and the success came, I allowed the vision to pale. For a time I was caught up in it all—the chaos and the excitement and the adoration of the crowds. Always somewhere to go, something to do, people demanding more and more from me. I suppose I grew to *need* it. Perhaps I even *fed* on it. It made me more *alive*, gave me that rush to the blood that can be a kind of...seduction. To my shame, I reached a place where the music no longer mattered nearly as much to me as what it could *provide* for me. Even my God, who *gave* me the music in the first place—he no longer mattered so much to me either.

"But eventually, something began to change. At first, it happened slowly, very slowly. At some point, I began to sense a need for something more important and fulfilling than the crowds and the fame and the money. The way I was living—the way *we* were living at that time—had become meaningless. Empty."

He stepped away from the fireplace and came back to his chair. Susanna couldn't take her eyes off him as he braced one hand on the table and let the other fall at his side. In that moment, with his tousled hair and commanding Mediterranean features, he seemed to belong to an older time, a different place. If he were to exchange his casual clothing for a cloak and a walking stick, he could easily be taken for an Italian prince from the remote past.

Perhaps Susanna should have been shocked at the things he was telling her. She could hear his voice, see his face, feel his pain—and his shame. And yet she took it all in as from a distance, all the while knowing that the man he *used* to be could never in any way diminish the man he had become.

The man she loved...

"There was much chaos in my life at that time, and in my marriage as well," he went on. "I almost became ill. Not physically, but in my mind and"—he touched his heart—"in my spirit. I could never seem to find a quiet place. I could never be alone. There was such confusion, such clamor all around me and inside me.

"And so I left. I went away." He shuddered. "I *ran* away."

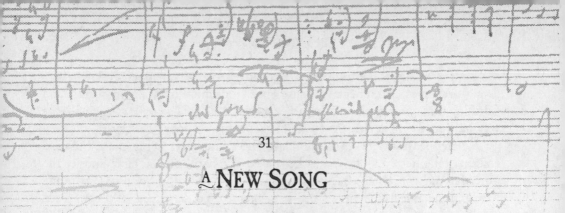

31

A NEW SONG

I cannot sing the old songs,
For me their charm is o'er
My earthly harp is laid aside,
I wake its chords no more.
The precious blood of Christ my Lord
has cleansed and made me free,
And taught my heart a new song,
Of his great love to me.

FANNY CROSBY

By now I was desperate," Michael said. "Desperate to find some peace, a quiet place. I needed to *think*. I needed to find God again."

He heard Susanna's sharp intake of breath. "You went alone? Without Deirdre?"

"Deirdre would not have gone, even if I had asked. But I *didn't* ask. She became very angry with me. But I had such an urgency, such a need to get away—I felt I had no choice. I canceled my performances. All of them. And then I left."

Michael's back knotted with tension, and he straightened, easing his shoulders before going on. "As it happened, I ended up staying away for a long time—weeks. But it was the best thing, the most important thing, I could have done." He paused. "It changed my life.

"A friend—another singer and a man of great faith—allowed me the use of his cabin in Canada. I took nothing with me except a few clothes, some food, my Bible—too long unread—and a collection of Mr. Moody's teachings and sermons that my friend lent to me…"

As he went on, Michael forgot his present surroundings, forgot even Susanna's presence. He was back in the lonely cabin in the Canadian wilderness, back to the time when he had still been able to see…but only with his eyes, not with his heart.

It had been agony...
And it had been glory.

Alone in that cabin in the woods, he soon discovered that he had almost forgotten how to pray. He was like a child who had to learn his letters all over again. At last, when he did manage to break through the clutter of his mind and soul, when he finally began to pray—haltingly at first, but honestly—he found himself speaking to silent walls.

God's only response had been *no* response.

Drenched in self-pity, drowning in desperation, he begged and raged and wept. He learned what it meant to "storm heaven." At times his words were little more than the babble of lunacy, but still he went on praying, trying to break through the wall his own foolishness and sin had erected.

Only years later did he recognize how troubled and tormented he had been. And only with the perspective of time did he come to understand what God had wanted from him: total brokenness. Nothing less could release him from his past so that a new heart could be born in him, a new life begin in him.

Days turned into weeks until one morning, shattered and bitterly disillusioned, he faced himself in a soot-clouded mirror and saw a filthy, unkempt, unshaven *husk* of a man with wild eyes and streaks of silver in his hair. An empty man: empty of pride, his will crushed, his hope abandoned.

A man in total despair.

Only then did God speak. Not with a shout of judgment or angry rebuke, but in a whisper that pierced Michael's spirit and stitched his very soul to eternity. In that isolated, wind-battered cabin, Michael found his mind opened to truth, his soul flooded with the healing, all-encompassing love of his Savior.

He remembered the moment, remembered the Word: *"But what things were gain to me, those I counted loss for Christ... What shall it profit a man, if he shall gain the whole world, and lose his own soul?"*

He also pored over the book his friend had lent him, the writings of the evangelist, D. L. Moody, a man known to despise the limelight. Moody repeatedly cautioned that one must *"sink the self"* and get rid of *"this man worship."* Man's desire, he wrote, is for *"the great and the mighty,"* but God's way is to use the *"foolish and despised things."*

One passage in particular reverberated in Michael. He read it over and over until finally it was seared into his memory forever. *"If we lift up ourselves and say we have got such great meetings and such crowds are coming, and get to thinking about crowds and about the people, and get our minds off from God, and are not constantly in communion with Him, lifting our hearts in prayer, this work will be a stupendous failure."*

That's what his work had become, Michael realized. That's what *he* had become. *A stupendous failure...*

And in the realization, Michael found new hope. God had broken his heart only to fill it with His own presence, His truth, and His love. At times, Michael thought he would surely die of the outpouring of such wondrous love.

A few days later, he went home: a new man, with a new heart, and a new life.

~

As Michael went on speaking, Susanna realized that he was not so much recounting the past as *reliving* it. She could see it in the tension of his hands, the tightening of his mouth, the disjointed frame of his words.

She could also sense what this was costing him. The pain of the account was chipping away like a sculptor's chisel at his reserve and composure. Once she was tempted to save him from the agony, to tell him he needn't go on. But her need to hear the rest—to hear *everything*—was too compelling. He was opening the door of his soul to her, and she had no intention of standing outside.

So she sat in rigid silence, her breathing shallow, her mind scrambling to imagine what he had gone through—all the while wishing she dared to touch him, to put her arms around him and comfort him.

"I tried to explain to Deirdre what had happened to me," he finished. "And the changes I needed to make in my life—in *our* lives. Foolishly, I believed I could persuade her to want what I had found."

"And you never went back to the opera?"

He shook his head. "No. I knew before I left the cabin that I was finished with that life, that I would never again go seeking after the world's idea of greatness. I knew that I would never sing again in public except to praise my Creator—and only then if God specifically led me to do so."

He grew still for a moment. "I think it might have been much like this for the great Jenny Lind. You know of her?"

"Yes, of course."

"She, too, left the stage at the height of her success and never returned. It is said that her reason for doing so was because her career had begun to draw her attention and her loyalty away from God. She feared it would consume her and eventually separate her from Him entirely. So she gave it up."

"But wasn't it nearly impossible to abandon all that? Your voice—it's such an incredible gift—"

"I still sing," he said before she could finish. "I simply sing a new song. The orchestra is my voice now, and the music I write—this is my song. A song from my own pen, from my heart—and from God's heart, of course."

Susanna gazed at him with dawning understanding. She couldn't begin to comprehend everything he had relinquished, even though she stood in awe of his willingness to surrender it. But she could see for herself that what he had renounced was nothing compared to what he had gained.

Michael had exchanged a crown for a Cross; the crown of celebrity for the Cross of Christ.

There was no doubting the serenity she saw in his face, the undercurrent of peace that emanated from him, even when life was at its most chaotic. The strength of his character and the power of his genius were tempered only by his submission to the God who had gifted him.

The life he lived was a victory, a tribute, a rare and continual blessing to everyone who knew him. Michael himself was a gift.

Finally, Susanna realized, she had met the man behind the music.

When he had completed his story, Michael's mood seemed to change. He rose, facing her. "Well, I've kept you long enough."

"Oh, no, Michael! I'm so grateful you told me. All this time I've wondered why…"

She stood, feeling the need to say more, to say something…meaningful. Instead, she was able to manage only a question. "Michael, will you ever sing again? In public?"

He seemed to frame his words with great care. "Only if I knew it was what God wanted."

"But how would you know?"

"I would know," he said after a moment, "because I would not be able to *not* sing. It would be…that I could not contain the joy, and so I would have to give it voice."

Susanna studied him. "Tonight, for the first time," she said, "I finally feel as if I know you."

"*Si?* And now that you know me, Susanna, I wonder—do you *like* me?"

"What? Of course, I—" She broke off. "What do you mean?"

He started around the table, then paused, a ghost of a smile touching his lips. "It's something Caterina said just the other day. She informed me that she loved you better than anyone else in the world—with the exception of her papa, of course."

Susanna warmed to his words. "Thank you for telling me that, Michael."

"And then," he went on, "she asked me if *I* liked Aunt Susanna. Naturally I assured her that I…like Aunt Susanna very much."

Susanna found it nearly impossible to swallow. He drew closer.

"She also asked if you are *aware* of how much I like you, and pointed out that I should make my feelings known to you, lest there be any doubt."

"*Did* she?" Susanna fought for breath.

"Oh, yes. Cati was very firm about that."

He came the rest of the way around the table and took Susanna's hands in his.

"Since I will most surely never hear the end of it if I don't act upon my daughter's advice, allow me to reiterate what I said to Caterina."

He squeezed her hands a little. "I like Aunt Susanna very much," he said, his voice scarcely more than a whisper. "Very much indeed."

Susanna's heart turned over as she saw the uncertainty in his expression and heard the tenderness in his voice.

"Cati also said that when you look at me, she can tell you like me, too."

Susanna inhaled sharply. "Did she? Precocious child, Caterina." She had intended to assume a light tone, but her voice wavered.

A look of surprise darted over his face. "Ah," he said. "Is it true, then?"

Susanna swallowed against the lump in her throat. "Yes...it's true."

When he opened his arms to her, it felt like the most natural thing in the world to step into his embrace and let his warm strength enfold her. And when he eased back enough to pass a hand over her cheek, not quite touching her but hovering as if he *wanted* to, Susanna had the strangest feeling that he could *see* her, that he was looking deep inside her.

She drew his head down to hers, closed her eyes, and with both hands began to trace the lines of his face with her fingertips, just as he had done the night he had first "looked" at her. He let out a long, shaky breath as she continued to mold his face with her fingers.

When she stopped, he touched his forehead to her forehead, then his lips to her lips. "Susanna?"

Again, Susanna squeezed her eyes shut, reveling in the sound of her name on his lips.

"Susanna," he repeated, "do you think you could ever come to love a hopelessly stubborn blind man who is probably too old for you and is given to long bouts of silence?"

Susanna framed his face between her hands. "I thought you knew," she said softly. "I already love such a man."

His smile was slow in coming, but infinitely tender. "And...do you know how I feel about you?"

"I think I should make certain, don't you? Caterina wouldn't want me to have any doubts."

"That's true. Ah...let me think: how do the Irish say it? 'I love you...more than anything.'"

"Everything," Susanna corrected. "'I love you more than *everything.*'"

"Sì! And I love *you* more than everything!"

He swept her into a dizzying embrace and kissed her again. And again.

"Do I make myself clear?" he asked.

"Perfectly," Susanna replied.

Epilogue

THE GIFT, THE GIVER,
AND THE GLORY

That Voice that broke the world's blind dream
Of gain, the stronger hand may win,
For things that are 'gainst things that seem
Pleaded, The Kingdom is within.

PERCY CLOUGH AINSWORTH

New York City
A week before Christmas

Backstage in the rehearsal room, a few minutes before the concert, Michael put his arm around Susanna and drew her aside. "How are you doing?"

"I'm…ill. Yes, I'm definitely ill. I'd really like to leave and go home now, please."

Susanna kept her tone light, but there was some truth in her reply. At the moment, she would rather be anywhere else than here, preparing to go onstage.

He smiled and clucked his tongue at her. "You're going to be fine, *cara*." He turned his head as if listening. "Are we alone?"

Susanna glanced around. "Yes, but I don't—"

"So, then—tell me again what you're going to remember if you get nervous."

"Michael, I'm more than nervous! I'm terrified!"

He lifted an eyebrow. "*Tell* me."

"Oh, all right! The *Gift*, the *Giver*, and the *Glory*."

"And explain."

Susanna glared at him. "I must remember that my gift is no greater—and no smaller—than any of God's other gifts." She paused, her voice a little stronger as she went on. "In playing the organ, I offer it back to the Giver of all gifts, who makes it shine with glory."

Michael lifted a hand to graze her cheek. "Tonight God will make your gift…*all* our gifts…shine with glory. You will see, *cara*."

He leaned down to kiss her—a gentle but lingering kiss.

"Ahem."

Susanna turned.

Paul Santi was standing there, his face the color of ripe beets. "*Scusi*, Michael, Susanna. It is time."

～

The lights dimmed. The velvet curtains opened. The audience vigorously applauded the orchestra, then waited amid rustling and murmuring.

Relieved that she'd actually made it to the organ without tripping, Susanna sat staring at the manuals. The stops. The music. Her hands.

There had been so little time, so few rehearsals.

She stared at the backs of the musicians and choir members. They were ready. Confident. At ease. Again she glanced at her trembling hands, then wiped them down both sides of her dress.

Paul stood with his violin and gave the musicians their note of A. He waited until the cacophany of tuning swelled and finally died away. Then he left the stage to get Michael.

Susanna forced herself to search the audience, her gaze traveling upward to Michael's private box where Caterina and Rosa Navaro were seated. Caterina saw her and waved, and Rosa smiled. Buoyed a little by the sight of them, Susanna took two or three deep breaths and wiped her hands again. Downstairs, in orchestra seating, she found Dr. Cole and Dr. Carmichael—newly betrothed, both their faces aglow. Beside them sat Miss Fanny Crosby, beaming in the direction of the orchestra.

A hush fell over the concert hall as Paul escorted Michael onto the stage, followed by an outburst of applause. A rush of pride and love swept over Susanna as she watched Michael acknowledge the audience's welcome with a small bow. Did others see him as she did—as elegant, as regal as a prince, achingly handsome in his black tails and snowy white stock?

He turned to the orchestra, touching his toe to the metal strip at the podium, the marker he used while conducting. Unexpectedly, he lifted his head and aimed a knowing smile in Susanna's direction, nodding ever so slightly, as if to reassure her.

And then it was time. Michael gave a light tap of the baton, squared his shoulders, and cued the organ's robust introduction to "Adeste Fideles."

A rich blast of sound rumbled through the concert hall as the mighty organ, the full orchestra, and three choirs announced to the audience that a celebration of joy had begun.

"*O come, all ye faithful...*"

～

What a glorious sound! Susanna had to remind herself that the music emanated not only from the organ, but from her, pouring out from the depths of her spirit and powered by the gift that had been given to her. Even so, she had to struggle to retain control and harness the power of the massive instrument she so precariously commanded.

She gave only an occasional glance at the music in front of her. Instead, she watched Michael: not the manuals or the stops or even her own hands, but Michael. She watched him so closely—every movement, every facial twitch, every lift of his head or sweep of his baton—that gradually she began to feel herself being melded into the orchestra, absorbed into the choirs. Under Michael's leadership, she became one with the musicians and the music.

So immersed was she in this festival of praise that she lost sight of her fears and inadequacies, forgot about notes and chords and arpeggios, no longer thought about crescendos and diminuendos or even stops and manuals. It was all a gift, and she was only one of the many givers.

Michael sensed the very instant when Susanna's panic gave way to command, her self-doubt to excitement, her fear to freedom. He knew, exactly to the beat, when she wrested control of the organ and conquered it.

It happened long before the children's lighthearted selections and the traditional carol singing had come to an end. The gate of her spirit opened wide, freeing her gift to rise above the concert hall, to soar beyond her self-limitations—even beyond his own expectations for her.

From the first impromptu passage through the unexpected improvisations, the angelic winging of the descants, the elegant, inspired transpositions—he knew the fire that fueled her brilliance was *holy* fire. Her fear was gone.

By the time they reached the "Hallelujah Chorus," Michael himself was on fire, and the audience with him. The "Chorus" was, in his estimation, the greatest, most divinely inspired piece of music ever written.

Handel's servants had often found the composer in tears and exultation as he composed *The Messiah,* a miracle of music. He became a captive of its creation, writing in solitary frenzy, never leaving his house, day or night, until the work was completed—in an unbelievable twenty-four days. And when the final triumphant note had been penned, Handel himself had proclaimed that he had seen "all Heaven before me, and the Great God Himself."

Of all tonight's selections, Michael knew that Susanna dreaded this one the most. She believed that in performing this incomparable work, one simply could not be anything less than brilliant, for fear of disappointing God Himself.

Michael, too, was feeling the pressure, despite the fact that he had conducted the "Chorus" numerous times. He heard the crowd stir, but he gave the musicians a few seconds to ready themselves for the coming effort before turning and prompting the audience to stand. Then he lifted his shoulders, drew in a long, steadying breath, and inclined his head slightly in Susanna's direction to indicate that she should lead them onward.

~

Susanna had thought she would have to call upon every ounce of strength and skill available to her just to do an acceptable rendering of this greatest of all choruses. Instead, she found herself lifted almost from the beginning, empowered with an ease, an agility, and a depth of emotion she could never have imagined.

It seemed she could do no wrong. Her hands had never held such power; her fingers and feet seemed to fly. She felt as if she were riding on the wind, and thought her heart would surely explode with pure elation before this was finished.

She caught the look on Michael's face—pure, unmeasured joy—and only then did she realize she was seeing him through a glaze of tears. For the first time, Susanna understood, at least in part, what Handel meant when he insisted that God had "visited" him in the creation of this greatest of all music.

And then, as they arrived at the final measures, she heard the glorious, incredible voice that had once thrilled thousands on a different kind of stage now rise above the other voices to fill the entire concert hall.

Michael was singing.

Susanna's gaze swept the sea of faces before her. All through the audience, people wept for joy as they lifted and clasped their hands in adoration. The hall vibrated with this thundering outpouring of music and praise and power.

Her eyes went back to Michael, and his beloved face filled her vision. He would sing in public again, he had told her, only when God called him to do so. Only when he could not contain the joy...

And He shall reign forever and ever.
King of Kings, and Lord of Lords,
Hallelujah!

The *Gift*...the *Giver*...and the *Glory*...
Oh, the glory!

BOOK THREE

JUBILEE

The world cries out
With a common voice:
"Is there Hope? Where can Hope be?"
To our wounded world,
God still replies
With the Cross of Calvary.

—BJ HOFF

Prologue

To Hold a Promise

I was made her guardian angel
And to me the charge was given,
Still to keep and shield her footsteps
All the way from earth to heaven.

FANNY CROSBY

Bantry Hill, Hudson River Valley
August, 1871

Michael Emmanuel held his newborn daughter with extreme care, as if she might break from the pressure of his arms.

The shallow, even breathing from across the room told him Deirdre, his wife, had fallen asleep, exhausted by the birth process. The doctor was gone, leaving behind the nurse to look after the mother and child. Michael heard the rustle of her skirts and the occasional clatter and dull thud of things being tidied up and put away.

Night had gathered in on Bantry Hill, a sultry, humid night that hung heavy over the grounds. In spite of the August heat that had scorched the valley for days, the stone walls of the mansion kept the rooms pleasantly cool.

Too cool for an infant? Immediately, Michael tested the thickness of the receiving blanket in which his daughter was wrapped. Satisfied that she was snug, he carefully got to his feet. He was eager to introduce his new daughter to the rest of the household, who would, he knew, be just as eager to welcome her.

Ordinarily, he would have taken the wide, sprawling steps on his own, his blindness no hindrance in his own, familiar home. But not this time, not with such a precious bundle in his arms.

"Nurse? Would you be good enough, please, to carry the baby downstairs for me? The others will be waiting to see her, and I don't want to risk a fall."

"Oh, of course, sir. I'd be happy to."

She came and took the child from him, leaving him with an unexpected feeling of emptiness. Already he missed the warm sweetness of her small form in his arms.

In the drawing room, as he'd expected, they found Paul, more brother than cousin, along with Liam and Moira Dempsey, the couple who had worked for Michael for years. Rosa Navaro, too, his good friend and neighbor, had been there throughout the day, waiting.

Michael thought his face would break from the fullness of a smile he could not suppress. Perhaps, though, he could be forgiven a touch of drama as he parted the blanket away from his tiny daughter's face, then lifted her for all to see. He was pleased by the ohs and ahs of admiration, the excited murmurings among them.

It was Rosa who firmly announced that the child "looks just like you, Michael! Your dark hair—and so much for one so tiny!"

Each of them had something to say, but it was Paul who most clearly voiced what was in Michael's heart. With a gentle hand on Michael's arm, his young cousin pronounced quietly: "She is your gift from heaven, *cugino*. You hold in your arms God's promise for your life, your future."

"What is her name to be, Michael?" asked Rosa.

Now he had to fight to keep his smile in place. His daughter's naming had been of little interest to Deirdre. Her indifference had been just one more wound among many.

"I don't care what you call her! I never wanted her in the first place, and you know it!"

Michael forced the memory of Deirdre's angry words out of his mind and drew his daughter closer to his heart. "Her name is Caterina. Caterina Saraid— Saraid after my mother."

There was another round of approving murmurs. Then, after a few minutes more, Michael tucked the infant snugly against his shoulder and left them. He wanted to be alone with his child.

Slowly and carefully, he made his way to the front door and stepped outside, onto the broad porch that ran the length of the house. The baby sighed against his shoulder, and he moved to cradle her in his arms, rocking her a little to and fro. The air was still warm and fragrant with the late summer roses from the gardens and the wildflowers on the hillside. No breeze stirred, and other than the usual night strummings of the crickets and the occasional screech of an owl, all was quiet.

There should have been nothing but joy and excitement in his heart on this night. A man should be filled with celebration at the birth of his first child. And indeed the incredible happiness of holding his new daughter in his arms was enough to nearly overcome all other thoughts, all other emotions. But somewhere beneath the joy was a place where an old pain dwelt, a weight of misery that even the elation of new fatherhood could not dispel.

His daughter, this small, incredibly perfect, and completely innocent infant, was unwanted—and unloved—by her own mother. As unwanted and unloved as he, her father.

She must never know, this baby girl sleeping so peacefully in his arms, that her mother had tried to abort her, that in a drunken rage—rage at him—she had attempted to lose their child by jumping from the high-pitched porch of the carriage house.

He had once thought there could be no pain more agonizing than that of living with a woman who despised him, who humiliated him at every opportunity, who continually sought to rub his face in her loathing of him. But he had been wrong. Deirdre's resentment of their unborn baby throughout the months of her pregnancy, her indifference to anything related to their child, and her refusal to even pretend affection after her birth was the worst pain he had ever known, the greatest heartbreak of his life.

And the greatest dread. For he knew his wife's animosity toward him and their daughter would not abate simply because the birth had been accomplished. If anything, it might become even more poisonous and vindictive.

Already she had refused to help name the child. She had also refused to nurse her, leaving them to either find a wet nurse or depend entirely on a nursing cup. In truth, had the doctor not unknowingly placed the babe in her arms after the delivery, Deirdre might not have held her at all.

Before Caterina was ever born, Michael had vowed that she would never suffer from her mother's coldness. Or her cruelty. Somehow he would have to become a buffer between the two, would have to give the child enough love that she would never suffer from neglect.

But how? How did a man become both father and mother to his child? How would he ever compensate for what Caterina might lack from her mother? With a blind man for a father and a mother who was at best cold and indifferent, how would his daughter ever experience a normal childhood?

His eyes burned, and his heart squeezed so painfully he caught his breath. The reality of his own helplessness suffused him, and he moaned aloud to ward off despair.

As if alarmed by the change in him, the infant in his arms whimpered. Michael drew her soft warmth as close to his chest as he dared without hurting her. He attempted to soothe her, crooning softly in the language he knew best, the tongue of his Italian father. He must not give in to this hopelessness. He could not, would not raise his child in the shadow of fear. He must seek only the good, the best, for his daughter.

What was it Paul had said?

"She is God's promise for your life, your future."

Michael passed a gentle hand over her tiny features, her crown of silken hair… like his, Rosa had said. He lifted the baby to press his lips against her cheek—so soft, so sweet, it made him ache.

Suddenly, he felt a tiny hand groping, then finding his index finger and closing over it. And at that instant he realized Paul was right. Here was God's promise; here was his future…his child, his daughter, his life. He had no idea how he would be all things to her, all the things she would need. But he would live his life trying, being as much as he could be, doing whatever he could to make sure this promise of God was safeguarded and fulfilled.

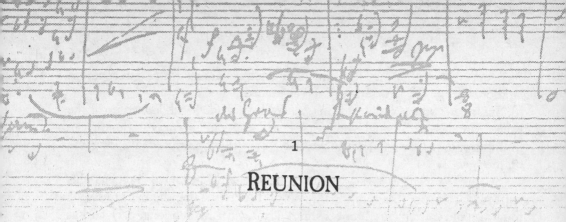

1

REUNION

Let my voice ring out and over the earth,
Through all the grief and strife,
With a golden joy in a silver mirth:
Thank God for life!

JAMES THOMSON

New York City
Late March, 1876

The first time Susanna Fallon saw Riccardo Emmanuel, she wasn't in the least surprised that he was weeping.

He had not seen his son, after all, for years. Not since the accident that had blinded Michael. It was all she could do to hold back her own tears as she watched Michael's father grasp his son by the shoulders, study him, then pull him into a long embrace.

Uncomfortable with the idea of intruding on such an intimate family occasion, Susanna had wanted to stay behind this morning. Despite the love that had blossomed and then deepened between her and Michael Emmanuel over the past months, she still found it hard to think of herself as his fiancée, not his dead wife's sister and his daughter's governess. Only at Michael's insistence had she agreed to come to the city with him to meet his father's ship. And so far she had managed to remain where she wanted to be—in the background.

Around them, all was confusion and commotion. The New York City harbor brought back memories of her own arrival in America: the fear she'd had to struggle against when she'd first stepped off the ship into the midst of the other immigrants milling about the waterfront; the tall buildings along the wharf that had seemed so forbidding; the mix of foreign tongues and English, spoken more sharply and harshly than she was used to; and the ever present runners, most of them Irish themselves, who preyed on their fellow countrymen as they hustled them off to disreputable shanties and dilapidated tenements where unscrupulous landlords would take advantage of them yet again.

Susanna shuddered and, shading her eyes with one hand, looked up at the bright March sky. Although winter still held the city in its tenuous grip, the late morning sun was clear and sharp, the bracing air full of promise that spring was on the way.

Susanna watched as Riccardo Emmanuel released Michael to draw Paul, his nephew, closer and kiss him soundly on both cheeks. Then he bent to sweep four-year-old Caterina up into his sturdy arms, tugging at a long, dark curl as she squealed with delight.

"Bella! Mia bella nipote! "

My beautiful granddaughter.

"But surely this cannot be your baby girl, Michael? Not this *bella creatura*! Why, she's nearly grown!"

Susanna smiled to see Caterina throw her arms around the neck of the grand-father she had never met, hugging him as if they'd been together forever. Clearly, this relationship held great promise.

Only when Michael called to her did Susanna finally step out and approach. Seeing her, Riccardo Emmanuel set Caterina carefully to her feet, then beckoned Susanna closer.

"Ah," he said softly, with a quick glance at Michael. "She is exactly as you wrote of her, *mio figlio*."

She had only a second to speculate exactly as to what Michael had written before Riccardo turned to her. After only a slight hesitation, he brought her hand to his lips, his keen blue eyes taking her measure in one quick but thorough sweep. Had it not been for the unmistakable twinkle in his eye, that sharply discerning gaze might have intimidated Susanna. As it was, however, Riccardo Emmanuel seemed more intent on charming her than intimidating her.

He was a big man, Michael's father—nearly a head shorter than his son but of broad, even rotund, girth. Like Michael, he sported a neatly trimmed beard and wore his hair, liberally streaked with silver, somewhat longer than fashion dictated. With his weathered, ruddy skin, he looked like a man who had spent much time in the Tuscan sun.

He was—dashing, Susanna decided. Impeccably tailored, freshly barbered. How had he managed that aboard ship? And where in the world had he found a flower for his lapel?

And then there was his smile. Brilliant. Irresistible.

Susanna liked him immediately.

He lifted his head, still searching her face as he said, in surprisingly good English, "I am delighted to meet you at last, Susanna. We will spend much time getting to know each other, no?"

"I'm looking forward to it, *signor* Emmanuel."

He shook a finger at her. "No, no! None of that. You are betrothed to my son. You will be my daughter, and so you must call me Papa." He said all this with an ingenuous smile and a certain good-natured presumption.

Well, then. In addition to being dashing, he was also adept at getting his way.

"Very well. Papa," Susanna said, aware that she was being dazzled and enjoying it immensely.

At that point, Michael cleared his throat as if vying for attention.

"We still have to take the ferry upriver, Papa. We should be going. Pauli will see to your luggage, and Susanna and Caterina and I will go with you through the registration."

Michael extended his hand then, reaching for Susanna. When he failed to find her, she moved closer and put a hand to his arm. She glanced at Riccardo Emmanuel and saw that he was watching his son with an expression of great sadness. In that instant, Susanna's gaze met his, and a look of shared love and understanding passed between them.

Then Michael's father squared his shoulders, renewed his smile, and again caught Caterina up into his arms. "So—let us tend to the necessary business and be on our way! I am eager to begin my visit!"

"And we're so happy to have you here, Uncle Riccardo!" Paul told his uncle. "We intend to make your visit so very pleasant you will decide to stay and make your home with us!"

"Ah, is that what you're up to?" said Riccardo Emmanuel, tweaking Caterina's nose. "Then the first thing you must do is to feed me as soon as possible! I thought I would most certainly starve on that ship's swill. I'm sure I've lost far too much weight."

Grinning at Caterina, he thumped his considerable stomach. "Why, I must be a mere shadow of myself by now!"

Caterina giggled and hugged him again.

After completing the registration process, Susanna and Michael led the way to the ferry while Caterina, her grandfather, and Paul followed behind. In their wake came a boy towing a luggage cart piled with Riccardo Emmanuel's trunks.

"So," asked Michael, his hand covering Susanna's on his forearm, "what do you think of my papa?"

"I think he's absolutely wonderful, and I couldn't be happier that he's come." Susanna paused. "Although it seems you may have a serious rival for your daughter's affections."

Michael lifted one eyebrow but smiled. "This is bad for me, I think. I am no competition for my debonair papa."

"Oh, I don't know. You do have a certain charm of your own."

"*Grazie*," he said dryly. "I must remember to use this to my advantage from now on. Just as soon as I discover what it is."

Susanna squeezed his arm. "You're a sweet man."

"Sweet?" He slowed his pace slightly. "What man wants to be sweet? You might just as well tell me I'm dull, I think."

"Hardly. I understand that Italian men are strong-willed, even stubborn at times. But always interesting. Never dull."

"A generalization," he pointed out, then amended, "though no doubt an accurate one."

"I'm sure that's true."

"It would seem that I am marrying a very diplomatic woman."

"Also true."

He seemed to have forgotten that they weren't alone, slowing his steps even more and nudging a little closer to her.

"Michael," Susanna warned, "your father—"

"—is no doubt pleased to see his son so happy," he said. "This is a happy day for me, *cara*."

Even in profile, Susanna could see the contentment ordering his strongly molded features. Gone—for good, she hoped—was the tightly drawn look of sorrow that had shadowed his face when she'd first arrived in New York the year before.

"That's what I want for you, Michael. Much happiness."

"Your love has already given me that," he said as they continued walking. "And now, to have my family all together, here—I could not possibly hope for more."

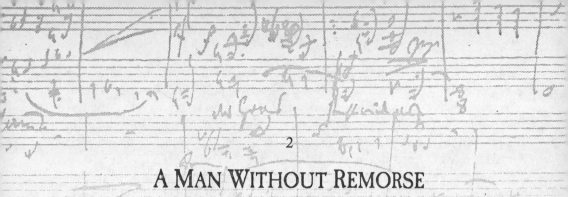

2

A MAN WITHOUT REMORSE

Man is caught by what he chases.

GEORGE CHAPMAN

The world occupied by the Women's Clinic and Convalescence Center was one of squalor and despair.

Prostitutes and thugs roamed the streets of the area freely, looking for their next "clients" or victims. Derelicts of all colors and nationalities—Negro and white, Irish and Slav, Italian and Bohemian—loitered in doorways, tin cups or bottles in hand, as they called out jeers and insults to the vehicle traffic rumbling by. Even now, well before the noon hour, men and women could be seen carousing and fighting, dancing and procuring, openly debasing themselves and their companions. Only the pigs and marauding dogs spilled out into the streets in greater numbers than the forgotten souls on Baxter Street.

Andrew Carmichael was always relieved to put the area behind him. Not so much because of the unfortunates who swarmed the neighborhood—he spent a large part of his life among the outcasts of the city, many of whom were worse off than these degraded residents of Five Points. But the narrow alleys and mud-slick lanes of the entire settlement gave off a miasma of wretchedness and corruption that seemed to cling to a man like a vile web from which he could not extricate himself so long as he was inside the infamous slum.

Today, however, it was worry, not relief, that fueled his hasty departure. Mary Lambert, a woman he had been treating since back in December, needed to be lodged in a facility where she could receive far more concentrated care and attention than the understaffed women's clinic could provide. Although she had come a long way in recovering from her opium habit, Mary was still indigent and homeless, her children lodged in two separate institutions. And the clinic would have no choice but to release her sooner than later. They needed beds too badly to allow a patient to stay once she was deemed "cured."

Andrew paid the young Negro boy he'd engaged to watch the buggy, then climbed in and sat thinking for a moment. Mary wasn't cured, not really. Her health had been shattered, her body wasted, and opium addiction was an insidious thing. Without a place to go and with her children taken from her, she was likely to fall back into her old ways as soon as she walked out the clinic door. He had to find the means to keep her in treatment until she was much stronger—and until there was something more waiting for her than misery.

Andrew felt that Mary would benefit greatly from the treatment at Prospect House, a private clinic with an excellent, highly experienced staff. But Prospect House was expensive, and there was no one to pay the bills.

His gaze flicked over the dilapidated tenements lining the street. A pack of ragged children charged in front of his buggy, chasing one of the countless pigs that roamed the filthy streets and alleys. A bearded drunk sprawled in the doorway of one of the many flophouses, bottle in hand, seemed scarcely conscious. From the upper floor of a nearby boarding house came a shriek and then a curse, followed by the sound of breaking glass.

Andrew shuddered, then retrieved a piece of paper from his pocket. There was someone in a position to aid the hapless Mary Lambert—someone who was obliged to help her, who owed the woman far more than the payment of her medical expenses.

Yesterday he had obtained the address of that someone.

And today he intended to use it.

He studied his own scrawled handwriting for another moment, then tucked the paper back into his pocket and drove away.

⌒

The impressive brick three-story was not quite a mansion. But with its high, narrow windows, graceful columns, and tastefully landscaped grounds, it made a statement of elegance and charm. Taken with the rest of the obviously affluent neighborhood surrounding it, the residence of the Reverend Robert Warburton stood in startling contrast to the squalid slum Andrew had just departed.

He hesitated, aware that what he was about to do would take him far outside the boundaries of his professional responsibilities, not to mention his usual nature. And that no matter how he might attempt to justify his intentions, he was acting out of anger—anger fueled by the resolve to right a wrong done to a patient.

Before he could talk himself out of the idea, he climbed down from the buggy and started up the walkway. By the time he reached the paneled double doors at the front of the house, there was a fire in his knees. Indeed, every joint in his body seemed aflame. The pain from his arthritis had been relentless all morning, so vicious that perspiration now dampened his face, and he blotted his forehead with a handkerchief before lifting the brass door knocker.

Perhaps he shouldn't have been surprised by the middle-aged Negro man who opened the doors. The neatly tailored dark attire and deferential manner marked the man as a servant, though to the best of Andrew's recollection, none of the clergymen with whom he was acquainted employed servants.

But then Robert Warburton wasn't just any clergyman. It was probably safe to say that no other churchman—except possibly for Henry Ward Beecher before the adultery scandal had shaken his ministry—commanded as much respect or wielded as much influence as Robert Warburton. Through his pastorate of one of the city's largest and wealthiest congregations and his extensive writings on morality issues in politics and human services, Warburton had established himself as a public figure of no small renown. He was generally revered among the Christian community as a man of God with a heart of gold, held up as one who typified true compassion and benevolence, especially where the lower classes were concerned.

Andrew couldn't help but wonder what Warburton's most ardent admirers might think if they were to discover that the man they held in such high esteem had sired three illegitimate children, only to abandon them and their mother to their own resources in a dilapidated tenement on Mulberry Street.

∼

The man at the desk rose as soon as Andrew was ushered into the library, coming to meet him with an outstretched hand and a cordial smile.

"Dr. Carmichael, is it? Please, come in. Have we met?"

Andrew was immediately thrown off guard, not only by the geniality of the other's greeting, but also by the man's appearance. He had expected something of an elder statesman, with an imposing physical presence. But the man who stood before him beaming and pumping Andrew's hand appeared to be no older than his late forties. He stood several inches shorter than Andrew, stoutly built and somewhat jowly, with a receding hairline and small, pouched eyes. His features were thick, almost coarse, his skin florid and somewhat mottled. His handshake, Andrew noted with some discomfort, was aggressive and energetic.

"Have we met, Dr. Carmichael?" the clergyman said again, finally releasing Andrew's throbbing hand.

"No, I'm certain we haven't."

"Well—have a seat, won't you?"

Warburton returned to his desk, motioning to a chair directly across from him and looking surprised when Andrew remained standing.

"Well," he repeated after a slight hesitation, "what can I do for you, sir?"

"I haven't come on my own account," Andrew said, recognizing that his tone sounded forced, stilted. "I simply wanted to make you aware of a certain…circumstance, one I believe you will want to remedy."

A look of uncertainty crossed Warburton's features, but the good-fellow smile remained fixed in place. "Really? And what situation might that be?"

The clergyman lowered himself into the chair behind the desk, again gesturing that Andrew should be seated. Again, Andrew ignored the invitation.

Now that he was face-to-face with Warburton, he felt a measure of doubt begin to blur his initial confidence and wondered if he might have undertaken a fool's errand after all.

"I'm here," he said, anxious to be done with this distasteful business, "on behalf of Mary Lambert and her children."

Warburton's expression never wavered, though he took his time in replying.

"Mary Lambert? I'm sorry, but I don't recall the name. Is she a new member of the congregation?" Warburton's smile actually widened. "The church has grown so quickly, I can't always keep up as well as I'd like."

The man's ingenuous manner grated on Andrew like a rusty file. "I believe you know who Mary Lambert is, sir."

Warburton now affected a gesture of impatience. "If you would kindly get to the point, Dr. Carmichael? I've a very busy afternoon ahead."

He was so sure of himself. It struck Andrew that taking the man down a peg or two would not be altogether unpleasant. But he hadn't come to satisfy his own resentment, acute as it was.

"Very well. I'll be blunt, Mr. Warburton. This patient of mine, Mary Lambert, and her children are in desperate need of assistance—financial assistance. It occurred to me that you might want to help alleviate their difficult circumstances, given the fact that the children I refer to are your children as well."

Warburton's good-natured expression suddenly flamed to a look of surprise, then outrage. He shot to his feet, the chair tottering with the force of his movement.

"Whatever are you talking about?"

Andrew clasped his hands behind his back, watching Warburton. "I am talking about a woman who bore you three children. A woman with an opium habit who is trying to put her life back together. A woman who has been receiving medical attention for some months now but who needs the care only a private clinic can provide—for an indefinite period of time. Meanwhile, her children have been taken from her and separated from one another. The boy—his name is Robert, as I'm sure you're aware—is presently staying at Whittaker House, and the two little girls, who were hospitalized for a time, are now being cared for at the Chatham Children's Home." He paused. "I thought you should know their circumstances."

At that moment, Warburton looked as if he might leap over the desk and assault Andrew. Instead, he lifted his chin, knotted his hands into fists, and said in a voice laced with an arrogant self-assurance, "See here, Carmichael—I don't know what sort of swindle you're attempting, but if it's money you want, you'd do well to remember that I'm a pastor, not a rich man. However, even if I *were* wealthy, I'd hardly fall for whatever absurd scheme you've concocted. I'll have to ask you to leave immediately."

This wasn't going well. Andrew had never been one for confrontation, and even though his anger had compelled him to come here, it was now beginning to interfere with his intent. Not that he was taken in by the other man's outrage; Warburton was furious, all right, but his fury was that of a guilty man unexpectedly exposed, not an innocent man wrongfully accused.

Even so, had he really thought that he had only to face Warburton with the evidence of his wrongdoing and the man would be so stricken with remorse that he'd immediately move to make restitution?

Robert Warburton's defiant stare made it clear there would be no softening of this man's heart, even toward a woman who had borne him three children or toward the children themselves. Indeed, Andrew sensed that Warburton had already turned his back on his mistress and his children, had put them completely out of his life, and was altogether capable of erasing the memory of them.

Despite Warburton's lack of response to the accusations, Andrew had no doubt whatsoever about the truth of what Mary Lambert and her son—*Warburton's* son—had confided to him. For one thing, Mary had revealed things about the clergyman that would have been known only by someone close to him, such as the fact that Warburton suffered from diabetes and an occasional flareup of gout.

Andrew had managed to verify the status of the clergyman's health through two of his professional colleagues, but only with some difficulty. There was simply no way that someone like Mary Lambert would have been privy to such information unless she had been well acquainted with the man himself.

No, however facilely Warburton might deny the truth, Andrew had no doubt but what the man was guilty of exactly what Mary had charged.

It was equally clear that Warburton would do whatever it took to make certain no hint of scandal touched him.

Revulsion rose in Andrew's throat. It was difficult to understand how a man could set himself up as a preacher of God's Word and a teacher of God's way—and still continue to live with such a blight on his soul.

But it wasn't his place to judge, he reminded himself sternly. And there was nothing to be gained for Mary or the children by pursuing this exchange any further.

He studied the other man's flushed features, then said, "My only reason for coming here, Warburton, was to make you aware of a deplorable situation in which you apparently played a crucial part. I had hoped that for the sake of the woman you've ruined and the three children who are also suffering the consequences of your behavior, you might accept your responsibility and do the decent thing for all of them. I can see I was wrong."

He paused, catching his breath against a stab of pain that radiated all the way up his arm. "If you should have a change of heart," he said, "you can reach me at my office."

He turned to go, but Warburton quickly rounded the desk and grabbed Andrew's throbbing arm hard enough to make Andrew lose his breath.

"If you have any intention of spreading this outrageous story, Carmichael, I strongly advise you to forget it."

Andrew shook off the other's grasp. "You needn't concern yourself on my part, Warburton. *I'm* not your problem."

A vein pulsated at the clergyman's temple. "Then don't give me reason to become *your* problem, Carmichael. Because if I hear so much as one word of this preposterous tale repeated, I can promise you'll regret it."

Andrew stared at the man. "You're *threatening* me?"

Something flared in Warburton's eyes. Then, as if he'd thought better of what he meant to say, he took a step back, his features clearing slightly. "A man in my position has to protect his reputation."

Suddenly his countenance settled into the same benign, good-natured expression with which he'd first greeted Andrew. "I'm sure you understand what I mean, Dr. Carmichael. After all, you are in a similar position, are you not? Your profession also demands the highest caliber of integrity. Men like ourselves cannot guard our character too carefully, now can we?"

The man *was* threatening him.

Something cold wound its way through Andrew at the hint of menace that lingered behind the other's genial gaze.

Momentarily at a loss, he turned away without a word and headed for the door, despising the painful stiffness in his limbs that prohibited any facsimile of a dignified exit, yet too eager to escape the corruption of his surroundings to delay another moment.

⁓

In his haste to reach the front doors, Andrew nearly collided with a woman entering the house. He mumbled his excuses, then stopped to stare. Even without the hooded wrap she had worn upon their first meeting, he recognized her: the mysterious woman who had appeared at his office late one winter afternoon months before, seeking treatment for Mary Lambert and her children.

The woman hesitated just inside the entryway, her eyes wide with obvious recognition. Just as she opened her mouth as if to speak, her gaze flicked past Andrew to the hallway behind him, and from her expression he realized that Robert Warburton had followed him out of the library.

Again the woman's gaze went to Andrew, her startled expression changing to one of appeal.

Understanding dawned, and Andrew knew she must be none other than the wife of Robert Warburton. He nodded to her, their eyes meeting and holding for only seconds before she dropped her gaze and passed by him.

Shaken, Andrew hurried down the walkway to the buggy.

What kind of woman, he puzzled, would approach an unknown physician in search of help for her husband's mistress and illegitimate children? Had her visit to his office been the altruistic action of a wife intent on compensating for her husband's sins? Or had she meant to protect Warburton's reputation by attempting to conceal the consequences of those same sins?

Whatever her motives, he reflected, she had saved the life of Mary Lambert and perhaps the lives of her children as well. Without intervention, they would probably not have survived the winter.

Something told him, however, that the man he had just confronted would not thank his wife if he were to learn of her extraordinary efforts—whether those efforts had been on his behalf or for the welfare of the woman with whom he'd been unfaithful.

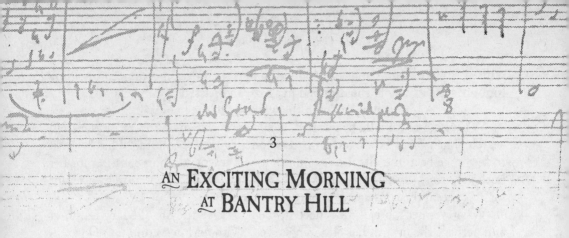

3

AN EXCITING MORNING AT BANTRY HILL

There are gains for all our losses.
There are balms for all our pain.

RICHARD HENRY STODDARD

The last person Paul Santi expected to see when he opened the back door off the kitchen on Friday morning was Conn MacGovern's daughter, Nell Grace.

He gaped at the vision she made, standing there in the doorway, a basket in her arms, the morning sun behind her gilding her auburn hair. She was like a painting. A poem. A song!

How fortunate for him that Moira Dempsey was occupied upstairs. Otherwise the housekeeper would have opened the door.

Finally, he realized he was staring. "*Signorina*—Miss MacGovern! *Buon giorno*! Come in, come in!"

He held the door, allowing her entrance. Once inside, she smiled at him, then quickly lowered her gaze. "I brought a gift for the poor wee girl. The one that's ill," she said, lifting a cloth from the basket so Paul could see.

He found himself peering into the amber eyes of a white-and-apricot spotted kitten. The creature's stare was surprisingly direct, seemingly unafraid, and openly curious.

Paul glanced up to find Nell Grace MacGovern studying him. "For Maylee?" he said.

She nodded. "'Tis one of the barn kits. We—Mum and I—thought perhaps she'd be good company for the child. Little girls almost always take to kittens, it seems."

Paul couldn't take his eyes off her face. *Bella!*

"Will she be allowed, do you think?"

"Allowed?"

The girl invariably had this effect on him. All she had to do was come near and he immediately became—how to say it?—"tongue-tied." His wits seemed to escape him. Either he stood mute and dry-mouthed or else he babbled like a great *stupido*.

"To have the kitten," the MacGovern girl prompted.

He did love to hear her speak! Truly, that Irish lilt was lyrical. Like a crystal stream splashing over small stones. *Si*, like music.

Again, her expression told Paul he was staring.

"Ah! The kitten. *Si*—"

He stopped. *Could* Maylee keep the kitten? He remembered Dr. Carmichael saying the child's resistance to illness was not as strong as that of a healthy child due to the cruel affliction that wasted her. Did cats carry germs? He had no idea.

The MacGovern girl looked so hopeful. He hated to disappoint her. Yet, the doctor had insisted that they must be very careful.

"We will speak with Miss Susanna," he finally said. "She takes charge of Maylee's care. She will know. And she will most likely be delighted with your thoughtfulness. We will go right now and find her."

The girl's face brightened.

He took the basket from her and gestured toward the door.

She smiled at him, and for a moment Paul felt like dancing. But he could only smile in return—the foolish, vacant smile, he feared, of one who had taken leave of his senses.

It was as he had told Michael some months ago: the thunderbolt had struck him at last. He could only hope it would not leave him such a fool forever. To be in love was a wonderful thing. He knew this, even though he had never been in love before. Love was supposed to be a grand adventure, a wondrous, exciting thing. He knew this as well.

What he had not known was that love might also render him a man without his wits.

At that moment Gus the wolfhound poked his head through the partially open door, then lumbered the rest of the way into the room, no doubt in search of Caterina. The big, fawn-colored hound—easily as tall as a grown man when he reared on his hind legs—started toward them, his tail whipping in circles. The kitten mewed, and the wolfhound stopped, his attention caught by the basket dangling from Paul's arm. He took a step back, then loped forward.

Paul tried to stop him, but Gus poked his big head into the basket, eliciting a demonic shriek from the small creature inside.

"Gus, get away—" Paul started to caution.

The kitten shot out of the basket, skidded across the slippery surface of Moira Dempsey's recently mopped floor, and hurled herself against the base of the pie safe before leaping onto the baking table.

The wolfhound charged in pursuit, barking as if he'd treed a squirrel.

Paul shouted a retreat, but Gus merely tossed him a look over his shoulder and continued to circle the table where the kitten crouched, back arched, claws digging into the wood as she hissed and spat at the dog.

The wolfhound howled back at her, then thumped one mighty paw onto the table, dangerously close to the small creature's neck. In a whoosh, the kitten catapulted from the table, over the wolfhound's back, and fused herself to the doors of the cupboard, where she clung, glaring behind her at the wolfhound.

The MacGovern girl hurried to retrieve her, but the kitten simply scaled the cupboard until she reached the very top, where she began to skulk from one end to the other, gloating down at the frustrated wolfhound.

Moira Dempsey chose that instant to come clomping through the door, fire in her eyes and a blistering stream of Gaelic on her tongue.

Paul groaned. Nell Grace MacGovern's face froze in terror. The wolfhound barked at the kitten, then turned to snap at Moira Dempsey, whom he had never much liked. The kitten hurtled from the top of the cupboard to the sideboard of the sink, landing smack in the middle of the crock of bread dough Moira had set out to rise.

~

Susanna got to the kitchen as quickly as she could when she heard the commotion. Her first thought had been that Caterina and the wolfhound had been up to mischief again. As a pair, they could be counted on to deliver trouble wherever they went—and Moira Dempsey typically blamed Susanna for any disruption. But Caterina had stayed the night with Rosa Navaro, her godmother, and was nowhere on the premises.

The scene that greeted her was such that she could only stand and stare. Across the room a small, yowling creature rose out of the bread dough, kicking and flailing the air with its paws. Like a miniature golem from the Hebrew legends, formed of clay and a secret spell, it struggled to free itself from its glutinous prison.

Gus the wolfhound yelped and snarled, jabbing his big head toward the sticky little creature as if to thwart its escape. Nell Grace MacGovern stood wringing her hands and gaping at the bread dough, with Paul pivoting from her to the hound, clearly stymied as to what to do.

Meanwhile, Moira Dempsey splayed her hands on her hips, scolding them all as only Moira could, the Irish shooting from her mouth like a barrage of hot coals.

Susanna turned to look as Michael entered, holding a sheaf of papers in one hand, raking his hair with the other hand as he added a spiel of Italian to Moira's run of Gaelic. Something to do with trying to work in a lunatic asylum.

It occurred to Susanna to be grateful that Papa Emmanuel had taken the buggy to collect Caterina from Rosa's house. One more agitated Italian male in the house right now might be one too many.

She put a hand to her fiancé's arm. "'Tis all right, Michael. Really. Just a small…incident with—I think it's a kitten."

"A *kitten*? All this noise from a *kitten*?" He paused. "What kitten? We have no kitten."

Susanna shooed him out of the kitchen, promising to get the situation under control "in no time," breathing a sigh as he went.

Moira seemed to have turned the full blast of her fury on the kitten itself for the moment, shaking her apron at it and screeching like a demented harpy. As if the housekeeper's harangue had sounded a clarion call, the poor creature suddenly gave a bloodcurdling wail and launched itself from the sideboard onto Moira's shoulder, from where it slid effortlessly down the gaping front of the woman's apron.

The MacGovern girl brought her hands to her face in a look of sheer horror. Paul had gone quite pale, his eyeglasses slipping almost all the way down his nose, no doubt from the perspiration dampening his face.

Moira whirled around in a mad little dance, trying to shake the kitten loose. But the creature apparently felt protected at last, even playful, as it began to pitch from side to side beneath the bodice of the woman's apron, eliciting a series of squeals and shrieks from the Irish housekeeper.

Good sense overcame a sense of hilarity as Susanna moved to loosen the ties of Moira's apron and in the same motion catch the kitten as it tumbled free. Taking the indignant little creature to the sink, she began to sponge it with a damp towel.

It took some doing, but Paul managed to coax Moira out of the kitchen, then came back to remove the reluctant wolfhound, leaving Susanna and Nell Grace to cope with the kitten and restore order to Moira's kitchen.

Susanna could not help but wonder what it would take to restore a measure of calm to Moira.

Only when Paul explained that the troublesome creature was meant as a gift for Maylee and would, if allowed, be taking up permanent residence did Susanna give way to the simmering amusement that had been threatening to explode almost since she first walked in on the bedlam.

Her good judgment dictated that under no circumstances should the fierce little feline be allowed to stay. But the thought of the pleasure such a gift would bring the ailing Maylee—instantly followed by the idea of the temperamental Moira Dempsey at the mercy of the small goblin—urged her to abandon, just for this occasion, her more practical nature.

"I think the kitten will be a lovely gift for Maylee," she told an incredulous Nell Grace, who stood cuddling the now clean and contented wee creature against her shoulder.

"She can't be allowed outdoors, of course—she'll have to be kept very clean. And we'll need to keep her claws closely trimmed. But with a little care, I'm sure she won't be a problem."

She smiled to herself as she recalled Moira Dempsey's demented dance.

⌒

Susanna stood just inside the doorway of Maylee's room, enjoying the girl's pleasure and excitement as she sat in the middle of her bed, holding the spotted kitten on her lap. Surely this unusual, delightful child deserved all the happiness available to her.

Maylee was a tiny, delicate girl who even from this short distance appeared more like a fragile old lady than the eleven-year-old child she actually was. The victim of a bizarre premature-aging disease, Maylee already exhibited the telling signs of the disease's escalation. Her wispy white hair scarcely covered her scalp. Her skin was dry, wrinkled, and unnaturally mottled in some places with "liver spots." Her joints were almost always badly swollen these days, and Susanna knew she lived in considerable pain most of the time. Yet when one asked after her health, Maylee invariably replied that she was "feeling very well today."

Abandoned by her parents while still a toddler, Maylee had spent almost her entire childhood in one of the city's institutions until Michael learned of her existence from Dr. Carmichael and eventually arranged to have her moved to Bantry Hill. Susanna liked to think that they were providing Maylee with something she'd never had: a real home. Certainly, the entire household had pitched in to help with the child's care in an effort to make her remaining time on earth—which according to Andrew Carmichael would almost certainly be brief—as pleasant as possible.

Even Moira Dempsey seemed to have developed a surprising tenderness for the girl. In spite of a routine that kept her constantly busy, the housekeeper had, from the beginning, taken charge of helping Maylee bathe, as well as seeing to the special diet that Dr. Carmichael had prescribed. More than once, Susanna had marveled at Moira's uncharacteristic gentleness with the girl; she clearly doted on her.

For Maylee's part, she seemed to have no conception of herself as a victim, although Susanna couldn't help but think of her as such: the victim of a merciless, punishing disease for which there was no known cure, not even medications to alleviate the worst of its plundering. Maylee, however, was unfailingly cheerful, genuinely appreciative of the smallest thing done for her, and, as Michael was quick to point out, an inspiration for them all.

Indeed, Michael seemed to have formed an uncommon bond with the girl over the past few months. Susanna knew he was determined that the ailing child should not suffer from loneliness in addition to everything else. He took special care to spend time with her each day, and his visits were more than duty calls. Susanna hadn't missed how pensive he seemed after being with Maylee and how attentive he was when she felt strong enough to take her meals with them.

It was disappointing that Caterina, at only four, was really too young to be a close friend to the older girl. Not that she didn't make an effort—she often played board games with Maylee, and sometimes the two enjoyed teatimes together with their dolls. But the age difference was significant, and no matter how conscientious Caterina tried to be, the gap between them most likely would not be breached.

Maylee had made another friend, however, one closer to her own age. Renny Magee, the young girl who had come over from Ireland with the MacGovern family, was spending more and more time with Maylee, who seemed to find her an entertaining companion. They spent many hours together talking and reading, with Renny almost daily bringing small items from outdoors to amuse Maylee.

Vangie MacGovern had no idea exactly how old the Magee girl might be—she had been alone, singing for her supper on the streets of Dublin, when Conn MacGovern found her—but both Vangie and Susanna had concluded she couldn't be more than twelve or thirteen. She was slight, exceedingly thin, with an unruly thatch of dark hair, a small space between her two front teeth, and a wiry energy that seemed in direct contrast to Maylee's gentleness. But unusual as the combination might appear to be, the two were apparently becoming great chums.

At the moment, however, a different combination drew her attention. Nell Grace MacGovern—as lovely a young woman as Susanna had ever seen—was sitting on the bed next to Maylee, showing her how the kitten liked to be held and stroked. At the side of the bed, Paul stood watching Nell Grace with an expression that could only be described as *adoring*.

Michael had alluded to the fact that Paul had been struck by "the thunderbolt" in regard to Nell Grace. Watching them now, Susanna had to concur. It seemed to her, in fact, that Michael's gentle cousin had not only been struck, but was still reeling from the impact. His dark eyes, which usually glinted with amusement behind his spectacles, now held a slightly dazed expression, and his slight, youthful body leaned toward the girl like a sunflower toward the light. And when Nell Grace turned to look at him in response to something he'd said, Susanna smiled to herself.

Clearly, this was a thunderbolt with a double edge.

4

AN UNEVEN MEASURE

That man is great, and he alone,
Who serves a greatness not his own,
For neither praise nor pelf:
Content to know and be unknown:
Whole in himself.

OWEN MEREDITH (LORD BULWER-LYTTON)

The day finally drew to an end, but it seemed to have taken an interminable time getting there.

Susanna and Michael sat before the fire in the drawing room, even though it was conceivably improper for them to be sitting here by themselves so late at night with everyone else abed—except possibly Paul, who was wont to roam about until all hours. Susanna reasoned that this was the first time today she and Michael had been alone, and they were both too much in need of the quiet and a few precious moments spent together in peace to fret about a proper chaperone.

Besides, even now they were busy. Michael had offered to help wind several skeins of yarn into balls for the blanket Susanna was knitting as part of a layette for the MacGovern baby, due to arrive near the end of April.

"There," she said, inspecting the looped ends of the skein draped over Michael's hands.

"This is all I have to do?"

"Mm. Just keep your hands as they are. Not too far apart. Not too close."

She took the loose end of the yarn and wrapped it around four of her fingers several times, then around the middle, and began to work the yarn, keeping a watchful eye on her helper's hands.

"How am I doing?" Michael asked.

"Wonderfully. Consider this a permanent position from now on."

"Ah. I learn quickly, no?"

"You learn quickly, yes."

Amused, she watched him smile as he continued to gently lift and dip his hands in a kind of rhythm while Susanna wrapped the yarn into a ball. In one way or another, it seemed that anything in Michael's hands turned into music.

"What color will this blanket be?" he asked.

"White. Most everything will be white."

"Everything? What else are you making?"

"Hopefully, an entire layette. Don't let that slip to Mr. MacGovern, though. I want this to be a surprise for Vangie."

"Ah. And how is she?"

Susanna reached to move his hands a little closer together. "Like that, Michael. You have to keep the tension the same."

She started winding again. "Nell Grace is concerned. She told me this morning that her mother hasn't been feeling all that well for days now. Vangie does look tired," she went on. "And much too pale."

Susanna supposed they really shouldn't be talking about Vangie MacGovern's condition. In truth, she probably ought to be downright uncomfortable discussing the subject with Michael. And yet it always seemed so uncommonly natural, so easy, to tell him anything. Everything.

She had never thought about it in quite this way before, but it occurred to her now that Michael had become her closest friend. Odd. She had never had a truly close friend before, not even her sister. And now that she'd finally found such a friend, he turned out to be her future husband. She thought it might be a very good thing indeed to be marrying her best friend. On the other hand, until they were married, it also made it somewhat more difficult to observe the proprieties.

Observing those proprieties hadn't been a problem until they fell in love with each other. Indeed, her initial feelings about Michael when she'd first arrived in New York had comprised distrust and suspicion. After all, he was the husband of her late sister, Deirdre, who in her letters had written almost nothing good of the man she'd married.

Susanna allowed herself a long look at Michael, his dark head bent over the dancing yarn, intent on doing even this homely task to the best of his ability. She shook her head in disbelief that she had ever given credence to Deirdre's rantings about his "selfishness" and "brutishness." Deirdre, who had never had a thought in her short life for anyone but herself.

But Susanna had believed those letters. And she would never have come to live at Bantry Hill were it not for two circumstances. One was that little Caterina, left motherless after Deirdre's accident, desperately needed a caretaker. And the second was the bitter reality that Susanna needed a home. After the death of her parents, facing the prospect of either a loveless marriage or working for strangers, she'd decided it would be better to care for her only surviving family member, her young niece—even if her niece's father was a brute.

But he wasn't a brute, of course. Far from it. And Susanna would be forever thankful she'd made the decision she had. For she had come to love Caterina as if she were her own child—and Caterina's father more than she'd ever thought she could love—

"You've slowed down," Michael observed, ever sensitive to changes in her mood. "Am I doing it wrong?"

"You're perfect," she told him, picking up the pace again—and acutely aware that it would be best to change the subject.

"I wish you could see Paul with the MacGovern girl," she told him. "He's absolutely enchanted with her."

Michael chuckled. "I don't have to see them. Pauli speaks of little else these days. And what of Miss MacGovern? Do you think she likes him?"

"Oh, indeed! She has the most marvelous eyes, you see, and when she turns them on Paul they positively shimmer. It couldn't be more obvious that they're very taken with each other. And they do make a handsome couple."

"Ah. You have this all figured out, it seems."

"And something else—" she went on. "Did you notice how many questions your father was asking about Rosa at supper this evening? He certainly took his time fetching Caterina home from Rosa's house. I wouldn't be at all surprised if your papa isn't a bit smitten himself."

Michael raised his eyebrows. "Papa? And Rosa?"

"Rosa Navaro is an extremely attractive, intelligent woman, Michael. And she and your father would have much in common, what with both of them being from Tuscany and loving music as they do. Think about it."

Obviously, he was doing just that. "Papa and Rosa," he finally said, shaking his head. "Would my father have—appeal—for a woman like Rosa, do you think?"

Susanna looked at him. "Your papa is absolutely natty. And yes, I should think women would find him most attractive." She paused, unable to resist. "And there's the Italian factor as well."

He frowned. "The Italian factor?"

Susanna smiled to herself. "Well, some seem to think there's a certain irresistible appeal about Italian men."

His hands stopped moving. "Oh? Irresistible, eh? And...what do you think?"

"Well—oh, Michael! Be careful. You're losing the—"

He grabbed at a loop to avoid dropping the yarn, but too late. The remaining loops slipped from his hands to the floor. He bent to retrieve it and Susanna reached to help, dropping the ball she'd been winding in the process. They bumped heads, laughed, but quickly sobered when Michael reached for her, touching her face and drawing her to him for a brief kiss. And then another. Susanna's gaze went over the darkly handsome Tuscan face, the black hair shot with silver, the quick smile that never failed to make her heart leap—as it did now.

"I believe I like this work," he teased. "Anytime you would like me to help, you've only to ask."

Flustered, Susanna tried for an even tone of voice. "You can help me untangle this mess is what you can do. Hold out your hands again."

He smiled and, like an obedient schoolboy, sat patiently as she draped the yarn over his hands and began to work through the snarled strands.

"What is this you are doing?"

Susanna and Michael both jumped at the sound of Riccardo Emmanuel's booming voice as he walked into the room.

"Papa," said Michael. "I thought you would have been asleep long ago."

Michael's father seemed to fill up any room he entered. He stood before them now, arms crossed over his sturdy chest, an imposing figure in a crimson dressing robe and matching nightcap.

"What are you doing?" he asked again, frowning as he stared at Michael's hands.

Michael kept his head bent over the yarn. "I am supposedly helping Susanna," he said lightly, "although I think I'm more trouble than help."

"May I get something for you, Papa Emmanuel?" Susanna asked him. "Some warm milk and biscuits, perhaps?"

He declined her offer with a wave of his hand. "No, nothing." He paused, still frowning, and only then did Susanna realize that he was, if not angry, at least annoyed.

Her instincts told her to leave the two men alone. "Well, I believe I'd like some for myself. Michael?"

He nodded. "That would be nice, *cara*. If you don't mind."

Susanna didn't mean to eavesdrop as she left the room, but Riccardo Emmanuel had the kind of voice that couldn't be ignored. She was no more outside the drawing room than she heard him proclaim, "I must tell you, *mio figlio*, it disturbs me to see you so. I hope you are not giving in to the blindness."

"Giving in?" Michael's tone was definitely puzzled. "What do you mean, Papa?"

Susanna stopped, unable to walk away until she heard Riccardo Emmanuel's reply.

"I find you sitting here, in front of the fire, working the yarn like a woman when I would expect to find you concentrating on your music."

Michael didn't respond right away, and when he did, Susanna could still hear the confusion in his voice, as well as the slight thickening of his accent that invariably came when he spoke with either his father or Paul.

"My music? But, Papa, always I work with my music. I spend hours every day—"

"*Uffa*! Your music should be the most important thing in your life, Michael! It is God's gift to you. You should have no time for trivial things such as—yarn."

There was a long silence. Susanna heard the sofa creak under Michael's weight as he shifted and stood. "Forgive me, Papa. I don't mean to be insolent, but you are wrong."

His father made a sound as if to interrupt, but Michael stopped him, his tone respectful but firm. "*Susanna* is the most important thing in my life, Papa. Whatever time I can spend with her is not trivial."

"Of course, of course! I understand about Susanna! She is a wonderful young woman, and you are most fortunate to have found her. But you must understand, Michael, that you are a very important man. A genius! Yet you have stopped using your voice, forsaken the opera, your singing—"

"Did I not explain all that to you in my letters, Papa?"

"*Sì*, you did, although I won't pretend to understand. Michael...only God can give a man such a voice. Do you truly believe that He would not want you to *use* that voice? Is this how God would expect you to use the gifts He has given you? Helping a woman roll yarn? Unthinkable!"

There was a long silence. Then, "I told you, Papa. I left the opera because it was...an obstacle, a hindrance to my faith. It was no longer a good thing for me. But I haven't abandoned my music. Surely you must see this. I work very hard. With the orchestra, the composing—"

With relief, Susanna heard his father's tone change to a reasonable note.

"I know, I know, Michael! Still, I see you—hiding away here, in this cold, dark place, like a—a hermit! Writing the music is good, *sì*, and your work with the orchestra is to be commended, but—your voice, Michael! To no longer sing—"

"I do sing, Papa," Michael said quietly. "I sing in worship. I sing for Caterina and Susanna, and sometimes I also sing with the orchestra. I sing...for God. And I'm not hiding away here. This is my home. I am at peace here. Finally, I am at peace. Please, Papa, this is not something I wish to debate with you. I made my decision, and I believe God led me to that decision. Please, you must try to understand."

His father said something in Italian, with Michael answering in kind, and at that point Susanna stepped away from the door and went on down the hall.

This was not about yarn, she realized. Nor was it about her. At first she'd felt guilty, mortified that Michael's father was blaming her for encouraging Michael to squander his time when there were more important things he should be doing. But now she sensed that Papa Emmanuel's pique had been triggered not so much by what Michael was doing as by what he was not doing. It had to do with Michael's turning his back on the stage, on the celebrity that had once been his. In the process, in Riccardo's mind, he had disobeyed—and disappointed—God.

More to the point, he had disappointed *Riccardo*.

Susanna ached for Michael. She knew how painful it must be for him not to have his father's approval or understanding. He loved his papa intensely. Even an ocean apart, they had remained close over the years. Now, to learn that after all this time, his father didn't accept the path he had chosen, that indeed he disapproved of that choice, perhaps even believed that Michael had betrayed his gift—this would cause Michael a terrible anguish.

Still, it was good that his father was here. Only by being with Michael on an everyday basis could Riccardo come to realize what a strong man—what a truly remarkable man—his son had become over the years.

Michael and his father loved each other—of that there could be no doubt. Surely this time together would not only help deepen that love, but would also restore Riccardo's pride in his son as he came to better understand the choices Michael had made and his reasons for making them.

But, please, God, let Michael not be too wounded in the process.

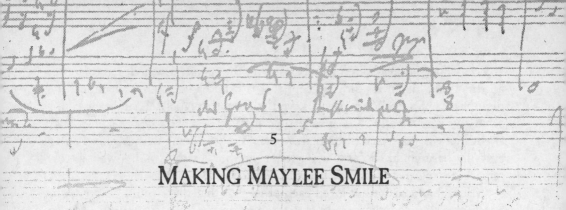

5

MAKING MAYLEE SMILE

Friendship improves happiness,
and abates misery, by doubling our joy,
and dividing our grief.

JOSEPH ADDISON

The best things about Bantry Hill, at least in Renny Magee's estimation, were its endless opportunities for exploring and the limitless treasures to be found within a hand's reach. To a girl accustomed to big-city slums—first in Dublin and then in New York—the open countryside held an irresistible appeal.

For the first few months of their resettlement on the river, Renny made it her business to spend nearly every free minute investigating her new surroundings. Now that the weather had grown milder, she could extend the scope of her kingdom, climbing trees the likes of which she'd never seen in Ireland, examining footpaths that led into forests so dense the daylight couldn't break through, scouting the wildlife—red foxes and black squirrels, owls that lulled her to sleep at night and delicate gray doves that woke her in the morning. She climbed massive rocks so high the view made her dizzy, and she walked crumbling stone bridges where the moss and lichen of another century had stamped their patterns for all time. She spied on giant elk and deer and every now and then engaged a moose in a staring match.

She had even gained a bit of familiarity with the Big House itself.

At first, the blind man's mansion had been off limits. Both Vangie and MacGovern had cautioned that Renny was not to go near the place unless invited. With the arrival of her new friend, Maylee, however, the situation changed. Because she and the wee girl—who in truth looked more like a little old lady than the eleven-year-old girl she actually was—had struck up well together from the first, Renny was soon invited to the Big House on a regular basis. So far these visits had taken place entirely in the frilly downstairs bedroom where Maylee had been ensconced, but Renny held hopes that she might one day see the rest of the rambling old mansion that reminded her for all the world of a castle in a storybook.

Today it was late afternoon before she arrived for her visit with Maylee. She'd taken time to collect a pouch of colored stones and an armful of pussy willow branches. Maylee liked to touch the catkins, and she would add the stones to the rest of her collection.

Inside the house, Renny found her friend waiting eagerly, sitting in the big rocking chair by the window with her new kitten on her lap. Renny darted a look to the bed where, sure enough, several books were laid out for her choosing.

She could scarcely wait to make her selection, but first she handed Maylee her "treasures," as the other girl called them. As always, Maylee's smile grew larger with each stone and branch she examined.

"Oh, Renny! These are the best ever treasures! Thank you!"

Although Renny pretended to shrug off the other's gratitude, in truth she was highly pleased. She liked doing things to brighten things up a bit for Maylee. The younger girl asked for nothing, but Renny had soon learned that these little gifts from outdoors or a tune played on the penny whistle would invariably bring a smile.

And making Maylee smile had come to be of special importance to Renny, who couldn't imagine what it would be like to be in the other girl's place. It seemed cruel beyond all understanding that someone so young should be afflicted in such a way. Miss Susanna had explained about Maylee's "condition," about the strange disease that somehow speeded the process of aging so that, although Maylee was only eleven years old, her body was much like that of an elderly woman.

At times Renny thought she could almost see her friend growing weaker and more frail by the day. Lately, she had felt a kind of desperation to bring whatever pleasure she could to the ailing girl. But it seemed almost like trying to stem a hemorrhage from a mortal wound. She had the sense that at any moment, despite her best efforts, the flow of blood might accelerate and drain the very life away from its host.

She shook off her gloomy thoughts when Maylee raised the question Renny had come to anticipate during each visit.

"Well, you're ready for a new book, Renny. Which one do you want to start today?"

Renny took her time making up her mind, finally settling on a book of fairy tales. Maylee had many books, some of which had been given as gifts while she was still at the children's home, others given to her by Miss Susanna or the blind man's cousin, Mr. Santi. Renny favored the small set of Bible stories with lots of pictures, though she also was partial to the books featuring animals that talked or particularly hateful people who got their comeuppance in the end.

"Oh, you'll like that one, Renny!" Maylee said, indicating the volume of fairy tales. "The brothers Grimm wrote some of the very best stories of all!"

Renny thumbed through the first few pages. "'Twas written by brothers?"

Maylee nodded. "Brothers from Germany. It's called 'collaborating,' Miss Susanna said."

"What's called collaboratin'?"

"When two people write a book together. Go ahead and start. I like to hear you read."

Renny cracked a small smile, trying not to show how pleased she was. "Could be because you taught me how, I expect."

Maylee was always telling her how quickly she learned and what a good reader she was by now. Renny still remembered the first time Maylee had loaned her a book in return for some stones and ferns Renny had brought her from the woods. Too ashamed to admit to the other girl that she didn't know how to read, Renny had simply taken the book with a mumbled thanks and made a hasty getaway. When she returned the book a few days later, Maylee insisted on sending another home with her.

For days afterward, each time Renny returned a book, Maylee pressed another upon her until finally, confused by the girl's generosity and at odds with her own pride, Renny had burst out with the lie that books were really of no interest to her, that she had more important things to do.

She cringed now as she remembered how Maylee's pointy little face had fallen, almost as if Renny had struck her. But after a moment she had simply tilted her head in that funny way she had and, with a long look at Renny, said, "Can't you read, Renny? Is that why you don't want the books?"

Something in that steady, kindly-natured gaze had made it impossible for Renny to deny the truth any longer. Her face burning, she confessed her secret.

Instead of looking down on her, as Renny expected, Maylee had taken it upon herself that very day to begin teaching her, assuring Renny that "as clever a girl as you are, you'll be reading everything in sight in no time."

Renny wasn't one to boast, but in truth she had learned quickly. And the more she read, the more she wanted to read. By now she and Maylee had a well-oiled system in place. Renny collected items from outdoors she thought Maylee would enjoy: pinecones, sprigs of greenery, shiny stones from the river, and anything else she thought would appeal to her friend. In return, Maylee would listen to Renny read, helping her where it was necessary, then send her off with a book or two until next time.

Thanks to Maylee, Renny no longer had to work to conceal her humiliation. Now she could take turns with Nell Grace and Vangie reading three-year-old Emma a bedtime tale, and when MacGovern was ready to relinquish his newspapers at the end of the day, she could pore over them the same as he, although not quite so quickly.

Maylee's teasing voice called her back from her thoughts. "Renny? Where have you gone? I asked if you'd play your tin whistle for me."

Renny nodded and pulled the penny whistle from the back pocket of her skirt. She had finally, albeit reluctantly, given in to Vangie's insistence that she do away with both pairs of her boy's trousers and don a skirt. In Renny's estimation, skirts were a big bother. Trousers were ever so much more comfortable for exploring and just about anything else—but Vangie had it in her head that since Renny was "growin' up," it was unseemly to run about "dressed like a raggedy plowboy." In truth, she had grown tall enough over the past few months that the one skirt she had brought from Ireland and the boy's trousers she had scrounged on the streets of New York were noticeably too short. So Vangie had had her way—as was generally the case.

Renny brought the whistle to her lips and began to play. Maylee was fond of the hornpipes and the jigs, and by the time Renny leaped into the latter she was dancing to the sound of her own music and her friend's chiming laugh. The kitten, however, had gone skittering across the room to hide under the chest of drawers.

～

At the sound of Renny Magee's tin whistle and Maylee's laughter, Michael smiled and stopped just short of the door to listen.

What a treasure young Renny had been to the ailing Maylee. With her music, her lively antics, her attempts to bring the outdoors inside—and her friendship— the Irish orphan girl had enriched Maylee's life and brought a note of joy to a child who presumably had known little before now.

Michael had quickly grown fond of both girls, appreciative of the youthful cheerfulness they'd brought to Bantry Hill.

As for Renny Magee, he had already concluded that the girl was musically gifted. She could do some extraordinary things with a common tin whistle, and the rhythmic stomps that punctuated the lively tune confirmed what Susanna had told him—that the girl had "flying feet" when it came to the old Irish dances.

According to Conn MacGovern, who had brought the girl with him when he and his family came to work on Michel's estate, Renny was inclined to be "saucy" and perhaps "too clever by far." But Michael had heard the note of affection in the big man's voice when he spoke of the girl and wasn't fooled by the feigned criticism. Conn MacGovern was fond of Renny Magee, even if he did disdain to show it. And according to Susanna, Mrs. MacGovern had more than once declared the girl a "fine helper" and a "good child at heart."

As he stood listening to the music of her tin whistle, it struck Michael that he just might be able to use the talents of this mercurial "good child" to his own ends—or, more accurately, for the purpose of his *American Anthem's* first performance. That would happen this summer, during a concert at Central Park celebrating the country's one hundredth birthday.

He wondered how open Miss Renny Magee, former street busker and vagrant entertainer, might be to performing in front of a far larger audience—say that of a few thousand people gathered to celebrate the centennial of the United States of America.

6

A Deceptive Contentment

Blessed are the souls that solve
The paradox of Pain,
And find the path that, piercing it,
Leads through to Peace again.

G. A. STUDDERT KENNEDY

Vangie MacGovern was enjoying a rare afternoon of peace and quiet.

As she sat in the sturdy, padded rocking chair at the open window of the bedroom, letting out hems on the twins' trousers, she caught herself whispering the same prayer over and over: a prayer of thanks for bringing them to this place called Bantry Hill, a place that only their Lord could have provided for them.

The day was uncommonly warm, one of those disarming afternoons when the trees were dotted with the first few speckles of blossoms soon to open and the air held a tempting hint of springtime. Had it not been for the nagging headache and the discomfort of her swollen limbs, she might have been lulled into a nap.

The house was completely quiet, a rare occurrence indeed. Nell Grace had taken Emma for a walk, and Vangie's husband, Conn, had taken the twins with him to clear some of the brambles and weeds from the fence line. Of course there was no telling Renny Magee's whereabouts, but most likely she had gone to the Big House for a visit with her friend Maylee.

Vangie leaned back, for the moment giving in to the aching heaviness in her abdomen and legs. Despite her increasing discomfort during the last weeks of her pregnancy, she lived with a sense of quiet joy these days. Indeed, were it not for the ongoing concern about Aidan, her eldest son, and when he might arrive in America, things would have been near perfect.

But surely Aidan would come soon, hopefully before the new babe arrived. How grateful Vangie was that her Conn had finally swallowed his pride and written Aidan, asking him to join them in America—and that Aidan had swallowed his own pride and accepted. What a gift it would be to have their firstborn under roof with their newborn at the same time—and her two grown menfolk finally at peace with each other.

She put a hand to her middle, thinking about the babe due to be born in just a few weeks. This child would be born into a real home, not a foul-smelling basement in the Liberties of Dublin or a tumbledown shanty off an alley in New York, but in a snug, clean house on a lovely piece of land where the only things one could see for miles were rich, fertile fields, the mighty river, and rugged mountains covered with forests. The younger children loved it here and she knew Aidan would love it, too.

Their house was small but cozy and nicely furnished with everything she and Conn needed to make a comfortable home for their family. She smiled at the thought of her husband. At last Conn had a job he loved, working for Mr. Emmanuel, taking care of the grounds and the horses and other livestock.

The children were thriving, the twins growing like healthy young colts, going to school and helping their father about the place. Little Emma, their youngest, had grown into a happy, spirited little tyke who scampered all over the place, especially delighting in chasing the chickens and playing with the cats in the barn. She was well out of didies by now, and that would be a help when the new wee one arrived. As for Nell Grace, the girl seemed to be content, though lately she'd had to assume more and more of the household tasks in Vangie's place.

Vangie couldn't think what she would ever do without the girl—or without Renny Magee as well. That one never ceased to surprise her. Renny seemed to be everywhere at once. When she wasn't working in the stables with Conn, she might be found helping Mr. Dempsey about the grounds. Other times she would go roaming through the woods or up on the hill, "exploring," or collecting items to take to the poor ailing child, Maylee, who lived in the Big House.

Only in the evenings, when the family had settled in for nightfall, were Renny's whereabouts predictable. Then she could almost always be found hunched over the table, removed from the rest of them as she pored over one of Conn's newspapers or yet another book lent to her by Maylee.

It was as if the girl could not get enough of the books. Nell Grace had been the first among them to realize that Renny couldn't read. Vangie still felt ashamed that she'd been too involved to notice. But what with the harrowing crossing, James's illness aboard ship, and the ongoing struggle just to survive once they arrived in New York, there had been no time to notice, no time for anything except for work and more work. When Nell Grace finally called Vangie's attention to her discovery, the child, Maylee, had already undertaken the task of teaching Renny Magee to read.

They had become fast friends, those two. Strange friends. One would have thought that Renny—the older—with her all her restless energy and gumption, might have seen fit to lord it over the younger Maylee. But in many ways, the more fragile Maylee seemed the elder of the pair. Vangie had not been around the ill child all that much, but she found it a bit surprising how Renny Magee, who was as stubborn as she was independent, invariably gave in to her.

Vangie ached for the girl, yet sensed that Maylee would abhor her pity. And sure, it was nothing like pity that Renny Magee brought to the friendship. Miss Susanna had remarked more than once on how well the two got on together, and Vangie had seen for herself that they gave each other something that might have otherwise gone lacking. In a way that perhaps only the Lord could understand, they blessed each other.

Almost lightheaded from drowsiness now, her vision clouding as it was wont to do lately, Vangie set the sewing aside and closed her eyes. She would rest, she decided, but only for a moment.

⁓

The house was quiet, the deep, heavy shadows of late afternoon drawing in when Renny Magee returned from her visit with Maylee.

She found it odd that she would be the first one home at the end of the day. Most often Nell Grace and wee Emma were in the kitchen when Renny walked in. She looked around, then went to the sink and pumped a cup of water, downing half of it before realizing something else was amiss. Her gaze went to the cookstove. It was cold. No potatoes cooking, no stew simmering, no water heating for tea.

A glance at the sink and the table showed no sign of preparations for supper. All this and an uncommon silence...

Renny slammed her cup down, wiped her mouth on her sleeve, and hurried out of the room, toward the back of the house.

She found Vangie dozing, slumped forward in the rocking chair by the bedroom window, her sewing bag on the floor.

Should she wake her? Vangie hadn't been sleeping well lately. She was too uncomfortable, she said. Still, she would be upset if the family came back to a cold stove and an empty table. Even now, when she was heavy with child and not feeling well, Vangie MacGovern took her responsibilities as woman of the house very seriously.

It seemed strange that Nell Grace hadn't started the supper. But then Vangie usually got things going and let Nell Grace tend to the rest.

Renny stood there, trying to think what to do. Finally she spoke Vangie's name. When there was no reply, she crossed the room and stopped in front of Vangie, whose arms were wrapped tightly around her abdomen.

Renny spoke her name again, louder this time, and Vangie raised her head. Her face was puffy and red, her features drawn. She stared at Renny with hollow eyes, as if she didn't really see her.

Fear squeezed Renny's spine like an icy hand. "Vangie? Are you all right?"

For an instant Vangie's eyes seemed to clear. She opened her mouth as if to speak but gasped and threw her head back against the chair. "Renny—get Conn! Tell him to...come!"

Renny saw the blood then. It was thin and watery, but it was blood all right, trickling down Vangie's legs and turning to a pool at her feet.

She began to shake. Oh, she was cold—she'd never been so cold! She stared at Vangie, unwilling to leave her alone, yet not having a thought of what to do. Her head felt like mud, her legs like useless sticks beneath her.

Vangie reached out with one hand as if to push her. *"Go!"*

Renny whirled and ran. She shook so hard as she charged through the house, she thought her bones would surely shatter like glass. Her chest was on fire, for she had no breath. She bolted out the door and onto the lawn—stumbling, nearly falling, straightening, and screaming for MacGovern as she went. Screaming for anyone who would come.

⌒

Nell Grace heard her before she saw her. Renny Magee, running straight at her and Emma, shrieking like a wild thing.

Nell scooped Emma into her arms and began running as well.

"What is it, Renny? What's wrong? Is it Mum?"

Renny stopped, nodding and gasping for breath, her thin chest heaving. "There's blood! I think she's in terrible pain! She said your da should come right away. Oh, she's bad, Nell Grace. She's in a bad way and no mistake!"

Nell Grace didn't hesitate but drew Emma tightly against her. "I'll go to Mum," she said, breaking into a run. "You go get Da!" she called back over her shoulder. "He and the boys are at the fence down by the creek. Go as fast as you can, Renny! Tell Da to come at once!"

Renny was already on the way. She had caught her second wind now, and her legs took on new strength as she ran. She seemed scarcely to touch ground as she went flying over the field and down the hill toward the fence line, calling out to Conn MacGovern as she went. She couldn't shake the image of Vangie clutching at herself, as if she were trying to hold herself together, the pain racking her face, the blood...

She took a furious swipe at her eyes and kept on running, willing herself not to think about the blood, not to think about anything but reaching Conn MacGovern.

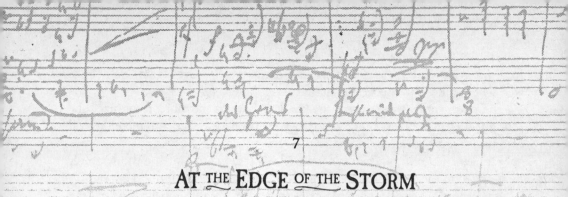

7

AT THE EDGE OF THE STORM

I hear all night as through a storm
Hoarse voices calling, calling
My name upon the wind—

JAMES CLARENCE MANGAN

Vangie thrashed her arms and legs, struggling to stay afloat as one red wave after another pounded her and pulled her under. Fierce pain gripped her, but more frightening than the pain was the angry, unknown sea in which she found herself.

Flashes of lightning, jagged and razor sharp, pierced the water, illuminating the raging current that swept her away from shore. She was caught up in a vortex, an undertow that threatened to drag her below even as the storm whipped her about, tossing her over the waves like an empty fish basket.

Between rolls of thunder, she heard her name called and looked back toward shore to see Conn and Nell Grace crying out to her. Miss Susanna from the Big House was there, too, with Mrs. Dempsey, the housekeeper, right beside her.

But where were the children? Wee Emma and the twins?

She reached out for Conn, as if he could somehow pull her back to the safety of land. But even as she thrust out her arm, she knew she was too far out for rescue.

She turned away, gasping when a babe suddenly appeared in view, bobbing and rocking as if he were riding the waves. A tiny infant, wrinkled and red, with only a wisp of hair but with great, sad eyes, his little arms and hands beckoned her forward, coaxing her to come now, come away from that other place, away from those calling her name—

An enormous wave slammed at her, hurled her up and over, as if she were but a weightless thing. As the sea dropped her again, Vangie glanced back toward the shore one more time. Conn's face was contorted with what appeared to be fear—or grief—as he continued to cry her name over and over again. Nell Grace was sobbing, her hands covering her face.

There were other voices, some she knew and others she didn't recognize. She thought they might be praying, but they were soon lost when a tremendous roll of thunder came barreling in on her.

Her legs felt so heavy, her arms as well. Any moment now she would surely be dragged to the ocean floor or flung wildly into the storm and lost at sea.

She ceased her efforts to turn back to shore, her strength too far gone to fight her way through the relentless fury of the storm. Besides, the babe with the sorrowful eyes seemed to be pleading with her to come to him. Aye, him—sure, the infant was a boy! And he so tiny and helpless! He needed her more than the others, his eyes seemed to say, more than those she was leaving behind.

❧

Susanna took one look at Vangie MacGovern and wanted to run from the room. The woman was obviously in excruciating pain. She didn't even appear to be conscious. At best, she was out of her head. Her usually lovely features were swollen almost beyond recognition, her eyes open but unfocused and so shadowed they looked to be bruised. She lay moaning and muttering, sometimes calling out or shrieking.

She looked as if she might be dying.

Was this what childbirth was like?

Susanna jumped when a clap of thunder shook the small house and a wicked bolt of lightning arced outside the window. For once, Susanna was thankful to have Moira Dempsey nearby. She felt helpless entirely, but the irascible housekeeper had already begun snapping orders to Mr. MacGovern and Nell Grace, sending them from the room while she turned back to examine Vangie with a confidence born of experience.

"Ach, this one needs more help than I can give, and soon!" she said, straightening and turning to Susanna. "Her waters have broke, and the babe's tryin' to come. And somethin's bad wrong."

"But the baby's not yet due."

"Due or not, it means to be born. Tell my man to go for a doctor. Someone should have sent long before now."

Susanna tried to think. "Dr. Kent is the closest, but he's never recovered from his stroke. There's no one else nearby."

Moira cast a look at the woman writhing on the bed, then turned back to Susanna. "I fear this babe will not be born at all, at least not alive, without a doctor." She paused. "I'll do what I can, but she's in for a long, hard time of it. I've never helped with such a birth, but I'll warrant the babe is turned wrong to begin with. And she has the look of one with the poison runnin' through her."

Susanna had no idea what the older woman meant about "the poison," but the look in Moira's eyes sent fear hurtling through her like a splash of icy water.

"What—how can I help?"

Occupied with elevating Vangie's upper body, Moira scarcely glanced at Susanna. "You shouldn't be in here at all," she said. "You're naught but a maiden. No need for you to watch this."

Susanna really didn't *want* to "watch this," but she'd be no help to Vangie MacGovern by playing the coward. "No, I'll stay. There might be something I can do."

The housekeeper turned now, her sharp gaze raking Susanna's face. "Be keepin' those children out of here, then. And the man as well. They shouldn't see her so."

Another slam of thunder struck just then. Vangie cried out, and Moira turned back to her, tossing instructions over her shoulder. "We'll be needin' plenty of hot water and towels. And if you think they'll come, send my man to the city after those doctor friends of yours. They'll never get here in time, but even so, we ought to try."

Susanna couldn't help but think that if someone had only sent for them sooner, Bethany Cole and Andrew Carmichael would have been well on their way by now. She knew they would come, for they were friends as well as physicians. Andrew had come in the middle of the night, after all, when Caterina was so terribly ill with the croup. But it would take hours for them to get here from the city. And watching Vangie MacGovern, she had a sick thought that neither Vangie nor her baby could wait for hours.

Ashamed of her own cravenness, Susanna knew she had to get out of the room or be ill. "I'll—have Nell Grace fetch some water and towels. Then I'll go and find Mr. Dempsey. There's that new telegraph office at Tarrytown. Perhaps he could get a wire off to Dr. Carmichael. That would save a great deal of time."

"If he can rouse the fool what minds the place," Moira grumbled as she heaped more pillows and a quilt under Vangie's torso. "From what I've heard, he's in his cups more often than not."

Susanna closed the door behind her as she left the room. In the kitchen she forced a smile for the anxious faces turned toward her, but she feared her voice was less than convincing as she attempted to reassure them. She managed to persuade Nell Grace to stay out of the bedroom, but Conn MacGovern would have none of it. Before Susanna could even protest, he was on his way back to his wife.

Once outside the cottage, she practically ran the distance to the house, heedless of the rain and the muddy water splashing onto her skirts. Heedless of everything except Moira's words, which continued to echo ominously in her head:

"They'll never get here in time…"

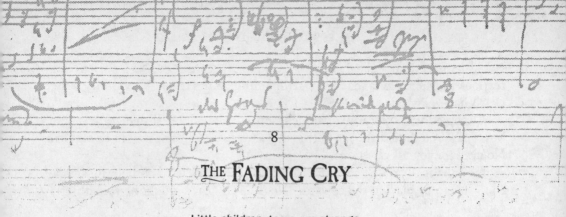

8

THE FADING CRY

Little children, tears are strange
upon your infant faces,
God meant you but to smile
within your mother's soft embraces.

SPERANZA (LADY JANE FRANCESCA WILDE)

Bitter cold engulfed Vangie, numbing her limbs and stealing her breath, while flashes of lightning bore down upon her in dizzying succession. Torn and battered by the force of the wind and brutal waves, she felt exhaustion take over and knew she could no longer keep herself afloat.

The cries from the shore were growing fainter now, the face of the wee baby boy fading from view. He was wailing, crying out for her, and Vangie extended her arms to him, knowing even as she did that the distance between them had widened and she had no real hope of reaching him. She hadn't the strength to go forward or backward, could do nothing but give in to the wind and let the sea carry her where it would.

A terrible grief seized her, but she was too spent even to weep as the storm made one last crushing assault on her. She had lost them all, lost her loved ones left waiting on the shore, lost the tiny babe now gone from her sight—the infant boy, her son, taken from her before she ever knew him. She could still hear his fading cry, a litany of loss, and it intensified her grief.

Suddenly, without warning, the wind seemed to turn. The angry roaring of the sea began to subside. The lightning dimmed, and the very air grew thick and still. Vangie felt herself lifted and held secure, cradled in the waves that only a moment before had threatened to destroy her. Released from the numbing cold, a gradual, renewing warmth began to spread over her.

But nothing eased the hollow anguish of her soul. Vangie was sure she could still hear the babe calling out for her. She searched her line of vision for the infant boy who had been there only a moment before, but there was no sign of him. Her arms—her heart—felt empty and bereft as the gently rocking waves carried her back to shore.

The weak cry of the babe seemed to echo over the water. He was near, as close as a whisper breathed softly upon her cheek...and yet beyond her grasp.

"Mother...Mother..."

No, this wasn't the cry of a babe, the voice of an infant. This was the imploring voice of a man, a man hidden in the mists that had settled over the sea at the edge of the storm.

"Mother...Mother, 'tis Aidan."

Not a babe, but Aidan, her firstborn son, a man grown.

And he, too, far beyond the reach of her flailing arms.

⁓

"Toxemia," Bethany Cole said, her voice tight as she straightened from her examination of Vangie MacGovern. "And the baby is breech."

Andrew Carmichael nodded, tossing his suit coat and rolling up his shirt sleeves. "Let's get a table brought in here. I don't want to move her."

"You're going to do a caesarean? Here?"

"I don't have a choice," Andrew said. "She's bleeding, and she's going to start seizing any moment. It's too late to try to turn the baby." He looked around him, assessing the resources available. "Why didn't they send for us sooner? She must have been this way for hours."

"Apparently they didn't send for Susanna and Mrs. Dempsey right away either." Bethany shook her head. "They're recent immigrants, don't forget. Everything is strange to them, and probably frightening. They most likely didn't know what to do. Actually, there wasn't much they could do. Susanna said the closest doctor is recovering from a stroke and may not return to his practice. That's why they sent for us."

Andrew expelled a long breath. "Well, she's scarcely conscious. This could hardly be a worse situation." He didn't so much direct his words to Bethany as to himself. He felt exceedingly frustrated by the circumstances and more than a little anxious about the treacherous delivery he was about to undertake.

He ran a hand across the back of his neck, knowing what he had to do but reluctant to do it. "I suppose I should speak with MacGovern."

"Andrew?"

He looked at her.

"Do they have a chance? Either of them?"

Did they? He didn't know how to answer her. He knew himself to be capable, but this would be no ordinary delivery. A breech birth. Toxemia. A mother nearing forty years. He shook his head. "The risk is as great for one as the other," he said. "I'll do everything I can, but we both know that ultimately it's in God's hands."

"Yes," Bethany replied quietly. "I know. Well, I suppose you should talk with Mr. MacGovern now. And Andrew—I expect they'll want to send for a priest."

He swallowed, finding it painful against the raw dryness of his throat. "Yes," he said. "They'll want to do that."

He turned and started for the door. There were times—and this was definitely one of them—when he wished God had called him to the ministry. Or the mission field. Anywhere but medicine.

～

Bethany brushed a shock of dark hair away from Andrew's face, then blotted the perspiration from his forehead with a towel. She had never been more impressed with the man who was her partner in medicine—and the man she loved—than during the long ordeal with Vangie MacGovern. Even in circumstances that could not have been much more trying, she could only watch him with admiration.

His long, lean face was set in intense concentration, his hands quick and sure. Working on a table that was solid but not quite large enough, with only the most rudimentary of necessities—including kerosene lamps for light—on a patient who was clearly in a mortal state, he performed a caesarean delivery that was nothing less than astounding in terms of brevity, control, and skill.

From the moment Bethany placed the towel soaked with chloroform to the mother's face until Andrew made the quick, deft incision, then lifted the tiny infant from the patient's open womb, he never faltered. Bethany knew his hands were giving him grief throughout the process—there was no mistaking the swollen joints and redness of his skin—but he remained steady, as calm and seemingly confident as if he had performed this sort of surgery numerous times under the same primitive conditions.

He was, in her eyes, magnificent.

He gave the baby's bottom a smart slap, which produced only the weakest of cries. Then he handed him into Bethany's waiting arms, draped by a warm towel.

This was by far the smallest infant Bethany had ever seen. "Will he be all right?"

She had to ask, even though she anticipated his reply.

"I honestly don't know," Andrew said, beginning to suture. "Cleanse him as well as you can, but try to keep him securely wrapped as much as possible. Massage his limbs, but very carefully." He glanced up. "You know what to do. There's only so much we *can* do."

The door opened just then, and a tall, silver-haired priest stepped inside. Andrew frowned and shook his head, lifting a hand as if to indicate "not yet," then went on suturing the incision. The priest nodded and moved to stand in a shadowed corner of the room.

After Bethany had washed the infant, she wrapped another prewarmed towel around him, hugging him close to her heart as she rubbed his tiny legs through the thickness of the cloth. He began to wail, a frail cry like that of an abandoned kitten.

As she cuddled the child, she watched Andrew close the incision, then lift the still unconscious Vangie MacGovern from the table onto the bed.

Her throat threatened to close when she saw Andrew motion for the priest. The man stepped out of the shadows and came to stand beside the bed.

Andrew glanced at the exhausted mother, then at the infant in Bethany's arms before he responded to the priest's unspoken question.

"I don't know," he said, his voice weary, his shoulders slumped. "I expect the mother would want last rites for them both."

Bethany drew the infant boy a little closer, as if she could strengthen his thin, fluttering heartbeat by pressing his tiny form closer to her own heart.

When the priest gently lifted him from her arms, it seemed that the baby's feeble wail continued to echo deep inside her own spirit.

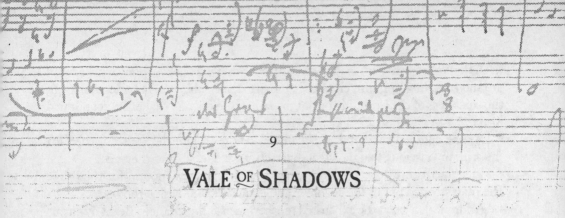

9

VALE OF SHADOWS

Lead me through the vale of shadows,
Bear me o'er life's fitful sea...

FANNY CROSBY

By midafternoon the next day, Susanna faced an unsettling certainty—that the previous night had changed her forever. It had evoked a formerly unknown fear that now threatened to shake a fundamental conviction about herself and what she wanted from life.

How would she ever again entertain the thought of giving birth without remembering Vangie MacGovern's swollen form, her distorted features, and the agonized cries that reflected a torment unlike anything Susanna had ever imagined? After this, how could she ever bring herself to give Michael the family he so desired?

He had made no secret of the fact that he'd always longed for a "house filled with children." He had grown up as an only child and was emphatic about not wanting the same kind of childhood for Caterina. Papa Emmanuel, too, often made mention of how *he* looked forward to more grandchildren, even hinting at the possibility that those grandchildren might be the very inducement that would keep him in the States.

As Michael's wife, Susanna would only naturally be expected to share this desire for a family. And up until now, she *had* shared it. Before last night, however, she had never given much thought to what exactly was involved in bringing a baby into the world. Even though she'd grown up on a dairy farm, her parents had done their best to keep her and her sister, Deirdre, fairly unenlightened about such things as mating and giving birth.

For the first time, Susanna realized that perhaps her mother—for it had been mostly her mother's doing, as she recalled—had done her no favors by sheltering her so closely. What she had witnessed with Vangie MacGovern might not have been such an immense shock had she been better prepared. Uninformed as she was, she had been badly shaken by last night's events. Indeed, she was still struggling to suppress the fear they engendered, along with her disgust at herself for reacting as she had.

She crossed her bedroom and sat down on the side of the bed, unable to stop thinking about Vangie MacGovern. Such suffering—and the poor infant might not even survive. Simply watching Bethany and Andrew with the MacGovern family after the delivery had confirmed her own suspicions that the baby's grasp on life was tenuous at best.

As for Vangie herself, Andrew Carmichael had not attempted to minimize the seriousness of her condition, although it seemed to Susanna that he considered the mother's survival more likely than the infant's.

Incredibly, as if there had not been agony enough for the MacGoverns during that dreadful night, in the early hours of the morning had come the devastating news that their oldest son, en route to America, had been lost at sea.

Susanna shuddered, her own personal anxieties receding in the face of the tragedy that had fallen upon the MacGoverns. How much more must that poor family bear? How much more *could* they bear, Susanna wondered, sick at heart for them all, but especially for Vangie, who might yet have to face the terrible blow of losing not only her firstborn son but her newborn as well.

And that was assuming Vangie survived to learn of her loss.

⌒

By sheer force of will, Conn MacGovern sat still as a stone, watching his wife sleep. He wanted nothing so much as to flee the small room that reeked of sickness and despair. The despair was his own, for Vangie was as yet unaware that the life of their tiny infant boy was in jeopardy and that they had already lost their eldest son to the sea.

Conn felt as if he were being torn in half, willing Vangie to come to while at the same time dreading the moment when she would revive.

If she revived.

And if she did, would she survive the dire news he must lay upon her? Weak as she was, the loss of Aidan, their firstborn and ever so dear to her heart, might be the final blow that would destroy her, even before she learned that death might also await the new babe.

He tried to reason with himself that perhaps, if the wee boy should live—perhaps that might strengthen Vangie's will enough to make *her* want to live.

As quickly as the thought arrived with its fragile trace of hope, just as quickly did it flee, leaving Conn's spirit as bleak and chilled as before. Even the doctors could not say whether the babe would last through the day.

How could he not fear the worst? Although Mrs. Dempsey had had some success in getting the infant to suckle from a knotted cloth soaked in sweet cream with a little sugar water, the babe appeared desperately frail, his blue-veined skin thin as paper and just as fragile. Even his wail was pitiful, as weak as that of a sick pup.

To lose two sons, their eldest and their youngest—why would he think that Vangie could bear it, in her own dangerous condition, when he wasn't at all convinced that *he* could?

He had tried to be strong, to cling to his faith, ever since his first glimpse of the babe after the birthing, and even after the word came about Aidan. No doubt Vangie's counsel would be the same steadfast reminder as was her custom to offer in a dark time such as this: "What seems a disaster when left to our own means," she would say, "can be turned to a glory when touched by our Lord." Or something to that effect.

But Vangie was the one with the faith of a saint, not himself. He did his best not to bring shame to his Savior, but the dear Lord knew his faith was a feeble thing indeed compared to Vangie's. She was the one who kept them all from flying apart when things were bad. Like any man, he liked to think he was the bedrock of his household, strong enough and brave enough to meet whatever might come. But in truth, Vangie was his bedrock. His flame-haired darling feared nothing. Well...except perhaps for bats and spiders.

His spirit groaned to think of ever living a day without her.

Oh, sweet Savior, what would I do...what would any of us do if You were to take her from us? Please, Lord, have mercy, not simply for my sake, but for the children. How could I possibly care for them all and give them what they need without Vangie? How would they ever manage without their mother?

Struck with terror at the direction his thoughts had taken, Conn felt he would surely strangle. He squeezed his eyes shut and began to knead his temples with his hands, hoping to relieve the ache that wreathed his skull.

The rain had finally ceased, but the wind was still up. Dazed with exhaustion and nearly numb with fear, he thought at first the faint moan was naught but the wind rustling through the great pines that ringed the property. But when it came again, he opened his eyes to see Vangie watching him.

He shot out of his chair and bent over her, catching her hand in his.

"Conn..."

Her voice was thin, scarcely more than a tremulous whisper, but to Conn it sounded like music. "I'll go and get the doctors, love! You must lie very still now."

"No...wait. The babe, Conn...is the babe—is he all right?"

Conn swallowed, squeezing her hand carefully. "He...he's a wee thing, love, but a fighter. Sure, he'll be fine in no time at all." He stopped, studying her. "How did you know we have ourselves another boy, Vangie?"

She gave the slightest shake of the head. "I just...knew. I dreamed about him. I...think I saw him."

Conn knew he should go and fetch the doctors, but still he clasped her hand, unwilling to leave her. "Well, your dream was right enough, love. And won't he be needing a proper name now? We'd not quite decided on that, so we'd best—"

Suddenly, she shook her hand free, grasped his arm and pulled herself up, clinging to him.

"Vangie, you mustn't—"

"Aidan! Oh, Conn, I dreamed of our Aidan, too! Has there been any word of him?"

Conn's blood seemed to halt its flow. His heart pounding, he sat down beside her on the bed, supporting her with his shoulder as she continued to cling to him. Her eyes burned with the flame of fever, and her hand on his arm was like a claw.

"Vangie, you mustn't do this, you must not strain yourself so—"

She ignored him, beginning to ramble as if she hadn't heard. "He was calling for me, Conn...on the sea. There was a storm...he kept calling but I couldn't reach him! At first I thought it was the babe, but it wasn't. It was Aidan! Oh, Conn, he was calling out for me, and I couldn't—"

She stilled, her sunken eyes enormous against the pallor of her skin. "Conn?" His name on her lips was harsh and laced with fear.

It was too soon to tell her...she wasn't strong enough...it might drain what little strength was left in her...

He tried to calm her, knowing as he did that Vangie, even weak as she was, could strip away all his pretenses like the skin of an onion and look into his soul. She knew him too well. She had seen what he could not say. Much as he longed to, he couldn't lie to her. Not now. Not ever.

"What is it?" she said, her feverish eyes searing his own, her grasp tightening on his arm. "The babe?" She twisted to better study him, and the panic in her gaze wrenched Conn's heart.

"No. 'Tis as I told you, Vangie. The babe is holding his own."

Her eyes darkened, and Conn saw her struggle, saw her dread of hearing the worst, her inability not to hear it.

"Aidan?" she finally choked out.

An entire world of grief hung over the name of their son like a shroud.

"So it is Aidan, then. Tell me," she said in a tone dull and thick with knowing.

Conn tried to pull her closer, but she gave a fierce shake of her head and lifted a hand to restrain him. "*Tell* me," she said again, her voice turning hard.

He was the one who had had to tell her each time they'd lost a child—the tiny girl who had died before being birthed, the infant son who had not lived past his first week. And each time, seeing the raw pain in her eyes and the terrible desolation that hung over her for weeks afterward, he had thought he could never bear to see such sorrow looking back at him again.

But this was a harder thing entirely, a far worse agony to thrust upon her. To lose one's firstborn—to watch him grow to manhood, love him and care for him for nearly twenty years, and then know he was gone forever—could there be a more grievous loss?

If only that loss could have been prevented...

But I begged him to come. For the sake of your mother, I told him, you must come so you and I can be reconciled and bring her some peace...and so we can all be together again as a family. She is fading here without you. You must come...

Worse yet was the bitter awareness that, had he not been so hardheaded, had not been such a bane to the boy all of those years of his young manhood, perhaps Aidan might have come across when *they* did, instead of waiting.

But he could not think of that now. That was *his* grief. He could not make it hers. Somehow, for now, he must put aside his guilt, his torment, and help her bear her own.

She was waiting, watching him, her blue eyes hot and shadowed with fear.

And so he told her, trying to ignore the part of himself that he could feel dying with every word he spoke.

~

In the kitchen, dim in the late afternoon light filtering through the small windows, Renny Magee sat watching Nell Grace try to feed her new baby brother with a knotted cloth dipped in sugar water.

The poor sickly little thing was doing its best to suckle, and Nell Grace actually seemed encouraged, but Renny wondered if her hopes might not be ill-founded. Ever since the priest had been summoned in the night—and soon afterward sent for the blind man to come and pray with him—she had feared the worst for the wee boy.

And for Vangie MacGovern as well, though Renny tried hard to shut *that* thought out of her mind. As yet she couldn't bring herself to think about Vangie dying. She *wouldn't* think about it.

The kitchen was hushed, as was the rest of the house. The twins and Emma had been put to bed. Miss Susanna and the Irish housekeeper had gone back to the Big House to see to Maylee and the blind man's little girl.

Two hours or more had passed since Conn MacGovern had shut the door of the bedroom, where he watched over Vangie. Only the low voices of the blind man and the priest, who had again come together to pray, and the sound of Nell Grace's crooning broke the silence.

Renny didn't like the quiet. It made it harder to ignore her own troubled thoughts. Because she wouldn't allow herself to worry about Vangie, and since Nell Grace had taken charge of the wee babe, there seemed no escaping the sickening waves of guilt that rode over her at frequent intervals.

If the MacGoverns' eldest son had only used his passage to America instead of giving it over for her, he would be alive now.

If Aidan MacGovern had come across with the rest of his family—if Renny had stayed in Ireland, where Conn MacGovern had wanted her to stay—then the dread news about their son's death would not have arrived this day. He would not have died in a shipwreck.

It was *her* fault. Hers. Never mind that Aidan MacGovern had chosen not to make the crossing with his family. Never mind that Conn MacGovern had failed to convince his son that he was being foolish entirely by letting a raggedy busker girl use the ticket in Aidan's place.

If she, Renny Magee, had not begged to come with them, grabbing at her chance for free passage as if it were her ticket to life itself, then perhaps the MacGovern lad would have changed his mind that day on the docks.

He might have, after all. Wasn't that so?

But the boy *hadn't* come across, and she had, in his place, and now Aidan MacGovern was dead. And even if Vangie survived her sickness and the birth of the babe, she might still die. She might die of the grief.

Renny's gaze went to the two men in the shadowed corner. The big blind man stood with a hand on the silver-haired priest's shoulder. Their eyes were closed as they continued to pray, but Renny could sense the sorrow in the blind man's face. He was a good man—a kind man—according to Maylee. Sure, and he must be, to spend the hours that he had praying for Vangie and the babe as if they were family.

Renny knew she should be praying, too. She had tried, earlier, only to stop when the few words she'd managed to force up from the barrenness inside her spirit sounded wooden and meaningless entirely. How could she pray about the dreadful things that had happened? What was there to pray for?

Besides, it seemed wrong somehow to pray about the MacGoverns' tragedy when she might have been at least partly responsible for causing it.

Without warning, a fierce cry from the bedroom shattered the quiet of the house. Renny jumped and turned toward the bedroom door, as did everyone else in the room.

The sound of Vangie's mournful keening stabbed Renny's heart like a dagger. All the pain of the night before and the long, sorrowful day now came thundering down on her like an avalanche, pinning her beneath it and crushing her with its weight.

She stumbled from the chair and, without so much as a look in the direction of Nell Grace or the two men in the corner, made a lunge for the door, practically throwing herself outside, into the night.

She didn't care where she went, as long as she couldn't hear the sound of Vangie MacGovern's heart breaking.

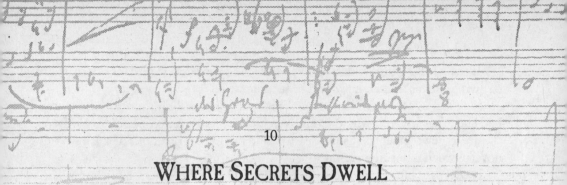

10

WHERE SECRETS DWELL

Where once she walked with graceful steps,
She falters now as blind.
She walks the way of hopelessness
Where guilt and secrets wind.

ANONYMOUS

Andrew Carmichael had seen only one patient with symptoms similar to those of Natalie Guthrie. And since he had not been the lady's physician at that time, but only a medical student tagging along behind the great Dr. Cyrus Cooper, he had gained little from the case other than the disillusioning awareness that some illnesses can frustrate even the finest of physicians.

Late this afternoon, he had been summoned to the home of Edward Fitch, where Mrs. Guthrie lived with her son-in-law and his family. The heir to Fitch's Department Store and a highly successful attorney in his own right, Fitch was also a former patient. Since recovering from a severe case of diphtheria a few years past, the man had been quite outspoken in attributing his rather startling recovery entirely to Andrew's care.

Andrew, who had simply been filling in during another other doctor's absence, had done his best to convince Fitch that the man owed his recovery to the grace of God more than to any "miraculous" cure effected by himself. In truth, there was little any physician could do in the face of such a virulent case other than to employ the usual treatment—which was often ineffective. The grateful attorney, however, had chosen to believe that Andrew had worked some sort of a providential healing on his behalf, and no amount of protests to the contrary could change his mind.

Consequently, Fitch had referred a half-dozen or so wealthy friends to Andrew's practice. A few had made generous donations to hospital wings or children's homes at Andrew's request, when they would have otherwise paid *him* exorbitant fees. Although not entirely comfortable with spending his time attending to the wealthy, who could afford any physician in the city, Andrew wasn't so foolish as to ignore the benefits of having a few patients who could afford to pay their bills on time—and make an occasional contribution to needy institutions as well. So when Edward Fitch's carriage arrived for him late Friday afternoon as arranged, he had gone willingly enough, leaving Bethany to see to their one remaining home visit for the day, an elderly widow on Houston Street.

Between Fitch and his mother-in-law, Andrew had by now made quite a few calls to the opulent, but not ostentatious, mansion. Although the residence itself seemed to sprawl over an enormous piece of real estate, it gave an unexpectedly warm impression of graciousness and family living. Andrew found himself relatively comfortable when he called, and he had come to like and respect the heavy-shouldered attorney who resided there. He had quickly learned that the perpetual frown on Fitch's broad face in no way indicated bad humor, but was more the expression of a man who was always thinking, his mind constantly turning ideas over for inspection. Fitch gave himself no airs. In fact, were it not for the reputation of his family and the genteel elegance of his home, one would never have recognized him as a man of wealth and influence.

Fitch rose from his chair behind his desk as soon as Andrew entered the study. The two men shook hands but wasted no time on pleasantries.

"How is she?" Andrew asked.

Fitch shook his head. "It's been a difficult week. And today—well, she's worse than I've seen her for some time. Earlier this morning she was so nervous she was in a shake. Pacing the upstairs like a caged cat, not eating—she wouldn't even speak to my wife or the children." He paused, looking at Andrew. "Her mood changes without any warning whatsoever. One hour she's in a fever; the next she's so enervated she can scarcely communicate with any of us. That's how she is now—or was, last time I went up to check. I tell you, it's as if she's simply—falling to pieces."

Andrew couldn't argue with Fitch's observation about his mother-in-law "falling to pieces." That seemed to be exactly what was happening to Natalie Guthrie, and for no apparent reason.

But there had to be a reason. Apart from her obvious weight loss, which was only to be expected since her appetite had drastically decreased, she seemed to be in good physical health. Yet emotionally and mentally, the woman was clearly deteriorating.

"When I was here last week," he said, "you mentioned a family vacation, to get her away from the city. Have you broached the subject with her yet?"

Fitch's expression turned sour. "You'd have thought we were trying to put her out in the street. She became almost hysterical. She used to love going to the lodge. Now she won't even entertain the thought of it."

He stopped, giving a shake of his head. "I'll admit I'm almost at my wit's end with her. And so's my wife. Why, the children are actually afraid of her. I can't bring myself to have her institutionalized, but she's having a disastrous effect on our home life."

He was looking at Andrew as though hoping for an answer, a solution, but Andrew had none. He had become more and more convinced that Natalie Guthrie's illness was emotional or mental in origin, but as to its specific source or treatment, he had no idea.

"I wish I had an answer for you," he told Fitch in all sincerity. "But I'm afraid I can only advise you to seek help from a specialist. Someone who focuses on... disorders of the mind."

Fitch scowled. "You mean one of those alienists? I'd never convince my wife to expose her mother to such a person. She believes it's all quackery. And I'm not so sure but what she's right."

Andrew tried for just the right words, for he understood the man's distrust of psychiatric treatment in general, even if he didn't entirely share it. Among the "better families" such as the Fitches, mental and emotional illness were subjects to be whispered about, not discussed openly. And physicians who aspired to treat those conditions were looked upon with either distaste or distrust. *Quackery* was a common epithet applied to those who practiced any kind of psychiatric care. Andrew himself had questions about some practices, yet knew of patients who had definitely benefited from attention to their mental state.

"Mr. Fitch—"

"Edward," the other corrected.

"Edward, I wish you and your wife would at least consider the possibility of psychiatric treatment. I'm at a loss as to what else to do for Mrs. Guthrie. And we both know she's getting worse, not better."

"Andrew, you're the only person outside the family who can even come near her these days. She won't leave the house, she won't accept callers—she won't even come downstairs if the children have friends in to play. Even if I could convince my wife to enlist psychiatric help for her, Mother Guthrie would most likely bar herself in her room and not come out."

Andrew knew Fitch wasn't exaggerating. He was certain he could arrange for a house call from one of the psychiatrists in the city, but that would avail nothing if Natalie Guthrie wouldn't see him.

"Well, let's go up," he said. "Perhaps I can at least calm her a bit."

~

Natalie Guthrie's condition appeared even more wretched than it had upon Andrew's last visit, two weeks previous. Despite her son-in-law's description of her earlier excitability, the woman slumped in a chair by the fireplace looked as if every last ounce of strength had been drained from her. A sickly pallor had replaced her usually flushed complexion, and her hair clearly had not been dressed that day. Her hands rested limply in her lap as if the bone structure had been liquefied and rendered useless. There was no hint of the self-possession or prideful posture that, according to her son-in-law, had once characterized her demeanor.

Her expression brightened only a fraction when Andrew entered the room, and her greeting was a lethargic, low murmur of his name.

He went to her and took her hand, which he found to be cold. She made no effort to return his clasp. "How are you, Mrs. Guthrie?"

She looked at him with dull eyes. "I am...very tired just now, Doctor. Very tired."

Andrew nodded, studying her dry skin, her slack jaw. It struck him that Natalie Guthrie had given up. There was simply no life about the woman; she was virtually fading away.

But why?

Edward Fitch stepped up just then. "Mother Guthrie, is there anything I can have sent up for you and Dr. Carmichael? Some tea perhaps?"

She gave a faint shake of her head but made no reply.

"Andrew?"

"No, thank you. I'll just visit with Mrs. Guthrie for a while."

Fitch glanced from one to the other, then excused himself and left the room.

"I'd like to examine you, Mrs. Guthrie. Why don't I have your daughter come in?"

She gave an idle wave of her hand. "Not today, Doctor. I don't want to be examined today."

Andrew tried to feign sternness with her. "You didn't want to be examined last time either. How can I help you, Mrs. Guthrie, if you won't even allow me to monitor your condition?"

To Andrew's dismay, she began to weep. He stooped low and took her hand. "I didn't mean to upset you, Mrs. Guthrie!"

She shook her head, the tears streaming down her cheeks. "I know you mean well, Dr. Carmichael," she said, her voice low and thick, her words coming slowly and in a monotone, "but you can't help me. You mustn't waste your time coming here. Please don't bother with me any longer. Just...give me something to help me sleep, won't you? Some laudanum or...perhaps something a little stronger. I'm sure that's all I need."

She had made this request before, and once—only once—Andrew had complied with a light sleeping potion, enough for two nights. But he sensed that giving her anything stronger could be a treacherous mistake. He knew all too well how an innocent act, even on the part of a well-intentioned physician who meant only to help, could turn a patient onto a path that led straight to destruction.

He also knew this was no time to allow his sympathy for the woman to override his better instincts. "I'm afraid I can't do that, Mrs. Guthrie," he said, straightening. "I don't believe it would be the best thing for you right now."

Unexpectedly, the dullness that had glazed her eyes only a moment before was replaced by a flash of anger. The woman's chin came up, her jaw tensed, and in that instant Andrew caught a glimpse of the pride and a certain air of condescension that, in a previous time, might have distinguished the woman's bearing.

"What exactly does that mean, Doctor?" Her voice was surprisingly firm all of a sudden. Firm and even haughty.

Andrew recognized that this Natalie Guthrie might once have had the hubris to intimidate her own physician. He wasn't about to let this unexpected show of strength divert him, however.

"Merely that a palliative isn't going to solve your problem, Mrs. Guthrie. I'm interested in seeing you well again, nothing less."

She stared at him. "And you don't trust me with laudanum," she said woodenly. Again her entire countenance changed. As quickly as it had come, the imperious dignity had fled. Her eyes glazed with tears, her shoulders slumped, and her chin fell.

"I will never be well, Dr. Carmichael," she said, not looking at him. "I want only to be less of a burden to my daughter and her family. Caroline is the very best of daughters, and Edward is as good to me as if I were his own mother. But they don't know what to do with me, and the children—" She broke off, shuddering. "—the children avoid me. I believe...I believe I must consider going away. An... institution, perhaps, or even...I don't know..."

She had begun to ramble and seemed to be growing more agitated.

"Mrs. Guthrie, that's not an answer," Andrew hurried to say. "And it's not what your family wants for you. They love you. They want to help you—"

"I'm not worthy of their love! They can't help me! And neither can you!"

With a strength that surprised Andrew, she half rose from the chair, her hands gripping the arms as if to steady herself. Even in her agitation, she was deathly pale and trembling visibly.

Andrew moved, meaning to catch her if she fell, but she groped her way to her feet and stood staring at him, wringing her hands, her eyes darting everywhere but at him. "I'd like you to leave now, doctor. Obviously, you're not going to do anything for me, so please go."

Andrew sensed the woman was on the verge of hysteria, that arguing with her or trying to placate her might merely serve to increase her distress. Besides, he had nothing to offer her at the moment but a solicitude that to Natalie Guthrie must seem empty and worthless.

But in that moment as they stood facing each other, the thought struck him anew that this woman, once so stately and self-controlled, was being destroyed from within. And not from any mortal physical ailment, for he had exhausted every test at his disposal for some insidious illness. No, whatever blight had descended on Natalie Guthrie might be every bit as malignant as a cancer and as brutal as a punishing disease, but he was convinced it had taken deep root in her soul and was now spreading over her entire being, eating away at her body, mind, and spirit.

To his silent despair, he had to admit that she was right—that he couldn't help her, except perhaps through his prayers. All he could do, it seemed, was assure the woman that he had no intention of giving up, that he was committed to her healing. She responded with an agitated twist of her hands, and after another moment Andrew left the room and went downstairs to take his leave of a badly disappointed—and exceedingly frustrated—Edward Fitch.

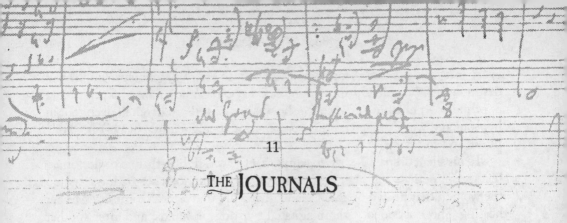

11

THE JOURNALS

Our deeds pursue us from afar,
And what we have been makes us what we are.

JOHN FLETCHER

By the time Andrew returned to the office, he was beyond tired. His joints had been aching since morning, his hands and wrists badly swollen. He'd even begun to wonder if the salicylates were losing their effectiveness. Had he used them so long and so frequently that their benefits were diminishing?

And if that were the case, then what was he to do?

He was too weary to think about that tonight. Yet he couldn't help but recall the plaintive expression on Natalie Guthrie's face when she asked him to give her "something to help me sleep."

Something to make the misery go away...

How well he knew that longing. And because he did know it so well, he also knew why he dared not give in to the disturbed woman's plea.

Andrew sighed as he turned the key in the lock. He would just collect the newspapers and go on upstairs to his living quarters to rest awhile. Please, God, let there be no late-hour emergencies tonight. He badly needed a full night's sleep.

He stood in the open doorway to the office waiting room, looking around. Everything looked perfectly normal, just as he'd left it. Yet as he closed the door behind him, he was seized by the peculiar sensation that something was different, something was wrong.

An irrational sense of invasion stirred in him.

So strong was the sensation that he delayed entering. When he finally crossed the room, he glanced at the counter that divided the waiting area from the offices and examining rooms. Because both he and Bethany had decided they could do without a receptionist, at least for the time being, only the two of them had access to the files and other papers neatly stacked in place on the desk. Their appointment pads were still open to today's list of patients. Clearly, nothing had been disturbed.

But even though he saw nothing out of place, Andrew still couldn't shake the unsettling feeling that something was amiss.

He went to the larger of the two examining rooms and found the door open. He was certain he'd closed it. Out of habit, he always closed the doors to both examining rooms and his office when he left the premises.

The last of the day's light was gone, so the room was dark. Andrew lit one of the two gas lamps on the wall, then turned to face the room.

The first thing he saw was the window on the back wall. Someone had broken it from the outside. Shattered glass was strewn on the counter below and across the floor.

An evening breeze filtered through the shards of glass left intact, cooling the room. Andrew's first thought as he looked around was that one of the countless stray dogs that continually roamed the city streets was responsible for the chaos. But dogs didn't break windows, and no dog could have left behind such destruction and debris. Only human hands could have plundered the room with such violence.

The examining table had been thrown onto its side, and trash from the waste barrel had been pitched every which way about the room. Cabinet drawers had been overturned, their contents strewn onto the floor, along with towels and surgery pads and instruments.

His gaze went to the storage cabinets above the counter. Their doors hung open, the locks broken and thrown aside.

Andrew stumbled the rest of the way into the room and found the medicines that he kept locked inside the cabinets—including narcotics and anesthetics—now in total disarray. Some bottles had been overturned, others broken.

For a moment Andrew could only stand in shock, staring at the ruin before him. A vessel at his temple began to throb with pain. He whipped around, his heart hammering at the idea of what might be lurking at his back.

Nothing was there, and the ominous silence told him he was alone. Whoever was responsible for this wreckage had come and gone.

Fear traced the length of his spine as he stood staring into the hallway and beyond, into the waiting room.

He was shaking like a palsied old man as he turned back to the cabinets and began to rummage through the medicines, trying to recall the contents. Even though his hasty, nervous inspection was far from precise, he was almost positive nothing had been taken.

Why, then, had the room been ransacked?

He went to the second examining room and found much the same scene he'd left behind him. Here, too, the cabinet doors had been forced open, the shelves cluttered with broken bottles and spilled powders.

Slowly, fighting for his breath, Andrew began to back away, trying to think what to do. His first thought was an almost overwhelming sense of relief that Bethany was out of the office. Who knew what some larcenous thug or half-wild addict might have done to her had she been here?

But this couldn't have been the work of an addict looking for drugs...nothing had been taken!

Completely bewildered, Andrew stood leaning against the frame of the examining room door rubbing his right shoulder, which was on fire with pain. Then his gaze went to the open door of the private study he and Bethany shared—the door he always closed behind him.

His heart hammered against his rib cage as he walked toward the darkened room. After lighting the lamp on the wall, he saw his fears realized. His desk was a shambles—papers tossed everywhere, the drawers emptied and their contents strewn about. Books ripped apart and tossed from the wall shelving.

Mindless destruction.

Somehow he managed to still the shaking of his hands. He dropped down onto his knees and riffled through the debris. Patient notes, unpaid bills, correspondence—everything seemed to be here, though much of it had been crumpled and torn.

His journals.

Panic squeezed his heart and churned his blood as he looked around, then slowly got to his feet.

He had kept the journals most of his life—year after year of daily entries that tracked his time at medical college and then his experience in private practice, first in Scotland, next in the States. Accounts of his successes and his failures. The cases over which he had puzzled and agonized. The patients who had both frustrated and challenged him. His struggles and his sorrows. His health problems. His growing love for Bethany. Intensely personal and private, more spiritual in nature than merely a day-by-day accounting of his life, those journals revealed the very essence of his life.

And its secrets. Including his earlier drug addiction, known by no one here in his adopted country except Bethany. Not even Frank Donovan, his closest friend, knew the terrible secret of that other, dark period of his life.

It was all there, in the journals.

And the journals were gone.

Only God knew who had taken them.

Or why.

The fabric of his deepest fears fell away, revealing in all its horror the long-confined but never quite suppressed dread that some day, somehow, his past would be found out and he would be known for what he had been: an addict. A weak, pathetic addict who had risked everything—and nearly lost everything—for the sake of the narcotics that imprisoned him and held him captive.

Cold rushed in on him like a howling wind. Over the thundering of his heart and the roaring in his head Andrew thought he could hear the door to his hard-won peace—and any hope for future happiness—close with a resounding thud.

⌒

Half an hour later, Andrew was still trying to dismiss his urgent desire to go to Bethany. He wanted to be with her—he *needed* to be with her. But he didn't want to alarm her. Besides, her landlady would certainly frown on the impropriety of his presence in Bethany's flat without a chaperone, especially after dark.

He knew it would be best to wait until morning to talk with her here, at the office. But oh, how he craved the soothing effect of her presence, her warmth, her good judgment, at this moment.

Instead, he decided to summon Frank Donovan. He needed a policeman, but not just any policeman. Frank was not only his friend, but was acknowledged even by his contemporaries to be one of the shrewdest and most dependable officers on the force.

There was no denying that things were not quite as comfortable between them as they once had once been. In truth, Andrew still smarted a bit from Frank's thoughtless opinion about Bethany's "unsuitability" as a wife, his assumption that she wasn't likely to be as devoted a wife as she was a physician.

That argument had been months ago. Frank had said too much; Andrew had taken offense; and for several weeks the two had avoided each other. Lately, however, they had taken to having a chat whenever they happened to meet, and Frank was again stopping by the office for an occasional cup of coffee. Most of the time things seemed almost back to normal.

Even if that had not been the case, Andrew knew this was no time to let pride get in the way of common sense. He would send one of the newsboys who lived on the streets to find Frank and fetch him here.

Frank would know what to do.

It occurred to him that he would have to tell Frank about the journals—and that in turn would necessitate telling him at least something about what was in the journals.

Andrew recoiled at the very thought.

A man knows when he has another man's respect, even his admiration. Andrew had long been aware that, in spite of his friend's barbed sense of humor and his bluff demeanor, Frank held him in high regard.

What would he think once he learned the truth?

As he went to find a messenger, Andrew was surprised how much it hurt to think of losing Frank Donovan's respect—or possibly even his friendship.

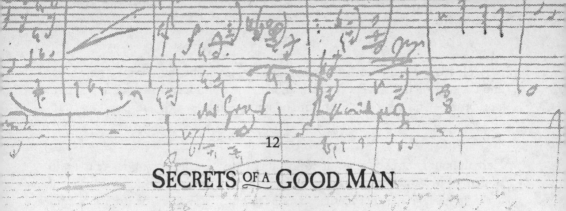

SECRETS OF A GOOD MAN

For the thing I greatly feared has come upon me,
And what I dreaded has happened to me.

JOB 3:25 (NKJV)

Andrew felt sheepish admitting, even to himself, how Frank Donovan's presence in the building eased his mind.

The big Irish policeman could be annoying, no doubt about it, with his ruthless sense of humor and his brash, jaded opinion of human nature. But at a time like this he was all business—deadly serious, with a keen, incisive way of assessing a situation for what it was. It didn't hurt that he emanated a kind of coiled strength, a powerful physicality that could explode any second with dire consequences. While this quality could be downright intimidating to those on his "bad side," Andrew found it reassuring to his own situation.

"You all right, Doc?" Frank said, taking off his hat and tossing it onto the counter in the waiting room.

Frank had spent only a few minutes inspecting the wanton damage of the office. Now he leaned against the counter in the waiting room watching Andrew, who had finally given in to the pain in his legs and sunk down onto a nearby wooden chair.

Andrew was anything but all right, but he merely nodded.

"Well, I'd say you got yourself an enemy. Any idea who it might be?"

Andrew looked up. "Are you saying this is not just a case of breaking and entering?" Even as he said the words, he already knew the answer.

Obviously, Frank did, too. He traced his mustache with an index finger, his dark eyes boring into Andrew. "No, I'm not thinkin' it is. Who's got it in for you, Doc? Any ideas?"

"You must see this sort of thing all the time—vandalism and the like. Why do you think this might be—anything different?"

"What do you think it was?" Frank said, his gaze never wavering.

"A patient who thinks his bill is too high, perhaps?"

Andrew's attempt at lightness failed badly. Frank's arched eyebrow made it clear he was not amused.

"So what's gone missin'?" Frank asked. "You said there was no sign of any medicines taken. No other valuables?"

"Not that I could tell," Andrew said, massaging his swollen knuckles. "Everything seems to be here except...some journals from my office."

Frank frowned. "Medical journals?"

"No," said Andrew with a slow shake of his head. "Personal. Quite a few, actually. They go back a number of years."

"A kind of diary, then?"

Andrew nodded. "Yes. I expect you'd consider it foolishness, but I've always kept an accounting of—things that happen in my life."

Frank was studying him—measuring him—with a speculative expression. "I don't find any foolishness about you, Doc, and that's the truth. So, why would somebody be interested in these journals, then? And do you have a thought as to who that somebody might be?"

Andrew looked at him. "No." At Frank's skeptical look, Andrew said again, "I've no idea, Frank. Really. And as for—"

He stopped, humiliation washing over him.

"Doc?"

Andrew put his head in his hands and pressed his fingers against his aching temples. "There are some intensely personal things in those journals, Frank," he said without looking up. "Things I'd not want...anyone to know."

There was a long silence. Then, "Tell me something, Doc. Whatever is in these journals, could it hurt you at all?"

Andrew looked up, then dropped his hands to his knees. "Oh, yes, Frank. It could hurt me a great deal."

Frank pushed away from the counter but remained standing where he was, arms folded across his chest. "Well, see here, Doc. I don't need to know what's in those journals to help you get them back. But it might make my job a sight easier if you could at least give me an idea as to who might want to hurt you."

"Who—"

"Don't you see, Doc? Somebody's gone to a lot of trouble here." Frank made a sweeping gesture to take in the waiting room and the entire expanse of the office.

"But if you're right and nothing was taken save for your journals, then I'm thinking they made the mess simply to put a scare into you or at least rattle you a bit. And as for the journals themselves, from what you're tellin' me, they'd not be worth much to anyone but you."

He stopped. "Unless someone is looking to hurt you. Maybe embarrass you somehow, if there's anything of a nature in those journals that would lend itself to that."

The ache in Andrew's skull now escalated to a nearly unbearable pain. Between the headache and the fire in his joints, he found it almost impossible to think clearly.

But he could reason well enough to take in the awful truth of Frank's words.

"It wouldn't just embarrass me," he said, his voice strangled. "It could ruin me."

He heard Frank Donovan draw a long breath, knew the man was waiting for him to say more. When Andrew remained silent, Frank finally offered what he undoubtedly intended as an encouragement, but it only served to make Andrew more miserable as he realized that he couldn't afford not to confide in his friend.

"Well, we can't have that, I'm thinkin'," Frank said with a forced cheerfulness. "You're a good man, Doc—one of the few in this wretched city, I'll wager. You don't deserve to be treated so. I'll take care of this—never you worry."

Frank sounded awkward—and uncertain.

"Frank—"

"Just don't fret yourself, Doc. I said I'd handle it."

"Frank, listen to me."

Again Andrew lowered his head to his hands. He didn't look at his friend, couldn't bring himself to face the disappointment and disillusionment—and the disgust—that would surely register in those dark, merciless eyes when Frank learned the truth.

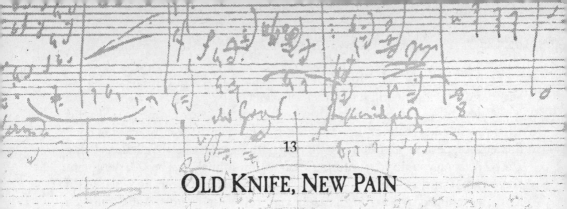

13

OLD KNIFE, NEW PAIN

Who made the heart, 'tis He alone
Decidedly can try us.

ROBERT BURNS

Andrew told Frank everything. He told him about his former drug addiction, making no attempt to soften his words when he described what he had once been, how low he had fallen, what a shameful wretch he was at that time. It occurred to Andrew that it was as difficult to relate his ugly story to Frank as it had been to tell Bethany.

But he went on, faltering only once or twice as he recounted how the addiction had been precipitated by a well-intentioned physician and instructor at the medical college who meant only to ease the agony of Andrew's rheumatoid arthritis. The hardest part came when he forced himself to describe, in some detail, what it had been like to give up the opium.

"You can't imagine," he said, his voice low. "No one who hasn't watched it or gone through it can begin to understand what it's like."

Frank broke in. "Doc, I've known my share of addicts. Don't put yourself through this. You owe me no explanations."

Andrew regarded his friend, tempted to take his suggestion, to stop right now and say nothing more. But that seemed too easy. For some inexplicable reason, he felt he needed to hold nothing back.

"You've known addicts, but have you ever watched one try to escape from the addiction?"

Frank hesitated, then shook his head. "No. Can't say that I have."

"I want you to know it all, Frank—every ugly, sickening detail. Maybe then you'll understand what those journals can do to me. Because it's all there, in black and white."

Frank said nothing, but his lean face went hard, and Andrew saw the mix of anger and pain glinting in his eyes.

"When an addict goes through withdrawal, he loses his personality, his self-respect, and whatever dignity is left to him, which in most cases is none. Sometimes, he loses his mind as well. He's nothing but a shell of a human being. The pain eats at your insides until you're a howling animal. You beg for the opium. You plead. You threaten. You pray to die. Every nerve in your body feels as if it's being stripped bare and set ablaze. Even your brain is pressed and squeezed beyond endurance. The pain—it's like nothing I can put into words."

He stopped. "And the worst of it is, you even lose the...the shame of what you've become. You lose everything, and yet you'd give up your soul for just one more time, one more hour, with the very poison that brought you to where you are."

"But you beat it, Doc," Frank said quietly.

Andrew shook his head. "Oh, no. I didn't beat it, Frank. An addict is never really cured. Just...rescued. God rescued me—is still rescuing me. Hour by hour, He sees me through a day. That's how it will always be for me. For the rest of my life."

Just as he had explained his deliverance to Bethany the night he asked her to marry him, he went on to relate to Frank how God had worked a miracle of healing through the caring heart and endurance of a friend, Charles Gordon. His roommate at medical college had eventually recognized Andrew's addiction and virtually forced his unwilling friend to accompany him to his family's home, where he proceeded to lock them both inside an attic room. For two weeks, Charles had prayed with Andrew, cared for him, and suffered with him through every stage of the torturous and demeaning withdrawal from the drug.

To this day, Andrew could scarcely bear to think of the abuse he heaped on his friend during that horrendous time. And yet his roommate had refused to give up on him. And because Charles persevered, Andrew had finally emerged from his private hell.

By the time Andrew reached the end of his account, he was so totally exhausted, so emotionally and physically drained, he could barely force the last few words out of his mouth. In the long silence that followed, he actually fought for his breath as if his heart and his lungs had been crushed.

He squeezed his eyes shut. "Everything I've told you...and more—it's all in the journals. It's all there."

So surprised was he to feel Frank's strong hand on his shoulder that he actually jumped, but he still couldn't bring himself to look up.

Frank cleared his throat. "Does Lady Doc know?"

Andrew nodded. "Yes, Bethany knows."

"And I'll warrant she thinks no less of you for it. Am I right?"

The memory of Bethany's quiet reassurance whispered at the edge of Andrew's mind as he shook his head. "Don't insult me, Andrew," she had said. "It would be a poor kind of love indeed that would allow the past to destroy the present and the future. It doesn't change the way I feel about you."

"Nor do I, Doc," he heard Frank Donovan say in a voice unnaturally soft and laced with an uncommon warmth. "Nor do I."

Andrew lifted his head. "What?"

"I think no less of you, Doc. In truth, though I'm sorry to hear you went through such a terrible time, I might even be a bit relieved to know you're not without a wart or two of your own, given the fact that I've so many."

Andrew stared at him, watching the familiar, thoroughly Irish smile spread slowly across Frank's features.

"You fuddled me something fierce, don't you know? It was never all that easy, seeing you as some kind of a blessed saint."

"Good heavens, Frank, I never intended you should think of me as any such thing!"

Frank's expression sobered. "But still, you're the best man that's ever crossed my path, and that's the truth. I expect that's why I had somewhat of a hard time with you—at first, that is. I kept looking for you to judge me."

Andrew uttered a humorless laugh. "I'd be the last to judge you, Frank—or anyone else, for that matter."

"Aye, in time I came to see that about you. All the same, Doc, mind what I say: You're a better man than you think, I expect. And sad to say, 'tis been my experience that there's no lack of scoundrels out there looking to bring down the really good men. No lack at all."

Frank dropped his hand away from Andrew's shoulder, pulled up a chair nearby, and straddled it, facing Andrew. "Now, then," he said, swiping a hand through his dark red hair, "I expect you've at least an idea or two about who might be behind this nasty business. So tell me what you think, Doc."

Andrew felt somewhat dazed—dazed and immensely grateful as it gradually dawned on him that both the woman he loved and his closest friend now knew the ugly truth about his past. They knew—and neither condemned him. Neither had turned away from him.

Once again, it seemed that God had poured His grace out upon an undeserving sinner's head.

The long, ragged breath of relief he pulled in was in itself a fervent prayer of thanks. He began then to tell Frank about Mary Lambert and her children. And about Robert Warburton, the well-known, much revered clergyman who had fathered those children—and threatened Andrew during a heated confrontation at Warburton's residence.

As he spoke, he saw Frank's mouth tighten, his eyes grow cold.

"But I can't actually believe Warburton has anything to do with this business," Andrew cautioned. "The man's threat was contingent upon my revealing what I know about him and Mary Lambert. But I've kept my silence, other than to tell Bethany and now you. I've given Warburton no reason to fear me."

He paused. "Besides, the man is a pastor. Even if he thought I'd spoken out about his affair, surely he wouldn't stoop to something so—sordid."

Frank's dark eyebrows shot up, then he scowled. "Doc, you'll pardon my saying so, but you can be terrible green sometimes. Didn't you just tell me this Warburton fella sired three illegitimate children?"

Andrew looked at him and nodded, feeling the heat begin to rise from his neck to his face as he realized what Frank was getting at.

"And didn't you say he treated this woman disgraceful and then abandoned her and their children?"

Again Andrew nodded. "I'm sure of it."

"And you don't think a man like that would stoop to something sordid?"

Frank shook his head, and Andrew felt thoroughly embarrassed now to realize how naïve he must seem to his friend.

"I take your point," he said before Frank could chastise him again. "I suppose it's possible."

"It's not only possible; I'd just about bet my badge on it, Doc," Frank said, getting to his feet and scooting the chair back to its original place. "A blighter like himself might not dirty his own hands in such a way, but there are those who wouldn't mind doin' it for him."

Andrew also stood. "Frank? What are you going to do?"

"I'll have to study on it for a bit," Frank said. His gaze flicked over Andrew. "You go upstairs now and get some rest, Doc. I'll bring a couple of the boyos over first thing in the morning, and we'll help you clean up."

Frank started for the door, then turned back to retrieve his hat. "Oh, and Doc? Watch your back, mind? Something tells me this isn't over."

He was almost out the door before Andrew stopped him.

"Frank—"

The other man waited.

"Thank you."

Frank gave a wave of his hat and closed the door behind him, leaving Andrew to marvel, not for the first time, that the Lord had chosen to bless his life with such friends as Charles Gordon and Frank Donovan. He hated to think where he would be without them.

⌒

The first article appeared three days later in the *Herald*. Andrew had finally settled himself at the kitchen table with a cup of tea and a piece of buttered bread for breakfast. He was thumbing through the pages of the newspaper when a letter to the editor caught his attention. After taking in the first few words, he set his cup of tea to the table with a trembling hand and read on.

Gentlemen,

It is with no small measure of distress that I feel it necessary to write this letter, in order to bring a matter of scandalous proportions to the attention of our unsuspecting populace. Were this not an issue that could endanger countless numbers of innocent people, I would choose to keep my silence rather than bring to light a situation that might better remain in the dark, where other unspeakable acts of like nature commonly dwell.

In this case, however, my great concern is to send a warning to those who might unknowingly fall victim to the unconscionable behavior of a practicing physician in our midst, a person of some reputation and distinction. The individual to whom I refer has under his care a significantly large and varied patient list, ranging from the shadowy and questionable inhabitants of the more squalid tenement sections of the city to the more respectable elements of our society.

This physician, who shall for the present remain nameless, while maintaining the appearance and pretense of being a qualified and conscientious medical doctor with only the good of his patients at heart, is in reality an addicted user of opium—a shameful, abominable narcotic.

Who can tell how many may have already fallen victim to the less-than-proficient skills and questionable morality of this individual?

Competent medical care is not only the right of every upstanding citizen; it is also a necessity. When one's physician, however, masquerades as an equal to those esteemed men of the healing arts while indulging himself in a degrading, despicable habit known to have enslaved its users by the hundreds—nay, by the thousands—a habit which causes erosion of all morals and the eventual devastation of the mind and body, it calls into question the trustworthiness of other members of his profession.

There is no telling what harm this particular "physician" could possibly inflict upon his innocent patients or the damage he might bring upon his noble profession. Just as shocking, if not more so, is the fact that he has recently associated himself with one of the disturbing number of female practitioners bent on carving out a place for themselves among the serious, conscientious members of the medical community.

I write with the genuine concern of a resident of our city who cannot in good conscience stand by in silence, for to do so is to encourage an insidious and potentially disastrous situation.

A concerned citizen

Andrew forgot his bread and tea. He sat motionless, staring at the newspaper page in front of him, his breath coming labored and shallow.

Deep inside him, something dark and cold and ugly began to tear and open, like a once-healed wound newly stabbed and savaged by the same knife with a different blade.

Clearly, the vandalism in his office had merely been the forerunner of an even more devastating attack. Now the real evil had been unleashed.

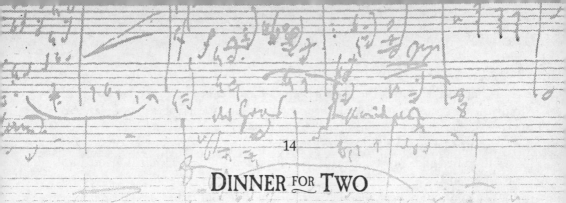

14

DINNER FOR TWO

She bid me take love easy,
as the leaves grow on the tree;
But I, being young and foolish,
with her would not agree.

W. B. YEATS

Susanna stopped the moment she stepped into the dining room and found no one there. The room was aglow with candlelight, the table set with the best china, sparkling crystal, and snowy white linen. At each end, blue violets spilled from white china bowls.

But only two places had been set.

Puzzled, she walked the rest of the way in and looked around. "What in the world…"

Her question died on her lips as Michael came into the room. Susanna took a second look at him, suddenly glad she'd changed into her blue silk instead of relying on one of her everyday ginghams. He had obviously gone to some trouble with his own appearance. His gray jacket was informal but, as always, perfectly tailored for his tall form, and he'd donned a pearl-hued cravat that lent a touch of elegance. His dark hair, which lately seemed to be taking on more and more silver, had been brushed into as much control as was possible, given its natural unruliness.

"Susanna?" he said. He invariably sensed her presence in a room—a fact which never failed to please her.

"Michael, what's going on? Where are Caterina and your father? And Paul?"

"Papa and Caterina dined early, while you were at the MacGoverns'. Papa is seeing to Cati's bedtime. And Pauli is attending the birthday party for his friend Enzo this evening, remember?"

He touched her shoulder and, with the accuracy of one who was perfectly sighted, pulled her chair out and waited for her to be seated.

"So, we're dining alone?" she said.

He nodded and took the place to her right, at the head of the table. "*Si*, it is only the two of us tonight. And since that makes it a special occasion, I planned a special meal for us—a traditional Italian supper."

Susanna looked at him. "*Moira* cooked a traditional Italian supper?"

He smiled and shook his head. "No. Papa and I did most of it. I wanted to surprise you."

"You and your papa? Well—I *am* surprised. But your father should be eating with us if he helped to prepare the meal." It occurred to Susanna that Michael's father had been puttering about Moira Dempsey's kitchen quite a lot since he'd arrived at Bantry Hill. Or at least it seemed that way. With Michael being one of the few exceptions, anyone who dared invade Moira's domain could count on being bullied off the premises. Either Riccardo Emmanuel had managed to ingratiate himself with the Irish housekeeper, or else he had somehow employed a few bullying techniques of his own.

"We prepared more than enough for Papa and Cati to indulge themselves earlier," Michael said. "They seemed pleased, so I hope you will be, too."

He found her hand and covered it with his. "I wanted us to have an evening alone for a change. It seems as though we're always hurrying to do something, you in one place, I in another. And always there are others with us. Especially over the past weeks."

"I know. But there's been nothing to do for it except—manage. What with Maylee needing more attention lately…and Vangie's illness…and looking after Caterina, and then with your father here—of course, he's wonderful with Caterina—"

"I'm not complaining, Susanna," he interrupted. "It's just that I've missed you. I need to have you to myself now and then."

Susanna's heart turned over as she studied the dark, handsome face she'd come to love. "I've missed you, too," she said softly. "And this is nice, Michael. I'm glad you thought of it."

Now that the surprise was wearing off, in fact, Susanna found herself exceedingly pleased. It was a rare occasion indeed these days when she and Michael found any time alone to just sit and talk for a few minutes, much less to enjoy a leisurely meal together. They worked together on the music, of course, but with Michael, work meant work, with little time spent on conversation. Besides, they were usually a trio, not a duet, for Paul almost always worked with them.

Just then young Rebecca MacBride, a local girl who sometimes helped Moira in the kitchen, appeared, balancing a tray with a soup tureen and bowls. Susanna discreetly slipped her hand away from Michael's and spoke to the girl before she left the room.

One taste of the smooth, clear broth and Susanna looked up. "Michael! This is delicious. What is it?"

"*Stracciatella*," he said, tasting his own. "Papa used to make this when I was a little boy. It's really just eggs and broth and cheese. A little parsley, some semolina. I'm glad you like it."

He took another spoonful of soup, then said, "So, how is Mrs. MacGovern getting along now?"

Susanna delayed her reply. These days, it seemed that any discussion involving Vangie MacGovern and her family was one marked not only by sadness and concern, but also by unanswered questions. It was difficult to gauge Vangie's condition, other than to observe that it wasn't good.

"Vangie is still—I don't know how to describe her, Michael. She's so awfully sad, of course. And physically, what with the difficult time she had—"

"With the birth," he put in.

"Yes." Susanna didn't like to think about that part of things, much less speak of it with Michael. She feared he might sense the apprehension that had taken root in her since the night she'd witnessed Vangie's ordeal.

Michael was keenly sensitive; he missed little, especially where she was concerned. Susanna would hate for him to learn that she was such a coward as to be frightened at the idea of bearing a child.

She wanted Michael's child—she truly did—and she knew she ought to be willing to give him as many children as he wanted. He was a wonderful father to Caterina. The thing with Michael was that he genuinely enjoyed being a father and treated the role not so much as a responsibility, but more as a joy, a delight.

If only she hadn't seen what Vangie went through...

"Where have you gone, *cara*?"

"What?" Susanna looked up to see him frowning, obviously waiting for her to go on. "I'm sorry. I'm really worried about Vangie, Michael. She doesn't seem to be regaining her strength as she should. But it's more than that—it's as if she's dead inside. She doesn't talk unless she absolutely has to, even to Mr. MacGovern. And the baby—she seems almost...indifferent to him. He's not thriving a bit, the poor wee thing."

She stopped. "Moira says a baby can sense when he doesn't have the mother's full attention or affection. It's a terrible situation, and there doesn't seem to be any help for it."

Again Michael found her hand—and again the MacBride girl interrupted them, this time to exchange their soup bowls for two small plates holding a variety of cheeses.

"You really cannot do anything more than you're doing, Susanna," he said after the MacBride girl exited the room again. "Andrew says the shock of losing the older son will most likely delay the physical healing."

Susanna sighed, pushing a piece of cheese around on her plate. "I keep thinking that if Vangie could only warm to the new baby, perhaps that would be the first step in healing her heart."

Michael nodded. "*Sì*, you may well be right. There is something about a child, a new baby—"

Again he reached for her hand. "We've never talked very much about our own children, *cara*. What are your thoughts?"

Susanna froze. *Not now*, she thought, struggling for a way to change the subject.

She expelled a quick breath of relief when Rebecca returned to collect their cheese plates and proceeded to serve the main course—delicately herbed roast chicken and a bowl of small potatoes in a white sauce with parsley.

"You do realize," she said lightly after the MacBride girl was gone, "that you may have to roll me out of the room after this meal? I'm eating twice as much as I should."

"Good. Papa thinks you're too thin."

Unreasonably irritated by this offhand remark, Susanna bit down a response. Lately it seemed that Michael's father found quite a few traits in her that didn't meet with his approval. She was too young to understand world events—and therefore Riccardo tended to ignore any comment she might offer on the subject. She spent too much time doing household chores—she should let the staff take care of the menial tasks so she could spend more time with Caterina. Her presence tended to divert Michael's attention from his work—perhaps Paul's assistance would be less distracting. On the other hand, she needed to spend more time developing her own musical gifts—so she could be of more assistance to Michael.

And now she was too thin—as if she needed to have that particular fact pointed out.

"Susanna? Papa meant nothing. Don't be offended."

"I'm not," she said too quickly.

"You should know," he went on, "that my mother was, shall we say, a *substantial* woman. Like Papa. He thought she was the most beautiful woman in the world. He is, perhaps, a somewhat old-fashioned Italian male in the respect that he appreciates, ah…ample-figured women."

"But your mother wasn't Italian. She was Irish," Susanna pointed out.

"True, but they spent most of their time in Italy. Papa sometimes joked that the Tuscan sun had boiled most of the Irish out of her blood."

Susanna made no reply.

"You *are* offended," Michael said after a moment. "I shouldn't have repeated his remark. I apologize."

"Really, Michael, don't worry about it. It's not as if your father isn't right, after all," she said, trying for a note of lightness. "Rosa has offered the same observation."

He stopped eating and raised his head with a look of displeasure. "I hope you will ignore both of them, then." He smiled. "To me, you are perfect just as you are."

Again he paused. "We should change the subject. Why don't we return to the pleasant topic of children? Our children."

Susanna looked at him, swallowed hard, but tried to keep her tone level. "I don't think I'm…comfortable with that, Michael. We're not married yet, after all."

She sounded priggish and artificial even to herself, but she was determined to deflect this conversation. She simply wasn't ready for it, not yet. He would hear the unease in her voice and be disturbed, perhaps would even be impatient with her.

"But we are betrothed." He hesitated. "You don't think it proper for us to discuss having children?"

"It's just that Rebecca will be in and out to continue serving, don't you see? Wouldn't it be better to wait for another time?"

"Ah, *sì*." Seemingly satisfied with her answer, he patted her hand. "Could we at least discuss the date for our wedding, then? Don't you think it's time we settled on it and announced it?"

His expression, endearingly boyish, even eager, warmed Susanna's heart. "I expect we should, but how on earth do I plan a wedding with everything else that's going on right now?"

"You don't," he said easily. "We let Rosa plan the wedding. She has already offered, no?"

"She has, yes, but even with Rosa taking charge, I can't possibly be ready before—fall, at least."

He arched an eyebrow. "I was thinking of next month."

"Next month? Michael, you know very well that's impossible! I couldn't begin to—"

A corner of his mouth turned up.

"Oh! You're teasing me again."

"*Sì*, but not altogether. I would marry you tomorrow if it were possible." He leaned toward her, his intention to kiss her patently clear.

Rebecca MacBride picked that moment to return, carrying a large plate of fruit and a smaller one of fruit tarts.

Susanna warned Michael off by clearing her throat and saying, "Good heavens, Michael, how many courses are we to have?"

He shrugged. "Papa and I might have gotten a little carried away."

"Well, I won't fault you for it. Everything is wonderful."

"We'll have our coffee in the drawing room," he told Rebecca, adding under his breath for Susanna's benefit, "where we will also discuss a date—in the near future—for our wedding."

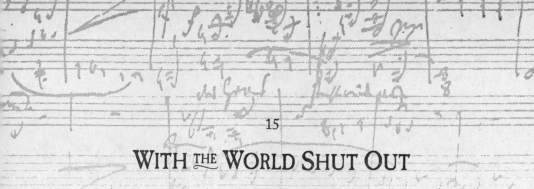

15

WITH THE WORLD SHUT OUT

We two clung together—with the world shut out.

ETHNA CARBERY

They sat together on the drawing room sofa. Michael reluctantly kept a discreet distance between them, sensing that Susanna might shy away from any real closeness with him tonight.

He found the thought particularly painful in light of his high hopes for the evening.

She had been distant for days now. He hadn't questioned her about it, instead had pretended he didn't notice.

But how could he not notice? It wasn't so much that she was avoiding him, but more that when they were together she seemed, if not exactly reserved, then at the least preoccupied, as if she always had something on her mind.

Something besides him.

The truth was that her uncharacteristic remoteness had been part of the reason he'd planned a private supper for tonight. He'd hoped not only to secure her undivided attention and set a firm date for their wedding, but also to discover whatever might be responsible for the peculiar way she was acting.

He realized it might be nothing more than the time she spent in caring for Caterina and looking after the many household and family affairs—including her efforts on behalf of Maylee and the MacGovern family. Not to mention the hours she spent each week helping him and Paul with his own music and the program music for the orchestra.

Still, he couldn't help but wonder if there was something more. He hoped it wasn't his father. The remark about her being "too thin" had clearly annoyed her. He should never have mentioned it. But Susanna had been withdrawn for days, not merely tonight, so any thoughtless comments on his father's part—or his own—couldn't be entirely responsible.

"Susanna? Before we discuss our wedding plans, there's something I need to ask you. And I want you to be very honest with me."

Even before he ventured the question, he could almost feel her tense.

"You seem—remote of late," he said carefully. "I'm wondering if something is wrong? Have I done something?"

There was just the slightest delay before she replied, only enough to let him know she was thinking about how to frame her answer.

"No. No, of course, not, Michael. There's nothing wrong."

"What is it then?"

"Nothing, really. I…suppose I've just been busy."

Her voice was thin, less than convincing.

"Susanna, I can't help but think it might be more than that. Hm?"

There was a long silence in which Michael found himself holding his breath. Was she already regretting her decision to marry him? Questioning her feelings for him? Had he rushed her into a relationship she now regretted?

He heard her sigh, and his chest tightened.

When she finally spoke, she sounded hesitant and strained—even somewhat ill at ease, as if she were trying to avoid something unpleasant. "I don't know exactly. I'm sorry if I haven't been very good company. Perhaps I am preoccupied. Lately, there's been so much to do. And there seems to be so much… unhappiness…all around us."

She paused. "With Maylee's condition growing worse and all that's happened to the poor MacGovern family, it's difficult to be…lighthearted. But it has nothing to do with you, Michael. Truly, it doesn't. I suppose it's simply affected me more than I'd realized. I'm sorry if I haven't been myself."

He let out an unsteady breath, unable to let himself completely relax, yet relieved to hear that he wasn't the problem.

"Don't apologize," he said. "I know it's been a difficult time for you. And no doubt I've put too much on you. I've let you do more than you should."

"No, Michael! It's not that. I do what I do because I want to, because I can't… *not* do it. I suppose I'm just a little tired."

He heard her attempt to force a little more brightness into her voice and realized that perhaps she *was* simply overtired.

"What can I do to make things easier for you, *cara*? I'll hire more help—"

"No, please don't, Michael! It would only mean more people about the house, and I honestly don't want that. Really, you're making far too much of this. I'm perfectly fine. Don't worry so."

He moved closer to her and took her hand. There was no response to his touch, but still he coaxed her closer. "It might be that we should at least consider hiring a nurse for Maylee. In the meantime, I'll see if Andrew—or Dr. Cole, perhaps—can come more often. Not only for Maylee, but for Mrs. MacGovern and the infant as well."

He hesitated. "And, Susanna? Please don't let Papa upset you. He means well, but he doesn't always think before he speaks. He adores you—I know he does."

He felt her tense, but only for a moment. "And I've grown very fond of him, too, Michael. Really, I have. I'm just not quite used to his ways yet. He's so… different from you."

He laughed a little. "Papa is different from anyone and everyone."

He took a deep breath, sensing that she'd begun to relax, at least a little. "So, then, you do still want to marry me?"

"Michael! You know I do. Why would you ask me such a foolish question?"

He drew her closer and pressed his lips against her temple, allowing himself to savor the warm softness of her skin, the sunny scent of her hair—Paul had told him it was the color of warm honey—the sheer happiness of holding her in his arms. "Then marry me soon, Susanna," he whispered. "We can be married here at the house. A simple ceremony—you said that's what you wanted, no? Nothing large or complicated. What do we really need, after all? Just you and me and our family."

He heard the smile in her voice. "A pastor, too, I think."

"*Sì*, all right. A pastor."

"And I'll need a gown. Nothing elaborate. But even so, it will take time."

He feigned a groan. "How much time?"

"Well, time for fittings, and the actual sewing—and alterations. It can't be done overnight, Michael. You see? One can hardly rush a wedding. You'll have to be patient."

He heard the note of teasing in her voice and felt something deep inside of him finally relax. She suddenly sounded happy—happier than he'd heard her for days.

"How patient?"

"Well…perhaps by late summer."

"That's months away!" he groaned.

A thought occurred to him. It would be just like her…

"Susanna…*cara*? Are you quite certain that you really want a simple wedding—a small ceremony? You're not just saying that because you believe it's what I want? Because of my…earlier marriage?"

She stiffened in his arms. "Your marriage to Deirdre has nothing to do with my wanting a small wedding, Michael," she said. "I simply don't want a large, showy ceremony with a lot of people. Only those closest to us." She paused. "I thought we'd agreed on that."

"*Sì*, we did. I merely want to make certain. I want you always to tell me what you want, Susanna, so there will be no misunderstandings between us. More than anything else, I want your happiness. Your happiness and your love."

He felt her hesitate, but then she surprised him by slipping her arms around his neck and drawing his face down to hers. "You will always have my love, Michael," she said softly. "And my happiness will be making you happy."

Michael thought his heart would explode. Gently, he framed her face with his hands, kissed her forehead, then found her lips. He kissed her and felt her breath quicken with his as he kissed her again, dizzy with the euphoria of her closeness.

He wished he never had to stop, wished he could keep her this close...closer... always. Suddenly, she released him, pushed him away. In that instant he heard his father's sharp voice and shot to his feet, bringing Susanna with him.

"Michael! Some wonderful news! You must listen to this! *Scusi*, Susanna, but this is very important!"

Shaken, Michael heard Susanna's gasp and knew she was mortified by his father walking in on them, finding them in such an intimate embrace. He reached for her hand and found it trembling.

He was both embarrassed for her and irritated with his father, who might have had the forethought to knock before bursting into the room.

On the other hand, he realized with some self-consciousness, it was he, not his father, who had put Susanna in this awkward position.

He felt Susanna try to tug free of his hand as if to flee the room, but he kept a firm grip. "No, stay," he said, his voice low. "Please."

"*Sì, sì*, Susanna! You must stay and hear this, too!" His father sounded unaware that he'd interrupted a most private moment. Or if he did realize it, he didn't seem in the least contrite.

"Here, now—listen to this," said his father. "From the newspapers. It seems that Giocomo Conti is planning a new production of *Lucia di Lammermoor* next fall. And this is what you must hear, Michael. In this interview, Conti states that he will settle for no lesser tenor in the part of Edgardo than 'the legendary Michael Emmanuel'! Here, there's more—listen to this: 'I shall do everything in my power to coax the great Emmanuel out of his premature retirement. I mean to have him as Edgardo. No one else will do.'"

Michael heard the rustle of pages as if his father were waving the paper about in the air.

"You see, Michael? This is what I have been trying to tell you. Even the great Conti knows you are without equal. He refuses to allow you to waste your gift. You belong on the opera stage, and he does not intend to let you forget it!"

Michael took a long breath, striving for patience. "Papa—I made my choice, and I have never regretted it. You know this. We have talked about it many times. I have no intention of going back to the opera. Not ever."

"You are not pleased that a musician of Conti's stature would demand you for his own production of *Lucia*? Do you not understand the magnitude of such a compliment?"

"Of course I understand, Papa. And I am honored that he thinks so highly of me. But I have no interest in doing this. It is no longer a part of my life."

Michael felt Susanna squeeze his hand and knew a quick rush of gratitude for her understanding. She, more than anyone else, grasped why he had left the world of opera and why he would never return.

"*Insensato!*" his father exploded. "Foolish! God created you with a voice unlike any other. A voice of angels! And you throw it away as if it is nothing but filthy rags! I do not understand you, *mio figlio*! I do not understand you at all!"

Michael gripped Susanna's hand even more tightly. "I'm sorry if I've disappointed you, Papa. But it's not as if I haven't tried to explain."

He could almost see his father shaking his head and waving a hand in the air.

"Explain, explain! There is no explaining how you could so carelessly discard such an opportunity. Such a great gift!"

And then he was gone, and Michael was left to feel an uncommon weight of guilt and anger. Guilt that he couldn't be what his father wanted him to be. And anger that he should feel guilty for following God's voice instead of his own.

～

Susanna watched in astonishment and indignation as Riccardo Emmanuel whipped around and went stomping from the room, slapping the newspaper against the palm of one hand. How dare he treat Michael as if he were nothing more than an obstreperous child? It was bad enough that he had degraded both of them by charging into the room unannounced, coming upon them in a moment meant only for the two of them. But to excoriate Michael for taking a path not of Riccardo's choosing, when Michael meant only to be obedient to God's will for his life—that was outrageous.

She fought to dismiss her own embarrassment. For Michael's sake, she mustn't let him know that his father had thoroughly humiliated her. But in truth, once again they had opened themselves to temptation by being alone so late, unchaperoned—and, admittedly, so in need of each other. Still, she wished it hadn't taken Riccardo Emmanuel to point out their folly.

"I'm sorry, Susanna," Michael said, his voice hoarse. "I should never have put you in such an awkward position. This is entirely my fault. Papa—I doubt he understands how difficult it is for us, living under the same roof, loving each other, yet compelled to avoid any real…intimacy. It won't happen again, I promise you."

Susanna reached to put a hand to his lips. "Don't apologize, Michael. You weren't alone in this, after all. I am just as responsible as you. I'm sorry for the way it must have looked to your father. If there's any fault in our behavior, it falls to both of us."

Oh, Father, forgive me for allowing this situation to develop in the first place.

She studied him, wondering if she should actually voice what she was thinking. "I'm far more concerned that he's hurt you, Michael. This matter with the newspaper—he was just excited. I'm sure your father didn't mean to denigrate your work. He's very proud of you. You must make allowances. He doesn't understand."

"He never has. I fear he never will. I've tried to explain, but he doesn't hear me. He doesn't *want* to hear me, I think."

"He is proud of you and your music, Michael—all that you've accomplished," Susanna repeated gently. "But he's also very proud of your voice. I think he's even in awe of it, and I can understand that. So am I. But he hasn't been here, to know what it's like for you, and so it's difficult for him to accept the choice you made. He'll come around eventually. You'll see."

He gave a short nod, but Susanna could tell he was still dubious.

He drew her closer, clasping her shoulders. "Susanna, I am truly sorry that he embarrassed you. I apologize for that. But I won't apologize for the way I feel about you, for wanting to be with you. I can't help being impatient to make you my wife."

Susanna searched his face, saw the depth of his emotion—the love and the desire shadowing his strong features—and realized they mirrored her own. "And I'm impatient to be your wife, Michael," she said softly. "But you have a child to consider. We have to guard our reputations, not only for ourselves, but for Caterina's sake. We've known each other less than a year, after all, and Caterina's mother was my own sister. In August, it will be a year since I came to Bantry Hill. I think we must wait at least until then to marry."

His expression and the long breath he expelled told her he was conceding. "I don't like it, but I suppose you are right." He dipped his head a little. "August, then. But no later."

"No later."

With one large hand, he cupped the back of her head, touching his lips to hers ever so gently, then brought his cheek to hers. "Susanna? Please understand—it isn't just physical need that makes me coax you to marry me soon. It's much more than that. I want to be with you. All the time. I want to know that you're my wife, that we belong to each other. I want you beside me every moment, in everything I do. I'm so eager to begin our life together, to be a family...you and me and Caterina...and our children. You do understand, don't you, *cara?*"

Susanna moved back just enough to bring a hand to his bearded cheek. "Yes, Michael. I understand. And I want...what you want. I truly do."

Even children?

For just a second, she felt the anxiety return to her in a flash of memory, an image of Vangie MacGovern in agony, a rush of fear and shame.

Then her gaze went over his face, loving the strength, the nobility of his features, the faint lines that webbed from his eyes, the humor and kindness about his generous mouth. And in that moment she knew that she loved this man so deeply, so completely, she would spend a lifetime giving him whatever he wanted from her.

Including a houseful of children, if that was his desire.

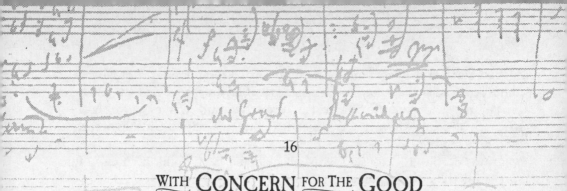

16

WITH CONCERN FOR THE GOOD

Peace does not mean the end of all our striving.
Joy does not mean the drying of our tears.

G. A. STUDDERT KENNEDY

Early the next afternoon, while Caterina was taking her nap, Susanna picked up the section of newspaper Michael's father had discarded in the library the night before. Papa Emmanuel had left it folded open to the article he had found so exciting the night before. She merely scanned the piece, since she already knew its contents. In truth, it brought an unpleasant taste to her mouth as she recalled her embarrassment from the night before and the scene the article had prompted between Michael and his father.

She opened the paper and flipped through another few pages until she found the editorial section and settled in to read the letters to the editor. She read this section regularly, in part because they were sometimes so foolish as to be amusing, but also because they pointed out legitimate issues that needed to be brought to public attention.

By the time she neared the end of the first letter, however, and found the reference to the "shocking" association with a "female practitioner," Susanna's heart was pounding painfully against her rib cage.

Surely she was jumping to conclusions. But was she? How many physicians in the city of New York worked in partnership with a woman?

But the writer couldn't be referring to Andrew Carmichael! How could anyone accuse him of such a horrible thing? Why, the Scottish physician was goodness itself. Next to Michael, Susanna had never met such a godly, kindhearted man.

She stood there, her eyes locked on the appalling accusation. Even if it weren't aimed at Andrew, weren't readers likely to believe it was? Just look at how quickly she had latched on to the assumption.

An accusation like this could be disastrous to a physician. It could ruin the man!

She grabbed the paper and hurried out of the room in search of Michael, almost certain he knew nothing of this as yet. If he did, he would have told her. If he didn't—and if indeed the letter was directed toward Andrew Carmichael—Michael needed to know. The two men had formed a close friendship over the preceding months.

It was possible, of course, that Michael would likely think her foolish for suspecting the letter referred to Dr. Carmichael.

And she fervently hoped he would be right.

~

When at home, Michael made it a regular part of his daily routine to visit with Maylee early in the afternoon. He found the child wise beyond her years and her company a true pleasure.

As was usually the case, her door was open. He rapped softly on the frame before entering.

"Oh, Mr. Emmanuel—I'm here, by the window! I just saw Mr. MacGovern take the black stallion out for a run. Isn't he wonderful?"

"Mr. MacGovern or the black stallion?"

Maylee giggled, and Michael walked the rest of the way into the room. He loved to make this child laugh. She had had so little reason for merriment in her brief, difficult life that to hear her break into genuine delight was a gift to his own heart.

"Do you have time to sit with me, Mr. Emmanuel?"

Michael felt for the chair across from her and sat down. "That's why I came, my young friend. And how are you this afternoon?"

He heard the slight delay before her reply. "I'm feeling very well, thank you."

Michael smiled a little. "Do you know, you always give me the same answer, Maylee? Now then, tell me—how do you *really* feel?"

"I feel…happy, Mr. Emmanuel," she said quietly. "Bantry Hill is so very beautiful, you see, and everyone has been so kind to me. It makes me happy just to be here."

Pleased, Michael leaned forward a little. "And it makes me very happy to hear you say that."

She was silent for a time, and Michael could almost hear her thinking.

Then, "I've been wanting to ask you if it's all right if I call you as others do—Maestro. 'Mr. Emmanuel' doesn't seem to suit you, but you're much too old for me to call you by your given name," she said, her tone altogether serious. "It would be disrespectful, I think."

Michael smiled at her directness. "I *am* very old."

"Oh, I'm sorry. I didn't mean that you're *very* old—"

Still smiling, Michael warded off her apology. "I'm teasing you. You may call me whatever is most comfortable for you, Maylee."

"All right, then. I'll call you *Maestro*, although I'm not exactly sure what it means."

"It's a word most often used for a conductor or a teacher, sometimes an expert in one of the arts, most especially music."

"That makes it sound just a little stuffy."

"Ah. Stuffy. That makes me feel even older, I think."

"But not as old as I, *Maestro*."

Michael winced at her soft reply. He extended his hand to her, and when he felt the small, fragile hand clasp his—the dryness of the skin, the fragility of the bones—he had to struggle to conceal the dismay that rose in him. "Is there anything I can do for you this afternoon, Maylee? Anything you need?"

She didn't answer right away. When she did, the brightness was back in her voice. "There is something."

"You've only to ask."

"Would you say a prayer for me? Like you did yesterday?"

"But of course." Michael leaned forward and extended his other hand to her. He was careful to apply only the slightest of pressure as she entrusted both her delicate hands to his much larger ones.

So dainty, these small hands, so tiny and fragile. The hands of a child, yet with the frailty of the aged.

Misericordia, Signore, misericordia. Mercy, Lord, mercy.

"*Gesu*, Lord and Savior," he prayed, "I thank You for my young friend, Maylee, for bringing her to us here, to our home, and for the inspiration of her faith, the light she has brought to Bantry Hill. Please may You wrap Your love around her and carry her through the hours of this day, close to your heart…warmed by Your grace. Let her heart sing with hope through the day—through all her days. Never may her spirit bow to anything but Your majesty and Your holiness, *Gesu*, and may her soul know no, ah…no boundaries save the fortress of Your love. Amen."

Maylee echoed her own amen, the sweetness of her voice warming Michael's heart.

After a moment, he pressed her hands ever so gently, then stood. "I must go to work now," he said. "I hope you have a good day, Maylee. Is your friend Renny Magee coming to call?"

"I think so. I hope so."

Michael started for the door, turning back when she said, "Mr. Emmanuel—Maestro?"

"*Sì?*"

"I—may I ask you a question?"

"You may ask me anything."

"Can you…see—in your mind?"

"In my mind?" Michael smiled and nodded. "Yes, I can."

"Well, then, what do you see when you pray?"

Michael hesitated, momentarily confused. "I'm not sure I understand."

"I wondered...can you see Jesus? When you pray, I mean. Can you see Him?

"No one sees Jesus, Maylee, except for the Father," Michael said, still puzzled. "Why do you ask this?"

Her reply was slow in coming, her voice quiet. "Because when you pray, I can almost imagine that *I* see Jesus. That's why I like it so much when you pray. It's as if He's right here, in the room with us."

Michael swallowed. "And so He is, child," he said softly. "So He is."

~

Michael was at the piano in the music room when Susanna found him, working on a theme she recognized from one of the chorales in his *American Anthem*. She hesitated before entering the room, willing to postpone her unsettling errand for a moment to enjoy the music.

Something was new about the piece, which Susanna and Paul had already notated several times. The motif was the same, both haunting and beguiling, but the harmonies were different. Richer, somehow. Susanna always marveled at how Michael could take a piece she believed was perfect and, with a little tinkering, make it even more wonderful.

Papa Emmanuel was surely right that his son had a gift, a gift from God.

What he couldn't see was that Michael, far from squandering the gift, was working hard to offer it back to the Creator in the most faithful way possible.

She gave a little sigh, but then the music ceased as Michael called out her name. Pushing back the bench and rising to his feet, he turned toward her with a smile. She sighed again as she went to him.

~

Moments later, after listening to Susanna read the letter from the *Herald*, Michael stood with one hand on the mantel, the other kneading the back of his neck. His face was creased with concern, but he remained silent.

"Michael? I'm sure I'm being foolish, thinking this could be directed at Dr. Carmichael."

When he still made no reply, Susanna went on, her words rushing out. "Since the two of you have become friends, I thought you needed to know about it, in the event that someone is trying to start some sort of trouble for him."

"I'm afraid it is about Andrew," he said quietly, his profile hard and still.

Stunned, Susanna stared at him. "What makes you think that?"

With a deep sigh, he turned slightly toward her. "Andrew confided in me some months ago that there was something…regrettable in his past. Something of a most serious nature. I believe he was about to tell me the entire story. He seemed to think, since he and Dr. Cole have become not only Caterina's physicians but ours as well, that we should know about…whatever it is. I told him it wasn't necessary, that we needed to know nothing more than what we already did—that he was an excellent physician, and a friend, and that we trusted him as such."

He stopped, indicating that Susanna should sit.

She sank down onto the chair by the fireplace. She suddenly felt as chilled as if a cold wind had swept the room.

Michael remained standing, his voice heavy, as though burdened with a great weariness. "This is a very ugly thing, this letter. It would seem that Andrew has an enemy. A dangerous enemy."

"Whoever wrote this is insinuating that he's an opium addict! Surely, you don't believe that!"

He shook his head. "I don't know what to believe. But certainly I'd not believe anything in that letter unless Andrew were to tell me it was true. And I have no intention of asking him about it."

"As if he doesn't have enough trouble, with that awful arthritis he suffers from. Bethany worries so about his health."

Michael didn't answer right away. When he finally spoke, he seemed to be speaking to himself as much as to her. "I understand that his condition is exceedingly painful, at times even debilitating. I suppose there's always a possibility that because of the pain—"

He stopped, letting his thought drift off unfinished. "We can't speculate about something so important. If there's any truth to this letter—and I'm not saying I believe there is—but if there is, I know Andrew will explain it to us. Until then, we will say nothing of it to anyone else."

"I couldn't agree more. But it's impossible for me to imagine Andrew Carmichael indulging in such a vile habit! He's such a fine man, Michael."

"He is indeed. On the other hand, none of us is so strong we cannot fall. But whatever is behind this, it's clear that someone means to malign him. Even if this letter is nothing but lies, such accusations could destroy a physician's career. We need to pray for him."

"I simply don't understand why anyone would want to harm such a good man. I can't believe that Andrew Carmichael has ever hurt another human being."

Michael shook his head. "Surely, you are not so naïve as that, Susanna. We both know that good men aren't exempt from the effects of evil."

"No, of course not. But it seems so different when something like this happens to someone you know. And respect."

"*Sì*, that's true. Well, Andrew and Dr. Cole will be here tomorrow evening. Perhaps he will want to discuss the matter with us."

"I can't think what we'll say to them," Susanna said, getting to her feet.

"We will simply let them know we care and want to help however we can. Susanna, before you go—"

He reached out a hand, and Susanna went to him.

"About last night," he said. "There was no time this morning to talk with you. But I know you were deeply upset—"

"Oh, Michael, please—forget about last night! I'm perfectly fine. It was you under your father's gun, not I."

She saw him wince at her thoughtless choice of words. "I'm sorry. I didn't mean it that way."

He shook his head. "No, that's how it felt. But that's not what kept me awake last night."

She looked at him more closely, seeing for the first time the evidence of sleeplessness—the dark shadows under his eyes, the faint pallor of his skin. "What, then?"

"I think—no, I *know* I did you a disservice last night, and it bothers me very much."

"A dis—what are you talking about?"

"I should never have put you in the position I did. Being alone with you, behaving as I did—it was wrong." He inclined his head in a brief, formal bow. "I ask your forgiveness."

Susanna studied him, touched by the genuine contrition so obvious in his expression, his posture, his tone of voice. Sometimes she forgot just how gallant Michael could be. For all his worldwide travel and experience, and for all the renown and celebrity he had once enjoyed—and despite what his father and others might view as his "Americanization"—Michael was still very much of the Old World. At unexpected moments, he could display a courtly, even quaint, sense of propriety.

Susanna loved him for it. She also knew it would be a mistake to take his apology lightly. He had in no way compromised her virtue. He had not, last night or at any other time, made the slightest attempt to seduce her or to lure her into an improper situation. There was no denying that she'd been embarrassed by his father's unexpected and brash appearance. But being alone with Michael—and in his arms—had been as much her doing as Michael's.

Even so, she knew that his distress was real, that she should be careful in her reply. "It's not necessary to apologize, Michael. But thank you for caring enough to be concerned."

He lifted her hand then and touched his lips to it, a gesture that never failed to make her legs go weak while endearing him just that much more to her.

"I promise you can trust me to keep a closer guard on my feelings from now on," he said solemnly, still holding her hand to his lips.

Then he flashed that quick, boyish smile of his and added, "But only until August."

On that note, Susanna reclaimed her hand and hurried from the room, aware of the need to keep a close guard on her own feelings.

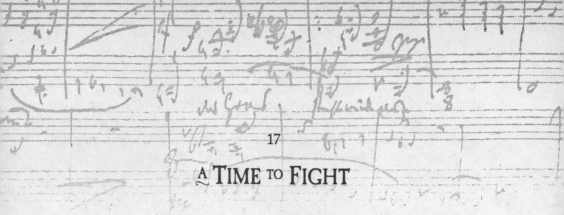

17

A TIME TO FIGHT

That my weak hand may equal my firm faith...

HENRY DAVID THOREAU

Within the week, it was painfully clear that the letter to the editor in the *Herald* was affecting the practice of Andrew Carmichael and Bethany Cole.

Fridays and Mondays were ordinarily their busiest days of the week. It wasn't unusual to find the waiting room filled to capacity on either morning. But when Bethany arrived at the office on Friday morning, she found only two patients waiting, both of whom appeared too destitute to be choosy about where they went for treatment. The patient count had been light yesterday as well, although neither she nor Andrew had remarked on it.

She greeted the patients, telling them they'd be called shortly, then went to find Andrew. To her surprise, he was seated behind his desk with Frank Donovan standing across from him. The latter seemed uncommonly serious when he greeted her. Andrew, too, had no welcoming smile, but then he'd been desperately solemn and tense ever since the ugly letter had appeared in the *Herald*.

"Frank saw the letter, too," Andrew said with no preamble. "He's convinced it was written by Warburton—or that he had it written."

Bethany glanced at Donovan and nodded. For once she agreed with the caustic Irish police sergeant.

"I still can't believe a clergyman would be capable of something like this. It boggles the mind, to think of a man of Warburton's prestige stooping to anything this low." Andrew stopped when the policeman uttered a sharp sound of derision.

"Many's the man who's plowed a crooked furrow in a straight field, Doc," said Donovan, crossing his arms over his chest. "Now tell me, what's the name of this woman Warburton was mixed up with?"

Andrew looked at him. "Lambert. Mary Lambert. But, Frank, you can't bring her into this! She's still too fragile."

Donovan pulled a sour face, then bent and splayed both hands on top of the desk. "Listen to me now, Doc. This bounder has brought bad trouble on your Mary Lambert as well as yourself. She more than likely knows the man better than anyone knows him, including his missus. And I can tell you that a woman who's been wronged by a man like Warburton is usually all too eager to pay him back."

Andrew shook his head. "Frank, Mary's not like that. And she's not well yet—"

Donovan's jaw tightened even more.

"Doc—have I ever tried to tell you how to do your job when you're sewin' someone up?"

"No, of course not, but—"

"Then don't be tellin' me how to do mine. I aim to take care of this nasty business, but you've got to trust me to do it my way. Now, where do I find this Lambert woman?"

Andrew hesitated another second or two. Then, "At the women's clinic on Baxter. I'd hoped to get her out of there before now, but there's no money to pay for a better place."

"And where are the younguns?"

Andrew frowned and leaned forward. "You leave the children out of this, Frank."

"I will if I can. But I want to know where they are, Doc."

"The boy's at Whittaker House," Andrew said after a heavy sigh. "The two little girls are at the Chatham Children's Home."

Donovan nodded, then straightened and left the office, his hat tucked under his arm.

Bethany turned toward Andrew, who sat holding his head in his hands, looking exceedingly weary. Her heart wrenched with worry to see him like this. And after what she had learned of addiction while treating Mary Lambert, she couldn't help harboring another concern. In light of this heinous attack and the effect it was having on their practice—on their *lives*—what if he simply gave up? Was there a possibility he could succumb again to his addiction?

She shook her head, as if to throw off the ugly thought. It sickened her that she had even allowed it into her mind for an instant.

"Andrew, he's right," she said. "We're in over our heads with this. Let Sergeant Donovan handle it his way."

He raised his head. "Frank can be ruthless, Bethany. Even the other men on the force keep their distance from him."

She laid a hand gently on his shoulder. "Maybe that's what it will take to put a stop to this nightmare, Andrew. And he's right about Mary Lambert. She would know more about Warburton than anyone else. She might be able to tell Donovan something that will help."

"But Mary is still so—"

"Andrew! Will you please just this once think of yourself instead of everyone else?"

He reared back as if she'd thrown a rock at him.

Bethany fought to curb her impatience. One of the reasons she loved this man was for his goodness, his genuine concern for others. But he could also be impossibly naïve, and right now he needed to face facts.

"You're in trouble, Andrew! You need help. Robert Warburton knows you can ruin him if you choose. He means to destroy you first—you must see that! And you've no idea what he might do to Mary Lambert—or the children. Do you honestly think they're safe from the likes of him?"

He went pale. "You don't believe he'd hurt his own children?"

"Oh, Andrew, I doubt this man even considers them his own. And with what he's done to that poor woman so far—and to you—I wouldn't put anything past him. Don't you see? Mary Lambert and those children are as much a threat to him as you are—even more so."

She hesitated, unwilling to cause him more pain but determined to make him see that he was in real jeopardy. "There's no telling what a man like Warburton might do to avoid the kind of scandal Mary could create for him," she said, softening her voice. "You've already seen that he's not going to stand by and let his reputation be ruined. Please, Andrew, if there's any way to stop him from ruining you, you have to let Frank Donovan handle this."

He got up—with some difficulty, Bethany noticed—and stood studying her with a worried look. Finally, he nodded. "I suppose you're right."

Pain ripped at her when she saw the hopelessness, the humiliation in his eyes. He was ashamed, she realized. Ashamed of a past he'd thought locked away, ashamed of what its revelation would mean to his patients, his practice—but most of all for what it would mean to her.

She moved closer and grasped his hands in hers. "Oh, Andrew! Don't look at me that way. We're not going to let this happen. We're going to fight it, and we're going to win! Don't you dare think anything else."

"Bethany," he said, his voice hoarse. "This isn't your battle."

Bethany lifted her hands to his shoulders and held him fiercely. "It's just as much my battle as yours! I'm going to be your wife, remember? Besides, where's your faith, Andrew?"

He frowned.

"I've heard you tell more than one troubled soul that we don't fight our battles alone, that the Lord is at the forefront fighting for us. That we've only to stand firm and believe, and He'll give us the victory."

A somewhat sheepish expression settled over him, and he even managed a faint smile. "Do you believe everything I say?"

"Do you?" Bethany countered.

He shook his head. "Hardly." He paused, searching her features. "But I do believe God's promises. And it seems you just reminded me of one of them."

Bethany framed his face in her hands and brought his head down to hers. "Then see that you don't forget it," she said, kissing him gently on the cheek and then the lips.

He pulled in a ragged breath. "Well," he said, his smile a little steadier now, "at least all this has accomplished one thing I never thought I'd see."

Bethany arched an eyebrow.

"You agreeing with Frank Donovan," he explained.

"It's not likely to become a habit."

"No," he said, cupping her chin in his hand. "I'm sure it won't."

He moved as if to kiss her again, but Bethany put a finger to his lips. "We have patients waiting. And we've kept them waiting too long."

He glanced toward the door. "Patients? Really?"

"Really," she assured him, freeing herself from his arms. "You take one, and I'll take the other."

~

Frank Donovan didn't give a second glance to the squalor surrounding the Women's Clinic and Convalescence Center. He knew it well. The area never changed, unless it was to grow even more disreputable.

He parted the boozers littering the street corner and dodged the debris—mostly broken bottles and animal waste—as he headed toward the steps. Inside, he paid little heed to the dingy surroundings, also familiar to him. Instead he went immediately to the matron, who sat at a table piled high with papers, dirty dishes, and a suspicious-looking pan covered with a towel.

There was a stench in the place that reminded him of a hospital smell but with some unidentifiable odor added—something sweet and putrid and unwashed. The woman at the table looked up as he approached. She wore a plain gray dress and threadbare white apron, and Frank noted that her hands were dirty. But then, in a place like this, perhaps it was difficult to keep them clean.

"Sergeant." The matron's tone made it clear she remembered him from their last encounter, which had been anything but agreeable. On that occasion he'd brought in a girl not yet sixteen years of age who had been repeatedly raped by a drunken stepfather, a piece of garbage who'd also passed consumption to the girl.

This particular matron had fought with Frank, insisting they could not take a consumptive patient who would likely spread the disease throughout the center. In the end, Frank had threatened to have the afflicted girl cough in the woman's face if she didn't find her a bed where she could be secluded from most of the other patients and see that she received the proper medical attention.

Her hostile glare didn't faze him now, although she gave herself airs as if he would be wise to show her some respect. To avoid laughing at the pretentious old scold, he fixed his stare on the sizable mole by the corner of her mouth.

"Where would I find Mary Lambert?" he said.

Miss Savage looked down her nose—no easy feat, Frank noted, since it was a long way down—and snapped her reply. "This isn't a hospital. We don't observe visiting hours."

"I'm not a visitor, darlin'. I'm the law."

If looks could maim, no doubt he would have found himself missing all four limbs. Miss Savage—a fitting name if ever he'd heard one—fixed a stare on Frank that sawed its way through every bone in his skull until it drilled a hole into his brain. He'd have thought the woman would warm to his endearment, for surely she would have heard precious few.

"Where," he repeated, "would I be findin' Mary Lambert?"

"Down the hall," she snapped, not looking at him. "Last room on the right."

"Ah. My thanks, dear."

Frank could feel the blade still slashing away as he turned the corner and started down the hall.

〜

He walked in without knocking and stopped just inside the room. Two sets of sagging beds faced each other on opposite sides of the room, indicating it was shared by four women. At the moment, only two occupants seemed to be present.

"Mary Lambert?" He addressed his words to the woman nearest the door. A somewhat blowzy sort, with wild black hair and knowing dark eyes—attractive enough if a man liked her kind—she looked him over and smiled. Frank smiled back, a firm believer in the old saw about catching more flies with honey than vinegar.

He was surprised when a soft reply came from the far side of the room.

"I'm Mary Lambert."

The woman curled in the chair by the window was small and fragile and looked much younger than she must be in reality, given Doc's account of the years she'd been Warburton's mistress. She had a cloud of fair hair tied back with a yellow ribbon and was swathed in a wrapper that looked to have belonged to someone twice her size.

She was not what he'd expected, to say the least.

He turned to her roommate. "Would you mind takin' a turn down the hall, lass? I need to be speakin' to Miss Lambert alone, you see." He made sure she understood he wasn't asking.

The woman got up, glanced from Mary Lambert back to Frank, then gave a lazy shrug and left the room.

Frank walked over to the window where Mary Lambert sat and took a closer look. She quickly uncurled herself and straightened, one hand gripping each arm of the chair—most likely, Frank speculated, to still their shaking.

She was slender, too slender by far, and had the fair, porcelain skin of a fine doll-baby. With her wide blue eyes and dainty features, she appeared impossibly young—and unmistakably frightened.

For a moment or more, Frank felt at a loss—a condition almost unknown to him. He had been prepared to either turn on the Irish charm and sweet-talk a fallen woman into telling him any and every tawdry little piece of information that might prove helpful in putting an end to that snake Warburton's shenanigans or, if need be, bully his way past her defenses until he had all he needed.

He was sorely afraid that this strangely childlike creature staring up at him with the fearful eyes was going to make either contrivance next to impossible. He suddenly felt as brutish as a wild boar. Even his size, which most often served as an advantage, now seemed to turn him into a great clumsy oaf, and he felt the irrational urge to keep his distance for fear his very shadow might somehow bruise the slight woman before him.

With some effort, he yanked himself back to his senses and pulled up a chair across from her. "We need to talk, Mary Lambert," he said, forcing a hard note into his tone. "My name is Frank Donovan—*Sergeant* Donovan—and I'm a friend of Dr. Carmichael's."

The apprehension in her eyes flickered and ebbed just a little, but she watched him closely, saying nothing.

"I need you to tell me everything you know about Robert Warburton," Frank said. He hated the way she seemed to crumple under the impact of his words, but she had flummoxed him just enough that he didn't quite know what tack to take with her.

"Everything," he said, doing his best to ignore the pain that had replaced the fear in her eyes.

"From what I understand," he added, "you would be knowin' him better than anyone else."

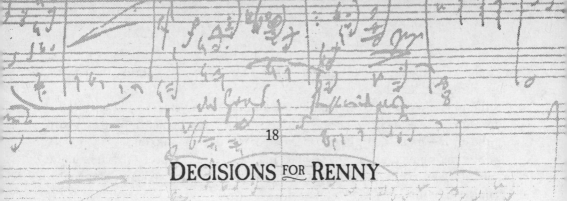

18

DECISIONS FOR RENNY

Behold me now,
And my face to a wall,
A-playing music
Unto empty pockets.

ANTHONY RAFTERY (TRANSLATED BY DOUGLAS HYDE)

Renny Magee walked the floor in the bedroom she shared with little Emma and Nell Grace, treading lightly to avoid waking the other girls. This was the second sleepless night in a row for Renny. Soon the sun would be up, and she had her chores to do no matter how poorly she was feeling. Her eyes were hot and sandy, and every few minutes her stomach roiled as if she might be sick. Was this, then, what it was like to be "flattened"?

Flattened was Conn MacGovern's word, and he used it often. It seemed to mean that he was either dead tired or famished to the point of queasiness.

Renny didn't think she was famished, although she hadn't eaten much at all yesterday, or the day before either for that matter. She definitely had that queasy, faint feeling that used to strike her when she was still on the streets of Dublin trying to earn enough coins for a proper meal.

The reason for her upset had nothing to do with hunger, but everything to do with the MacGoverns. Last night she had posed the question to herself as to whether she should leave. Sure, and no one in the family wanted her around any longer, since more than likely each of them blamed her for the death of their son and brother.

After all, she would have never made it to America in the first place had she not used Aidan MacGovern's passage to get here. Hadn't she begged to come in his place when he announced he'd not be using it? And hadn't Conn MacGovern argued up one end and down the other with Vangie that they shouldn't waste their son's ticket on the likes of Renny Magee?

But Vangie had prevailed. It had been Vangie who made the final decision to allow Renny to board with them.

By now, no doubt, Vangie surely regretted that decision.

The thought of Vangie sharpened the sickness in Renny even more. Vangie had been near to dying for days, lying still as a stone, ignoring the new babe—not eating, not talking, but simply…existing.

Even when she'd roused a bit and finally begun to nurse the infant, she paid him little heed, as if she would do what she must to keep him alive but no more. She scarcely looked at the poor wee thing. Indeed, Vangie hardly noticed anyone or anything these days, other than to give a nod by way of reply or a dull word of instruction. Even Conn MacGovern had had no success in coaxing her back to some semblance of the way she had been before their eldest son's death.

When Vangie spoke to Renny these days, which was seldom enough, she didn't actually look at her, just said what needed doing as she stared across the room or down at her hands. She didn't seem angry so much as merely…absent.

Renny thought angry might have been easier to take.

She supposed she would have to leave soon. Every day she thought to do it. But then would come the question as to how she could leave Nell Grace with most of the work of running the household and taking care of the new babe.

And how could she leave her friend, Maylee, the only true friend she'd ever had? Maylee was fading more and more every day. Lately it seemed to Renny that she would simply continue to fade until there was nothing left of her, not even a shadow.

Maylee depended on her, Renny knew—her visits, the "treasures" from outdoors, the foolish old tales and ditties from Ireland with which Renny often regaled her. How could she turn her back on Maylee?

And how could she ever bear to leave Vangie? Especially Vangie, who had become, at least in Renny's imagination, the mother she'd never had.

A mother who didn't want her, who in truth must resent her something fierce.

But, oh, wouldn't it be a terrible grief to no longer be a part of Vangie's life—of the MacGoverns' lives?

Renny looked around the pretty room with its big windows letting in the first light of dawn, and the thought of leaving it to again go on the streets was like a knife to her heart. But wasn't it more painful to live in a household where she wasn't wanted than to live on her own in a city of strangers?

Abruptly, she stopped pacing and went to wash her face. She had her chores to do, and the rest of the family would be up before long.

A few minutes later, she left the house quietly—and unnoticed.

〜

That afternoon, Renny found Maylee waiting for her. The younger girl looked a bit better today, less pallid and tired. She also looked excited. She was propped up on a huge mound of pillows with another plump cushion at her midsection. On this the kitten—Maylee had named it Cookie—was curled up in a ball, sleeping.

Renny grinned at her as she handed over the day's "treasure"—a small glass jar that held a few marbles contributed by the MacGovern twins and a scrap of pale rose material with a faint green stripe. Nell Grace had sent the latter, thinking it might be just the right size for Maylee's doll bed.

"Oh, Renny, marbles! I've never had marbles before. And this material—it's so pretty! Are you sure Nell Grace meant for me to keep it?"

Pleased by Maylee's response, Renny perched on the side of the bed. "It was her idea. And the boys have plenty more marbles."

The dozing kitten stirred, stretched, and yawned, her attention immediately fastening on the piece of material in Maylee's hands. She batted at it a few times, then lost interest and tried to poke her head down in the jar of marbles.

"No, Cookie," Maylee scolded. "You'll get stuck, you foolish kitty. Here," she said, handing the jar to Renny. "Set it on the windowsill, would you, Renny? That way the marbles will catch the light."

When Renny returned to the bed, Maylee was looking at her with an odd expression, and again Renny thought she seemed excited about something.

"The maestro wants to talk to you!" Maylee blurted out. "You're to go down the hall to his study before you leave."

Renny's hands turned clammy. What had she done?

"Why does he want to talk to me?" she croaked.

"Don't worry, Renny! It's a surprise. You'll see!"

"You know what he wants, then?"

"Yes..."

Renny could see that Maylee was both eager and reluctant to tell.

"Well?" she prompted. "What?"

Still the other girl hesitated. "Well, I don't know if I'm supposed to tell you..."

"Sure, you are!" Renny eyed her warily. "Am I in trouble for something?"

"No! Why do you always think you've done something wrong, Renny?"

Renny gave a shrug. "I used to get in trouble now and then." She paused. "Before, when I was a lot younger."

"Well, you're not in trouble now."

"I expect I can't be sure of that, now can I, since you won't tell what this is about?"

"Oh, all right! It's something really, really good, Renny! The maestro is going to ask you to play your tin whistle in the Independence Day concert! In the park!"

Renny stared at her friend. "What concert? What park? What are you talking about anyway?"

"On the Fourth of July—America's Independence Day—the maestro and his orchestra are going to perform in Central Park. It's a special celebration to celebrate the country's one hundredth birthday! And the maestro wants you to take part in it. He wants you to play your tin whistle! Aren't you excited, Renny?"

Renny made a face. "You must be mad entirely. Or else you're funnin' me. Conn MacGovern says the—maestro—is famous. Him and his orchestra both. Now just why would a man like that be wantin' anything to do with the likes of me?"

Maylee's expression turned sober. "Why are you always so hard on yourself, Renny?" she said.

"I'm not hard on myself. I'm just trying to figure out what you've been eating that's made you crackers."

Maylee shook her head. "You're forever making light of yourself. Sometimes I just can't figure you out, Renny Magee."

Renny tapped her head and grinned. "'Tis because I'm smarter than you, don't you see? Now, what brought on this foolery about the blind man and my tin whistle?"

Maylee frowned. "He has a name, Renny. Don't call him 'the blind man.' Most folks call him Maestro because he's a great musician."

"Oh, he's a great musician, is he?" Renny shot back, enjoying a chance to tease her friend. "You wouldn't be sweet on him, now would you? I'd watch out for Miss Susanna, if I were you. She won't like you taking a fancy to her sweetheart!"

"Oh, Renny, you're...incorrigible!"

Renny hadn't a thought as to what *incorrigible* meant, but she could tell that Maylee wasn't really upset with her.

"Are you going to be serious or not?" asked Maylee.

"Yes, ma'am. Please, ma'am, go ahead with your story."

"This will be a very important concert. The maestro and his orchestra will be performing some special new music he wrote in honor of the United States. There will probably be thousands of people there, according to Miss Susanna."

Renny studied her friend. Confusion and disbelief warred with a flare of excitement. Maylee couldn't know what she was talking about. Could she? Why, the blind man—the maestro—had never even heard her play the whistle.

She didn't realize she'd voiced the thought aloud until Maylee replied.

"He has so heard you, Renny. Plenty of times. When you visit me—and outdoors too."

Still skeptical, Renny didn't reply. The man was Conn MacGovern's employer, after all, and MacGovern was her employer. That being the case, the maestro was the head of this whole place and the boss of them all. Why would he even give her a thought?

Still, she'd have to say that he was always kind enough when they chanced to meet—which was seldom indeed. He never treated her like most of the grownups back in Ireland had, as if she were no more than a troublesome dog on the street. To the contrary, he was politeness itself. He would give her a smile and a funny little bow and call her "Miss Renny," almost as if she were a lady.

Ha! That was because he couldn't see her. One glance would tell him Renny Magee weren't no lady! Though Vangie had done her best to tame her hair, it more often than not stuck out like a destroyed bird's nest. And although she had taken to wearing a skirt now and again—only to humor Vangie, of course—she wore a pair of boy's trousers under the skirt so she could climb a tree whenever she wanted or go hiking in the woods without scraping her legs.

Maylee's voice jarred her back to her surroundings. "Renny? You're not afraid of the maestro, are you?"

Renny straightened. "I'm afraid of no man," she stated. "And certainly not a blind man."

Maylee looked hurt, and Renny instantly wished she could take her words back. "I didn't mean anything," she muttered. "But I'm not afraid."

In truth, she wasn't afraid of him. It was just that she never quite knew how to act around the man or what to say. It was strange, even uncomfortable, knowing he couldn't see her, when she could see him.

"Well," she said, giving a small laugh, "perhaps you ought to tell the maestro what I look like. That would take care of this peculiar notion of his, I'll warrant."

"See," said Maylee, "you're doing it again."

"Doing what?"

"Making light of yourself. The maestro wouldn't care what you look like, even if you were ugly as an old witch—which you're not. He wants you for the music you make with your tin whistle, not for the way you look." She paused. "You don't even know how pretty you are, do you, Renny?"

Renny burst out laughing. "Now I know you're crackers! You're touched in the head for certain, girl!"

Maylee just shook her head. "You ought to appreciate what you have, Renny. You could always look like me, you know."

Renny swallowed, suddenly feeling awful. Poor Maylee, too thin by far, and with her almost bald scalp and peeling skin and old-age spots all over her hands and arms. There was no denying that she looked more like a little old lady than a girl of eleven years.

"You're pretty, too," she lied without a qualm.

Maylee smiled at her. "No, I'm not. But I will be someday."

Renny cocked her head and looked at her.

"Some day I won't look like my own grandmother anymore. I'll have a perfect body, and I'll be strong and healthy. Like you."

It dawned on Renny then, what the other girl was getting at. "You're thinking about heaven," she said.

Maylee glanced toward the window, where the late afternoon sun had struck the glass jar of marbles with shafts of light that made them sparkle and flare. "Yes," she said softly. "I think about heaven a lot."

When she turned back, there was a look in her eyes that squeezed Renny's heart and yet made her wonder at the stillness her friend seemed to wear like a cloak.

"Sometimes," Maylee went on in the same quiet voice, "I can't wait to get to heaven, so I won't look like this or hurt anymore or be a bother to others. Some day I'll be out of all this."

She glanced down at her frail body. "Someday I'll be able to be myself, the way I really am inside, instead of what people think I am now, when they can only see the outside of me. I'll be able to run. I could even challenge you to a race—what do you think of that? Or maybe I'll even be able to fly." She smiled. "I think it would be the finest thing of all, to be able to fly. To just throw off this ugly old body and fly free."

Renny didn't know what to say. She simply stood, staring at the floor and trying hard not to think about the day Maylee was referring to. Because that day would mean her friend would be gone. Gone forever.

"Now, then, Renny Magee," Maylee broke into her thoughts, her tone now brisk and matter-of-fact. "You just march yourself down the hall and listen to what the maestro has to say. I promised I'd send you to him when you arrived, so you mustn't wait any longer. Besides," she added, "I'm very busy. I'm making you a present for Easter."

"You're making *me* a present?"

Maylee nodded. "Easter Sunday is next week, and I'm making something I think you'll like. It's not much, of course, since I can't go out to get what I need. But Miss Susanna is helping me." She paused. "I love Easter, don't you? I love hearing about the empty tomb, how Jesus escaped from being dead and came back to life, to live forever."

Renny liked the story about Jesus rising from the dead, too, but right now her mind was racing, already trying to think of a gift—something special—she could get for Maylee. Only when the other girl gave her a stern look and wagged a finger at her, ordering her once more to "go," did she start for the door.

⌒

More than an hour later, Renny practically flew down the hill between the Big House and the MacGovern cottage.

Maylee had been right! The maestro had asked her to play her tin whistle at the concert.

There would be two fiddles, he'd said. Two fiddles, an Irish drum—the *bodhran*—and herself, with her tin whistle. She would be playing his music—music he'd written himself. A "selection" he'd called it, with an Irish "motif," whatever that meant.

He and Miss Susanna would help her with the music, he'd told her. "Although I expect you'll pick it up quickly, gifted as you are," he'd said.

Gifted. A great musician like himself had called her "gifted"!

Faith, and her not knowing the first thing about the dark squiggles on the paper he'd showed her or the fancy words he'd used in that Eye-talian way he had of speaking.

And she was to be *paid*, he'd said! She would be paid to trill a tune or two with some fiddlers and a drum.

Renny was tempted to pinch herself to make sure it was real!

She was nearly wild with excitement, so much so that not until she reached the back door did the thought of the MacGoverns and their troubles come barreling in on her. But the minute she stepped into the kitchen and heard the babe wailing in the bedroom and saw Nell Grace all teary-eyed with wee Emma squirming in her arms, it all came rushing back.

She felt a sting of guilt for allowing herself such happiness when the people she loved more than everything in the world were burdened with so much trouble.

Only then did she remember that she probably wouldn't even be here for that foolish concert in July. More than likely, she would be gone by then.

And so, more than likely, would Maylee.

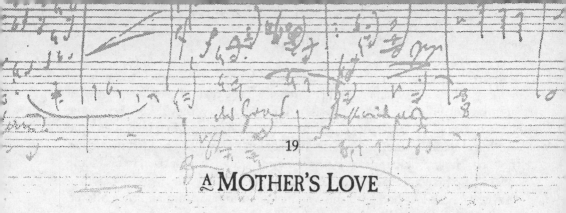

19

A MOTHER'S LOVE

If I were drowned in the deepest sea,
Mother o' mine, O mother o' mine!
I know whose tears would come down to me,
Mother o' mine, O mother o' mine!
If I were damned o' body and soul,
I know whose prayers would make me whole,
Mother o' mine, O mother o' mine!

RUDYARD KIPLING

Conn MacGovern had known few days without worry over the past twenty years. Lately, he had known not even one.

Pitchfork in hand, he straightened, catching the perspiration on his brow with his shirt sleeve. He stood leaning on the door of Amerigo's stall, breathing in the pungent odors of the stables and the horses, staring at nothing, worrying about everything.

Behind him, the big black stallion threw his glossy head over the door of the stall, snuffled Conn's neck inquisitively, then snorted and returned to his restless pacing. They got along well, the big horse and the big Irishman. In a sense, they'd rescued each other—Amerigo from the brutal treatment of his previous handlers, Conn from a life of jobless misery in the slums of New York. Their chance encounter at the harbor, when Conn had managed to calm the frantic stallion and earned himself a position on Michael Emmanuel's estate, had seemed like a new beginning, a harbinger of hope.

But in just a few months—half a year—it had all gone sour.

Conn's stomach clenched and burned with the sense of dread that had hounded him for days. What with the pitiful look of his newborn son, the long faces of his other children, and his wife's unrelenting sorrow, he felt himself engulfed by despair. Even Renny Magee seemed hard-pressed to force a true smile these days, a stark departure from her usual tomfoolery.

Scarcely an hour went by these days when Conn wasn't struck anew by the memory of how he had failed his wife throughout the years of their marriage—all the times when he couldn't put food on the table, when they'd lost their home because he couldn't find work and had no money for rent, when he couldn't prevent his children's illnesses because they couldn't afford the needed medicines. Those past failures, bitter as they were, seemed small in comparison to his failure now to help his Vangie in her time of need.

Always before, it had been she who managed to buoy him and the children, to rally their spirits and keep their hopes high. No matter how hard things were, Vangie's strong faith invariably had held desperation at bay for them all.

But now it was Vangie who was drowning in despair, and he seemed helpless entirely to save her. Nothing he said, nothing he did, made a difference. It was as if her grief at the loss of Aidan was gnawing a hole in her spirit, eating her up from within, where no healing could reach the wound.

Conn had tried everything he could think of, but most of the time he had all he could do to keep from giving in to his own grief and sense of hopelessness. In front of the children, he did his best to hide his pain and keep a cheerful face. The children needed a strong father they could depend on, a father with a backbone, not a weak-kneed whiner as fearful as a child himself. But the truth was that without Vangie's unflagging faith and optimism, he knew himself to be pitifully weak, a man undone.

The stallion made one more circle of his roomy stall, tossed his head, and gave the walls a purposeful kick just to make the point that he could escape the stable if he wanted.

"Ah, my boy," Conn told him with a rueful smile, "we'll be havin' none of that. It's wantin' your own way so strong that gets you in trouble."

He leaned both elbows on the top of the stall and reflected, "Guess it's what gets us all in trouble."

There was no escaping the fact that their son's death was, at least in part, his own fault. If only he hadn't waited so long to write and make peace with the boy, Aidan might have made the crossing sooner, thereby avoiding the doomed ship that had cost him his life. Or, if only he hadn't been so hardheaded and, as Vangie often accused him, bent on asserting his will with the lad all the time, perhaps Aidan would have come across with the rest of the family and they wouldn't have been separated to begin with.

If only…if only…

Conn knew no good could come of thinking this way. It did nothing but deepen the despondency in which he already felt trapped. What he needed to do was act, take steps to make things better. There must be something that would rouse Vangie from the state she was in, something that would make her smile again, allow her to hope.

But what?

He had asked himself that very question over and over again throughout these oppressive days, but there was never a reply, nothing but a cold and heartless silence.

The thought occurred to him that perhaps he and the children had depended too much and too long on Vangie. And now that she needed them to be strong for her, they didn't know how to begin.

Perhaps for the time being the best they could do was to lean on each other. If they could be strong for one another, then perhaps some of that strength would eventually find its way to Vangie and she would see that this was her time to depend on them.

Sighing deeply, Conn MacGovern picked up his pitchfork and opened the door to the next stall. Even when he didn't know what to do, he always knew how to work.

⁓

Vangie MacGovern stared down at the small red face at her breast. His tiny fists were clenched as if in anger, and he jabbed at her and the air even as he nursed.

Weak as she was, she tried to summon some nudge of feeling, some vestige of tenderness and maternal affection for the wee, wrinkled babe in her arms. A vague memory stirred in her, a remembrance of how, with the other children, she used to love this time of warmth and closeness.

These days she felt nothing—nothing but the inertia and fatigue and… deadness…that had become second nature to her. What was meant to be—and once was—an act of love and nurturing was now nothing more than routine, a task to be tended to, a duty.

Even though she knew she might be inflicting harm on her own child, Vangie found it impossible to shake herself free of the numbness that held her captive. The Wise Women in the village of her childhood believed an infant could sense the rejection or the indifference of a mother and claimed that such a child wouldn't thrive, but instead would eventually grow ill and perhaps even die.

But somehow even the memory of those horrible tales couldn't stir her to more affection for this babe. It was as if the part of her that had once held the capacity to mother a child had died in the same cursed shipwreck that took the life of her eldest son.

A cold shudder racked the length of her body, and the babe jerked and wailed. Automatically, Vangie placed him back at her breast, where he suckled even more voraciously, as if he feared that any moment she might cast him away.

She studied the babe, guilt clawing at her soul like a deranged buzzard. Not merely the guilt occasioned by her lack of feeling for her newborn son, but a guilt prompted by her previous resentment of Conn for not trying to make peace with their firstborn son—a resentment so fierce she had delayed telling him she was with child again until she could no longer hide her condition. And there was also the ever-present suspicion that, by allowing her bitterness and unhappiness to show, she had driven her husband to finally write Aidan in an attempt to reconcile and coax him into make the crossing to America.

If she hadn't made her misery known to Conn, he might never have written to Aidan, and if he hadn't written...

She choked down the acid taste of her misery, her heart seizing with another twist of grief. Weakness swept over her and, trembling, she called for Nell Grace to come take the babe.

~

After walking the floor for over an hour with her fretful baby brother, Nell Grace sighed and carefully put him down in his cradle, waiting to make certain he wouldn't wake.

Even sleeping, he seemed restless and agitated, as if he could find no comfort, no real peace. His teeny mouth twitched, his little hands knotted and unknotted, and his legs jerked beneath the blanket with which she'd covered him. Already his few wisps of hair revealed the same red hue as his mother's, the fiery red that all of the MacGovern children had inherited. And he had the high, broad forehead of their da.

And of Aidan as well.

Nell Grace shook her head. She wouldn't think about her older brother right now. Aidan was lost to them. Baby Will—William, named by Da with no input from their mother—was here. He needed her attention, needed the attention of all of them.

What he needs is his mum.

The thought wrenched her heart. Her mother had no interest in the infant boy who lay sleeping so restlessly in the same cradle Emma had used only three years before.

Her mother had no interest in anything these days. Mum had taken to depending on her for everything, especially anything to do with the baby. It was left to Nell Grace to comfort him when he cried, which was most of the time, to change his didies and give him his baths—indeed, to see to his every need, except of course for his feeding.

It just wasn't right. Nell Grace loved the poor wee boy dearly, but he needed more than a big sister. He needed his mother. But his mother—well, she just couldn't be bothered.

Nell Grace knew it was wrong to think so harshly of her mother—the woman who only weeks ago had evoked nothing but feelings of affection and admiration. But she couldn't help it. Of late it was difficult, sometimes impossible, to realize that the frail, lethargic woman sleeping in the bed nearby, indifferent to her own newborn son, was the same woman who had once loved her children so fiercely, sacrificing her own needs and desires to fulfill their wants and needs.

Aidan's death had turned her once beautiful, fiery mother, so filled with a zest for life, into a listless, mourning shadow of herself. Nell Grace could almost see her fading, slipping away from them like a cloud of smoke, carried out to sea by the wind.

Something had to be done. There must be a way to bring her mother—her real mother—back to them.

Nell Grace touched one finger to her tiny brother's smooth cheek. His mouth pursed, but he didn't wake. Tears scalded her eyes as she watched him. He was so precious, so perfect, so sweet.

So tiny...so fragile...so needy.

Abruptly she straightened, stalked across the room to the piled-up laundry basket, and began folding clothes with far more energy than the job required. She had to do something. There must be something that would draw her mother back to reality, force her to see how much Baby Will needed her.

How much they all needed her.

And then, as she was shaking out one of William's little didies, an idea slipped into her mind—so quick it surprised and unsettled her. The fabric hung limp in her hands as she turned the idea over in her head.

Could it work? It wouldn't be easy. It would depend almost entirely on Miss Susanna and Mrs. Dempsey—would they be willing to help? And Renny Magee would have to do her part. But Nell Grace sensed that Renny would do anything to help, anything at all.

The real question in Nell Grace's mind was whether she could carry it off. She was terribly soft where both her mother and Baby Will were concerned. Could she really go through with such a thing?

There was only one way to find out. But first, she must talk to Miss Susanna.

In the meantime, she could only hope she knew her mum as well as she thought she did.

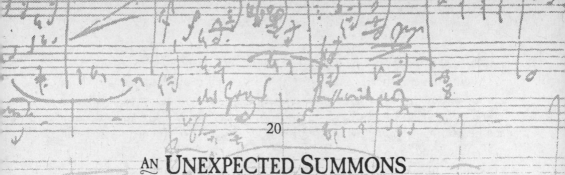

20

AɴN UNEXPECTED SUMMONS

God of mercy! God of peace!
Make this mad confusion cease;
O'er the mental chaos move,
Through it speak the light of love.

WILLIAM DRENNAN

A few minutes after seven that evening, Andrew opened the door of his flat to find Edward Fitch's driver standing there, hat in hand.

"It's Mrs. Guthrie, sir," the man told him. "Mr. Fitch apologizes for the lateness of the hour, but requests that, if possible, you come right away."

Andrew was surprised but didn't hesitate. Mrs. Guthrie's condition must have worsened significantly for Edward to send for him so late in the day.

He fretted all the way to the Fifth Avenue mansion, trying to think of something he could do for Fitch's mother-in-law that he hadn't already thought of. He had exhausted every medical avenue he knew, and she had often been in his prayers, but her condition had steadily worsened. At this point, he was at a loss as to how he could help her.

Despite this frustration, he felt a measure of relief that he'd been summoned. Given the rumors that were spreading in certain circles, he wouldn't have been surprised if Edward Fitch had joined a number of his other patients—former patients—in shunning him.

Another letter had appeared in the papers just two days ago—this time in the *Tribune* and even more vitriolic than the one in the *Herald*. Without actually naming Andrew, this second letter left no doubt as to the target of its accusations, describing him as a "physician from the British Isles" and again making reference to his "female associate." Although it had been written in such a way as to make it seem penned by a different hand, Andrew was convinced the same person was responsible for both letters.

Predictably, Andrew and Bethany's patient load had dwindled still more following the appearance of the second letter. Humiliated by the venomous letters, the reduced practice, and the cold shoulder he was receiving at the hospital, it was all Andrew could do not to give in to the depression that lurked continually at the edges of his spirit.

A part of him was enraged by the unfairness of it all. Warburton, if indeed it was Warburton behind this heinous campaign, seemed invincible in his efforts to destroy him, while Andrew felt virtually helpless to defend himself.

He couldn't deny the charges completely—not when his journals partially confirmed them. In order to make a rebuttal, he would have to admit that he had been an addict at one time. And such an admission, for many, would do nothing but confirm the allegations. Among some of his colleagues and his patients, there would be no forgiveness, no quarter given—only the speculation that one was never free of such an addiction.

And in all honesty, he couldn't refute that charge either. Who knew better than he that, for an addict, there always loomed the danger of falling from grace?

Why had he ever been so foolish as to confront Robert Warburton? That singularly unpleasant visit had accomplished absolutely nothing for Mary Lambert and her children. It had incurred immeasurable trouble—and quite possibly total ruin—for himself. And Bethany, who had worked so hard and made so many sacrifices to practice her chosen profession, was in danger of being ruined as well.

She tried to appear untouched by the whole wretched business. But he had seen the pain in her expressive blue eyes, even when it was masked by anger. He would die before he'd hurt her. And yet she *was* being hurt, and hurt badly, by these malicious attacks. She didn't deserve what he had brought down upon her—any more than he deserved her and her love.

The idea of giving Bethany up for her own sake occurred to him daily, even though he couldn't bring himself to entertain the thought for more than a moment. If he were a stronger man, a better man, he would free her from her promise to marry him. Instead, he needed her more than ever.

He hated himself for it, but he couldn't help but wonder whether Bethany would, given a choice, altogether reject the idea of bringing their engagement to an end.

～

He found Natalie Guthrie noticeably weaker. The deterioration of both her physical health and her mental stability was so dramatic that Andrew, who thought he'd seen her at her worst, was shocked.

She was a forlorn figure, her shoulders hunched as she sat on a small chair near the fireplace, where, in spite of the mildness of the evening, a fire blazed. She looked up as her son-in-law left the room and Andrew walked the rest of the way in. Every vestige of the dignity and pride that once lined her elegant countenance had disappeared. Her skin was ashen and her hair had gone almost white. The combination gave her a bloodless, almost ghostly appearance.

He could tell she had been weeping, and the moment their eyes met, she began to weep again, a racking, punishing seizure of sobs that shook her entire body. Andrew quickly went to kneel in front of her, taking her hand to steady her, but saying nothing.

When she finally quieted, she motioned for him to pull up the chair from beside the bed. "Please sit with me for a while, Dr. Carmichael. There's something I must tell you."

Andrew seated himself and leaned forward a little, waiting.

"Today—" She looked at him, her eyes glazed with a hint of the familiar wildness he'd come to expect in her. "Today I decided to…end my life."

Alarmed, Andrew again reached for her hand, but she shook her head. "No, it's all right. I'm telling you this so you'll know how desperate I've been. Besides, as you can see, as with everything else I've attempted, I lost my nerve and couldn't do it."

She paused, gave a small sigh, then went on. "I was able to pray today," she said, wringing her lace handkerchief into a rope. "I haven't prayed for a long time, not really *prayed*. I've…'said my prayers,' given lip service to the effort—that's all. For so long, the words have seemed meaningless, as if they simply bounced off the walls and fell back at me.

"But today—I don't know why, but today was different. When I tried to pray, I…I simply fell apart. It was as if I were breaking into pieces. It was actually painful. Physically painful. I finally just…threw myself at God and begged Him to take me, to put me out of this unbearable misery. I did, Doctor—I begged Him to let me die. I suppose that was a terrible sin, but I just felt I couldn't go on any longer."

Again she broke off and sat watching Andrew, her eyes now clear. She was obviously gauging his reaction to her words.

"Something…happened," she whispered. "I can't explain it—I don't understand it. But I tell you, Doctor, that God spoke to me in that moment. He somehow—I don't know how else to say this—He broke through to me, through the cloud of sickness in my soul. He stayed my hand from harming myself. And He impressed upon my heart that I was to send for you."

A chill edged its way down Andrew's spine. That something had happened to Natalie Guthrie, he didn't doubt. And there was no doubting the fact that she meant to make him a part of it.

But why?

"I delayed, not wishing to bother you," she continued. "But the more I hesitated, the more desperate I felt. Somehow I knew I must confide in you."

Andrew swallowed, for the life of him unable to imagine what could be driving the woman—and a little reluctant to find out. Yet he couldn't doubt her earnestness. He knew that whatever had possessed Natalie Guthrie to summon him here this evening was of monumental importance to her.

She leaned closer, still studying him with a peculiarly intense expression.

"Tell me, Dr. Carmichael," she said, her words coming slowly now, her voice thin and strained. "Do you believe that a secret sin can drive one to the edge of madness?"

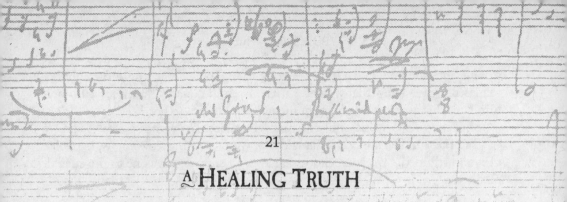

21
A HEALING TRUTH

Thou must be true thyself
If thou the truth wouldst teach;
Thy soul must overflow if thou
Another's soul wouldst reach!

HORATIUS BONAR

Andrew sat staring at Natalie Guthrie, shaken by the blunt and entirely unexpected question that hung between them. He had to remind himself that the woman was obviously speaking of her own sin, not his.

He formulated his reply carefully. "Yes, I suppose I do believe that. It seems to me that sin is very much like acid."

She was still watching him closely. "Acid?"

"Yes. If sin remains unconfessed and unacknowledged, I think in time it—in a manner of speaking, of course—can burn a hole in one's spirit. And that, in turn, it can quite possibly lead to all manner of illnesses, including disorders of the mind."

Natalie Guthrie looked strangely satisfied by his reply. "Yes! Yes, that's it exactly! And I believe that's what has happened in my life, Doctor! My sin has finally eaten a hole in my spirit, and perhaps in my mind. Oh, I knew you'd understand!"

She was growing quite agitated, and Andrew put a hand to hers to try to calm her. "Mrs. Guthrie, what is it? What do you want to tell me?"

"Oh, Dr. Carmichael! You have no idea of the dreadful thing I've lived with all these years. You can't imagine—"

She stopped, again wilting into the demoralized woman he'd seen upon entering the room. Andrew gave her a moment, and eventually he could see her making a determined effort to pull herself together.

"My daughter must never know," she said, searching Andrew's eyes. "Neither Caroline nor Edward can ever know what I am going to tell you."

Andrew gave a nod of assent. "You have my word that whatever you say to me will remain strictly between us."

She waited two or three seconds more, then glanced away, toward the other side of the room. "Caroline is…illegitimate," she said heavily. "My late husband was not her father. He never knew. Caroline doesn't know. I've never told a soul the truth until today."

Somehow, Andrew wasn't surprised. This wasn't the first time it had occurred to him that Natalie Guthrie's condition might be prompted not by a disease of the body, but by a sickness of the soul—a condition he understood all too well. He made no reply but simply waited in silence for her to continue.

Her voice grew a little stronger as she went on. "It doesn't really matter who her father was. I don't want to talk about him, not even to you. It's enough to say I was…infatuated. I was quite young, and he was an older man, very cosmopolitan. I told myself he took advantage of my almost ludicrous naiveté. The truth is, I was flattered by his attention, and I'd been daydreaming about romance, as girls of that age will sometimes do, and—well, it happened, that's all. Only once. But—" she shrugged. "Merritt, my late husband, had been courting me for more than a year, and when I first realized I was going to have a child, I agreed to marry him. I…also agreed to a very brief engagement."

The tears were falling again as she lowered her head. "I never told Merritt about the…the other man. If he suspected, he kept it entirely to himself. He was a good man, my Merritt," she said, her voice unsteady. "He really did love me, and in time I grew to love him. After a while, I couldn't bear to hurt him, and if he'd known the sordid truth about my…indiscretion, it would have hurt him. Terribly.

"So I've lived with the knowledge of my sin and with the harshest kind of self-reproach every day of my life since. Truly, Doctor, especially in this past year, I have longed for death, just to be free of the guilt."

She covered her face with her hands, her shoulders shaking as she lapsed into another bout of weeping.

Andrew knew this was no time for platitudes, so he simply waited for her to regain her composure. And while he waited, he prayed for her.

When she finally dropped her hands away from her face to look at him, her features were contorted by exhaustion and grief, her eyes red and swollen from unrelieved weeping. But Andrew thought he detected a new clarity and even a kind of strength in her gaze.

"Mrs. Guthrie? I must ask you: Why do you think it was so important that you tell me about this?"

She unknotted her wrinkled handkerchief and wiped her eyes. "I'm not sure," she said. "I thought perhaps you might know."

Andrew shook his head, trying to digest what he'd heard and why he'd been… selected, if that were the case, to hear it.

"I believe I've finally been forgiven."

Her words fell quietly between them, like drops of rain on soft ground.

"I'm so glad, Mrs. Guthrie," Andrew said, greatly pleased but still puzzled.

She nodded. "I've asked forgiveness before, of course. But to tell you the truth, I never once believed God had forgiven me. In fact, I was convinced He wouldn't forgive me. I had no excuse for what I'd done, and I'd deceived my husband and my only child all those years. Why should God show me any mercy?"

"Why should God show any one of us mercy?" Andrew said. "But go on— please."

She leaned forward. "Something happened today, Doctor. I don't understand what it was or why it happened. But while I was praying this afternoon, something changed. It was as though God put His arms around me and told me all was well. And I was forgiven—I just knew. But I also knew that I had to...to confess to someone else. I had to tell someone the truth, the entire ugly, terrible truth. But I couldn't tell Caroline or Edward. I simply couldn't. And then your name came into my mind like a banner and wouldn't go away until I convinced Edward to send for you." She paused, then added, "And I think I know why."

Andrew smiled a little. "Then I must admit you are a ways ahead of me, Mrs. Guthrie. Why?"

"Because," she said, again worrying her handkerchief between her hands, "I know you're a very wise man, Doctor—a godly man. I need your advice as to whether I must tell Caroline or if I may simply keep my silence."

Andrew ran a hand over his forehead. The woman was asking for wisdom he didn't have. How could he possibly answer such a question?

"Mrs. Guthrie, I don't see how anyone can decide that for you. You can only act on what you truly believe is best—for you, and for your daughter."

He almost added that she'd also need to be ready to bear the consequences if she did tell her daughter she was illegitimate, but he caught himself. Now wasn't the time for such a caution.

"But what do you think, Doctor?" Before he could reply, she went on. "I have to admit I'm terrified by the very idea of admitting my sin—and my deceit of all these years—to my daughter," said Mrs. Guthrie, her voice trembling. "I don't know if I can actually bring myself to hurt her in such a terrible way, and I can't see how such news could benefit her. But I suppose I'm also being selfish. I can't imagine how I could possibly endure—the loss of her love."

This was definitely not his province. Natalie Guthrie was an intelligent woman. She would have to think this through for herself, and Andrew didn't envy her dilemma. But the Lord had brought her to this place. Surely He would also guide her to make the right decision about what, if anything, to tell her daughter.

Suddenly, he remembered the night he told Bethany about his opium addiction—how frightened he'd been that he would lose her once she knew about his past.

But he didn't lose her.

"I can't tell you what to do, Mrs. Guthrie," he finally said. "I'm not nearly as wise as you seem to think. But let me try to reassure you of one thing. Sometimes we badly underestimate the people we love. I don't know your daughter very well, but I have seen the love and devotion she feels for you. Please understand, I'm not suggesting that you necessarily need to tell her the circumstances of her birth—that's for you and the Lord to decide. What I am saying is that if you reach the point where you believe you must tell her, then try to have enough faith in her—and in her love for you—not to expect the worst. Naturally, it will be a tremendous shock. But I truly believe that love is almost always strong enough to bear the truth."

He reached to free one hand from the handkerchief she was wringing. "It's fair to say that the truth can hurt," he admitted. "But it's just as important to remember that the truth can also heal."

In that instant, Andrew sensed something trying to work its way to the surface of his own mind, but it disappeared as quickly as it had come. He gave her hand a gentle squeeze, then stood. "I'll stop in to see how you're doing tomorrow. In fact, I'll be sure to do just that, because somehow I don't expect you'll need me much in the future."

A hesitant smile slowly broke across her face, and she got to her feet. "Even if you're right about that, Doctor," she said, her voice still somewhat tremulous, "please don't ever think you need a reason to stop by and see us. You will always be welcome in this house."

As he started down the hallway, Andrew was surprised to realize just how much her words had meant to him. It had been quite a long time, he thought, since he'd felt really welcome anywhere.

With that thought, he recognized the beginnings of an unwelcome burst of self-pity and shook it off before it could tighten its grip.

～

Downstairs, he spent a few minutes with Edward Fitch, trying as best he could to explain the change in his mother-in-law's condition without revealing anything Natalie Guthrie had told him in confidence.

"You honestly believe she's going to recover?" Fitch asked hopefully.

"I don't think there's any question," said Andrew.

"Was this—was it all in her mind, Andrew? Some kind of hysteria?"

Andrew thought for a moment before replying. "No. Not entirely. Mrs. Guthrie has also been suffering from exhaustion and anemia—mostly because she hasn't been eating or sleeping as she should. She's had a difficult time of it, so her body's resources have been fairly depleted. But I believe you'll see a marked improvement over the next few weeks. Just be patient with her."

The other man studied him closely. "You're not going to tell me what that 'difficult time' was all about, are you?"

"Can we just accept the fact that Mrs. Guthrie has turned a corner and leave it at that?"

"How very cryptic of you, Andrew."

Andrew managed a smile, but it quickly fled at Fitch's next words.

"I'm deeply grateful to you for your help—and for your patience with us. Especially since I'm aware that you've been going through your own, ah, difficult time."

Andrew had no intention of getting into his personal problems with Edward Fitch, but the other wasn't to be put off.

"Gratitude aside, I just want to say that the calumny presently being attempted on you and your reputation isn't going to work. I can't imagine anyone who knows you believing a word of it."

Moved by the attorney's show of trust, Andrew said awkwardly, "Thank you, Edward. I appreciate that. But—"

"All the same," Fitch interrupted, "I'd strongly suggest that you make a public statement and defend yourself, even bring suit against the perpetrator of this outrage." He cracked a sly smile. "And I just happen to know where you can find yourself a good attorney, should you decide to take such action."

Caught off guard by the suggestion, Andrew stumbled over his reply. "Why—I hadn't even considered such a thing. Besides, the truth is—"

Fitch made a dismissing gesture with his hand. "You owe me no explanation, Andrew. All I need to know is that you are most definitely not guilty of what this lunatic is accusing you of. If you ever had such a problem—well, that's past history, and quite frankly I couldn't care less. But again, I hope you'll at least consider a public defense of some sort. You're an excellent physician, and you're a good man. But you're in a position where doing nothing could conceivably cost you your reputation and your career. If there's anything you need to divulge about your past, I'd urge you not to be afraid to do so. Whatever it is, it couldn't be worse than the garbage these scandalmongers are dishing up."

Fitch paused, then added, "The truth can be a formidable weapon against these kinds of tactics, you know. And don't forget the words of our Lord—that the truth will make us free. The Gospel of John, chapter eight, as I believe you know."

Surprised, Andrew looked at him. "You're a believer?"

Fitch burst out with a laugh. "Don't look so shocked! Even lawyers can be saved!"

Embarrassed, Andrew tried to cover his gaffe, but Edward Fitch wouldn't have it. "It's all right, Andrew! I'm used to getting that look when I step onto my soapbox. But nevertheless, I hope you'll consider what I said. Now, I know you need to get home to your supper. I believe Thomas is waiting to drive you back. And, Andrew?"

Andrew waited.

"Thank you. On behalf of Caroline and her mother—and myself—thank you."

Andrew thought he might have a little more spring to his step as he left the Fitch residence and started for the carriage. Despite the troubles that had been wearing so heavily upon him for days now, he was acutely aware he'd been doubly and richly blessed in the course of just one evening.

He was also aware that he had some very serious praying and reflecting to do about the discussion that had taken place tonight regarding truth. More than once he'd felt that familiar nudge that signaled that the Holy Spirit was trying to get his attention.

And somehow he couldn't quite shake the feeling that Natalie Guthrie's unexpected summons this evening had been as much for his sake as her own.

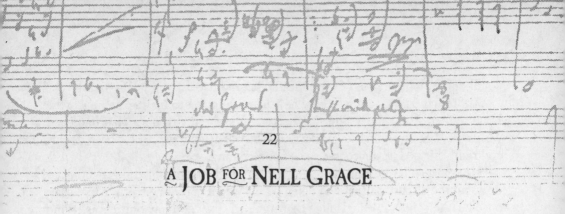

22

A JOB FOR NELL GRACE

There is always hope
for all who will dare and suffer.

JAMES CLARENCE MANGAN

Caterina was one step away from being completely out of control.

"I'm going to the circus—the circus—the circus—"

"*Caterina*! Either you take five deep breaths," Susanna cautioned, "and stand perfectly still until I finish your braids, or else I'm calling your papa in here to settle you."

Had she ever seen the child this unruly?

Only at Christmastime, she decided, and the day of her grandfather's arrival. Well, there was also the day of her own arrival, Susanna remembered. But surely all children didn't turn into such monkeys over a circus, did they?

As she attempted to secure her niece's right braid for the third time, Susanna realized that most children probably did.

"There," she said, giving the stubborn braid a final tug. "You are ready to go."

That was the cue Caterina needed to begin chanting and bobbing up and down again. Susanna turned her around by both shoulders, unable to suppress a smile at the girl's high spirits as she held her firmly in place.

Papa Emmanuel and Rosa Navaro were treating Caterina to a day in the city, which would include the child's first visit to P. T. Barnum's "Greatest Show on Earth." She had been practically wild for over a week now, ever since she'd learned of the outing. Indeed, Susanna had announced to Michael more than once that, in the future, any plans that might lead to excitability were to be kept secret until the very hour of the big event.

Caterina threw her arms around Susanna's neck and pulled her forward for yet another hug. "I love you, Aunt Susanna! Is it time to go yet?"

Susanna tugged the child's other braid, laughing at the little minx and her exhausting energy. "I do hope so!" she teased. "Otherwise, I'm going back to bed and hide under the covers."

Caterina kissed her on the cheek and then, with surprising strength, tugged at Susanna until she got to her feet. "Let's go downstairs and see if Grandpapa is ready!" she urged. "I hope he knows we can't be late for the circus!"

Downstairs, to Susanna's huge relief, they found Papa Emmanuel ready and waiting. Michael and Paul had come to the door to see them off, and when Caterina saw her father she practically leaped into his arms.

"Papa! Don't you wish you were coming with us?"

Michael hoisted her a little higher and smiled at her excitement. "Of course, I do. But cousin Paul and I have much work to do before our concert next week, so we must stay at home." He kissed her soundly on the cheek, then set her to her feet.

"You are going to have a wonderful day, Cati. Nothing is more fun than the circus. You're a very fortunate little girl, to have a grandpapa who takes you to such special events."

Susanna was surprised to see Caterina suddenly grow solemn. "I wish Maylee could come with us, Papa. I feel so bad for her, having to stay in her room all the time now. She can't even come to the table with us anymore."

Her niece's words brought an ache to Susanna's throat, and she noticed the flurry of pain that crossed Michael's features. He stooped to his daughter's level and pulled her into his embrace. "I know. But Maylee wouldn't want you to be sad on her account. You go with Grandpapa now and enjoy yourself. Perhaps you will say a prayer for Maylee on the way to the ferry. And, Cati?"

"Yes, Papa?"

"You make me very proud, to know that you remember someone less fortunate even when you are so happy. I know Jesus is pleased, too."

Caterina hugged him once again before turning to her grandfather and taking his hand. By the time they stepped out onto the porch, she was singing again.

Both Michael and Paul turned to go back down the hall, but Susanna stopped them. "Michael, wait. I know you're busy, but I need to ask you about something."

When Paul made as if to leave them alone, Susanna said, "No, that's all right, Paul. Please stay. I'll only take a moment."

She explained then that Nell Grace MacGovern had been to the house early that morning, asking if there might be work for her to do through the day.

"Here?" Paul said, his eyes wide. "At the house?"

Susanna curbed a smile. Paul was so badly smitten with the MacGovern girl he could scarcely speak her name without stammering.

"Yes. For a few hours a day."

"But isn't she very young?" said Michael.

"Not too young to work. And she implied that she needed the extra money."

Michael frowned. "The MacGoverns need more money? I'll raise MacGovern's wages. I should do so anyway. The man deserves it."

"Wait, Michael," said Paul, putting a hand to his cousin's arm. "Perhaps Nell—perhaps Miss MacGovern is wanting to earn money of her own. She's not a child, after all."

"So I am told," Michael said dryly.

"Well, just so you know," Susanna put in, "Moira could certainly use the help. And so could I, " she added.

"What about Mrs. MacGovern?" Michael said. "Is she well enough now to do without the girl's help?"

"I asked Nell Grace that very question. She told me that Renny Magee is willing to take on extra responsibility so that Vangie won't need to overdo."

"There!" Paul said. "It will all work out, no? Don't you think it's a good idea, Michael? Since Susanna and Moira are in favor of it?"

Susanna looked at Michael and saw the slight twitch at one corner of his mouth. "Obviously, you are in favor of the idea, Pauli," Michael said. "All right, then, it's fine with me. You decide on her wages, Susanna." He stopped. "Does Moira know about this?"

"Yes, and she actually seems pleased," Susanna replied. "Moira is slowing down, Michael. I really do think she needs the extra help."

He nodded. "Good, then. And, Pauli?"

Susanna knew he was feigning the stern expression he suddenly adopted.

"You be very careful around this girl. She is quite young—"

"She is a young woman," Paul offered.

"—as I said, she is quite young, and I suspect Conn MacGovern is not one to tolerate a man playing light with his daughter."

Paul's face flamed. "You know I would never do that! Not with any woman! And especially not Nell Grace—Miss MacGovern."

"I rather imagine that in the case of Conn MacGovern and his daughter, Pauli, you must avoid even the appearance of dallying. I have the distinct impression that he is most protective of his family."

Paul sighed. "Sì, Michael. You do not have to warn me of this. I know the man." He brightened. "But surely there can be no harm in my speaking with his daughter from time to time? And now I must leave you. I have much to prepare for our day's work."

Susanna watched him as he turned and went down the hall. "He's practically skipping," she said to Michael.

"Love will make a fool of the best of men," Michael offered just before kissing her on the cheek and following his cousin.

~

"I'm sorry, Mum, but I have to do this. We need the money."

Nell Grace MacGovern had steeled herself for an argument from her mother. She'd known this wouldn't be easy, especially since she was already dodging volley after volley of guilt. But something had to be done, and she could think of nothing else.

"We don't need the money so badly that you should hire yourself out as a servant! And how am I to get along while you're up at the Big House all the time?"

"You'll be fine, Mum. And I won't be there all the time. Only a few hours a day. Da says he can check on you often, and Renny is going to assume more chores. She's already doing a great deal as it is, you know. She's a good worker, Renny is. And the twins will help as well."

"The twins will be at school most of the day," her mother pointed out, her tone bitter. "And Renny's not one to handle the babe. She says she doesn't feel easy with such a responsibility."

Nell Grace knotted her hands behind her back, bracing herself as she said, "Well, but you're doing so much better, now, aren't you, Mum? You don't need Renny or me as much as you did. This will work out just fine, you'll see." She paused. "It's important that I do this, Mum."

"Important to who? That cousin of Mr. Emmanuel's? He's the real reason you're going to work up there, isn't he?"

Nell Grace felt the heat rise to her face. "No, he is not the reason!"

It was the truth, she told herself. She knew Paul Santi was sweet on her, and she liked him well enough. Maybe a lot more than well enough. Every time she was around him, she took on the strangest feelings, and her brain seemed to turn to pudding.

But she wasn't doing this because of Paul Santi. She was doing it for her mum—and for Baby Will. She knew it might not be the best idea in the world, but it was her only idea for the time being, and she was going to try it.

Her mother was silent, and Nell Grace thought perhaps this wouldn't be as difficult as she'd feared. She was wrong.

"I'm going to talk to your da about this, Nell Grace. I don't think for a moment he'll go along with your foolishness."

"I've already talked to Da. He said it's all right."

Something flared in her mother's eyes—something Nell Grace had not anticipated. She realized then that what she was seeing was fear. Her mother was actually afraid.

But afraid of what?

"I can't—I can't take care of the baby by myself," her mother argued, not looking at her. "I'm not strong enough yet, Nell Grace. I can't—manage alone."

"You won't be alone, Mum. Besides, didn't the doctor say that the more you do from day to day, the sooner you'll get your strength back?"

"He doesn't know everything. What does a man know about having a baby? The birth was so hard...and after losing Aidan..."

Her mother's words drifted off, unfinished. She made a weak gesture with her hand and slumped back in the chair.

She was actually whining.

Vangie MacGovern whining—Nell Grace could scarcely believe it. Her mother had always been death on whining. The MacGovern children simply were not allowed to whimper or complain. If they did, they'd be taken to task as soon as word reached Mum's ears.

More to the point, the whining was working, and Nell Grace could feel herself about to relent. Any minute now she'd give in and say she was sorry and she wouldn't go to work at the Big House after all.

No! She wouldn't give in. She couldn't. If there was a chance at all of helping her mother and her wee baby brother, she had to take it. No matter how difficult Mum made it, she must stand up to her.

"Well, Mum, we'll work it out, I'm sure," she said before her resolve failed her entirely. "I start tomorrow, so I'll spend this afternoon tidying the house and cooking something ahead."

Before her mother could protest further, Nell Grace hurried out of the room and went in search of Renny Magee.

~

"Are you clear, then, Renny? About what you're to do—and what you're not to do?"

"Aye," said Renny. She was clear about it all, she thought, except why exactly she was doing it—or not doing it, whichever the case might be.

"Tell me again," said Nell Grace. "Just to make certain we haven't forgotten anything."

Renny dug at the floor with one foot. "I'm to keep the house clean and tidy and keep the kettle on at all times."

"And set the table as well, Renny. Don't forget that. But I'll be home in time to make supper in the evening. And I'll fix extra to tide you over for the midday meal next day."

Renny nodded. Nell Grace ought to know by now she wasn't no eejit. She could remember a few simple chores in the girl's absence, now couldn't she?

"And what else, Renny?"

"I'll be feedin' the chickens and emptyin' the slops and carryin' anything heavy in or out, should your da or the twins not be here to do it." She grinned. "And make sure to keep the creepycrawlies away."

Nell Grace allowed herself a smile. Her mum's fear of bugs was a constant source of amusement to Renny Magee, who found it hard to believe that such a strong woman could quail and quake at the sight of a spider or a cockroach. Renny had long ago appointed herself in charge of bug-busting in the MacGovern household and had dispatched many a creature to its reward—or captured it in a bottle and taken it up the hill to show Maylee. Nell Grace, being none too fond of crawling things herself, was happy for Renny to take care of such chores entirely.

"Very good," she told her. "Now tell me, what are you not to do?"

Renny shot her a dubious look. "I'm not to take care of wee William. Even if Vangie should ask me to."

"That's right. And that's the most important thing of all, Renny, as I explained. Do you understand?"

"Aye. But what if Vangie insists?"

"You just keep telling her you can't. Tell her you're afraid, that you don't know how to care for a baby and you simply can't do it. And look…frightened if she tries to coax you."

Renny frowned. This was the part that had her worried.

"Renny," said Nell Grace. "I know you care deeply for Mum."

Renny looked up, reluctant to have her deepest feelings known even by Nell Grace.

"I know you care about Mum, Renny," she said again, "but don't you see? That's why we're doing this. It's to help her. She's unhappy, Renny. She's miserable. It's not like her to ignore a babe—any babe, not just her own. More than anything else, she's a mother. A good mother. The way she is now—it's not natural for her! She's just not herself, don't you see? I know losing Aidan broke her heart. But she can't go on ignoring Baby Will. He needs her."

Nell Grace stopped and took Renny by the shoulders. "I know I'm asking a lot of you, Renny. I'm putting more work on you—"

"I don't mind the work, Nell Grace."

"I know you don't. And I know you hate saying no to Mum. But if this works, it won't be for long. And then we can all get back to normal." She paused. "So, you'll do it then, just as we agreed?"

Renny found it almost as hard to say no to Nell Grace as she did to Vangie. Especially when the girl insisted they were doing this to help Vangie.

She nodded. "I'll do my best."

"Thank you, Renny! And, by the way—"

Renny had turned to go, but stopped, waiting.

"Pray, Renny," Nell Grace said, her gaze as intent and solemn as Renny had ever seen it. "Pray really, really hard. For Mum. And for Baby Will. For all of us."

Renny gave a nod. Nell Grace needn't worry about that part of things. She'd be praying, all right. Amongst everything else, she'd be praying that Nell Grace knew what she was doing.

For heaven help them all if she didn't.

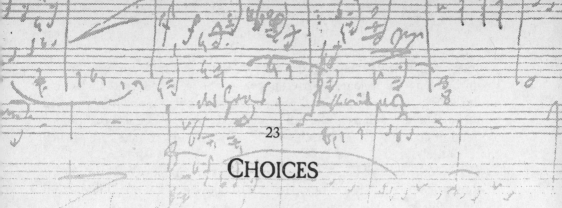

23

CHOICES

The tissue of the life to be
We weave with colors all our own,
And in the field of destiny
We reap as we have sown.

JOHN GREENLEAF WHITTIER

Susanna was doing her best to keep the house quiet for the day.

With Papa Emmanuel and Caterina away, she thought it should be relatively easy to give Michael and Paul several uninterrupted hours in which to work. She knew Michael was hoping to spend most of the afternoon on his *American Anthem* suite, once he and Paul ironed out a few items in the upcoming concert program. Later, she would go in and do whatever she could to help, although at this point he kept insisting he wanted to keep the finishing touches a surprise to her.

She was in the drawing room, trying to mend a pull in one of the sofa's antimacassars when she heard a crash in the music room and went running. She met Paul midway down the hall. His face was flushed, his eyeglasses riding low on his nose, the collar of his shirt slightly askew.

The moment he saw her, he threw both arms in the air in a gesture of futility.

"Paul? What's wrong? What was that noise?"

"*That*," he said with marked emphasis, "was the sound of my genius cousin—and your usually good-natured betrothed—making a profound statement of dissatisfaction with his own work." He stopped. "In other words, he barely missed my foot with one of those river rock paperweights from the mantel."

She stared at him. "Michael threw a paperweight at you?"

He waved a hand. "No, no, not at me! He was aiming at the floor, I believe. My foot just happened to get in the way."

"Good heavens! Why was he throwing a paperweight?"

Paul shrugged. "The music is fighting him, he says." He glanced around, then turned back and lowered his voice. "Between you and me, Susanna, I think it is Uncle Riccardo fighting him."

"What do you mean?"

"I don't think Michael is concentrating so well these days. Uncle Riccardo keeps shooting these little darts at him, you know?"

Susanna shook her head. "I don't know. What are you talking about?"

Again he glanced behind him to make sure Michael hadn't come out of the music room. "He sometimes says things that disparage Michael's music. He insinuates that Michael should be doing more…important work."

Anger swept over Susanna like a fever. For an instant she felt like throwing one of those paperweights herself. "And this is affecting Michael's composing?"

Paul lifted his shoulders. "Something is. He tries not to show his irritation with Uncle Riccardo, but I believe these remarks are hurtful—and discouraging to him. He's, ah, stuck, he says, in the last movement. He says it's going nowhere." He stopped, looking at Susanna as if considering whether he should say what he was thinking.

Apparently, he decided to risk it. "I've never before known Michael to be… temperamental." Unexpectedly, he grinned at her. "He's behaving like a musician."

Susanna was unable to manage a return smile. "Is there anything I can do?" she said. "Or perhaps you could speak with Michael's father?"

He looked at her over the rim of his glasses, eyes wide. "It is not my place, Susanna. And besides, it takes more than talk to change Uncle Riccardo's opinion once he sets his mind to a thing."

That didn't surprise Susanna. In the brief time Michael's father had been with them, she had already learned that he could be frustratingly stubborn.

She sighed, wondering how such a likable man—and she did like Riccardo Emmanuel—could also be so aggravating.

"Well, I'll at least go and talk with Michael."

"Keep your eye on the paperweight," Paul said dryly.

⌒

She found Michael slumped on the piano bench, one hand thumping idly on the keyboard. His hair was wild, his mouth set in a hard line. He looked for all the world like a great black bear with a thorn in its paw.

In front of the fireplace, Gus the wolfhound, looking somewhat wary and at loose ends without Caterina to tend to, sat watching his owner. At Susanna's entrance, his tail began to whop in a circle, but he remained where he was.

Michael gave no indication that he heard her enter, which wasn't like him at all. Usually he responded to her presence the moment she walked into a room.

Susanna came up behind him and put a hand to his shoulder. "Michael?"

After a slight hesitation, his only response was to reach back and cover her hand with his.

"I heard a terrible crash. Paul said you dropped a paperweight." She glanced around and spied the large piece of polished rock still on the floor.

"*Sì.*"

His tone was as petulant as his expression.

"Is there anything I can do?"

He shook his head, then sighed and straightened a little. "No. But I should go and apologize to Pauli. He probably thinks I'm upset with him."

"What *are* you upset with?"

"Myself," he said flatly.

She squeezed his shoulder. "The music isn't going well?"

"The music," he said somewhat caustically, "is not going at all. It's a dead thing, like an animal shot and skinned."

Susanna cringed at the analogy even as she fought to suppress a smile at his flair for the dramatic.

"Your music is absolutely brilliant, Michael," she said calmly. "Don't you even think of belittling it. Now, why don't you tell me what's really wrong?"

Again he shook his head. "I'm getting nowhere. I knew the last movement would take much time, but this is ridiculous! And it's not even because of the music itself. It's because I've simply…stopped. I can't seem to get past the point where I am now."

Struggling to find just the right words, Susanna clasped his shoulders with both hands. "I've heard what you're doing, you know. Right up to this…stopping place. And it's wonderful, Michael! Truly, it's an incredible work. Surely you haven't lost your passion for it?"

When he didn't answer, Susanna gripped his heavy shoulders a little more tightly. "Michael?"

He startled her by shooting to his feet and whipping around to face her, practically flinging her hands off his shoulders. "It's not so simple, Susanna! It's—I don't know what it is! What I do know is that at this rate, I'll never have it ready for the Centennial concert."

"That's still months away—"

"And I'm still months away from completion," he countered.

He turned his back on her and paced over to the fireplace. Hurt, Susanna stayed where she was. She had never seen him like this. It was a good thing that Riccardo Emmanuel was out of the house. Had he been here, there was no telling what she might have said to him.

"Well, then," she said uncertainly, "I suppose I should leave you alone."

Before she could go, however, he turned back to her. "Susanna, I'm sorry," he said, raking a hand through his hair. "I didn't mean to take my frustration out on you. Don't go. Please."

Susanna watched him, still keeping her distance. "Michael, this has something to do with your father, doesn't it?"

A muscle near his eye jerked. "Of course not."

"I think it does. What has he been saying to you, about your music?"

For a moment she thought he wasn't going to answer. He stood with one arm propped on the mantel as if he couldn't decide what, if anything, to tell her.

Finally, though, he pushed away and came to stand closer to her. "You already know what he wants for me."

Irritation flared in Susanna again. "Yes, he wants you to return to the opera. But that's not what you want." She paused. "Is it?"

He started to speak, then stopped, giving a slight shake of his head. "No, you know it's not. But...what if he's right and I'm wrong, *cara*? What if I am, as he seems to believe, wasting my gift?"

Susanna studied him, then tugged at his hands and led him to the sofa, coaxing him to sit with her. "Michael, don't you see what's happening? Your father is trying to influence you. He's attempting to change your mind about what direction your music should take. And I can't help but wonder if it might be working."

He frowned. "Don't be upset with him, Susanna. He genuinely believes I'm wrong. He means only to help me."

"But he's not helping you," Susanna pointed out. "In fact, he's hurting you. I've no doubt that your father means well, Michael. He loves you dearly, and he believes wholeheartedly in your gift—your voice and your potential. But it isn't right, what he's doing. He's confusing you. I think he's actually making you question your decision to leave the opera. How can you let him do that?"

She paused. "After everything you went through to make that decision, how could you be anything but convinced it was the right one, the choice God wanted you to make?"

Silence, in which Susanna sensed he didn't know what to say.

"Think about this, Michael. Had you ever at any time, before your father came to visit, questioned your decision?"

His response took some time in coming. But the shake of his head was firm and final. "No."

Susanna squeezed his hands. "Then it seems to me there's only one reason for your questioning it now. Oh, Michael, I know it must be incredibly difficult to stand up to your father when you know he wants only what's best for you! Papa Emmanuel genuinely believes that you might be squandering a God-given gift. And your former success in the opera world would even seem to confirm—to him, at least—that he's right. But how many times have I heard you say that one's success in a chosen field doesn't necessarily mean God's blessing is on that choice—or the success?"

He raised his face. "*Sì*. From my own experience, I know that to be true."

Susanna didn't move, said nothing, and simply waited.

He turned his head as if to ease the tension in his neck. "So, then, you're saying that I'm allowing my father to divert me from what I know in my heart is right?"

Susanna felt his hands tighten on hers. "I'm saying that you made your choice once, and I believe it's still your choice. Michael...darling...it couldn't be clearer. You must choose to please either your earthly father...or your heavenly Father."

With that, she felt she had said enough. She leaned toward him and very gently kissed him on the cheek. "I'll leave you alone. I want to speak with Nell Grace before she leaves and see how her first day in the house went for her— especially how she and Moira got on together."

Even as she was still speaking, the wolfhound came to rest his head in Michael's lap. The two were still sitting there, both quiet and seemingly contemplative, when Susanna left the room.

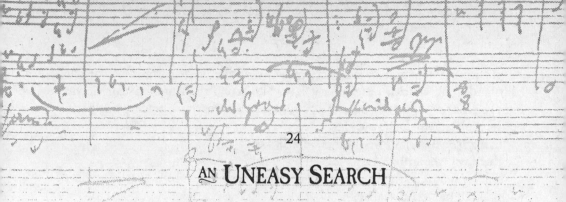

24

An Uneasy Search

All day long, in unrest,
To and fro, do I move.

OWEN ROE MAC WARD
(TRANSLATED BY JAMES CLARENCE MANGAN)

The rain was already picking up again when Frank Donovan walked into the Women's Clinic and Convalescence Center for the third time in a week.

Try as he would, he couldn't altogether ignore the snide voice—a voice remarkably like his own—that had taken to questioning the motivation behind these frequent visits. Then he reminded himself that the good name and even the very future of his closest friend might be riding on what he could learn from Mary Lambert.

The very sight of Miss Savage—"the Matron from the Pit," as he'd come to think of her—immediately soured his stomach and his mood. Even so, he wasn't going to miss a chance to get under her skin as much as she got under his.

"Ah, Miss Savage," he said cheerily, doffing his rain-drenched hat and putting on the Irish, "Wasn't I hopin' you'd be here?"

He knew from the instant the smirk appeared that she was going to give him trouble. Normally, she reserved her fiercest glare for him. Not today. She was definitely smirking, all right, and it was the kind of knowing, mean-spirited smirk the woman might wear to the execution of an archenemy.

Someone like himself.

In an attempt to thwart whatever the harridan might have up her sleeve, Frank shot her a smile of his own, guaranteed to melt her resistance.

In return, he received a thoroughly venomous scowl.

There would be no melting of the Iron Matron today.

All right, then—back to business. "I'll just be speakin' with Miss Lambert," he said, starting down the hall.

"Not today, you won't," she said, stopping him on the first step.

Surprised—for he'd already determined that the woman was a coward at heart and would quickly retreat in the face of an actual challenge—Frank slowly removed his hat, tucked it under his arm, and leaned forward, bracing one hand on the table at which she sat.

"Is that so? And why would that be, Miss Savage?"

There was the smirk again. "Because she isn't here."

She leaned back and crossed her arms over her bony bosom, watching him with a kind of gleeful malice.

Caught off guard, Frank straightened. "What do you mean, she isn't here?"

"Miss Lambert had already exceeded the time allotted for treatment. She was checked out this morning."

"By whose orders?"

Her eyes glinted. "Mine, of course. I am the head matron. Or weren't you aware of that—Sergeant?"

The wicked old fishwife was clearly indulging in some sort of unholy amusement at his expense. Frank wanted to go across the table and snatch her by her wattled throat. Instead, he checked his temper and favored her with a tight-lipped smile.

"So then, where would I be findin' Miss Lambert?"

Her eyebrows shot up in a look of mock innocence. "Well, how would I know that? The clinic's responsibility for a patient ends when she walks out the door."

Despite Frank's resolve not to let the woman provoke him, she was doing an admirable job of just that. "You set her out in the rain, not knowin' if she has a place to go?" he said, his tone hard with an edge of warning.

"As I told you, Sergeant, we can hardly be responsible for every addict we treat after they leave the premises. Now if you'll excuse me, I have other patients who require attention."

She made a show of gathering up some charts, and now Frank did go across the table. He slammed his hat down, sending her charts flying in all directions and, bracing both hands on the scarred wooden top, he leaned forward until he was in her face, close enough to smell her stale breath.

"You don't want to aggravate me, Miss Savage," he bit out with deliberate menace. "Really, you don't. If you have a thought as to where Mary Lambert might have gone, it would be in your best interests to tell me and not make me ask again."

At least he had the satisfaction of seeing her shrink from him. To her credit, however, she recovered quickly. "I told you. I have absolutely no way of knowing where the woman might have gone. Now I suggest you leave, Sergeant, or else—"

"Or else what?" Frank countered, digging his fingers into the desk to keep from shaking the old witch. "You'll call the police?"

He could feel the rage boiling up in him but knew he'd accomplish nothing by exploding, so he contented himself with taking a swipe at the row of tins and bottles on the table and knocking them to the floor with a terrible clamor. Then he straightened, pointed a finger at the furious matron, and issued a warning: "You'd best hope I find Mary Lambert, woman! She's at the heart of a criminal investigation. And if I don't find her and find her soon, I'm coming back here to haul your sorry self straight to the Tombs for obstructing that investigation."

As he went tearing out the door and down the steps into the rain-slick streets, it crossed Frank's mind that he hadn't a hope of doing any such thing. He could hardly lock up a clinic matron for discharging a patient—though he doubted Miss Savage knew that.

Besides, he had no intention of carrying out his threat.

He would find Mary Lambert, and he would find her today.

⁓

The thought of that poor woman walking the streets of New York—homeless, defenseless, in a sorely weakened condition, and in this weather—rode Frank's back like a devilish buzzard. He practically pounced on every slight figure with fair hair until each turned around with a look of wanting to slap his face or else take off running.

He didn't dare question himself too closely as to why one small woman with an opium habit should be important enough for him to lose a full day's work in an effort to find her. True, she was crucial to his efforts to rescue Doc from that barrage of vile attacks and clear his good name in the process. But was that the only reason for his dogged search?

Some carefully guarded place deep inside him was trying to force itself open and entice him to search among the secrets hidden there, along with the possibilities and forgotten dreams. But Frank Donovan had long ago learned to keep that place securely bolted even against himself. Once again he deliberately closed his mind to it—refusing to think, refusing to question, as he continued to roam the teeming streets of the city.

All day he walked in the rain, pressing his way through the crush of other pedestrians and vehicle traffic, finally taking to his department's mount, the dun-colored Attila, in an increasingly desperate search for Mary Lambert.

If an occasional uneasy thought nagged him about the reason for his tireless pursuit, he reminded himself it would take more than a frail, flaxen-haired woman to bring down the walls of that well-guarded chamber in his heart.

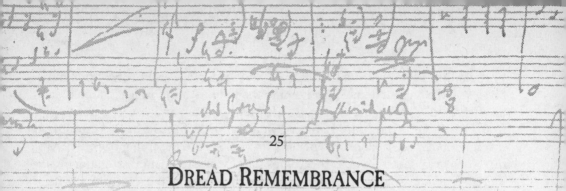

25

DREAD REMEMBRANCE

Sad are our hopes,
for they were sweet in sowing
But tares, self-sown,
have overtopp'd the wheat.

AUBREY THOMAS DE VERE

The rain was steady now. It would soon be dark, and Mary Lambert still had nowhere to go.

Many hours had passed since she had been dismissed from the Women's Clinic. Morning had turned to afternoon, and afternoon to evening. The rain poured down in cold sheets and Mary fervently wished she had a coat. When Miss Savage discharged her this morning, she'd said Mary wasn't wearing a coat when she was admitted, and since it was April, she wouldn't be needing one anyway.

It might be April, but Mary was cold. Cold all the way to the bone.

Her dress was sopping wet and clung heavily to her body. Her hair hung in sodden ropes. It was a miserable evening, and she glanced longingly into the shop windows that displayed their various wares in the warm radiance of gaslight and candle glow. She wasn't exactly lost, but she was frightened and trying not to show her fear lest some of the bounders roaming the Bowery try to take advantage.

Her first thought when she was released was to go and find her children. Robert and Lily and Kate. She longed to see their faces, tell them how sorry she was. But although Dr. Carmichael had told her where they were staying, in the fog of withdrawal from the opium, she had forgotten what he said. So she had gone to the old flat on Mulberry Street, knowing her hopes were foolish but still compelled to see for herself that her children were no longer there.

Not only were her babies gone, but so was everyone else she had known in the neighborhood. She should have expected as much. Renters came and went in waves in the tenement districts.

After that, she'd set out to find the doctor's office. Surely he would help her. He was a kind man, and Dr. Cole was such a fine lady. Good people—and Mary hadn't known many good people during the time she'd lived in New York.

The trouble was, she couldn't remember which street the doctor's office was on, if indeed he had told her at all. So she'd wandered aimlessly for a while, feeling weak and numb and increasingly ill. Despite all the misery she'd gone through to shake her opium habit, she knew that if she had any money at all she would go looking for the evil stuff.

But she had no money. She had nothing. Growing desperate now, she stopped a middle-aged man who wore the clothing of a laborer and appeared a decent-enough sort. He eyed her somewhat curiously, but his voice was kind when he directed her to Dr. Carmichael's practice.

The moment she spied Elizabeth Street, she began to run, the water squishing out over the tops of her shoes as she went. At the sight of the shingle announcing the doctors' offices, she slowed, then flung herself against the door at the side of the building—only to find it locked. She went around to the front and peered through the window, but there was no light, no sign that anyone was inside.

At that point, Mary could bear no more. She went back to the side door and inched herself under the narrow overhang of the tin roof. Exhausted and weak to the point of collapse, she slid down onto the stoop and began to weep.

What a miserable failure she was. She had failed everyone who ever loved her. She had failed her children most of all. Oh, what she had done to them!

She had failed her parents as well. They had begged her not to leave their home in Ohio. But, oh, she would come to New York, for she was going to be a great stage actress. That dream had faded in a cloud of smoke before her first year in the city had passed. She was "too small," they said, "too childlike," and her voice wasn't "right."

She'd been left to support herself by washing dishes in a Bowery tavern during the afternoons and checking coats and hats in a "gentlemen's club" at night. The trouble was that many of the "gentlemen" picking up their outerwear after a night of drinking and gambling were interested in picking her up as well. She'd been dismissed from that place after slapping a horse-faced young dandy with bold hands and a filthy mouth who was intent on dragging her into the coat room.

That was when she'd gone to the mission house seeking assistance. And that was where she had met Robert Warburton.

~

She'd been so naïve all those years ago. Even after a year in the city, she still thought a properly dressed gentleman with a *Reverend* before his name, a man with a kind smile and a "God bless you!" for each unfortunate in the food line, could be trusted.

Robert was volunteering that day, helping to serve meals alongside some of the women from his congregation's benevolence committee. He seemed to take a personal interest in everyone he served, coming around to the tables, introducing himself, and visiting with each one individually.

He was a plain man, not the sort to fancy himself irresistible to women, and he had an amiable, almost an avuncular manner that set her at ease from the first meeting. His concern for Mary appeared to be sincere and immediate, and when he appeared the next afternoon at the tavern where she washed dishes she was genuinely glad to see him. Then when he offered her employment as assistant manager of an apartment building he claimed to own—a position that included free rent and furnishings—she nearly fell at his feet and wept.

If it struck her as curious that a man of the cloth would own an entire apartment building—much less more than one—she didn't bother to question it too deeply. After inquiring among a few of the regulars at the mission, she soon learned that Warburton's congregation was one of the largest and most prosperous in the city. It was said that his wife was also an heiress, a very wealthy woman in her own right.

Even when he began to drop by the apartment just to "check on the building" and see how she was faring, Mary suspected nothing improper. He was a clergyman, after all, and she was one of his employees. It never occurred to her to question whether his other employees were treated as well as she.

As time went on, he began bringing her gifts, small things, at first—a tin of sweetmeats, a canister of coffee, a loaf of bread from the nearby German bakery. Later, when the visits became more frequent and the gifts more lavish, he dismissed her protests with the explanation that, not having children of his own, he took great pleasure in "fussing over" his younger employees.

Over time, Mary actually grew fond of him—not in a romantic sense, but as she might have developed affection for an older friend or relative. She looked forward to his visits with an eagerness that had nothing to do with the gifts he brought or any sort of interest in a clandestine relationship, but much to do with her need for human companionship. She was lonely, and he was kind to her, and she was willing to overlook the questionable propriety of his visits for the simple pleasure of his presence.

Then came an evening when she was feeling particularly isolated and downhearted. Robert came around later than usual, bearing a small velvet box in which rested a delicate gold and pearl locket, the loveliest piece of jewelry Mary had ever seen. As she knew she must, she refused to accept it—and continued to refuse until, crestfallen, he appeared to wipe some suspicious dampness from his eyes. At that moment she softened, and he declared his affection for her, slipping the locket around her neck and begging her to listen as he explained, haltingly at first, the true state of his marriage. A wife who was no helpmate, a sickly older woman whom he respected and would never embarrass or humiliate, but whom he could not bring himself to love.

Mary realized later that the whole tale was taken straight from the pages of the most lurid dime novel, a story that countless men before him had no doubt used to win over an innocent. But she was young and admittedly foolish, and he had become more important to her than she'd realized.

That was the night she became his mistress.

Robert continued to be good to her as time passed. Indeed, when they were together, no husband could have been more devoted.

She knew all along that he wouldn't marry her, of course. He'd made that perfectly clear from the beginning of their affair. He was a widely known, influential member of the clergy, a respected community leader, and an esteemed author and speaker. He told her clearly that he would never do anything to hurt his wife or disappoint or disillusion his "flock." The Lord was depending on him to further His kingdom, and no hint of scandal must be allowed to touch him or his expanding ministry.

Mary understood. For the most part, she was glad of his attention and company. He brought her books and newspapers, told her she was beautiful and talented, made sure she had what she needed. The security of knowing he cared for her outweighed the nagging shame of being a kept woman.

Gradually, however, things began to change. He didn't come to the flat as often, and when he did come, he seldom brought a gift. He also began to exhibit certain behavior during their intimate times together that disturbed her slightly. For the most part, however, she managed to dismiss her disappointment and uneasiness.

Besides, she was expecting a child.

Not long after their son was born, Robert moved them to a larger flat. For a time, he seemed to lose interest in the physical side of their relationship. He spent an afternoon or an evening with them once a week or so, but seemed content merely to have dinner, play with the baby for a while, and then leave.

Most often he appeared to be tired and preoccupied. But because Mary knew how involved and busy he was—and because she had no real choice—she never complained.

For over a year they existed this way, more as companionable friends than as lovers. Then everything changed, and the undercurrents she'd sensed earlier in their relationship came to the surface. Little by little, his demands turned aberrant—or at least what Mary sensed to be aberrant. She was ignorant for the most part about such things, but despite her naiveté, she knew that much of what Robert Warburton required of her was unnatural. Unnatural and degrading.

In a matter of months, he had involved her in practices that made her lose all respect for him and even begin to hate him. She learned things about him she would have never dreamed of—horrid things that both astonished and sickened her.

She began to plot and scheme about getting away from him, taking little Robert and escaping to a place where they couldn't be found. She had no money—he kept close watch on the meager "household funds" he allowed her. She was desperate to leave, but with no independent income and little Robert just past two, there was little hope of escape. She was trapped, at least for the time being.

She decided to stay and make the best of it, at least until her son was older. But the months turned into years, and eventually she found herself with child again—and again, for within months of giving birth to Lily, she discovered that Kate was on the way.

The only thing that kept her from completely going to pieces at this point was her fear for her children—and the fact that at least when she was pregnant, Robert left her alone. It was as if he was repulsed by her condition. The respite from his deviant physical demands was such a relief that she dreaded the day when the child would be born.

As it happened, the baby came early. Another little girl. Kate was a sickly infant from the beginning. She couldn't seem to nurse properly, and she suffered so badly from colic that at times Mary thought she would go mad with the infant's incessant screaming.

This time, when Robert began to insist on "his rights" again, Mary fought him and refused any further physical intimacy. She also made the incredibly foolish mistake of threatening to make his wife and even his church congregation aware of what she knew about him.

It was the worst thing she could have done. Robert was not a tall man, but he was thickset and brawny, and he found it nothing more than an inconvenience to force himself on the much smaller Mary, especially as weak and ill as she was at the time.

The encounter was so fierce that Mary thought she would surely die of it. Robert actually seemed remorseful that night, and before leaving he coaxed her into trying some "medicine" he'd brought with him. Knowing how "delicate" she was and how difficult it seemed to be for her to contend with his "admittedly strong passions," he explained that he had procured something for her that would not only ease her "discomfort," but would also counteract those "terrible black moods" from which she seemed to suffer more and more.

That was the night Mary first discovered opium.

That was the night she sold her soul to hell.

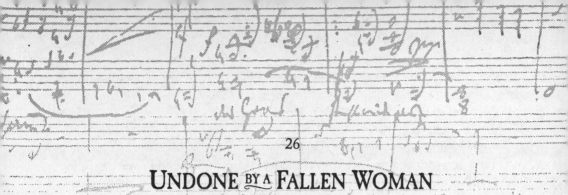

26

UNDONE BY A FALLEN WOMAN

A pity beyond all telling
Is hid in the heart of love.

W. B. YEATS

Frank found Mary Lambert huddled under the overhang at Doc's office.

His eyes never left her as he dismounted Attila and tethered him. She was soaked through and shivering with every breath, for she didn't have so much as a sweater around her thin shoulders.

And she was crying. Crying like a lost child.

Frank was unprepared entirely for the effect the woman had on him. The sight of her hit him like a blow to the stomach, shocking him out of his resolve to stay detached and throwing every bolt that held in place his deepest feelings. He would never have admitted it to a living soul, but the force of his reaction almost frightened him.

He knelt beside her, rainwater streaming off his hat and face, and for an instant he had the oddest feeling that he was weeping with her.

He shook his head to dispel the foolish notion, then put a gentle hand to her shoulder.

"Mary," he said, his voice raw with the swelling in his throat. "It's all right now, Mary."

Her head came up, her eyes wide and frightened as she flinched and shrank from him.

The idea that she was afraid of him turned in Frank like a jagged blade. "Don't be afraid, Mary. I mean only to help you."

She was all in a tremble, shaking fiercely and hugging her arms to herself as if to keep from falling apart.

Frank shrugged out of his raincoat and pulled it around her. It was heavy with rainwater, but it would at least keep the worst of the wind off her.

She tried to say something but was shaking so hard the words wouldn't come.

"We need to get you inside. Doc's door is locked, is it?"

She nodded.

"Well, I know where he keeps the key."

Frank straightened and went to the door, running his hand over the lintel until he found the extra key to the office. He unlocked the door, then helped Mary to her feet and took her inside, tossing his hat behind him on the floor of the entryway.

After settling her on a chair near the iron stove in the waiting room, he went to start a fire, working it and punching it up until he had a good, vigorous blaze going.

One glance back at Mary, wrapped in his wet coat and still shaking, sent him in search of a towel and a blanket. He found both in the linen closet between the examining rooms and, after easing his wet coat from around her shoulders, did his best to dry her hair before wrapping her snugly in the blanket.

This would help some, but it wasn't enough to keep her from getting pneumonia. She needed a thorough change of clothes and something warm to drink.

The entire time he was working with her, she said nothing, but merely watched him through those deep-set, sorrowful eyes. Finally, he stood back and tried to think. He didn't know quite what to do with her. He could keep her here for a while, but sooner or later he'd have to report in, or the captain would set him to cleaning up horse droppings in the Bowery for the next week. She needed somewhere to go, somewhere she could stay.

For now, he sat down in the chair next to her. "Is the fire helping?" he said.

She nodded. Frank reached for her hands, and she jerked at his touch until he shook his head, saying, "You're too cold, Mary. I mean only to warm you."

She relented, and Frank managed to keep his expression impassive as he took in the smallness of her hands, the fragility of her bones. He could have crushed them with his own big paws with no effort at all. No wonder she was afraid of him.

He looked up to find her watching him, and when their eyes met she didn't glance away but continued to search his gaze. Her eyes were filled with questions, and Frank realized then she wasn't accustomed to having someone fuss over her or take care of her. The realization caused his heart to wrench, and he was surprised at the strength of his desire to protect her.

She glanced away, but not before he saw that she was weeping again, large tears that tracked slowly down her face. This silent evidence of the depth of her despair nearly undid Frank. Overcome by a fierce desire to gather her into his arms and provide a fortress of protection for her, he shuddered.

He had to stop this. The woman who was turning his mind to mush was an opium addict. A kept woman, a woman who had allowed herself to be used by the same man who meant to destroy Andrew Carmichael. And Frank's one purpose where she was concerned was to elicit any information she could give him about Robert Warburton.

Never in all the years he'd been on the force had Frank Donovan allowed personal feelings to interfere with his work. And he wasn't about to start now.

But he couldn't ignore the rasp he heard in her breathing or the bluish tinge to her lips or the hard shaking that still wracked her small frame. He couldn't question—or bully—a sick, shivering woman, could he?

There was no help for it at present. He had to do what he could for her until she was up to another round of questions. So he disregarded the instinct hammering at him that he should release her hands now and go sit across the room from her. Indeed, he was still warming her hands between his own when Doc and Bethany Cole walked in.

~

They stopped just inside the doorway and stood staring with bewilderment and disbelief.

Frank had no doubt that the last thing the two doctors expected to find was himself and the miserable-looking Mary Lambert sitting by the fire in their office waiting room.

He realized then that he was still holding Mary's hands, and he dropped them as if her skin had suddenly scalded his own.

"Frank?" Doc said, looking altogether baffled.

Frank stood. "Doc," he said, then inclined his head to Bethany Cole. "Dr. Cole."

Doc had already come across the room and was now standing over Mary, taking in her wretched appearance. "Mary? What's happened? What are you doing here?"

She sat staring at him but made no reply, instead looking to Frank.

"The clinic turned her out," Frank said. "Sent her packin' in the rain, with no coat and nowhere else to go."

"What!" Dr. Cole now came to stand on the other side of Mary. "Oh, Mary, you're absolutely drenched!"

"Do you think you could find something dry for her to put on, Dr. Cole?" said Frank. "She's chilled bad."

Doc took over then. "Bethany, please take her in back and get her as dry as you can. I'll go upstairs and find a clean nightshirt for her."

"Can I do anything, Doc?" Frank asked, watching Bethany Cole help Mary from the waiting room.

Doc turned and eyed him with a dark look. "You can tell me what's going on! I'll be surprised if the woman doesn't have pneumonia. And look at you—you're as soaked as she is! Where have you been, Frank?" He paused. "Tell me you're not still harassing Mary about this Warburton matter."

Frank ignored the bit about his "harassing" Mary. "Well, it's like this, Doc. As I said, that terror of a woman at the clinic—Miss Savage is her name, and a fitting one it is—set your Mary Lambert out today with nothing but the clothes on her back. And since I figured she had no business wanderin' about in the rain, I've spent a good part of the day trying to find her. And where I found her was here—sittin' out there by your door, as drenched as a sewer rat and pretty much undone."

He saw his friend wince. "This is my fault. I knew they wouldn't keep her much longer, and I've been so—involved with my own affairs I neglected to find another place for her. This is my fault," he repeated.

"Seems to me it's the fault of the clinic, Doc," Frank pointed out. "And I'd say you've had enough to handle lately that you can't be expected to remember everything. Will she be all right, do you think?"

"Well, I need to examine her before I can answer that. But you can see for yourself that her condition is anything but good."

Frank nodded. "I'll just wait out here while you check her over."

Doc looked at him as if he'd lost his wits entirely. "You surely don't mean to bother her yet tonight? I'll not hear of it."

Frank hitched his thumbs in his belt loops and met Doc's look straight on. "Beggin' your pardon, Doc, but it's not up to you to tell me when I can question her."

"Now see here, Frank. Mary Lambert is my patient, and I will tell you when you can see her. Besides," he added, "you don't intend to just talk with her. You mean to ply a sick woman with questions about something she had nothing to do with."

"I mean to question Warburton's sick mistress," Frank growled. "Now I'll wait just as long as I need to. But I *will* wait." He paused and let out a long breath. "Look, Doc, this woman has already told me plenty about the good Reverend. But I know in my gut she's holdin' back more than what she's told me—and I intend to get it all. I'm convinced this woman is the best chance we've got of stopping Warburton and his dirty tricks."

He stopped, then put a hand to the other man's shoulder. "In case you haven't noticed, Doc," he said, lowering his voice, "things are getting worse for you by the day. I don't see too many patients in your office anymore, and I hear plenty of talk around the streets that isn't exactly favorable to your reputation, if you take my point. And so you see why I need to know everything Mary Lambert knows about Warburton. If I'm right, I can fix him so he won't be doin' you any more damage."

Frank could see the other man fighting with the urge to tell him to get out— and he also knew the instant Doc's common sense won the battle.

"All right," Doc said, clenching his swollen knuckles into fists. "If I decide that Mary's up to speaking with you, you can talk with her. Briefly. But if she's simply too weak—or, worse, yet, if I find evidence of pneumonia—you're leaving, Frank. I mean it. I won't let you badger her if she's as ill as I think she might be."

Frank had no intention of "badgering" the frail Mary Lambert. All his better instincts clamored for him to protect her, not mistreat her. But he merely grinned and said, "I get the picture, Doc. For the time being, you're the boss."

Doc made a small sound of disgust, and on the way out the door muttered something about a "hardheaded Irishman."

"Sour-tempered Scot," Frank fired at his back.

Doc kept on going, as if he hadn't heard, but Frank knew he had.

~

More than an hour later, Doc having given his reluctant consent, Frank again found himself in the role of Mary Lambert's merciless interrogator. He had all he could do not to back off entirely from the woman. He found the whole process loathsome, and the longer he went at her with his questions, the more he disgusted himself. But he sensed that he finally had her where he wanted her, ready to spill everything she knew about that snake, Warburton, and so he would continue his unrelenting drive for the truth.

After examining Mary, Doc had taken her upstairs to the sofa in his apartment, where he'd wrapped her snugly in blankets. A fire was crackling and hissing in the grate. Indeed, the room was so warm that Frank longed to stick his head out the window and cool himself off in the rain.

The woman was weeping again, and Frank thought he would strangle on the sight of her misery and humiliation. Instead, he bent over her, swallowing down his own shame and self-disgust as he repeated his last question, the one that had triggered this fresh bout of tears.

"You told me he was a terrible man, Mary, but you haven't told me why. I need to know more than that. There's an entire host of terrible men walking about town, but without evidence as to what they've done, there's no stopping their mischief. What is it about a man of the cloth that would make you say such a thing?"

She stared up at him, the blankets tucked all the way up to her chin, looking more like a girl than a grown woman.

He yanked himself back to reality by remembering where she had been and what she had done. Mary Lambert was no innocent child.

"Mary?" he prompted her.

She squeezed her eyes shut. "He's not a man of the cloth," she said in little more than a whisper.

Frank didn't move. "What?"

Mary opened her eyes and looked at him. Frank bent lower.

"I said he isn't really a man of the cloth. He…a long time ago, he was a kind of…salesman. Then, later he took up with a…with one of those…tent healers. The ones that travel around the country holding revivals. Robert used to laugh about it, how he got his preacher training in the back of a wagon and the front of a tent."

Frank straightened, his mind racing. "He's a charlatan, then? A confidence trickster," he said quietly, more to himself than to Mary.

She nodded.

Frank imagined he felt like a man might feel who'd been holding his breath under water and suddenly came up for a lifesaving gulp of air.

"You're sure of this?"

Again she nodded. "He seemed…proud of the fact. He swore me to secrecy, of course, warned me not to tell even the children. But I believe he liked to think he'd pulled off something clever."

"All these years," Frank said, his mind scrambling to take in what he'd just heard.

He stood looking down at Mary Lambert, who had turned her face away from him. "How could he pull it off as slick as he did? The man is famous—practically a saint in this town. How'd he fool so many for so long?"

She shook her head. "To hear him tell it, it wasn't all that difficult. And I told you, he'd been a salesman. He has…a way with people. He could make you believe anything he wanted you to…"

Her voice broke, and Frank felt a pang of sympathy. This might be good news for him, but Robert Warburton had been nothing but bad news for her.

She drew in a breath. "Robert's a smart man. Educated. He used to read the newspapers, and he could read the entire paper in the time it would take me to read one page. And he remembers everything." She paused, her voice quaking when she repeated, "He's very smart."

The bitterness in her voice caught Frank's attention. Looking at the woman on the sofa, her eyes again glazed with tears, her body so slight as to almost disappear inside the blankets, Frank saw something more than the humiliation of a woman taken in and used by a consummate deceiver. Something more dreadful had happened to her than falling victim to a corrupt man and an addictive narcotic. It was as if something had snuffed the light from Mary Lambert, had battered her and bruised her until there was nothing left in her except shadows. She was…fading. Draining away.

"What else, Mary?" he said, dropping down to his knees beside the couch.

"Nothing," she said quickly. Too quickly.

Frank touched her hair. Something like pity, but stronger, more personal, gripped him, and he had to fight the impulse to gather her to himself and try to dispel her shadows with his own life force.

Deliberately, he softened his voice. "Mary," he said. "You must tell me."

She turned to look at him. "You said before…you said that Robert is making bad trouble for Dr. Carmichael."

Frank nodded. "I know he is, but I have to prove it. If there's anything else you can tell me—anything—I need to know what it is, Mary."

She closed her eyes. "I can't." Her voice was hoarse.

"Please, Mary. Doc—Dr. Carmichael has been good to you, hasn't he?"

She nodded, the tears now spilling from her eyes.

"He's a good man, Mary," said Frank, reaching to stroke her hair away from her face. "You know that. He's…more a man of God than most preachers, I'm thinking. I'm proud to call him my friend. And Warburton is close to ruining him."

He told her everything that had happened, from the vandalism of Doc's office to the letters in the papers, the rumors, the scandal, the outright shunning of Doc by some of his colleagues and many of his patients.

Her expression was stricken. "No." The word caught like a sob.

"Oh, I mean to stop him, Mary. I *will* stop him. And I can with your help. But you have to tell me everything. Everything you know about him. Anything I can use."

"I can't." She sounded as if she were choking on the words. "I *can't!*"

She looked up. Frank followed the direction of her gaze to the doorway, where Doc and Dr. Cole had come to stand like silent sentinels.

Mary looked at them for a long time, then turned back to Frank. "I can't tell you," she said. "But…I'll tell Dr. Cole."

Frank held her gaze, then slowly nodded and got to his feet and crossed the room. "She has something she won't tell me," he said to Bethany Cole, who glanced toward Mary. "She says she can't tell me. But she'll tell you."

Dr. Cole looked at him, then back at Mary. She seemed uncertain, hesitant.

Frank put a hand to her arm. "Whatever she means to tell you, it's almost sure to be…ugly. But I have to know what it is. No matter what she tells you, you'll have to tell me. For Doc's sake."

Bethany Cole searched his eyes, and for the first time since he'd met the woman, Frank saw something besides dislike or irritation at him. Finally she nodded, and Frank dropped his hand away from her arm. She started toward the couch, then turned back.

"Andrew," she said evenly, "you and Sergeant Donovan will have to leave the room now. I want to speak with Mary."

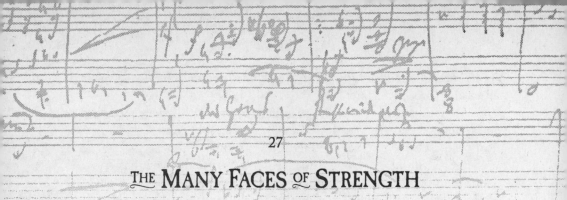

27

The Many Faces of Strength

There is no healing
for one who has known no pain.
There is no darkness
for one who chooses to in the light remain.

ANONYMOUS

More than an hour later, Andrew Carmichael was still sitting in the kitchen of his flat with Frank Donovan.

Darkness had drawn in on the night, and a kerosene lamp flickered on the table between them. Frank was clearly growing more and more impatient with the waiting. He would sit for a while, then get up and pace the room. Andrew had lost count of how many cups of tea they'd consumed between them.

When Bethany appeared in the doorway, her appearance triggered an urgency in Andrew to go to her, lest she faint. He did get to his feet, as did Frank, but something in her expression warned him not to approach her.

She looked…ill. Tendrils of her fair hair had escaped the confines of the neat little knot at the back of her neck. Her porcelain skin had turned ashen, and her eyes deeply shadowed, with an almost startled expression. But even more stark was the mask of pain she wore.

"Bethany?" Andrew suddenly wished he had tried to stop her from talking with Mary Lambert. Whatever she had heard had left her…different. Changed.

Clearly shaken, she seemed not to hear him. She leaned heavily against the door frame, staring into the room but obviously not seeing them.

"Dr. Cole? What did she tell you?" Frank's voice, stronger and not so cautious as Andrew's, seemed to snap her out of her peculiar state. Slowly she raised her head, lifted her shoulders, and walked the rest of the way into the room.

She faced them both at the table. Andrew hoped he would never again see such a look of anguish on her face as he saw in that moment. Her hands trembled when she gripped the back of the chair, and when she spoke, her lips trembled, too.

She looked from one to the other, her countenance still taut with distress. "I'm so ashamed," she said, shocking Andrew and, from his expression, Frank, as well.

Andrew reached to cover her hand with his, but she pulled away from him and shook her head. Although hurt and confused by her appearance and her behavior, he stood very still, sensing her need for quiet.

"I judged her, you know." Her voice was unsteady, yet there was no sign of wavering. "The first time I saw her, when we went to that awful tenement building and found her and her children in such wretched circumstances, I was so angry with her. I thought she must be a terrible woman, to degrade herself and allow her children to live in such squalor."

"Bethany, don't—" Andrew tried to interrupt, but she raised a hand to silence him.

"No, let me finish. I want to say this before I tell you anything else." She seemed to gain strength as she went on. "I judged her to be a weak and selfish woman. A woman with no morality, no self-respect."

She moistened her lips, then swallowed, as if she were finding it extremely difficult to get the words out. "I was wrong. Although Mary Lambert may have been naïve and too trusting for her own good, she wanted out of her situation. But she believed herself to be trapped—by the three pregnancies and later the addiction—and Warburton threatened her and the children if she should try to leave him." She paused. "I've only now come to realize that, in her own way, Mary Lambert is a very strong woman."

She stopped to pull in a deep, ragged breath. "At least she survived, and that makes her stronger than I. I would never have survived what she's lived through."

She locked eyes first with Andrew, then with Frank, and the pain in her expression reflected the hideous nature of what she had heard from Mary Lambert.

"I...wanted you to know that before I tell you anything more. You mustn't make the same mistake that I did. You mustn't judge her. She doesn't deserve that."

There was still horror in her eyes, but her features softened when she turned to Andrew. "I can't talk to you about this, Andrew. Please understand. You and I, we're—" She shook her head. "I...couldn't bear to tell you the things she described to me. But Sergeant Donovan—" She glanced at Frank. "He's a policeman. I'm a doctor. And he needs to know...what Warburton really is."

She touched Andrew's hand, her gaze meeting his in a look of appeal. "Perhaps you could check on Mary while I speak to the sergeant?"

At first he didn't understand, and he was about to object, but something in her eyes told Andrew not to press. Apparently, Frank sensed the same thing, because he was quick to chime in. "Why don't you do what Dr. Cole suggested, Doc? You stay with Mary for now and let us talk."

Andrew didn't like it. If what Bethany had to tell was so horrible she couldn't repeat it to him, how could she tell Frank—a man she scarcely knew and didn't even like?

He knew if he voiced what he was thinking, he would risk sounding peevish. As it happened, Frank offered an answer before Andrew could ask the question.

"There's no shockin' a copper, Doc. What I haven't heard most likely hasn't happened. But there's some things a woman shouldn't have to discuss with the man she's going to marry, and I'm thinkin' what Dr. Cole has to say may just fall into that category. So you go on now and tend to Mary while Dr. Cole and myself have a chat."

Andrew glanced back at Bethany, and when she nodded he took his cup of tea and started for the bedroom.

～

Frank Donovan sat drumming his fingers on the kitchen table, staring at the flickering flame of the oil lamp. He was aware that Bethany Cole, seated across from him, was avoiding his gaze, and it wasn't difficult to understand why. She might be a doctor, but she was also a lady. As a physician, she'd doubtless encountered a number of situations that would have horrified other women. But that didn't mean she found it easy to confront the sort of ugliness she had just related to him.

He cringed to think that Mary Lambert had lived with this sort of ugliness for years. The very thought kindled a hot flash of anger.

With more than two decades under his belt as a policeman, Frank had known surprisingly few individuals he would have categorized as altogether evil. There had been some, of course, but even they had rarely evoked in him the dark bloodlust that ran through him now, the kind that makes one man feel as if he might murder another.

At the moment he was trying to figure whether the urge to hurt Robert Warburton, to destroy him, was due entirely to the unqualified evil the man seemed to personify. Or was it more because Warburton had inflicted that evil on Mary Lambert?

An equal dose of both, most likely. But whatever the reason, it in no way lessened the fury building in him that made him want to grind Warburton under the heel of his boot like the vermin he was.

The man was a plague, more vile than he'd even thought.

"So he's a pervert as well as a charlatan," he muttered, speaking aloud what he was thinking.

"What will you do?"

Bethany Cole's strained voice yanked him back to his surroundings. He looked at her, and saw, not as he usually did, a woman physician—and a testy one at that—but a woman. A woman who was tired and still badly shaken from sharing the confidence of Mary Lambert.

"Nothing near what I'd like to do," Frank bit out. "And he's just snake enough to get away with it all."

"That can't happen! The man is a monster! You're going to arrest him, aren't you?" Outrage had stained her pale skin an angry crimson.

"Oh, I'll go after him, all right. But don't be surprised if he never sees the inside of a cell. In fact, I expect he'll be gone like a shot as soon as word leaks out."

"What do you mean?"

Frank leaned forward a little on his elbows. "What brings down a man like Warburton is a public scandal. Once it gets out that he's not and never has been what he's passed himself off to be—well, that'll be the beginnin' of the end for him, don't you see? His fancy church will throw him out on his ear, and all the speeches and the book writing will come to a halt, so there'll be no more funds coming in. Now, if Mary's right, it's Warburton's wife who holds the purse strings. So just how likely is it that she'll be spending much of it on him once she knows what he's been up to all this time?"

"I think she does know. Or at least knows in part. It was his wife who first came to Andrew and asked him to make a call on Mary Lambert. Andrew recognized her the day he went to Warburton's house."

Frank lifted both eyebrows. "Is that a fact now? Then that means she must be a decent enough sort. All the more likely that she'll send him packing."

Rather enjoying the scenario he was painting for Bethany Cole, Frank went on. "New York will wash its hands of him, and he'll simply pull out some night when no one's about to see him go. And no one will care."

"That's too easy for him!"

"I agree with you, Dr. Cole, but I know how things are done in this city. And though I'd like nothing better than to walk him to the hangin' tree myself, I'm about as sure as I can be that he'll disappear before I have the chance." He drew in a long breath. "He'll more than likely just pull up stakes here and start all over again somewhere else."

"But if you arrest him—"

"His fancy lawyer will have him out before the sun goes down. So far as we know, he hasn't murdered anyone, and there's no clear evidence of fraud or theft—at least not the kind you can prove, the kind that will put a fella behind bars. No, listen to me now. As much as I'd enjoy cleaning the city streets with his bare hide, I'm more interested in undoing the damage that's been done to Doc. That's what I intend to take care of before anything else."

Bethany frowned. "But how? Warburton has all but ruined Andrew with these fiendish attacks. What can you do?"

Frank stood. "I'll have to work on that, Dr. Cole. But don't you worry—I'll think of something."

He braced his hands on the table and leaned toward her. "Something I want to know first. What can you and Doc do to help Mary Lambert?"

She looked surprised. "Why…I'm not sure." She paused, studying him with an intensity that made Frank squirm a little. The woman had a way of looking right through a man.

In spite of the sadness engraved upon her face, a slow smile began to tug at the corners of her dainty little mouth. She looked as if she'd just realized something of great interest. "Don't you worry, Sergeant," she said archly, repeating his own words to her. "We'll think of something."

"Well," he said gruffly, "if there's a question of money for any special care she might be needin', you've only to ask. I've a bit put by."

Her smile grew even wider, and, tired as Frank knew she must be, for an instant her eyes took on a peculiar shine. "That's very generous of you, Sergeant— Frank. Andrew will be pleased to know you want to help."

Eager to escape that curious look, Frank started for the door. "Tell Doc I had to go," he said. "I'll stop by tomorrow."

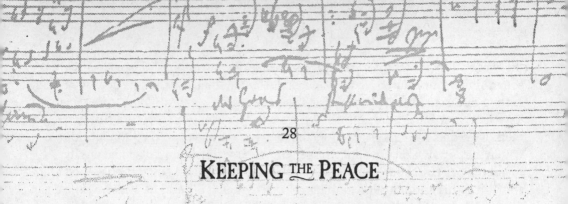

28

KEEPING THE PEACE

My crown is in my heart, not on my head;
Not deck'd with diamonds and Indian stones,
Nor to be seen: my crown is call'd content;
A crown it is that seldom kings enjoy.

WILLIAM SHAKESPEARE

On the Wednesday before Easter, chaos reigned at Bantry Hill. Michael was working in a frenzy on his *American Anthem* suite in addition to preparing for two concerts before the Independence Day event. His calls for help were frequent but erratic, and he seemed to expect Susanna and Paul to anticipate each request. He was usually more reasonable than this, but, as Susanna was learning, he was by nature a musician, and as such tended to isolate himself in his own world when the pressures of his work engulfed him. Until, that is, he needed something—when he had a way of bursting forth from his world and rocking the axes of other worlds. Of course, when he was actively composing, he really did require assistance—and these days, he seemed to be composing most of the time.

Then there was Caterina, who was in a fret, insisting that her dress for Easter Sunday needed the hem let out and the shoulders eased. Susanna found this hard to believe since the dress had been finished only six weeks before. When she tried it on her niece again, however, she realized Caterina was right. The child had grown just enough that the garment was too short and needed more give in the shoulders. There was nothing to do but alter the dress before Sunday.

Moira Dempsey and Nell Grace, who seemed of one mind these days, especially in regard to the extra cleaning and preparations required by the Easter season and the approach of spring, were dashing about from one task to another, attacking each with great energy. Susanna could not have been more grateful for the addition of the MacGovern girl to the household staff, for Moira seemed to have taken a liking to her and was happy to share the work. The negative aspect of this was that there seemed to always be someone dusting or polishing or cleaning something in any room Susanna happened to enter. There was simply no way of getting out from underfoot wherever she went.

Papa Emmanuel tried, in his own way, to be of help, but he had his own method of doing things—and unfortunately his way never seemed to coincide with Moira's way. Consequently, he spent much time following individual family members or staff about the house, offering his unsolicited suggestions—and sometimes his criticisms—regarding their activities. To Susanna's dismay, the two people he most closely adhered to were Moira and Michael.

Riccardo Emmanuel and the Dempseys had known each other forever, of course. Michael and his parents had often spent weeks with his mother's family in Ireland, and the Dempseys had been friends and neighbors of his grandparents. Although they had not seen each other for several years, one would have thought that Papa Emmanuel and Moira had never been apart, so familiar were their habits to each other and so personal and heated—and frequent—their disagreements.

In the midst of all this pandemonium, too, ran a somber undercurrent: Maylee's obvious decline. While everyone else in the house was running about in a constant flurry, Maylee lay abed almost all the time now, watching through her window as winter ended its last dance to make way for spring. Dr. Carmichael had cautioned them all during his last visit that these were almost certainly Maylee's final days.

Given this painful reality, when Susanna was tempted to grumble about the extra work and confusion, she tried to stop and give thanks that she and the rest of the family had been blessed with the strength and the good health to carry out their daily busyness. At the same time, in light of what the ailing child in the front bedroom had to endure, she found the household skirmishes and everyday irritations increasingly difficult to tolerate.

More and more, she understood why Michael had such a deep need for peace in his home and in his life, and why he so often went out of his way to thank her for whatever she managed to do to keep the peace at Bantry Hill. What he didn't know was how often she had to pray for patience with those who sometimes seemed intent on disrupting that peace.

～

Papa Emmanuel could easily be heard throughout most of the first floor when he raised his voice. For that matter, so could Moira Dempsey when, as Michael put it, "her Irish was up."

That being the case, Susanna didn't feel too guilty when she happened to overhear the argument taking place in the kitchen that afternoon. In truth, she was tempted simply to walk in on the fracas and hope that her intrusion would put a stop to their bickering, which of late seemed to be an almost daily event. But when one heard one's name being bandied about by raised voices, it was awfully difficult not to listen.

So she stopped just outside the door long enough to hear Riccardo Emmanuel pronounce her "too young," and "possibly too far removed from the music world to understand Michael's genius," and to know "what was best for him in his career."

Susanna bit her tongue, fully expecting Moira to agree with Michael's father. It hadn't taken her long to realize that she wouldn't have been Moira's choice for Michael. Nor had she forgotten another conversation she'd overheard some time back—goodness, she'd been eavesdropping then, too; she really mustn't allow this to become a habit. During that exchange, Liam Dempsey had been defending her to his wife, while Moira insisted that 'even if she means well, she's too young. A girl like that is not going to tie herself down with a blind man and a child for long!'"

All the more reason she was caught completely off guard by Moira's next words. "Aye, she's young, but she understands more than you think. I say she's been good for the lad. You haven't been here long enough to notice the difference she's made in him."

Riccardo made the sound he typically uttered when he disagreed or was put out with someone. Susanna likened it to an audible breath with a nasty edge. "*Sì*, she is a pleasing girl," he said, "and perhaps she, too, has the gift of music— my son tells me this. But I think she is not so wise—or she would want him to return to his first love, the opera. She should want him to accept Conti's offer for *Lucia*."

Susanna's eyes widened at Moira's retort. She could almost see the housekeeper waving a kitchen utensil at Michael's father as she took him to task. "He had that world, now didn't he? And what good did it do him is what I'd like to know? Why can't you get it through that thick Eye-talian head of yours that the lad was sick of all that? Didn't he give it up? And it seems to me that should be his business! Sure, it's not yours!"

Susanna took a sharp breath. Michael's father would never stand for such disrespect.

As she'd expected, his rebuttal was harsh with anger as his accent grew stronger. "I am his father! My son's welfare—it is my business! And who are you, you Irish...*busybody*, that you should talk to me in such a way?"

Silence. Susanna waited, her nails digging almost painfully into the palms of her hands.

"Well, this Irish busybody has spent a good deal more time with your son than you have these past years," Moira shot back. "I saw what he went through when he lost his eyesight—you didn't. And I saw how that other one—that *Deirdre*—nearly unmanned him with her wanton ways and her drunkenness and her mean-spirited devilment. You didn't. And I've seen how much happier the man is now. Miss Susanna might be young, but she's good for him. And what's more, she'd be the first to encourage him if she thought he wanted to go back to that other world, that opera. But she's smart enough to know that has to be his choice, not hers."

Moira stopped, then added in a tone as cold and hard as a gravestone, "And it's for certain not your choice, Riccardo Emmanuel. You best stop tormenting that girl—and stop interfering in your son's life!"

The sound that came rumbling up from Papa Emmanuel's throat sounded almost dangerous. Susanna decided she'd heard enough. Besides, she fully expected Michael's father to come charging out of the kitchen like an enraged bull at any moment. With no further delay, she gathered up her skirts and hurried off.

Halfway down the hall, however, she caught herself smiling. The very idea—Moira Dempsey defending her! She would never have dreamed such a thing could happen.

~

Michael's morning had gone reasonably well so far. There had been few interruptions in his work, and his session with Renny Magee had been pure pleasure.

The girl was extraordinarily gifted in a number of areas, not the least of which was her perfect pitch and an innate, precise sense of rhythm that was impossible to teach. She had only to hear a tune once, and she could duplicate it almost note for note on that tin whistle of hers. Michael was already planning to try her on a flute and then a piccolo; he wouldn't be at all surprised if she didn't take to both like an eagle to flight.

His one failure with her seemed to be the ability to cheer the girl's heart. She and Maylee had become so close, such extraordinary friends, that Renny was grieving the other child's deteriorating condition. He had hoped that the music would in itself work to brighten Renny's spirits, but although she breezed through the music like a professional and did everything as she was told, Michael sensed that her heart wasn't altogether in her performance.

He, too, grew saddened when he thought about Maylee. He had grown quite fond of the girl. He admired her courage, her optimism, her faith, and her indefatigable sense of humor. The child could find at least a touch of lightness in almost anything, including her own condition.

He was still thinking about Maylee when his father walked into the room. It was almost as easy to identify Papa's entrance as it was Susanna's. Riccardo Emmanuel didn't so much enter a room as sweep into it. Surprisingly light on his feet for a man of his size, he never moved slowly. Every step seemed propelled by the man's enviable energy.

"Papa," Michael greeted him.

"Ah, at least my son concedes the fact I am his father."

Michael groaned, but silently. His father's tone as much as his words pointed to a fit of pique. No doubt he and Moira had been at it again.

"That—woman," his father declared, "is *una minaccia*!"

A menace. So he *had* been arguing with Moira.

"I don't understand why you put up with her!"

"If you're referring to Moira, Papa, you know very well why. She and Liam are family to me. As they were to Grandmama and Grandpapa. I can't think what I'd do without them."

His father uttered a sound of disgust. "I never did understand your grandparents'—and your mother's—affection for the woman."

"You've been arguing again?"

"Ha! There is no arguing with that one. She is always right. I am always wrong. She is—" Michael could almost see him tapping his head. "—the great sage!"

"Papa—"

"Never mind, never mind, is not important. I have an idea and would like you to consider it."

"Of course. What kind of an idea?"

"I think we should invite *Signor* Conti to supper one evening soon. After all, he has paid you high compliments, and it seems we should at least be gracious to acknowledge his interest in you."

A sharp pain stabbed at Michael's right temple. He pressed a hand against it, clenching his other fist. He would not let his father anger him or put him out of sorts—not this morning. But the headache had already begun.

"I think not, Papa. At least not anytime soon. Things are far too hectic as it is right now."

"But I think perhaps you misunderstand me. I know what you've said about not returning to the opera, and it is, of course, your decision. I mean only to be courteous to the man. Giocomo Conti is most important in the music world, yes?"

"*Sì*, he's a very important man, Papa. But I must remind you that I have no intention of performing in his *Lucia*—or in any other opera ever again."

"Michael—"

Michael heard the frustration in his father's voice and knew he was in for yet another debate about his decision to stop singing. He pulled in a long breath, bracing himself. At the same time, the pain in his head intensified.

"*Mio figlio*, why are you being so stubborn about this?"

"Why am I being so stubborn?" To give himself time to cool his irritation, Michael got up from the piano bench and walked to the mantel, keeping his back to his father for the time being.

"I am suggesting only a friendly meal, Michael. Nothing more."

Michael turned around, not speaking until he was sure he could do so without being argumentative. He loved his father too much to wound him or insult him, but lately Papa was trying his patience to the limit.

"Papa, don't dissemble with me. I think you're hoping that if I share a meal and a little friendly conversation with Signor Conti, I'll agree to perform again."

His father tried to interrupt, but Michael warned him off. "No, let me finish, please. If I'm right, if that's your intention, it would be a complete waste of his time—and ours—to invite him here. Please, Papa, hear what I am saying. There is nothing you can do to change my mind. Nothing."

Somehow he must convince his father to accept the fact for once and for all that he was finished—for good—with the world of opera. Papa's incessant harping on the subject was driving him to the end of his patience, and he knew Susanna was exceedingly tired of it as well.

"Michael, you are not being reasonable, I think—"

"Papa!" Michael cringed at his tone—when had he ever raised his voice to his father before today?—but what with the headache and Papa's obstinacy, he was finding it nearly impossible to curb his impatience. With great effort, he lowered his voice, but he was still rigid with frustration. "Papa, I love you, and I respect you—more than any man I know. But I must demand the same thing from you. I need you to accept the decisions I make regarding my own career—and *any* other area of my life. You must believe me. If I had any doubt in my heart—any doubt—that I made a mistake by leaving the opera and turning to composition and conducting, I would admit it. And I would carefully consider your opinion. But I have no doubt."

He stopped long enough to think. "I am a man, Papa, not a boy. I haven't been a boy for a very long time. You must begin seeing me as a man—your son, yes—but a man. And as a man, I believe that God has called me to this...place in my music—where I am today. You have no right to interfere with God's will for me, Papa. And with all respect, I must say to you that you are attempting to do just that."

He heard a sharp intake of air from his father, but he could not, he must not, relent. "Papa, don't you see? I had that other world once. I had it all—the crowds, the celebrity, the money, the...excitement. And I found it worthless. It gave me no peace, no joy—only emptiness. It turned me into a man I didn't even like, a man I couldn't respect."

Michael paused, struggling to find the words that would pierce his father's intransigence. "I don't regret for a moment leaving that world, and you must stop trying to make me want it again. I want you to be proud of me, Papa, to be proud of my music, what I am doing now. But I can't be what you want. I have to be what I am."

The throbbing in his head had built to a crescendo. Again he pressed his hand against his temple, trying to ease the pain. "There's one more thing, Papa. I need to say this. You have been critical of Susanna, and that, too, must end. This is the

woman I love, the woman I have chosen to spend my life with. Susanna is a wonderful person. She has brought peace and love into my world, and I had almost
given up hope I would ever find either. She loves me, and she loves Caterina—
and Caterina loves her as well. And she will love you, too, Papa, if you let her.
I'm asking you, for my sake, to please…accept Susanna as she is. Stop looking
for her failings. Instead, get to know her. If you do, I believe you will find much
that you approve of, much to love. But even if you don't, I cannot allow you to
be disrespectful of her—you must see that. It must end."

The silence was unnerving, especially since Michael couldn't see his father's
face or interpret his response. For a moment he thought he might have left the
room. But, no. Michael heard a slight movement, then the sound of his father's
voice, uncommonly hoarse and broken.

"Oh, my Michael…you cannot think I'm not proud of you? Surely not! *Mio
figlio*, but of course I am proud of you! No man ever had such a son—such a fine
son! You are my greatest pride, my deepest joy, in all the world! I would be proud
of the man you are even if you could not—what do they say in the English?—
carry a tune. You are my *son*!"

Caught completely unaware, Michael suddenly felt himself embraced—
vigorously embraced, and held so tightly as to make him lose his breath. His
father's hands were on his head, his face, his shoulders, and when Michael
skimmed a hand over the other's face, he felt the dampness of his father's tears.

"Forgive me, Michael! I am a terrible man!" A dramatic explosion of Italian
followed these words, along with another hard embrace, and Michael suddenly
found himself comforting his father.

"Papa, no, you are not—"

Their reconciliation was abruptly interrupted by a growling, barking wolfhound who bounded into the music room and threw himself at Michael's father.
Apparently Gus had heard the commotion and, believing his master to be in
danger, had rushed to perform a heroic rescue.

Now Michael had to turn his efforts to convincing the great hound that he
was in no jeopardy. It took both of them, Michael and his father, to calm the
dog and assure him the ruckus had been friendly and nonthreatening. Soon the
wolfhound was waltzing back and forth on his hind legs between the two of them,
and Michael and his father were laughing like two mischievous boys at play.

Susanna picked that moment to come hurrying into the room to see what all
the noise was about. Almost instantly, Michael found himself deserted as the
wolfhound and his father went to Susanna.

Her cry of surprise told Michael that it was her turn to receive the attentions
of Gus the wolfhound, along with one of Papa's bear hugs.

And her laughter told him she didn't mind in the least.

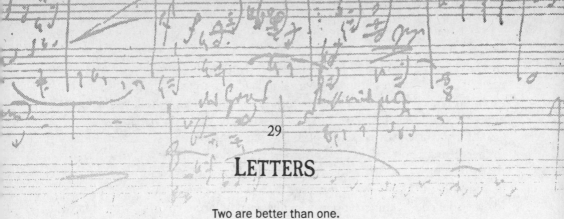

29

LETTERS

Two are better than one.

ECCLESIASTES 4:9 (NIV)

Frank Donovan took a friend with him when he called on Robert Warburton.

Well, not *his* friend exactly—but a friend of Doc Carmichael's. A friend who wanted to help.

Doc had been reluctant to mention Edward Fitch's offer to help. But once he did, Frank had decided the prominent attorney might be just the ticket for getting rid of that snake. Not only could Fitch fill Frank in on the finer points of the law; his reputation was bound to carry weight with a social climber like Warburton.

So dressed in his best uniform, his badge polished, his gun on full display, and Edward Fitch at his side, Frank paid a visit to the *Reverend* Warburton.

A dignified-looking black man opened the door. When he hesitated to announce them, Edward Fitch pulled a calling card from his pocket and put a foot in the door. "Just tell your employer we need to speak with him on a most important police matter. We'll wait until he's free."

Warburton was a surprise to Frank, to say the least. Though he hadn't exactly expected the man to have horns and breathe brimstone, he wasn't looking for him to be as unimpressive in appearance as he was. He was short—a fact Frank appreciated, having found he could intimidate some blokes just by glaring down on them. The man also had a bad complexion and eyes that reminded Frank of a pig.

Clearly, he meant to keep them standing in the fancy hallway, but Frank thought he might change his mind when he heard the nature of their business. This wasn't a fella who'd want his wife listening in on what Frank and Fitch had to say.

"How can I help you…gentlemen?" Warburton asked.

"You might want to talk with us in private—*Reverend.*" Frank made absolutely no effort to conceal the contempt in his tone.

Warburton's gaze flicked over him, then Fitch. He lifted his eyebrows and smiled. "Goodness, what does a clergyman do to rate a call from a policeman *and* an attorney?"

He thought he was slick, Frank decided. Well, they would just see *how* slick.

"For starters, he commits fraud and defamation," Frank replied in a voice just as oily as Warburton's. "Oh, and then there's also the matter of breakin' and enterin' and vandalism of private property."

He stopped, smiling grimly at the other man's red-faced look of outrage.

"You want to talk privately now, Reverend?"

"In here," Warburton said, his tone sharp. He marched in front of them and opened the doors on a room Frank assumed to be a study, though quite a swanky one for a "preacher."

Warburton went to the other side of his mahogany desk and sat down. He offered no indication that Frank and Edward Fitch should do likewise, but when Frank plopped down in one of two chairs across from him, Fitch followed suit. As previously agreed, Edward Fitch took up the conversation by citing the crimes Warburton could be charged with.

It didn't take long for the man on the other side of the desk to jump to his feet, his face livid. "This is the most ridiculous thing I've ever heard! It's ludicrous! Why would you even think of accusing me of such—atrocities? Don't you know who I am?"

Edward Fitch rubbed a finger across his upper lip, staring at Warburton. "We know exactly who you are, and you're no more clergyman than I am. You're a two-bit salesman with a clever tongue and a fast pitch. You learned whatever you might know about religion in a traveling tent show."

He paused, and Warburton tried to jump in, but Fitch stopped him with a snap of his fingers.

"We also know about Mary Lambert and your illegitimate children," Fitch went on. "Oh, and I'd rather not go into detail about this, but we've come up with a fairly clear idea of your sexual perversions. You really are a disgusting man."

Frank thought he might have enjoyed this if he didn't have to look at Warburton. But he couldn't seem to stop thinking about that snake touching Mary Lambert, putting his hands on her. The idea that a loathsome piece of rubbish like Warburton had humiliated her—and hurt her—made him itch to get the man's throat between his hands.

He gave himself a mental shake. Fitch was the best one to handle this. He knew the finer points of the law, and he could outtalk Warburton without batting an eye.

In fact, he had him squirming like a worm on a hook already, although the man was doing his best to wiggle free.

"I won't hear another word of this," Warburton sputtered. "I don't know this... Mary Lambert person. And all this nonsense about vandalism and such—I don't know what you're talking about! You simply cannot come in here and insult me with this corruption."

Frank could no longer hold his tongue. "Ah, but we are here, and if it's corruption you want to talk about, let's us have a talk about what you did to Mary Lambert."

Fitch reached over and put a hand to Frank's arm. Frank straightened a bit and closed his mouth.

"Sergeant Donovan here is prepared to take you with us as we leave," Fitch said, his tone casual. "You'll be charged and held, you understand, until you can hire yourself an attorney."

Then he stopped and locked eyes with Warburton. "But whoever you hire won't be able to help you very much if we produce a witness who can substantiate most of the charges brought against you. The breaking and entering might be a bit shaky, although I imagine it won't be all that difficult to locate the thugs you hired for the job."

Warburton twisted his mouth into an ugly scowl. "If you're so sure of yourselves, why haven't you arrested me already?"

Again Fitch smiled. "Is that what you really want? We'll be glad to oblige if you do."

Now it was Frank's turn. He got to his feet and pulled himself up to his full height. "A couple of things you need to know—*Reverend*. Doc Carmichael is a good friend of mine—my closest friend, as a matter of fact. And Doc is a real good man. I mean a *good* man, not that you'd know much about the breed."

Frank shook his head. "But me—I'm not a good man at all. In fact, I can be a very nasty fella altogether, and I'd just as soon make mutton out of your face as anything I can think of right about now. I just plain don't like you. And if I thought you were going to be locked up, out of my reach for any length of time, I'm afraid I'd have to at least settle my differences with you before they threw you in the cell. But Mr. Fitch here, he thinks there's a better way to maybe save your skin and work things out for all concerned. If you're interested, you might want to hear him out."

Warburton settled a killing glare on Frank. "Why should I be interested?"

Frank lowered himself back to the chair as Edward Fitch took over. "It might keep you out of jail, for one thing. Oh, by the way, I don't think I've explained that, like Sergeant Donovan, I'm also a good friend of Dr. Carmichael. He once saved my life. So you can imagine that I'm grateful. That's why I'm here."

Fitch dusted a speck of lint off his suit coat before going on. "Here's what I think might help your situation. You'll make a complete, detailed statement of your involvement in the vandalism of the doctor's office. You'll confess to the outrageous letters that have been appearing in the newspaper defaming Dr.

Carmichael—you'll send a copy of that admission to those same newspapers, by the way."

"I didn't write those letters!" Warburton burst out.

"If you didn't," Edward Fitch shot back, "you know who did. But you'll confess to them, all the same—and retract the accusations. Then you'll admit to your abuse of Mary Lambert and make arrangements to pay for the support of your illegitimate children—say, through a trust fund. I can assist you with that matter this very afternoon."

Warburton looked as if he might keel over from a massive stroke at any moment. Edward Fitch, however, was not quite finished. He made a clucking sound with his teeth, then said, "You know, Warburton, you very likely could have saved yourself a great deal of trouble by simply agreeing to what Andrew Carmichael asked of you in the first place. If you had consented to pay for the support of your own children, more than likely no investigation would have ever taken place. I must say, that was quite foolish on your part."

By now, Frank was growing impatient with all this gentlemen's blather. "So what's it goin' to be, Warburton? A cell or a retraction?"

Warburton ignored him, directing his reply to Edward Fitch instead. Frank decided that he must like lawyers better than cops.

"If I do this, I'll lose everything," Warburton whined. "I'll have to leave town, my ministry—"

"Your *ministry*?" Frank burst out. He couldn't help himself. The man was either a fool or a lunatic.

Warburton leveled a look of pure hatred on him, but Fitch redirected the man's attention. "Well, you're right about losing everything, of course. And as you might have realized, that's exactly what we want and expect."

Warburton sat leaning on his elbows, his fingers laced in front of his face. "You'll guarantee I can...leave...if I do what you ask? There will be no jail time?"

Fitch sat forward a little. "You can leave. About the jail time—well, that depends on what you get yourself into wherever you land next, now doesn't it?"

The man's shoulders finally sagged, as did his features. "All right. I'll do it. Not because I'm guilty, you understand, but I can see you're resolved to frame me."

"Whatever you say," Fitch said. "Now, I don't believe either Sergeant Donovan or I are in any particular hurry. We'll wait for you to write your statement. We'll need two signed copies, by the way. But take your time."

Warburton obviously knew he'd lost. Fishing some stationery from his desk drawer and a pen from its holder, he began to write. Frank sat watching, knowing Fitch had been right about the probability of Warburton's getting off. A sharp lawyer in New York City could get a man acquitted of just about anything, including murder. But he didn't like letting this slime get away with what he had done.

On the other hand, perhaps losing his reputation, his fortune, his fancy house—maybe even his rich wife—might be more punishment for a man like Warburton than a jail cell would ever be.

Frank fervently hoped so.

~

In his study, Andrew Carmichael prepared to write a letter of his own. He had known for some time now that he had to do this. The way the word *truth* kept insinuating itself into his life and his thoughts was no coincidence, he was certain.

He had seen the way lies had nearly destroyed Natalie Guthrie. And deceit—along with some abnormal appetites—had turned Robert Warburton into a veritable monster.

But that wasn't all. On a daily basis now, every Scripture Andrew turned to, every book he read, seemed to emblazon the word *truth* on his conscience and in his heart. How much clearer did God have to make it?

The Lord was relentlessly pressing the need for this letter upon him, and he dared not delay any longer. For Bethany's sake, he dreaded its almost inevitable consequences. To spare her the shame and humiliation, though she would certainly object, he would try to convince her to break their engagement.

That prospect hurt most of all. Andrew thought he could lose everything he had without half the pain that losing Bethany would bring him. But if he kept Bethany and continued to live in the shadows of a sordid past, wouldn't their relationship eventually suffer from it? No, he had to tell the truth, no matter the cost.

He saw now that the damage to him and his reputation wasn't entirely due to the rumors or the accusatory letters. It came from half-truths and his unwillingness either to deny the accusations—which of course he couldn't do—or else bare his soul and admit there was indeed some truth in the letters and the rumors. He needed to tell the whole story and trust the Lord for what would happen next—though he was fairly certain he already knew.

With a heavy heart but a convicted conscience, Andrew Carmichael locked his study door, sat down at his desk, and began to write.

~

Bethany knocked lightly on the closed door to Andrew's study, but there was no response. She waited another moment before trying again, thinking he might be in conference with a patient. When there was no answer to her second attempt, she spoke his name.

"I'm busy right now, Bethany. I'll be out later."

His voice sounded weak and tight, as if he were either ill or under a great deal of strain.

"Are you all right, Andrew?"

In the same peculiar tone, he replied, "Yes, of course. I just need some time alone, please."

Disturbed and a little hurt, she hesitated, then finally walked to the waiting room door and ushered an elderly woman, one of their two waiting patients, into the examining room. By the time she'd completed the examination and that of the next patient, a young woman from Russia who spoke only a few words of English, Bethany expected to find the door to Andrew's study open.

But it wasn't. By now she was growing uneasy. Andrew had never shut himself off from her this way, not for so long a time and certainly not without an explanation. After everything that had happened over the past few days, she didn't know what to think. Andrew had been so different lately. And despite her earlier resolve, she couldn't keep the doubts from her mind.

She hated herself for doing so, but she went to check the pharmacy cabinet in his examining room. Before she could unlock it to see if anything was amiss, however, she pressed her face between her hands and ordered herself to stop.

She deliberated only a few more seconds before again going to the closed door of his study and knocking firmly. "Andrew? Please, may I come in?"

After a long hesitation, he replied in a voice so quiet she had to strain to hear. "Not just yet. I've something I need to finish."

Now she was frightened. In spite of the disgust she felt for what she was about to do, Bethany went back to the examining room and unlocked the cabinet that held their supply of narcotics and other drugs. There didn't seem to be anything missing. But something was obviously going on in Andrew's office—something he didn't want her to know about.

She stood in the hall, staring at the closed door. Then, her decision made, she tossed off her apron and left the building.

~

Frank Donovan had returned to the station house with one of Warburton's signed confessions in hand. The knowledge that the lying trickster would be out of town before the week ended was little comfort, but he knew he had to let it go. At least this guaranteed that no silver-tongued attorney would get the serpent off scot-free.

And maybe, just maybe, once she realized Warburton was out of her life for good, Mary Lambert would be able to heal and begin a new life. He was considering asking Miss Fanny Crosby to call on her. The woman made him uneasy with her constant urgings to "accept the Lord," but Frank somehow knew Miss Fanny would do everything she could to help Mary. It was known all about the city that the little blind woman was more than a famous writer of hymns. She was also a good one to call if you needed help.

Come to think of it, maybe he'd best pay a little more attention himself to what Miss Fanny had to say. It couldn't hurt. He'd been so mired of late in the disgusting goings-on of the likes of Robert Warburton and some of the other filthy rabble he encountered on his job that he was beginning to feel a bit soiled himself. And it wouldn't be making any sort of commitment just to listen, after all.

He was leaning back against the counter, reading through the confession for the third time, when Bethany Cole walked in.

"Well, now," he said, straightening and doffing his hat. "I'd ask what a lovely lady like yourself is doin' in a place like this, if I didn't know that you often venture into worse places, Lady Doc. To what do I owe the pleasure?"

He took a closer look at her and saw that she was in no mood for his teasing.

~

When Bethany saw Frank Donovan leaning against the counter in the crowded police station, his usual smirk in place, she had to remind herself of everything the big Irish policeman was doing to help Andrew. Even so, at the moment she had no patience for his sarcasm.

"I think I might need your help," she said.

Donovan stood watching her, twirling his hat on the tip of one finger. "You'll understand if I seem a bit surprised to hear that, Dr. Cole. By the way, the Warburton business has been taken care of. Doc's going to be all right. But what is it that brings you here?"

"It's Andrew," Bethany said, so tense she was sure her nails must be drawing blood from her clenched hands.

He stilled, his expression instantly changing to one of concern. "Something's happened to Doc?"

"I don't know," Bethany said, fighting to keep the tremor from her voice. "I need you to come with me. I'm afraid there's something wrong. Will you come? I'll explain on the way."

Donovan's dark eyes probed hers as he pushed away from the counter. "Is Doc all right?"

Bethany looked at him, fighting to hold off the fear closing in on her. "No. I mean, I don't know."

Donovan caught her arm and shouldered their way through a group of officers gathered by the door. "Over here," he said, propelling her toward a police wagon directly across the street.

~

Andrew stared in confusion as Bethany and Frank Donovan came bursting through the door of the waiting room and stood looking at him.

"Bethany?" She had the most peculiar look.

"Frank?" His friend, too, appeared somewhat bewildered.

"Andrew, are you all right?" said Bethany.

"Of course, I'm all right," he answered her. "Why?"

"You sure, Doc?" Frank put in before Bethany could reply.

"What's going on with you two? You look as if you've seen a ghost. Do I look that bad?"

He watched as Frank took a deep breath. "You look a bit peaked, to tell you the truth, Doc."

"Well, I might be a little tired, that's all," said Andrew. "What are you doing here, Frank? Aren't you on duty?"

"Oh, aye. I am. But—" Frank stopped, darting a glance at Bethany, who was still studying Andrew.

"Are you quite sure nothing's wrong, Andrew?" she said.

He frowned, then decided to go ahead and tell them about the letter he'd just posted.

Frank looked as if he might be sick, and Bethany turned pale.

"Doc," Frank said, "there was no need to do that. We've got a full retraction from Warburton. The papers will print it, I'll make sure of that. You needn't have written a word!"

Bethany said nothing, but simply stood watching.

"I had to, Frank," said Andrew. "I couldn't defend myself as things were. Part of those letters to the editor were true. You know that. I was an addict."

"Even so, Doc, nobody ever had to know, not with Warburton owning up to what he did. And he'll be gone—out of your life—in a day or two." Frank actually looked woeful when he repeated, "Nobody would have had to know, Doc."

"I knew," Andrew said. "And I'm asking both of you to try to understand. I couldn't live with myself any longer. I've concealed this part of my past for years. I've let it eat at me too long as it is. I think it would eventually have poisoned me."

He turned to Bethany. "I'm so sorry, Bethany. I know this is going to make things harder for you, but I simply had to do it."

To his amazement, a slow smile broke over her face.

"What?" he said.

She shook her head. "I'm just so—proud of you."

Andrew stared at her. So did Frank Donovan.

"Proud of me?" Andrew said.

"Oh, yes," she replied, still smiling. "Very proud. It took real courage to write that letter."

Frank looked from one to the other. "It wasn't necessary," he insisted sourly.

Bethany turned to him. "I think it was, Frank. For Andrew, it was crucial."

"So you do understand," said Andrew.

She nodded and stretched to kiss him on the cheek. "I understand. And I think you're the bravest, most honest man I've ever known."

"Too honest for his own good, I'm thinkin'," groused Frank Donovan.

"Oh, stop it, Frank!" said Andrew. "You big phony. You don't fool me anymore. You're not half as tough as you want everyone to think. At heart, you're just like me."

Frank Donovan couldn't have looked more surprised if Andrew had struck him. The look of total incredulity on his face actually made Bethany—and then Andrew—laugh.

"Well," Bethany said, "I don't know if I'd go that far."

Frank's ruddy face had turned a deeper shade than usual. He put on his hat, then took it off again. "If you think you had to do it, Doc," he finally said, "I suppose that's good enough for me." He hesitated, then said, "When are you two getting married anyway?"

They both spoke at once.

"Soon," said Andrew.

"Next week," said Bethany.

"Time to go," said Frank Donovan as he hurried out the door, banging his shoulder against the wall in his rush.

Andrew turned to Bethany. "Next week?"

She nodded. "Absolutely."

Andrew took her by the shoulders and allowed himself to be drawn into her gaze. "Next week," he said. "Absolutely."

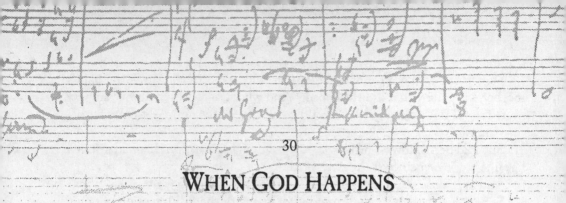

30

WHEN GOD HAPPENS

Through many dangers, toils, and snares,
I have already come;
'Tis grace hath brought me safe thus far,
And grace will lead me home.

JOHN NEWTON

"No, Mum! I can't stay home today. I already explained all this to you. I promised Mrs. Dempsey and Miss Susanna I'd for certain work today, tomorrow, and Saturday. There's extra to be done for the family because of Easter."

Vangie MacGovern threw up her hands in resignation—and no small measure of frustration—at her daughter's reply. "What about your family? Or don't we matter at all, now that you've got yourself such a fine job up at the Big House?"

She was irked by the way Nell Grace stood looking at her, hands on her hips, her mouth pursed in impatience.

"Am I not giving you enough of my wages, Mum? You know very well I'm not doing this for myself!"

Not waiting for Vangie to answer, she grabbed her sewing bag off the kitchen table and left the house, letting the door swing shut behind her with a thud.

Vangie tried to ignore the sense of shame that stole over her in the wake of their argument. In all fairness, Nell Grace had been more than generous with the money she earned. The girl hadn't a selfish bone in her body, and that was the truth. She helped fix breakfast for the children before she left for the hill in the morning, and after working a full day, she would come home to start supper for the rest of them, help the twins with their homework, bathe Emma, and do whatever was needed until bedtime.

But the girl was no help at all with the baby. And that was the source of Vangie's resentment, although she wouldn't have admitted it to anyone but herself. It seemed that everyone in the family was usually too busy to help with the babe, leaving almost the entire responsibility to her.

Something at the edge of her thoughts whispered that *she* was the baby's mother, after all. What did she expect? And what was wrong with her anyway, that after all this time she still hadn't the energy—or the desire—to care for her own child?

She told herself it was the fatigue, the continual exhaustion that had gripped her like a vise ever since she'd given birth.

And ever since she'd learned of Aidan's death.

Some mornings she actually got out of bed with the full intention of doing better, telling herself that today she would get back to being the kind of wife and mother she had once been. She vowed she would clean the house and cook Conn a nice noonday meal and spend more time with the babe and little Emma. Perhaps she would even fix herself up a bit, put on a pretty dress that Conn favored.

And in truth, she should have been able to do just that. She was stronger now. She could feel her health coming back. But by midmorning, after nursing the baby and putting him back to bed, her good intentions would disappear. The weariness and feelings of infirmity would send her back to her chair by the window, where she would sit and watch Emma play for the next few hours until Conn came in. Then she would get up and fix him and Emma a bite to eat, tend to the babe again and, after Conn was gone, put both little ones down for a nap. And then she would sleep—that is, when the baby allowed her to sleep.

The trouble was, the wee mite was restless and slept only fitfully. Lately he'd been colicky, and Vangie sometimes caught herself pressing her hands over her ears, unable to bear his feeble but piercing cries another moment. She would even shriek at him to be quiet, but the sound of her raised voice only made him scream that much louder. Yesterday he'd scarcely slept at all, and every time he cried, Vangie had also dissolved into a fit of weeping that left her limp as a scrub rag, her nerves completely raw, by suppertime.

Even then, Nell Grace made no attempt to take over the wee one's care. She busied herself in the kitchen after their meal, leaving the babe to Vangie.

As for Renny, she was worthless entirely where the babe was concerned. How a girl almost grown could be afraid of a tiny babe was beyond understanding, but that was definitely the case with Renny Magee. She simply wouldn't hold him at all unless she was forced into it, much less change a didy or give him a bath.

Lately, Vangie had grown so desperate that she sometimes caught herself intoning a monotonous prayer, over and over again like a chant, a plea that the Lord would help her see the babe with love rather than as a kind of...parasite, which was how she sometimes viewed him. Then her blood would chill as she realized what an unnatural thing this was, having to plead for the capacity to love her own child.

And then there was Conn. The man had been more patient with her than any woman deserved. But if she sometimes felt ashamed of the way she was hurting him—deserting him, in truth—she also felt helpless to do anything about it. She hated the pain in his eyes when he looked at her, so most of the time she simply turned away from him, refusing to look.

The awareness of what she was turning into made Vangie retreat even more deeply into herself. At times she felt as if she were buried, hidden away from everyone she knew. Indeed, the deadness of spirit with which she'd lived since losing Aidan seemed to be spreading over her like some dark creature of the sea, its tentacles choking off every part of her.

There were even moments when Vangie caught herself listening for her heartbeat to stop.

And moments when she thought she would welcome the silence.

⁓

Nell Grace felt as if she were drowning in the torrent of feelings that rushed over her as she climbed the hill toward the Big House. Never had she felt such a mixture of desperation and anger and helplessness.

Her grand plan wasn't working, that much was obvious, and she was beginning to feel like a fool for ever believing it would. Her mother might be going through the routine of caring for Baby Will, but anyone could see that's all it was to her—a routine. If she had any feelings for the poor wee babe at all, she seemed intent on not showing them, especially to him.

What else could she do? She couldn't force Mum to love the baby. No one could do that. Except perhaps the Lord.

But in spite of all her asking—and she had asked, countless times—He didn't seem to be listening.

She was beginning to get really angry with her mother, who shouldn't have made Aidan her whole life, after all. She had five other children, including herself, who needed a mother's attention and affection. And Da—well, he was about as helpless as a man could be in the face of what was happening. Every time she tried to talk to him about Mum, he would mumble something about her not being completely over William's birth yet or her not having all her strength back or how much better she would be once winter was gone and she could get outside and work in her garden. Nothing but excuses, and so far as Nell Grace could see, none of them credible.

But Da had always been a bit soft where Mum was concerned.

No, Dad was a *lot* soft where Mum was concerned, and in truth, would she want him to be any other way? Besides, she knew he felt as helpless as she did, and that must be terrible for a man when he loved his wife as much as Da obviously loved Mum.

She looked up to see Paul Santi standing in the backyard of the Big House, watching her. He removed his eyeglasses, smiled, and waved at her, and Nell Grace's heart lifted. They talked almost every day now, not for more than five or ten minutes, but she was learning to like him ever so much. He was the nicest young man. So polite and thoughtful and funny.

Da, of course, would take none of these things into account once he learned that she was interested in an Italian gentleman. She could almost hear him calling Paul just that, in that way he had of drawing out the words that made it sound as if he were saying something bad: "that *Eye-talian* fella."

Well, Da would just have to learn that she wasn't going to be ordered around anymore like a schoolgirl. She would soon be eighteen years old, the age of a woman, not a child. She had a job. She was an adult. She liked Paul Santi—and he liked her, she could tell. She thought he liked her a lot. And if she was old enough to work full-time for Mr. Emmanuel, help keep house and stand in for her mother with Baby Will—not to mention raising the other children at least a part of the time—then she was old enough to talk to the young man of her choice, whether he happened to be Irish or *Eye-talian*.

So full of her imaginings about a coming conflict between her father and Paul Santi was she that, for a moment at least, she nearly forgot her sadness and discouragement about her mother and Baby Will. When she remembered, she said yet another prayer for the both of them, then quickened her steps to meet Paul at the gate.

~

By midafternoon, after Conn had gone back to work and Emma had settled for her nap, Vangie felt the old, familiar lethargy begin to seep through her. The sky, earlier bright with sunshine, had darkened now, with clouds quickly moving in. The encroaching gloom seemed to reflect her mood.

She had heard nothing from the baby for over an hour. Although she was grateful for the quiet, she supposed she ought to go and check on him.

She found him lying quietly in the crib Conn had originally made for Emma. He wasn't sleeping after all, but wide awake, lying quietly and staring at the foot of the crib. Vangie watched him for a moment, and for the first time she seemed to really see his thinness, the nearly translucent quality of his pale skin, the red-gold highlights in the puff of downy hair that covered his head. So delicate, so frail...

Her other babies, the ones who had lived, had been sturdy little things with rosy cheeks and plump limbs and round tummies. Aidan, especially, had been unusually large and robust. "All boy," she remembered Conn saying, pride evident in his tone and in his eyes.

The memory of her firstborn hit her like a hammer blow. Her eyes filled, and she was about to turn and leave the room when her attention was caught by the baby's faint gurgle and the way his attention seemed to be locked on his own feet.

She followed his gaze. There, inching its way toward one tiny foot, was the largest, most terrifying spider she'd ever seen. It was black and covered with fur and obscenely ugly.

Vangie cried out, and the baby snapped his head to look at her. He wailed, kicking his feet and flailing his fists. Vangie grabbed him, whisked him up under one arm, and frantically called for Renny Magee.

She had always been terrified of spiders. Even the small ones. She could imagine unknown horrors at the very sight of one. Indeed, she would shriek for Conn or Renny at the sight of a dark blot on the wall that turned out to be nothing more than a smudge. But this—this *thing* was the worst she had ever encountered.

And it had been in her baby's crib—it had threatened her child.

Renny was not to be found. Then Vangie remembered the girl had gone up to the Big House to visit her ailing friend. And Conn was down at the stables well out of earshot. Vangie paced the floor, holding the babe securely against her as she frantically tried to think what to do. Finally, drawing a determined breath, she hurried to fetch the broom from the kitchen pantry.

When she came back, the ugly thing was still squatting in the crib as if looking for new prey. Plopping wee William in his basket by the window, she swept the horrible creature through the rails of the crib onto the floor, where she proceeded to beat it with the flat of the broom as hard as she could until it finally gave up its struggle and shriveled into a lifeless blot on the floor.

Still shaking, she stared down at her grisly work with a peculiar sense of triumph, then set the broom aside and retrieved the babe from his basket.

She looked down at the baby boy cuddled against her shoulder. He was watching her with wide eyes but no sign of fear. Indeed, his expression was curious, as if this might be some sort of game devised for his entertainment.

Vangie carried him into the bedroom. Not until she collapsed on the rocking chair by the window did she begin to weep—softly at first, then harder. All the guilt and the anguish of the past weeks came rushing in on her like an avalanche, dislodging the wall she had set around her heart.

She saw it all now, saw what she had done, what she had allowed to happen—and it was a bitter awareness entirely. She had been so unfair to Nell Grace—to all of them. She had forsaken her own responsibilities as a mother and hardened her heart not only to the wee boy in her arms, but to her other children…and her husband, her faithful, long-suffering Conn. She had absented herself from the ones who loved her best. Because of her grief for the one lost, she had grieved the ones who needed her most.

Had it not been for the baby in her arms, Vangie thought she might have broken in half with the weight of her selfishness, her sin. She leaned her head back against the chair and squeezed her eyes shut and wept.

"*O God, O Lord God, forgive me!*"

Only then did the babe begin his own surge of wailing. Realizing that she'd startled him, Vangie quickly gathered him closer and began to soothe him, pressing her cheek against his as she patted his back and rubbed his silken head.

"Shush now, sweet William," she crooned softly. "You're safe now. Mother's here. Don't cry. Mother's here."

After a moment, he stopped. With her own tears still tracking down her face, Vangie turned him onto her lap, on his back, so she could study him. His soft white nightdress was too big for his teensy body, but he was growing some, she noticed. He had long fingers and long toes for such a wee thing, and she saw now that his ears stuck out just as the twins' had when they were born.

"Never you mind about those ears," she told him. "You'll grow into them soon enough."

She continued to look him over, each tiny part of him a discovery. "Why, he's perfect," she murmured, running a finger over the tops of his toes. So tiny, but perfect indeed. He quirked his fair, red-gold eyebrows as he examined Vangie's face, and what appeared to be a smile in the making appeared, tugging at the corners of his mouth.

Vangie's tears fell over him, and he lifted a wee fist to touch the dampness on his cheeks. She lifted him then and buried her face in the softness of his flannel-covered body and then, just as she had with her other babes, she inhaled the warm sweetness of him, breathing deeply of the promise and the glory a new babe had always held for her.

A few minutes later, little Emma came shuffling into the room, rubbing her eyes. She had obviously slept right through all the excitement but now intended to claim her place with her mother and baby brother. Thumb in mouth, she crossed over to the rocking chair and climbed up beside them.

⁓

That was how Nell Grace and Renny Magee found them when they came home later that afternoon—Vangie, Baby Will, and wee Emma all cuddled together asleep in the rocking chair by the bedroom window.

Nell Grace stood watching her mother with her baby brother, her little sister huddled close to them. After a long moment, she brushed a tear away, then turned to look at Renny.

Renny met her gaze, and Nell Grace smiled at her. "Mum will be all right now, Renny," she said.

"Aye," Renny said, her voice hushed, her own eyes damp. "So it would seem." She turned to again look at Vangie and the baby. "I wonder what happened."

Nell Grace, too, returned her attention to the scene by the window. "God," she said to Renny Magee. "I'm thinking God happened."

⁓

Late that night, with the moonlight streaming through their bedroom window, Conn MacGovern lay drinking in the sight of his wife and the infant in her arms, both sleeping soundly.

There could be no more beautiful sight in the world, he thought, swallowing hard against the swelling in his throat. Vangie, her riot of dark red hair fanned out over the white bedsheet, the wee boy tucked against his mother's heart.

Contentment. Peace. Beauty.

All the lovely words he could think of, the words that spoke of God's blessing and a man's joy, went drifting through his mind. He was growing drowsy, yet was reluctant to sleep. He could be a happy man just lying here the rest of the night, watching the woman he had loved for more than twenty years and the tiny, newest evidence of that love.

Here, tonight, in this room that looked out on the place the Lord had brought them to, was everything a man could ever want, ever need. Oh, they'd been through their valleys, that was true. They had known hunger and homelessness and sickness and the loss of loved ones—*oh, Aidan, my son!* They had met with disdain and contempt and outright hatred in some places of this country they now called home. He supposed they'd experienced just about every hurt, every heartache, every loss, that human beings could know.

But in the midst of it all, they had also known grace. God's grace. That's what had brought them this far. And as he watched his sleeping wife and child, and as the years of their lives played through his memories and his thoughts like a continuous river of dreams, Conn MacGovern knew that in the years to come they would know that grace again. And again.

And again.

31

BEYOND THESE WALLS

When my spirit, clothed immortal,
Wings its flight to realms of day,
This my song through endless ages:
Jesus led me all the way.

FANNY CROSBY

Maylee died on Easter Sunday evening.

Miss Susanna had sent for Renny Magee late in the afternoon, so Renny was there when Maylee drifted quietly off to sleep and didn't wake up.

Up until then, she read to her from Maylee's favorite book, the Holy Bible, pausing once to remind her friend that the only reason she was able to read anything was because Maylee had taught her. She didn't know if Maylee heard her or not, but she felt the need to thank her one more time.

She also played her tin whistle, because Maylee always urged her to do so during their visits. She played Maylee's favorite hymn, one written just recently by Miss Fanny Crosby, a friend of the maestro and a frequent visitor to Bantry Hill. Renny knew she would never play or listen to that hymn again without hearing Maylee's pure, high voice singing the words as she almost always did when Renny played it:

> *All the way my Savior leads me;*
> *Oh, the fullness of His love!*
> *Perfect rest to me is promised*
> *In my Father's house above:*
> *When my spirit, clothed immortal,*
> *Wings its flight to realms of day,*
> *This my song through endless ages:*
> *Jesus led me all the way.*

Before she left, Renny looked back one last time at the room where she had spent so many hours with her friend. Cookie, Maylee's kitten, was peeping out at her from underneath the bed—Miss Susanna had promised she would take good care of her. The jar of marbles Renny had given Maylee still sat on the windowsill, but their sparkle was gone without the sun to cast its light on them. The Easter present she'd given Maylee, a paperweight she'd made of multicolored, carefully polished tiles—now rested on the bedside table. Maylee's eyes had been heavy when Renny helped her open the package, but she had smiled at the sight of all the colors.

Renny managed not to weep until after she left the Big House. Even when Miss Susanna led her from the room after Maylee died, and even when both she and the maestro gave Renny a hug and told her what a good friend she had been to Maylee, she remained dry-eyed.

She was able to hold back her tears because she knew Maylee would have scolded her for weeping. She would have reminded Renny that she had been eager for this day for some time now and welcomed it when it came.

Outside the house, as she started home, Renny wondered if Maylee was flying now. The younger girl had always been keen on the idea of flying and talked about it often, especially when she talked about heaven.

Renny had never thought much about heaven one way or the other until she became friends with Maylee. Even though she had given her heart to Jesus several months before, heaven just didn't occupy much space in her thoughts. In truth, it was a subject that seemed to be reserved for old people.

But Maylee wasn't old, not really, even though her disease had made her look and feel old. Even though she was only eleven—almost twelve, as Maylee liked to say—she didn't mind talking about heaven at all. In fact, she liked to talk about it. She was always wondering if she really would "wing her flight" to get there.

"Even though I'll have a new and perfect body, I hope I'm not confined to just walking around all the time," she'd said to Renny during one of their conversations about heaven. "I hope I'll be able to just fly around with the angels and go everywhere and see all the wonderful things they see. I get so tired of never being able to go anywhere or see anything but walls."

The memory made Renny choke on a sob, and she stopped where she was, plopping down on the side of the hill toward home. No longer able to contain her grief, she finally let the tears flow. She wept until she thought her heart had been wrung dry and there could be no more sorrow in her.

Nell Grace found her there and eased down beside her. After a moment she put her arm around Renny's shoulders. And as the twilight crept in on the hillside and the stars began to fire the evening sky, the two girls sat and quietly wept together.

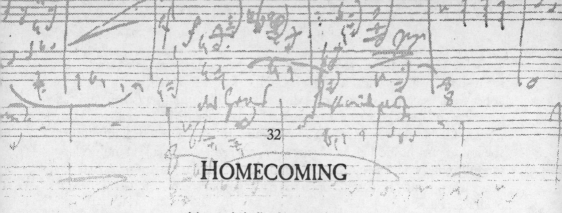

32

HOMECOMING

A house is built of logs and stone,
Of tiles and posts and piers;
A home is built of loving deeds
That stand a thousand years.

VICTOR HUGO

Two weeks after Easter, Renny Magee was finishing up the ironing—a task she actively detested and rarely undertook voluntarily. Today, however, she had offered to do at least a part of it in order to help out Nell Grace, who was working all day at the Big House.

As she ironed, she was watching over Baby Will and Emma so Vangie could finish hanging the freshly laundered curtains in the twins' bedroom. The monotony of heating the iron and pressing the clothes gave her too much time to think, and since she'd mostly been thinking about Maylee, her mood had become increasingly somber.

Although the day was golden bright and warmer than any weather they'd had so far this spring, to Renny everything seemed faded and dull with the ache of Maylee's absence. Sometimes on days like this she still caught herself anticipating her afternoon visit with her friend. Then she would remember that there would be no visit with Maylee ever again, and the raw place deep inside her would burn with pain.

On this afternoon, too, there was something else on her mind, something that carried with it its own pall of gloom. With Maylee gone and Vangie back to her old self, there was really no need for Renny to stay on with the MacGoverns now. She had already stayed past the time she'd committed to work for them, delaying her departure as long as she could out of sheer reluctance to leave.

As crowded as things were in the small MacGovern house, more than likely they would be relieved to see her go. What with her having used their Aidan's passage to come across and then him later lost at sea, she couldn't fault them for any hard feelings toward her, though if such resentment existed among them, she'd seen no sign of it.

Even so, they no longer seemed to need her help as much as before, and there was really nothing to hold her here any longer. Nothing except her feelings for them all. And they wouldn't be knowing about that—or caring, even if they did.

Renny glanced at Emma, who was trying to get her wee brother's attention by shaking a baby rattle in his face. The baby, however, seemed more interested in what Renny was doing as she set the iron on its heel atop the stove.

He was a cute little fella, with those funny ears and the thatch of strawberry-blond hair on top of his head. It was a relief to see Vangie now so wrapped up in the new baby that she hesitated to let anyone else tend to him. Once Renny had overcome her initial nervousness, she'd discovered she actually enjoyed holding him now and again. And when he clutched at her shirt front with his wee fingers and studied her up close, as if he found her highly fascinating—well, she liked it well enough, she had to admit. On occasion she even fantasized about what it would be like to have a baby brother of her own, not that there was any chance of that ever coming to pass.

For another moment, Renny stood watching a squirrel scurry down the oak tree outside the kitchen window. Then she turned, gathered wee William up in his basket, and took Emma by the hand.

"Let's go change your baby brother's didy," she said, wrinkling her nose at the little girl to coax a smile. "Everyone will be in for supper soon, and we can't have him disgracing himself, now can we?"

⁓

It seemed to Renny that Conn MacGovern and Vangie were acting strangely over supper tonight. For that matter, Nell Grace also appeared to have something on her mind. There was much glancing back and forth across the table—long, meaningful looks accompanied by a smile or even a giggle now and then—and the twins were more rambunctious than usual. Their da had to quiet their whisperings and foolishness more than once.

When Renny scraped her chair back from the table after the meal and asked to be excused, she was caught unawares entirely by Conn MacGovern's reply. "Not just yet, lass. We've been wanting to talk with you, and now would seem as good a time as any."

Something shattered inside Renny. So it had come, then. They were going to ask her to leave before she could make the decision herself. She ought to have expected it. She should have been steeled for it. But she wasn't. She had all she could do to keep from blubbering like a wee tyke as she scooted her chair back up to the table and glanced around at the faces that were now all turned toward her, watching her.

Conn MacGovern cleared his throat—always a sure sign that he had a serious topic on his mind. Renny sat up a little straighter, forcing herself to look him straight in the eye.

"No doubt you'll recall that when we agreed to bring you across with us, we had an agreement," he began.

Renny nodded, and he went on. "You were to earn the price of your passage by working for us no less than six months after we arrived. Do you recall that?"

"Aye," said Renny, her mouth so dry she could scarcely get the word out.

"Well, then, as I'm sure you're aware, you've fulfilled your commitment and then some."

Again, Renny nodded. *Say it. Just say it, won't you? Let's have it over with.* She wanted to run from the room screaming. She wanted to be alone so they wouldn't see her pain. She wanted to shut her ears entirely and pretend this wasn't happening...

"Well, we've been thinking, lass, that although your work has been exemplary—"

Conn MacGovern did love his big words, Renny thought bitterly, squeezing her arms around her middle to keep the pain from stealing her breath.

"—and in truth we have no complaints, none at all, with the arrangement as it is—"

"Oh, for goodness' sake, Conn!"

Renny darted a look at Vangie, who was wiping her hands on her apron and frowning at her husband. She turned to Renny, her frown giving way to a smile. "What the man is trying to say, Renny—though why he's having so much trouble getting it out, I can't think—is that we've talked with Mr. Emmanuel, who knows about these things. And he's agreed to help us go through the proper channels—if you're willing, that is—to adopt you."

Renny gaped at her, then at Conn MacGovern, who was grinning like a fox. To her dismay and utter humiliation, she felt her face begin to crumple. She blinked furiously, knotting her hands beneath the table so their shaking couldn't be seen.

"Adopt me?" she croaked, sniffing a bit to keep her nose from dripping.

"Yes, Renny," Vangie said quietly, still smiling. "We'd like it very much if you were to be our daughter. How would you feel about that?"

How would she feel about it? She would feel as though the angels were dancing on her shoulders—that's how she'd feel!

"You—you don't want me to leave, then?"

"Leave?" Conn MacGovern and Vangie and Nell Grace all voiced the word in unison. It was Vangie who answered her first.

"Oh, Renny! Of course, we don't want you to leave! You're one of the family!"

"You're like a sister to me, Renny," said Nell Grace. Emma clapped her hands and squealed, "Sister! Renny my sister, too!" The twins nodded their agreement. Then Johnny poked James and James punched his arm in retaliation—and Vangie shot them one of her looks.

Renny turned then to Conn MacGovern, who, slightly red-faced, glanced around the table at his family, then lifted his tumbler of water high, inclining his head toward her. "We all agree that you're as much a part of our family as is any one of us, lass, and we wouldn't like to think of your leaving. We'll do whatever it takes to make it official for you to be our daughter, Vangie's and mine—and sister to the rest of these rascals."

He paused, his expression gentling as he locked eyes with Renny. "So, what say you, Renny Magee?" he said softly. "Will you have us?"

There had been a time when Renny would have countered with a cheeky, impudent reply as a way of masking any trace of sentiment or her true feelings. But at this particular moment, she could think of nothing to say. It seemed that every broken thing in her was coming together and being made whole…that every cold, lonely place inside her that had never known the security of acceptance or the warmth of affection suddenly seemed aglow…that every wound, every empty space, in her heart of hearts began to heal and fill to overflowing.

She took a swipe at her eyes to blot the dampness, then lifted her face to Conn MacGovern. "Aye," she said, her voice hoarse but strong. "And it's proud I am to be asked. There's nothing I'd rather be than a MacGovern."

"Well said," proclaimed the head of the family.

~

The letter arrived the next day. The twins brought in the post, tossing the few pieces of mail on the table and immediately running back outside. Vangie called after them, as she always did, to stay clear of the creek.

She went to the table and thumbed through the mail. Her eyes came to rest on the envelope at the bottom, and she pulled it free for closer inspection. In that instant her pulse set up a roar in her ears that sounded like thunder, and her heart threatened to explode inside her chest.

Too stunned to cry out, she could only stand and stare at the writing on the envelope. Aidan's handwriting—but how? Had there been a terrible mistake? Was he alive after all?

Excitement flooded her. The questions came arrowing in on her like jagged bolts of lightning. Finally she managed to get to the kitchen door and then to the porch, where she began to scream for Conn.

~

At the sound of Vangie's screams, Conn MacGovern ran as fast as he could toward the house. Something must have happened to one of the children, something bad. The baby was hurt…or wee Emma…or Vangie herself.

Oh, merciful Lord, what now, what now?

The instant he reached the porch, Vangie threw herself against him. She had a letter in her hand and was waving it in the air, shrieking something about Aidan, but Conn could make no sense of what she was trying to tell him.

He managed to get her inside to the kitchen, where he helped her onto a chair.

"You open it, Conn," she said, thrusting the letter in his face. "I can't."

"Vangie, what—"

He took the letter from her, then saw for himself why she was raving. It was Aidan's handwriting on the envelope.

Hope flared in Conn as he ripped the letter open. After all this time, could it be? Was it possible?

His eyes went to the top of the page, where the date was written—and his hopes collapsed and died.

"It was—he must have written it just before he left," he said, his voice shaking, his hand trembling as he reached to touch her.

Vangie moaned as her own hopes came crashing down.

She reached for the letter, but he stopped her. "Wait." He scanned down the page, and his heart slammed in shock, then began to race as he read on.

"Read it to me, Conn," Vangie said, her voice little more than a whisper.

Conn had reached the end of the letter. His throat was so swollen he didn't know if he could read it to her. His emotions rioted, pain warring with a growing wonder, even a bittersweet kind of joy.

"Conn—"

He scraped a chair up close to hers and faced her. "Our Aidan wrote this just before he left Ireland," he explained. "Probably posted it on his way to the harbor. All right, love, here's what he says." And he began to read:

Dear Da and Mother,

> *I know this will come as an enormous shock to the two of you, and I'm sorry for that. I planned to tell you myself when I arrived in America, but then I got to thinking perhaps I ought to write and tell you now, just in the unlikely event that something might happen to me during the crossing. Once you read this, I am sure you'll understand why I would rather be telling you these things in person. On the other hand, I don't want to take any chances on something happening to me and you not knowing about this.*

> *What I'm trying to say, and I might just as well say it, is that I am a married man. I wed my Riona O'Donnell nearly four months*

past—you'll remember Riona from her family's booth at the Summer-fest, sure. We have just learned she is carrying my child. Although we've known each other a long time as friends, we were surprised to finally realize we wanted to be more to each other.

And that's a part of the reason for my delay in coming, you see. I was trying to raise the money for our passage. As it turned out, I'll be coming alone, for we simply couldn't manage the funds we'd need for both of us to make the crossing. We also feared that the crossing might be too difficult in her delicate condition, after all, so she must stay with her family in Enniskerry.

I plan to find a position right away and save everything I earn to bring Riona and our child across as soon as possible. I don't know how well you'll remember Riona, but I do know you'll both love her. She is beautiful and courageous, like Mother, and has an unshakable faith, also like Mother. I'd give anything if she were coming with me—I can't think how I'm going to bear being without her, I love her so. But I will be working hard, and I will have you and the rest of the family to keep me company until I can send for her, so that will help to get me through, I'm sure.

I beg you both to forgive me for putting this in a letter, but I also beg you to be happy for me. There's one thing I must ask of you. If something should happen and I don't make it to America, please, out of your love for me, please contact Riona and bring her and our child to you and give them a home. I want you to know my beloved and her to know you. And I want my child raised as a part of the grand family I belong to.

I love you all, and I can't wait to see you.

Until we're together again.

> *Your devoted son,*
> *Aidan MacGovern*

By the time Conn had finished reading the letter, he and Vangie were both sobbing.

"Do you think he knew?" Vangie said. "Do you think he might have had a...a warning or the like?"

Conn thought about it, then shook his head. "Don't you hear the happiness in him, love? He was full of joy when he wrote this letter, not the kind of joy a man would know if he were afraid of dying. He was just being right smart, taking precautions, you see."

"I suppose you're right," Vangie said, lifting the hem of her apron to dry her eyes. "Oh, Conn, think of it—our Aidan married to Riona O'Donnell—and with a child. Our son has a child."

A child he'll never see, Conn thought, the taste of sorrow almost choking him.

But then something else struck him. He looked at Vangie and saw her watching him. "You know what we have to do, of course?" he said.

Slowly, she nodded. "We must find Aidan's wife...Riona...and bring her here. Of course, if she's too far along with the child, she may have to wait until after it's born. But we must bring her to us. It's what Aidan wanted."

Conn put aside the letter and took both her hands in his. "And isn't it what we want as well, love? To have our son's wife here—and his child—where we can give them a proper life and look after them?"

Her eyes still glistening with tears, Vangie squeezed his hands. "Oh, yes, Conn! It will be almost like having Aidan with us." She paused. "Conn, have you realized? We'll have two babies in the house! We're going to be grandparents!"

He stared at her, then got to his feet, tugging her along with him and gathering her into his arms. "Aye, so we are, love. But I must tell you, Evangeline Mary Catherine MacGovern, that you don't look like any grandmother I've ever seen."

She lifted her head and smiled through her tears at him. "We're going to be all right now, aren't we, Conn?"

He cupped her chin with his hand and kissed her gently on the forehead. "We are definitely going to be all right, love. And not just for now. With God and our family, we will always be all right."

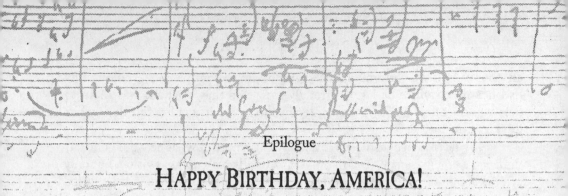

Epilogue

HAPPY BIRTHDAY, AMERICA!

Let music swell the breeze,
And ring from all the trees
Sweet freedom's song.

SAMUEL F. SMITH

July 4, 1876

For this one occasion, Susanna was pleased to be a member of the audience instead of a part of the performance.

Tonight she wanted to see not the backs of the orchestra members, but the faces gathered in community. She wanted to feel the thrill, the surge of excitement that she knew would energize the crowd at any moment.

That excitement had already begun to permeate the vast gathering of spectators waiting for Michael and the orchestra to appear. Indeed, Susanna had never seen such heightened anticipation among so many. She could actually feel the expectation stirring throughout the park, as if all there sensed that something that had never happened before was about to take place.

Susanna could scarcely control her own eagerness. After all these months of working with Michael and assisting him in a dozen different ways with the music—playing parts, sorting through page after page of notation, or at times simply supplying an opinion—she had yet to hear the entire suite orchestrated and in full.

The *American Anthem* had taken its toll on Michael. Some days she had almost feared he would have to give it up altogether, so frustrated was he with its progress and drained of his own physical energy. He had gone without sleep, even lost weight. But something had kept him going.

No, not something, she amended. *Someone.*

She believed that with all her heart.

Michael himself was convinced that this was not just another score, not merely another work to be performed, but a kind of divine commission. And Susanna had heard enough to be just as strongly convicted that what she was about to hear was the offering of a man anointed by God's Spirit, a vision fulfilled by His guidance and grace.

As a child, Michael had been given only a glimpse of what he would one day undertake as a musician. As a man, he had finally realized that vision, but only after overcoming obstacles that might have felled one less driven, less dedicated to the Lord of his life.

Central Park seemed ready to welcome the event. In the early dusk, lanterns glowed like fiery stars throughout the entire area, even on the hillside rising above the park itself. A special bandstand had been erected to accommodate the full orchestra, and here, too, lanterns cast their twinkling lights among the red, white, and blue bunting and countless flowers woven through the trellises framing the platform. Gas lamps highlighted the American flag raised just beyond the bandstand. In the distance, the elegant Bow Bridge had been decorated as well.

Earlier in the day, families had gathered in the area for picnics and games, speeches, and other Centennial events. But now adults and children alike had come together to wait in smaller, more intimate groups, their voices lowered, their laughter subdued.

Suddenly, the drone of a bagpipe was heard. A piper in full regalia marched slowly across the field, approaching the bandstand with great dignity and solemnity as he intoned the melody to a work Susanna recognized as a part of Michael's *Anthem.*

A riotous burst of applause followed, and the audience of thousands rose to their feet as Michael and the members of the orchestra approached from the other side of the bandstand and began to file up the steps to the platform.

Michael stood waiting until every musician was in place, then turned to the audience. He was greeted by wave after wave of applause and raucous whistles. Somewhere a child shouted "God bless America!" and Michael's face broke into an unrestrained smile.

He finally had to lift his arms to quiet the crowds. A hush fell over the audience, still standing, the silence a kind of tribute. They were keenly aware that, although they could gaze upon him with respect, he could not see them, and that his blindness was only one of the many difficulties he had faced and overcome.

Caught up in an overwhelming range of emotions, Susanna began to weep before Michael voiced even his first words.

She could sense his emotion in his thickening Italian accent as he finally spoke. "I would like first to say, 'Happy Birthday, America.'"

The crowd erupted into more applause as children blew whistles and one of the trumpets in the orchestra blasted a brief fanfare.

Again Michael had to quiet the crowd before going on. "During the time I worked with the music we will play for you tonight, I was aware, painfully so at times, that there was always some vital element that eluded me. At times I feared I would never discover what was missing, and I knew that without it, the music would be less than it was meant to be."

He stopped, as if to consider his next words. "Finally, when I least expected it, God revealed to me that I was too, ah, intent on making everything perfect, making everything fit just so, as musicians are wont to do. I began to understand then that I must do with the music what we are meant to do as Americans. I was to celebrate the many voices of America, the differences that make our nation what it is."

He opened his arms in an encompassing gesture. "We are different kinds of people, we Americans. We come from different countries. We share different beliefs, different traditions, different dreams, and different music. But one thing we share in common. We are all God's children, all blessed by His love and His grace. For truly God has bestowed grace to this nation and its people, so that with all our differences, we might yet exist in unity. May we never cease to be mindful that we will exist as a great nation only as we are faithful to our great God."

Had Central Park ever been as silent as it was in that moment? Susanna's heart swelled with so much love and pride she thought she couldn't contain her feelings for another instant.

"So please, as we first sing America's song, our national anthem, and then as the orchestra offers you my own *American Anthem*, join with us and let us celebrate the birthday of the greatest nation in the world."

After the most rousing rendition of "The Star-Spangled Banner" Susanna had ever heard, the crowds made themselves comfortable, some sitting on chairs, some on benches, most on blankets covering the ground.

Paul Santi, dapper and dignified in his dark suit, rose from his concert-master's chair to supervise the discordant process of tuning. Susanna felt the crowd's expectation go up another notch as they waited through this necessary preliminary.

Then Michael tapped his baton, and the celebration began.

Susanna glanced around at those nearest to her. Caterina, her face rapt with attention and love for her father. Papa Emmanuel, who had pulled from his pocket a huge handkerchief and was wiping his eyes with it. And the elegant Rosa Navaro who, Susanna noticed for the first time, seemed to have her arm tucked snugly inside Papa's arm.

Moira and Liam Dempsey were there as well, and Miss Fanny Crosby, seated on a blanket, was smiling as always. The newlyweds, Andrew and Bethany Carmichael, sat close together on a quilt, their faces aglow with love and deep contentment. Close by, his eyes continually sweeping over the crowd, stood the gruff Irish policeman Susanna had met during her first few weeks in America—Sergeant Donovan, she recalled. And he was not alone. A small, fair-haired woman held tightly to his hand, and three children Susanna had never seen—a gangly boy and two younger girls—clustered around them. Susanna made a mental note to ask Bethany who they were.

The MacGoverns sat together on the lawn nearby—all of them, even the baby. Baby William sat in Nell Grace's lap, his round blue eyes taking in everything around him. But then, seeing his mother, he stretched out his little arms, and Vangie reached to gather him close. Nell Grace, her eyes fixed on the violin section of the orchestra, barely seemed to notice. Then Conn MacGovern leaned over to whisper to his wife, and the smile that Vangie gave him warmed Susanna's heart.

It seemed right, somehow, to gather here with family and friends, loved ones and neighbors—plus a few thousand of the folks who filled this remarkable and varied land. Her land, too—the new home that had given her so much. Thankful to share this experience with all of them, Susanna settled back to enjoy the *American Anthem*.

She wasn't in the least surprised that the suite was a work of genius. She had already accepted the fact that the man she loved, the man she would marry in just a few weeks, possessed a gift of which others could only stand in awe. But she was surprised at the length to which Michael had gone to incorporate into the music the many voices of which he'd spoken. She knew about the Negro choir he'd engaged. He had told her about the piper and the elderly Italian street vendor with his accordion. And she was eagerly anticipating Paul Santi's brief but haunting violin solo based on an old Tuscan theme—a little gift from Michael to his father. But, adamant that he would at least withhold some surprises from her, Michael had not divulged the appearance of the children's choir from the Cathedral or the Swedish vocalist or the Irish stepdancers or the Spanish guitarist.

There was no describing the music. Mere words couldn't possibly begin to define or describe the magnitude of what Michael, with God's guidance, had accomplished. *Overwhelming* was the only word that came to mind, and it was a poor substitute for what Susanna was feeling.

Partly because of her own Irishness but more because of her fondness for the girl, one of the brightest highlights of the evening for Susanna was when Renny Magee swept out from behind the orchestra onto the platform, her tin whistle spilling out Irish tunes like silver coins tumbling down a waterfall, her feet flying as she dazzled the crowds.

As the music slowed and grew softer, the girl stooped to exchange her tin whistle for something else. Susanna was close enough to see the tears tracking down Renny's face as she scurried down the steps from the platform and ran into the crowd. As she ran, she released a multicolored kite, fashioned in the shape of a butterfly, into the air, where it rose high and sailed free on the summer breeze.

Few here tonight would know that Maylee, with Susanna's help, had begun the kite as an Easter gift for Renny. Maylee had died before she could complete the gift for her friend, but Susanna had gone ahead and finished it, holding it back just for this occasion. Only this morning, she'd presented the kite to Renny in memory of Maylee, who had often spoken of flying free of her poor, frail body, and also to commemorate Renny's performance in tonight's concert. The kite was constructed from every colorful scrap of material Renny had ever given Maylee. More than anything else, Susanna thought, it reflected the friendship of two very different—and very wonderful—children.

Somewhere tonight, Susanna thought, *Maylee's spirit is flying.*

Darkness had completely settled over the park when the fireworks began to flare above the hill. Now Michael unleashed the full force of the orchestra for the monumental finale. The combined experience of the explosion of music and the fireworks brought the audience to their feet—but almost sent Susanna to her knees.

She could only stand in wonder of the spectacle playing out before her and the thunderous riot of music under Michael's baton. She was weeping, she was praying, she was laughing as Central Park erupted in celebration and praise.

When the music stopped and Michael turned to face his audience, he appeared dazed, as if stunned by his own achievement and its effect on those before him. His face was wreathed in perspiration and an exhausted smile, his lightweight black suit hanging limply on his tall form.

But his words came ringing out over Central Park like a holy benediction when he opened his arms as if to embrace the audience and cried, "May God... forever...bless America—and all her many voices!"

In that moment, that sanctified moment, Susanna's heart whispered a fervent *amen*.

DISCUSSION QUESTIONS

For *Prelude*

1. *Prelude* is not only the beginning novel of a trilogy, but it's also an account of "beginnings" for most of its main characters. Do you think starting over is more difficult for women than for men, and, if so, in what ways? In what significant ways does Susanna's new venture differ from the "new beginnings" of Bethany Cole and Vangie MacGovern?

2. How do you feel about Michael's attempts to keep the truth about his marriage from Susanna? Do you believe he's being fair, protective, or deceitful? Do you think Paul is justified in finally telling Susanna the truth? How can loyalty to a friend or family member sometimes intrude upon the well-being or even the safety of a third party?

3. When did you first sense that Susanna's doubts and misgivings about Michael, based on Deirdre's letters, might be unfounded? Have you ever formed an opinion about someone based solely on information supplied by another, only to learn that the person was far different from what you'd been told? How did you move past the temptation to let your judgment be clouded in the same way again?

4. Do you agree with Vangie that the comforting figure she witnesses in the harbor just before they leave Ireland is a godly "promise?" Have there been times in your life when God has somehow manifested to you a sign or a promise of His presence and His safekeeping? How did you respond?

5. In your opinion, is the young street musician, Renny Magee, a tragic figure or a survivor to be admired? What are her strengths? What are her weaknesses? Why do you think Vangie is so drawn to the girl, and Renny to Vangie?

6. One of the epigraphs in *Prelude*, written by John Boyle O'Reilly, reads: "Our feet on the torrent's brink, Our eyes on the cloud afar, We fear the things we think, Instead of the things that are." Which character do you think this most applies to: Vangie, Susanna, or Renny Magee? Why?

7. When Andrew tells Bethany that he believes the kind of healing being effected by D. L. Moody and Ira Sankey in their evangelistic campaigns is more important than what he can offer as a physician, what is he getting at? Do you think he's being wise or foolish to subject himself to elements—such as prolonged cold and dampness aboard ship—that he knows could aggravate his poor health? Do you agree with his reasoning about this issue?

8. As one of the early women physicians in the United States, Bethany faces a number of obstacles in gaining the respect of her peers and her patients. What do you believe

accounts for Andrew's immediate acceptance of her as a member of his own profession—and a partner in his medical practice? What makes him different from most
of his colleagues? Have you ever felt the resistance of your contemporaries in relation
to your occupation or your field of study? How do you deal with the problems you
encounter without becoming bitter or resentful?

9. What other significant elements besides music did you find woven into the story of
   Prelude?

10. Toward the end of the book, Susanna realizes that she stands at a "crossroads," that
    she has a choice between holding onto the past or moving forward in faith. Have
    you faced a similar crossroads in your life? How did your decision affect your walk of
    faith, your spiritual journey?

For *Cadence*

1. One of the few times Susanna manages to let go of her feelings of inadequacy is when
   she's at the piano, absorbed in the music of a "great composer"—or in Michael's original compositions. Not only is she swept up, beyond her insecurities, when she plays,
   but she also seems to gain a strong sense of the composer's heart. When God gifts
   a person with an exceptional ability or talent, do you feel that others can actually be
   drawn, moved closer, to God by exposure to that gift? How do we define "talent" as
   opposed to "gift?" What do you think accounts for the way some seem possessed of
   many gifts and abilities while others seem to excel at very little, if anything?

2. Just when his future couldn't look more bleak, Conn MacGovern rushes to rescue a
   terrified stallion on the docks of New York City. For the first time since their arrival
   in America, hope for a better life for him and his family seems within reach. This one
   impulsive act—coming to the aid of a suffering animal and those placed in charge
   of the animal—leads to events that only hours before couldn't have been imagined.
   While some might tend to see this occurrence as coincidence, what do you think? Is
   there such a thing as coincidence in the life of a Christian?

3. After meeting Maylee, a child afflicted with a premature aging disease, Dr. Bethany
   Cole confronts her associate, Andrew Carmichael, with a question similar to one
   asked throughout the ages by non-believers and believers: "He (God) may not have
   caused it (the disease), but he could prevent it! If God loves her so much, then why
   doesn't he simply take it from her? Or at least provide a means of mitigating the
   symptoms and easing her misery?" Have you ever struggled with the question of why
   God doesn't intervene to spare the suffering—or the life—of one of his children? Do
   you believe it's wrong to question why God does or doesn't act in certain ways? How
   do you think God views our doubting and questioning of his will?

4. Although Michael loves his young cousin, Paul, "like a brother"—and though he
   despises himself for the jealousy that has begun to plague him in regard to Paul and
   Susanna—he can't deny the fact that he is jealous. He recognizes the destructiveness

of this emotion and is determined not to let it gain control of his feelings again, as it had during his marriage to Susanna's sister. Is there ever a time when jealousy is "acceptable?" What does the Bible mean when it calls God a "jealous God?"

5. What do you think accounts for Michael's reluctance to move beyond friendship with Susanna, when he knows he loves her? Is he merely being protective of her, or is it something else?

6. What was your first reaction to the following: Upon "meeting" the opium-addicted mother of young Robert Warburton and his small sisters, all illegitimate? Upon hearing the boy's angry accusations, that their father was a highly respected, prestigious clergyman? Upon hearing Andrew Carmichael's charge that people—including "good people," Christian people—are inclined to forget the "Mary Lamberts of the world," that their problems often seem "so overwhelming that one person couldn't possibly make a difference?" Can you think of any situations, either from personal experience, or perhaps in your own community or church, that would contradict this assumption?

7. Susanna was quick to believe that Michael had been deceitful, had deliberately attempted to dupe her into playing the organ for his Christmas concert even though he knew she didn't want to. Why was she so quick to suspect him of duplicity? Have you ever reacted in a similar manner—made assumptions, suspected someone of trying to deceive you based on past experience or because of something you thought you knew? How did you feel…and how did you react…when you realized you'd been wrong?

8. What does Susanna finally realize about her lifelong avoidance of the "limelight," her preference to remain "backstage?" When she finally admits that her humility might have been a kind of false humility, she asks herself the question: "How did one distinguish genuine humility—a virtue God not only approved but even commanded—from a desire to be 'safe,' a deliberate attempt to stay backstage out of fear of failure?" How would you answer that question?

9. What does Vangie mean when she finally admits to Conn that her reason for keeping her pregnancy a secret was because she meant to "punish" him? Have you ever done this—withheld something you knew would bring joy to a person you cared about as a means of "punishing" or "getting back" at that person? What do you think the real motivation for this kind of behavior is?

10. In Susanna's eyes, Michael had "exchanged a crown (the crown of celebrity) for a Cross, the Cross of Christ." What are some of the pitfalls of celebrity? What is the Christian's perception of "success" and "celebrity" to be?

For *Jubilee*

1. When Andrew Carmichael first goes to the home of Robert Warburton, he's aware that he's exceeding the boundaries of his profession. He senses that anger—an anger

stemming from the determination to right a wrong inflicted on a patient—motivates his behavior. Do you agree? Is this a case of "righteous anger" or are Andrew's actions prompted more by a kind of carnal outrage?

2. When Susanna realizes that Michael has become her closest friend as well as her husband-to-be, she's somewhat surprised by the thought. Yet, friendship can be the very cornerstone of a marriage. What other elements can work together to strengthen and enrich a husband and wife's life together?

3. Is Riccardo Emmanuel, Michael's father, genuinely concerned that his son might be wasting a God-given gift (Michael's singing voice), or does his frustration have more to do with his own pride? Is his refusal to accept his son's retirement from the opera world truly motivated by a conviction that Michael has made a terrible mistake? Or is he merely unwilling to see Michael give up his former celebrity and success?

4. In your opinion, is there any basis for Renny Magee's feelings of guilt about the death of Aidan MacGovern? Do you believe, as Renny seems to believe, that if she had stayed behind in Ireland, she could have spared the MacGovern family the pain of losing their first-born son?

5. What do you think accounts for Frank Donovan's obvious resolve to protect, first, Andrew Carmichael, and, later, Mary Lambert, at all costs? Is this tendency to "guard," to "shelter" those he cares about a contradiction to his real nature? Describe, as you see it, the true character of the Irish police sergeant.

6. How does Susanna handle the challenge of not allowing her own frustration with Michael's father to overshadow her efforts to understand him, and at the same time attempt to keep peace between the two men?

7. What do you think Maylee means when she tells Michael that, when he prays, she can almost imagine that she "sees Jesus"?

8. How does God use Natalie Guthrie, one of Andrew's patients, to bring healing into the beleaguered physician's life?

9. After hearing Mary Lambert's incredible story about Robert Warburton, Bethany Cole seems almost dazed by the horror of the situation. At the same time, when she returns to face Frank Donovan and Andrew Carmichael, she's obviously overwhelmed by something more than the awareness of Mary's torment. What emotion is responsible for her shocked condition?

10. We've seen evidence in our own lives that although God sometimes takes away, He also gives. In what ways do you also see the truth of this at work in the lives of some of *Jubilee*'s characters, particularly with Conn and Vangie MacGovern, Michael and Susanna, and Renny Magee?

BJ Hoff's bestselling historical novels continue to cross the boundaries of religion, language, and culture to capture a worldwide reading audience. Her books include such popular series as The Riverhaven Years, The Mountain Song Legacy, and An Emerald Ballad. Hoff's stories, although set in the past, are always relevant to the present. Whether her characters  move about in small country towns or metropolitan areas, reside in Amish settlements or in coal company houses, she creates communities where people can form relationships, raise families, pursue their faith, and experience the mountains and valleys of life. BJ and her husband make their home in Ohio.

To learn more about books by BJ Hoff
or to read sample chapters, log on to our website:

www.harvesthousepublishers.com

HARVEST HOUSE PUBLISHERS
EUGENE, OREGON

FICTION AT ITS BEST FROM BJ HOFF...

SONG OF ERIN

The mysteries of the past confront the secrets of the present in bestselling author BJ Hoff's magnificent *Song of Erin* saga.

In her own unique style, Hoff spins a panoramic story that crosses the ocean from Ireland to America, featuring two of her most memorable characters. In this tale of struggle and love and uncompromising faith, Jack Kane, the always charming but sometimes ruthless titan of New York's most powerful publishing empire, is torn between the conflict of his own heart and the grace and light of Samantha Harte, the woman he loves, whose own troubled past continues to haunt her.

Originally published to strong sales nearly a decade ago, this new edition combines two of BJ's best novels into one saga–length volume.

"The *Song of Erin* contains some of my favorite characters. This story—and its people—hold a very special place in my heart."

BJ HOFF

...a brilliant saga that powerfully depicts the struggle and uncompromising faith of an entire people who helped build America."

CHRISTIAN RETAILING MAGAZINE

GREAT REVIEWS FOR BJ HOFF'S MOUNTAIN SONG LEGACY TRILOGY...

BOOK ONE...*A DISTANT MUSIC*

"BJ Hoff always delights readers with her warm stories and characters who become part of your 'circle of special friends'."

JANETTE OKE,
BESTSELLING AUTHOR OF *LOVE COMES SOFTLY*

"For this Kentucky woman, reading *A Distant Music* was like driving through the eastern hills and hollers on a perfect autumn day, with the scent of wood smoke in the air and the trees ablaze with color. BJ Hoff's lyrical prose brings to life this gentle, moving story of a beloved teacher and his students, who learn far more than the three Rs. I brushed away tears at several tender points in the story and held my breath when it seemed all might be lost. Yet, even in the darkest moments, hope shines on every page. A lovely novel by one of historical fiction's finest wordsmiths."

LIZ CURTIS HIGGS, BESTSELLING AUTHOR OF *THORN IN MY HEART*

"As always when I open BJ's books I'm drawn into a place that is both distant and at home...as I tell my husband, I wish I could create the kinds of characters B.J. does because I fall in love with them and want them always as my friends."

JANE KIRKPATRICK, AUTHOR OF *LOOK FOR A CLEARING IN THE WILD*

"In some ways, *A Distant Music* is reminiscent of the 'Little House' series. Each chapter recalls the details of an event or some character's dilemma. Eventually, though, Hoff connects all the threads into a solid story whose ending will deeply touch readers. *A Distant Music* should find an eager audience."

ASPIRING RETAIL MAGAZINE

BOOK TWO...*THE WIND HARP*

"BJ always does a great job of drawing her readers into the lives of her characters. I'm sure that there will be many who will be eagerly pleading to know 'what happens next.' I will be among them."

JANETTE OKE, *LOVE COMES SOFTLY*

"BJ Hoff continues the story of Maggie and Jonathan, who must endure their share of trials before reaping their reward. Though this novel is historical, BJ Hoff deals with issues that are completely contemporary...Kudos to the author for charming us again!"

ANGELA HUNT, BESTSELLING AUTHOR OF *THE NOVELIST*

BOOK THREE...*THE SONG WEAVER*

"Like a warm visit with a good friend over a hot cup of tea, *The Song Weaver* offers comfort and satisfaction...and you don't want the visit to come to an end."

CINDY SWANSON

"BJ Hoff is a master at characterization, and her stories are rich with insight. I love the historical setting and learned something new about the role of women in that society."

JILL E. SMITH

"*The Song Weaver* is the last book in the Mountain Song Legacy Story, and I hate to see it end. I'll miss Maggie and Jonathan and all the others...A very satisfying end to a special series. She never disappoints."

BARBARA WARREN

RACHEL'S SECRET

Bestselling author BJ Hoff promises to delight her many faithful readers with her compelling new series, The Riverhaven Years. With the first book, *Rachel's Secret*, Hoff introduces a new community of unforgettable characters and adds the elements readers have come to expect from her novels: a tender love story, the faith journeys of people we grow to know and love, and enough suspense to keep the pages turning quickly.

When the wounded Irish American riverboat captain, Jeremiah Gant, bursts into the rural Amish setting of Riverhaven, he brings chaos and conflict to the community—especially for young widow, Rachel Brenneman. The unwelcome "outsider" needs a safe place to recuperate before continuing his secret role as an Underground Railroad conductor. Neither he nor Rachel is prepared for the forbidden love that threatens to endanger a man's mission, a woman's heart, and a way of life for an entire people.